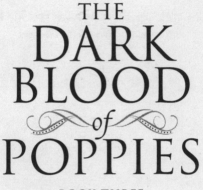

THE
DARK
BLOOD
of
POPPIES

BOOK THREE
of the
BLOOD WINE SEQUENCE

ALSO BY FREDA WARRINGTON
and available from Titan Books

A Taste of Blood Wine
A Dance in Blood Velvet

COMING SOON
The Dark Arts of Blood

THE DARK BLOOD of POPPIES

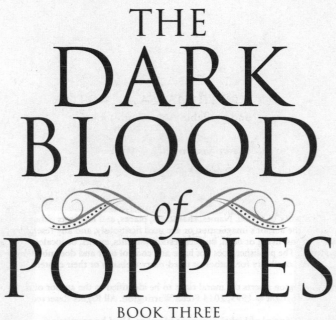

BOOK THREE
of the
BLOOD WINE SEQUENCE

FREDA WARRINGTON

TITAN BOOKS

The Dark Blood of Poppies
Print edition ISBN: 9781781167076
E-book edition ISBN: 9781781167274

Published by Titan Books
A division of Titan Publishing Group Ltd
144 Southwark Street, London SE1 0UP

First edition: May 2014

1 3 5 7 9 10 8 6 4 2

A CIP catalogue record for this title is available from the British Library.

Printed and bound by CPI Group (UK) Ltd, Croydon, CR0 4YY

Did you enjoy this book? We love to hear from our readers.
Please email us at: readerfeedback@titanemail.com

To receive advance information, news, competitions, and exclusive
offers online, please sign up for the Titan newsletter on our website:
TITANBOOKS.COM

This book is dedicated to our friends,
the Warringtons in the USA:
Freda and Ralph, Danny and Alisa and their families,
with love and thanks.

CONTENTS

PRELUDE

IRELAND, 1704

On the night the vampires came, Sebastian Pierse was thinking of vengeance, grief and fire. Perhaps it was his anguish that drew the vampires to him. He gripped his injured right arm but hardly felt the pain, or the hot blood running from the gash to mingle with rain on the cobblestones. With sweat and rain running into his eyes, he put back his head and uttered a raw scream of desolation.

His cry rang off the walls and was swallowed in the downpour. The courtyard was the heart of the magnificent house he had built for his wife, Mary, but in darkness it was forbidding: a roofless prison.

Eight years he had worked to create the mansion beside the River Blackwater: the grandest house County Waterford had ever seen. He'd dreamed of taking Mary from their draughty tower house to the residence she deserved. The house was days from completion. And now he was going to burn it to the ground.

He'd planned to name it Mary Hall after her. Not now. They would never live here now.

Nothing left but to reduce the dream to literal ash.

Sebastian stared at rows of lightless windows above him. His overwrought mind played tricks; he saw shapes moving across the panes. *Who's inside? Those damned shadows again!*

What will it take, he wondered savagely, *to set this place afire? An English army, Cromwell's or William's, adepts at gutting tower houses and castles – where are they when they're needed? Can one man do this alone, with only peat and firewood to set the blaze?*

Yes, he told himself. *I'll burn the place, whatever it takes.*

But he could barely move his arm. He was shivering. His shirt clung to him, linen and lace soaked with watered blood.

When Mary had told him the truth in the old house, that primitive stone pile, he felt no urge to punish her physically. Nor even to seek out her lover and take revenge with a sword-thrust. No, his first thought was the house, symbol of their future. But in a few words his wife had turned the future to winter.

The child isn't yours, Sebastian.

The sight of her haunted him: her long, wheaten skeins of hair, the curve of her belly under a white chemise, her face blanching as she confessed. Her hand had groped for a pair of scissors, as if to defend herself, even though he'd never once shown her violence. Instead he'd run out into the night, across the fields and woods of his estate, as if running could purge the grief of betrayal.

Shadows followed him, like shapes cut from the night. All his life he'd been self-contained, unemotional – until tonight. Tonight he'd gone insane.

He had tripped on a rock, gashing his forearm. The cut went to the bone but he didn't care.

After all we did, he thought, *to keep our property out of English hands*! His ancestors were Anglo-Normans: Catholics who'd come to Ireland in the twelfth century and intermarried with the locals until their English overlords saw them as indistinguishable from the native Irish. Yet Sebastian's family had resisted all attempts to confiscate their lands.

My forefathers bested Elizabeth and Cromwell, he thought. *God forgive me, I even turned Protestant to outwit William of Orange. So much effort and sacrifice – for nothing! But if I have no descendents to inherit this house, I'm damned if anyone else shall have it. Not Mary, not my brothers, not some accursed English nobleman.*

He swayed, his vision blurring. Now the shadows were moving around the courtyard walls.

They'd haunted him for years. In the corners of the tower house, flitting between trees when he rode to see his tenant farmers, even writing on the freshly plastered walls inside the mansion after the artisans had gone home.

Sebastian planted his feet wide apart to keep his balance. His heart pounded. The eternal presence of the shadows had shaped him into a brooding introvert who showed his wife too little affection.

"You are never here!" Mary had cried. "Always on your farms, or cloistered with your architects and builders. No wonder I couldn't get with child. I never see you!"

What defence was that against the sin of adultery?

Set the fire, he thought. *Quickly, while I can still stand.*

The black sky split open and the rain became a deluge. Cursing, he ran, his boots slipping on cobblestones, to a cellar door behind the kitchen. There were logs and kindling in the cellar, he knew. *Wait until the rain stops*, he thought, lifting a latch and stumbling down the steps. *Then I'll do it. And with luck I'll die in the blaze.*

Inside the darkness was absolute, but he knew the cellar's shape: a chamber like a long, curved tunnel with recesses for storage. Racks were set ready for beer barrels and wine. Just a store-room... yet it held an atmosphere of intense menace, like an ancient torture chamber. Sebastian sank against a wall, cradling his right arm. All he could see was a patch of stormy sky outside.

Then someone shut the door.

Hinges creaked. The strip of grey gloom narrowed and vanished.

Sebastian scrambled to his feet. "Who's there?" He spoke in English and again in Gaelic. No reply. He started forward, then heard a footstep.

He was trembling as much with rage as fear. How dare anyone interrupt his plan? And why had he been foolish enough to rush out without a sword or pistol?

His arm was very bad now. He'd lost feeling in his hand.

"Sebastian," the intruder whispered. A woman's voice, with an unknown accent.

"Who is it? Show yourself!"

He saw eyes in the dark, a faint gold aura... Then came a wash of candlelight, painting the walls ochre and throwing lurid shadows from the feet of three overwhelming figures.

Sebastian couldn't breathe. In that annihilating moment, all human concerns fell away.

Standing before him was a magnificent golden man with extraordinary yellow eyes, like a cat. He shone.

"Sebastian." His voice was beautiful yet metallic. "I am Simon. Don't be afraid. We have come only for your blood and your being."

In blinding terror, he *knew*. This was a fallen angel, Lucifer robed in glory. And for his sins, they were about to dispatch him to hell.

He crossed himself with his good hand. The golden man laughed. His gaze fastened on Sebastian's bloodstained sleeve.

"What have you done to your arm?"

In panic Sebastian looked around and saw the other two behind him, trapping him in the centre of a triangle. One was an attenuated man with snow-white skin and hair. The third, who held a candle, was female. He'd never seen anyone like her, even in Dublin or London. Her skin was dark brown like a nut, her hair a long fall of blue-black silk.

They wore satin robes, heavy with embroidered symbols, befitting their unearthly nature. They were *too* perfect, frozen in beauty like painted statues. Yet, paradoxically, they appeared so vital and full of fire that humans were flabby sleepwalkers by comparison.

Sebastian's mind evaporated.

"Is this punishment for what I did?" he breathed.

"What did you do?" said the golden one, Simon, amused.

"Renounced my religion. Became a Protestant. A sin, I know, but the only way to keep our estate out of English hands!"

"We have nothing to do with that," said Simon. He came closer. "God recognises no sects. No, Sebastian, we are not here to punish you. We have watched you for a long time."

Simon placed his hands on Sebastian's shoulders. His eyes were new-minted sovereigns, spellbinding. He lifted the injured arm, peeled back the wet sleeve and began to lick the wound. Sebastian, horrified, could do nothing to stop him.

"Why?" he whispered. "What are you?" But as he spoke, he knew. Not angels or devils but the faerie folk, the old Irish gods who existed for thousands of years before Christianity drove them out. Children of the goddess Danu...

"Vampires," said the woman. From behind, she put her arms

around his lean waist. "Immortals. Others. My name is Rasmila and our friend is Fyodor. Don't be afraid. Why are you here alone, in such pain?"

Hypnotized, Sebastian answered. "Tell me, how better could I love my wife than by building her this house? But she says I never loved her. Ten years we've longed for a child. When she gave me good news, I was so happy, I wanted her to live like a duchess as she deserved... until I found out the babe isn't mine. A servant told me she has a lover in Dublin, that she took him because I couldn't give her children. So I asked, and she confessed. She says I'm at fault, that I'm never with her, that she had to prove she isn't barren. But I was working for her while she acted the brood mare with another man! And now she loves him and I have no wife, no child, nothing. I built the house for nothing. Now it must be destroyed."

"Poor Sebastian," Rasmila said into his shoulder.

"But what are you thinking?" said Fyodor, stroking his neck. His eyes were silver, pitiless. Their hands felt hot like the sun, cold like porcelain. "Destroying this house is not revenge. Bloodshed is revenge!"

Simon lowered the arm from his lips. Sebastian looked at the torn, discoloured skin as if it did not belong to him.

"Fyodor is right. The house is innocent. If you burn it, you only hurt yourself. But if you desire true revenge – we'll give you that."

"How?" Sebastian shivered with awe and fearful excitement.

"Give yourself to us, and receive all the power you desire," said Rasmila.

"What's the price? My soul?"

"You think you possess a soul?" said Fyodor contemptuously. "You are only a thought in God's head."

"But His thoughts can live forever." Simon's large hand, with fingers like gold rods, hovered over his chest. Sebastian felt his life caught in a metal-cold balance.

"You were my choice," said Rasmila. "Mine. You are beautiful and perfect. We love you, Sebastian. Whom do you love? Mary?"

"I love..." His knees buckled. "This house."

Fyodor grinned. "Then sweep your enemies from your path, and you'll be free!"

"Free?"

"To follow another path," said Simon.

"I don't understand."

"Give us your body and your blood. In return we shall grant life eternal."

"No," he said weakly. "No."

He knew they would have their way. Yet he sank into their embrace still half-resisting, thinking, *God help me! Save me!*

God remained mute.

"We are the wings of heaven," whispered Rasmila. Her kohl-lined eyes ensorcelled him; her warm mouth met his, igniting all his nerves. As she began to make love to him, he couldn't resist, even with Simon and Fyodor watching. He let her unlace his shirt and breeches, barely aware of his injured arm. He felt her fingers slide against his bare skin; he kissed the silky flesh of his neck and breasts. Astonishment and desire took him in a flash flood, extinguishing all the frustration of his poisoned love for Mary. In an unholy dream he pushed her down onto the flagstones, running his hand along the firm thigh beneath her robe. Underneath she was softly, sweetly naked.

Oh, she was human. Oh God, she was.

He entered her urgently, oblivious to the fact that two deities, like gold and silver flames, bore witness. Perhaps he was failing some test, giving in to temptation, but he didn't care. The fire was everything. She clutched him, kissing his throat, laughing and gasping encouragement. He could not hold back.

The fire peaked, so complete and perfect that he sobbed. But it was over too soon. Then his whole body ached with cold, and terror reclaimed him. His only impulse was to haul himself out of her arms, out of this madness.

Rasmila held him fast, seeming angry. Such strength, for a woman! He hadn't satisfied her but he didn't care, only wanted to escape the eerily dispassionate ferocity with which she gripped him, her arms around his back, her legs locked with his. Then – she bit his throat.

The attack came from two directions. Rasmila's teeth sent pain plunging so deep that it pierced his heart. And the pale one, Fyodor, closed his mouth on Sebastian's arm. He did not lick the wound as Simon had done, but savagely re-opened it and sucked hard until blood flowed again.

Sebastian began to choke for breath. He knew this faintness was the beginning of death. He tried to fight, but couldn't. He was fading. Dying.

"Yes, you will die." Simon's voice echoed down a great tunnel. "But you will live again. You will be like us."

A god, he thought, as he was jerked out of his body and into a burning, gold and purple firmament. *A milk-skinned betrayer with the jewelled eyes of a saint.*

When Sebastian returned to the old house, he found Mary fully dressed in her room, throwing clothes into a trunk. Her lover was there: a thin-faced, overdressed milksop of a man he'd never seen before. He'd come to take Mary away. Cheek of the Devil!

Seeing him, they both shrank in terror, clutching each other. How cold and bare was this stone chamber, but Mary had forfeited the luxury of the new house. He wondered how he looked; demonic, he imagined, his clothes ragged and bloody, his face luminous with the light of undeath.

"There's nothing to fear," Mary told her lover. "My husband can't stop us. Tell him I'm going with you!"

Sebastian killed the man before he opened his mouth. Simply tore out his throat with his fingernails, stating, "I'd rather she'd had some peasant under a hedgerow than you."

Mary screamed. She tried to escape but he held her easily with one hand, even though she was a tall, strong woman. Even though his hand had been useless a few hours earlier. Now there was no sign of injury on the flawless skin.

Sebastian felt completely calm. Unmoved by her terror, or even her infidelity. Such human concerns no longer mattered. Only her beauty moved him; she was still magnificent with her luxuriant hair and the sweet rosy glow of her skin…

"All I wanted was to give you a son!" she cried.

"I would rather have had you, and no son."

"I loved you, but you never wanted me!"

"You are mistaken," he said quietly. "Let me show you how I

wanted you." And he bit her throat. Tore her abdomen, until his whole world was a scarlet sea.

Then he wept. His tears flowed out with her blood; and all the passion he hadn't realised he felt, all the passion he'd neglected to show her, was distilled in the crimson heart of that moment.

His need sated, he let her lifeless body slip to the floor. Servants came running in, screaming, but he walked past them as if nothing had happened. Walked into the darkness and vanished.

Afterwards, he stood on a hill with Simon, Rasmila and Fyodor, looking up at the stars. Nets of light webbed a clear deep sky. Never before had he seen with such clarity, never dreamed that such crystalline beauty was hidden from mortal eyes. He could see for miles: northwards to the River Suir, the towers of Cahir Castle, the Golden Vale of Tipperary and Cashel of the Kings. Close at hand lay his own estate: the stump of the stone tower where Mary lay dead, and the unnamed Hall, a great, pristine mansion like a gold casket swathed in deep blue twilight. He saw the River Blackwater flowing on its dark way; the peaks of the Galtee and Knockmealdown mountains; and in between, a quilt of pasturelands and luxuriant woods, steeped in tints of green and violet and silver. Night-colours he'd never seen before. The air was sweet and icy, like wine.

"And was your revenge satisfying?" Simon asked.

"It was meaningless," said Sebastian.

Simon nodded as if he understood, but Fyodor said, "To milk your enemies of their blood – meaningless?"

"I thought it would be a great, affecting tragedy, but it wasn't. The only thing that mattered…" He struggled to explain, as much to himself as to them. "All that mattered was the blood. I realised as I drank my wife's blood that no other affection, nothing can hold a candle to that red passion."

"Exactly." Simon spoke intensely. "And now you're free of your earthly bonds."

"Free?" He looked at Simon; awed by his beauty, yet no longer afraid. "What does that mean? I don't care about Mary, I don't care about the house or anything, not even the dead infant. If the price of revenge is to care for nothing but blood for eternity, I might as well be dead. You three have done this to me, and I don't even know why!"

"Don't be angry." Rasmila slipped her hand through his arm. "You'll find other passions. What will you do now? Stay here, or leave?"

"What?" Sebastian looked at her, amazed. "I thought you meant to take me with you."

"Ah, no," said Simon. "We are immortals, not nursemaids. We've bestowed glorious powers on you, but to learn their use – you are alone."

"You can't leave me like this!" Sebastian felt the absolute terror of abandonment. "Why have you done this to me?"

"Once or twice in a century," Rasmila replied, "we choose an individual worthy of our gifts: power over humans, eternal life, a glimpse of heaven. You were my choice, Sebastian. You will be a wonderful immortal. Don't let me down."

Terror subsiding, he realised he was glad. He did not want these divine, malevolent creatures around him. More than ever, he wanted solitude.

"You want me to prove myself? Or rather, prove to your comrades that you made a good choice?"

"Of course," she said stiffly, withdrawing her hands from his arm.

"Well, you can go to hell, all of you," he said. He became aware of his blood thirst as a sprawling, uncontrollable entity, his future a wasteland. He sensed nothing of paradise or the faerie realm. "Hell. That is surely where you're from, is it not?"

They looked at him with hard, cold eyes, displeased by his ingratitude. He thought, *Perhaps they could kill me as easily as they changed me, but I don't care. I'm not afraid of them anymore.*

"We did not transform you to win love or hate," Simon said sternly. "Your feelings mean nothing. We are only God's instruments. You'll learn that this existence is both a blessing and a curse. The pleasures of immortality carry a severe price: to be alone forever."

"Good," Sebastian said harshly. "You have it the wrong way round, my friends. Solitude is the blessing, blood-hunger the curse."

Simon and Rasmila looked at each other; exquisite demons

with eyes of flame, disappointed yet amused by his insolence. Sebastian decided to leave before they abandoned him. A small act to show he was not their victim. He walked away through the long grass into the endless dark...

No one came after him, not even Rasmila.

He already knew he must leave Ireland. A new world was opening up to him; no longer the one he knew, but a dark twin of its daylight self. So before he left, he paid a last visit to his mansion.

How often had he walked through these cavernous rooms? First, the entrance hall and kitchens; then up sweeping stairs to the great salon with a double row of long windows, then the library, drawing rooms and dining rooms, and up again to the bedchambers, the nursery... All silent, shadowy, empty. Scents of fresh paint and new timber infused the air. The workmen's clutter was gone and the rooms were naked, aching to be filled by carpets and furniture, paintings, books and ornaments. To receive the imprint of a new family.

He'd strolled these rooms with pride. He'd run through them in anguish, cursing as if Mary's infidelity were their fault. Now he haunted them in a quiet reverie, saying goodbye.

Someone will live here, he thought, *but not me. Some other family will shape these spaces to their own design and it won't meet with my approval, but...*

A revelation. He still cared about the house after all. The human urge to destroy it had passed. He didn't even begrudge the place to strangers.

Euphoria gripped him.

"It doesn't matter," he whispered. "This house still belongs to me. It will always be mine in spirit. Whoever lives here will never be at ease. They will know they are only tenants of an unseen landlord."

Time to leave, he thought, *but one day... I shall return.*

They'd seduced him with the Devil's promises, the old gods, then flung him into purgatory. He brooded as he walked away from his house and lands... but in truth, he realised he had wanted this. He'd invited it, drawing the three to him with his love of solitude, the heat of despair and his yearning for fire and vengeance.

Sebastian was new-born, but he felt ancient. The vampires had only given him what he needed.

PART ONE

Man's daughter she is not, nor Angel's bride:
beyond paradise's prolific marshes
waiting to be milked
the unicorn
carries her, Lilith, who already knows
the mysterious form of the mandrake root
and the golem that grows in the kernel. She knows
that jasper placed in henbane
causes a mortal sleep, drier and stranger
than the one fastening on Orpheus' back
that in the starred moray's vulva
there is a mermaid's embryo
in the tiger lily the latex
that will beget Amazons, and one hundred
female deities are waiting in the steeped firtree
in the shape of gold ducklings
another hundred female deities
will be nursed by unicorns and their blood
will be white to contagion, prescient to fire.

ROSANNA OMBRES
"THE SONG OF LILITH"
TRANSLATED BY EDGAR PAUK

CHAPTER ONE

1926: CRUEL ANGEL

Violette Lenoir, *prima ballerina assoluta*, was not proud of her ability to inspire terror.

Of course, it has its uses, she thought as she watched her *corps de ballet* daintily traversing the mirrored studio. *I need their respect; without it, I'd have no authority. Perfection requires discipline.*

Sometimes, though, she would go too far. If she involuntarily let her vampire nature show through the human facade and frightened some poor girl or boy, afterwards she would feel mortified. So she was always on guard. It made her a ruthless taskmaster, never cheerful, never relaxed.

Violette stood at the barre, supervising rehearsals for *Coppélia*. She was dressed like her dancers in practice clothes: leotard, skirt and tights of grey wool. She was of average height but appeared taller, being very slender and long-limbed. And she looked like Snow White, with alabaster skin and black hair – now gathered in a loose bun – and her claret mouth and large, knowing eyes. Their colour was startling and changeable, from deep blue to violet, like the iridescent wings of a butterfly.

As a human, she had been as beautiful and graceful. Adored for her talent and notorious for her perfectionism, she'd always commanded respect. Outwardly, nothing had changed.

No one has guessed, she thought. *None of my dancers, musicians or staff, not even Geli, has any suspicion that a few months ago I became a vampire, or something worse…*

I can see it in my own eyes, she thought, *but they can't. Thank goodness vampires cast reflections after all, or I really should be in trouble.*

The ballet was still her life. So, if she was to continue working in the human world, the truth must remain secret. Such a struggle, though, against the blood thirst, the raging entity within her. A perpetual strain to keep it in check.

Pushing these thoughts aside, she watched the dancers with intense concentration. Their synchronisation was imperfect. One girl, Ute, usually flawless, had been making mistakes all afternoon.

"No!" Violette snapped. The pianist stopped abruptly. "We changed that step. Can't you remember anything? Like this!"

Moving to the centre of the studio, she demonstrated *en pointe*, her blocked shoes barely making a sound. The girls watched raptly, desperate not to fall short of Madame's expectations.

"Try again," Violette said crisply.

She knew they were tired, but she felt no pity. Her own teachers had never shown her any. "If you cannot stand hard work, leave," she told any dancer who dared complain. Harsh, but realistic.

This time, the *corps de ballet* was perfect... until Ute went wrong again.

Violette felt like shaking her. Such feelings were dangerous, threatening to unleash the floodgates of vampire thirst. She must always hold herself like stone against emotion.

"Ute!" Her voice made the mirrors ring. "If this is your best, perhaps you'd better give up your role to someone who can concentrate."

The girl, thin and elfin with honey-blonde hair, looked at the floor. She was a fine dancer and should make a prima ballerina one day. Violette saw that something was badly wrong. The long curve of Ute's neck held her attention...

"What is the matter?" she asked more gently.

Ute's reaction was to flee the studio in tears. The others shifted uneasily. Madame Lenoir had reduced them all to breaking point at some stage. They were better dancers for it, but never forgot the pain. Violette knew they nearly hated her sometimes.

"Continue," she said, and the long-suffering pianist began again. She knew she pushed them too hard. She'd forgotten how it felt to battle with aching muscles, to rehearse until she was near-blind with exhaustion. Now her limbs were always strong and supple, and she could have danced for days if she'd wished. That made her impatient with human frailty.

A few months ago, she'd been fighting arthritis that was slowly eroding her joints and spine. *Would I still be dancing now, if not for Charlotte? No, I would have been facing life in a wheelchair. But the price I'm paying...*

Rehearsal over, she went to her office and found Ute outside, her face drawn and eyes bruised from crying. Violette took her inside, sat her down on a hard chair, and gave her a handkerchief. Lamps under blue glass shades cast a harebell glow.

"I don't mean to upset you," Violette began. "Anyone can make mistakes. But with three weeks until we sail for America, and two ballets to perform, we can't afford to be less than perfect. You understand why I am so strict."

"Of course, Madame," the girl whispered, her head bowed. "It's not the discipline, I'm used to that."

"What, then? Are you ill?"

"No, Madame. It's my father... he wants me to go home. He insists I give up my career to look after him."

"Why? Is he sick?"

"No, he's in perfect health. He misses me. He doesn't think a girl should have a career, especially not on the stage. He always disapproved of me coming to you, Madame. I don't know what to do."

"It's simple. Stay here."

"But, Madame, you don't know him!" Sobbing again, Ute explained her father's arguments. Utterly ludicrous and selfish, they sounded to Violette. But the girl was weakening towards his demands. Her weakness made Violette furious.

She felt herself becoming Lilith, regarding the young dancer through cold and ageless eyes. *Ute must be forced to face her own stupidity.* Violette could not suppress the impulse.

"Are you mad?" She walked around her desk and gripped Ute's shoulder. The girl's head jerked up in shock. "You would sacrifice a career as magnificent as yours will surely be, deprive the world of your talent, just to satisfy the whims of a selfish old man? What do you want to be, when you are sixty?"

"Madame?"

"An embittered old woman, living in obscurity in some Bavarian village – or sitting behind this desk in my place?"

Violette saw the pulse jumping in Ute's neck, felt it accelerating under her fingers. She caught the scent of fear. And then she committed the sin. Gave in to Lilith's thirst.

That night Violette stalked the deserted rooms, a creature condemned never to sleep. She was still in her practice clothes. Clawing her arms like an abstracted Lady Macbeth, she stared into the darkness, stricken.

Her apartment above the studio was no longer a place of refuge and sleep, merely somewhere to keep her possessions. Space to be alone, yes, but she felt alone everywhere, so it made no difference. Her maid, Geli, must have noticed the changes, and wondered why she no longer suffered backache or demanded ice packs on her knees. Violette had made no attempt to explain, and Geli was too meek to ask.

Charlotte had insinuated herself into Violette's life without invitation. Unwelcome at first, she became irresistible. A strange and lovely creature, sweetly old-fashioned with her demure manners and a gorgeous wreath of tawny-bronze hair. Deceptive Charlotte; a demon who drank blood. And who, for all her promises of restraint, had eventually slaked her thirst from Violette's veins. It had seemed a violation, a betrayal of trust... *but I encouraged her*, Violette thought. *I was as much to blame. And afterwards, we still couldn't leave each other alone.*

Violette had not consented to becoming a vampire – not until the very last moment, at least. It was Charlotte who insisted. Violette had fought, though not too hard, because it felt inevitable. Her fate, if such a thing existed.

In the moment of transformation she'd become someone else. Someone who knew too much, whose talent was to corrupt and ruin and transmute.

That other being's name was Lilith.

Now Violette's life was one of conflict with her other-self. She found the state of vampirism hateful. Her desire for blood was agonising, the bliss of sating it, loathsome. Violette fought for creativity, to preserve her ballet, and never to take a sip of blood from any member of her company.

Lilith's intentions were the opposite.

You cannot be a vampire and live like this, Lilith would whisper. *You cannot resist your instincts. Listen to me.* Oh, the seductive whisper in the night. *Listen, and you'll know everything. Look into their pitiful souls and show them the truth!*

Violette tried to turn away, but when the hunger rose, she *was* Lilith. At those times, to protect her dancers, she would usually leave the premises and wrestle with hideous urges alone in the darkness. Until today, with Ute…

Now, her blood thirst guiltily sated, restlessness brought her to the empty studio. On the polished floor, lit by long rhomboids of starlight, she began to dance in meditation.

A chill washed over her, as if someone were watching.

She sensed human presences in the building, asleep. She perceived inhabitants in houses along the riverbank, and across the river, where the domed and spired city of Salzburg slumbered. Sleeping mortals. Lilith's prey.

What can I do? she thought. *How do I find a way to bear this?*

Ute, too, lay in her little attic room, perhaps troubled with bad dreams. Violette would never forget the flat astonishment in her eyes, or the searing tang of her blood. She could only pray that the girl would forget. Ute had been dazed, stunned… wide open to the suggestion that nothing had happened.

I drank only a little, Violette told herself. *The physical harm will pass – but what have I done to her mind?*

However strict and aloof she appeared, the truth was that she cared passionately for her dancers. She would lay down her life for them.

When Violette-Lilith took a victim, it was not just to satisfy thirst. There was a deeper compulsion. Her bite was transformative, forcing her victims to see themselves all too clearly. The results could be disastrous. Violette hated the responsibility, but Lilith would have her way.

Outside, the river flowed softly and a cold breeze off the Alps ruffled the forests. Violette thought of entering the Crystal Ring, but the other-realm of immortals held no respite. Wherever she went, Lilith went with her.

So she danced slowly, her hair flowing loose.

If Lilith existed only in her imagination, this might be easier. She could accept herself as mad. Nothing could be that simple, however: others had seen Lilith in her, too. Three enigmatic vampires had captured and delivered her to Lancelyn, a human and self-styled magus. He'd addressed her by many titles: the Black Goddess, Sophia, Cybele. He had offered hope that she was not evil. *We can empower each other*, he'd said. *Your darkness is the veil of Wisdom; let me lift the veil and become immortal through you. Then we will both find the truth.*

She'd almost succumbed. In her despair, Lancelyn seemed the only one who could help. But in the end, his desires had been selfish. He wanted to possess her, to marry her and achieve magical communion by consummating the marriage.

Everyone wants to control me, as if the force inside me is too terrifying to be let loose.

Violette had always rejected men, from her father onwards. Many had wanted her, several had dared to try, but she'd never given in. She found their lusts repulsive. It was a matter of pride to stay forever immaculate and self-contained.

So Lilith had risen up and destroyed Lancelyn, before the violation – magical or not – took place.

I had to do it, she thought. *Could he have taught me anything? He was the only one who even partly understood what I am. However, because he chose to put his own selfish whims before true understanding – he paid the ultimate price.*

One thing helped her cope: the self-discipline of her lifelong ballet training. She forced herself to think of nothing but her steps.

As she danced, she became aware of shadows solidifying around her. Watching her. Judging.

The three angels again? She thought she'd seen the last of them. Anger rose in her chest. *No*, she thought. *You can't return to haunt me again! Your power over me is gone. You no longer exist.*

She danced wildly, as if to repel them, experiencing a sense of danger so extreme that at last she stopped dead.

Blending partway into the Crystal Ring, she saw the intruders vividly. Five elongated, jet-black demons, glittering dimly against the distorted cobweb walls. Vampires.

Not her three former persecutors... but who were they?

As Violette slipped back into the solid world, they came with her, taking human form in the studio. Four men and one woman, with radiant skin and the mesmeric stillness of cobras. Violette recognised two of them: Charlotte's friend, blond Stefan, and his mute twin Niklas. Stefan had assisted Violette's transformation. She was unsure whether that made him her friend or her enemy.

Facing her, they gave minimal nods of respect. Their eyes were guarded, impassive and accusing all at once, like those of a hostile jury. She was intimidated, outraged.

"Violette?" Stefan said softly. He had the grace to look apologetic, at least. "Please forgive the intrusion. My companions wish to speak with you. I don't think you've met Rachel –" he indicated the woman, a tall, thin creature with hair like apricot flames "– and this is John, and his companion, Matthew."

John and Matthew were small, slight and pale, with dour faces and dark hair cropped short. They had the look of monks from medieval portraits, and they stared at her with suspicion and loathing. *Witch-finders*, she thought.

"What do you want?" There was no courtesy in their invasion, so she showed none in return.

"Madame Lenoir," said Rachel. Her polite tone was razor-edged. "You don't know me, but you knew my closest friend. Katerina."

A flash of ghastly memory. The screech of train wheels, sparks, blood smeared on a steel rail...

"You killed her," said Rachel.

"I don't deny it," Violette said thinly. "But she was trying to kill *my* dearest friend, Charlotte. Have you come for revenge?"

"No." Rachel's face was like ice, translucent, her lips vivid scarlet. "Only justice. We want you to do the right thing."

"Which is what?"

"To give up your ballet and your public appearances."

Violette laughed in astonishment. "Why in the world should I do that?"

"You are breaking the laws," Matthew said harshly. He was smaller than John, more belligerent.

"What laws?"

"The laws of God, of Satan, and of our nature."

"Oh, do tell me about Satan!" Violette said with rising anger.

"As vampires, we are possessed by the Devil," stated Matthew. "You must know this! We are being tormented for sins we committed in life. As Satan's instruments, therefore, we serve and appease our master until it pleases God to release us – because, you understand, even the Adversary is part of God's great plan. We submit in humility to our role. But you, Lilith – you serve neither God nor Satan. You are outside. You are too arrogant, too dangerous."

"Females of our kind are more deeply corrupt than males. They lack humility or a sense of duty," said John, his voice quiet yet harsh. "But you are the worst, Lilith. It ill befits our kind to make lascivious displays in public."

"Immortals should vanish from mortal eyes and prey upon them at night," said Matthew. "You are not like us."

"Of course I'm not like you," Violette said contemptuously. "You two haven't left the thirteenth century."

Rachel said, "You may think John and Matthew old-fashioned, but they have a point. Vampires are designed to be discreet, yet every other person in the world knows your name. Your photograph appears in newspapers. How long can you sustain this charade? Someone is bound to notice that you are not growing older, or that your nocturnal habits are strange. Some sharp-minded victim will recognise you."

"None of this is your concern." She gazed at the golden-haired twins. "Stefan, you don't agree, do you? I thought you were my friend!"

"I am," he said softly. "But they have a point. You can't go on trying to live a human life." Although he had the grace to look shamefaced, he held her gaze steadily.

"It is our concern," Rachel said coolly. "You could bring disaster to all of us. We're not infallible. You cannot go on flaunting yourself."

"Can't I, Rachel?" Rage filled her. Their impudence! "Who are you to come here uninvited and dictate how I behave? I don't believe you're frightened of humans. We can disappear; what can they do to us? No, it's something else."

"You killed a vampire." Rachel compressed her lips.

Violette moved closer to her. "Are you afraid of me?" She looked hard into each face in turn. Their nervous response both excited and alarmed her. Provoking them was unwise, since she was outnumbered, but she had to speak her mind. "Do you think I'm trying to be another Kristian? Is that what this is about?"

"Kristian also broke the laws!" Matthew exclaimed. "He, too, was arrogant! That was why he had to die."

Rachel turned and glared to quieten him. Then Violette knew for certain. They were afraid of her. So afraid that they wanted her dead. Even kind Stefan!

"How dare you assume I would want to emulate Kristian! Or that I'm remotely interested in your concerns!" As she spoke, Violette-Lilith was filled by strange energy. Their primitive fears and threats inflamed her.

"You must obey God's law," said John.

Violette shivered. Talk of God made her ill. It brought back memories of three dark shapes standing over her, the wings of cruel angels beating around her.

"So, you want me to disappear, but what if I refuse?"

No one answered. She sensed their combined will weighing her down. Did they speak for all vampires, even for Karl and Charlotte? Lilith would not submit. She rose like a great shadow in Violette's soul, ready to fight or flee.

Lilith did not need to ask why they dreaded her.

"Well, you've asked and my answer is no," said Violette. "Now if you would kindly leave?"

Matthew looked at the ceiling, his face ghastly in the starlight. "Sweet mortals, sleeping peacefully above. Have you never partaken of their blood? You must have been tempted."

She thought of Ute. Painful shame suffused her. "I've sworn not to touch them."

"You can protect yourself, but you cannot protect them," Matthew said softly.

"What?"

"Matthew," Stefan chided, but it was too late, the threat had been uttered. Violette felt her fury gathering in a great wave.

"I can disregard threats to myself," she said, "but not to my company."

The wave of fury broke, exploded through her.

She lunged and seized Matthew by the throat. He tried to slip into the Crystal Ring but she went with him, dragged him back. His sombre expression flashed into hideous panic as she squeezed his neck, shook him, pierced the skin with her nails.

John, Rachel, Stefan and Niklas grabbed her. She threw them all off with one hand, heard them spinning across the floor, colliding with the mirrored walls. Lilith's strength seemed limitless.

Tightening her grip on Matthew's neck, she snapped his spine, wrenched back his jaw until the skin ripped. Muscles and fibres tore, blood oozed from the wound. Vampires clung to life like cockroaches. She strained until the vertebrae parted and the spinal cord finally broke with a dull, moist popping sound. Then she bent and drank from the stump of his neck.

Blood flowed through her like sexual pleasure – only for a second or two. Her victim was dead.

Violette flung him aside in disgust. Lifting her head, she saw the others staring, their eyes glazed with horror. Stefan put his arms around Niklas, as if to protect his mute and near-mindless twin.

Then Violette realised what she'd done. Decapitated a vampire with her bare hands.

But Lilith had not finished.

She went after Rachel next. The woman tried to flee but Violette was too fast. She snagged the flame-red hair and wound Rachel towards her. Biting into the white neck, she sucked hard. Scarlet light filled her. Rachel thrashed in helpless terror.

All the time, Violette moved with the weightless grace of her art. It wasn't that she felt unnaturally strong, more that the others seemed as fragile as paper in her grasp.

John ran past her. Still feeding, she grabbed him one-handed. Over Rachel's shoulder she saw Stefan flee into the Crystal Ring. Dragging Niklas with him, he glanced back in horror – then they vanished, as if the mirrors had swallowed them.

If they hadn't fled she would have attacked them too, friends or not. Lilith had no pity.

Now she held Rachel and John together, one in each hand, writhing helplessly against her. Both were spattered with their own blood. She did not bite John, only ploughed his flesh with her fingers.

Then Violette found herself descending from fury into shock. As the fever subsided, she emerged shaking, aghast at herself. *What have I done? Dear God, it was so easy!*

She shook her two captives. They were like sacks of flour in her hands.

"Now leave my property," she hissed. "If ever you return, or threaten any human associated with me, if I so much as *see* you near this place, you will think Matthew fortunate." She raised her voice. "Do you understand?"

"Yes," Rachel gasped. Her face hung with fear, colourless.

Then Violette flung her and John on top of Matthew's body. "Get out. And take that thing with you."

John's eyes lanced her with venom. Now she'd slain his friend, as well as Rachel's. Now she had two mortal enemies. It would have been safer to decapitate them too, but her killing frenzy had subsided. She couldn't do it.

"We can't take a corpse into the Ring," Rachel whispered.

"Then leave by the back stairs. Just go!"

They obeyed. John hefted Matthew's body over his shoulder, his face a mask of blood and tears. Rachel took the head, a grisly burden. And with blank looks, like two demons carrying a soul to hell, they fled.

Violette listened to their soft footsteps descending, an outside door opening and closing. Their auras dwindled along the riverbank until she could no longer sense them.

She was alone. Silence settled like snow around her.

She wanted to weep, but couldn't. Her reflection showed not a winged and clawed monster, but a young ballerina: composed, beautiful, incapable of harming a soul.

Violette went to the mirror and stared at her *doppelgänger*. Their fingers met and trailed across the glass; their faces bore the same cool expression. The mirror held no answers.

"Help me," she said to no one in particular. "Help me."

Her gaze moved to the smears of spilled blood on the floor, thick and luscious as berry juice. She caught a succulent aroma. *Oh God, blood...*

As if pulled by puppet-strings she knelt, arching down to breathe the scent, to touch the blood with her tongue...

Movement made her freeze. A large black-and-white cat strolled into the room and began lapping at the same deep red stain. Suddenly Violette saw herself as a beast, part-serpent, part-wolf... She leapt up in horror, panting for breath.

"No," she gasped, digging her nails hard into her own arms. "No, I am not an animal!"

The cat lost interest in the blood and came to Violette, mewing and weaving around her legs. Violette bent down and scratched the top of her pet's head.

"Magdi," she whispered. "Tell me it didn't happen."

Then Violette went to the dressing room and filled a bucket with water and detergent. With the same diligence she applied to perfecting her ballets, she dropped to her knees and began scrubbing the bloodstains out of the smooth, varnished floor.

CHAPTER TWO

FRIENDS AND STRANGERS

On clear cold nights, when a full moon hung over the Swiss Alps, Karl and Charlotte often walked for hours through the magnificent peaks. In temperatures no human could endure, they climbed impossible slopes with ease. Anyone seeing them would think they were ghosts.

As compensation for the darkness of immortality, Charlotte reflected, this was among the greatest: to stand on a mountain summit with the world rolling away in white silence below, Karl's arm around her, their coats blowing in the icy wind.

Below the peak on which they stood was a straight two-hundred-foot drop. Irresistible. Detaching herself from Karl, she went to the very edge and hesitated, drunk with euphoria. Then she spread her arms, and dived into space.

Freezing air made a banshee wail in her ears. She felt weightless and completely at peace. *This is what it means, to be mortal no longer...*

She landed in deep soft snow. Plumes of white powder rose and blew away on the wind. She lay on her back, staring at the sky: a glorious arch of black velvet clustered thickly with stars. There was another explosion of snow nearby; Karl had jumped after her. Finding his feet, he waded towards her.

"Charlotte!"

She accepted his hand and stood up, shaking snow from her coat. The spark of anger in his eyes startled her.

"Have you gone mad?" he said, staring hard into her eyes. "If you want to fly, enter the Crystal Ring. Don't attempt it on Earth."

His fervour took her aback. "I wanted to see how it felt to jump. I knew I couldn't kill myself."

"No, but you might have been badly hurt. Our flesh can tear and our bones can break. We heal, but the pain is terrible."

"I know." She lowered her eyes. "I'm sorry. But there's no harm done."

He relented with a rueful smile. "You must forgive me, also, for being overprotective. Sometimes I think you are still human."

"Well, I'm not."

Karl shook his head, more amused than annoyed. Her beautiful demon lover.

"Shall we go home?" he said. "Now we've taken the shortcut."

On a winding path though a pine forest, they walked arm-in-arm like an innocent couple out for a stroll. Charlotte loved these times when she could forget the blood thirst. Simply bask in the pleasure of being alone with Karl.

Both sensed the presence before they saw her: a peasant woman, heavily wrapped up against the cold, walking towards them. Charlotte smelled animal blood on her, and guessed she'd been up half the night helping cows to calf. Now she looked forward to her warm bed.

In the two years that Karl and Charlotte had been together, they preferred to hunt separately. Both felt that the drinking of blood was too personal to be witnessed. Perhaps it was a form of denial. To hunt together would have been conscious collusion, a step too far across the borderline of evil.

Normally they would have let the woman pass by. Nothing was different this evening...

Yet something happened.

Unbidden, mutual need flowed between them. No word was spoken. As the peasant woman reached them they stopped, blocking her path.

She appeared to be in her thirties, fresh-faced and charming in her headscarf, shawl and long skirts. A benevolent soul. But Charlotte, seeing her through a mist of hunger, perceived her as prey; as meaningful and precious as a sacrifice, but prey all the same. And Karl, his eyes like flames behind amber glass, no longer looked human at all.

The woman froze in shock. Gently they closed in, embracing her with tender hands. Charlotte fed first, then held her while Karl sank his wolf-teeth into the plump throat. Moving behind the victim, Charlotte fed again, breaking the virgin skin on the other side of her neck.

Her hands met Karl's around the human's hot body as they fed. They clasped each other with the victim between them. The moment was eternal, primal, throbbing with heat and blood. Transcendent.

It was the first time they'd fed together like this. More than lust, this was a blood-ritual, connecting them to the darkest side of their natures. Entwining them in wordless ecstasy... and damnation.

Afterwards, they carried the woman to the edge of a farm to be found, either to live or die. Then they went home without a word.

What was there to say? They were both shocked to the soul, swimming in the same shadowy lake of passion. Moved, excited, afraid.

Home was an isolated black chalet poised high in a pine forest beneath the Alps. The peaks of the Eiger, Mönch and Jungfrau floated on the horizon. Within, the rooms had a timeless, faded luxury. Dark pine walls and high ceilings supported by rafters. Persian rugs, panels of muted floral wallpaper, elegant furniture; a library lined from floor to ceiling with books; a music room; a kitchen used only by their housekeeper, who climbed the steep hill twice a week to clean the house. If she thought her employers strange, she was too well paid to ask questions.

Vampires had few material needs – only human blood was essential – so they could have lived naked in graveyards, if they wished. Charlotte did not know of anyone who did. They still preferred to live like humans. The trappings of ordinary life were a fascinating luxury to some; to others, a poignant connection to their lost humanity. In this, Charlotte and Karl were no different.

In the drawing room, Charlotte forced Karl to look at her. He seemed hardly able to do so. His exquisitely sculpted face, dark eyebrows giving bewitching intensity to his lovely eyes, his soft full hair of darkest mahogany – black in shadow, red where the fire caught garnet lights on the strands – still stopped her heart with their beauty. But sometimes he scared her to death. Tonight had added another irrevocable layer of darkness to their relationship.

"Now do you believe I'm not human?" she whispered.

Charlotte lit candles on a low table, each flame adding a new wash of light to her golden-pale skin. Fragrant incense smoke coiled through the glow.

Karl watched her. There was silent reverence between them, for what had gone before and what would surely follow.

The drawing room took on the feel of a church prepared for midnight mass. This was a kind of ritual; dream-like, unplanned, but inevitable. A celebration, or wake, for the death of delusion.

Karl, seated in an upright chair, felt the familiar curves of the cello between his knees. Scents of old, varnished wood mingled with the peppery incense. He set his bow to the strings and began to draw out deep, warm notes. He played a nocturne in a minor key, mournful and evocative. Charlotte, arrested, blew out her match and closed her eyes. He saw her body tauten, saw the tip of one fang indenting the rose-red curve of her lower lip.

The solitary line of music expressed all that had happened this evening. The mad leap from the mountain, the mutual bliss of killing. *How easy it was*, he thought, *when we hunted alone, to pretend we're better than we really are. Until thirst comes in a primitive rush and we fall on our prey like animals... And, dear God, it was so like making love. Devouring each other while that poor woman faded between us...*

As Karl played, Charlotte rose to her feet and began to dance. So hard, even now, not to see her as the sweet young mortal he had first met. So hard to believe she had shared the kill with him! In a dress of cream, rose and gold lace she was slender and graceful, her upright back and neat square shoulders swathed by waist-length hair. Her hair was a shimmering wreath of soft brown and gold, framing her lovely, ageless face. She smiled as she danced. She looked so carefree, so heartbreakingly pretty, no one would believe that blood had ever touched her lips.

Only her eyes had changed. The amethyst-grey irises were layered with experiences and sorrows that no mortal could imagine.

She was an elemental, a nymph, an enigma. Karl watched her rippling hair, the subtle roundness of her breasts, hips and thighs moving beneath the lace. He felt an intense longing to make love to her... but that could wait. They had all night.

The nocturne wound to its sombre end. Charlotte curtseyed, her arms stretched behind her like wings.

"I'm not Violette," she said apologetically.

"Thank God for that," said Karl.

She came to him and stroked his hair. "Do you still dislike her so much?"

"*Liebchen*, as I keep telling you, I don't dislike her. I meant that I want to be with you, no one else. And I do not want to talk about Violette."

"But we must."

"Why?"

"Well, we can't talk about..." She gestured at the window, meaning the outside world, the forest, the shared feast. "Can we?"

He folded his fingers around her hand. "Not yet."

"I'm sure Violette will be all right. As long as she goes on dancing, there's hope."

"That she won't destroy us?"

"That she'll keep her sanity, and not be unhappy."

"And not carry out her threats against us?" Karl said.

"Dear, she wasn't herself."

"Yet she said it. She threatened to take you from me, and change us both into people we would not recognise. I can't afford to ignore that."

Karl wished Charlotte would forget Violette, but it was Charlotte's obsession that had made her into a vampire. Now she felt endlessly responsible for the dancer.

"However," he went on, "I won't live under the shadow of any threat. I had enough of that with Kristian. We're free now. I refuse to fear Violette."

"I'm not afraid of her. I made her." Charlotte knelt beside him, her face shining in the candlelight. "She's like my mother, daughter, sister –" Karl was glad she didn't add *lover* "– and I won't turn my back on her."

"Of course not, but that doesn't mean she's not dangerous. The last time I saw the three supposed 'angels', they warned me against her. Although I don't trust them, I think the warning was genuine." Memory enveloped him. He felt the frost-burn of the *Weisskalt* and saw the three – angels or devils, they had been more than vampires – leaping like jets of fire into the black cauldron of space. Simon, Fyodor, Rasmila – who also called themselves by mythical names: Senoy, Sansenoy, and Semangelof.

Karl wondered what had become of them.

"We should be cautious, that's all."

Her hand, rosy with stolen blood, rested on his thigh. "Yes, but we must remain friendly with her. If we avoid her, that may make her more dangerous."

She looked anxious for his reaction, but for once he agreed with her. "You're right, beloved. Safer to keep an eye on her, no?"

Charlotte relaxed. "It will be all right, Karl. Play for me again."

This time she remained beside him, sitting on the carpet with her head resting on his thigh as he played. The strings were responsive under his fingers; he'd lost none of his once-human touch. The slow melody drew them deeper into the lake of sensuality. Sharing a victim had generated a richer desire that they could only sate on each other. Each felt the moment drawing nearer... the unutterable joy of fulfilment becoming deliciously, languorously inevitable.

Karl played the last note, and leaned down to kiss Charlotte. Her tongue touched his lips, parted his teeth; he tasted blood in the sweetness of her mouth.

"I always remember the first time you kissed me," she whispered. "Do you?"

"In the garden at Parkland Hall, on the bridge. I had tried for so long not to give in."

"And you said that you were bound to hurt me."

"But that night you came to my room anyway," he said, his words running into hers. "I knew that if we went any further I might be unable to control the blood thirst, but I couldn't stop."

"Nor could I. I didn't care about the consequences, my reputation or anything. Even when you said you couldn't marry me. The secrecy was terrible. It almost broke my heart, knowing it couldn't last, but not knowing why."

"I could hardly have told you I was a vampire."

"I wish you had, instead of the way I did find out! But I can't regret it. The secrecy was also delicious, knowing we shared a bond that no one around us guessed."

"Your father would have wished to kill me," Karl said, smiling.

"And I thought David *had* killed you. Gods, when I thought I'd never see you again – I've no idea why I didn't die of a broken heart."

"Because you're strong."

"No... because I couldn't bear to believe you were gone forever. I thought if I hung on long enough, I could will you back into existence."

"In a way, you did. Ah, but I would not have put you through what happened for anything."

"But it was inevitable," she said, "from that moment on the bridge..."

Their mouths touched. A faint, unwelcome sense of intrusion made Karl draw away from her. He sat back in the chair, sighing.

"What is it?" she asked, puzzled.

"You are not concentrating," he said. "We have visitors."

Not visitors, but a deputation, Charlotte observed, trying to be as effortlessly courteous as Karl. Ilona, Karl's wayward daughter; blue-eyed, callous Pierre; Stefan and his mute twin, Niklas. With them came two immortals whom Charlotte had never met: Rachel, a white, rarefied creature with scarlet hair, and a small, monk-like man named John.

Charlotte was always pleased to see Stefan. She greeted him with a kiss. He smiled, but his bright, cornflower-blue gaze avoided hers.

"What brings you here?" she asked.

"This is a little awkward," he said softly, moving to Niklas's side. Both blond and china-skinned, their only physical difference was eye-colour. Niklas's irises were pale gold. His movements echoed Stefan's in mindless, silent reflection of his twin.

"Don't be coy," Ilona snapped. "We're here to talk about

Violette Lenoir." As always she looked exquisite, a perfect fashion plate with her bobbed hair, a sleek unstructured dress of dusky red flowing to just below her knees, a black silk rose on one hip.

"What is there to say about her?" Charlotte was instantly defensive. Karl quietly took the visitors' coats, betraying no reaction.

"You tell us," said Ilona, "what there is to say about Violette."

Without asking, Ilona wound up the gramophone and put on a record. The thin, cheerful lilt of a jazz band made an incongruous background as the vampires seated themselves around the drawing room. How awkward, Charlotte thought, that they had no social niceties to ease the atmosphere; she couldn't even offer them a drink. Like birds of prey they settled and gazed unblinking from lovely, piercing eyes. All watching her.

Charlotte busied herself stoking the fire and lighting lamps. As she finished, Karl came to stand beside her near the fireplace. Rachel, too, remained on her feet. She seemed restless, repeatedly touching her neck with both hands.

"Do you really think it's fair," Charlotte said, "to discuss Violette when she's not here to speak for herself?"

"You wouldn't want her here," said Rachel. "Believe me."

"Why?" Charlotte glanced at Karl, chilled.

John, the hard-eyed stranger, said, "Tell them."

Again Rachel scratched at her throat. "A vampire who places herself in the public eye is unnatural. We should exist as chameleons in the dusk. No human should know our faces or names. She's breaking the laws."

"There is no law," Charlotte said impatiently. "What does it matter if she's famous? No one will guess what she is."

"Someone might, if she reaches seventy or eighty without a line on her face," Pierre drawled. He didn't appear to be taking this seriously. Rachel shot him a vicious glance.

"It's not just that," she went on. "There's something wrong about her. It's no secret that she believes herself to be Lilith, the progenitor of all vampires. She's plainly mad and too powerful for her own good."

Charlotte's anger was fuelled by guilt. She feared Rachel was right, but couldn't accept it. "You don't even know her! At least give her a chance before condemning her."

"Oh, we gave her a chance," said Rachel. "We went to see her. We asked her politely to stop dancing, to stay well away from humans and vampires alike."

"Well, I can imagine how she reacted to that. Who went, exactly?"

Stefan answered uneasily, "Niklas and myself, Rachel, John and Matthew." Cautiously he met Charlotte's eyes. She glared, but he held her gaze.

"Not Ilona and Pierre?"

They shook their heads. Ilona said, "We're only here now because Stefan seems to think it's so important."

"Much ado about nothing," Pierre added, "but amusing."

"Nothing?" Rachel's chalky face lengthened. "I tried to set aside the fact that she murdered my friend Katerina –"

"Katerina could be *very* provoking," Ilona put in flippantly. Charlotte could have struck her for saying this in front of Karl, who had loved Katerina.

"I tried to be fair," Rachel continued, "but she wouldn't listen. John, you tell them. I can't."

John leaned forward, his eyes black with hatred. His modern but shabby suit hung on him like a stage costume. "Matthew is dead. She killed him. He was the dearest companion of my heart, my only refuge from the madness of this century, and she slew him. She tore off his head with her hands."

Charlotte gaped. "How? *Why?* What did he do?"

"Nothing!" John flared. "She flew into a rage and attacked him for no reason!"

Stefan added quietly, "Actually, Matthew suggested that unless she took our advice, her ballet dancers might be in danger."

"Oh, God," Charlotte gasped. "He threatened their lives, and you're surprised that she reacted? She would give her life to protect them!"

"But it was only a threat, mere words," said Rachel. "She didn't argue, she *tore off his head*. And that proves my point. She's insane, capricious, a danger to all vampires." Again she rubbed her neck, fingers tangling in her flame-red hair. "She attacked me, too... and I've lost myself. I'm so afraid."

A long, heavy silence. Charlotte watched Rachel in dismay,

realising she was not merely agitated but in torment. She thought, *Violette has done this*.

Controlling her emotions, she said, "What do you expect us to do?"

"You made her immortal," said John.

"But I didn't act alone." She willed Stefan to come to her defence, but he only shook his head, looking helpless.

"It's no good appealing to him," Ilona said tartly. "Stefan may have helped in the transformation, but we all know you initiated it. And the fact that Katerina also took part did not inhibit Violette from slicing off her head."

Charlotte couldn't look at Karl. "She acted to save my life. And I can't know the truth about Matthew unless I hear Violette's side of the story. Why are you trying to turn me against her?"

"We don't want another Kristian!" said Rachel.

"Don't be ridiculous. She's not seeking to rule you." As Charlotte spoke, a ghastly memory rose of the way they'd banded together to assassinate Kristian. She felt Karl's hand on her shoulder and knew he was sharing her memories. Gods, were they proposing a similar lynch mob to destroy Violette?

John said, "We need to know why you transformed her."

"What business is it of yours?" Charlotte said indignantly, but Karl's hand grew heavier.

"Tell them," said Karl. "We have nothing to hide."

"All right." Charlotte composed herself, determined to outface them. "It was my fault. I forced her. I can't justify what I did. As a human she was beautiful and I was drawn to her... you know how it can be. But I never planned to change her – until I learned she had arthritis that would eventually stop her dancing. I couldn't bear her talent to be lost, or to see her grow old and crippled. Was I selfish? I wanted her to stay perfect forever."

Karl's fingers were now so tight that they hurt like the kiss of fangs.

"And then she went crazy," said Pierre. "Stefan told us."

Charlotte felt betrayed that Stefan had told others about such intimate and painful events.

"Which of you didn't go mad in the first moment of becoming undead?" she said. "Who wasn't horrified by the blood thirst, who didn't believe themselves damned?"

"Damned, yes," John said thinly, "but none of us became Lilith, the queen of vampires."

Charlotte said helplessly, "I can't explain. It's too complicated. I could theorise all night, but I have no answers."

"When you made her," said John, "every vampire felt a darkening of the ether. Everyone knew! She's sown a seed of darkness in the Crystal Ring that will destroy us all."

Charlotte didn't reply. She had noticed changes in the Crystal Ring but couldn't talk about them, even to Karl.

"And what of you, Karl?" said John. "Have you nothing to say?"

"Like Charlotte, I prefer to reserve judgement until I've spoken to Violette," Karl said like the diplomat he was. Charlotte wished he would defend her wholeheartedly. She understood his distrust of Violette, but all the same, she hated it. He added, "Violette may present danger. However, I trust that you are proposing caution rather than assassination. We are not extremists, and like Rachel we all prefer a quiet existence. That is why we opposed Kristian. Let's remember that we're all on the same side."

"Of course we are!" said Stefan. John's expression remained closed.

Charlotte decided to speak plainly. "Yes, it's my fault Violette was initiated, and I take full responsibility. You don't know her! Until you understand her reasons, don't pass judgement on her. All she cares about is dancing; why should she be remotely interested in any of you? Don't pester her, and she won't touch you. But if you approach her with threats, what do you expect? Leave her in peace and you'll be safe. You have my word."

"You must be very sure of your influence over her," Rachel said acidly.

"I cannot forget Matthew," said John. "An eye for an eye…"

"If you go anywhere near her –" Charlotte flared, close to losing control.

"I support Charlotte," Pierre broke in. "The whole thing is ludicrous. What's become of us, that one neurotic fledgling sends us screaming for *maman*? Grow up and leave Violette alone."

Charlotte ignored him. Why was it callous, sarcastic Pierre

who came to her defence, not the ones she really cared about, Stefan and Karl?

"Do whatever you like," Rachel said, her voice faint. She leaned against the windows, ghostly pale against the night. "I want nothing more to do with Violette. I want…"

"Where are you going?" John cried.

"I don't know. Away."

And she vanished into the Crystal Ring.

"It appears the case for the prosecution is collapsing," said Charlotte, looking pointedly at Stefan. "I think you'd all better leave."

Karl, expressionless, brought their coats and distributed them without ceremony.

John left without a word, but the look he gave Charlotte was sourly threatening, almost deranged. He seemed entrenched in age-old dogma of God and Satan, as Kristian had been. *I don't know you,* she thought. *I don't care what you believe, just get out of our house and leave us alone!*

Ilona, unperturbed, presented herself to Karl. He kissed her forehead. Charlotte was learning to read his feelings, for all his skill at hiding them. She saw his ancient sorrow and the bittersweet love he felt for his daughter.

Charlotte said, "Ilona, you don't agree with them, do you?"

Ilona turned to her with a cool smile. "Very little frightens me, dear, except Violette. For some reason she scares me to death. But I won't give in to her."

The admission floored Charlotte. Before she could respond, Ilona melted into the Crystal Ring. Pierre gave a sardonic bow and followed.

Stefan glanced at Charlotte, as if intending to leave without saying anything. She said, "Wait a moment."

He came to her, Niklas a silent mirror image at his side. His hair was a white-gold nimbus, his eyes angelic. His was a teasing cruelty: he loved to rouse affection before he stole blood.

"Are you angry with me?" Stefan said. "H'm, silly question."

"How could you turn against Violette, when you know what she is to me? You helped to transform her!"

"Charlotte." He touched her arm lightly. "I haven't turned

against her. I only said what I believe."

"And so did I." She looked sideways at Karl. He was watching her, one side of his face lit by fire, the other in shadow.

"You know my feelings," said Karl. "I don't trust Violette, but there are very few whom I *do* trust."

"When I came into the Crystal Ring," said Charlotte, "I signed no agreement that I must answer to other immortals."

"We answer to no one."

"Then why do I have to suffer crowds of them coming here and threatening my friend?"

"I didn't threaten her," said Stefan. "I'm truly concerned about her, and have been since the moment of her transformation, as you know perfectly well. If anything, I was trying to protect her. I went to her in friendship; unfortunately, the others had different ideas and things got out of hand. It was meant to be a friendly warning, because if she doesn't take herself out of the public eye and live a quiet life, she is going to make enemies far worse than John and Rachel."

Karl was alone in the library, near dawn, when another unwelcome visitor came. Charlotte had gone to rest in the Crystal Ring; they each needed time to gather their thoughts. Karl sat looking through a large volume of mythology, searching for references to Lilith. Now and then he made notes on a writing pad.

He thought about Benedict and Lancelyn, two human occultists who'd foolishly tried to claim power over vampires. Karl, in trying to limit the chaos they caused, had almost lost Charlotte to Violette.

I understand Charlotte's fascination with her, he thought ruefully. *It might be easy to dismiss Violette's belief that she is Lilith as a delusion... if it hadn't been for the angels.*

Simon, Fyodor and Rasmila had appeared to be vampires like any other, until revealing themselves as dual beings: heavenly envoys whose purpose was to tame Lilith. *So*, Karl wondered, *were they all suffering the same delusion?* Lancelyn, too, had seen extraordinary qualities in Violette. Calling her the Black Goddess, he had sought immortality and enlightenment through her. *And*, Karl reflected, *he would have made a formidable immortal...*

But Violette had left Lancelyn writhing in madness. Devastated by his brother's fate, Benedict had turned away from the occult.

And the angels?

They'd been ruthless in helping Lancelyn to control Lilith. They'd kidnapped her, tortured Karl, almost killed Charlotte and Stefan. Yet when Violette-as-Lilith rejected their authority, they had fled.

Karl recalled his last encounter with Rasmila, Fyodor and Simon in the *Weisskalt*, the highest glacial layer of the Crystal Ring. Before vanishing, they had delivered a simple warning: *"For as long as she roams free, Lilith will cause untold harm and sorrow... One day you will have to stop her."*

He wished Charlotte had never met her. But perhaps the Crystal Ring – or Raqia, as Benedict called it – had used Charlotte as a catalyst in Violette's fate.

"That would make sense, if I believed in such things as fate," he murmured.

An oil lamp burned; beyond its glow, the library lay in shadow. Suddenly aware of an intruder, Karl looked up and saw a gilded figure manifesting by the far window. The newcomer's clothing was modern, unremarkable, but his appearance was striking. Golden skin, a bright halo of hair, topaz eyes. He looked like a Grecian deity, or a lion in human form.

After their last encounter, Karl had neither expected nor wanted to see him again. The intruder smiled as he approached.

"Simon," Karl said, sitting back in his chair. "I would thank you not to walk in unannounced."

"My dear fellow, what sort of greeting is this? You surely don't expect me to knock at the front door like a human?"

"It would have been courteous."

"Then I apologise for violating your privacy," Simon said with apparent sincerity. "What are you writing?"

"Nothing that concerns you."

Simon chuckled. "Be careful what you write, Karl. It may come back to haunt you."

"What do you want?" Karl couldn't forget that Simon had tortured and tried to kill his friends. "I thought I'd seen the last of you."

"I hoped so too." Simon gave him a cool look. "But things change."

"Where are your companions? I thought you were inseparable."

Simon wandered to a bookshelf and chose a book at random. "After the matter of Lilith, we had a difference of opinion and went our separate ways."

"And I thought you had ascended to heaven."

"There is no need for sarcasm, Karl." He flicked through the book without interest, pushed it back on the shelf. His presence was intimidating, dazzling like the sun, but Karl suspected he was troubled. "No, we returned to Earth."

"In what sense?"

"In every sense. When we failed to tame Lilith, God had no further use for us. He abandoned us. Fyodor and Rasmila blamed me."

"How unfair." Karl rose and moved in front of the table, half-sitting on its edge. "So, are you still the angel Senoy, or a mere vampire?"

Simon looked away, brooding. "I don't know. Can you imagine how it feels, having looked upon the ineffable face of God, to be cut off from the light?"

Curiosity got the better of Karl. "To be honest, I can't. What happened?"

To his surprise, Simon was in a confiding mood. He answered, "After we left you we flew above the *Weisskalt* as if we were invincible... Perhaps euphoria made us overconfident. We became cold and lost our way. The light blinded us. We fell a long way back to Earth. Fyodor almost died. And we realised that God had forsaken us. To teach us humility, I suppose."

"That must have been devastating," Karl said without inflexion. "But before, how did it feel to be an angel?"

"'Envoy' is the more accurate term."

"Less romantic."

Simon looked up. His eyes were sunlit orbs: single-minded, pitiless, alien. "How to describe it? I simply *knew*. God spoke to us from within the light. We had power, and knew many things that ordinary vampires did not: how to find individuals with special gifts such as Sebastian, Kristian or Lancelyn. I always knew what to do. Make Kristian a vampire and he'll be a magnificent ruler. Watch over Lancelyn because he has a destiny. Watch Violette because she is God's enemy... Even while we slept in the *Weisskalt,* we remained sentient. Isn't that proof of God's existence?"

"I have no idea," Karl said flatly.

"When we woke and became whole again, we became the angels tasked with taming Lilith. Such deep knowledge can't be explained. But Karl, it was glorious!"

"And then it ended."

"Rasmila and Fyodor were ready to accept defeat," he said with contempt. "They were lost souls. They clung to me like children, as if I could restore our status! And I grew sick of them."

"Callous," said Karl.

"Am I? Are angels callous, even disempowered ones? Perhaps. I need vampires around me..."

"As an audience? Lovers? Slaves? I suppose Rasmila and Fyodor were all of those."

Simon's eyes glinted. "I need to be at the heart of events! I can't bear to see everything fall apart."

There was naked pain in his voice. Karl felt no sympathy. "Go back to sleep in the *Weisskalt* then. Your suffering will be over."

"I find your attitude unhelpful."

"So you've lost your friends and your power? I fail to see what I can do about it."

"But it's partly your fault, Karl." Simon came closer. "There's a task I must complete before God will let me back into the fold. It's a test. I must prove myself to Him."

Karl laughed. He had no time for God. Simon's pupils contracted to points.

"You could have been my equal, Karl. Confronting the three of us in the *Weisskalt,* you showed no fear, only world-weary insolence. That reveals incredible strength! You slaughtered Kristian and almost killed me. Other vampires saw this power in you and begged you to lead them. You could have been great, yet you threw the chance away. Diminished yourself for the sake of a quiet life. Is this really what you want?"

Karl observed Simon carefully, gauging whether he might turn violent. "I have no interest in the power that Kristian or Lancelyn craved. I don't see it as diminishment, but even if it is, what does it matter?"

"Ah. So you're content for vampires to remain a leaderless rabble?"

Karl laughed. "Quite so."

"You find this a joke?" Simon said, raising his eyebrows. He walked in a slow loop around the table, glancing at Karl's book as he passed. "*Myths of Babylonia and Assyria*," he read. "How interesting. Lilith as wind-hag."

Karl, normally placid, was growing irritated.

"I see," he said. "You're here to establish where I stand on the question of leadership. But why?"

"Things are going wrong, Karl. Raqia is growing hostile. You might say that heaven has turned against us – and this is Lilith's doing! We had to tame her, but we failed. Without control, she creates chaos. We gave you a very clear warning, but you've done nothing."

"Violette's only interest is ballet. I don't think touring *Swan Lake* or *Coppélia* is going to destroy the world."

As he spoke, Karl thought of the visit from Stefan and the others, their description of Violette's behaviour. *She tore off Matthew's head with her bare hands*. Karl recalled the steel-calm way in which she'd dispatched Katerina under the wheels of a train…

"And you approve, do you?" said Simon. "A vampire flaunting herself in public?"

"God, I've heard enough of this," Karl murmured. "It's up to her."

"But it isn't. You think she's harmless? She will ruin us all!"

Karl knew Violette was far from harmless. Even Charlotte's resolve to remain friendly with her was a subtle attempt at control.

"Vampires need unity," Simon went on. "Fragmented, we cannot defend ourselves against her. We need a focus."

"I hope you are not asking me to be this focus."

Their eyes met. The look was a mutual challenge, the repulsion of opposites. Then Simon's expression changed, softening to one of earnest hope, reconciliation. "Karl, don't let us argue. We had such a fight, you and I; the torment you endured was tremendous. Yet you survived. I admire you greatly for that. Can you accept my apology?"

Karl stiffened. "It is hard to forget that you starved me almost to death, and made me attack my own friends. I admit, you seem more tolerable for not being drunk on power. If I were you, I'd leave it that way. Why do you suddenly want forgiveness?"

"You have such strength, Karl! Kristian's followers offered you leadership, because they saw qualities in you that you can't see for yourself."

"I've given you my answer. No. If you're so obsessed, why not seize power yourself?"

"Perhaps I should." Simon leaned close to him, his tone passionate. "However, it's not my vocation. If I tried, I'd be failing the test. God's role for me is to be the kingmaker, not the king. That's what we did with Kristian, and almost succeeded with Lancelyn. That's my duty: to make the best choice. This time, I must not fail."

Karl drew away. "Ah. The puppet master. Lancelyn empowered you by calling on your help. Now you want the same of me, while I become your puppet?"

"It's not like that. You're missing the point. I act for God, not for myself. We need a leader for the benefit of vampire-kind."

"Even though these would-be leaders have caused all our troubles?" Karl said acidly.

"So take on the role and make it what you want!" Simon turned scornful. "I find you incredible, Karl. You do momentous things like murdering Kristian, creating Charlotte, protecting Lilith – then you sit back and say you want a quiet life?"

"You make it sound as if I've earned it," Karl said mordantly.

"If I go to someone else, you will be sorry."

"Please tell me you are not considering Sebastian Pierse."

Simon grinned viciously. "Now wouldn't he make a leader to be reckoned with?"

"He'd be worse than Kristian. At least Kristian had a code of behaviour, albeit warped."

"You had the choice, Karl." Karl sensed frustration behind the grin. And fear, perhaps. "One last chance to change your mind."

"No. I won't be blackmailed. You'll never find Sebastian; even Kristian couldn't track him down. No, I won't change my mind. I once thought we might be friends," Karl said sadly. "You reminded me of a human I once knew, a brave and decent man, a war hero. But you're a liar. You enjoyed tormenting us. You speak of God's plan, yet all you care about is getting your own way. You're no archangel, never were. Don't talk to me about the good of vampire-kind, when you secretly despise us all."

Simon glared. Karl saw crimson fire behind his golden eyes, the worm eating at the rose. Finally he said grimly, "No, you're right. You wouldn't make a suitable leader. You're weak. Love for Charlotte has blinded you to Lilith's evil. I should have known better than to try reasoning with an atheist."

"I'd sooner go to hell than bow to your cruel God," Karl retorted coldly.

"How can you not believe?" Simon gathered himself like a tiger ready to pounce.

Yes, Karl thought, *I was right. He's deluded and dangerous – but he'll never intimidate me.*

"Many folk claim that God speaks to them," Karl said. "Strange, that he says something quite different to each one."

"I'll find my way back to Him, and your blind heresy will not stop me, friend-of-Lilith. Traitor."

Simon's hands rose in claws and his fangs extended to their full length.

"Don't," Karl said quietly.

Simon ignored the command. Swift and savage, he lunged, struck Karl across the face, seized his throat two-handed. Wedged back against the table, Karl could not dislodge him. Simon gripped him by the collarbone and the chin, stretching Karl's throat between his hands. His staring eyes were like Niklas's; the iced-gold, mindless eyes of a *doppelgänger*.

"If God creates angels like you," Karl rasped, "we are damned, for certain."

He thrust his hands upwards in prayer position between Simon's arms and stabbed his fingers at those glorious eyes. Simon loosed his grip to defend himself. Karl kicked his legs from under him and dropped on top of him, his hands clamping Simon's elbows to the floor, the tips of his canines touching the angelic neck. The flesh was peach-soft.

Karl did not bite. Instead he pulled back. "I don't want a single mouthful of your blood. I remember what happened when Rasmila so generously gave me hers. A trap to put me in your control."

Simon looked defeated, furious. Karl thought, *He's lost his way and he's frightened of something. Very frightened.*

"You should leave," said Karl. "If you wish to discuss anything in a civilised fashion, by all means call again. But if you threaten me, or lay a finger on my friends, I'll bury you with Kristian."

He rose to his feet, letting Simon up.

"You've made a grave error," said Simon, "but then, I suppose you've had a lot of practice." The vitriol of his stare could have melted glass. He pushed past Karl, looking back over his shoulder as he faded into the Crystal Ring. "You're going to hell with Lilith, for certain."

CHAPTER THREE

THE CLAWS OF THE OWL

Kristian was dead, but Schloss Holdenstein remained: an age-raddled pile of brown stone on a ridge above the river Rhine, crowned with decaying roofs and turrets. Its silhouette crouched like a beast against the creamy sky. Rocks and ancient trees crusted its flanks. The hillside below fell steeply to the river, fell again into the green mirror of the water.

Isolated in its forest wilderness, the castle lived under no human laws.

It lived once, thought Cesare, *but now it is dying*.

Every day Cesare would wander the tortuous corridors of the castle, the cramped, windowless chambers, the staircases leading up or down at mad angles. Sorrow and desolation breathed from the very walls. How empty, how drear this place was without Kristian, their master. Deserted and dying of grief...

He would always pause in the meeting room, the large chamber where Kristian had held court. The ebony throne remained. Cesare imagined Kristian's presence everywhere, as if to will the master back to life. He dreamed and mourned, dry-eyed.

And then he would return to his own cell, and meditate on the futility of existence.

There were a few vampires still left in the Schloss, but he might as well have been alone. They never spoke to each other. There was nothing to say.

When Kristian first disappeared, Cesare and the other disciples had tried to carry on as normal. Almost two years they'd waited, held together by faith that Kristian would return.

Instead, Karl had come to tell them that Kristian was dead.

Devastation. Knowing they were lost without their leader, he had told Karl – as if yielding to a new king – "You took him from us, so you must take his place!"

Karl had refused. In his anguish, Cesare had tried to kill him. Karl had won, almost severing Cesare's head in the process.

After the wound healed, Cesare changed. He no longer cared. Without Kristian, there was nothing to live for. Now he and the others, remnants who couldn't face the world beyond the castle, merely existed. They went out at night to drink human blood or energy, rested in the Crystal Ring, prayed to their cruel God. The rest of the time, all those interminable hours, they huddled in their cells, questioning nothing. No one new came or went. Nothing changed.

Cesare drifted through eternity in the depths of misery, dead inside.

When dawn found him one morning, cross-legged on the flagstones with a book of Kristian's writings in his lap, he thought he was imagining a new presence in the castle. He felt a shadow brush his mind, walking the corridors towards his cell...

"Cesare," said a raw, whispering voice.

He looked up, saw a vampire in a shabby dark suit. Colourless face, eyes pouched with grief, short hair standing on end. A sack dangled from his left hand.

It was a face Cesare hadn't seen for a hundred and fifty years. Impossible. He put the book aside and stood, shaking creases out of his robe. "Who are you?"

"You know me."

Cesare frowned. "John?"

"Yes, I am John. You must help me!"

Memory woke, and a splinter of black anger pierced the greyness. "But Kristian put you in the *Weisskalt*."

"I woke up." John's eyes were glassy, maniacal. "Kristian's death woke us and we escaped."

"You were Kristian's enemies, you and that traitor Matthew." Cesare's anger surged, exhilarating and uncontrollable. *So I'm not quite dead, after all.* "You attacked him."

"And we were punished. Don't turn me away."

Cesare was so stunned to be thinking, feeling, talking, that however deeply he'd hated John, he wanted to keep him here. "What do you want?"

John lifted the sack and thrust his hand inside. Then he let the sack fall to the floor. Between his hands he cradled a severed head.

Cesare stared at the distorted features. Its mouth and eyes drooped with sour pain. The neck stump was horribly ragged. "What happened?"

Tears ran down John's face. Finally he whispered, "It's Matthew. Someone – she –" He shook his head, swallowed. "I heard that Kristian could bring vampires back to life if he had the head. Do you know how?"

Cesare pondered, his own misery forgotten. "Why should I help you? I loved Kristian, you despised him. We can't be friends."

"Please!" John was trembling.

Cesare thought, *How pleasing to have this creature at my mercy!* "Why did you reject Kristian? Tell me!"

"He was arrogant." John hugged the repulsive head to his chest. "He wouldn't see that vampires are the Devil's possessions and must submit to God's punishment. Kristian dared to invoke God as if we were blessed, not damned. Blasphemous arrogance!"

Cesare broke in impatiently, "Not blasphemy. God has a use for us. We are not the punished, but the *punishers*. Our purpose is to visit God's wrath on mankind! This is a noble duty, not an evil one. John, we hold the same beliefs. The only difference is that Kristian's followers take pride in what we are."

"Pride is a sin."

"Very well, believe you're damned, if you must. But even the damned have a place in the Almighty's plan."

John's face lengthened with desperate hope. "If I could only believe you."

Then Cesare no longer felt hostile towards him. He felt fatherly. John's fault was ignorance, which could be remedied. Cesare gripped his shoulder. "We can debate to our heart's content. It's too long since I had the chance of a theological argument!"

John stared, his eyes wild. "So you'll help us?"

Cesare lifted the grotesque burden out of his arms, as tenderly as if it were a baby. "Come, let's begin. The head must be immersed in blood every day. Fresh human blood."

Vampires neither sleep nor dream, Violette had been told. So what were the nightmares that assailed her in the Crystal Ring?

Although Raqia terrified her, she couldn't stay away. She tried to resist, but a masochistic urge would overcome her, like dark music enticing her mind and body. The sidestep she made into the vampire realm was as easy as breathing. The world faded. Her own cells seemed to melt and form a new shape as she found herself in a wind-blown forest of shadows, under a sky of purple flame.

The sky drew her. She climbed a coil of cloud that frayed into nothingness under her thin, taloned hands. Black, her hands, with skin like a lizard: each scale a flake of jet. She felt as thin and hard as a whip, weightless.

If my body is so changed, she wondered, *is my face that of a demon, with eyes like red braziers? I can never see my own face here!*

She let go of her thoughts as she climbed. She was all sensation, a dancer. Her hair writhed like Medusa snakes.

Raqia was not a true sky but a strange multi-layered dimension. Mountains sailed in the void, but they were insubstantial, dissolving and reforming like clouds. Tonight they were bruise-coloured, racing on a mad wind, crimson light pouring down them like blood.

Occasional lightning bleached the void from indigo to pale amethyst. She heard thunder.

How cold it was. Desolate, vertiginous. All this sweeping emptiness without a soul to be seen. So much beauty and energy wasted. The emptiness chilled her.

She struggled to climb above the storm, but wind currents flung her around like a twig on the ocean. She stretched out on a cushion of air and closed her eyes, giving herself up to the rise and fall of turbulence. She was frozen to the bone, but didn't care.

In the Crystal Ring she could forget her thirst.

The trance came swiftly. Floating in Raqia gave immortals respite from perpetual consciousness. At least, that was how it should be – but Violette experienced a leering carnival of memories. She could remain alert and fight the blood thirst, or rest and face her visions. The choice crushed her between millstones and ground her flat. But she chose the trance.

At first she was on stage, dancing, carefree. The green cave of scenery was a self-contained world, while the audience, unseen beyond the spotlights, did not exist. This was her solace and her purpose. Her addiction. Dancing took away her pain.

But three shadows waited in the wings.

She danced harder and faster but could not drive them away. Her chest ached with exhaustion. She couldn't breathe. There were hands on her throat, a distorted male face glaring into hers.

Her father's face, his rasping voice. "This black hair is from the Devil, Vi. All women are bloodsuckers. All women belong to the Devil."

She couldn't answer this injustice. His belief infected her as his hands squeezed out her life... then suddenly he was torn away. She watched him borne into the distance by asylum attendants, but the horror stayed inside her.

He metamorphosed into someone else, another man whom she'd driven mad. Not intentionally, never that. It happened without her willing it. And this irascible and obsessive goat, a self-styled magus named Lancelyn, had called her Goddess.

Goddess, devil... no one knew who she really was.

Her father, Lancelyn, Janacek and others... they loomed over her, these men of power; covetous, possessive, lustful. She cowered and obeyed, hating them... until something inside her lashed out, a reptilian tongue of flame to scorch them and free herself.

Can't I have freedom without destroying them? Why could they not love me without making me hate them? Yet it couldn't be otherwise. They needed to control me but I am too strong. A demon.

The three shadows watched and smiled.

Violette stood by her mentor Janacek's grave and saw a woman watching her from the trees... Charlotte was demure in mourning black, her eyes clear and steady under the brim of her hat.

Come to me, Violette, said her eyes. *I'll change you into what you are meant to be. I killed Janacek to free you!*

Charlotte came out of the shadows to lure Violette into

darkness... but Violette's soul was already darker than a vampire's. It was she who swallowed Charlotte whole.

She was dancing again, but struggling now. Her chest hurt. She couldn't feel the stage beneath her toes, and with every step she stumbled. Looking down, she saw that her feet had become owl claws.

Violette shook herself out of the hallucination, trying to scream. She couldn't make a sound. Even if she could, there was no one to hear.

Her panic subsided as swiftly as it had struck. She was used to this now. The visions were tormenting, but she'd learned not to fight them.

The Crystal Ring flung her down the rolling flank of a cloud. God, she was cold. And the pain was still there, a cruel hand squeezing her throat. Fire, from mouth to heart to abdomen.

The thirst.

It had shocked her awake with nightmares of strangulation, and now it forced her down towards the Earth.

Night closed over her. The Crystal Ring melted away, and the mortal world reappeared, warm and solid. Violette felt stone beneath her feet, looked down and saw ordinary feet in button-strap shoes. She was back in human form. She stared at her calves in silk stockings, the hem of her dark blue coat. Her cloche hat half-covered her eyes. She hoped no one would recognise her.

How tempting to imagine a miracle; that the Crystal Ring didn't exist, that her bad dreams of being owl, serpent, Lilith, vampire, had never happened. But the thirst remained to mock the wish.

I must feed, she thought.

She found herself near the Mirabell Palace, an iced cake of a building set in formal gardens. She heard the soft dance of fountains. All around her stood elegant square houses of the eighteenth century, and beyond, forested ridges rose against the midnight sky. A chamber orchestra played in a house nearby; there was always music in Salzburg. Violette pictured the musicians in the golden warmth of some salon, and her hunger leapt.

She walked towards the river.

Halfway across a bridge, she stopped and leaned on the parapet. People glanced at her as they passed. She needed their blood but she held herself rigid, staring at the river, thinking, *Soon, but not that one... not him... not her.*

Reflected lights hung in the water. To her left, a hundred yards along the bank, stood the pale green mansion that housed the Ballet Janacek. Some windows in the top storey were still lit up. Not all the *corps de ballet* had gone to bed. *Bad girls*, she thought. *We're soon to begin our American tour and you need your rest!*

Amazing that she could think of anything beyond the hunger.

I won't feed tonight, she thought. Her lip stung, nipped between her teeth. *I won't.*

On her right lay the old town, sheltered by the Mönchsberg Ridge. She could see lovely colours, invisible to humans, in the darkness. All the scintillating roofs, domes and spires of endless churches... She'd sought solace in them once, but what had they done to save her? And what would their priests do now, but denounce and revile her?

Her eyes, as she gazed at the beautiful churches, were cold.

Footsteps approached. Something felt wrong... The steps were slow, soft, yet oddly emphatic. The presence came towards her, but no human heat came with it.

A vampire.

She looked round. A man in a dark, expensively tailored coat and a cashmere scarf stood regarding her brazenly. He was good-looking, she supposed, in an insolent way; his hair was brown and curly beneath his hat, his eyes very blue but a little too large and widely spaced. He had the look of a charming sadist.

He said in French, "Madame Lenoir? I have been looking for you."

"Well, you've found me." She answered in the same language, but he detected her accent and switched to English.

"Forgive me, I'd assumed you were a compatriot."

"English names aren't the fashion in the ballet world," she said tartly, "but we can talk in English, French, German; whatever you wish, assuming we have anything to talk about, which I doubt."

His eyebrows lifted with amusement. "Madame, I am Pierre Lescaut. No doubt you have heard of me."

"Not that I can recall." This wasn't true. Karl often spoke of his wayward friend.

Removing his hat, he bowed extravagantly, then kissed her gloved hand before she could avoid him. "Well, now you have. I'm enchanted to meet you. I am a friend of Karl von Wultendorf. You know him, I understand?"

"Slightly."

"I find it incredible that he has not mentioned me."

"Perhaps you are of less importance to him than you realise."

Pierre's smile thinned. He leaned on the parapet beside her. He stood too close and she wanted to draw back, but pride would not let her give ground to him. "And you know Charlotte, Stefan, Niklas?" He sounded sarcastic. He must know that Charlotte and Stefan had initiated her.

"Of course," she said thinly.

"They are all talking about you – except Niklas, of course, who has very little to say about anything." He grinned, but his eyes were cruel. "That's why I had to satisfy my curiosity about the new immortal who is creating such interest. You know, you have not many friends, Madame Violette."

That made her look hard at him.

"Might we stroll together?" he added. "I think we should talk."

She thought, *Why? I have nothing to say to you.* But she glanced back at her ballet premises and imagined an unscrupulous vampire such as Pierre preying on her darlings. The idea filled her with fury. So she slipped her hand through his proffered arm and led him in the opposite direction.

"Let's climb to the Fortress," she said. "There is such a lovely view of the Alps from the other side of the ridge."

Rain began to fall as they walked. The pavements shone. The steep cobbled path that wound up between the trees towards the Fortress Hohensalzburg seemed to run with mercury.

Pierre held Violette's satin-sheathed hand in the crook of his elbow, congratulating himself. What superstitious fools had Kristian left behind? How could they be afraid of this lily?

Pierre thought he was falling in love. He actually felt protective towards her, when in the past he'd never given a damn for anyone but himself.

She was stunning, a goddess among mortals and vampires alike. The combination of pale skin and black hair was irresistible, like an exotic Beardsley drawing. Her large eyes, enhanced by the velvety strokes of her brows and lashes, were truly violet; not amethyst-grey like Charlotte's, but the luminous indigo of the Crystal Ring itself. She seemed both delicate and strong. Imperturbable – but hardly likely to perturb anyone else.

He said, "I believe you need to feed, Madame."

"You're observant."

"It's obvious from your pallor, your whole demeanour. I know this… tension. You should not wait too long."

Her face transformed. Her serenity became rage, blazing from her eyes. He actually recoiled.

"Don't tell me how to conduct myself," she said.

One glimpse, then the shutters folded down once more. Pierre exhaled. Shocked at first, he felt a frisson of excitement.

"I pity the poor human who runs into you, *chérie*."

"Don't pity them," she said tightly. "I can control the thirst, if you can't."

"Can you?"

"And I am not your *chérie*."

"Forgive me, Madame. I did not mean my idle remarks to offend you. *Mon Dieu*, perhaps there's something in what they say after all."

"What do they say?"

They had reached the Fortress. The walls stood dark and impenetrable against the sky; trees rustled in the darkness, alive with the patter of raindrops. The air smelled deliciously earthy.

The gates were locked, but the Crystal Ring let them pass through barriers of wood and iron, and into a huge corridor that curved steeply upwards. Behind immense walls, the museum and staterooms lay in darkness. Tour guides and staff slumbered, a troupe of boy scouts slept in the old barrack rooms. A succulent treat for later, Pierre mused. The few sentries who kept watch were oblivious to the vampires' presence.

"Well, certain immortals believe you are mad, although who they are to judge, I've no idea," said Pierre. "They claim that you tore off a vampire's head with your bare hands – frankly incredible. They have paranoid conviction that you are… how can I put it? Not a conventional vampire, if such a beast ever existed."

"Who said these things?"

"Oh, everyone."

"Stefan?"

They crossed a courtyard and descended some steps to a terrace with a waist-high wall. The Fortress rose in all its masculine weight behind them. In front lay a sweeping view of the valley, sky and mountains.

"Yes, Stefan, Niklas, Karl, Rachel, Ilona, John. They went to Karl and Charlotte's house yesterday evening, to tell Charlotte that she's created a monster."

"And you happened to be there?"

"Only because Ilona insisted I go. For Ilona to be so concerned is quite out of character. You have certainly stirred them up."

"If they think I'm a monster, what do they intend to do about it?" Her voice was paper-thin and soft, and like paper it could cut without warning.

"No decision was reached."

"Do they mean to kill me?"

"Perhaps."

She leaned on the wall, silent. Across the valley, the Alps pushed up from the Earth's crust under a frost-white web. The peaks were immense yet they seemed to float, as if weightless. The sky was dark, cloudy. Rain fell steadily, but Violette seemed oblivious.

Pierre watched her, fascinated. She had a true ballerina's neck, long and slender. He studied the creamy curve of her throat – as much of it as her black fur collar revealed – and felt a perverse desire to kiss her there.

After a time she asked, with evident difficulty, "What did Charlotte say?"

A breath flickered in Pierre's throat, not quite a laugh. "Oh, she defended you with passion, but it was a case of 'the lady doth protest too much.' She was panicking, because in her heart she agrees with them."

Violette bent her head. "Even Charlotte," she murmured. "So, I have no friends in the world, then?"

Pierre shrugged, lifting his hands. "It's a cruel world, Madame."

"It means nothing. I'd guessed, anyway."

He moved closer. "Surely it means something. I came to warn you."

"Why?" Seeing deep suspicion in her expression, Pierre felt wounded.

"I refused to believe them, Madame, until I could make up my own mind. Now I have met you, my opinion is that they are a bunch of hysterics. Clearly you are a gracious and gentle creature who harbours ill intentions towards no one. *Ma chérie*, you won't even feed on humans until the need nearly kills you – will you?"

He ventured to put a hand on her shoulder. She looked at the hand, then at him. "What are you doing?"

He placed his other hand over hers, where it rested on the wall. "You have one friend."

He leaned towards her. Couldn't resist. Her scent was gorgeous: floral perfume mingling with satin, rosin dust, wood polish from her studio. But no taint of blood. She was clearly starving, her flesh drawn against the bones. Pierre shook with excitement. How could another vampire be as alluring as a human victim? He reminded himself that she wasn't human, that he must approach her not with his usual gleeful confidence, but with delicacy.

"You, my friend?" she said. "I think not."

Her coldness dismayed him. "But I have –"

"You have done nothing but mock me since we met. I've no idea what you're playing at, Monsieur Lescaut, but it is nothing kind. Nothing sincere."

"I am not mocking you." His hand slid along her shoulder and rested on her spine. *Careful*, he told himself. *Use all your charm.* "Why did you walk here with me, Violette, if you did not see something to your liking? We are not human, we need not pretend. Nor waste any time."

"What do you want?" She looked alarmed. That was good. It meant he'd got the upper hand.

"To kiss you."

"Oh," she said softly. "So you want to kiss me, do you?"

Oh God, yes, he thought, but she put a finger to his lips. Her whole manner changed; seductive softness came to her mouth and eyes. "Wait. Let me kiss you."

In an ecstasy of excitement, Pierre smiled and closed his eyes. "Whatever you say."

He knew he'd made a mistake, half a second after it was too late. Her hands slid softly over his shoulders. She leaned into him, her face questing towards his. Then, in a flash, her fingers became steel traps, and her mouth slid along his jawline and fastened on his throat.

His eyes flew open. He gripped her wrists, couldn't shift her. Her fangs darted into him and he felt her shudder from head to toe, felt the unvoiced release rumbling through her like the purr of a lioness.

Other vampires had fed on him before; it wasn't so bad, could even be pleasurable. But this was hideous. The first taste of blood seemed to madden her, and she unleashed all her pent-up hunger on him. She pushed him back across the terrace wall, almost cracking his spine, and came down on top, tearing at his neck, sucking.

Helpless at first, Pierre began to struggle. His surrender should have been divine. Instead it was horrific. There was nothing sensual about her. She wasn't like Ilona: beautiful, savage, but still womanly. No, Violette was elemental, covering him like the wings of a vast, sharp-taloned owl.

She blocked his instinctive escape to the Crystal Ring, held him in place. Pain ran molten from his throat to his spine. Already she'd taken too much blood.

How intimately he knew the compulsive power of the thirst. He knew she would not be able to stop... And his own response, even through his agony, shamed him. An urge he rarely felt because blood thirst was everything to him, a need he despised as human: sexual desire.

Suddenly the pain ceased and her face rose over his. Blood gleamed on her lips. Her mouth and eyes were purple caves.

"Do you want to kiss me now, Pierre?" she said throatily. "You think me some pliant doll you can jeer at, then have just for the asking? My friend? You liar."

Her contempt quenched all desire. Panicking, he thrust his foot under her ankle to wrench her off-balance. Then he was away, evading her clawing limbs, taking long strides that brought him to his knees on the ground, his legs were so weak.

Pierre staggered up and ran on.

He crossed the courtyard to another open corridor, and found himself in a maze. High walls rose on all sides and steps led in three different directions. No sign of a way out. The Fortress was vast and he had no idea of its layout.

He felt her following him. Heard faint sounds like wingbeats, claws scraping the cobbles, an animal panting after its prey.

Pierre made another wild leap at the Crystal Ring, fell back like a bird with clipped wings. How had she stolen his strength so quickly?

He ran into a dark archway. She was behind him, playing cat-and-mouse, laughing. His heart pounded and he turned clammy, like a scared human.

She can tear off a vampire's head with those little hands...

He broke a lock, burst into a tower room, and ran up flights of stairs to the top chamber. On the far side was another door. He flung it open, found only a small flat roof beyond, just a lookout place, a dead end. He weighed his chances of simply throwing himself off the edge. A long fall down the outside of the Fortress... That appeared his only escape, and wouldn't kill him, but this was his inadmissible weakness: he hated heights.

Trapped in the chamber, Pierre could hear Violette climbing the stairs quite slowly after him. There were old weapons displayed on the walls for sightseers. Pierre grabbed a spear and crouched in an alcove to wait for her.

His fear turned to anger. This had happened too many times, a stronger vampire feeding on him, stealing his pride with his blood. Usually Kristian, sometimes Karl. Perversely, he hadn't minded so much – but from a female, it was insufferable.

An owl screeched far away in the forest. Dull light fanned through a leaded window and through the open door. She would probably sense his presence, but if she didn't – if her senses were dampened by her blood-feast – she might assume he was out on the roof.

He watched the stairwell, listening... and realised he could no longer hear her.

She's in the Crystal Ring, he thought, shivering.

The hairs rose on his neck and his head whipped round. She appeared – not from the stairwell but in the roof doorway, a silhouette in the dark-blue arch.

"I haven't finished with you," she said.

She glanced dismissively at the spear, and began to approach.

Pierre would not give her a chance to get near him. With a shout, he leapt up and charged, aiming the iron tip at her heart.

Startled, she hesitated. The tip passed between the long fur reveres of her coat and made contact. He felt the fabric of her dress tear, felt her flesh break, bone splintering. She gave a cry. He smelled blood, saw a dark stain growing between her breasts.

Fevered, he ran her into the opposite wall and pinned her there.

Her eyes were white orbs, her mouth open. Blood ran from her lips. She spoke, her voice bubbling through the fluid. "A stake through the heart, Pierre? You know you can't kill me like that."

"Run away into the Crystal Ring, then, *chérie*," he grated. "I will destroy you, one way or another."

"For making you feel foolish?"

He stabbed and twisted the spear. "They were right about you! You are insane, you're the thing that mortals daren't name!"

"Satan?"

"Cancer!"

He pushed the spike deeper, feeling horribly exhilarated, yet helpless. She was in pain but she wasn't dying. And why didn't she escape into the Crystal Ring? Was it pain that stopped her, or was she mocking him further?

The metal slid deeper. He felt it break through the heart to touch her spine. She groaned, and her hands came up to grip the shaft, forcing it out of her body. Her gloves were wet and black with blood, yet her grip was solid. He pushed, she resisted. They struggled against each other, static, and all the time her gaze held his.

Mon Dieu, her expression! A blank, sightless look, as if some demon had possessed her and all she could do was observe its actions, aghast. Her horror infected him and he wanted to scream.

Then she wrenched the spear out of her chest and lifted it with terrible strength, swinging Pierre clear off his feet. Taken by surprise, he couldn't let go. She swung him in an arc, rushing forward as she did so. He was borne backwards at speed, felt the window at his back, the impact as the leading burst and the glass shattered around him.

He was out in thin air. The maw of the valley tilted beneath him. Frantically he held onto the shaft of the weapon, his legs jerking for a purchase on nothingness. He glimpsed Violette's face above him, a white gargoyle, an ice-queen.

"Please—"

She let go of the spear. Cast it away, as if releasing a dove.

He fell, limbs flailing, down the high grim walls of the Fortress, down into the trees, and onwards down the sheer side of the Mönchsberg Ridge.

Cruel rocks bruised him until at last he slammed into a hard surface. The momentum of his descent translated to shivering waves of agony. He slid over a curved ridge and came to rest in a niche, with saints looking down at him. Curving above him was the copper-salted cupola of a church. He'd landed on its roof.

The feel of broken bones made him cringe. Ribs, an arm, his left leg in two places. He stared up at the clouds, at the louring presence of the fortress high above. *Is she still up there*, he thought, *laughing at my distress?*

Pierre knew he must lie here until his unnatural body began to heal. He wouldn't die... but after a while, he wished he could. He wept with pain.

God, what's she done to me? Something more than physical injury, worse than humiliation.

A clawed creature with an owl's predatory eyes and a serpent's body swooped down, brushed him with dark feathers, covered him with a mantle of bitter darkness. Then it was gone.

Cesare found John sitting beside the sarcophagus, his head resting on his fists on the rim. He'd been there for days. The stone coffin was half full of blood, a glossy maroon blanket through which Matthew's head showed like a death mask.

The abattoir stench that filled the chamber was, to Cesare, rich and sweet.

"Well?" he said.

"The same as yesterday, and the day before, and the day

before," John answered dully. "Nothing is happening."

Cesare swept blood away from Matthew's cheeks and studied the sunken, slate-blue skin. No sign of regeneration. If anything, it was beginning to decay.

He sighed. "If there is no improvement by now, there's no hope."

John's fists tightened. "Why isn't it working?"

"I don't know." Cesare licked his bloodied hand clean. "Perhaps Kristian had some secret knowledge we lack. Or the head has been too long severed. It's no good, John. Let Matthew go."

He expected denial and grief, but to his surprise John whispered, "Very well. Would you do one thing for me? Take Matthew's head and bathe it. I can't bear to."

"Of course." Cesare scooped the head from its clotted caul and took it to a corner of the chamber, where a bowl of water stood on a table. With his back to John, Cesare rinsed stringy blood from the heavy waxen head. It took time. The hair was matted solid.

As he worked, John said, "I believe you."

"About what?"

"We belong to God," John said softly. "I believe it."

Cesare smiled. The words thrilled him. He'd converted a lost soul! "That is wonderful."

"It's not your fault Matthew can't return to life."

"You're being very gracious," said Cesare, drying the head on a square of sacking. "I expected you to blame me, although I'm sure we did everything right. I thought you would be distraught. You're taking this well, John. I'm impressed."

"No, it's *her* fault," John breathed.

"Who?"

"Lilith."

The name struck Cesare like a whip. It plucked a discordant memory from his own mortal life, centuries past; himself as a scared boy, his mother standing over him with a rod in her hand and the burning pain, tears, terror...

John went on, "Lilith, the mother of vampires. She killed Matthew and prevented his rebirth. She, far more than Satan, is our enemy. She will destroy us all."

Angered, Cesare wanted to silence him. He turned, only to find he couldn't speak. He could only stare at the thin figure hunched beside the coffin.

John had pulled out half his hair, leaving his scalp a mosaic of welts and glistening red holes; and as he went on raving in the same flat voice, he tore out a handful with every other word, as if to tear out his grief by its bloody roots.

CHAPTER FOUR

MOON IN VELVET

"Charlotte?"

The familiar, light voice sent an eerie thrill through her. Charlotte saw Violette appear in the doorway, pale in a dress of beaded ivory silk.

Violette stepped into the firelight. Her dress sparkled but her face and arms were matte, like velvet-white petals. With her black hair coiled under a bandeau, she held herself with all her natural balletic poise.

Charlotte put her book aside and stood up. "Violette, this is a lovely surprise. How are you?"

"I..." The dancer fell silent and stared into the fire. Her posture was defensive, as if to fend off any kiss or touch of greeting. Charlotte had no idea how to broach the subject of Matthew's death, or the complaints of the other vampires.

"I waited until Karl had gone out," Violette said finally. "I need to see you alone. Do you mind?"

"Of course not! Please, sit down."

"Thank you, but no." Violette clasped her hands across her waist. "I can't sit still. I should be helping the wardrobe mistress with the costumes for the tour, but..."

Charlotte, moving closer, was shocked by her pallor. "Have you fed tonight?"

"Not yet," Violette said brusquely.

"Are you still finding it hard to hunt?" She spoke gently, but her heart sank. Violette looked desolate. Charlotte's gaze was arrested by a pearly mark over her breastbone. "What's that on your chest?"

"This?" Violette smiled without humour, and drew down the front of her dress to reveal a ragged scar between her breasts. "Isn't it wonderful, how fast we heal? Last night it was almost through to my spine."

"Who did this?" Rage electrified her. To think that some idiot had actually tried to kill Violette! "Was it John? I'll tear him apart!"

"I think you would." Violette walked away into the dark library. As Charlotte followed, she added, "Something happened."

"Tell me."

Violette paused by a table, lowering her head. "There was a girl called Ute," she began softly. "One of my *corps de ballet*, gifted enough to become a soloist. She told me she had family problems. Her father was putting pressure on her to return home. He thought her place was to be a *hausfrau*, not a performer. She was so upset, poor angel, and she came to me for advice. Wise counsel." The ballerina touched her breastbone as if the wound was sore. "I am responsible for all my dancers, especially the girls. Some of them are very young and I am everything to them: parent, teacher, guardian. Ute trusted me in her distress, and I... I hadn't tasted blood for three days."

"Oh, Violette," Charlotte sighed.

"It was more than thirst. I wasn't sympathetic, I was furious with her for giving in to a selfish old man. And all the time I was sucking her blood and swooning with pleasure, I loathed myself. This thing that takes over..."

"It's hunger. If you'd drink when you feel the need, you wouldn't become so desperate that you lose control."

"No, it has a name. The demon that takes me over is Lilith."

Charlotte said nothing. Pursuing this subject never achieved anything. Violette flexed her shaking hands.

"I become Lilith, yet I don't know what she *wants*. I wish she'd let me in on the secret. I only know that she's driven. Like me."

"What happened to the girl?" Charlotte asked.

Violette moved towards a stained glass window at the far end of the room.

"Ute lived. I wasn't crazed enough to kill her. Do you remember that other young woman I attacked, Benedict's wife, Holly? That my bite seemed to break her child-like dependence on her husband? Well, something changed in Ute too, but not for the better. She didn't remember what I'd done, but she had nightmares. I watched her trying to sleep, her pale little face on the pillow..."

Charlotte recalled Rachel's distress and agitation. Lilith's judgement, it seemed, did not discriminate between vampires and mortals.

"But she stayed with the ballet?"

"Of course not," Violette said with contempt. "She ran home to her father the next day. I can't blame her. Who'd stay with a madwoman like me? But how could Lilith..." Her voice became anguished, "How could *I* do that to someone in my care?"

The window was violet, with winter trees traced in lead, and a moon of thick white glass caught in the branches. Violette was an inky-haired shadow against it. She turned and opened the window, and the scene outside was the same; the violet sky, the moon.

"They are out there," said the dancer. "Humans. Prey. All I have to do is leap over the sill and find them."

"Yes," Charlotte said without inflexion. "That's all."

Violette's hard white fingernails scraped the sill like a bird's claws. She released a short breath. "But I can't."

"Why not?" Charlotte watched her guardedly, unable to bear her pain. She wanted to soothe Violette, but daren't try. The dancer still terrified her.

"Always the same damned reason! This demon inside me..."

"Close the window," said Charlotte.

"I'm not cold."

"Close it anyway."

"Do you think I'm about to start baying at the moon and growing hair on my palms?" Violette banged the window shut. "Nothing would surprise me now."

"But the moon influences everything, even us. Aren't you more restless when it's full? I don't believe you haven't noticed."

"Just tell me, Charlotte, what am I to do? I swore that if ever I harmed one of my company, I'd find a way to destroy myself. It must be possible." Abruptly she extended her left wrist, palm up, and sliced the tender flesh with a fingernail. A slit appeared, red as poppies.

Charlotte ran to her and prised her hands apart. "Don't!"

They held each other's gaze. Even so close, Violette was icy, remote, not human. She looked ready to attack Charlotte without a moment's reflection. She'd certainly threatened to do so in the past.

Charlotte knew enough to dread the consequences. Lilith's bite brought unwelcome transformation... perhaps even the death of her love for Karl.

Still, she held her ground.

"I've told you the answer. Stop trying to resist the thirst."

"You don't understand. I can't simply give in to Lilith. I can't feed on just anyone, Charlotte. I'm compelled to choose my victims. And choosing them is agony. So, whether I defy the hunger or not, it's a fight that nearly kills me."

Growing braver, Charlotte touched the scar that peeked above Violette's neckline. "Why ask my advice when you won't listen? This scar, who inflicted such an injury?"

A pause. "You know Pierre Lescaut?"

"Yes, I know Pierre." Understatement.

"It was him."

"What?" Charlotte was mortified. Pierre had been the only one to support her at the meeting. It didn't make sense.

"You might have told me," said Violette, "that a group of vampires came here complaining that you'd created a homicidal lunatic, and to discuss what should be done about me."

"I'm sorry. I didn't know how. I hoped it would blow over. I would have come to you tonight..."

"Well, you're too late. Pierre reached me first. He suggested that, far from speaking in my defence, you supported them against me."

"That's a lie!" Charlotte didn't want to argue, but mixed emotions got the better of her. "I was on your side, even after what they said about Matthew. Is it true? Did you kill him?"

Violette's eyes betrayed no shame. Instead Charlotte saw Lilith's soul burning behind the sapphire irises. She recoiled.

"It was a warning," Violette said grimly. "No one threatens my ballet, *no one*."

"And Pierre?" Charlotte almost lost her voice. Perhaps the dancer had slain him, too. Obnoxious as Pierre could be, she did not wish him dead. "What happened?"

As Violette related the story without emotion, Charlotte turned away and leaned on the table. Pierre's behaviour left her incandescent – but Violette's retaliation had been extreme. Charlotte thought, *Gods, what have I created?*

"The worst thing," Violette finished, barely above a whisper, "is that I felt nothing. I wasn't angry or vengeful, I felt no pity or pleasure. I feasted on his blood, fought him and thrust him through the window, and I didn't care about any of it."

Charlotte was trying to form a response when Violette rushed at her. She was too shocked to defend herself as the dancer gripped her shoulders and slammed her back against a bookshelf. Tears glittered on Violette's long black lashes. "Have you some magic formula to make me *care* about anything, dearest?"

Her mouth came down on Charlotte's collarbone, burning. She tried to side-slip into the Crystal Ring, but Violette held her in place without effort. Charlotte closed her eyes, petrified. *This is it*, she thought. *This is where she takes my blood and destroys my soul.*

Stefan and the others are right. Violette is insane, a danger to us all. Why have I tried to protect her?

She felt the pressure of fang tips – then a rush of air where the mouth had been. Karl was there, gripping Violette's shoulder. His usually calm eyes were ablaze.

Karl hadn't stopped her, Charlotte realised. Violette had stopped herself when she felt his presence in the room.

"Get your hands off me," she said.

"When you let go of Charlotte," he replied softly. "Do you wonder that you've made so many enemies?"

Charlotte held her breath, certain Violette would attack Karl instead. But the dancer lifted her hands and stepped lightly away.

"What's the matter?" she said with venom. "It's only what you've done repeatedly, even when she was an innocent human girl. The same violation, Karl. Do you think it's worse for me to do it? Double standards, or jealousy?"

Trembling, Charlotte peeled herself away from the bookshelf. "Violette, I think you should leave."

The ballerina stayed where she was, glaring at Karl.

"This time, I stopped. But when the proper time comes, you won't be able to stop me. No one will."

"Do you imagine you can take Charlotte from me?" Karl's expression turned shrewdly thoughtful but his eyes were auburn fire: a disturbing combination. Charlotte couldn't bear their mutual hostility.

"What do you think?" Violette almost smiled.

"That you would try, not because you love her, but to defeat me," Karl said levelly. "Am I right?"

"Don't turn everything to yourself. You fear me, don't you? I don't know why. I only prey on the weak."

"I know," said Karl. "The legends say you take infants whose parents have neglected to leave an amulet in the cot with the magic names, Senoy, Sansenoy, and Semangelof."

"And the words, 'Out, Lilith.' Don't forget that." Violette gave him a bitter look. She came back to Charlotte, rested both hands on her left shoulder, and kissed her cheek.

Charlotte tensed. Incredible to think that those gentle hands were capable of such violence. As a human, Violette had never hurt a soul.

"I'm sorry, my dear," said the dancer, stroking her cheek. "I didn't intend to harm you. That's not why I – you understand, don't you?"

Charlotte nodded, her throat thick. She understood. The desire for blood dressed up as love, lust, affection; anything but cruelty. Yet, in the end, it could only be cruel. She still adored Violette. After all, only love could make her friend's behaviour such torment.

"We want to help you, but you're impossible. Don't you need any friends?"

"I need you," Violette whispered. "Don't desert me."

Charlotte clasped her wrist. The self-inflicted wound had already healed. "We won't."

"I'd like you to come with us on our American tour."

"Why?"

So lovely, Violette's cloudy-crystal face; powerful, fragile, compelling. "I won't survive without you."

Charlotte knew Karl would not want to go. Aware of his gaze on her, she put Violette gently away from her and said, "We'll talk about it. Now, for heaven's sake, go and hunt. Find someone and take them. Don't hesitate."

"I think," said Violette, "that I should do that."

She vanished. The Crystal Ring received her with a faint hiss, like snow crystals vaporising. Charlotte was alone with Karl.

Shaken, she wanted to run into his arms, but a mixture of anger and shame held her back. She met his eyes, wondering, *Does he think that Violette attacked me – or that I invited her embrace?*

Karl only said, "Dearest, are you all right?"

"No, I'm not." She made to sit down at the table, but he intercepted her. One hand went around her waist, the other enfolded her head. She felt his long, delicate fingers sliding through her hair. Divine. She leaned her head into his shoulder, certain he was about to say, *I told you so.*

"I thought she'd be happier," said Charlotte, "deciding to stay with the ballet."

"Obviously she isn't."

"Oh, but it's worse! Pierre sought her out last night, apparently to warn her we were conspiring against her. I don't know why. He was just being Pierre, too clever for his own good. But he offended her, so she attacked him. They had a dreadful fight, but he came off the worst. So yes, before you say anything, everyone was right. She's a threat. She feeds ruthlessly on other vampires."

Karl was quiet, eyelids falling, his lashes forming dark crescents against his cheeks. "Pierre has a talent for doing precisely the wrong thing. Yet he survives. It is the sordid truth that some vampires prey on others to establish their power. It's our most tangible proof of superiority. Violette steals Pierre's strength with his blood, rendering him subservient to her. That's how Kristian controlled us."

"You can't compare her to Kristian!"

"No. She is an anarchist, not a megalomaniac."

"I suppose Pierre will come here complaining about the injustice," she said tightly. "But you didn't see the wound he gave her! I can't forgive him."

"Even if he acted in self-defence?"

"Are you defending him?"

"Not at all," Karl said calmly. "But, *liebling*, Kristian's bite was a crude demonstration of power. Violette's bite is something more. That's why I fear her. Anyone she touches is never the same afterwards."

Karl could admit, "I fear her," with unaffected honesty, and yet he had the steadiest nerves of anyone she knew. She loved his courage.

"Well, if she ever harmed you, Karl..." A chill flashed through her and she dug her fingernails into his arm.

"She won't. She claims we can't stop her – but Kristian also thought himself invincible."

Memories made Charlotte catch her breath. Although Karl had loved Kristian, albeit in a twisted way, in the end he had slain him without pity.

"Swear you won't hurt her!"

Her vehemence appeared to startle him. His eyes were solemn, questioning.

"Charlotte, how can I promise that? I know you love Violette, but you don't imagine I would put her life before yours, before Ilona's or Stefan's? *Liebe Gott*, it doesn't bear thinking about. If she placed you in danger, I'd defend you. I'd have no choice."

"I know." Charlotte felt a wave of emotion crest and fall away, but the dilemma remained. "I'd do the same if she tried to attack *you*. You know, dearest, don't you? I set you above everyone else, whatever the cost."

"And it has proved expensive for you, beloved," Karl said softly. "Almost more than conscience can afford." He slid his fingers along her cheekbone. "I promise one thing: I will not harm her, as long as she leaves us in peace."

"And if someone else threatens *her*?"

"Then I would try to protect her – if she needs anyone's protection."

Charlotte embraced him in relief. This was the best assurance she could hope for. He added, "Well, I suppose we should accompany her to America. I believe it's safer not to let her out of our sight."

"Oh, that will be wonderful," she said, her heart lifting. "If only to get away from other vampires for a while! God, what else can happen?"

"Ah." Karl smiled wryly, resting his hands on her hips. "Let me tell you about Simon."

* * *

By the following night, Pierre had crawled down from the church roof and found a shrub-covered cleft between rocks in which to curl up with his suffering.

He was a victim of the unfortunate fact that, while a well-fed vampire would heal fast, one who'd been drained – as Pierre had – would find the process long and excruciating. Searing pain immobilised him, with no escape into unconsciousness.

Sometimes he hallucinated, and was glad when pain shocked him back to reality.

He hated Violette with passion. He must survive, if only for the pleasure of vengeance.

On the third night, despite his body's agonised protests, hunger drove him from his refuge. He hunted successfully. First a sour-faced old woman, then a succulent pair of young lovers.

Pierre felt no better.

Blood seeped into his cells like sap through a spring flower, swelling each tiny sac with life and growth. He began to heal so fast that he felt his bones creaking as they fused.

But something was wrong. He remained dizzy and weak. He had terrifying fits in which he would claw at his own body, choking for breath, trying desperately to escape something that wasn't there.

He realised with disgust that these were attacks of fear.

Soon he recovered his ability to enter the Crystal Ring, only to be seized by vertigo that drove him back to Earth. An oppressive shadow hovered over him, watching. He was afraid to hunt, afraid to enter the vampire realm that was his natural element!

Pierre was disgusted with himself.

He'd never sought help from anyone, but he needed it now. Habitually living between hotels and his victims' houses, he had no home of his own. Where to go? Kristian, the dogmatic yet comforting father figure, was gone. He couldn't go to Ilona or Karl in this state – the humiliation would be insufferable! Stefan, perhaps – but Karl would find out. *And all Karl will say*, thought Pierre, *is that I brought this on myself! Sadist.*

Kristian was gone, but his castle was still there. However bleak, it still bore a faint concept of "home". Pierre began to head there, like a wounded animal going to ground.

The meadows of Austria blended into those of Bavaria, Germany, the Rhineland. He wound his way through pine forests by day, passed like a ghost through villages by night, oblivious to the charm of the old timbered houses around him.

Sometimes he ran. At others he fell and could not move. He forgot to feed, then wondered why he was so weak. His finely tailored clothes became crumpled and dirty. Anyone who saw him in daylight would stop and stare. A tramp or a lunatic, he must be, this white-faced creature with maniacal blue eyes.

This was Violette's curse.

Reaching the Rhine, he followed the iron-grey flow north past the Lorelei, where banks rose steeply above the sinuous water. At last he saw Schloss Holdenstein, a cluster of brown turrets and tiled roofs standing desolate above the vineyards.

Afterwards, Pierre didn't remember entering the castle. One moment he was staring up at its rain-drenched roofs. The next he was inside, lying face down on chill flagstones, arms outstretched, like a child clinging to an indifferent mother.

Cruel twist. Of all people who least deserved a mother's love... For his first ever victim had been his mother.

"But it wasn't my fault," he moaned under his breath.

Something moved in the rushlit corridor. Looking up, Pierre saw soft black sandals, the hem of a dark robe. Standing over him was a monkish figure of medium height, with a cherubic face, cropped fair hair, pale grey eyes with pinpoint pupils.

"What has the storm blown in?" said the figure. "Have you come back to us, Pierre?"

"Cesare," Pierre groaned. He had despised Cesare, Kristian's lapdog, but in despair he reached up and tugged his hem. "You must help me."

"Must we?" The bland face contemplated him. Pierre half-expected a kick. Instead, to his amazement, Cesare bent down and helped him to his feet. "What brought you to this state, my friend?" He smelled of the castle, of dust, damp, nothingness. "Well, you're safe now. We'll look after you."

Placing a tight, possessive arm around his shoulders, Cesare led him deep into the Schloss. Pierre wanted to pour out his story, if only he could control his chattering breath.

Along the corridor he saw another vampire he knew; a Cinderella figure with straight dark-gold hair and a broom in her thin hands. Maria, another of Kristian's brood. Others were gathering to witness Pierre's arrival. It seemed only a few were left – the core of Kristian's most devoted followers. They lingered in Schloss Holdenstein like a sect awaiting the Second Coming.

No one ever came here now. Pierre supposed his arrival was quite an event.

Things were hazy for a time. Vampires in umber robes moved around him. Someone brought him a human, a small creature that squawked and fought while Pierre fed. Luscious blood, washing away all pain. The body was removed before he even noticed whether it was male or female, adult or child. It didn't matter.

When his head cleared, he was lying on a couch in a bare stone chamber lit by flaming torches. How familiar it was. There was the tall black chair on a dais where Kristian had sat to hold court. Cesare stood touching the chair, but didn't occupy it. To do so would be sacrilege.

The other vampires, ten in all, stood grouped around Pierre. Bleached faces, drab robes, no spark of humour. Yet their attention pleased him. They could almost be courtiers, attending a sick monarch.

Pierre felt stronger. He was safe here, certain that Violette could not breach the thick walls. His fear hardened to anger – and now he had an expectant audience to play to.

"What happened to you?" said Cesare. "You were babbling until we fed you."

"Babbling?" Pierre was affronted. He tried to sit up, but fell back onto the musty cracked leather. Then words started to tumble out. "There's a new vampire, created only a few months ago, a madwoman called Violette. Long black hair, black like a raven. Loveliest creature you'll ever see, but she's crazy, she tried to murder me…"

"Our father Kristian said that a woman's outer beauty was a sign of inner depravity," said Cesare. "It seems she has addled your mind."

"Yes, she has," Pierre said savagely. He stretched out a hand. "Look how I'm shaking. She did this to me!"

Horror overcame him and his head rolled back. Through a yellow mist he heard the murmur of concerned voices. When his sight cleared, Cesare was standing over him.

"Her name is Violette?" Cesare's pupils bored into Pierre's. Beside him, another vampire leaned down. Pierre took a moment to recognise him as John. He had changed drastically since their last encounter. A medieval robe had replaced his modern clothes, and all his hair was gone – ripped out, it appeared, leaving his scalp a bald, livid mass of scars. Soul-sickness pulled his priest-like face into ugly lines.

"He's talking about Lilith," said John, before Pierre could ask what had happened to him.

At her name, dread transfigured Cesare's face. Superstitious revulsion.

"Is it so?"

Pierre nodded mutely. "Has she been here?"

Cesare ignored the question and turned to the others. "Behold, the second one to come here complaining of Lilith!" he exclaimed.

"What does it mean?" said a slender male with yellow hair and black eyes.

"I don't know yet. But now we have a purpose again. We must find out who she is."

"John didn't tell you?" said Pierre. "You've never heard of Violette Lenoir?"

They all looked blank. John shook his ravaged head. "The human persona she puts on is a mask. She is Lilith, the demon mother who must be destroyed before she consumes her own children."

Pierre threw his hands up in exasperation. He liked the modern world. How he loathed all this medieval nonsense of gods and demons, how wretched that he needed the help of these fools!

"When did you last leave the castle, Cesare? If you live like hermits, it's no wonder you know nothing. You haven't a clue what goes on in the real world!"

"Of course we leave the castle," Cesare said thinly. "We have to feed. But your so-called 'real world' is one of shadows. Kristian rightly taught us to shun it."

"I remember. You only go out at night, like the ghosts of monks haunting graveyards. Very gothic. And do you sip only your victims' life-auras, or have you lapsed from Kristian's path? Do you steal a little taste of their blood?"

Cesare was thin-lipped. "Kristian was exceptional. Very few can match his high standards of austerity. Tell us of this female, Pierre."

"She's a famous dancer. If you ever went out, you would know. She became a vampire because Charlotte – Karl's companion?"

"I believe I saw her once," Cesare said dismissively.

"Charlotte became obsessed with her, and brought her into the Crystal Ring. But she came out of the initiation mad, convinced she's Lilith. I don't know her intentions, but I do know she's crazy. She's already killed two vampires and had a damned good attempt on me! You know who Lilith is?"

"As John said, the Mother of Vampires." Another spasm clouded Cesare's face. "Kristian spoke of Lilith as God's instrument. Her dark thoughts spawned us, and she will reappear at the end of time to destroy us. To cast her own children into hell. Unless..."

The hush that followed his words was charged with fear – and, if Pierre was not mistaken, a bizarre, hungry excitement. He closed his eyes, wishing he'd gone to Ilona after all. Her ridicule would have been comforting compared to this. Cesare's vehemence was shredding his last hold on sanity.

"Unless we can defeat her. That is our great test! And we can, if we hold true to our faith."

"Kristian's great purpose for us!" exclaimed the yellow-haired male, and the others all began talking at once, in a rushing murmur of joy as if everything had fallen into place.

Cesare clasped Pierre's shoulder. "You can help us, Pierre. Show us where to find her."

"No!" he cried. "No, I can't. I'm ill. Just let me stay here. Please."

"Vampires don't suffer illness."

Pierre loathed Cesare's condescending tone, but he'd asked for it by coming here. *I believe in nothing*, he thought. *I don't care what this means, as long as I never see Violette again. I'll do anything for Cesare, sell myself to a man I abhor, if it means gaining protection from the witch!*

"The question is this," Cesare went on. "Is Violette really

Lilith, or is she insane? Either way, she must be dealt with. She's committed heinous acts... Of course you can stay here, my dear friend. And I think that you are right."

"About what?"

"That I've been cloistered here too long." Cesare's eyes were unfocussed, his dread of the unknown becoming a hard light of defiance. "It's time I went out and re-acquainted myself with the world."

Charlotte and Karl still went their separate ways to seek blood, as if their mutual feast on the peasant woman had never happened. The incident went unmentioned. On her own after Violette's visit, however, Charlotte delayed her hunt. Instead she travelled through the Crystal Ring to Vienna, in search of a friend.

She found him quickly. He was on his way home, strolling alone through one of the public gardens. She went ahead, and waited under a tree. Tall and slim with thick grey hair, his face still leanly attractive at sixty, he had the melancholy, self-contained look she remembered.

Josef.

As he drew level, Charlotte stepped into his path. He stopped, raising a hand to his chest; for a moment, she thought the shock had stopped his heart. Then he breathed out and smiled. His grey eyes, behind black-rimmed spectacles, gleamed with wry pleasure.

He was in no danger from her. Josef was her only mortal friend.

"I'm sorry," she said. "I always startle you to death."

"That's uncomfortably close to the truth," said Josef. "You never knock on my front door, like a normal visitor. But, my dear Charlotte..." He kissed her hand, then held it between his palms. "Such a sweet death I would welcome."

"No, you wouldn't."

"Maybe not, but let me dream. Then you frighten me less." He tucked her hand through his arm, and they walked together. Light from the street wove green webs in the foliage.

"I never mean to alarm you, Josef, truly."

"But you can't help it. I still see you as the little daughter of my good friend, George Neville, yet here you are, a ghost..."

Josef knew what she was: an unholy creature in a human shell. When they'd met by chance last year, he'd recognised her because she looked so like her mother: deep-lidded expressive eyes, sombre mouth, warm brown hair that turned to gold leaf in the light. Learning the truth about her had shocked him, naturally; that behind the veil of feminine softness, she now lived beyond death, watching humans with the radiant eyes of a goddess and the red tip of her tongue poised in hunger.

Josef had watched Charlotte end his sister's life. Lisl had been desperately ill, dying, and he'd wanted her suffering to end. Charlotte knew the memory would never leave him. No haze of illusion shielded Josef from the horror of what Charlotte was.

And yet he murmured, "Men would give their souls to be haunted by such a dear and beautiful ghost."

"They say vampires can't befriend humans without causing disaster, but we keep trying. I've something to ask you, but your soul is safe, I promise." They passed through an arbour of honeysuckle. The scent filled her head, making the world timeless for a lovely moment. "It's a friend of mine."

"Your vampire friend, Lilith? I remember."

"I'm still worried. She's so disturbed, I'm afraid she'll harm herself."

"Don't vampires harm others? I don't see what I can do."

"But you know the mythology and how to interpret it. You've studied psychology."

"Charlotte, after I moved from the science of physics to that of the mind, I worked as a psychoanalyst for a time, until I retired to nurse Lisl. Yes, I study and write, but I've had no practical experience for years."

"You don't forget, though. If you could observe her, perhaps talk to her if she'd permit it, you might gain some insight that would help."

He halted, a light breeze blowing his coat and scarf. Lights through the bushes made a silver mosaic around him. "Charlotte, my friendship with you is one thing. But to give help to another of your kind... I don't know."

"I know it's a lot to ask, but it means everything to me. I don't know what else to do." He was shaking his head, troubled. Out of desperation she added, "Josef... It's Violette Lenoir."

His head came up and he stared. "*The* Lenoir – the ballerina? You wouldn't joke about such a thing, would you? Of course you wouldn't."

"It goes without saying that you mustn't tell anyone."

"Who would believe me? But I've seen her dance many times." He waved vaguely in the direction of the theatres. "And now you tell me she's –?"

"Disturbed. Unhappy," Charlotte said quietly. "Perhaps this will help you to understand. What if I said that the 'collective unconscious' is perceived as a real place by vampires?"

"Is it?" He looked sceptical.

"Well, there is an otherworld that only we can enter. Some believe it's the mind of God, and that we are his angels of punishment."

"Do you?" Josef raised his thick grey eyebrows.

"No. I believe it's the subconscious of mankind. I mean the massed electrical impulses of all their thought-waves and dream-waves. Energy becomes matter and vice versa. This is a question of perception. Vampires perceive thought-impulses as matter, an ethereal double of this world; and I mean *ether* literally, as a medium through which we can move like fish through water..."

"Charlotte, stop," he exclaimed. "This sounds almost scientific, but..."

"I was a scientist," she said tightly. "I didn't just make my father cups of tea and type his notes. I understood and participated in his work."

"Forgive me, I didn't mean to sound condescending. It's hard to conceive of such a place, though." He took her arm and they walked onwards.

"I know, but please suspend disbelief for me. I'm telling the truth. We call this otherworld the Crystal Ring, or Raqia."

"Ah, I know that word!" said Josef. "A Hebrew word from the Bible, meaning firmament, or expanse, or heaven, or simply the sky... An appropriate word to borrow."

"And Raqia creates vampires. If a human is taken there on the point of death by other vampires, he or she becomes a vampire too."

"Rebirth," said Josef thoughtfully, "not from the energy of the real world but from that of the collective mind. Is that what you're saying?"

"Yes. I've no proof. It's what I feel to be true."

"But then... Why vampires? Why not – oh, anything the human mind can conjure? Monsters, dream lovers, figures from mythology? Archetypes, as we Jungians say."

She laughed. "But we are monsters and dream lovers, Josef. And what is Lilith but a mythical figure? But we must be vampires, we couldn't be anything else, because we represent the very extremity of human fears and hopes."

"The fear of death and the hope of eternal life," said Josef, nodding. "Yes, you are almost making sense!"

"Thank you," she said wryly. "But you've left one out: fear of the dead coming back to life and feeding on the living. Isn't that the deepest terror of all? The breaking of nature's laws. We can't be defined scientifically, because the laws of physics, chemistry and biology break down around us. We come from the lawless realm of dreams."

Josef was quiet for a while. "So vampires have theories and theologies," he said. "Amazing."

"And we argue about them as much as humans do."

He was fascinated now. She saw the glow in his face. "Let me propose a theory," he said. "Archetypes are motifs that crop up everywhere. Lilith appears in every mythology under many names; a primordial image. It sounds as if Violette has absorbed an archetype that has particular resonance for her. It may be a complex – that is, a fragment of the psyche that's broken away due to some past trauma."

"I'd say she's had her share of those," Charlotte murmured. "So if she thinks she's wicked and destructive, she separates that part of herself and calls it Lilith?"

"Possibly. In the voices heard by the pathologically insane, the complex can take on a separate character. Does Lilith talk to her?"

"I don't know." The words *pathologically insane* reverberated. "She speaks of Lilith *compelling* her... But Josef, I'm convinced you could help her. We're vampires, but we are still – well, human, in a way. If I can persuade her to speak to you. That's the difficulty."

"I'm not sure." Josef looked at the ground. His hands were in his pockets, shoulders hunched. "I'm tempted. It would be fascinating. But if she won't talk to me..."

"Surely you could learn something from observing her? Don't turn me down flat! Wait, before you answer, here's an enticement in return. The Ballet Janacek will be touring America soon. Karl and I are going. We're patrons, of a sort. There's a spare berth on the ship, so it would cost you nothing to come with us."

His face softened, and he smiled. "Why would I want to go to America?"

"The tour opens in Boston."

"Ah." His eyebrows rose.

"I've seen photographs of your niece Roberta on your desk. You said she lives in Boston and that you haven't seen her for years...?"

"Oh," he said, moisture filling his eyes. "Oh, this is quite a bribe. My little Roberta. I called her Robyn, with a 'why', because she was always asking questions."

"And wouldn't she love to see her uncle?"

His face was tender, lined with old sorrows. "Extraordinary, that a vampire should care for the happiness of a mere mortal."

She shrugged. "Most don't. Yes, it's a bribe, but please say yes."

He tried to look grave, but couldn't keep the joy from his expression. "Yes, I'll come. Dear God, I am going to see my Robyn! Thank you." He bent and kissed her cheek. A kiss of friendship – but the kiss lingered a moment too long. She had to suppress sudden, treacherous thirst.

Time to end the meeting before it went too far.

She knew that the words she'd spoken earlier had already come true. *Vampires cannot befriend humans without causing disaster.* Josef was in love with Charlotte, even though he knew they could never be together. But that was keeping him from finding someone else.

She had never taken his blood, never would. But still she was insidiously picking his soul apart.

CHAPTER FIVE

ANGELS FALLING

Sebastian avoided other vampires, as he had done for decades. They had nothing he desired or needed. He wanted the citadel of night entirely to himself.

He loved America for its size and grandeur. Forests, lakes and mountains where he might track a single victim across the wilderness. Cities, seething with the rich and poor of all nations, where he could pass from slum to glittering skyscraper like a chameleon.

Sebastian loved his ability to go unnoticed by humans. He would leave them with no memory of his presence, with only a feeling of unease as if shadow wings had brushed them. He could even pass unseen by other vampires, a rare gift. Immortals usually sensed each other, but they never noticed Sebastian unless he willed them to.

This confirmed his sense of being unique, superior.

Over two hundred and twenty years had passed since Simon and his companions had drawn Sebastian into their dark world. He hadn't seen them since. Sometimes he wondered why they'd chosen him. The fair folk, it seemed, had a grim sense of humour.

You will make a wonderful immortal, Rasmila had said. Sebastian knew from the start that he was an orphan in the darkness. Yes, it was purgatory, but his only possible fate: the natural extension of his solitary, dark character. He relished both his own pain and the evil he visited on others. His revenge against the faithless Mary had only been the beginning.

How very far away that night seemed now. Meaningless. *I didn't love Mary as I sucked out her life. I loved only her blood...* And yet, on a deeper level, the act hadn't been meaningless at all, but the profound sealing of his vampire nature.

After he left Blackwater Hall – as later occupiers named it – he'd taken ship to America. He wanted no more of Ireland's shadowy magic, its religions and superstitions, war and the endless struggle to hold onto his birthright. In the early years of his new existence he was savage, bitter and self-absorbed. As time passed, though, he discovered that vampires were not frozen in one mood forever. Bitterness passed. He gained control of his blood thirst and his fear of eternity. Then he began to think of the house again.

Eventually, some sixty years after he'd left Ireland, curiosity drew him back. He discovered that the scandal of the landowner who'd murdered his wife and her lover, then vanished, was local legend; a folk tale told by old men in their cups. The estate had passed to the Crown, then been awarded to a Protestant family in gratitude for their loyal service to William of Orange. Sebastian felt no resentment. He simply wanted to see who the family were, how they kept the place. Blackwater Hall: a good, plain name stating that the house belonged to the river and the land. Self-important noblemen came and went, but the land endured forever. And the family was pleasant enough, fair to their tenants. Sebastian approved of the way they looked after his demesne.

Yet he owed it to the house, and to himself, to haunt them a little. To frighten the old men, to feed on the young and strong. To turn a capable wife into a crazed neurotic, or seduce a virgin and ruin her for marriage, to kill a first-born son here, a beloved small daughter there. Just to darken their lives once in a while, as generations came and went. America remained his hunting ground, but every few years he would revisit Ireland and listen with pleasure when people said, "That Blackwater Hall is haunted; it's cursed the family!" And he would slip silently into the house and torment the hapless inhabitants a little more.

Sebastian had seen off the last of them, an eccentric old bachelor, in the 1860s. Blackwater Hall had stood empty ever since, which gave him immense satisfaction.

The house was his once more.

These days, however, he rarely dwelled on the past. He lived in the moment, drinking sensation as if it were blood. Tonight he was in New York, moving through the soft sparkle of lights in search of human heat, the shimmer of music and laughter. How the New World had changed since he'd first arrived! Ah, the Jazz Age. Since the Great War, cities had mushroomed: skyscrapers soaring up everywhere, motor cars with long bonnets and wire-rimmed wheels crawling nose-to-tail through the streets. Dirt and fumes, noise and energy. He loved the mood of criminality engendered by Prohibition, a law that enticed more people than ever before to imbibe the forbidden fruit of alcohol. Wild music, outrageous clothes, a new cult of youth. And yet the modern age still had romance, a kind of innocence.

Sebastian drifted through the streets with a sense of ennui that had possessed him for months, years. He was an observer, distant from the world but connected to it by a cord of ravenous thirst.

Losing himself in crowds on their way to parties or theatre shows, he observed the women with their furs and pearls and sleek hair. He sensed them watching him as he passed, captivated by the treacherous beauty of a vampire. Later, he would find one to invite him home... The only difficulty was choosing between them.

He realised suddenly that he was bored.

All too easy to find prey. They would meet and part – if the victim survived – as strangers. Years had passed since he'd indulged the pleasure of cultivating a relationship, teasing and torturing his lover for months before the final, fatal betrayal.

He thought, *have I become too isolated? When a vampire possesses too much power, no challenges remain and he must go to ever greater lengths to find pleasure...*

Lost in reflection, he paused outside a theatre to watch the audience streaming in. Yellow light spilled over the sidewalk. Sebastian walked between white marble pillars to look at posters in glass cases, advertising future shows. Musicals, plays, operas, concerts.

Could human entertainments relieve his weariness of spirit for a while? *And then I'd slake my thirst on some lovely woman from the audience... or, even better, one of the performers.*

But is this anything I've not done before?

A photograph caught his eye. The poster beside it announced

that the Ballet Janacek would be performing *Swan Lake* and *Coppélia* at the Manhattan Opera House... And the face, in grainy tones of grey, captivated him. "*Prima ballerina assoluta* Violette Lenoir, the greatest dancer of our time," read the caption. She had long hands folded over her breastbone, a divinely curved neck, white feathers clasping a face of exquisite, fairy-tale beauty.

Sebastian smiled. Now, to indulge the pleasures of seduction and treachery with this goddess would be a game worth playing!

A month before the ballet came to New York. He couldn't wait, he wanted her now... A glance at the list of cities and dates revealed that the tour opened in Boston in two weeks' time.

Yes, he thought, *I'll go to Boston!*

He had affection for the city, with its sophistication and wealth. He felt at home there, among the Irish exiles; he felt such empathy as he drank their blood, as though the smoky richness of the old country ran in their veins.

A voice said over his shoulder, "Beautiful, isn't she?"

Sebastian hadn't sensed anyone approaching. The entity behind him felt dimensionless, a shadow. Annoyed, he swung round and found himself staring into the lion-golden eyes of Simon.

Simon leaned on a pillar, arms folded, statuesque in a beige mackintosh. A faint shimmer cloaked him, but he wasn't the terrifying angel of two centuries ago. Sebastian was shocked, dismayed to see him.

"Well, it has been quite a time," said the apparition. "I suppose you thought you'd never see me again."

"I've not been holding my breath, I assure you. I thought you were dead. There was a rumour that Kristian destroyed his creators."

The angel-demon smiled. "We slept in the *Weisskalt* for a time, that's all. Now I am back."

"Without your companions?"

"I had a difference of opinion with Fyodor and Rasmila. I work alone now."

"How did you find me?" Sebastian was furious that another vampire had tracked him down. "Even Kristian never found me."

"You have quite a reputation for being elusive, my dear friend," said Simon. "But don't forget that I created you. That made an insoluble link between us."

"A shame you didn't stay in the *Weisskalt*, then," Sebastian murmured. Humans bustled around them, but he and Simon were isolated as if in a glass bubble. "Why now, after two centuries? What do you want?"

"Only to talk," Simon said, shrugging. "You haven't changed a bit. As suspicious and misanthropic as ever."

Sebastian laughed. "So, you don't approve of Rasmila's choice? You prefer men of Kristian's calibre. I gather he was your choice: Kristian, that saint of compassion."

Simon's smile vanished. "You knew him?"

"Yes, I had the misfortune to meet Kristian." Sebastian exhaled. "In the 1850s I met a vampire called Ilona and, out of idle curiosity, I let her take me to Schloss Holdenstein. What I found there was a despot, tyrannising other vampires in the name of God. I was disgusted. How could beings like you and I, strong and deathless, bring themselves to worship such a tyrant?

"Yet I understood, in a way. When you transformed me, you flung me into the unknown. Some vampires must find it intolerable. Kristian maintained a hold on them by saying, 'I am ordained by God!' They were prisoners of their own fears. They clung to a self-appointed prophet rather than face the dark on their own."

"You dismiss them with such contempt," said Simon, "but don't underestimate Kristian's sheer strength. Didn't he try to win you over?"

"Oh, he tried," Sebastian said grimly. "He treated me like visiting royalty. He must have thought me a gift from above – the challenge of subduing an immortal as strong as himself! He soon deteriorated from flattery and persuasion to arguments, threats, and violence. Finally he tried to imprison me in the *Weisskalt* but I escaped. He tried to find me and failed. He must have given up in the end. But I'll tell you this, Simon: I could have killed him if I'd chosen. I could have taken his place."

He thought Simon would be angered by his boast. Instead, his expression was strangely intense. "Why didn't you?"

"Because I don't care. Their power struggles and passions were too human, an irrelevance that corrupts the purity of true vampire nature."

Simon gasped. "What a beautiful sentiment!"

"Besides, other vampires tried to involve me in a conspiracy against Kristian. They saw my strength and wanted me to kill him. I refused; why should I do their dirty work? I let Kristian live, because his followers deserved him. Karl was the worst. He hated me for not helping, and loathed me more for supposedly corrupting his daughter."

This made Simon laugh. "Did you?"

"Ilona needed no encouragement to indulge her natural depravity. But she was as deeply entwined with Kristian as the rest." Sebastian spoke with disgust. "No, the whole episode only confirmed that I want no business with other vampires."

"But your house in Ireland – you go back there, don't you? Why not reclaim it, make it your own?"

Sebastian looked coldly at Simon, wondering how he knew so much. "It was never taken from me. Do you understand? It's mine in spirit, so the deeds to its fabric are irrelevant."

"Yes, I understand." Simon looked warmly at him now. "And I believe Rasmila chose well, after all."

"Did she?" Sebastian wanted to end the conversation and leave. "Does it matter?"

"Oh, yes. It does. I bring news, dear fellow, unless you already know. Kristian is dead."

Sebastian, who'd barely thought of Kristian for seventy years, experienced a twinge of delight. "He is? How splendid. Are you heartbroken?"

"Don't attribute human emotions to me," Simon replied, unmoved. "Karl killed him. I punished Karl, then forgave him. It's done. The point is that vampires are leaderless."

Sebastian leaned against the theatre wall. "So?"

"Like Karl, you think you're above such concerns, but you're not. There is a new immortal at large, too dangerous to be allowed her freedom. If she isn't stopped, everyone will be affected. Even you." Simon stepped closer and placed a hand on his arm. Sebastian endured the touch with annoyance. Angel or not, Simon was still intimidating. "You have magnificent qualities, Sebastian. You've had two centuries to grow into your full strength and you are more than ready. Come with me, take control and unite your immortal kin against the danger."

If Simon expected him to be flattered and overwhelmed, he was disappointed. All Sebastian felt was cynical dismay. He drank in the warm night air and the surging life in the street, the towers rising towards heaven shining with thousands of lighted windows. He thought of Boston, of human blood and the cruel game he was planning. To exchange that for the cold company of vampires was laughable. "Why not do it yourself?"

"It's not my role. I serve God, which means I observe and guide on His behalf. Angels may offer wisdom, but they don't come to Earth and rule men."

"Ah. So you're actually *too important* to be a mere pack leader?"

"Someone must choose a leader, by God's will," Simon retorted, "because, frankly, vampires cannot be trusted to choose for themselves."

"I see," Sebastian said evenly. "Well, it's a generous offer but I must decline."

The fiery eyes narrowed. "Why?"

Sebastian felt dark emotions rising. "You, a supernatural creature from whom I seem to have no secrets, should know that I've always loved solitude. Why do you expect me to have changed?"

Simon drew away, looking sideways at him. "Because you've a duty to use the gifts we gave you! You'll make such a leader, Sebastian; wise, strong, beautiful as an angel. What harm have I done you? All I offer you is power."

"I know," Sebastian said softly, "but I don't want it."

Simon laughed, exasperated. "It's not a question of what you want. You have been chosen by God! You cannot refuse!"

"I don't believe in your God."

"Nor the Devil?"

"I believe in the older gods," Sebastian said darkly, "and I fear them, but I won't bow down to them – especially not to one who doesn't even recognise what he is. You came from nowhere and thrust this existence on me; now you appear after two centuries and expect me to welcome you like a saviour? Go to hell, Simon. Sort out this mess yourself. I won't be used."

"You sound like Karl!" The gilded face hardened.

"Oh, I see." Sebastian read meaning into the oblique insult. "So, you asked him first, and he also refused?" He leaned closer

THE DARK BLOOD OF POPPIES

to Simon, fired by the thrill of defying his creator. "Is that why you transformed me? Insurance? I was second in line, in case the mighty Kristian was assassinated? Or forty-seventh in line, for all I know."

Simon stared into the middle distance, as if all the world's troubles lay on his shoulders. Sebastian felt nothing: no sympathy, no interest, nothing.

"No," Simon answered. "Even God's plans go awry. That's the price we pay for the gift of free will. All we wanted was to create immortals worthy of their Creator."

"So what will you do if I refuse?"

"Don't refuse."

"I already have." He shrugged. "Kill me, if you can. I won't be your puppet. You brought me into this, Simon. At least have the decency to leave me alone."

A shudder went through Simon from head to foot. Anguish? It passed, and he was the serene, burnished demi-god again. He pressed his fingers to the glass that encased the photograph of Violette Lenoir.

"Very well, have your way." His tone was icy, dangerous. "Enjoy the ballet. But afterwards, think about what I've said – then decide whether I am right or wrong."

Simon left New York in a state of despair. Although he'd known Sebastian might refuse, he couldn't accept that his powers of persuasion had failed – not once now, but twice.

I have to find someone, he thought as he soared through the Crystal Ring. *I must appoint the saviour, or God will never let me back into His circle!*

He couldn't admit it, but his powers were collapsing. He felt like a creature of spun sugar, left out in the rain. Yes, he could impersonate the golden seraph to vampires like Karl and Sebastian, but inside he was falling apart – and they knew. Secretly, they knew.

Even his journey from America to Europe was a struggle. Once – with his trinity – they could speed through the Crystal Ring in a few hours. Not now. He had to work his way north through Canada, occasionally slipping into the real world to feed. By the time he reached Greenland, he was so chilled that the snowy landmass felt warm by contrast.

Simon rested again in Iceland. Having sucked the life from a farmer and his daughter – prettiest girl he'd ever seen, such a waste – he climbed a glacier and sat in white silence, praying. Below the glacier's rim lay a brown wasteland strewn with boulders. To the south, the black cone of a volcano stood on the horizon. North lay the Arctic ocean, like bright blue silk. Yet the stark beauty meant nothing.

We made a mistake, Lord. We let Lilith escape. Now we're being punished, and rightly so. I understand. I must tame her – but how? Who is to help me? Why are Karl and Sebastian blind to the danger? Oh, they'll be sorry on Judgement Day, but that's no consolation now. Lilith is the Enemy. Until all immortals unite in your name to revile her, Lord, she will work to destroy us. Am I the only one who sees it?

Simon had deliberately not told Sebastian who Violette Lenoir was. If he'd said, "There is your Enemy!" Sebastian wouldn't have gone within a hundred miles of her. His only hope now was that if Sebastian met her – if he survived – he would learn the hard way that Simon was right.

A thin hope. *Dear God, if you'd offer me a mandate to seize power, I'd do it! But I can't. I'm only a messenger. I need someone like Lancelyn or Kristian. A ruthless, efficient brute to carry out my will.*

Alone, I am nothing. Lord, have mercy.

God, however, was mute. Simon's God was not the merciful deity in which humans put their faith, but a demanding, punishing God. He had no pity, not even for his angel Senoy.

Two figures dropped softly onto the snow-crusted ice before him. He started. One pale, the other near black. Fyodor and Rasmila.

He glared at them, ice stinging his eyes. They'd let him down, yet they kept following him with their pleading eyes.

"Simon!" Rasmila cried, falling to her knees in the snow. "What are you doing here? You look so unhappy."

"Leave," said Simon.

"No," Fyodor said fiercely. "Not after it took so long to find you."

They were dressed in thin clothes in which a human would

freeze, Fyodor in a modern shirt and trousers, Rasmila in a midnight-blue sari. The garments were ragged with wear. Their long hair was wild and they looked mad, demonic, and incredibly beautiful.

"How many times have I commanded you to stop pursuing me?" Simon asked thinly.

"We'll follow until you give in," Rasmila said, grasping at his hands despite his efforts to shake her off. "Simon, please! You can't abandon us after we were together all those years."

"But I can and I have." Her pleading made him furious. "Do you have someone else now? Is it Karl?"

"I love only God."

"What God?" Fyodor exclaimed. "Imagining we were angels – delusion!"

"No, never," said Simon.

Fyodor gripped Simon's shoulder and shook him. "Give up this idea of being God's envoy! It's over. Come with us and revel simply in being vampires. To drink human blood, to glory in your savage power – isn't that enough?"

Rasmila argued, "No, Fyodor, it's not over! If we join again, our power will return."

"No," Simon said grimly. "It won't."

"What can we do to prove our love?"

"Nothing. I don't care."

"You must care!" Rasmila clung to him, but he endured her embrace like a rock. "Remember how we first became angels?" Her voice dropped, becoming softly melodic. "Fifteen hundred years ago we were lost souls, wandering the world feeding on humans, with no memory of how this curse fell upon us. And then we met, the three of us, and fell so deeply in love we could never bear to be apart."

"I never loved you," Simon said callously.

Rasmila would not be stopped. "You don't mean it. I left my own gods and culture for you. For a thousand years it was always we three, no one else… and then the light spoke to you! God spoke through you, Simon, and told us to guide other immortals, to choose humans worthy to join us. The light and power were so beautiful! We were together, three in one. Waiting for the Enemy,

Lilith, to reappear so we could fulfil our purpose and chain her before God. We haven't finished, Simon. You are still Senoy. I am still Semangelof and Fyodor is Sansenoy."

"No, you're not," Simon said woodenly. "You let me down! You weren't strong enough to hold Lilith. You were vessels for the light but too fragile. You broke and the light spilled out, gone."

"Past repair?" Fyodor said bitterly. "Was it God who drove us to create other vampires – or vanity and boredom? Immortality, love, power; nothing was ever enough for you. You had to metamorphose into something more important, and you need others to feed your great importance."

"Stop. I've heard enough."

"And then you grew bored with us!" Fyodor cried. "Well, forgive us for being constant in our love! But you despise your own imperfections, and blame us. Yet, damn you, we still need you."

Ice speared Simon's heart. "All that matters is destroying Lilith. Don't you see? Unless we defeat her, we won't be *here* to love or hate each other! You can't help, so leave me alone."

"I wish we'd stayed in the *Weisskalt* forever," Fyodor murmured.

"We can help. We'll prove it," said Rasmila. "Only don't send us away again."

They grasped him and hung on his neck, weeping. Infuriated, Simon tried to prise them off. And then he did something he'd never done before. He attacked them. Tore Rasmila off him, struck her so hard she spun away across the ice. He bit a great hole in Fyodor's neck and flung him aside.

Yet they went on reaching out like wounded children, weeping bitter tears of rejection. And still Simon felt nothing, nothing to the frigid core of his soul.

Pierre was a realist. He hadn't expected anyone to look for him, so it was a shock when Ilona arrived at Schloss Holdenstein. She was dressed in the height – or depth – of fashion, in a coat of maroon velvet and black fur, a scarlet dress dripping with beads, rubies and red gold flashing on her wrists and encircling her hair. An affront to the sombre memory of Kristian – but Cesare, fortunately, was not there to chastise her.

Pierre greeted her with world-weary flippancy, but his acting was lamentable. Fear had gnawed holes in his sanity. As she looked around his dank, rushlit chamber, he suffered an unravelling sensation that felt suspiciously like an urge to embrace Ilona and cry his eyes out.

"It's taken me an age to find you," she snapped. "What the devil are you doing here?"

"Exactly what there is to do here," he retorted. "Nothing."

"What's wrong with you, Pierre?" She moved closer, studying him shrewdly. "You weren't in your usual haunts. I can't believe you're here, but I had an intuition... Have you lost your mind? You hate this place."

"What do you want?" He was fractious now. Since Violette's attack, everything irritated him.

"There have been rumours," she said, "about you and a certain ballerina."

"Rumours? The bitch tried to kill me!"

"Shame she didn't do a better job," Ilona said crisply. "So you ran to Cesare?"

"Not to Cesare." He almost enjoyed the familiar joust. Anger was easier to manage than fear. "He doesn't own this place. I had to go somewhere."

"To hide?"

"You didn't see her! She was crazed!"

"I've met her. She *is* crazy, but really, Pierre, she's only a slip of a thing. How did she reduce you to this state? You don't look fit to scare the birds out of the fields."

Pierre lacked the strength to answer. He sank down onto a bench, where he'd been trying to read some rambling religious tract left behind by Kristian. Ilona stared at him with contempt.

"Where is Cesare, by the way?" she said. Her tone softened, as if she were genuinely shocked by Pierre's appearance.

"He went to look for Violette. He's been gone for days, so perhaps she's slaughtered him too."

"You told him about her?"

He shrugged. "Yes, everything. Why not?"

"Well, he won't find her. She's in America. Karl and Charlotte went too, to keep her out of mischief."

"Good luck to them," Pierre whispered. "She should be kept out of trouble. Permanently."

She sat beside him, her velvet-brown gaze fastening on his. "Do you really think so?"

"Do you?"

She didn't answer. He wondered if Ilona, cavalier as she was with human life, had it in her to kill another vampire... then he remembered Kristian. *We are all capable*, he thought. *But not acting alone.*

"What does Cesare say?" asked Ilona.

"He's been quite agitated. John got here before me."

"I know. I saw him on my way in." Ilona pulled a face. "What has he done to himself? He could star in *Nosferatu*."

"He's sick. They're all sick here. Cesare wants to launch a crusade against Lilith."

"He wouldn't dare set himself against the supposed Mother of Vampires, would he?"

"Oh, he has an answer for that," said Pierre. "Lilith is the demon mother who will devour her children at the end of time, unless the sons of God defeat her, or something."

"Aha. Of course. Matricide. I can see Cesare as someone who hated his mother."

At her words, Pierre wilted. He remembered a conversation with Karl. *"I was not like you, Karl, wanting to stay human for love. I was greedy for what Kristian offered... My first victim was my mother, and I fed on her without a qualm. The silly witch had already made herself a martyr for me, so what better way to go than to give me her last drop of blood?"*

Oh, how flippantly he'd uttered those sentiments! Now they haunted him. What he felt was long-delayed guilt, a horrible, twisting pain imposed on him by Violette-Lilith.

"Are you listening?" said Ilona.

"Yes," he said savagely. "Could you feast on your own mother?"

"I don't know," she said in a thin tone. "I never knew her. Kristian had her murdered when I was a few months old, so that he could take Karl away. So I have no feelings about mothers, though I have often felt like strangling my father. I once thought I'd like to become a mother, but what's the use, when your children turn on you?"

"You sound like Violette." Her words filled him with creeping dread. "Stop."

"My God, she's really got to you, hasn't she?" Ilona touched his shoulder. "Poor Pierre. You so badly wanted to be heartless and gloriously wicked like Sebastian, but it's not in you."

"Oh, yes, him," Pierre said, stung. "I should like to see how Sebastian gets on with her. She'd tear him to shreds."

"Why didn't you come to me, instead of baring your sorry soul to Cesare?"

"Thrown myself on your sweet sympathy? I think not. Why the hell does it matter?"

"Because Cesare's deranged, and so is John. Couldn't you leave this band of halfwits to fester in their ignorance? Why stir them up? We have enough troubles without them blundering into our world."

"Cesare's harmless. He's actually been quite nice to me."

"Well, I can't see him joining forces with Stefan; they loathe each other," said Ilona. "The opposition to Lilith seems to have collapsed. Everyone she touches falls apart. Matthew's dead, Rachel's vanished, and here are you, cowering in this pit."

"Don't be kind, Ilona. Gloat a little."

"You used to like being teased."

"I've lost my sense of humour."

"I'm not surprised, in this place." She stroked his cheek. "Good God, you're freezing! Come with me and hunt."

"No, Ilona…"

"You need blood."

Pierre shrank back, shaking his head. "I can't leave the castle."

"Why not? Do you need a note from Cesare? I see no shackles or locked doors."

"I can't, because I'm frightened." His words crackled like dry leaves.

Ilona stood, looking at him in disgust. "I thought you were like me, Pierre, but you're a coward. I know she's dangerous, but we can't let her win! She humiliated you, that's all. That's what you can't face. Ooh, bruised pride."

When he didn't reply, her face darkened.

"This is my plan," she said. "I'll follow her to America, on a later sailing so Karl and the others won't know I'm there. And I'll prove, to myself and everyone, that she's no one to fear. Talk of destroying her is exactly the same as hiding from her. It gives Madame Lenoir power and status she doesn't deserve."

"Be careful," he said, with a touch of his old mockery. "Stefan says she has a grudge against you."

"Oh, that. She claims I attacked and mutilated her father, years ago, which drove him out of his mind. So I am responsible for all the family problems that sent her mad. Have you ever heard such nonsense? She has no proof that I ever met her damned father, but if I did, he should have been grateful I didn't kill him. Men," Ilona spat. "Boys!"

She vanished abruptly into the other-realm, but not before Pierre had seen the look in her eyes. For all her brave words, Ilona, too, was terrified of Violette. And that made him want to huddle around his own fear and beg her not to leave him alone.

As the ship surged across the Atlantic, Charlotte found relief in being among strangers, journeying to a new land. No other vampires – apart from Violette – were here to come between her and Karl. Kristian, Katerina, Andreas, Ilona, Pierre, even Stefan and Niklas, had all tried to weaken the bond between Karl and Charlotte. How good it was to leave those struggles behind.

Neither she nor Karl had been to America before. Karl had said that travelling through the Crystal Ring was impractical. A long, exhausting journey through the firmament would put them at risk of starvation and becoming too weak to return to Earth. Charlotte had broken impatiently into his explanation.

"It doesn't matter. We're going to another continent! I want to experience the journey in earthly time and reality, otherwise it won't seem… real."

All the same, she'd nearly swallowed her words. Charlotte was used to skimming from one place to another through the unearthly Ring. She was aghast to discover how unbearably slow the liner's progress seemed. At first she was agitated, impatient to dive into the sky and fly ahead.

After a few days she attuned to the gentle pace. She began to relish the ship's steady progress, the daily rhythm of life in this elegant, self-contained community. Her anticipation of America heightened to an exquisite degree.

She delayed telling Karl that Josef was on board. It was a delicate subject. The liner was so large she could probably avoid Josef for the whole voyage – but she wanted to be honest with Karl. *I'll tell him soon*, she kept promising herself.

She and Karl fed discreetly and sparingly on the other passengers, leaving members of the ballet company strictly alone. There was a minor outbreak of "illness" causing lassitude and fever, but no deaths.

Violette, meanwhile, was barely seen throughout the voyage. She remained in her suite, attended only by her maid, Geli, who was used to her odd behaviour. Presumably she attributed it to Madame's artistic temperament.

Violette appeared twice a day to supervise a ballet class – essential to keep her dancers in peak form – then retired again. Even Charlotte barely spoke to her. She knew that Violette's turmoil over taking blood was worse in the confines of the ship, and that she was starving herself. Nothing Charlotte said made any difference. Eventually Violette lost patience and refused to see her.

The talk among the passengers was of the legendary Madame Lenoir. Greatly excited at the prospect of meeting her, they were to be disappointed. Charlotte gave up hope of Josef even glimpsing her before they reached New York.

Some months ago, Charlotte had told Karl about Josef. "A friend of my father," she'd said. "We met by chance and he recognised me. I tried to pretend he'd made a mistake but he saw through me... and yes, he knows I'm a vampire."

Karl had warned her against making human friends, so she'd been nervous of his reaction. To her surprise, he'd been sanguine about it. She was touched that he still trusted her, after her relationship with Violette. But that was Karl.

For him to be confronted by Josef in person, however, was a different matter. She dared not tell him before the ship sailed, in case Karl persuaded her to leave Josef behind. So she'd said nothing.

No use delaying any longer, though. On the fourth night, at a cocktail party in a large mirrored stateroom, with the floor rocking gently beneath them, she took Karl to meet Josef.

Josef greeted her warmly, his kind face suffused with pleasure. If Karl was disconcerted by this show of affection, he didn't betray it. Smiling to hide her apprehension, Charlotte said, "Josef, may I introduce Karl Alexander von Wultendorf. Karl, this is Dr Josef Stern."

The men's reaction to each other was formal and guarded as they exchanged pleasantries. Watching them together, Charlotte's head swam. Both lean and elegant in evening dress, they could almost have been father and son.

She only wished they liked each other. They clearly did not.

As Karl didn't know why Josef was here, nothing important could be discussed. Instead, a neutral conversation about the ship's magnificence concealed an ice-edged game. Josef knew Karl's true nature, which made the exchange even more difficult. And Karl, aware that this stranger knew his secret, was also wary. They were polite, but she saw the icy gleam in their eyes.

When Charlotte found an excuse to end the exchange, the two men parted with the impeccable courtesy of old friends.

Then Karl took Charlotte's arm, led her through the crowd and up on deck. The ocean wind was damp and chill. No one else braved the night air.

"So tell me, dearest," Karl said lightly, "What is Josef doing here?"

"I should have told you."

"Ah, so it's not a coincidence." His eyes were dryly reproachful.

"No. I invited him." She looked sideways at him, gauging his reaction. "I thought he might help Violette."

Karl rarely showed any immortal arrogance – the assumption that humans had nothing to teach vampires – but she sensed a touch of it now. "In what way?"

"He was a physicist – that's how he knew my father – but he also worked in psychology and he's familiar with Hebrew writings about Lilith."

"And this qualifies him to psychoanalyse Violette? I wish him luck."

"What else can we try? He might perceive *something* we hadn't thought of." Charlotte felt defensive, and wished she didn't. "Also, he has a niece in Boston. This is a perfect chance for him to visit her."

"You are very considerate."

"Are you jealous?" she said, suddenly amused.

Karl smiled, almost. "Charlotte, the man is in love with you."

"Perhaps," she said, with a slight shrug. "But he knows we can only be friends. He accepts it."

"A mortal friend," he said gravely, "who knows what we are."

"I hope this isn't another lecture about the dangers of human friends."

"No lecture. Have I not left you to learn by experience?"

The remark was subtly barbed. Her friendship with Violette had proved disastrous. "You can be such a beast, Karl, without even trying."

"Not to you, beloved." His tone softened. "I wish you'd told me of this plan, that's all."

"I meant to. But I knew you'd warn against it, and of course you're right. I shouldn't have involved Josef. Should never have let him see what I am. But he seemed able to accept it without horror, that's all."

Karl leaned on the ship's rail, arms folded, eyelids veiling his seductive eyes. "And it means so much, to be accepted by one mortal?"

"Of course." She laid her hands on his sleeve. "Did you never need a human to accept you?"

"Only you." He trailed one hand gently down her back. His touch made her shiver with pleasure, like the very first time he'd touched her.

"He isn't my secret lover, Karl. Perhaps he'd like to be – but he isn't."

"I'm glad to hear it," he said with a wry smile. "But my concern is for him. I welcome anything that could help Violette, but how will she react if you present her with a psychiatrist?"

"She'll be furious. That's why I must handle this with extreme care."

"Quite," said Karl, "because Josef is the one who'll suffer if Violette reacts badly. You've put him in danger."

"I know." She exhaled. "But I've warned him, and I'll protect him."

"I hope so." His long fingers pressed into her shoulder; the fingers of a musician, precise and strong. "For his sake."

In the hour before dawn, after Charlotte had fed, she stood alone at the rail, cold salt spray on her lips echoing the hot salt of blood. Watching the waves, she thought about her family. Those few words, "He was a friend of my father," led her along a thread of memories. She remembered her father, a gruff and imposing figure in his shapeless tweed jacket; a man with the modern mind of a scientist and a Victorian heart. She recalled quiet, happy times in his laboratory, Charlotte assisting as he teased out the secrets of the atom. His laboratory had been her refuge from the outside world.

She and her father had been close, yet unable to communicate. He couldn't endure losing his beloved daughter to Karl... and how could she justify her decision to put her love for a vampire before her own family?

Her behaviour had been unforgivable. She knew her father's health was poor; part of her was still human enough to worry. At least he wasn't alone. Her younger sister Madeleine, their brother David and his wife Anne, once Charlotte's best friend, would always take care of him. She still loved them... But she'd hurt them too badly ever to go back.

The price of being with Karl was to leave my human life behind, she told herself. *Oh, why's it still so hard to let the memories go? But I can and I must.*

This is where I belong. Leaving the past behind. Travelling to New York, Boston, a new world.

She watched the grey-green waves rising and falling, drawing the ship slowly towards the horizon. She let her imagination flow forward in time to the grey bowl of the harbour, towers rising through the haze, and the great oxide-green statue in all her grace, the flame of liberty making its eternal promise.

The real world came as a massive shock to Cesare.

With every step he took from Schloss Holdenstein, he became more aware of his own naivety. All his vampire life he had sheltered in the monumental dark temple of Kristian's theology. After the master's death, he'd stayed there, believing that one day

Kristian must return, or eternal life had no point.

For centuries Cesare had seen the world only by moonlight. He'd seen his victims as prey, lacking inner life. He knew nothing of world events, war or politics. He was unaware that fashions had changed, that the motor car was supplanting the horse, that women were questing towards equality with men.

Even without Kristian, in his steady state of despondency, he had been at peace. He'd lived a monkish life. His mind had become small and cramped, a walnut shell sealed around nothingness.

But the shell was cracking.

Venturing from the castle was like walking on knives. How the sunlight dazzled. How strange people looked in daylight, busy and oblivious to him. He was used to being his victim's universe, the last thing they ever saw! He hated being ignored. Yet he bore it, forcing himself to observe and learn.

A dreadful feeling grew inside him. *Fear*. His ignorance was a thick fog between him and the unfamiliar world.

Cesare knew Violette lived in Salzburg, but he didn't wish to face her without an armoury of knowledge. Instead he travelled through Switzerland to Italy, once his native land. There people took him for a priest and called him Father. Cesare liked that. It restored his sense of self.

The world dismayed him. Decadence, promiscuity, weak and faltering governments. He decided that a new order was sorely needed, among mortals and immortals alike.

But how little I know, he thought. *How much I have missed!*

These small admissions shredded his complacency until, close to his birthplace in northern Italy, despair overcame him. He broke down before the altar of a tiny village chapel and wept, dashing his head on the flagstones.

Kristian is gone. He is never coming back! Who is there to carry on after him?

No one but me.

A life-sized crucifixion, crudely carved and brown with age, hung above the altar. It represented a faith he'd forsaken long ago to follow the true saviour, Kristian. A soft human belief that sentimentalised meekness and mercy. But now the figure portrayed something else. The rigid arms nailed to the cross, the agonised face under a crown of thorns – all expressed Kristian's own anguish at his betrayal.

In his grief, Cesare leapt onto the figure and clung to it, tearing its shoulder with his fangs. No one was there to witness the bizarre scene. Wood splintered, the foul taste of sap and old paint filled his mouth. Yet he went on in his frenzy, as if clinging to Kristian and punishing him at the same time.

The storm in his skull overcame him, and he fell. As Cesare lay on the flagstones, God showed him a nightmarish vision. A blond child curled up under the wrath of a witch: a vast, ragged figure with wings and claws, wild black hair. She was beating the boy with a rod, lashing the tiny tender body with glee. Her hair flapped in a gale from hell.

Cesare knew that she was both the child's mother and the universal mother – the goddess of destruction, bride of the Devil, the Enemy.

Terror overwhelmed him. He wept for the tiny golden boy, but couldn't move. He knew that the child was secretly a cherub, immortal.

Next he saw a bright gold figure with white wings and a fiery sword. Cesare saw himself at a door with a key in his hand. And he understood.

I must open the door to God's army. Let them through and they will slay the witch-mother and save the sweet child of immortality!

The vision ended. He rose to his knees, gasping with terror and hope. He laughed and cried. "Forgive me, Father," he said, clasping his hands. "I doubted you, but now I understand. Kristian died to test me. Use me, Lord. Let me be your sword in the war against the Enemy!"

Presently Cesare walked out into the sunlight. As he emerged, he saw lines of soldiers marching along the dusty, bright road. It was the most beautiful sight he'd ever seen: light filtering through the green leaves, gilding these brisk rows of disciplined, strong young men.

Cesare felt new-born.

Now, he thought. *Now I am ready to face Lilith.*

* * *

Cesare arrived at the Ballet Janacek's house in Salzburg by night and entered, feeling all-powerful and disdainful, as if this act of stealth were below him. With heaven on his side, Violette could not touch him. The prospect of confronting her filled him with fire.

The house, save for a sleeping caretaker, was deserted.

Cesare's first thought was that Violette had deliberately, spitefully thwarted him. Then he felt relieved. He thought of killing the caretaker as a small warning, but a letter on a desk distracted him. It concerned a tour of America, making it plain the company would not be back until autumn.

But this is excellent, he thought. *I have time to plan.*

Cesare's new interest in the world led him to explore storerooms and offices, kitchens and rehearsal rooms. He lingered in an empty dance studio, then ascended to the private apartments.

Photographs of Violette were everywhere. Other dancers, too, but her face held him. Blanched skin and huge dark eyes, black feathers clasping her head. Even in monochrome she was enchanting. "Odile, 1925," read the caption. Cesare had no idea who Odile was. A witch, clearly.

Here she was again, in loose white chiffon, her hair unbound. "Giselle, 1923." A glacial sylph under a mantle of soot-black hair. Cesare stared, trembling. Through her terrifying eyes, her soul lanced straight into his, and he recognized her.

Oh yes, she was the witch of his vision.

She was the Enemy.

She was everything Kristian had fought against, an affront to God. Alien, impure, uncontrollable, irreverent, wicked. She would bring degradation and death.

He backed away, transported by the pure fire of hatred. Then he knew. Pierre and John had spoken the truth. Lilith was real and at large in the world, more terrible than even John had suspected.

"And you're mine," Cesare whispered to her frozen face. "Mine to deal with."

He raced back to Schloss Holdenstein as if winged. No good to wallow any longer, hoping in vain for Kristian's resurrection. He knew he must take up the holy work in his own way. Destroy the Enemy, Lilith, and create a new order.

Cesare thought of the strong and joyous young soldiers he'd

seen. *They were only humans*, he thought. *I am immortal, God's chosen. I have a battle to fight, a golden world to create – and never again, as I build the new empire, shall I walk in another's shadow.*

He'd stolen a small framed photograph. Inside the castle, he drew it from a pocket and gazed on the insolent face of chaos. Violette was in a daring, tight-fitting costume of glittering jet scales, not unlike the changed shape of a vampire in the Crystal Ring. The caption read, "The Serpent, *Dans le Jardin*, 1925."

"If you think you can slaughter the chosen of God," he whispered, "you are very wrong, Lilith."

He smashed the glass with his knuckles. His blood smeared the dancer's image, dripping over her throat and breasts, obliterating her eyes.

CHAPTER SIX

APPEASEMENT

In her elegant house on Beacon Hill, Roberta Stafford lay beneath her lover, expertly coaxing his excitement to a peak while her thoughts wandered elsewhere. His back felt hairy, damp, and crepey with age, but she never let her distaste show. She was an accomplished actress. Thankfully, because he was not young, his demands were modest.

At last he convulsed, grunted, and rolled aside with his wrist flung across his flushed forehead. Roberta immediately threw back the covers to let cool air onto her body.

"Wonderful, wonderful," he said. "I must remind myself of why I'm keeping you in luxury more often."

She laughed, stroking his cheek. "Whenever you like, Harold. I'm always here."

"Was it wonderful for you, my dear?"

"As ever," she said ambiguously. He fumbled for her but she evaded him and went to open a window, reaching between curtains of creamy lace. The afternoon was golden. When she turned, Harold was out of bed and getting dressed. She regarded the doughy folds of his skin, his paunch ballooning over his sparrow legs, his heavy jowls and sparse grey hair, with affectionate tolerance. Harold wasn't so bad. His love-making might be inept but it was financially rewarding. After all, he was no worse than any other man she'd had, and one of the few she did not actively despise.

"So, I hear you threw him over," said Harold, tying his shoelaces.

"Who?"

"Your young beau... Russell Booth?"

"Oh, him." Still naked, she helped him to fasten his gold cufflinks. "He wasn't my beau. He was getting altogether too serious. I had to end it."

"Word is you broke his heart."

"He'll get over it."

"Word is you also broke *him*."

"He must have thought I was worth it. He had a damned good time in the process. He has a rich daddy, he'll be all right." She sat at her dressing table and began to brush her thick, waist-length hair.

"He's not the only one with a rich daddy, is he?" Harold leaned on the back of her chair, the respectable businessman in his old-fashioned suit and wire-rimmed spectacles. "You're a tough woman, Robyn."

"You don't mind, do you?" She glimpsed her reflection. Her eyes were soft and mischievous, her face glowing, her smile fresh and without artifice. She might be uncomfortably close to forty, but could still pass for twenty-seven. "He knew the conditions, and so do you. No wedding bells, no exclusive rights."

"Oh, I'm not jealous, my dear. Have as many boyfriends as you like, as long as you don't throw me over for any of them."

"I couldn't afford to, don't worry."

In fact, she had money of her own, but preferred to spend Harold's. She turned her head and kissed the back of his hand. The white hairs were dry against her lips.

"Well, I have to go," he said. "But I got you a present."

Robyn gave a soft laugh, pleased. He always brought an offering, even when he only came to rant about his problems and drink her illicit brandy – which, of course, his money had bought.

His hands slipped under her hair and attached a sparkling band round her neck. A diamond choker. "Just a little something," he said. His "little somethings" were always worth a fortune.

"I guess this means you bought your wife a present too."

"Oh, sure," he said, "but yours cost more. Actually, the diamonds are kind of a peace offering. I wanted to take you to the ballet, but my wife wants to go, so I have to take her instead. I'm sorry."

"Oh, never mind," Robyn said, indifferent. "You're very sweet.

When have I ever been angry with you?"

"Never. Why d'you think I keep coming round? You're the nicest woman I ever met."

He patted her shoulder and left.

When he'd gone, Robyn took off the choker and dropped it on the dressing table. The tiny hard gems clicked as they folded onto the polished wood. Her depression lasted only a few seconds. Then she shook herself out of it, rang for her maid to run her bath, and began to coil her hair onto her head.

Her hair was the one thing about herself she admired. Heavy, thick and glossy, a deep glowing brown threaded with the gorgeous fall colours, her hair wove the power that attracted men to her. And she was pretty, she knew, but scores of Boston women were prettier, and younger. She saw the subtle ravages of maturity in her strong-featured face. Her allure came from a deeper level. She had a quality of repose, of warmth and tolerance. Men felt they could talk to her, that she'd welcome them, faults and all.

At the same time they found her mysterious. The combination seemed to be irresistible. And Robyn had learned to take full advantage of her appeal.

Some men only wanted sex; they were fun, because she could pick apart their egos with exquisite subtlety over months. But the best ones were those who fell in love and begged her to marry them. Those she could destroy utterly, especially if she got them to leave their wives before she rejected them.

There were two or three a year, not droves, but each one was a work of art. She was selective, choosing men who had the most to lose. And it was particularly satisfying to follow her vocation in Boston, that most puritanical and stratified of societies.

For each man who fell, there was another to replace him. She could have drawn up a waiting list. They never learned. Her reputation was known, but each new lover thought he'd be the one to change her.

That was her weapon. She made them believe her when she said, "You're different to all the others. I never loved until I met you."

Some of them she had quite liked, superficially. But deep inside, she despised their schoolboy infatuations, their arrogance. They deserved punishment.

Sometimes she hated her existence, but mostly she drifted through it with the same placid optimism that drew lovers into her trap.

The Irish maid, Mary, came to say the bath was ready. Robyn slid into the perfumed water and lay in contemplation of steam beading the marble tiled walls. Pleasantly tired, she was soothed by the sounds of Mary tidying the bedroom.

Her housekeeper, Alice – more companion than servant – entered the bathroom through wreaths of steam.

"Would you like your back washed, madam?" she asked, calling her "madam" with affectionate insolence. Robyn sat forward, enjoying the soapy sponge on her back. Alice's hands were firm and soothing. She was the same age as Robyn but looked older, her round, kind face still handsome in a cloud of dark hair. Over the years that she'd kept house for Robyn, they had grown close. Robyn considered Alice her only friend and ally against the world.

"Would you like to go to the ballet?" Robyn asked. "There's a company here from Europe. You probably saw it in the *Evening Transcript*. Harold mentioned them, too."

Alice paused in her task. Streams of hot water coursed deliciously down Robyn's spine. "The ballet, h'm? I would love to, but surely some gentleman –"

"To hell with them," Robyn said decisively. "Harold wanted to take me, but of course he can't be seen with me in public."

"Well, if you've no one else," Alice said darkly, rising to her feet. She was never impressed by any favours that Robyn offered, aware they could be withdrawn without notice. "I need to send Mary for fresh towels."

While she was out of the room, Robyn heard the doorbell. She cursed. A long pause, then Alice returned with an armful of white towels.

"There's a gentleman caller for you, madam." She seemed to be suppressing a smile.

"Oh, damn. I'm tired," Robyn sighed. Then she remembered her heartbroken beau. "It's not Russell, is it? Tell him to go away."

"No. He asked me not to say. It's a surprise."

"Oh, Lord, tell me it's not my father!"

"No. It's someone you'll want to see, I promise."

Robyn rose from the water, creamy and long-limbed, and let Alice wrap her in a cloud-soft towel. "I hate mysteries. All right, tell him to wait, then come back and help me do something with my hair."

Robyn took her time dressing, unable to think of a man she actually wanted to see. On entering the parlour, she almost did not recognise the tall, slight man who rose hastily to his feet to greet her. Years had passed. How grey his thick, unruly hair had turned! But the kind, chiselled face behind the black-rimmed spectacles was the same.

"Uncle Josef!" She flung herself into his arms, laughing.

He hugged and kissed her with delicate reserve. They'd met only three times; once when she was a child and Josef had visited her family, again when her parents had taken her to Europe. The third time had been after her wedding, seventeen years ago. Such a long time. But they'd always kept in touch.

"Forgive me for not announcing myself," he said. "I wanted to surprise you."

"Oh, you certainly did that!"

"My little Robyn." He held her at arm's length. "You look so lovely. Glowing."

"So do you, Uncle." She laughed again in amazement. "But you're in Vienna! What are you doing here?"

"A long story. A friend was travelling to America and asked me to come with her."

"Who is she? Come on, do tell."

He looked away, as if embarrassed. "It's not what it sounds like. She really is just a friend. She's with the Ballet Janacek and there was a spare berth."

"A dancer?"

"No... some sort of business partner."

Amused, Robyn shook her head and opened the French doors to her garden terrace. Ivory nets fluttered like bridal veils in the breeze.

"Do you believe in coincidence? I was just talking to Alice about seeing the ballet. Now I've heard them mentioned three times in one day. That's an omen, don't you think? Come see the garden."

Josef followed her out onto the terrace. A flight of steps led down to a tiny walled garden filled with shrubs and ferns, honeysuckle spilling over the walls, plants in terracotta tubs, a lemon tree in the centre of a handkerchief lawn.

"Where are you staying?" she asked.

"At a rather grand hotel on Tremont Street. Oh, I'm not here to impose on you, don't worry."

"I never thought you were, dear."

"But this is a lovely house," he said.

"Thank you." She added silently, *and so good to be mistress of my own domain.*

Robyn was proud of her home, one of a row of town houses that stepped gently up Chestnut Street. Built of soft russet brick, it had long leaded windows with white shutters, black railings tipped with gold, a flight of steps up to the front door. The rooms were big and beautifully kept, with polished floors or pale jade carpets, carefully placed antiques. Visitors always remarked how elegant and friendly the house was, how at home they felt there.

"Well, there's plenty of room with just Alice, Mary and me," she said. "I have the Wilkes, too, a married couple, but they don't live in. Mrs Wilkes cooks, Mr Wilkes is my chauffeur and gardener. They're very sweet."

"You are not lonely," he said, "since your husband... passed away?"

"Not at all."

"It's wonderful to see you," Josef said with feeling. "The last time was..."

"My honeymoon in Europe," she said flatly. "Before the War."

He gave her a rueful look. "You write less often than I do."

"I'm sorry, Uncle. I'm a dreadful letter-writer. But I do send photographs every Christmas."

"They are all framed on my desk."

"And I wrote several times last year, when Auntie Lisl died. I'm so sorry, I know how much you loved her."

Pain crossed his face. "She was terribly ill. Her death was a release."

"So now you're all alone... or are you?"

"All alone," he said resignedly.

"How have you have escaped all the women who must have fallen for you over the years?"

"Because I could never make a choice." Her teasing made him grin. "I know myself well enough not to make any woman unhappy by marrying her. Well, now I've grown up enough to tire of being a bachelor, I find it's too late. There is someone, but she's half my age and doesn't love me, so…" He shrugged.

"She must be mad."

"I am quite happy," he said, "apart from missing you."

He held her hands and they looked at each other, taking in every new line, every sadness. Josef meant more to her than her own father. "Have you seen my mom?"

"Yes, I felt I should, out of courtesy," he sighed. Although Robyn's mother was his sister, he didn't get on with her any more than Robyn did.

"Then I'm surprised you're here," she said lightly. "They've quite disowned me, and I'm sure they told you why."

He sounded more sad than disapproving. "Robyn, your letters give away more than you realise. But are you really happy, living like this?"

"How would you like me to live?" The anger that sprang into her voice startled her. "My parents wanted me to live as the wife of a rich, respectable, churchgoing Bostonian, happy ever after. So much for that!"

Josef looked startled and concerned. "You must miss your husband. Even if you were unhappy, it's harder being alone."

"Miss him?" she gasped. Josef didn't know the whole truth. No one did, except Alice – and her mother, who'd refused to listen. She wanted to tell Josef, *I danced on his grave!* – but movement in the parlour stopped her.

"Here's Mary with the tea," she said, letting anger go with her breath.

Stepping back through the fluttering net curtains, he caught her elbow. "My dear, I didn't mean to upset you. If I've offended you, I'm sorry."

"You haven't. Who am I to take offence at anything? Truly, I'm fine. My life is under control."

"Robyn," he said, fixing her with compassionate grey eyes, "you don't have to justify yourself. I'm not your father. I have only one demand to make of you."

"Which is?"

"That you do me the honour of accompanying me to *Swan Lake*."

The dancer in white was an avatar of perfection.

In the enraptured eyes of her audience, Violette Lenoir's genius made her more than human. Amid the painted sets, swelling music and lavish costumes, she was in her true place. An enchanted higher world, an aquarium of light separate from reality.

Only a few knew Violette's true nature. Strip her of her satin and tulle, feathers and greasepaint, and she would still shine like porcelain and ebony. The stage was camouflage. Take her out of context, and her otherness would still glow like a torch.

This was *Swan Lake*'s opening night. Charlotte watched from a private box with Karl beside her, drinking Violette's magic.

As Odette, the dancer was all innocence and flowing delicacy, radiating passionate warmth. Yet it was only as Odile – Odette's evil counterpart – that she was truly in character. She didn't have to act. She became a pillar of glacial fire contained by the luscious black of her jewelled and feathered costume. Her powerful fluidity was stunning.

In the darkness, Karl reached out and took Charlotte's hand.

It will be all right, Charlotte told herself. *As long as Violette goes on dancing, she will be all right.*

The story wound to its poignant climax. Violette danced her curtain calls, while the audience showered her with flowers and applause. When the house lights came up, Karl said, to Charlotte's surprise, "I think we should go and see her, don't you?"

She agreed, with a dart of apprehension. How ridiculous to fear Violette! But she couldn't help it. The dancer had barely spoken to her since leaving Europe. Images of Violette cutting a red line across her wrist... seizing Charlotte, poising fang-tips on her throat, then confronting Karl with twisted rage in her eyes...

Her morbid isolation throughout the journey.

As they crossed the foyer, the body scents of the crowd woke Charlotte's thirst. This pressing desire was no longer a shock. She drew it in like breath. The prospect of sating it later – outside, in some dark place without witnesses – was exciting.

Nothing obvious marked Karl and Charlotte as predators. Someone who looked for too long might consider them almost too perfect in their soft radiance to be human. Film stars, perhaps? The onlooker would never guess that their allure was a jewelled trap.

Backstage, dancers, musicians, directors and scene-shifters milled around the brick corridors. The theatre staff, with their American accents, their exuberance, their different fashions and manners – all struck Charlotte as fresh and strange. Even the lowliest errand boy was cheerfully impertinent, to her delight.

The ballet company members were more reserved, acknowledging Charlotte politely as an enigmatic patron of the Ballet Janacek. She returned their greetings, her focus on the door of Violette's dressing room.

"Come in," she called before Charlotte knocked. Exchanging a look of unease with Karl, she went in.

The dancer sat at her dressing table in a cream satin gown, her hair coiled around her head. The cold cream she'd used to remove her make-up gave her skin a glassy shine.

She stood and greeted them with real warmth. "I'm so glad you came. Did you enjoy it? Didn't they love us?" And she clasped both Charlotte's and Karl's hands, laughing.

After their recent encounters, Charlotte was taken aback. She'd seen Violette in distress so often that this innocent glow of happiness was astounding. Karl, for once, was lost for words.

"I told you *Swan Lake* was the one," said Charlotte, relaxing a little.

"And you were right. Ballet Janacek, the toast of Europe; soon to be the toast of America." Turning to the mirror, she unpinned her luxuriant hair to unravel in fronds around her shoulders. "I noticed a man in the front row," she said lightly. "Grey-haired, quite handsome, staring at me as if analysing my performance more than enjoying it. Do you know who he is?"

Shocked, Charlotte didn't know whether to lie or not. The man might not have been Josef. She tried diplomatic evasion. "A reporter, probably."

"Perhaps, but he was on the ship with us. He was watching me then, too. Tonight there was a woman with him, brunette, very striking." Violette's happiness was a veneer, Charlotte noted sadly. Her eyes in the mirror were haunted.

"If you see him again, point him out and I'll tell you if I know him," said Charlotte. Karl's face was immobile. She was grateful when he changed the subject.

"If they'd seen you tonight, even your opponents would be convinced it would be a tragedy for you to stop dancing. You must go on, Violette, if it's what you want."

"It is." Her joy resurfaced. "Mortal or immortal, the ballet is still my life. At least that hasn't changed. If Charlotte hadn't transformed me, I would still be waking up half-crippled every morning, wondering how long I could stay out of a wheelchair. Instead I can dance forever, as if my shoes are possessed by the Devil. I know I've been a little wild at times…"

She left the thought unfinished. Karl kissed her hand in a token of truce, a mere courtesy. But when the dancer came to embrace Charlotte, there was terrible electricity between the two women. Charlotte, who often wished Violette would be less sparing with affection, suddenly wanted to escape.

"The good people of Boston are giving a party in our honour," she said into Charlotte's ear. "Please come. You know how I hate these affairs."

"Of course we will. We're always here if you need us."

"Oh, I do," she said with sudden intensity. The tip of a fang grazed Charlotte's earlobe. "You and Karl. I need you."

Sebastian looked forward to *Swan Lake* with keen anticipation. Boston struck him as fresh and tranquil after New York. He decided to stay a while. And by the week's end, the ballerina would be his.

He viewed the imminent game with sombre passion rather than glee, as if it were a duty to his dark vampire nature. How else should the Devil behave?

My attentions will put paid to her dancing, of course, he thought as he took his theatre seat. *It could destroy the company; and by the time I've finished with her – days or months, depending on how amusing I find her – she will of course die. What a waste.*

But how glorious, to extinguish such a light!

Sebastian loved needless tragedies. They moved him unutterably.

He settled down in the back row to await Odette – but within seconds of her bewitching entrance, he was sitting forward in astonished horror. The ballerina in white net and swansdown was a vampire!

The pearly glow of her skin, the lustre of her eyes and the fluidity of her dancing; everything gave her away. Sebastian was appalled. Recalling his encounter with Simon in New York, he thought, *Did Simon know about her? He certainly knew that if he told me, I'd never have come near her.*

Sebastian almost walked out, but suppressed the impulse and forced himself to watch, nails digging into the plush arms of his seat.

Violette Lenoir. A slender-limbed weaver of enchantment. Had her rapt audience the faintest idea of what they were worshipping? Of course not. If she'd been human he would have found her captivating. Instead she stirred nothing in him, beyond detached appreciation of her skill. He saw her for what she was, a savage, heartless creature of ice. Like him. But to brazen it out before a human public –!

It's one way of attracting prey, he thought cynically. *Well, if I cannot feed on her, I'll find someone else. Another dancer, perhaps, less famous but lusciously human...*

He sighed. It wouldn't be the same. A cloud of desolation descended.

But... did Simon want *me to discover that Lenoir is one of us? Why? He told me to reconsider what he'd said after I'd seen her... He should know that manipulating me won't work. I've no interest in my kind. I refuse to rule or be ruled. How much more plainly could I have stated it?*

With distaste, he sensed two other vampires in the audience. He couldn't see them. He could only feel their presence, like two cool gems in a sea of sweltering humans.

He left before the end, not wanting to risk meeting them. The foyer of rose marble and gold leaf was quiet. The street, with tall brownstone and Victorian buildings, was gently busy with the moving lights of cars. Hands in pockets, Sebastian walked towards the Common and the Public Garden. This was Boston's heart, the green land between the old town and the wealth of Beacon Hill.

Warm spring air brushed his skin. He was so deep in meditation that he hardly noticed the warning sign, a glass dagger pricking his mind...

Suddenly alert, he looked ahead to locate the vampire. Too late: the woman had seen him and stood on the sidewalk, smiling. Waiting for him. He couldn't avoid her.

She wore a coat of black figured velvet and fur, jet beads twinkling on her ears, her dark fire-tinged hair frozen in a precise curve around the pale heart of her face. She studied him with the amused disdain he remembered from Kristian's castle, many years ago.

"Sebastian!" she said, her eyes shining. She'd retained her charming Austrian accent. "This is the most wonderful surprise!"

"Ilona." He inclined his head, polite but cold.

"Is that the best you can do? After all these years!" Without waiting for an invitation, she pressed close to him and clasped her hands behind his neck. With an inward sigh he relented and embraced her, pressing his lips to her cold skin.

"How did you know I was here?" he said.

"I didn't. Don't flatter yourself into thinking I crossed the ocean to look for you. I saw you in the theatre, but you were too busy staring at Violette to notice me. I have a little advantage. Like you, other vampires tend not to sense me until I'm right in front of them."

Ilona slid her hand through his arm, and they crossed the road into the Public Garden. He couldn't shake her off without resorting to violence. At present he lacked the will even to argue.

"I guessed you would leave early," she went on, "so I came out and waited for you."

"So, are you here with the other three?" he asked. "The enchanting Lenoir and her companions... I didn't stop to see who they are."

"One of them is Karl."

"Oh, I should have known," said Sebastian. They entered an undulating green space full of trees. On the nearby lake, the swan boats were moored for the night. "It goes without saying, I've no wish to see him."

"His companion is Charlotte, some human he took up with

about three years ago. She's a sweet immortal, but too soft for her own good."

"Ilona," he said, "I am not interested."

"You haven't changed, have you?" she said with relish. "Still the loner, the fastidious vampire-hater. You even made love to me as if you hated me."

"Wasn't that the way you preferred it?" he said acidly.

Laughing, she rested against a broad tree trunk. Sebastian reflected that Ilona was his equal, not a human to be ensorcelled, played with, tormented. Unrewarding. Yet he still found her attractive. He stood close, one hand resting on the trunk above her shoulder.

"I'm not with the others," she said. "They don't know I'm here. And I doubt they've noticed you, either." Her tone was conspiratorial. Similarities in nature had drawn them together, although they'd nearly torn each other apart during their brief, fierce liaison.

"Ah, I remember," he murmured. "You're the main reason I prefer solitude."

"You sure know how to hurt a girl." She mimicked a New York accent. Then, in a rush of feeling, she said, "But of course, you don't know! Everything's changed. Kristian's dead!"

"Aren't you the bearer of glad tidings," he said coolly, deciding not to admit he already knew.

"Perhaps, but some think Violette might be worse."

Simon's warning again. *A new immortal at large, too dangerous to be allowed her freedom.*

"Violette?" He felt his patience evaporating. "If this is another attempt to involve me in vampire affairs, don't waste your breath."

She blinked, uncomprehending. "Not content with humans? You want to kill the art of conversation as well?"

"I've already had Simon plaguing me with cryptic remarks about doom and destruction. Get it over. Tell me about Violette."

"Charlotte transformed her. Couldn't leave her alone. She looks harmless enough on stage, doesn't she? But a number of vampires are working themselves into a frenzy of terror over her. She's certainly crazy. She has two immortal heads on her belt already. Or more, for all I know."

"What's your opinion, Ilona?" he said, impatient. "I can't

believe you're frightened of her. You're like me; you don't really care, do you?"

She shrugged. "She doesn't like me, but she's never threatened me. However, she attacked an acquaintance of mine, Pierre. The effect on him was alarming."

"In what way?"

"She reduced him to a trembling heap, afraid to set foot outside the dubious sanctuary of Schloss Holdenstein. Pierre is a coward, but only in the sense that he prefers an easy life. If anything, he has a positive taste for being abused and humiliated. So tell me, what power does Violette possess, to dismember his personality as Kristian never could?"

Sebastian's indifference was shaken by unease, as if a huge crow had swooped over him. "I've no idea. As I said, I don't care about the petty infighting between you and your kind."

"My kind?" Ilona glared at him. "Dear God, do you really think yourself so superior?"

"Not superior. Separate. That's how I prefer to remain."

"Have it your own way." Her rage cooled to disdain. "No one missed you when you left Schloss Holdenstein. Why should we need you now?" Her mouth, a perfect plum-red bow, curved into a smile that said firmly, *You cannot hurt me*. She was lovely, but his desire for her was passionless, purely physical. "There's something else. You must have noticed changes in the Crystal Ring. Doesn't it seem stormier? Hostile, as if it doesn't want us anymore?"

Her tone chilled him. Although she mocked other vampires' fear of Violette, he sensed that she was secretly terrified.

"I rather like it," he said.

"You would. Well, the rumour is that it's Lilith's fault. Her presence has warped the Ring. She could be our doom, they say, unless..."

"You called her Lilith," Sebastian broke in.

"Did I? It's what she calls herself. I told you she's crazy."

The name stirred an inky stratum within him. A formless shape rose, dissipated, vanished. "But you don't believe this nonsense?"

"I can't stand hysteria," said Ilona, sliding her arms around his waist under his coat. "I'm here to prove it's not true. And you, why are you here? Toying with some human?"

"You remember me. How touching." He kissed her. Her mouth opened to his, warm and eager. Then she drew back and smiled, stroking his cheek.

"Confess," she said. "You look miserable. You're bored, aren't you? Let's forget all this. I'm taking you to a party."

"Will Karl and the others be there?" He rested his hands on her shoulders. His need to be alone was proving stronger than his lust for her.

"Of course. It's in honour of the Ballet."

"Where?"

"Some grand house on Commonwealth Avenue."

"Good. I shall avoid Commonwealth Avenue like the plague."

She frowned. "Why? They needn't see us. And there will be humans, an ocean of fascinating strangers to plunder." She pressed her slender body against his, her mouth curved in invitation. "I thought we could amuse ourselves together, as we used to."

"Well, you thought wrong," he said icily. "I don't want to be with vampires, Ilona. I don't want to see Karl or hear another word about Violette. I hate vampires, Ilona – and that includes you."

"You arrogant bastard!" She glowered venomously at him, her head tilted. Then she showed the tips of her fangs.

Sebastian's hands tightened on her shoulders. His mouth fell to her throat, his lupine teeth springing through her flesh. Ilona yelped, tried to struggle, then clung to him, groaning with mingled pleasure and pain. After a few seconds – realising he was doing this not in desire, but as a reminder of his strength – she began to fight again.

Sebastian was not angry. It was only the bleak, lightless vista within him, demanding its solitude. Its autocracy.

He took a last swallow of her burning blood and withdrew, leaving Ilona more indignant than hurt. She began to speak but he pushed her away, slamming her back into the tree so hard that she gasped and fell to her hands and knees on the tree roots. Oblivious to her curses he left her there, and walked softly away into the darkness.

CHAPTER SEVEN

HOUSE OF THORNED VINES

Charlotte's father, a philosopher and scientist, had used to say that the microcosm contained the macrocosm; that if they could understand the physics of the atom, they would understand the universe itself. This theory, Charlotte thought, also held true for social gatherings. Several times in her life a party had become a central event, a small universe complete in itself, its relationships and emotions forced in a hothouse of artificial contact.

As a human she'd hated these events. Tonight, though, as she and Karl entered the mansion, the prospect of the evening ahead excited her. They would move among unsuspecting humans, who would be captivated without knowing why. They would have innocent conversations with mortals while acutely aware of the blood beating beneath their fresh, unbroken skin. Such electrifying pleasure. And Charlotte would think, *All I'd have to do is say the word and you'd gladly permit an embrace that might end your life…* Yet she would spare them.

Most of them, at least.

Karl met her eyes, and she saw her anticipation mirrored there. Often she was still shocked to know that he shared her passions, that his gentlemanly detachment was a mask. This unity was only a step away from their shared feast; wondrous, horrific, forbidden.

The party followed the first performance of *Swan Lake*, the one night that suited the ballet's schedule. Karl and Charlotte were introduced to the host, an imposing patriarch named James

Wilberforce Booth, patron of the arts and a major figure in Boston society, so Violette said. Then they entered the ballroom, a grandiose marble hall that sparkled with mirrors and chandeliers. The space was already crowded, dancers mingling with wealthy socialites. Glass doors stood open to the garden.

"I like this city," said Charlotte. "It feels familiar, yet so different."

"I love the subtlety of the differences," Karl said softly. "Their accents, the way they dress and move. These old Bostonians pride themselves on being of English stock yet they are completely American. Here we are in this aristocratic fortress, but we could walk outside and enter a different world: Irish, Italian, Chinese. There's such energy here." He paused, as if contemplating all that seething human heat, life and blood. "This land seems full of possibilities that have died in Europe. They are not jaded by the weight of history."

"When we walked down by the harbour," Charlotte murmured, "I imagined immigrants walking off the ships through the sea fog. Like ghosts, but full of hope. Everything is so different and exciting, but it feels like home."

The gleam of fascination in Karl's eyes reminded her that vampires thirsted for more than blood. She'd seen that look when he helped her father with his research. Karl often warned her against befriending humans, but the truth was that the mortal world intrigued him.

"Did you invite Josef?" he asked as they wove between guests.

"Of course. Tonight's ideal for him to meet Violette. She might even be receptive."

"And have you told her about Josef?"

"No." Charlotte sighed. "I'll say he's a friend, that's all. He may learn something from talking to her. I don't like subterfuge, but if I tell her the truth – I can imagine how she'd react!"

Karl shook his head. "You do like playing with fire, beloved, don't you?"

"I can't see either of them, anyway. Violette's bound to be late."

"If she comes at all," said Karl.

"Oh, she will. She has a strong sense of duty towards her admirers."

"True," he said. "She is never ungracious to strangers; only to her friends."

Charlotte ignored this barbed remark.

Glancing towards the doors for a sign of Violette, she saw Josef with an attractive woman on his arm. She caught his eye and he came over, introducing his companion as his niece, Roberta Stafford.

"Call me Robyn," she said. "Josef gave me the name, that's why I like it." And she smiled affectionately at her uncle.

Charlotte liked her immediately. She seemed friendly, mischievous and irreverent.

"I hope you won't find us all as dull and proper as our hosts," Robyn said, looking pointedly at Mr Booth senior and his sons, two rigid, unsmiling men in their twenties. "No liquor in the fruit cup, no champagne. You must think we're hideously uncivilised."

"Isn't Prohibition a civilising influence?" said Karl with a half-smile.

"The exact opposite, if you ask me," said Robyn. "Oh, liquor can be had at a price. But the Booths are teetotallers. If they can't enjoy themselves, they're darned if anyone else will!"

"I hope we're allowed to dance," said Karl.

"Oh, sure; dance, smoke, anything." She touched Karl's arm conspiratorially. "Just don't look as if you're enjoying it."

While Karl spoke to Robyn with his usual charm, Charlotte watched keenly for her reaction. His effect on women could be devastating. Charlotte herself had fallen heavily, after all. Robyn, though, seemed too worldly – or cynical – to be easily impressed. Her manner was relaxed: friendly, not flirtatious. Only a flicker of her eyes betrayed uncertainty.

I knew Josef wouldn't tell her what we are, Charlotte thought. *She senses an indefinable strangeness about us, has no idea what it is.*

Josef was the one who reacted. As Robyn touched Karl's arm and he laughed with her, Charlotte saw Josef turn white. She knew he was suddenly seeing Karl as predator, Robyn as prey. Taking his niece's arm in mid-conversation, Josef stammered an excuse and steered her away.

"A shame," Karl sighed. "Even if I reassured Josef that I've no intention of touching her, he wouldn't believe me."

"Not in a million years," Charlotte said wryly, "because you were tempted, weren't you? And so was I."

The image of the shared feast blazed like blood-red flame between them, and when their hands met, the touch was like lightning. But no one around them suspected a thing.

Despite what Sebastian had said to Ilona, he found himself walking along the broad, imposing Commonwealth Avenue until he found a grand red-brick house alive with light and music. THE CITY OF BOSTON WELCOMES THE BALLET JANACEK announced a banner draped above the front door.

His intention to avoid the party had been genuine... yet now the idea drew him like an oasis. A sea of fascinating strangers. Arriving early, before any other vampires appeared, he circulated freely for a time. He watched the women, listened to their chatter and breathed their perfume. In New York he'd been intrigued by the so-called "flappers", their unstructured, revealing dresses and the undignified exuberance of their dances. The ladies of Boston and their debutante daughters were more conservative. He took in the subdued brilliance of their jewels and beaded gowns like an observer from another age.

Sebastian felt like a foreign visitor, unsure of the customs, but he liked the feeling. That was as it should be. How easily women fell for a mysterious stranger.

Presently the dancers began to arrive. Women and men alike rushed to them in a fawning flock. Sebastian decided to stay, and enjoy the party from a distance, from the shady recesses of the house.

Leaving the ballroom, he went to explore, stepping in and out of the Crystal Ring to avoid being seen. He could tolerate crowds for only a short time. Sometimes he craved solitude more than blood.

On an upper floor, his attention was caught by a lone human in a nearby room. Curiosity drew him. He opened a door and found a young man sitting in a darkened study.

Sebastian walked to the leather couch where the man sat. Faint light from the windows sheened expensive dark furniture, the man's hunched shoulders and his thick, light-brown hair.

He was quite handsome, Sebastian noted, and very unhappy. A gold cigarette case lay at his feet, cigarettes scattered on the rug.

"Are you not in the mood for a party?" Sebastian asked softly.

The man looked up, as if resenting the disturbance but too depressed to care. His collar and tie were undone, and he gripped a glass of gin on his knee. The smell was distinct. *So much for Prohibition*, Sebastian thought, amused.

"I tried, but I couldn't face it. Someone turned up who... I know I ought to show my face for my father's sake, but I can't. My brothers said it would cheer me up, but..."

"The contrast between their happiness and your sorrow is unbearable."

The man uttered a huge sigh. His face was flushed, his eyes lifeless. "Yes, unbearable. You put that well."

Sebastian bent down, gathered the spilled cigarettes into the case, and handed it back to him. "Thanks," said the young man. "Clumsy, my hands were shaking."

"Shall I light one for you?" the vampire asked.

"I'd appreciate it." Sebastian obliged; the man sucked deeply and blew out clouds of reeking smoke. "Thanks. You?"

Sebastian declined. He sat on the rolled arm of the couch and looked down at the bowed head. "Would it help to talk about your troubles?"

"Did my father send you up here to persuade me out?"

Sebastian had seen the moustachioed patriarch greeting guests in the ballroom, flanked by his wife and two humourless sons. This wretched creature, he guessed, must be the black sheep. "No, but I'm sure he's concerned."

"Concerned, hell. You won't tell him about this, will you?" He held up the glass. "He thinks liquor is the devil's work."

"Our secret," said Sebastian. He thought up a false name and said, "I'm John Waterford."

"Russell Booth." They shook hands. The young man named Russell took a loud swallow of his drink and stared at nothing. Then he said, "It's a woman, what else?"

"And she let you down."

"That's an understatement. Bitch! No, no, I take it back. I

loved her. She was older than me, a lot older, but I didn't care. I wanted to marry her. My family were dead against it. Said she was married before, as if that matters! Said she had a reputation, but I wouldn't listen; I thought she'd be different with me. God, I worshipped her. The clothes I bought her, jewels, a car. Even made business investments for her."

"Ah. That sounds like a bad idea."

"Sure, she took me for a fool. I think she would've stayed as long as my money lasted, if I hadn't found out she was seeing someone else. Not just one man, a string of them. She can pick and choose, and she only chooses the rich." He laughed bitterly, on the edge of tears. "I make her sound like a whore, but she's not. I can't explain. You'd understand if you met her; men'd just die for her."

"So, has she ruined you?"

"Oh, the money doesn't matter. Father isn't speaking to me, but he'll come round. I loved her, that's the problem. When I found out about the others, I went crazy. You know what she did? She laughed. Can you believe it? After everything, she called me an idiot, said I'd got what I deserved. It's her living, see; she bleeds rich men dry, and if she breaks their hearts in the process, that makes her even happier. My brothers tried to warn me, she's done it countless times. What she likes best is to take fools like me and ruin them for any other woman."

"She sounds charming, and not especially unusual." Sebastian was growing interested, despite himself.

"She's one on her own, I'm telling you. But the thing is..." He paused, struggling. "She's here. Came with the ballet folks. After what she did, she walks in with her head in the air, laughing at us!"

"What a nerve," Sebastian said admiringly. "So that's why you're hiding?"

"Couldn't face her."

Sebastian shook his head. "You should have done, to show you don't care."

"But I do! I still love her." Russell looked up with hollow, desperate eyes. "I hate her too. I'd like to kill her, then myself."

"Romantic."

"If you think this is funny, you can go to—"

"Please, my friend." Sebastian took Russell's clenched fist and pushed it away. "I feel for you. But you've made yourself her victim, when you should forget this sentimental nonsense of love and think instead of cold-blooded revenge."

Russell stared at Sebastian, jerked out of his self-absorption. Then he slumped. "I can't. It's pathetic, but I'm beyond it."

"Then perhaps I could do it for you."

"You?" Another flash of life, tinged with alarm. "How?"

"I could do to her what she has done to you. A taste of her own poison."

The man's eyes were huge, his mouth slack with astonishment. Sebastian smiled. Russell plainly realised that it was not an empty threat. Terror sobered him. "No. I couldn't do that to her."

"Describe her and tell me her name."

"No. No."

"Why not? How will she understand what she's done, unless she suffers as you have?"

Russell hesitated, trembling. Sebastian saw an instinctive desire to protect his ex-lover warring with unholy excitement. Then he whispered, "Her name's Roberta Stafford. She lives on Chestnut Street. You'll know her – she's so beautiful, with brown hair like all the colours of fall. Her friends call her Robyn, with a 'y'." He caught his breath, as if to suck back the information he'd spilled.

"I look forward to meeting her," said Sebastian. His hand slid along Russell's shoulder to the damp skin of his neck. "No regrets, now. Remind yourself that she deserves it."

"Yes. But…" There was desperate anxiety in his eyes. "You won't hurt her? Physically, I mean."

"No more than this." Sliding down on to the couch, Sebastian covered the strong young body with his own. He felt his fangs spring through the tender skin.

"What–?" One feeble protest, then surrender. Sebastian was already drinking his hot, pulsating blood, absorbing the ambience of smoke and stale alcohol and despair.

I doubt they'll find the body until after the party, thought Sebastian. *And they'll think the poor heartbroken boy drank himself to death.*

* * *

Robyn was happy tonight. She'd been content on her uncle's arm as they'd taken their seats for *Swan Lake*; nothing to prove, no one to impress. The ballet was a delight. As for her guilt about letting Alice down, she'd assuaged it by buying Alice tickets for a different night.

Leaving the theatre afterwards, she saw Harold with his wife in the crowd. Robyn amused herself by catching his eye. How satisfying to see his eyes bulge in sudden terror, blood engorging his face! She heard his wife – a formidable matriarch – exclaim in annoyance as Harold steered her at an abrupt right angle.

"Someone you know?" asked Josef.

Robyn laughed. "Not officially."

Harold, thankfully, was not at the after-show party.

Although Robyn was unimpressed by status, money or talent, she found the idea of mingling with the dancers oddly thrilling. On stage, they'd seemed too ethereal to be quite human... particularly Violette Lenoir.

"This is wonderful," she whispered as she and Josef entered the ballroom.

"Very impressive," said Josef, looking around.

"No, not the room. James Wilberforce Booth has three sons: Russell, Victor and William. I had an affair with Russell. Now his family loathes me. Watch them looking daggers at me! I shouldn't be here, but there isn't a damn thing they can do."

"Oh, Robyn," her uncle said sadly. The narrow eyes of Victor and William poured venom in her direction. "Don't you mind them glaring?"

"No, I love it. They're the ones tearing themselves apart, not me."

"But what if you bump into Russell?"

"What if I do? I might lead him on and drop him all over again. Don't look at me like that! I am joking."

"Are you?" said Josef, shaking his head. She only smiled, knowing he loved her too much to condemn her.

Russell, however, did not appear. The Booth family ignored her, as if it were beneath their dignity to make a scene. Robyn relaxed.

There were people here she knew. Some shunned her, but there were plenty of others prepared to overlook her scandalous reputation, simply because she was attractive and good company. They found genuine sweetness in her character, and couldn't believe the worst.

The evening was convivial, until Josef took her to meet his friends. The moment she saw them, the atmosphere changed.

The strangers made a strikingly attractive couple. Charlotte was the daughter of an old friend, said Josef, but his excuse was transparent. *So*, Robyn thought, *this is the mystery woman! How sad that he loves her without hope...* Robyn read their stances and gestures like an adept. Charlotte, although clearly fond of Josef, had an unbreakable bond with the man at her side. Meanwhile, Karl and Josef quietly resented each other.

Her impressions went deeper. Karl and Charlotte were not merely beautiful but curiously vivid. Charlotte's solemn face and violet eyes were wreathed by gold-frosted hair, her arms pale and slender against the russet velvet of her dress. And Karl could well be one of the male dancers. He had that slender strength and grace, a dark presence that was quiet yet overwhelming. To Robyn it seemed the ballroom and guests were sketched in watercolour, while these two were painted in rich oils. They had luminosity, beauty and depth more extreme than reality.

Unnerving. Accustomed to being the centre of attention, for once Robyn felt invisible. She made light-hearted conversation, trying not to give away how irrationally disturbed she felt. Perhaps Josef sensed it too. He ended the exchange abruptly and led her away, suddenly pale.

"What's wrong, dear?" she said. "Are you unwell?"

"No, no, I'm quite all right. But we can't keep them all evening, they have to circulate."

Robyn didn't argue. There were too many people, introductions to be made, one conversation spilling into the next. The dancers, mostly female, were noticeable for their swan-like grace. A wealth of human beauty. Robyn became languorously enchanted, seeing the room through a crystal haze. Everyone seemed to move slowly, like swimmers through a flooded temple, their pearly flesh adorned with silk and jewels.

Through this uncanny light, she watched Karl and Charlotte from a distance.

Together or apart, they kept exchanging glances as if passing thoughts by telepathy. Always observing others, too, like spies. Emotionally, they were wrapped around each other like vines. With strangers, they were friendly but unreadable. With each other, their faces became radiant, expressive, conveying a hundred thoughts without words. Karl's long dark lashes lowered as he spoke softly to Charlotte; her expression ignited into sunlit charm as she responded.

Watching them, Robyn burned. *Oh lord, not jealousy*, she thought. She despised romantic love as a lie, yet it hurt to be reminded that for some, it was true. *Even if it's not forever*, she thought cynically. *However strong, there's always something that might break it. Oh, but to feel such passion, if only for a month, a year, a day! If I could be seventeen again and unbruised...*

A rise in the level of conversation jolted her. There was a flurry of excitement, a wave of applause. The *prima ballerina assoluta* had arrived.

Like worker bees around their queen, everyone began clustering around Violette Lenoir. Minutes passed before Robyn even saw her.

Then she glimpsed a small woman, a sylph in ashes-of-roses silk and silver lace, lilies in her coiled black hair. On stage she projected a commanding presence; in life she looked softer, more delicate, and wholly a star. A weird shiver went through Robyn: a shocking recognition of another creature like Karl and Charlotte.

But recognition of what? Robyn wondered, disturbed. She felt Josef's hand on her elbow. He too was staring at Violette.

"Well, there she is," Robyn said cheerfully. "The star of the show. Do I get to meet her?"

"No, I..." Josef took out a handkerchief and wiped his forehead. "I don't think so."

"Uncle, are you sure you're not ill? Do you want me to take you home?"

"No, but I think you should go." He tucked the handkerchief away.

"Why? I'm enjoying myself."

"Some of the people here... they are not so nice."

She laughed gently, imitating his Viennese accent. "Oh, Uncle, what makes you think I'm so nice?"

"I mean it. They may be... dangerous."

"Ballet dancers? What are they going to do, pirouette us to death?"

"I'm serious, Robyn. I shouldn't have brought you here. I didn't think."

"Well, if you won't explain, I'm going nowhere. Don't worry, I can take care of myself."

His expression closed and he gave a small, resigned shake of his head. An autumn-clad figure slid quietly to his side: Charlotte.

"May I steal your uncle for a while?" Her voice was lovely, Robyn noticed, with its English delicacy. She gave Robyn a look of genuine warmth. "Do you mind?"

"Of course not. Go ahead," Robyn answered with a smile. She watched them walk away, the golden-brown head tilted towards Josef's shoulder.

Within seconds, a man – one of her hopeful admirers – cornered her, but others joined them so she was able to excuse herself and edge around the dance floor towards the beckoning peace of the garden.

What's the matter with everyone tonight? she wondered. *Me, especially. I need air.*

Heads turned as she passed but she took no notice. They were like dream figures. Her sense of unreality verged on euphoria. And... yes, a twinge of jealousy that Josef was privileged to meet Violette Lenoir.

Why? she thought. *Some of the people here may be dangerous? How in heaven's name am I supposed to take that?*

As Charlotte led Josef to the corner where Violette was holding court, he said, "Won't she be suspicious of your motive for introducing me?"

"Oh, probably," Charlotte replied. "She misses nothing. But I won't let her hurt you, Josef, believe me. Talk about the weather, ballet, anything, but observe her and tell me what you think. And be careful what you say to me, because we have sharp hearing."

His expression was dark with misgiving. "Really, I don't know that I'll be of any use."

"Nor do I. It's just a feeling that you might see *something* we've missed."

"Ah. There is a name for this exercise," he said.

"Yes?"

"It's called clutching at straws."

Violette sat in an alcove between marble pillars, embowered by green ferns, receiving a stream of admirers. No one tried to monopolise her, Charlotte noticed. Violette leaned forward in her chair, hands folded in her lap, her ankles crossed. A defensive posture. Yet she sounded relaxed as she spoke to a middle-aged couple.

"Our daughter just loves the ballet," said the wife. "We wondered, Madame, if you would be so gracious as to see her dance, tell us if she has a future? You must be dreadfully busy, I know."

"It's no trouble," Violette said kindly. "Bring her to the theatre tomorrow afternoon." And the couple gushed in gratitude.

Charlotte knew that Violette had once hated this attention, the unavoidable by-product of her talent, but her transformation enabled her to endure it. Easy for an immortal to act the gracious goddess – and Violette was nothing if not an actress.

Too many people wanted to meet her: introducing Josef was impossible. Instead, Charlotte and Karl found chairs, and the three seated themselves at the edge of the group. Josef turned even paler. He removed his spectacles, polished them, replaced them on the long blade of his nose.

"What is it?" said Charlotte. Karl's face was impassive.

Josef replied quietly, "It's like the first time I saw you, Charlotte; I mean, the first time I realised what you are." He glanced uneasily at Karl. "Now I can hardly fail to see the signs in others. It's disturbing, to put it mildly. But she is... oh, more than beautiful. Divine and terrifying. What else could Lilith be?"

He spoke in a whisper, but the word was a soft hiss. *Lilith*. As he spoke it, Violette looked up, her gaze travelling past her immediate companions and locking on to Charlotte's. Eyes dark with anger, she rose from her chair. "If you would excuse me..." she said, weaving through her admirers.

She came towards Charlotte, Karl and Josef like a serpent poised to strike. Josef's hands tightened on the arms of his chair. Violette fixed Charlotte with a glare, as if to demand, *How dare*

you bring some human to stare at me as if I were a specimen?
Then her glance flicked away. She glided past them and vanished into the crowd.

Josef wilted with relief. Charlotte touched his arm, aware that she, too, had been rigid from head to foot.

"Charlotte?" Karl said softly.

"Damn it," she said. "I should know Violette well enough by now! Why does she still make me feel like this?"

"I'd say you have good reason to be afraid," Josef said heavily. "I can't explain, but she terrified me on a level that even you have never touched. What I can make of this, without speaking to her, I don't know."

"We shouldn't have involved you, Josef," said Karl. "This is not for humans to deal with."

"Karl's right," said Charlotte. "I'm sorry."

"No, no." He waved a dismissive hand. "I don't give up so easily."

"I'll go to Violette." She made to stand up, but Karl's hand pinioned her.

"Don't," he said. "You know how unpredictable she is. Leave her. She'll come to you soon enough."

"Very well," she said, knowing he was right. "Josef, you should go back to the hotel."

"Nonsense. I'm perfectly all right." Josef looked gravely at her. "It's Robyn I'm concerned about. I was a fool to bring her." His glance flicked to Karl and back.

Charlotte saw the look, and sighed inwardly.

"Robyn is not in danger," she said firmly. "Don't worry about her. You're safe, and so is she, I promise."

Robyn was pleasantly surprised to find the garden almost deserted; a handful of guests were smoking on the terrace, but no one took any notice as she passed. How lovely to be alone in the night, with the scent of honeysuckle and orange blossom floating around her. Passing a couple who were pressed between an ivy-covered tree and a wall, she started. In shadow she saw a man's back, a mass of dark hair, the woman's hands like pale sea anemones against his evening jacket. For a moment she thought they were Karl and Charlotte – but no, she'd left them inside with Josef. Only a courting couple, wrapped up in each other. She passed quickly, pretending she hadn't seen them.

Robyn found a tree to hide her from the house and leaned against it, feeling the bark imprinting her bare back. *I must shake off this foolish mood. Why is Josef being so mysterious about his friends?*

"I guess he'll tell me in his own good time," she murmured aloud. She stretched, breathed the sweet air, exhaled.

"Will he tell you?" said a voice in the darkness. "Men tell women so little. It's their last weapon, keeping us in the dark."

Robyn jumped. The voice was English, as delicate as frost-feathers, sharp as a sliver of crystal. Holding herself steady, she called, "Who is that? How do you know so much?"

There was movement, and Robyn saw the woman framed in a trellis arch against scattered light from the house. A dancer's silhouette in an ashes-of-roses dress like a dewed cobweb, witch-black hair. Robyn couldn't see her face.

"I'll tell you what I know," said the dancer, "if you'll tell me."

Detaching herself from the tree, Robyn approached her.

"Sure, would you like to hear some stories?" said Robyn. Incredible excitement and pain fountained inside her, none of it betrayed by her casual tone.

"Oh, yes. Tell me," said Violette, holding out a hand – the hand that had earlier described Odette's grief and Odile's malevolence so eloquently.

So began their conversation, without preliminaries or awkwardness. There were no social barriers in the darkness, only empathy.

"I'm Violette," said the dancer.

"I know who you are, Madame."

"You have the advantage, then." Violette slipped her hand through Robyn's arm; how deliciously soft their flesh felt, pressed together. "Even I don't know who I am. But please call me Violette."

"I guess all that attention must be… exhausting. I'm Robyn."

"I'm pleased to meet you, Robyn."

"You found it a little crowded inside?"

"Too hot, too crowded. I need to get away sometimes."

"Away from their eyes," said Robyn. They walked side-by-side along paved paths, between neat rows of trellis hung with roses, honeysuckle and vines. At intervals there were arbours with clipped bay trees in tubs. Robyn was slightly above average height, and felt clumsily large beside the petite dancer.

"Thirsty eyes," Violette agreed. "They have eyes like vampires, even the women, though the men are the worst. You're right, it is tiring, trying to satisfy their demands. The social demands, I mean."

"What about other demands?" Robyn risked impertinence. "Or don't they dare?"

"A few have tried." The dancer's tone was chilly. "Not many. But I want to hear about you, Robyn. Tell me." She spun round in front of her, took both her hands and pulled her along as if dancing. Robyn saw her eyes: expressive blue-violet jewels caged by black lashes and arched black brows. Hypnotic with light and life, yet strangely hard, as if they contained a vast and ruthless soul.

Violette led her to a bench under a cavern of Virginia creeper. Robyn felt drugged, dream-laden. She was acutely aware of being in the company of a virtual goddess, at a loss to understand why the ballerina had chosen her to the exclusion of all others – but rather than making her feel awkward, this enhanced the weird thrill of their encounter. It was so easy to talk to Violette. She unwound Robyn's story like silk.

"It was my father's fault," Robyn began. "I'm nothing to him. He must have been capable of love once, when he met my mom. He met her in Vienna, married her there and brought her back to Boston. Unfortunately, he didn't realise she was Jewish – or rather, he realised, but didn't understand that marrying an outsider would stop him taking his place in society. She wasn't a girl from the right Boston family, you see. He should've known, but he was young, hot-headed. So he had to work extra hard to achieve his goals, and it left him a little bitter because he was *very* ambitious, had to be the biggest man in town. To him, his children were... how can I put it? Commodities." She leaned back on the creeper-covered wall, feeling the tender leaves against her skin, aware of Violette's cool radiance beside her. "Wasn't so hard for my brothers; they only had to succeed in business. But my sisters and me... well, we were all pretty, and that made us valuable. So he sold us."

"Sold?" Violette sat forward, her face intent. Robyn was amazed to have shocked her.

"You know, business deals. Favours. 'Sign this contract and your son gets my beautiful, rich daughter.' That's how I came to marry Samuel James Stafford."

"And you had no say in the matter?"

"You don't know my father. He always gets his own way. I was young and scared of him, and Mom always took his side. So I decided to make the best of it, convinced myself I loved Samuel. He was handsome in a cold, Harvard sort of way, and completely obsessed by me. Wouldn't take no for an answer. So everything was fine," she said sarcastically.

Violette leaned towards her, holding Robyn's bare arms, and something eerie and inexplicable happened. Her magnificent, luminous eyes captured Robyn's. It seemed they entered another place together, where no one else existed, and Robyn's life was unreeling in a necklace of images.

Her husband's jealous cruelty. Sexual degradation that escalated to brutality. His bouts of drunkenness, beatings from which she barely emerged alive. And then, webbing her into the sticky prison of deceit, his apologies, his endless promises to change, his pathetic declarations of love... and the cycle began again.

"I could do nothing. No one would have believed me. Divorce would bring disgrace on my family and wreck my father's most important business connections. That was the truly horrible thing," she whispered, her wrists now resting on Violette's shoulder, their faces close together. "That both our fathers had sold me into this, because they both knew what Samuel was like before he married me. *They knew*. And I was a slab of drugged meat to tame the hyena, to keep him from damaging his family's status. They all knew, these men. What could I do against their silent conspiracies, their handshakes and deals, when a daughter or a wife is just a thing to be bought and sold?"

Tears of rage ran down her cheeks. The wind rustling the creeper sounded like rain. "I conceived and miscarried five times. Three of those were because he'd hit me or knocked me downstairs, the others out of despair, I think. I never conceived again. So he decided I was the devil because I was barren. Eight years of hell, and then heaven smiled on me. The bastard died of a heart attack.

"When we came home from the funeral, my housekeeper Alice and I locked the doors. I tore off my widow's weeds and we danced and laughed like a pair of mad witches. And then... I set about taking revenge."

"Against the men you hated?"

"Against all men. Couldn't do much to my own dad because it would've hurt Mom, but I got Samuel's father; I seduced him, ruined his marriage and business within a year. And then others. Young and old. I decided that no man was ever going to use me again. Never."

"Do you hate them all?" Violette spoke with an urgent hunger in her voice that startled Robyn.

"Not *en masse*," she said thoughtfully. "Some of them have good hearts. Harold's not so bad, too old to be any real trouble. And my uncle, and Wilkes, my driver. H'm, that's three; can't think of anyone else."

She smiled wryly, but the dancer's face remained intense. Unnerving, for all its beauty.

"So you don't believe in love?"

"Do you?" said Robyn. "Here I am, talking about myself all night, not giving you a chance. Why do I get the feeling that you feel the same, that things have been just as bad for you?"

"Not quite as bad, because instinct made me keep them at arm's length before they got the chains on me – but bad enough," Violette murmured. Her hand slid over Robyn's shoulder, down her upper arm. How cool her touch was, how sensuous. "We both knew the moment we saw each other, didn't we? Like knows like. The same bitterness, the same suffering, even though we've lived our lives thousands of miles apart."

I can't believe she's telling me this, Robyn thought, electrified. "It's a pretty common experience."

"I know," said the dancer. "I see it everywhere, this hideous weakness that makes men into monsters and women into victims – and the other way round. It enrages me. No, I don't trust love, even when I see a couple doting on one another. What are they trying to hide?"

"Who are they trying to fool?" Robyn added, thinking of Karl and Charlotte.

"But have you ever wondered," Violette said, her voice softening, "how it would be with a woman instead?"

This is getting out of hand, Robyn thought. Yet she was seized by the thrill of trying something new and forbidden. "Oh, Lord," she said, embarrassed. "Thought about it, I guess, but never –"

The dancer leaned in and pressed her lips to Robyn's. The kiss was cool, dry, brief – and completely unravelled her.

"Never?" Another kiss. "Never at all?" Another, another. Robyn was shaking. This was awful and yet tantalising... why not a woman, after all... no one, male or female, could resist Violette... Her hands crept onto Violette's shoulders, slid into her luxuriant hair. She was scared to go further, worried that Violette was not sincere, and that if she betrayed any feelings the dancer would pull away and mock her.

Violette's mouth met hers, parting her lips and teeth. Her tongue felt shockingly hot. What Robyn felt was not exactly sexual, for she had suppressed those feelings for too long. It was generalised heat, sensation rippling over her skin, an unbearable sensuality flowing from Violette's fingers, her lips, every point where their bodies touched... a red excitement building in her spine... yes, sexual after all, but also frightening.

Violette pushed her into the wall, her kisses growing more fervent. Robyn felt trapped. She tried to loosen the dancer's grip, to convey that this was too much, too soon – she'd expected gentleness; shouldn't women be gentle with each other? – but Violette was too strong. As she pressed Robyn down, her passion seemed single-minded, blind. Like a rapist.

"No, don't. Stop, please stop," Robyn tried to say, but Violette's hand was on her windpipe and she was choking.

"You deserve it," Violette murmured. Her lips slid hotly down Robyn's throat, came to rest on a throbbing vessel just above her collarbone. "Yes, you deserve it."

Teeth nipped the skin, making her nerves leap with pain. She shivered with fear, yet something within her yearned outwards, surrendering to this dark entity. *Yes... do it...*

Cool air rushed between them. Violette pulled away and

the pressure vanished. She was looking across the garden, as if distracted; then she turned back to Robyn, and pressed one hand lightly between her breasts.

"But not yet," she said, eyes glazed. "Excuse me."

She stood up coolly, as if nothing had happened. She slipped away into the darkness, leaving Robyn confused, breathless, bereft. Unable to move.

As she sat there, nearly catatonic, she saw the distant silhouette of a woman on the terrace, light spinning a golden web through her hair. And she heard Charlotte call out softly, imbuing a single word with concern, warning and rebuke.

"Violette!"

After Sebastian left his victim cooling in the study, he had a decision to make. He was eager to meet the unique Roberta Stafford, but if he rejoined the party he was bound to be recognised by Karl and the others. They might not *sense* him as such, but once they saw him, they'd know. He wasn't afraid of confrontation; he simply couldn't be bothered with it.

So Sebastian delayed the moment. No hurry, after all. He haunted the edges by keeping to the terrace, moving in and out of the Crystal Ring, listening to conversations. He quickly identified Robyn, even without a clear view of her face: there was only one chestnut-haired woman with any presence about her. The anticipation of meeting her was torment.

He knew she would be beautiful. Unusual beauty, perhaps. Someone special, a worthy substitute for Violette.

Those other vampires had better not make a claim on Robyn, he thought. *If they try, that would be a confrontation I'd relish.*

As he watched from a distance through the glass doors, his thirst stirred. So warm and alive she looked, the opposite of Violette. Laughing, confident, seductive in her gleaming world. The centre of attention.

Ah, the first glimpse of her face! A surprise, as he'd anticipated. Not a fragile or simpering beauty. Her features were emphatic: a strong nose and chin, soft brown eyes that narrowed with mischief when she laughed, a mobile, deep red mouth. She looked warm, kind and poised: a strong character. People accepted her, despite her reputation, because they *liked* her. And she was lovely. A shaft of creamy fire, tipped by the chestnut jewel of her hair.

His disappointment over the ballerina was dust.

Sebastian wanted Robyn fiercely, but he wouldn't go inside. No, he'd wait in the shadows, at one with the night that was his soul's twin: dispassionate, brooding, limitless.

"So, you came after all?" said Ilona's voice a few feet away.

He turned, saw her leaning against an ivy-covered wall. Although her composure appeared undamaged by his earlier attack, her eyes had an icy glitter.

"I knew you couldn't resist," said Ilona. "I'm glad we met: I was just growing bored. So, here we are, both hiding and spying. Pathetic, isn't it?"

Sebastian looked stonily at her, folding his arms. "You're free to leave."

She frowned. "Are you still being a swine?"

Sensing a human nearby, he pushed Ilona behind a tree. "Why pester me," he said, "unless I broke your heart when I left Schloss Holdenstein?"

"Don't flatter yourself," she whispered. "I enjoy getting on your nerves, that's all."

"You always did."

The human passed by. They pressed into the darkness, faces hidden, like lovers. Sebastian caught Robyn's perfume: jasmine, rain-soaked flowers, the secret heat of her body, and the pull of her blood...

In his desire for Robyn he held Ilona tight, feeling her stiffen and gasp with pleasure.

"Be nicer, Sebastian," she said softly, "or I'll tell Karl you're here."

"Oh, and what could Karl do about me?"

"Well, he has interests in certain humans and he knows what you're like. He'd want to protect them, which would rather cramp your style. And you don't want to tangle with Violette, believe me."

"She's nothing," he said. "But you don't want Karl catching you, either, do you? The threat works both ways."

She shrugged. "No, it doesn't. He'll notice me soon enough. His attention matters less to me than to you."

Ilona reads me too well, he thought with an inward sigh. "And if I'm nice to you, dearest?"

She smiled at his mordant tone. "No one will ever know you were here. Our little secret."

"You have a point," he said, warming to her more from increasing lust than friendship. Her body felt firm and lithe against his. "We're too alike to tell tales."

"That's right," Ilona breathed. "Don't spoil my fun and I won't spoil yours." Her mouth glistened dark red, succulent. Her hands moved over his chest, tantalising. Now her presence was no longer unwelcome. "We should find somewhere quieter, don't you think?"

And if Sebastian was aware that Robyn met another woman in the darkness, the impression was no more than the flutter of leaves.

As Violette reappeared from the garden, Charlotte took her arm and steered her into a verandah, a cool square room with marble benches and potted ferns. The party shimmered beyond the pillars, while this space was deserted, dim and echoic.

"How could you, Violette? If I hadn't called just then, you would have fed on her, wouldn't you?"

Violette jerked her arm from Charlotte's grasp, her eyes glacial.

"I find you incredible. After months of pleading with me to accept my thirst, as soon as I find a victim, you interrupt and lose your temper! How dare you?"

"I dared to stop you," Charlotte said furiously, "because you attacked someone I promised would be safe."

"Do you imagine you're responsible for protecting individuals? That's dishonest."

"No, it isn't! Anyone else, Violette – but not Josef, and not Robyn! He's my friend. She's his niece."

"I know. I saw them together."

"But you don't care?"

The lapis eyes widened, star-flecked. "Who is this human friend, Charlotte? I told you he was aboard the ship, and at the ballet, and you wouldn't admit you knew him! Then you bring him to stare at me, like a doctor assessing me for an asylum. Why?"

Charlotte looked down, embarrassed. Nothing escaped Violette. "Because that's what he is, in a way."

"What?" The frost in her eyes turned to flame.

"He studies mythology and psychology. I hoped that if we understood why you think you are Lilith, it might help. I wanted to tell you. I didn't, because I knew you'd refuse to see him."

"So instead you lie, and sneak him into my presence?"

"I'm sorry. But... I knew you'd react like this."

The last words, spoken quickly, seemed to defuse Violette's rage. She laughed, but her face was colourless.

"What do you expect? How many times must I say, stop trying to help me? You're as bad as the others, who would burn me at the stake! Anything to deny what I am – but at least my enemies are honest!"

Charlotte turned away and sat on a bench, one hand clasping her bowed head.

"Is that why you chose Robyn – to punish me?" she said.

"For heaven's sake," said Violette. "You should know me better! It was nothing to do with you or Josef."

Charlotte looked up. As always, the sight of Violette – a birch-pallid figure contrasted by the sooty blackness of her hair – stirred her deeply. "Why, then?"

"Because I saw a mass of pain and mistakes inside her. Her soul is webbed with bitterness... and I wanted to tear it all out."

Still angry, Charlotte was disinclined to listen.

"This is the thirst, Violette. It finds any tortuous route to be satisfied."

"No. I see *inside* people. I don't want to, I hate it! But when I meet someone like Robyn, I have an urge... to bite. To suck out the poison, make her see what a fool she's been." She paused. A caprice of light made it seem that a demon shone like a dark skeleton through the fabric of Violette's clothes and flesh, as if she'd become translucent. The impression was horrific.

Violette said lightly, "This conversation is a waste of time. Let's return to the party."

"Will you speak to Josef? Give him a chance, at least."

"No, I won't," Violette said imperiously. "And don't ever try such a trick again! Come, Karl will wonder where you are."

For once, Charlotte had no desire to prolong the argument. "You're right," she said coldly. She stood up, not even wanting to look at Violette. But as they approached the ballroom, the dancer stroked her arm with sharp fingernails.

"You didn't stop me feeding on Robyn. If the moment had been right, I would have taken her there and then. I'll do so eventually. And when the time comes, Charlotte, I'll do the same to you."

Robyn was recovering, trying to rationalise what had happened. *A woman made a pass at me! Why am I surprised? After all, I've a shrewd idea of why Alice is so devoted to me, although she'd be mortified if she knew I guessed, poor puritan soul... No, it was her blatancy, and the fact of who she is.* Violette Lenoir!

She stretched, leaning back into the ivy. *I need a drink*, she thought, *a real one. I'll go find Josef... God, what a strange evening!*

I think I was willing to let her seduce me.

A sinking sensation went through her. An ache. *I never thought of women that way but, God, I'm so sick of men, anything would be better. Yet I had a feeling Violette didn't really want me. She wanted me to want her, so she could reject and humiliate me. Was that her game?*

Robyn's heart hardened. *So, the great dancer has problems? Well, Madame, you can leave me out of them.*

Bitterly amused, she began walking back towards the house. A tunnel of climbing roses led to a pergola with a little fountain dancing in the centre. On the far side, blocking her path, stood a man, a stranger.

She stopped, annoyed. Retracing her steps would look ridiculous. Besides, a gentleman would step aside and let her pass.

"Good evening," she said, walking around the fountain.

"Good evening." He didn't move, so she had to stop awkwardly in front of him.

"Excuse me, please."

He only looked at her, eyes half-veiled. He was a little under six feet, no more than five inches taller than her, but he seemed to be looking down from a great height. In the shadows, she could hardly see his face. Only the hint of a firm chin, an unsmiling, sculptural mouth, those disdainful eyelids. Dark, thick hair. Elegant bearing... another dancer?

Then the feeling hit her again, setting her nerves aflame. He was too vivid, too overpowering. *This man is another like Karl and Charlotte and Violette.*

"Would you please let me pass?" she said tightly.

"Forgive me, madam, but are you Mrs Roberta Stafford?" The voice was quiet with coiled strength, the accent soft with a hint of Boston Irish. A neutral voice, fitting a creature who blended with shadows.

"I am," she said guardedly.

"I've been looking for you."

"Well, I was at the party all evening..."

He cut across her. "I have some news. Bad news."

"What is it?" Chilled, she felt a rush of dread.

"I regret to say that your ex-lover, Russell Booth, is dead. He took his own life, Mrs Stafford. He killed himself because of you."

The garden tipped and slanted away beneath her.

When she revived, she was on a wooden seat under the pergola. The stranger was beside her, holding her arm. His fingers felt like cold satin.

"Are you all right?"

"I never faint," she said, drawing deep breaths. The cause wasn't the news itself, but his gentle, dark voice: a stab of guilt, as if Death itself had pointed an accusing finger.

"You're in shock," he said. So sombre: a spirit from the shadow-world, unreal yet electrifying. She pressed her fingers to her temples.

"Wait," she said. "He can't possibly be dead. He lives here. If he'd committed suicide, I hardly think his family would be throwing a party."

"Perhaps they don't know how depressed he is – how much he's drinking because you came here tonight."

"He can't be dead."

"If not, it's no thanks to you," said the soft voice. "If he is – you're responsible."

"This is crazy. Help me inside, please," she said sharply. Perhaps if she saw him in electric light, among other people – but he didn't move. Robyn began to shiver. The detached faceless presence of death... she felt herself fading again, blood rushing from her head.

Collecting herself, she spoke in anger. "Sir, I'm terribly sorry to hear about Russell's problems, but my contact with him ended weeks ago. This is nothing to do with me. You have no right to make such insinuations!"

"I stated a fact. In his eyes, your callous treatment destroyed him."

"How do you know?" She sat forward, gripping the edge of the seat, preparing to run. "Who are you?"

"Only the messenger, Mrs Stafford."

Impossible, but – he was transparent. She could see the bench and the climbing roses right through him.

Her head swam. Gasping, she shut her eyes.

When she looked again, she was alone. Air stirred softly in the space where he'd been: a ghost, her own conscience, or an actual spectre from limbo seeking revenge?

Impossible.

Robyn stood up. Walking as briskly as she could without actually running, she gained the columned verandah. Great squares of blond light swam in her vision. On the steps she missed her footing, and collapsed into Karl's arms.

CHAPTER EIGHT

PRAYERS AND CONFESSIONS

Cesare found John at a table in his cell, his bald, scarred head bent over a book. Pierre was there too, slumped on a pallet as if he'd lost all interest in living.

"The world of mortals is a terrible place," Cesare said gravely from the doorway. "A sewer."

"What?" Pierre looked up, his face skull-hollow and waxen. Candlelight gleamed horribly on its starved planes. His eyes were bulging orbs, his unwashed hair straggled in matted curls. Cesare regarded him with both pity and irritation.

"A sewer," he repeated, "infested by vermin who squabble without dignity to survive, who breed without discrimination, maim and kill each other for entertainment, and worship depravity. Who think that, for a stab of remorse and a prayer, God will forgive them."

"This is news?" Pierre said wearily.

Cesare stiffened with rage at his insolence. *However, a leader must tolerate petty faults in his followers,* he thought. *I've endured the world's horror, but I can and I will do something about it!*

These two victims of Lilith filled him with sudden sympathy. John, no longer the self-contained monk, appeared demented and monstrous. His scalp would have healed if he'd let it; instead, he continued to mutilate himself, as if in penance. On the corner of the table sat Matthew's head, like a grisly candle welded there by its own wax. The flesh was beginning to desiccate, lips drawing back in a ghastly grin, fangs hanging at full length. Vampire flesh, it seemed, did not decay like that of humans, but turned slowly to dust.

Yet John could not let his friend go.

To Cesare, this symbolised the way vampires would cling to the past unless he – the new prophet, dare he think it? – could turn their thoughts to the future.

"And you, Pierre," Cesare murmured, looking down at him. "Once so bold and cruel. Now you cower here, afraid of your own shadow. It's pitiful."

"Whose fault is that?" Pierre snarled. "Yes, I'm scared!" He waved a hand at John. "I spend time with vampires I hate, rather than be alone. Violette's crippled me." His eyes grew wild. "I daren't enter the Crystal Ring because she's there. I see her eyes in the clouds, and her hair like a great black shadow. The strangling knot of her hair. Why am I so afraid? Why?"

He lurched forward and clung to the front of Cesare's robe.

"Because she is the Enemy." Cesare eased him back onto the pallet. "Don't be ashamed of your weakness, my brother. You have faced our greatest threat."

"I have?" Pierre blinked.

John, meanwhile, only stared at Cesare from dead eyes. He spoke little these days.

"Look at you two and Matthew: this is only the beginning of her evil," said Cesare. "The darkness of the Crystal Ring is Lilith's shadow falling between us and God. It's her fault that we could not bring Matthew back to life."

At that, John's eyes flared with poisonous light.

"Perhaps Kristian protected us from her before," Cesare went on with passion, "but Kristian is gone, and we must protect ourselves. The Almighty has revealed His purpose to me. I am the one chosen to unleash the forces of heaven against her."

Far from seeming impressed by this statement, Pierre groaned, "*Mon Dieu*." He covered his face with his hands, muttering.

"What are you saying?" Cesare snapped, gripping Pierre's shoulder.

One blue eye blazed up at him from the tangle of hair and fingers. In it, Cesare saw the cynical spirit of the atheist. Pierre, though, seemed to think better of arguing.

"Nothing, nothing. I don't care what you do. Dress this up as a religious crusade if you like – only please get rid of that damned woman! I see her in the corners when the candles burn out. Please."

Cesare let go, and smoothed Pierre's crumpled shirt as if petting a dog. How pleasing to see Pierre with his blasphemous insolence knocked out of him. Like a bud, a tiny hope for the future.

"I'll crush her like a wasp." Cesare dropped his hand on Pierre's head in benediction. "Come and pray with me, my brothers."

Pierre shrank away, shaking his head.

"John?" Cesare held out his hand.

The other vampire came to Cesare, pausing only to glance at Matthew's head. Pierre, too, stared at it as if to say, *Don't leave me alone with that thing!* But as John and Cesare left, Pierre did not follow.

"Let him be," said Cesare. "I'll make a believer of him eventually."

Cesare led John to Kristian's inner sanctum, a cell tucked beside the meeting chamber that contained the ebony throne. Inside, he knelt on the bare stone floor, John facing him. *This is now* my *sanctum*, Cesare thought.

"Concentrate," he whispered. "Let your mind flow towards God. This is our prayer for guidance, and more: a call to his messengers. A summoning!"

The chamber was lightless, but with vampire acuity, Cesare saw the livid red scabs on John's skull, the raddled hollows of his face.

"This is blasphemy," John whispered. "We've no right to call on God's name. We'll be struck down!"

"Still clinging to your old ways? Find some pride, some courage! John, I never questioned Kristian's doctrine." As Cesare spoke, tears flowed down his cheeks. "But Kristian died to force us to think for ourselves! And I'm so happy."

"Happy? When we're in hell? We're damned souls; silent penitence is our only hope of redemption. We must submit to His will, not demand help!"

Cesare looked into the baleful eyes. "You're wrong! Very well; let this prayer be proof. If angels come and strike us down, then I am wrong. But if they answer and help us, then you'll know that I am right! Do you agree?"

The swollen skull dropped in acquiescence.

"Good. Pray with me."

Cesare let his vampire sight dim. He drifted into the Crystal Ring, hovering between the two realms. The flagstones seemed to soften, holding him like an ant in molasses. The sanctum became featureless, like the inside of an egg, flushing from black to deepest purple.

Cesare began to pray silently. Very far above, he felt a cold black energy gathering, feeding him. He thought, *I could begin a new religion here and now. Kristian could be the vampires' Saviour: a prophet murdered by his enemies only to live again. But with no resurrection...*

He began to tremble. In truth, Cesare no longer wanted Kristian reborn. His own ego had flourished too vigorously to tolerate competition.

He chastised himself for this heresy.

A compromise, he thought, bowing his head. *I'll call on God to send a sign. If Kristian appears, I'll submit to his will and establish the Church of Kristian. But if not – dear Lord, send me guidance!*

His lips began to move.

"Almighty God, Lord of All, Creator and Destroyer, hear me. In the name of Kristian our Father, I beg for guidance. I am thy humble servant, a thought in thy great Mind. I beg thee, send forth thy thoughts as envoys to do thy will in the world..."

Something happened. The purple glow above him flushed to gold.

"Oh, Kristian, beloved Father, manifest unto me, tell me how best to continue thy work. In the name of God, appear!"

The light swelled to a sphere, and Cesare's heart swelled with it. John groaned.

"God hears us!" Cesare cried. John moaned in terror and keeled over, face down, arms outstretched.

The light birthed a shape, a long glowing figure that hovered before Cesare's wondering eyes. A force pulsed from it, invisible but icily bright. Cesare pressed his hands to his chest, overawed.

"Kristian?" he whispered.

"No, not Kristian," said the light. "I am your holy messenger, your sword of flame."

"God be praised!" Cesare cried. "Speak, tell us who you are!"

"My name is Simon." The light dissipated to reveal – not an angel, but a tall blond man in modern clothes: white shirt, fawn trousers. Yet his eyes were suns, and he was as golden as Cesare was colourless. "Although I have been called Senoy."

To Cesare's astonishment, this glowing creature gathered both him and John in his arms and hugged them hard to his chest.

"God be praised, indeed," Simon-Senoy whispered, biting into Cesare's neck.

Simon had felt the call as he wandered through the Crystal Ring, brooding on his losses and failures.

To be needed, he was thinking, *that's the essence.*

Fyodor and Rasmila begged me to take them back but they're children; they need a nursemaid, not a soldier of God. And Sebastian never needed me, but perhaps it's for the best. He is a loner, and I need a pair to recreate the magic trinity.

Yes. The alchemy of three.

He thought of Karl again.

I need...

He floated in silence, wrapped in violet clouds, webbed by rainbow lines of magnetism. He watched a knot of darkness far above, perceiving it as a hole through which all the energy and beauty of the Ring was leaking away.

Panic and despair flashed through him...

And then he felt the pull. The magnetic lines thrummed like violin strings. The ether shuddered. He felt his hands turn hot, and saw that they were glowing, as they used to when he was God's envoy.

Simon gasped. "Dear God, what is this?"

He felt power returning. Not a blaze of ineffable light this time, but enough to prove that he was still an angel, that someone on Earth had empowered him by *needing* him.

And Simon went with the call, diving towards the source as if winged. He heard the prayer, bathed in the beseeching, honeyed words, slipped softly to Earth to greet his summoners.

His glorious manifestation was an act, for his new-born

strength was fragile. Still, it was enough to convince them that he'd answered their prayers.

A sword of God to slay Lilith.

So someone had finally realised the danger and called for Simon's aid! He was so grateful, he couldn't help but embrace them in his joy.

When Simon stood back, he was far from enraptured by what he saw. A mousy choirboy with a visionary light in his eyes, and a mutilated little man like a leper from a medieval woodcut. No beauty here. Yet there was *something*, a feeling of inchoate power that excited Simon beyond reason. So he clasped them, bit their throats and swallowed their blood in ecstatic greeting.

Because it was better than nothing. It was a start, at least.

The day after the party, Robyn walked to the Public Garden and sat under the willows by the lagoon. The gold-leaf dome of the State House glinted through the trees, bright against an overcast sky. She wished the sun would shine. The weather was so capricious in early June, changing from chilly to hot in an hour. Still, the park was always green and lush; the dogwoods laden with blossom, purple beeches and maidenhair trees shimmering all around her.

Robyn watched the swan boats circling the small lake. Round and round they went in genteel procession, each with a man pedalling stoically between the wings of a carved white swan, families seated in rows on the benches, children throwing bread to the ducks. She stared at the boats until she was hypnotised.

She'd put off Harold, invitations to lunch, everything, saying she was unwell. She wasn't lying. She was in a state of shock.

When Karl caught her on the terrace, she'd put on a show of levity. *"Oh, how foolish of me to miss the step, no harm done, how lucky you were there..."* But he knew there was something wrong; she saw concern in his eyes. God, Karl's eyes... too much like those of the stranger in the garden for comfort.

He and Charlotte had been solicitous, as if they feared she'd been in danger. Robyn, however, said nothing about Violette or the strange male. None of their business, really. She only wondered why they were so concerned.

Josef wasn't himself, either. Preoccupied, he'd insisted on leaving the party early. So Robyn asked Wilkes to drive him back to his hotel, but Josef wouldn't say what was wrong, only that he was tired.

Now she wished that she'd dispensed with social niceties and asked Karl and Charlotte directly, "What exactly is going on?"

At the time, though, it had been impossible. Why, when they were so lovely, so charming and kind, had she felt so uneasy with them?

After seeing Josef safely to his hotel, she'd gone home and to bed. No hope of sleep. In the middle of the night, she'd gone to Alice's room and woken her.

"I met a ghost last night," Robyn had said. "Or an angel of death, maybe. He told me that Russell Booth intended to commit suicide. Or already had."

Alice sat up in bed, half-asleep. "You woke me to tell me this?"

"Did you hear me?" She told her bemused companion everything.

"But, madam, if he'd killed himself, they wouldn't be holding a party, would they?"

"That's what I said." Robyn exhaled. "I know what it was – his god-damned brothers playing a sick joke on me! Funny. I never took any of that family to have a sense of humour."

Later, as Robyn ate breakfast, Alice went out to visit a friend. She returned within minutes, looking stunned.

"I just met the housekeeper from the house next door to the Booths. First thing this morning, the family found Russell dead in his study."

Now Robyn sat by the lake, her stomach a cold knot. Russell's death, however tragic, barely touched her heart, but last night's eeriness persisted.

Maybe I imagined the man after all. Some ghastly premonition?

Josef's hotel on Tremont Street was only minutes' walk away, but she suspected that even if she asked him outright who his strange friends were, he wouldn't give a straight answer.

As she sat watching the swan boats, she became aware of a shadow in the corner of her eye. He appeared as suddenly as before: a dark figure in a black overcoat, his face pale against the material. He stood beside her bench, hands in his pockets, silent as the air.

Robyn looked at him in a mixture of shock and relief. Her heart was pounding. *So I didn't imagine him!*

"Good afternoon, Mrs Stafford."

"Good afternoon... I'm afraid I don't recall your name," she said, with all the poise she could gather. She wouldn't let any man think he'd unsettled her.

"I am Sebastian Pierse," he said, "and I owe you an apology."

His words, spoken in a low, contrite tone, took her aback. She studied his profile and saw a high, curved cheekbone, well-shaped nose and jaw, long black lashes. Features a sculptor might have moulded with idealistic fingers – but they told her nothing about his character. The distant look in his eyes could have been arrogance, or something subtler and darker.

"Yes, perhaps you do."

He only stood there, watching the swan boats as if transfixed. Eventually she said, "Why don't you sit down, Mr Pierse?"

"Because I wait until I've been invited." He came to sit beside her with a dancer's effortless grace. As he half-turned towards her with one arm along the back of the bench, she saw him clearly for the first time.

"It was unforgivable of me to approach you without warning," he said.

Difficult to tell his age; he might be anywhere between twenty-five and forty, a world away from the brash, scrubbed American men who were considered handsome. His was an old-world beauty, chiselled but not polished, the fair skin radiant with a particular Celtic translucency. Despite his pallor, he seemed all shadows. His hair – darkest brown, soft, formless and too long – shaded his forehead. Dense black eyebrows and lashes gave alluring depth to his eyes. The irises were hazel-green, like woodland pools.

"You must understand," he went on, "I was upset about my friend's death. That is no excuse –"

"No, it isn't," Robyn said coolly. "You were rude, and I certainly did not deserve your insinuations."

"I know. I'm sorry." The timbre of his voice lulled her towards forgiveness.

"Was he dead when you came to me?"

"Yes."

"How did you know before anyone else?"

"Others knew," he said. "They didn't want to distress the party guests by announcing it."

This statement didn't quite ring true, but she let it pass. "Did you know Russell well?"

"As I said, he was a friend. I know nothing about you, Mrs Stafford, except what he told me."

"And what did he tell you?"

"That without you, he had no reason to live."

His head was turned slightly away, but looked sideways into her eyes; aware of her, but inwardly distracted. Certainly not attempting to flirt. She was irritated yet intrigued.

He was beautiful, in his understated way, like a creature of another race, another time. Not unlike Karl... different, but with the same ability to confuse and captivate...

Oh, no, she told herself firmly. *He won't get me like that. I'm immune.*

"Look, Mr Pierse, I know you're upset by Russell's death. So am I. I was fond of him." Half-truths and lies slid out with equal ease. "But our relationship had no future. He was so young. I was hardly the ideal daughter-in-law. So I had to end it, for his sake. I thought he'd get over it, never dreamed he'd..."

Sebastian sat forward, looking straight at her. "Would you have acted differently, if you'd known how desperate he was?"

"Why should I?" A smile iced her lips. "A threat of suicide would have made our liaison no more feasible. I have an aversion to emotional blackmail."

"Quite so. All the same..." As he spoke, she received the impression that Sebastian Pierse actually did not give a damn about his so-called friend. "I can see why he felt as he did."

This remark took her off-guard. Not that she was unused to compliments, but she hadn't expected them from someone so aloof. "I beg your pardon?"

"Now I've compounded the sin," he said. "Mrs Stafford, would you consider forgiving me over dinner?"

His lovely eyes were suddenly all over her. Robyn felt a dart of triumph. It seemed she'd misread him. He was no phantom, only a man, and he was falling for her after all, so predictably, like all the others.

In that moment, a delightful intention uncoiled like a snake's tongue inside her. *I've got him*, she thought. *And he thinks it's so easy. But I'll have him, and I'll make him pay for thinking he can manipulate me.*

"I hardly know you."

"All friendships have to begin somewhere. Please," he said with endearing sincerity, "let me make amends."

"Well... all right." She spoke with careful indifference, letting her eyelids fall. Then she looked up with the innocent, enticing expression that made idiots of most males. "If you think we have anything to discuss."

"As long as we've laid Russell to rest, we can begin again with anything in the world." He sounded positively tender. "Anything you desire."

Alone in his hotel room, Josef felt at home. The solitude of a plain, comfortable room, a lamp pooling yellow light on the desk, an open book; all pleasantly familiar. It was his habit to read long into the night. He sat in shirt-sleeves, reading about the long-haired demon of the night, Lilith.

He felt certain that Charlotte would visit him tonight.

The previous night at the party, she'd admitted that Violette had met Robyn in the garden.

"Nothing happened," Charlotte had tried to reassure him. "And I've told Violette to leave her alone."

"Will she?"

"Yes. She doesn't take victims indiscriminately. She has no reason to attack you or Robyn."

Josef was not reassured. The danger had come too close. Robyn alone with a vampire, all unsuspecting... the thought chilled him. Charlotte's attempt to placate him only underlined how dangerous she felt Violette to be.

His head ached. He pinched the skin between his eyebrows. *If anything happens to Robyn, if Karl or Violette touches her, it will be my fault! God, how did I get into this?*

Everything in his research portrayed Lilith as an uncontrollable, negative force. The dark side of the psyche. How could anyone contain a creature as wild as Lilith, except by destruction? The word of God, or a stake through the heart?

Josef, despite everything, still believed in the forces of good and evil.

He willed Charlotte to arrive, wanting to emphasise his concern for Robyn. She always arrived without sound. He should be used to her by now, yet it was always a shock: the spidery realisation that he was no longer alone.

Now he felt her standing behind him, more tangible than a ghost. He caught a hint of perfume, a soft footstep on the carpet. Without looking round, he drew and released a controlled breath.

"*Guten Abend*, my dear," he said warmly. "I hoped you would come."

"I'll bet you did."

The voice was not Charlotte's. It was low, accented, sharp as glass. And her perfume was wrong, too heavy...

He twisted round, one arm gripping the back of his chair. The slight figure at the foot of the bed was Charlotte's opposite. A bright young party creature, dressed in sparkling crimson. Her face was a bleached heart under a feathery bandeau, but her beauty was distorted by the livid black hunger in her eyes. Dark roses, the same red as her hair, trailed over the shoulders, suggestive of congealed blood and sweet, musky decay...

He'd never seen her before, but she reminded him of Karl. Did Karl have a sister, another member of the dark clan?

Gripping the chair to steady himself, he said, "Can I be of assistance, Frau –?"

"Oh, you're a calm one, Herr Stern."

She came towards him. Before he could stand, she somehow twined herself around him and was on his knee. Her hands caged his neck, thumbs on his windpipe. God, how cold she was! When Charlotte touched him her hands were sometimes warm, sometimes cool, but this creature was like iced wax.

And she was heavy for someone so slender, like cold stone leeching his warmth.

"What is this?" Josef whispered.

"I think you know, vampire-lover." Her smile was a parody of tenderness. She pulled off his spectacles and threw them onto the desk. Because she was so close, he saw her in clear focus. He stared in flat terror and fascination. Flawless, her skin, and radiant. The eyes were drowsily luminous... pupils expanding, drawing him in. Her mouth glistening. When she spoke, he glimpsed her teeth and the red tip of her tongue.

"I thought you were a little old for Charlotte... but no." Her fingers travelled over his cheeks and forehead, burning him with trails of frost. "You are very attractive, old man, like a magus with your silver hair and troubled eyes. You've seen a lot of life, haven't you? Too much. And now you're tired. So tired."

She was hypnotising him, but he couldn't stop her. A dream-state fell on him. He struggled to move but his body was anchored...

Suddenly she twisted round and slammed one hand onto the book, making him jump.

"What do you know about her?"

One moment, seductress – the next, interrogator.

"Who?"

"Lilith, of course. Otherwise known as our mad genius Violette."

"Only what's in the book. Take it, read for yourself."

She turned back, enveloping him again. "Well, it doesn't matter. You'll tell me eventually. Do you love Charlotte?"

He couldn't hold back the truth. "Yes."

"And does she do this to you?" With her left hand, the vampire broke the buttons from his shirt, slicing threads with her fingernail. Now her hand was exploring his ribs, sliding down over his lean abdomen, stealing warmth. Her lips touched his cheek, travelling in light kisses towards his mouth.

Josef's hands came forward to grasp her hips. He couldn't help it. Fear flowed through him as he realised what a fool he'd been, welcoming Charlotte into his life as if to say, "See how courageous and knowing I am, not like the superstitious fools all around us!"

Because, even though Charlotte was gentle and kind to him, she was still a vampire. She had to restrain her hunger to spare him. And this fiend who now devoured him was the dark side of the same coin. She was the danger he'd refused to acknowledge.

And still he welcomed the pressure of her lips as their mouths parted in a mutual "O" of lust, their tongues meeting, tasting—

She tasted of blood.

Ending the kiss, she whispered into his ear, making him shiver. "You want me, don't you?"

He nodded, eyes closed, mouth awash with fear and desire.

"On the bed or here on the chair?"

Her matter-of-fact crudeness stunned him. Drugged by the need for release, he tried to say, "the bed," to maintain at least a semblance of decorum, but before he could speak she swung one leg across to straddle him, her dress ruching around her thighs. Her hands worked at his trouser buttons. Then she slid forward and he felt the naked heat of her.

He groaned. The ache was unbearable.

"You want me," she whispered into his neck, "even though you know what will happen." And she laughed, a ripple of malice.

"Why are you doing this?"

"Because Charlotte values you. It pleases me to destroy what others value." As she spoke she lifted herself onto him, sheathing him in her moist, tight flesh. She wasn't cold there but hot, burning. The pulsing rhythm began and Josef's head fell back. Couldn't see, couldn't think. Only this excruciating ecstasy, building even through the web of terror.

She tore his shirt off his shoulders. Her nails ripped slits in his chest, drawing blood. She licked the drops away. Then she began to bite him, bruising without breaking the skin; pausing now and then to lap at the bloody nail wounds.

He cried out with pain. Heavy agony twisting tighter...

His climax was like an artery bursting. He felt as if he were pouring blood inside her. Turning dizzy, he slumped back, trying to push her away with strengthless hands. He couldn't breathe.

But he was lost under the fervid bud of her mouth, as it nipped its way towards his neck. She was like a lush jungle vine consuming him, a purple-tongued flower scented with musk and blood...

"Well, that was not your best effort, was it?"

Her voice shuddered with her own excitement. His eyes opened and met her gaze. Her pupils were sightless with thirst, her mouth open, the canine teeth lengthening until they locked into place with a ghastly faint click.

"Relax," she said sarcastically. "I'm not going to kill you."

Let it end. Why does she hesitate?

In a final peak of horror, he knew that it wasn't his throat she wanted. Instead she slid off his lap and knelt between his feet.

"You should have remembered," she hissed, "to attend to my pleasure before your own. One chance only."

The vermilion mouth with its ivory daggers came lancing down. Blackness exploded around him like the wings of a thousand crows.

Violette haunted the alley behind the hotel like a stray cat at the kitchen door. She felt restless to the point of distress. The thirst again, the damned thirst.

Three hours ago, she'd been a swan-queen commanding a stage. Now here she was, huddled in a black coat and cloche hat pulled down to hide her eyes, pacing the backstreets like a vagrant alcoholic.

That's what I am, she thought. *An addict.*

If the audience could only see me now!

I'll have to do it. Take a human. I could go to Robyn... no, not yet. I'll find a stranger.

Or I could resist... Until my control breaks and I take someone at random; oh yes, my male principal perhaps, or another of my poor girls! No. She bit her lip. The tang of her own blood tormented her.

Do I have to endure this every night to the end of the world? Why can't I be like Karl and Charlotte? Just... do it.

Or... feed on other vampires. It isn't the same – but it's better than nothing, better than this agony.

She looked up at the long rows of windows. Most were dark, but a few showed strips of light between the curtains. She knew which room was Josef's.

Violette had been furious with Charlotte for bringing Josef, a mortal, to study her like a specimen. Later, though, her anger had faded.

What do I know, after all? I feel Lilith in me like the raging cruelty of nature. The lioness bearing down the weakest quarry.

The cuckoo pushing babies from the nest. Nestlings left to die, like little children caught in wars. And through her I remember things that could not possibly have happened. I remember them like dreams with gaping holes where the cold gales of the Crystal Ring rush through.

I know nothing of who I really am. But perhaps Josef knows. Perhaps he has wisdom like Lancelyn... and even though Lilith's instinct is to mock and revile the wisdom of men, I think that I should swallow my pride and ask for help...

Charlotte and Karl weren't far away. They'd been out to hunt and were returning to the hotel; she sensed them, faint but clear, drawing closer. She had a few minutes before they appeared: time to see Josef. Not to harm him. Only to talk.

Violette entered the Crystal Ring and floated through steel-grey layers that were the kitchens, the foyer, stairs and corridors. The humans she passed were shimmering hairpins of fire, oblivious to her.

As she approached Josef's room, she knew something was wrong. The atmosphere warped with a heat-haze of fear, pain and excitement. As she reached the door, the scent of blood uncoiled to torment her. The thirst responded, drawing her fangs to full length against her will.

Someone had reached Josef before her.

The door dissolved, letting her through. As she snapped into the real world, she saw a hideous scene: the human on a chair, head back, hair dishevelled, face contorted – and the vampire straddling him. She was dressed in blood-colours, her face and hands dripping gore.

Ilona.

Violette heard her own father's voice from years past, "She was a lamia... hair the colour of blood..." She remembered the horrible injury he'd exposed to her in his madness, the mutilation that in the end had destroyed not only his life, but her mother's and her own.

For years, she'd believed her father to be insane. Only through meeting Charlotte had she come to understand that he hadn't been mad after all. He truly had been the victim of a vampire. And his attacker had been Ilona.

As Ilona slid off Josef's knee and lowered her savage mouth

towards his groin, Violette swooped. In an ecstasy of rage, she seized Ilona and ripped her bodily off her victim.

Josef slumped to the floor, unconscious.

Ilona twisted, eyes blazing, to see who'd thwarted her. "Oh, you!" she spat. Her hands whipped out in attack, but Violette was faster. Catching Ilona's wrists, she pulled the woman towards her, regardless of her furious struggling.

Ilona didn't try to escape into the Crystal Ring. Apparently she preferred to fight. But if she had, Violette would have gone with her. No one escaped the wings and claws of Lilith, not even Karl's daughter.

Violette's hunger was urgent, but Ilona clearly hadn't satisfied her own thirst. She jerked a hand free and seized Violette's hair, pulling hard to keep the dancer's mouth away from her throat. They were both strong and ruthless. There was a touch of sadistic delight in their conflict.

Violette broke the grip and her mouth clamped to Ilona's neck. How sweet the firm body felt against hers, taut with emotion. Need overwhelmed Violette and she sank her fangs. Ilona went rigid. The blood was dense, a little sour in a delicious way, like crisp apples. Pleasure throbbed through Violette from throat to loins.

Relief. Release, at last.

Ilona was cursing in her ear. "You – bloody – *witch*!"

And she broke free with an explosion of strength. From the corner of her eye, Violette saw Josef on the floor, huddled and groaning. There was blood all over him… human blood, which she still needed, despite the fluid she'd taken from Ilona. The hunger incensed her beyond reason.

"What did you call me?" Violette said thinly. She advanced on Ilona, who was backing away, her face feral.

"You heard." Ilona clawed at the wound in her throat. "How dare you touch me!"

"How dare you hurt *him*!" Violette pointed at Josef. "He was mine."

Ilona dodged the lash of her hands. "What's this, a new rule that we must put our names down for victims?"

Ilona was fast, but Violette surpassed her. She grabbed the bony shoulders and began to bite anywhere she could reach: face, neck, shoulders, arms. Ilona shrank away, mad with pain, defending now instead of attacking. Violette flung her down and pinned her to the floor, spattering the carpet with blood. "This isn't for Josef. It's for my father."

The impudent face glared into hers. "Not your bloody father again! Haven't you got over it yet? For God's sake, you're a vampire now! You'd do this to him *yourself*!"

Violette gripped her arm and jerked her onto her feet. Ilona began to look genuinely afraid.

"Look to yourself, before you talk of fathers," said Violette. "I see into your heart, Ilona, though I've no wish to look into such a foul pit."

And she struck the heart-shaped face, hard. Ilona reeled away but Violette followed, striking again and again. "Why don't you fly away into the Crystal Ring?"

"I can't, damn you! Stop it, leave me alone!"

But Violette-Lilith, caught up in the dark ritual of vengeance, could not stop. She pursued Ilona round the room in a cruel dance, blows becoming slashes. She tore Ilona's dress and broke her long necklaces, scattering beads everywhere, then gouged wounds all over her back and chest. When Ilona's cries turned from protests to pleas for mercy, Violette finally ran her up against the wardrobe and held her there, nails sinking deep into the flesh of her arms.

"You bitch," Ilona gasped. "Pierre was right. I'll never forget this."

"No, you won't. You hated Karl for making you into a vampire. Do you want your existence to end? Because I'll oblige, I'll snap your spine and tear off your charming head, and it will all be over. So, do you want to die?"

"No. No." Blank terror in her face.

"How surprising." Violette opened her mouth on Ilona's soft neck, sucking and tasting the skin. Thrusting her fangs deep into a vein she drew hard, working her tongue to increase the flow so the wound would not heal too fast...

She was drifting away. This victory was empty, actually. It meant nothing. There was something above her that she couldn't grasp, a mass of darkness floating in the Crystal Ring that seemed to be a house with blind windows and locked doors...

Hands fell on her shoulders, a massive sensory shock. Someone tore her from her prey, as she'd wrenched Ilona off Josef. The hands, transmitting rage, turned her round like pincers in her flesh.

She found herself looking into Karl's face. His anger, cold and ferocious, was alarming. She'd never seen such rage in his eyes before.

"Leave my daughter alone," Karl said quietly.

Charlotte was behind Karl, staring at Violette. She looked shaken, but said nothing. Instead she went to Josef and dropped to her knees beside him, her head bent in concern, more like a daughter than a vampire.

Ilona was leaning back against the wardrobe, white. Her neck, bent to one side, was jewelled with blood.

"The protective father," Violette said wearily. Her fear evaporated as Lilith's rage stirred again.

His fingers tightened. "What have you done to her?"

"Ask her what she was doing to Josef."

"As if you care about him," Karl said grimly.

Despite his fury, he seemed very controlled. So it was to her astonished horror that he bared his fangs and lunged at her throat.

"Karl, don't!" Charlotte cried.

Violette sprang to life, broke Karl's grip and thrust him away. Lilith's strength returned and she knocked him halfway across the room. There was a moment of stasis, black and distorted. Violette surveyed the scene as if watching a play: Karl, holding onto the chair that had arrested his fall, Charlotte hovering, not knowing which of them to protect.

Poor Charlotte, thought Violette, *forced to watch her loved ones trying to destroy each other.* Ilona struggled like a broken-winged bird, while Josef curled around his anguish and shame. How wretched this was. How ghastly.

Even Karl is not physically stronger than Lilith, she thought. *Perhaps no one is. And this gives me no pleasure. It is meaningless.*

She wanted to flee. Instead she stayed, held by their unearthly stares. Karl circled her, as if giving a wide berth to a snake, and gathered Ilona in his arms. Violette heard her whisper, "Get off me!" The remark brought a cold smile to her lips.

"You'd better take Ilona away, Karl." Charlotte's voice was low, shaky. "I'll look after Josef."

"And Violette?" No inflexion in his voice, but Karl gave Violette a look of wintry contempt. Her own emotions withered to grey stillness. She loathed herself.

"And Violette," Charlotte said firmly. "She won't hurt me."

Charlotte was so angry, both with Violette and Ilona, that she could barely speak as she helped Josef into bed. He stumbled as he went, clutching his torn clothes around him with both hands. His face was white. He would not meet her eyes.

"Are you all right?" Charlotte asked gently.

"Yes. Yes. She took no blood." Lying back on the pillow, Josef closed his eyes, pain ploughing his forehead. "Not much, at least."

"I'll send for a doctor," she said, looking at the wounds all over his chest. The punctures from a vampire's fangs healed quickly, but Ilona had made most of these with her nails.

"No!" he exclaimed. "No doctor, please."

"But some of these might need stitching."

"And how in heaven do I explain how I got them?" He shuddered. "She – Violette stopped her before it was any worse – Oh, my dear, I am so sorry."

Seeing his distress, and knowing Ilona's habits, she could guess what had happened. Dismay washed through her. Ilona liked to seduce before she drank. Although Charlotte could not rationally hold Josef to blame, she felt a pang of disappointment that he hadn't resisted.

She'd idealised him, but he was only human.

"No, it's my fault, Josef. I put you in danger. I meant no harm, but one vampire draws others." She went to touch his forehead, but he jerked away.

"Don't touch me," he said.

"Why not?"

"Because I'm ashamed of what happened," he said hoarsely. "So ashamed."

"Do you want me to send for Robyn?"

"No! She must never know."

"But your wounds need dressing. If you won't have a doctor or Robyn, there's only me."

He turned away, folding up around his pain. "I know you mean well, but leave me alone, please."

Sighing, Charlotte left him and went to Violette. The dancer was sitting in an armchair, legs crossed, one foot pointing and flexing in the air. Extraordinary that she could switch from violence to repose so quickly.

"Is it true?" Charlotte said. "Did you save Josef from Ilona?"

The vivid blue-violet eyes came into focus. "I was saving my father," she said.

Charlotte caught her breath. "Dear God."

"Yes, I caught her about to do what she did to him. The same mutilation. I had a crazed idea that if I saved Josef, I'd somehow save my own father. As if I could turn back time and prevent the trauma that ruined our lives. That's why I went crazy with her."

"Were you going to kill her?"

"I was tempted." Violette opened her expressive hands. "I was very close."

Charlotte put her hands to her face. "Karl would have loathed you for all time."

"I think he does, anyway. I don't suppose he'll ever forgive me, but I don't care."

"Don't you?" Charlotte flared. "I can't bear this. You're both impossible!" When Violette didn't reply, she continued with less heat, "He wanted to help you. Now you've made two more enemies, when you might have had two friends."

"Oh, should I have left Ilona to her feast?" Violette said frostily. "Can you not understand the reason for my anger?"

"Of course, but Ilona is still Karl's daughter! He couldn't stand by and say, 'She deserves it.' God knows, it's hard to feel sympathy for her – but how can I feel any for you, having witnessed what you did to her? If you and Karl go on fighting, it will kill me."

The lovely eyes widened. "Tell *him* that. He attacked me, Charlotte! I wouldn't kill him, for your sake – and how else could I really harm him?"

"You change people."

"Anything I've done to Ilona can only be an improvement, then."

Silence. Violette turned away. She was beautiful in the half-light, the quintessential ballerina in black. Charlotte worshipped her, even while she felt like strangling her. And she feared her, always.

"Why were you here, anyway?" Charlotte snapped. "Hoping to destroy Josef, whose only crime was to trust me?"

Violette's eyes and voice softened. She looked down. "No. I came to talk. To see if he really could tell me... what I am."

"Leave me alone!" Ilona repeated the words fiercely as Karl helped her along the hotel corridor. But she uttered them as if saying a rosary, trembling and boneless in his arms.

A short man with round glasses emerged from a room, stopped and stared. Karl cursed: he wanted no witnesses to his daughter's distress. He met the man's eyes; the man gazed back mindlessly. Then a change, a dreadful realisation, came over his face. Paling, he gagged as if his heart had stopped, and stumbled back into his room.

Karl gained the door to their suite with no further intrusions.

Vampires often fed on each other. This act expressed anything from love to dominance. It could be a divine exchange or savage violation. Karl suspected, though, that Ilona was in distress due to something deeper than blood-loss.

In the room, he let her go and she sat on the edge of the bed, arms folded tautly on her knees. Karl put no lights on. The room was cavernous in darkness, his daughter rimmed by a fragile pearly glow. Karl found a towelling bathrobe and draped it around her.

Despite the state she was in, he felt angry. Decades of pain they'd caused each other. Always this implacable conflict between them. Every time he thought the battle was over, it flared up again.

He sat beside her, pushing his anger aside. "Why didn't you let us know you were here?" he asked, falling into the *Wienerisch* dialect of the last century; a language they seldom used these days. A rare intimacy. "Why are you always doing this?"

"What?" Her words escaped through a knot of pain.

"Following us. Saying nothing. Destroying people in order to hurt us."

"You know why."

Karl placed his hand on her cheek and made her face him. Her cruel spirit seemed quenched. In her eyes he saw fear, confusion, thoughts dwindling to points of fire in an abyss. The revelation shook him. He hated what she'd become after he transformed her – but seeing her like this was worse.

"Did she take much blood?"

"Enough, thank you, *Herr Doktor*," she said. He offered his wrist. She stared at the tender flesh, turned her head aside. "I don't want yours."

"But you need it."

"Not from you. Why don't you just –"

"Leave you?" He spoke coolly. She could not know the pain she inflicted by refusing his help. "No. Not until you tell me what Violette has done to you."

"Isn't it obvious?"

"I mean mentally."

Ilona shuddered. "You know why I'm compelled to torment you." Her self-control seemed to collapse like a dam before a flood. Karl realised that he'd never seen her cry since she was a human child. Never, until now. As she leaned into his shoulder, he held her as if she were a stranger. As if some terrible contagion would soak into him with her tears. "You took my life from me. I wanted my husband and my child. You took them away from me. You even took Kristian! You wanted me to be a vampire, so that is exactly what I became."

"But Ilona," he said gently, after a moment, "you had no child."

"But I would have done. I was pregnant when you came for me. The transformation killed it, of course. *You* killed it." And as she spoke she collapsed against him, sobs convulsing her like dying breaths. Karl's hand played absently with her hair. He felt numb, the revelation a distant thorn-prick.

"You never told me." His voice was hollow.

"I never meant to. I told Charlotte once, to explain why I hated you so. I made her swear not to tell you."

"Charlotte knew?" The thorn-prick became an ache. He gripped her arm. "Why didn't you tell me at the time?"

"How could I? I didn't know what you planned to do, until it was too late. What difference would it have made?"

"I don't know," he said truthfully. "I don't know."

"None, because you were too wrapped up in what you wanted to consider my wishes."

"It's true." The ache reached his throat and eyes. He could hardly speak. "I was only thinking of myself. I wanted you with me forever, not growing old with some mortal man."

"Yes, jealousy, too; you think I didn't know? You didn't only kill the child I was expecting, but all the potential children. Our descendents. You didn't ask, you didn't give me a choice!"

"I know," he whispered. Ilona had never spoken so openly before. He'd longed for her to confide in him, but now she was doing so, he could hardly bear to listen.

"And my husband – after I became a vampire, I went back and killed him. You didn't know that either, did you? I sucked him dry, because it seemed the only thing to do. Strangle my mortal connections, cut them dead so I didn't keep wanting to go back. I can't remember what he looked like, actually."

"God, Ilona..."

"But none of this occurred to you. Even if it had, you'd have taken me anyway."

"Not if I'd known it would cause you such pain, a century later."

"But it doesn't." Her tone was thin, chilling. "Don't you understand? That's why I'm crying. Because I feel nothing."

Karl's grief hardened. It wasn't sympathy Ilona needed; she never had. "If that's true, why do you still want to punish me? I'm hopeless at being a martyr to guilt, however bad a father I have been."

"Did I spring fully armed from your head?" she cried. "Because you never talk about my mother, never!"

"Would you want me to? When I told you that Kristian had your mother killed, you fawned on Kristian all the more, knowing I'd hate it. There's nothing to say about our mortal lives, Ilona."

Her sobs ebbed away. She lay across his lap as if she'd disgorged all her strength. "I'm not weeping for my mortal life, Father. I'm weeping because I swore I'd never tell you these things, and now I've broken my oath. It's the humiliation. *This* is what Violette has done to me."

He lifted her up and cradled her against his side. Her slender body fitted along his chest and shoulder. And for once she neither teased nor reviled him, but simply rested there.

"I was wrong to make you a vampire," Karl said. "But if I hadn't, you would be dead by now. Perhaps your great-granddaughter would be here with me instead. Would you really have preferred that?"

She gave him a poisonous look. "Oh, I'm a consummate hypocrite. You know how I feel about you. Don't humiliate me more by forcing me to say it. You know."

"Why is it humiliating to admit you love me? Why does it almost kill you to weep in front of me, or admit that I hurt you? I was your father. You once said we can't retain human relationships, but I disagree. If you can't trust me, who else is there? But that's why you torment me, isn't it? Because you know you are safe to do so."

Karl expected vehement denial. Instead, her reaction was a shaky laugh. "You frightened me once," she said. "The time Kristian brought you back to life and you found that I'd come back to him? You looked straight through me and it was the first time I felt you'd stopped caring. Oh, I would hate it if you didn't care."

"And do you think my patience is infinite?"

"No, but I know you'd always save me from danger, as you did tonight. You even braved the *Weisskalt* to save me!"

"So we understand each other, then," he said gently.

Ilona raised a hand to stroke his neck. The hand pulled off his tie, undid the collar of his shirt. Like a cat she slid her cheek over his ribs and collarbone, nuzzled into his throat, then bit him. Her canines were so swift and sharp that Karl felt little pain. He let her drink, cradling her, his head tipping back a little, eyelids lowered, lips parted. Not breathing. As he looked down on her raptly bent head, he envisioned a baby's head, with a mop of the same plum-dark hair, suckling at her mother's breast. And this grotesque parody represented exactly what they were: a reversal of nature.

When Ilona raised her head, her brown eyes had turned molten, like a sated lover. Her fingers pressed into his neck; her robe and torn dress fell away from her milky shoulders. It took Karl all his willpower not to feast on her in turn.

"I'm going back to Europe," she announced. "I wanted to prove Pierre wrong about Violette – only to discover that he's right. She has to be stopped."

Karl's mood darkened. Violette had become an insoluble problem. Much as he distrusted her, for Charlotte's sake he did not want her harmed. In any case, she seemed indestructible. *But,* he thought, *how long can I stand by while she attacks people like Pierre and Ilona? How long before she turns on Charlotte?*

"That will only create more trouble," he said. "More grief."

"So? I have to prove that she *hasn't* changed me, that she can't turn me to a gibbering wreck like Pierre." Ilona seemed her normal self again. Karl didn't know whether to be pleased or dismayed. "Behaving vilely and destructively, tearing apart everyone she meets – that, my beloved Karl, is my job."

Sebastian knew that Roberta Stafford lived on Chestnut Street, Beacon Hill. Discovering her address had been simple: after they parted in the Public Garden, he secretly followed her home.

Tomorrow night he would take her out to dinner, like the gentleman suitor he played so well – but tonight he haunted the street outside her house as his true self, a malevolent predator in the darkness. How pleasing, to spy on his prey in her natural setting.

Leaning against a tree trunk, Sebastian felt rain pattering softly through the leaves. The drops wove webs of light from the lamps, made the road surface glisten. A lovely street, with cobbled sidewalks, gas lamps and rows of red-brick houses stepping gracefully up the hill. So quiet, folded discreetly on its riches like a hen on her nest. The lindens, maples and maidenhairs that lined the sidewalks were so lush that the buildings were barely visible. No two houses were alike: each had its own architectural quirks. Robyn's was particularly charming: four storeys high, tall windows framed by white woodwork and black shutters. A narrow front garden lay behind railings, with vines smothering the lower brickwork, wisteria twining around the arched doorway. The railings were topped with gold leaf, the steps whitewashed. The home of a rich widow, perhaps, utterly respectable.

And yet, defying propriety, this extraordinary woman lived like a courtesan in the grand old style. Sebastian, despite his world-weariness, was intrigued. He wanted to savour this.

He found his way around the row of houses, along an alley and into her walled garden. He noted kitchens on the ground floor, a flight of steps up to a terrace where lights shone from the parlour.

Thick lace curtains were ideal to shield a vampire from sight, even if he pressed right up against the glass.

Four people were in the room: a puffy-faced businessman, a middle-aged woman with dark hair, a maid serving a tray of drinks, and Roberta herself. A cosy, happy gathering; even the maid joined in the talk and laughter.

Roberta was seated, facing away from the window. Sebastian took in her sleek brown hair, the curves and angles of her shoulders under the thin straps of her dress... and her neck, peach-soft, pleading for the touch of his fingers and lips.

The anticipation was exquisite.

None of them saw his face, half in shadow under a mass of dark hair, lace-patterns icing one high cheekbone and the sharp line of his jaw, catching one point of light in a darkly introspective eye. They didn't sense him watching, nor notice him withdraw and vanish. He had learned enough for now.

The business type was called Harold and was apparently one of her lovers. *How many does she have?* he wondered. The two women were her maids, Mary and Alice. Roberta treated them more as friends than servants. Clearly they were loyal.

Interesting, Sebastian thought. He already knew that his victim-to-be was far from the cold *Belle Dame sans Merci* whom Russell Booth had described. She was kind to her servants. She was ordinary. Hidden, then, the real poison of her heart.

He began to smile, but his pleasure hardened into black thirst. He'd had too much sadness in the past to feel joy now. He was not a gloating killer. He simply obeyed the grim urges of his nature; his passion for blood was bleak, ruthless and absolute.

Tomorrow. But he would not take her immediately, because he'd learned that her uncle was in town, and that he knew Karl. So he couldn't fulfil his plan until the uncle and the other vampires left Boston. Still, he had time in abundance. He'd taken a risk, telling her his real name, but a little risk spiced his anticipation.

So hard to wait, so tantalising.

As Sebastian walked down Spruce Street towards the Common, he met an Irish housemaid with autumn hair like Robyn's. Did she feel safe alone, so late at night? he asked her, effortlessly imitating her brogue. Charmed, she smiled and blushed. Quite safe, sir. I'm only after visiting a friend. But, he said, will you let me walk you home?

She let him, and they talked about Ireland as they went. As always Sebastian felt the strange conflicts of memory. Savage pain no longer... yet there was still something, the deep green pull of the old land and the house...

The Irish girl trusted him, and flirted shamelessly. She led him to the back of a big house on Marlborough Street, more old Bostonian wealth and grandeur. In the shadow of the kitchen door, they stood like young lovers who weren't quite sure how to proceed.

"Well, goodnight, sir," she said, looking at him expectantly.

He kissed her. "I'm superstitious," he said. "I won't come in until I'm invited."

Her eyes were huge, dew-soft. He had not mesmerised her. "Would you like to?" she whispered.

They crept along corridors and up the back stairs to her attic room. As soon as the door closed he pulled her to him, scaring her a little. His hands travelled over the cheap material of her coat, ripping off the buttons in his excitement. She was compliant, not as inexperienced as a good Catholic girl should be. If they were really frightened or unwilling, which was rare, he would content himself with their blood. Sebastian was not a rapist – only of their veins, at least.

But she responded eagerly as he pushed her down onto the narrow, lumpy bed, tearing away her skirt and undergarments. He loved physical passion, albeit with a kind of grim detachment. She tried to kiss him but he turned his face away; that was not the intimacy he wanted. She was wriggling beneath him, gasping for breath.

"Slow down," she said, voice high and faint. "What's the hurry? Please, slow down!"

But he could not. All that mattered was his blind urgency as he thrust himself into her warm moist flesh, the shuddering build-up of fire.

How he loved this. Sometimes blood itself was not enough. Blood was the necessity, not sex – but to feed like this, in full, aching possession, gave the act an edge of unparalleled rapture.

His fangs entered her neck and hot fluid surged into his mouth. He was only half-aware of his victim's mingled pleasure and pain. She was only a vessel, the source of the ruby heat building within him. He raked his hands through her hair and dug his fingers into her skull, imagining...

Imagining that she was Robyn.

"Robyn," he murmured through the blood. "Robyn."

His climax was a lava-surge that went on and on as her blood flowed to quench the searing thirst... until it slowed to a trickle of pleasure, and the girl's body lay cooling beneath him.

Once it was over, he immediately wanted to escape. Leaving the house through the Crystal Ring, he strolled to the Charles River and stood looking across the dark water towards Cambridge. Anyone seeing him would have thought he looked too genteel to harm a soul. He was satiated, at peace; slightly depressed, perhaps, but nothing to cause pain.

The river's wide flow filled him with tranquillity. Only the faintest ripple of hunger troubled him: the desire not to take a substitute, but to seduce and possess the one who really mattered.

CHAPTER NINE

RED LIKE THE ROSE

"Where's Ilona?" Charlotte demanded.

She switched on a light as she entered the suite, but Karl was there alone. He stood at the window, looking out at the street. Outside, she glimpsed traffic crawling between tall Victorian buildings, lights flickering on darkness; heard trolley cars rattling, motor horns, drunken voices singing in the distance. American cities never slept, it seemed.

"She's gone," he said.

"Oh, has she?" Charlotte couldn't hide her anger. "She must know I'd like to tear her limb from limb."

Karl turned to her. His shirt was undone, his skin pale as if he needed blood. His eyes were cold. "Don't you think Ilona has suffered enough at Violette's hands? What reason have you to vent your anger on her?"

Charlotte gaped in disbelief. "She attacked Josef and nearly maimed him for life!"

"But you took this risk when you brought Josef with us." Karl's usual impartiality seemed to have deserted him.

"So it's not Ilona's fault? Karl, I know she's your daughter, but you can't condone her attacking Josef!"

"But you condone Violette's behaviour?"

His hostility floored her. In his eerie beauty, with his soft, dark hair and compelling eyes, Karl always wielded heart-stopping power over her. To see that beauty glazed with something of

Kristian's bane frightened her.

"Violette was protecting Josef," she said."

"Simple restraint would have sufficed. To attack Ilona so viciously was uncalled-for, yet you still insist that Violette is misunderstood? What must she do to make you admit that she is evil and beyond control?"

"Evil?" Charlotte trembled, enraged. They'd never quarrelled like this before. She'd never seen Karl so implacable. Often she'd wished he were not always so good-natured and reasonable – she took back the wish now. "Ilona deserved it! Violette reacted as she did because, years ago, Ilona attacked her father and sent him mad."

"I don't want to hear it."

"You tried to feed on Violette," Charlotte said in a low voice. "You attacked her. I'm not sure I can forgive you."

"Can't you?" Karl smiled thinly. "Still so distasteful, to be reminded that I am not always a perfect gentleman?"

She turned away, furious with him, but hating the feeling.

"Charlotte," he said, starting after her. She made for the door, but Karl caught her before she reached it. Then he held her hard, his chin on her hair, his body moulded to hers from chest to thigh. "We must stop this."

"How?" she whispered. "I've never known you to take sides before."

"I know. But I told you, I can't stand aside if Violette threatens anyone I love. Not even for your sake."

"And Violette would probably have killed you, Karl, not the other way round," she said bitterly. "And it destroys me to see you at each other's throats – literally. What am I supposed to do?"

"To begin with," he said, his mouth near her ear, "we must not quarrel."

She sighed, still aggrieved, but unable to disentangle herself from his seductive embrace. "Why not?"

"Because that's precisely what Ilona and Violette would want," he said. "Imagine how delighted they'd be to know they had driven us apart."

Karl's arms were now so tight that she couldn't draw breath. Almost desperate, his embrace. Charlotte gave in, and they held each other in the pure relief of reconciliation.

Yet she thought, *How close we came to letting this tear us apart! My terror of losing Karl is too painful to bear... So, maybe Violette's right. I should submit to her, and let her bite cure my fatal dependence on Karl's love. Let her take this merciless fear away.*

When Robyn visited Josef at his hotel late the next morning, she found him in bed with the covers drawn up to his chin.

He hadn't responded to her knock. She'd had to ask a porter to unlock the door. As she approached the bed, her heart rose into her throat in fear that he was unconscious or dead.

He looked grey, but his eyes were open, gleaming dully.

"What are you doing here, child?" He sounded weary.

"You were meant to call on me today," she said cheerfully. "When you didn't arrive or send a message, I was worried. What's the matter?"

"Nothing." He breathed out heavily.

"Come on, you don't fool me. Aches, pains, fever? Have you seen a doctor?"

She made to touch his forehead, but he jerked away. His brow contracted. "Don't touch me."

"Why not?" She sank down on the edge of the bed, puzzled and alarmed. "I've never seen you like this before. What is it?"

"Nothing. A headache."

He was lying. The sheet gripped around his throat concealed something.

"Do you often have headaches?"

"*Liebe Gott*," he whispered. "I tell you, I just need rest. Would you please leave so I can?"

"If you insist. But what is it, Uncle, really?" She put her hand on his, felt him flinch. "Tell me."

He gave her a long, candid look. Regret, guilt, awful secrets swam in his eyes. Then he said, "There are vampires..."

"Vampires?"

"They suck your blood, but they take your mind as well."

"Uncle, are you in trouble?" Robyn made a worrying deduction. "Is someone extorting money from you?"

"No, my dear, nothing like that. I'm rambling, I must have a fever."

"Well, that's it," she said briskly. "You're obviously in no fit state today, but tomorrow you're coming to stay with me. No arguments. If you don't co-operate, I'll get nasty; I'll send Mother round with chicken soup."

"Not that." He tried to smile.

"Have you eaten? I'll call room service. I'll be back later to see how you are."

"There's no need." He patted her hand. "Charlotte is looking after me."

Light from the corridor fanned into the semi-dark room. Robyn looked up and saw Charlotte in the doorway, a silhouette. Robyn approached her with a weird sense of unease, as if the air shimmered with secrets.

"What's wrong with him?" Robyn asked, her tone sharp.

"A slight chill," said Charlotte. Her violet eyes were warm, innocent. "No need to worry."

"Nevertheless," Robyn said firmly, "I'll see Josef this evening, and tomorrow I'm taking him home."

"I thought you were not coming," said Sebastian.

"I am rather late." Robyn offered no apology. He stood to meet her as she approached. The simple luxury of the restaurant – marble pillars, potted ferns, swirly red carpet – seemed a faded backdrop to Sebastian's dark and vivid presence. Dressed in black, he looked old-fashioned, yet he carried off his disregard for fashion with ease.

A waiter took her coat. "I was with my uncle at his hotel," she continued as they were shown to their table. "He's not well."

"Nothing serious, I hope." They sat, separated by white linen and silver, candlesticks and flowers. Voices murmured around them. A pianist played popular melodies on a white grand piano.

"I'm not sure." She fell quiet, preoccupied. She was so concerned about Josef that her appetite vanished, and she wished she wasn't here. Then she collected herself and shone her full attention on her companion. "I found him in bed with the covers up to his chin. He claimed it was a headache, but he was acting oddly. He wouldn't talk and didn't want me there."

Sebastian looked amused. "Were there shapes in the bed that should not have been? The chambermaid, perhaps?"

Robyn laughed, despite herself. "He's no angel, my uncle. Maybe that's why he understands me. Anyway, he seemed better tonight, but still won't talk. Sat there with the weight of the world on his shoulders, but won't say why. We almost argued. That's why I'm late."

"Did you think I would not wait?"

His eyes, under the dark combs of his lashes, woke a wave of feeling that she distrusted. "Oh, no," she said with cool sweetness. "I knew you'd wait."

"And you won't brood about your uncle all evening?"

"It's absolutely not in my nature to brood," she said.

"Nor in mine." There was a flash of something in his expression that disturbed her, as he had at the Booths' party. Gone.

Robyn took tea with her meal. Wine was prohibited, which was not helping the restaurant trade – or her state of mind. She wanted a drink to relax her – but with Sebastian, perhaps it was better to stay alert.

Afterwards, she had little recollection of their conversation. Inconsequential chat about Boston, the weather, the charms of New England, the theatre. One thing was certain: they never once mentioned her deceased lover, Russell. A taste of lobster woke her appetite and she enjoyed the food. Perhaps that was why she never once noticed Sebastian eating.

By the end of the meal, he was still a mystery. Obviously he liked her. Yet he was detached; friendly enough, but making no attempt to impress her.

She liked that. He was refreshing. He'd saved her from having to parry the syrupy clichés of seduction that most men thought made them irresistible. She could just be her good-natured, slightly acidic self.

"May I escort you home?" he said, as their coats were brought and doors held open.

He sounds, she thought, *like he's parodying polite behaviour.*
"You may."

Perhaps he's like me. He lives in society, but despises it.

From the restaurant near the harbour, they walked arm in arm

past Faneuil Hall and the market, and across the Common towards
Beacon Hill. Little lights shone in the trees, and the paths were
darkly inviting. The evening had a strange atmosphere that made
everything shimmer. Unreal. A dreamy excitement that threatened
to edge into nightmare. Sebastian was so unusual, almost too
vivid: beautiful, different, warm one moment, a thousand miles
away the next.

Robyn wasn't sure she liked him. Not that it mattered. She
never became emotionally attached to her victims.

He might induce obsession in a more vulnerable woman; a
wanton addiction, like opium. The thought repelled her. This
would not be easy... but challenge was preferable to boredom.

"You know, Mrs Stafford," he said, "you are not at all what I
expected."

She began to laugh. She tried to stifle it, but couldn't.

"What is it?" he said.

"Oh, they always say that. I'd taken you for being less predictable."

For a second, she sensed him turn hostile. Lights moved over
his face as if it were ice. Again she felt an echo of dread, but
when he spoke, his voice was warm, satirical. "Who are they, who
always say it?"

"Men. They've always *heard* about me, you see. They expect
some red-taloned vamp, Cleopatra with a poisoned dagger. So it's
a shock when they find out I'm... ordinary. Then they say what
you said."

"Well, I'm sorry to be predictable, but I'd hardly call you
ordinary."

"I won't ask what you would call me." She smiled at him. Her
smile had power, and she saw him respond. "However, I have a
suggestion."

"Yes?"

"You may call me Robyn."

She hadn't been concentrating on their route. Without thinking,
she'd let Sebastian lead her to the top of the Common, across
Beacon Street and along Charles. She was stunned when he took
the correct turning into Chestnut Street and headed straight to
her house.

She hesitated on the doorstep, shivering.

"I don't recall telling you where I lived."

"You didn't," he said. "I let you lead me."

With one hand curved around a railing, he gazed at her. He was lean and dark, his hair swept untidily back from his crystalline face, eyes gleaming. He made her think of a night-hunting cat, eager to be on its way. He made no attempt to kiss her.

This was the moment when Robyn must always make a decision. With those who were too eager, it was best to act aloof. Reducing them to a fever of unrequited passion made them simple to manipulate. With resistant men, however, she found it paid to go for the kill. Show them what they'd be missing if they lost her. The velvet snare: worked every time.

Sebastian belonged in the second category. She was about to invite him in when he took the decision out of her hands, leaving her both annoyed and relieved.

"I hope we'll meet again," he said, kissing her hand. Through the leaf-laced shadows of Chestnut Street, she watched him walk away.

Whatever had ailed Josef, he recovered quickly once Robyn settled him in her house. Her maternal side had a rare outing, fussing over him. Although Josef insisted that he had no need to be cosseted, his protests were half-hearted. He seemed glad of her attention, as if he'd been in danger and felt safe here.

Robyn didn't press him on the nature of his illness. He was subdued, as if his spirit was wounded. Restless, too; he went out often, perhaps to visit his strange friends, Karl and Charlotte.

"Why don't you invite them here?" she asked on the third morning, as they sat at breakfast in the parlour.

Alarm flashed over his face. "Oh, they are busy. The ballet leaves Boston the day after tomorrow."

"Too busy to spare an hour? What exactly do they do?"

"Well, they are... Madame Lenoir's business partners. Patrons of the ballet. I'll ask them, but I doubt –"

"Uncle, stop. If you don't want them here, that's your choice. Kind of a shame, though," she said, watching his expression. "I'd like to have met them again. And Violette."

"Violette?" he said, flinching.

"Yes, why not? Although I guess she really *is* too important to take tea with the likes of me," Robyn said caustically. "So, the ballet is leaving?"

"Yes, a week in New York, four days in Philadelphia and so on; it's an exhausting schedule."

"But what will you do, dear? Are you going with them or staying here?"

He folded his hands, gazing at the fire screen and dried flowers on the grate. "I don't know. I only came with them to see you. I think I'll stay here a few more days, do a little sightseeing, perhaps go to New York, and then sail back to Europe. If I am not imposing? I can go back to the hotel."

"Nonsense." Robyn thought how tired he sounded. "Stay here as long as you like."

"A few days only, I promise."

Much as she loved his company, she was secretly glad that he'd be leaving. His presence forced her to suspend her usual lifestyle. She could not in all decency receive Harold with Josef here, nor cultivate new admirers – nor see Sebastian.

In fact, Sebastian hadn't contacted her since their dinner date. Hadn't even sent flowers. Robyn had a feeling she would never hear from him again. His silence disappointed and offended her. Robyn had to be the one to end liaisons. She couldn't tolerate being treated so casually.

"You can't until you're fit to travel," she said firmly.

Josef breathed out as if heart-sore. Instead of brushing off her concern, he spoke kindly. "Robyn, I owe you an explanation."

"You don't, dear. Whatever's troubling you – well, I'm here to help, but if it's private, that's fine." She spoke sincerely, inwardly willing him to confide.

"The night I was ill..." He cleared his throat. "Well, I was ashamed of the whole affair, but it was caused by... a difficult situation. Charlotte invited me on tour because she was concerned for Madame Lenoir's state of mind."

"Oh!" Robyn was shocked. A recent memory unwound.

"You understand, it's delicate. I could hardly walk around telling people that Madame is..."

"Crazy?"

"Must you be so outspoken?"

"So, you came along as her personal psychologist?"

"Not exactly."

"I'm not surprised, to be honest. I spoke to her at the party. She was strange." The memory brought a wistful smile to Robyn's lips, a thrilling shiver. "I'd say that lady has troubles... but talented people are often eccentric, aren't they?"

"I wouldn't dream of passing such judgement on her," Josef said sharply. "The point is that we acted behind Madame Lenoir's back. When she found out, she was enraged and refused to talk to me. So, no point in me travelling with the ballet. All very embarrassing, combined with the fact that... I have great affection for Charlotte. Therefore Karl and I are not exactly friends."

"And he's not someone I'd want as an enemy," she said quietly.

He gave her a quick, keen glance. "Why do you say that?"

Robyn shrugged. "He struck me as an exceptional personality, that's all. A sweetheart – unless you cross him."

"Yes, well." Josef exhaled. "When you came to the hotel, I was the worse for drowning my sorrows the night before. I couldn't tell you because I was ashamed. That's all. Foolish old man."

He looked anxious for her to believe him. Actually she didn't, but she tried to take his story at face value. After all, what could he possibly be hiding?

"Are you telling me that I've pampered you over a *hangover*?" Her teasing drew a smile from him at last.

"Can you forgive me?" He leaned forward. "But tell me, what happened with Madame Lenoir at the party?"

"Not much," Robyn said, off-hand. "I was in the garden and she appeared and began talking to me. I ended up telling her things I wouldn't normally tell anyone. I don't know why. She seemed to understand, and she was... fascinating, really. And then... well, I think she tried to seduce me."

"Seduce?" Josef turned red. "Are you sure it was not... an attack of some kind?"

"What?" She was amazed. "Why would a ballerina go around attacking people? Oh, no, it was sexual," she said, not sparing his blushes. "You know, kisses, touches. I was so stunned I couldn't stop her. Almost scary..." Memories again; Violette's lips branding her neck, the soft-breathing night air, the sensation that some unearthly creature, half-bird and half-serpent, was possessing her... Robyn shook herself. "I don't know how serious she was, because she suddenly stopped and walked off, just left me there. Very weird." A thought struck her. "Is this why everyone's concerned about her? Uncle, you don't think that having sapphic tendencies is a form of mental illness? Do you?"

His silver eyebrows jerked up. "Not at all. I hadn't even thought of it."

"Most men prefer not to think of such things, but they happen all the same. I wasn't shocked. I'm broad-minded."

"Tolerant, Robyn," he said, his voice softening. "Well, some might not agree, but I assure you I do. No, her problems are..." More evasion. "Creative. To do with her art. She, er, works too hard for her own good."

"Stop struggling, dear," Robyn sighed. "If you can't tell me, just say so. I don't expect you to divulge professional secrets."

"I'm sorry. It's very delicate. Anyway, it's academic, since she won't see me."

No more was said on the touchy subject of the dancer. They spent a pleasant morning together and were discussing the best place to go for lunch, when the doorbell rang. Mary came in to announce the visitor.

"Ma'am, there's a lady to see Dr Stern. Madame Violette Lenoir."

Robyn saw her uncle's face turn the colour of ash.

"I hope you don't mind me coming to see you," said Violette.

She felt nervous; ridiculous, but she couldn't help it. The maid had shown her and Josef into a morning room on the ground floor; a small, light space with a writing bureau, bookshelves, two armchairs, a towering rubber plant. Robyn was absent. Violette had asked to see him alone.

Josef was an ambiguous figure in Violette's eyes. Slender, stooping a little as if he felt too tall, he seemed a silver-haired sage, full of wisdom.

He was not Janacek, who'd been a manipulative bully: simply a kind academic with a weakness for women. Also, she couldn't help

THE DARK BLOOD OF POPPIES

comparing him favourably with the self-styled magus Lancelyn, whose overconfidence and goatish sexuality had repelled her.

Josef was clearly uncomfortable in her presence. After all, she'd caught him in the most compromising position imaginable with Ilona. Then he'd witnessed their bloody fight – parts of it, at least. He'd regained consciousness in time to see Violette's wild assault on Ilona.

"I've had time to think," she said. "I've decided I should hear whatever you can tell me about Lilith."

"Madame, I am honoured. Shall we sit down?"

They settled in leather armchairs, a few feet apart with a rug between them. She had refused the maid's offer to take her coat and hat; irrational, but the garments were a layer of protection between her and an intrusive world.

She said, "There was another man who claimed to know my secrets. His name was Lancelyn. He tried to help, but he went too far and I destroyed him. He's in an insane asylum. He might be dead by now, for all I know."

"Is this a warning?" Josef asked gravely. "You cannot expect me to speak freely if I am afraid of what you might do if I offend you."

"No, I want the truth," she said. "I appreciate your taking a risk for my sake. Don't be afraid. I'm here only to talk. That was why I came to your room before. Please understand, it's extremely difficult for me to ask for help. I'm at your mercy."

He appeared to relax a little. "All I demand is that no harm comes to my niece."

"I promise."

Josef cleared his throat. She felt as if she were in a psychiatrist's office.

"Lilith is a figure who occurs in most mythologies, under different names, usually as a wind-hag. For instance, in Sumer she was Lil, a storm spirit, while the Semites of Mesopotamia called her Lilith, a night demon who lays hold of sleeping men and women and causes erotic dreams. In Syria she became a succubus and a child-killing witch. But she is best known from Jewish holy books, the Zohar and the Talmud, as the first wife of Adam."

Unpleasant memories flared in Violette's mind. She gave herself

189

up to them, letting Josef's voice soothe her. She said, "Yes, I was in the Garden, a disgustingly fecund garden crawling with life... The man lies over me, he won't accept me as his equal, he tries to force me but I refuse. I call the secret name of God to free myself, and I flee to the desert. God sends three angels after me, but I won't go back with them."

"Their names?" Josef sounded intent, fascinated.

"Senoy, Sansenoy, Semangelof. I'd never heard those names until my transformation. The knowledge came from inside me, not from books."

"Well, there are various stories of Lilith's origins that sound archaic and strange to us now. The Zohar says that the Left, the side of Darkness, 'flamed forth with its full power, and from this fiery flame came forth the female moonlike essence.' Two great lights arose, the Sun and the Moon, but they quarrelled about their power and God settled the dispute by diminishing the Moon and sending her to rule over the lower orders. The dominion of day belongs to the male and night to the female."

"And the female is dark," Violette murmured. "She belongs to the night. She has been diminished and from that comes her anger..."

"And gives birth to the evil that is Lilith."

Perhaps Josef used the word without thinking, but her tormented mind latched onto it. "Evil."

"But the Zohar teaches that knowledge of her is essential to self-development," Josef said hurriedly. "It speaks of two intertwined shoots, red like the rose, male and female. The male is Samael the Devil, the female contained in him is Lilith. The female is always contained within the male, as God contains the Shekinah –"

"The pair above and the pair below." She already knew the words. The images they conjured were not memories but dream-shadows, indefinable and threatening. "Samael of the dark side and his female, Lilith; the Serpent, the Woman of Harlotry."

"Do you really need me to tell you anything?" said Josef.

"Yes. I don't always know until you tell me, but everything you say, I recognise. I feel the weight of these men's writings, holding me down. Go on."

Josef's words, too, weighed on her like chains. "Cast out of heaven, she becomes the bride of the Devil. In psychological terms, you could say that men experience her as the witch who seduces then kills..." He struggled for a moment. *Remembering Ilona*, thought Violette. "Or as a succubus, or the mother who kills her own young. And to women she is the dark side of the self that desires to be joined to the Devil."

The essence of evil, she thought, shuddering. No redeeming features. "She was the first Eve," said Violette. "The demoness who was usurped by the second Eve. And the second Eve was good until the first, Lilith the Serpent, corrupted her."

"Yes, the Serpent is often identified with her. Medieval woodcuts show the Serpent with Lilith's face, whispering in Eve's ear. Then the Zohar says that after the Fall, God brought Lilith from the depths of the sea and set her to punish the children of men."

"Like Kristian," she breathed. "An instrument to wreak God's vengeance on mortals. That's what he believed vampires were, and perhaps he was right. Lilith, Mother of Vampires and the lash of God." Rage seized her and she sat forward. "Who is this punishing God, who so hates his own children? Is this what you believe?"

Josef flinched, colour leaving his face. Did he think she would attack him? She was close, but mastered the urge and sank back.

He breathed out raggedly. "The God I trust is a gentler being, but my opinion is irrelevant. It's what you believe that matters."

"You call it belief, I experience it as reality. Lilith is inside me. She hates men for their so-called 'wisdom' and their rejection of her. She hates women for their child-like dependency on men. She hates life, but loves the pure sterility of the desert."

Josef put in, "She chooses to create art rather than nurture a husband and children?"

Anger again – how dare he judge her? – but she controlled herself.

"She sees into people's souls, sees their foolishness and wants to tear it out... My conscious self wants Lilith to reveal herself fully to me, but I daren't let her. All I hear of her tells me she's evil. She is the destructive storm, the hag of death. I can't tell where I end and Lilith begins any more, I can't live with this dark fire inside me. There's no escape unless I end my own life – or others end it for me. Perhaps that's what I'm trying to do: drive someone to kill me. Karl, Ilona, John, Rachel, even Charlotte – but the harder I try the more I frighten them, and their fear makes Lilith insane with rage." Her voice fell. "She is going to do something terrible if she doesn't stop."

Josef went quiet in thought. He was very much the psychoanalyst: the sort who asked questions, nodded, but never gave any answers. Her despair deepened.

"In a sense," he said, "you could see Lilith as God's equal, in that her rejection of the angels creates an impasse between the upper and lower powers. She is the counterbalance to God's goodness and maleness. In Jungian terms you could describe her as God's anima, his dark, avenging female side."

"Oh, good," said Violette. "Now we know something about the men who wrote about her, but nothing of Lilith herself."

Another pause. "Tell me, did you have any foreshadowing of this before you became... a vampire?"

"Yes. All my life. My father taught me that women are intrinsically wicked. He said I destroyed him. My birth tore my mother open, so she would never sleep with him again, and that drove him to other women. One of those women was Ilona. She didn't kill him, but the physical mutilation drove him out of his mind. I believe you understand."

Josef groaned, tried to turn it into a cough. She sensed his shuddering horror at the fate he had narrowly avoided. And she thought, *men are so vulnerable, really. Can't I feel a touch of pity?*

"He said I was from the Devil," she went on. "He blamed everything on me. Ridiculous, I know. But now I am like Ilona, so who's to say he was wrong? Perhaps he foresaw my fate. All my life, the angels were waiting: three shadows, waiting for Lilith to possess me. I tried to obey them! I tried to renounce the darkness and walk in the light, but Lilith wouldn't let me. Charlotte insists there is no God... so why do I have these memories? Other people's visions, maybe... Therefore I'm mad, but what does my madness *mean*? I still reason and think and suffer. This may not be real to anyone else, but it's real to me."

"I suggest that Lilith represents the woman who refuses to obey," said Josef. "She chooses flight to the wilderness, rather than the safety of obedience to God."

"Outcast."

"There are forms of conduct that must be cast out in order for society to function," Josef said gravely. "If all women behaved as Lilith does, there would be chaos. You want me to tell you that Lilith is redeemable, that she is not completely of the darkness, but I can't. Perhaps her feelings are understandable, but that does not excuse them. You must make peace with this or you'll never recover."

"Recover?" His answer incensed her. "You are male: wise, pure and spiritual, created in God's image. Lilith is female: bestial, unclean and destructive. Whatever modern ideas you profess to hold, that's what you feel in your heart, isn't it?"

"Not at all." She saw he was struggling now. Josef had said nothing she wanted to hear. He'd only confirmed her fears. He forged on, "I can only theorise, but I believe that Lilith is a 'complex,' a psychic fragment that's splintered off and behaves as a separate and complete personality. You have absorbed the primordial image of Lilith from Raqia, and projected upon it the side of your personality that you find unacceptable. You can't live with this, so you divorce her from your other persona, the ballerina, and name her Lilith. But you are battling your own shadow. If you are to become whole, to achieve individuation, you must accept this. Call Lilith into yourself and face her. It's the only way to vanquish her."

"Oh, to vanquish this blood thirst would be a fine trick!" she hissed.

Josef shifted uneasily, looking dismayed and anxious.

"So, you maintain that it's all in my mind? How do you explain the fact that the three angels who pursued me were real, physical entities? Ask Charlotte, ask Karl. Explain how Lancelyn knew what I was without being told. You can't, can you?" She stood up, ready to leave.

"No, I can't." He rubbed his forehead. "I'm afraid I haven't handled this well. Please, Madame, don't go. We've barely scratched the surface. We might need hours, days of talking to unravel this."

"No," she said, reverting to the imperious ballerina. "I don't have days. I've heard enough. Thank you for seeing me, Dr Stern. I'm grateful to you for trying, but you've only confirmed what I already suspected. I am damned."

* * *

Robyn curled up with a book, trying to forget that Violette was in her house. Insatiably curious, she longed to eavesdrop, but her conscience would not let her. Fearing for Josef's safety was irrational – how could a petite ballerina possibly harm him? – yet she couldn't help linking Violette with his illness and disturbed state of mind.

Half an hour passed. Then a strange sensation made her look up. Violette Lenoir was standing by her armchair as if she'd materialised from nowhere.

Robyn started violently, dropping her book. She laughed, trying to make a joke of it. "No wonder you're renowned for your light step, Madame."

She made to stand, but to her surprise, Violette knelt beside her and put a hand on her arm. "Don't get up. You weren't so formal when we met in the garden."

Robyn, at ease with men, had no idea how to behave towards this woman. Her presence was uncanny. She wore a black cloche hat, glossed with feathers and jet beads. Under its deep crown her face was a lily, accentuated by dark lashes and brows. Her irises were startling, deepest violet-blue.

"Where's my uncle?"

"Downstairs. The ballet is leaving soon. I came to say goodbye."

"Oh." Robyn's mouth went dry. She remembered how Violette had embraced her, the strength of her fingers, her mouth, gentle at first, then demanding. Such thrilling terror... Now she felt as jumpy as a thirteen-year-old girl. "Would you like some tea, Madame?"

"No, thank you. And please, call me Violette. Don't say anything until you've listened to me." Her demeanour, Robyn saw, had changed from their first meeting. She seemed softer, even anxious. "There are certain things of which I can't speak. Dangers. Your uncle knows. He's been afraid for your safety."

"What are you talking about?"

A brief hesitation. "Oh, ballet company politics. Jealousies. Conflicts."

"What on earth has that to do with me?"

"I asked you to listen, Robyn. Please. This is hard for me. Almost impossible, actually." Violette's hand, gloved in black leather, grew heavier on her arm. "I frightened you in the garden. I didn't mean to; it's something I can't always control. But the strangest thing is that I've been completely unable to stop thinking about you since."

Robyn, taken aback, managed to suppress any sound she might have made.

"I couldn't bear it if any harm were to come to you."

"Why should it?" Robyn exclaimed. "Do you have a jealous admirer who might shoot me?"

Violette exhaled, at a loss. "I wish I could explain, but I can't. I simply wanted to apologise for frightening you. I didn't realise how badly I'd behaved until afterwards. I suppose this comes too late. I hardly know you, yet I feel I can tell you..."

"Anything."

"Then don't be too hard on me. You need not even reply. I have never in my life made a confession like this; never thought I'd need to. I love Charlotte but she's too much like me; our passions are like ice-thorns to tear each other apart. But when I met you... I saw someone with all the warmth and strength I lack, who could perhaps heal me. I despised love, until I met you! No, I'm not asking anything of you, Robyn. I simply wanted to tell you. You make me feel human. I've never felt human before."

"Oh, my God," Robyn said softly.

Violette looked steadily at her. Her presence uncoiled all Robyn's certainty about the world. Her allure would have captured anyone. Robyn realised that if she chose, Violette could seduce her into anything – but she held back, respecting Robyn's choice.

To be wanted by this goddess was too dazzling to bear.

"Are you horrified?" said Violette. "I don't blame you. Please don't be polite. Don't say, 'I'm terribly flattered but I prefer men,' or any of that. All I want is for you to remember this: you are the first person I ever felt I could love, and probably the last."

She began to stand up, but Robyn caught her hand and said, "Don't go."

An incredible wave of excitement was rolling through her. She saw a way to leave everything behind, to shed her tawdry life like a snakeskin: Harold, the endless string of victim-lovers, the bitter scars, the hollow tedium of waiting for Sebastian to call. All of it.

Replace it with an affection that was new and tender and clean.

"Violette," she said, her voice shaking, "what if I say I'm not horrified? Quite the opposite. If I say I want to come with you when you leave…"

Violette went paler, if that were possible. She looked dumbstruck. Robyn saw that this was the last reaction she'd expected. She'd spoken in the certainty of rejection. Finding acceptance, she was utterly bewildered.

Tears brimmed in her eyes. The tears, Robyn saw, were tinged faintly red.

"Oh, Robyn, no. It's impossible."

"Are you worried about people talking? No one need know. Don't you need a 'personal assistant' or whatever?"

"It's not that. God, I'd love to… but I'd destroy you."

"I'm not so easy to live with, either. Ask my housekeeper."

She spoke lightly, but Violette didn't smile. Her eyes glared with sudden annihilating menace: arctic ice steeped in blood. "No, I mean it. I would destroy you."

Violette dropped her gaze. Robyn's heart began to beat again. She felt angry, bereft and cheated. "So after all that, you're turning me down? Good grief, what do you want?"

"I'm sorry," Violette whispered. "I had no idea you would… No, it's impossible."

"If you leave here now, we'll never see each other again, will we?"

"I doubt it."

"I don't understand!"

"Forgive me." Violette leaned down and pressed her lips to Robyn's. She was trembling. Robyn thought she was about to break down, but when she slid her hands onto the dancer's slim shoulders, Violette immediately pulled away. "Please forgive me. I'll never forget you."

"Likewise," Robyn said stiffly. She watched as Violette let herself out. "Goodbye, good luck and…"

Go to hell! she added silently, her jaw clenched, her body rigid with emotion. Where the gloved hand had touched her arm, her skin tingled and burned.

* * *

196

"What did she want?" Robyn and Josef said in unison as they met in the parlour. Then they laughed uneasily. Violette was gone but her shadow hung between them.

"Have you been crying?" he asked.

"I'm just being silly," she said, sniffing. "So, what happened? You go first."

"Oh, nothing," Josef said, stroking her hair. "Well, not quite nothing. She decided to talk to me after all, but... I didn't say what she was hoping to hear. I wish I knew what she does want."

"You and me both!"

"Why, what did she say to you?"

Robyn tried to make light of things. "She made declarations of undying love, would you believe. I must have gone clean out of my mind for a few minutes, because I asked her to take me away with her."

Josef's face dropped in horror. He actually grabbed her shoulders and shook her. "Dear God, you mustn't go!"

"Uncle!" She stepped back, shocked. "Why not?"

"Because..." He pushed a hand through his hair, leaving it even more untidy.

"Come on, tell me."

"To spend too much time with her might not be... healthy. She's demanding. Can you imagine what force of personality it takes to train and discipline all those dancers? You would lose your own self to her."

"You make her sound like a vampire."

"Robyn, please..."

"It's all right, I'm not going. She wouldn't let me, and you know why? She said the same thing, that she'd destroy me. As if she was trying to protect me."

Josef sank onto a sofa, holding his head in relief.

"But it would have been fascinating!" Robyn said. "I could have written a book about her! 'My life with a mad genius'."

"Don't joke about it." He settled his spectacles on his nose. "Well, it's almost over. Once the ballet's left town, you'll be –" She thought he started to say, *safe* "– I'll be on my way and your life can return to normal."

"Won't that be fun," Robyn said aridly. The prospect was

dreary. "Without people like Charlotte, Karl and Violette around, I think I shall die of boredom."

"It's you, Cesare," said the angel, Simon. "You are the one chosen to lead us against the Enemy."

They clasped hands. In the gloom of the inner sanctum, yellow light flared from their palms, knifing between their entwined fingers. Power. Cesare looked into Simon's wondrous eyes and laughed, intoxicated by hope.

They'd talked endlessly since Simon had arrived. Cesare longed to ask him, *Were you ever human? Can I, too, achieve angelic status?* But it was too soon, too presumptuous.

John was silent, but at least he was with them, an essential part of the triumvirate.

"Join us," said Cesare, and John came to complete the circle. The energy he added was dark, like iron; but it was power, all the same.

"I came here because you understand," said Simon. To Cesare he was a seraph, too bright and cold for humans to bear. His face was gold ice, ravenous with immortal hunger. "Lilith is the Enemy. You know, as Kristian taught, that God is not the forgiving deity of mankind's belief. He visits vampires as a plague on mortals. He might equally visit Lilith as a plague on straying vampires."

"So we must warn them," said Cesare. "Bring them back to the true path."

"Yes!" Simon said fervently. "We're in perfect agreement. And you will be a worthy successor to Kristian, our beloved lost brother. Are you ready?"

Cesare had been awed to learn that Simon had helped create Kristian. Not that anything this angel did would surprise him. To be raised up in Kristian's place was an honour almost beyond comprehension.

"Can I make the others believe how dangerous Lilith is?" Cesare met Simon's dazzling eyes. "Will they accept me as their leader?"

"You can, and they will. Am I not your mandate from God? Come, it's time."

THE DARK BLOOD OF POPPIES

Cesare squared his shoulders. "I am ready."

In the assembly chamber, the other vampires waited sullenly in their hooded robes. There were only a few left now: he counted eleven. Maria alone looked at Cesare with respect. The others, including Pierre, reminded him of unearthed moles, blinking resentfully at the daylight.

Cesare stood near the throne-dais, not on it. John and Simon flanked him. In a low-key, conversational tone, Cesare began to talk.

He told them of his journey through the outside world, its depravity and corruption. He spoke passionately of Kristian's holy life and death. He held up the photograph of Lilith, still in its broken, blood-spattered frame.

"This is our Enemy," he said.

Did they believe him?

Not at first. They didn't care, but Cesare forged on like a true orator until he *made* them care. He brought John forward to display Matthew's severed head. He summoned the wretched Pierre to describe Lilith's violent cruelty.

"This is what she'll do to us all if she is not stopped!" Cesare's voice rose. "We've all seen and felt the growing darkness of the Crystal Ring. It is Lilith's doing. Unless we act, she will be the death of us."

The vampires had drifted into a tighter group. Now they were paying attention.

"Remember the story of Noah: God in his rage destroyed the human race, saving only a few. Well, Lilith is the new flood – sent to punish vampires for turning away from God. She is the Dark Mother who consumes her own children."

His flock listened with parted lips and staring eyes. Terrified.

"But there's hope. Schloss Holdenstein will be our Ark. We are the chosen few – if we work together." Tears flowed from Cesare's eyes as he walked among them. "You know I loved Kristian faithfully. I *never* turned against him. When I asked Karl to lead us, I made a vast error of judgement, for which I repent. I've learned so much since then. Instead, I offer *myself* as your leader. Your guide, your servant."

How bright were their eyes now, how beautiful their faces that regarded him from within their hoods! Like young priests and nuns.

"You all loved Kristian too," he said. "That's why you stayed. And it's very hard to bear eternity without him. So I prayed, and the Almighty answered. He sent Simon, His envoy, Kristian's creator. Simon is God's promise that I am destined to lead you against the Enemy. I am the soldier-priest whose sole purpose is to destroy Lilith and lead vampire-kind to salvation. Behold, at my side – the flaming sword and the hammer of God, our beloved comrades, Simon and John."

Suddenly the eyes all around him were full of tears. Cesare found himself half-smothered by embraces, voices clamouring, *"Yes, lead us, Cesare. Save us! We'll do anything, everything."*

No apathy in their faces now. He'd restored them to life.

Wondrous feeling.

"We'll draw other vampires here to share the truth and the light," he declared. "But any who refuse, any who shelter Lilith – they too are the Enemy."

Cesare was shocked at his own harsh assertiveness. Where had it come from? From above, of course! He moved among his followers in a state of near-ecstasy. He walked in a halo of golden light and his feet were winged.

This adoration might become addictive.

Simon watched beatifically, thinking, *Do you think you are safe, Violette, in your little world of human adulation? Do you imagine that the theatres in which you escape reality are any less fragile than eggshell?*

He wondered where Rasmila and Fyodor were.

If they find me here, I'll make them stay and serve Cesare. How hard are they prepared to work to win me back? He grinned. *Would they bring Lilith to me in chains?*

Their passion is there to be used, like that of Cesare and John. I'll use every one of these fools in God's service.

Yes, let Cesare stoke the furnaces of their hearts, that I might feed on their energy. I need all the light I can consume to burn away the shadow between myself and heaven.

The thought of Lilith made Simon freeze briefly, like a mouse in owl's shadow. But the dark wings passed, and his inner sun shone again.

You'll do for now, Cesare. You'll last for as long as you feed me with the light of your vision.

PART TWO

Use both your hands to hold me
Tight! Tighter than you should
My heart is coldest steel
But my body's flesh and blood,
Walking hand in hand with silver,
Close as gold to kiss,
Only lovers left alive
And they're swallowed in the mist.

I'm your Sword of Light
Won't you be mine tonight?
I'm your Sword of Light tonight
Going to scorch you deep inside
Make you glad to be alive
Because I'm your Sword of Light.

Wrap tight your cloak around me
And I'll whisper close my dreams.
My home is such a long way
And I'm older than I seem.
I've come a long way
With the good news;
See you need my help.
But don't ask me to be your guide
I'm a stranger here myself.

I'm your Sword of Light...

HORSLIPS, "SWORD OF LIGHT"

CHAPTER TEN

SWORD OF LIGHT

"I went to see Josef after all," said Violette, as they sat on the train that was taking the company to New York. A week at the Manhattan Opera House, then on to Hartford, Philadelphia, Baltimore and the southern states.

"What happened?" Charlotte already knew – Josef had told her when she'd wished him bon voyage – but this was the first time she'd heard it from Violette. They were alone in the compartment.

"Nothing." Violette stared listlessly at the landscape rushing past. "He told me things I'd rather not have heard."

"And then?"

"I thanked him, and left. What else? Do you think I attacked him?"

"Of course not. So, he was no help?"

"Lilith is an aspect of my personality, he implied, that I must learn to accept and control. Some hope of that."

"Isn't that partly true?"

"Perhaps. He was very kind. I know you had my interests at heart when you brought him, but he couldn't help. No one can. Except…"

"What?"

A pause. Then she spoke, very low. "Josef's niece."

"Robyn?" Charlotte said anxiously. "I asked you not to –"

"I don't know what possessed me. I've always been alone, that is Lilith's nature. But when I saw her… Oh, I love you, Charlotte,

205

but you're a golden ice shard. You began our relationship by scaring me witless, and it went downhill from there. But Robyn is human, soft and warm. And innocent. She's the only person I've ever met who is capable of making me act against my nature. Alarming, isn't it?"

"Violette, don't." She gripped the dancer's arm. "You'd kill her. Vampires and humans can't—"

"Do you think I don't realise?" Violette said coldly. "Did it ever stop you – with Karl, or with me?"

"No," Charlotte breathed. "Dear God, don't –"

"What?"

"Don't do to her what I did to you! This obsession, it's lethal."

"What's wrong? Are you jealous?" She spoke sharply. Charlotte couldn't answer. "Well, don't worry. She wanted to come with us, but I said no. I told her how I felt, but that nothing could come of it." Violette turned away and leaned her forehead on the window.

"Why?" Charlotte asked softly.

"Because what I feel is an illusion. Of course I know what would happen if I let her join me. So I ended the affair before it began."

She was expressionless, but Charlotte felt her suppressed emotion: a shattered heart.

"Oh, Violette. I never had the strength to resist my passions like that."

"Not strength. Just realism. You and Josef should be happy at least, because all the vampires have left Boston and Robyn is safe again."

The day after Josef left, Sebastian came to Robyn's house, as if he'd been waiting for her uncle to leave.

His unexpected visit displeased Robyn; she'd planned a quiet evening with just Alice for company. Still, his courtesy disarmed her. He invited her to dinner, but she had already eaten. Instead, she asked him in and they sat in the parlour with glasses of illicit wine, while Alice withdrew to her own room – with ill grace, Robyn thought – to sew.

Robyn tried to make conversation, but there was dreadful tension between them. Sebastian's dark presence and his bewitching eyes assailed her physically, like heat. And she thought, *why are we holding back? This is what I wanted, isn't it – to seduce him?*

Eventually Sebastian said, "I don't know why we're wasting time talking."

"Nor do I." She stood, holding out a hand. He accepted the invitation. As he rose and put his drink aside, she noticed that the glass was still full.

The bedroom, all heavy cream lace, was pale gold in the lamplight. Robyn had designed the décor to be luxurious, pure and inviting. Rose petals, with an underlying note of musk, perfumed the air. They'd said nothing as they climbed the stairs and Sebastian made no attempt to touch her. Was he feigning indifference, or here out of idle curiosity?

"I won't be long. Make yourself comfortable," she said as she entered her bathroom.

Sex itself meant nothing to her. It used to, in the early days of her marriage, when she'd imagined herself happy. Betrayal had murdered her physical desires. Now she would never allow them to reawaken.

She undressed and put on a robe of oyster satin. When she emerged he was already in bed, his hair almost black against the big pale cloud of the pillow, one bare arm resting on the cover. Fine dark hairs shadowed his forearms, she noticed, but his chest was as smooth and beautifully moulded as a statue.

Robyn felt businesslike as she approached, letting her robe slide to the floor. A tiny spurt of apprehension jolted her, as it might an experienced swimmer who dislikes the first chill kiss of the water; then, nothing.

She needed this passionless clarity in order to put on the act that men loved. She was like Violette, in that she prided herself on her choreography. Her emotions went into the art, not the act.

The bed was soft, dew-clean and enveloping as she eased herself in, Sebastian holding up the covers for her. She always kept her setting perfect. A jewel should be shown off to its best advantage. Her house, the extension of herself, was almost as seductive as her body.

"You know, I thought you would take more persuasion than this," he said. His fingers touched her cheekbone. Her heart jumped into a harder rhythm.

"I'm not open to persuasion," she replied. "Either I will or I won't." She stroked his breastbone with her fingernails. "I decide."

"So I meet your approval?" He was half-smiling. His subtle contempt for everything increased her determination to conquer him.

"Obviously." She reached up and removed the single comb that held her hair in place. Autumn-brown waves spilled over her shoulders. She wasn't sure the trick would work on him, so the change in his face was as startling as it was gratifying. His languid mockery vanished. He became sombre, rapt.

"Your hair," he murmured. His fingers played in and out of the long skeins. Smiling, she moved towards him, her hands travelling slowly over the firm chest, down the long flat abdomen, teasing and coaxing. Her mouth followed in a trail of kisses. She made circles and S shapes with her tongue. She found herself almost enjoying her work; she'd never seen such an aesthetically pleasing body before, so lean and silky, almost luminous.

Men, in her experience, were amazed by a woman who took the initiative. Presumably their wives just lay there, which was unsurprising in most cases. Amazed, then brainlessly intoxicated by her skill.

Yet as she reached the sable curls between his thighs, he caught her chin and stopped her.

"No," he said, "wait." He drew her up so they lay face to face. "Let me make love to you."

"If you prefer."

"It's only courtesy." He played with her hair again. "All you have to do is respond, however you wish."

She maintained her inviting smile, but her heart sank. She preferred to be active and in control. If he couldn't wait, though, at least this was unlikely to last long.

Sebastian was in no hurry, however. He began to caress her as she'd caressed him, and she looked at the ceiling in dismay, thinking, *Oh great. He's one of those who likes to go on all night.*

He paused, one cool hand enfolding her left breast. "I see

through you, Robyn. You do this for a living, do you not? You don't really want to be here."

She snatched a breath to retort, but he pressed a fingertip to her lips. "Never mind," he said. "Indulge me. I don't want to hear any pretend moaning. Just relax. Trust me... as if I were a friend."

His eyes were beautiful. Perfectly shaped and so clear, two woodland pools under the long lashes. Such a lovely colour, soft green edging into brown. Almost feminine. Eyes to die for.

Robyn sank back on the pillows in languorous resignation. *Why not relax?* she thought. *Let him do what he wants. Float away.*

She closed her eyes. His hands wove patterns over her arms, shoulders and breasts, absorbing heat as they worked. This was incredibly soothing. A warm feeling woke under her heart, a fluttering ache.

Instead of kneading her with frantic hands, as other men did, his touch was gentle. When his lips touched her collarbone, she stiffened with pleasure, suppressing any sound lest he think she was acting. His mouth alighted here and there on her face, avoiding her lips until she was ready, desperate for the kiss.

As her mouth opened under his, thirsting for the hot pressure and the taste of him, he slid one hand over her stomach and thighs. How gorgeous his hand felt. The warm ache flared and spread, tingling down the insides of her legs to her toes.

Now he pulled her on to her side, slipping one long leg between hers. Close as velvet, this intimacy, yet still he did not enter her. He was teasing her. And she was shaking now with the effort of denying her own arousal.

The yearning became sweet agony. *Oh God, he knows exactly what he's doing. How... this is cruel, he can't do this to me!*

But her head fell back and she groaned. He was going to hold back until she became so desperate that she made him...

The sensations deepened. At last, at last he slid into her. She could have cried at his gentleness, the incredible sensuality of his flesh against hers and inside her. *To do this to me when I won't find any release... he'll finish and roll off happy and just leave me...*

But instead of pushing blindly after his own pleasure, Sebastian found hers; found the exact place and drew her expertly along a mercuric path.

She clung fiercely to him, rocking with him, willing him not to stop. The barriers she'd set in place for years melted. Flames fluttered through her, feathers, chains of red jewels, building towards the single point of fire. She couldn't stop, couldn't even think. And suddenly, violently, the fire broke.

The sensation was so powerful that it was close to pain. It was an opening, a surrender, the honeyed stab of absolute release. The waves pulsed on and on, stealing her voice and soul, stranding her in blackness. Warm, satiny blackness filled with red stars.

"No one," she gasped. "No one has ever—"

She lay drained, unable to move. Sweat sheened her limp body. And her lover, the stranger, looked down at her with pleasure and affection.

"Well?" he said.

"How did you do that?" she exclaimed.

"You sound a little angry with me. Was it such a terrible shock?"

He moved gently inside her as he spoke, waking tiny flames of pleasure. She wanted to consume him, to possess him forever; and for making her feel those emotions, she hated him. Then he began to withdraw. With a cry of protest she clasped him, saying, "Don't."

But he turned onto his side, leaving her empty.

"Oh, you like me now?" he said, teasing. He stroked her hip. She arched towards his touch.

"What do you think?" she whispered.

"And your other lovers never give you such pleasure? Is that not part of the bargain?"

She didn't answer. *I shouldn't have given myself away*, she thought bitterly, *should have pretended it happens all the time.*

"Most men are selfish fools," he added.

"Oh, tell me."

"But all it takes is a little consideration." He caressed her cheek, smiling with infuriating self-satisfaction. But he was so lovely...

Her hand slid towards his thighs and grasped the satiny penis, still erect and slick with her fluids. Disturbing, that he'd held back while she had lost control.

"And what about you?" she said, coaxing him towards her.

"Why so impatient?" The dark amusement on his face

tantalised her. "We have all night, surely?"

Again he held back and began to kiss her with tormenting delicacy. He kissed her forehead, cheeks, nose. His lips printed her jaw and neck with heat. He seemed to love her throat most of all, though he lavished attention everywhere. Worshipping her. His touch pulled her down into the whirlpool again.

The bed became a secret otherworld in which it no longer mattered that Sebastian was winning the battle. Here was safety. No one would know if she gave herself up to him in the sweet darkness.

Her body opened to his, and wild feelings took her again. Again the red claws of joy pierced her and she writhed as her spasms lifted her up and hurled her into the universe.

Her eyes came open with wonder. She saw Sebastian's face above hers, not amused now but intent, his eyes blank with lust. She wanted him to share her fulfilment, even though the look disquieted her a little. She gripped his buttocks, thrusting hard against him.

When he spoke, his voice shocked her. He sounded different, not lost in passion but as steel-hard as a knife. "Is this what you wanted, Robyn?" he said savagely. "To find out... how your victims feel?"

A moment of primal terror. She went rigid, but all was swamped in chaos and she couldn't think, let alone escape. His head dropped so she saw only the mass of dark hair shimmering. He groaned and cried out, "Oh God. *Robyn.*"

She wanted to hold him through the convulsion, his rapture provoking another aching response in her – but the echo of his hard words stopped her.

Then he seemed to undulate, his head rearing and swooping down to her neck. Pain flared in her throat. Dull at first, like a wasp sting it grew more intense, throbbing, burning, pulling.

He was biting her. She heard him swallowing, felt her veins leaping and her heartbeat thundering in her head. A dim but overwhelming horror filled her.

He's drinking my blood!

It wasn't pleasant, not a bizarre heightening of their ardour. It was vile. Her hands tingled and her ears buzzed with blood-loss. She was pinioned, as if being held under swirling water.

Now she saw the appalling truth: that she'd been tricked. That he was taking revenge for Russell's death. *But this is not fair,* she raged silently. *You'll pay for this, Sebastian. You will pay!*

She believed this, until she realised she was dying.

No panic. Just slipping away.

Seeing their eyes and their spell-woven hair all around her. Sebastian. Charlotte. Karl. Violette. Was this their horrible secret? *No, oh God, impossible, no...*

Robyn wasn't dead yet. Something nudged her back to consciousness, and she realised that Sebastian was no longer drinking. His teeth were still in her neck, two hard rods impaling her, but he paused with the faintest sigh against her skin, raising gooseflesh all over her body. Then he released her. His fangs slipped out of the wounds. Pain receded.

As he lifted his head, mouth open, she glimpsed the sharp canines. Worse, she saw them retract until she thought she'd imagined their sharpness and length. Blood glossed his tongue and lips. Sickened, she wanted nothing but to escape.

He held her down. Their bodies were still joined... how terrible the betrayal seemed then. But his face!

Not the cruel, triumphant expression Robyn had expected. Instead he looked as she felt: confused, stricken, angry. At last she found her breath.

"You bastard!" she exploded. How weak her rage sounded. She craved words to wound him like bullets, but none existed.

"What did you expect, beautiful child?" His face lifted into more composed lines, but she sensed effort in his mockery. "If you play in the forest, you are bound to meet a wolf."

Her anger gathered strength. She made a concerted attempt to push him off. Her only desire now was to expel him from the house, without rousing Alice or Mary. "Get off me! Get out."

She slapped him – a foolish risk, but instead of retaliating he slid lithely out of bed. His face was icy as he gathered his clothes.

"I have no wish to stay, believe me," he said.

He dressed swiftly. Rage stung her eyes as she watched him. He possessed the cheating beauty of the Devil. And she hated him.

"Get the hell out of my house before I call the police."

And he was gone. He simply vanished from where he stood.

Robyn flung a pillow through the space where he'd been, as if to exorcise him. The pillow bounced off the dressing table and hit the floor with a *flump*.

"You don't frighten me!" she said aloud.

She meant to get up and wash, perhaps make a hot drink to calm herself.

Then she found she was too weak to move.

A chill wind rushed in and blew out her anger, followed by fever and nightmares.

Cesare walked with Simon and John through a pine forest on the banks of the Rhine. The tree trunks were dark pillars in a navy-blue night. Cesare felt at peace. It seemed only right that an angel had come to him. Confident, Cesare felt that he was marching to war with his warrior-comrades of gold and iron beside him.

And now he dared to ask Simon a question. "Were you ever human?"

"Once," Simon answered. "Thousands of years ago. The centuries wear us thin, until we become glass vessels for the light of heaven to shine through."

"So a vampire such as myself could become God's envoy too?"

"You might not wish to. It can be a great trial." Simon sounded weary.

"But not a burden, surely?"

"It is never a burden to serve God," Simon agreed.

"But there aren't enough of us," Cesare said thoughtfully. "We need new blood, a new race." He became more animated. Simon and John gazed at him; he'd caught their imaginations. "New vampires, untainted..."

Cesare stopped. A female was walking towards them, regal in a fur cape, jewels and feathers in her hair, an acidic smile on her lips. Ilona.

"What's going on?" she said. "I've seen Pierre. He told me to find you three. I've just returned from America because..."

She hesitated, her smile vanishing. Cesare had always disliked her, with her insolence and wanton femininity. He held her eyes, impressing his newfound power upon her.

"Go on," he said.

Her eyes flicked to Simon, John, and back to Cesare. "I've been Violette's victim. She almost tore me to pieces. I'm here to say that everyone is right. She's dangerous."

Cesare was thrilled. For this, he would set aside his distaste. "So you fled to us for sanctuary."

"Sanctuary?" Ilona tilted her head in disgust. "Hardly. Yes, Violette attacked me but I'm still on my feet. I intend to show her that she can't destroy me. However, I'm not such a fool as to tackle her alone. Pierre tells me you're joining forces against her, so anything I can do to help – I'm at your disposal."

Cesare wanted her help, but first she must learn humility.

"Lilith must have brought you down hard," he said softly, "for you to offer us help. Go and find Maria. She'll give you suitable clothing and instruct you in a few simple duties."

Ilona's gaze was steady. "It must be galling," she said sweetly, "to be fifth best."

"What do you mean by that?"

"I'm glad to see Simon found someone at last, even if he is scraping the bottom of the barrel. He lost Kristian and Lancelyn, and surely you know, Cesare, that he was recently begging both Karl and Sebastian to take this position before you? He came to you only because they turned him down. Maybe he asked others; I don't know. Still, I suppose that for you, fifth best is quite an achievement."

Ilona turned and stalked away: a spider-queen retreating from her prey.

Stricken, Cesare watched her go. His rage was so extreme that he was close to a seizure. Words, the sharpest of all weapons, slid unnoticed into their target and caused no pain until it was too late.

Lilith's power, he thought. *That's the power of all women: to take everything from you with a single lie.*

He turned to Simon and found his voice. "Is it true? You asked a dozen others before me?"

"Only two." Simon, for all his self-assurance, seemed embarrassed.

"Then you lied to me!"

"No! What lie have I told you? Yes, I asked Karl and Sebastian,

THE DARK BLOOD OF POPPIES

but you must understand that this is God's role for me, to choose immortals with leadership qualities. And I've made mistakes, I confess, because only God is perfect. I went to them before I knew about you. A ruler needs the *desire* to rule – something Karl and Sebastian both lack. But you, Cesare, have vision. You weren't my first choice, I admit – but you are the best."

Simon's gold eyes were mesmeric. Cesare, somewhat mollified, spoke stiffly.

"We need all the help we can muster, but I won't tolerate Ilona's insolence. She represents the very anarchy we're fighting to obliterate."

"I'll go after her," said Simon. "She'll behave, don't worry."

As Cesare watched Simon's athletic figure striding away through the trees, he said softly to John, "I don't trust him."

John stared from blood-rimmed eyes in a grim, gaunt face. Cesare thought, *He thinks I've uttered blasphemy. How dare I say I don't trust an angel of God?*

John only replied, "I trust no one."

Another revelation hit Cesare.

"I think Simon needs me as much as I need him," he murmured. "I think I could become stronger than him."

Afraid of saying too much, Cesare kept the rest of his thoughts to himself. *To create a new race of vampires, yes... Ones who won't look at me with the jaundiced eyes of those who think me inferior to Kristian and Karl and Sebastian. Ones who will worship only me. Yes, to create new ones...*

And then, to destroy the old.

Simon caught up with Ilona and placed an arm around her resistant shoulders. Although furious with her for nearly wrecking the delicate balance between him and Cesare, he hid his anger and became the essence of sweet reason. They strolled along the hillside, a forested slope dropping towards the dark mirror-plane of the Rhine.

"What's going on, Simon?" she demanded.

"Obvious, isn't it?"

"So, Cesare's the latest victim of your games? A little gold dust on your skin and hair and oh, you're an archangel. You don't fool me."

"Don't underestimate him." Her impertinence amused Simon. "He's not as stupid as you think."

"No one could be *that* stupid," Ilona said tartly. "You weren't happy at my mentioning Karl and Sebastian, were you? Delicious to hear you scrambling for excuses as I walked away. 'Not the first, but the best'? Really, what idiot would fall for that?"

Simon would not let her provoke him.

"Where did you see Sebastian?" he asked casually.

"In Boston. He's a virtuoso! Karl, Charlotte and Violette were there too – sometimes in the next room – yet they never noticed him. But I did. After Violette attacked me I almost ran to Sebastian for help."

"What stopped you?"

"I know what he's like," Ilona said bitterly. "He loathes his own kind. He'd have told me to go to hell – despite all the fun we had the previous night – and I will not be spoken to like that, Simon dear."

Simon caressed her cheek. "I wouldn't dream of it. It's a shame you didn't tell Sebastian, though. You might have made him stop and think about Lilith, after all."

"Surely you can manage without Sebastian's help?"

"Of course," Simon replied lightly. *But perhaps we can't,* he thought. *We need every strong immortal there is.* "I'm glad you came to us – but you must stop upsetting Cesare here and now. This is a warning, not a suggestion."

She pursed her lips, defiant.

"What's more important?" Simon asked. "Your pride, or defeating Violette?"

"The latter."

"Then learn to co-operate. You won't be consigned to sweeping floors with Maria, believe me. We'll find a meaningful use for your talents. Cesare has vision; wouldn't you like to help create a beautiful new race of vampires?"

"Like John?"

"Our kind should be beautiful." Simon shook his head. "It pains me to see John disfiguring himself, but he must grieve for

Matthew as he will. Even John has vision. You could share it, if..."

Ilona gave a baleful smile.

"Don't worry," she said. "I'll crawl to Cesare. If it means revenge on Violette, I'll swallow rivers of pride as if they were blood."

Robyn felt life flowing out of her throat, relived it over and over. She burned and shivered. Her eyes bulged, blood-rimmed... she saw a ghost-face grinning at her in the darkness. Her hands fluttered like moths.

The bed was awash with crimson. She lay drowning in her own life-blood.

Yellow lights swerved towards her, terrifying. Alice and Mary came rushing in, staring down at her, their faces hideous with horror. They looked like crones, like funeral mourners.

They dropped their lamps and screamed.

Robyn woke.

With a silent snap the world returned to normal. Morning light glowed through the thick lace curtains. The room was tranquil and friendly. And although her bed was rumpled from love-making and restless dreams, there was no blood. No blood!

She got up, found her robe and slipped into it as she went to the dressing table. Dizzy. No strength.

Her face in the mirror looked drained, with blue crescents under her eyes. On the right of her neck was a bruise, jewelled by two faint, pinkish moons.

Is that all? she thought, probing the place with her fingertips. It felt sore. Nothing serious. Almost healed.

She sat for a long time, staring at her reflection, fingers moving lightly over the wound. Just below was a slight crusting of dried blood, another on her cheek like the imprint of lips. *Did he kiss me after he fed on me?* she thought.

She rubbed away the dried blood. Soon all physical evidence would vanish.

The real damage is inside me.

Why didn't he kill me? I'm sure he meant to. I don't know why he stopped.

I don't think he'll come back.

She leaned on the dressing table, dropping her head onto her forearms with a huge sigh. She no longer felt afraid, only betrayed, humiliated to the centre of her being.

Mary came in with tea, plainly shocked by Robyn's face. "Oh, ma'am, you don't look well at all. I think you should get yourself back into bed."

"I think so, too." Robyn smiled. Speaking was an immense effort. "Run me a bath and change the sheets, there's a dear, then I'll have a lie-in."

Robyn's lie-in lasted four days.

Alice and Mary were continually at her side. They insisted on calling the doctor, who was brisk and unsympathetic. He concluded that Robyn was anaemic. *Tell me something I don't know,* she thought.

Yet Robyn couldn't describe precisely what was wrong. Lassitude, a dream-state in which life had no point. Nightmares of blood and betrayal; in her febrile slumber, every friend was revealed as a vampire. Alice and Mary, Josef, Harold... Violette.

She dreamed in glaring, fiery colours that she was copulating with priests who turned into demons. She would wake up suffocating, then lie awake, too languid for tears or anger. Simply brooding on Sebastian. Remembering his dark, deceptive beauty. His hands on her body. The soaring fire he'd awakened... she could never forgive him for that, either.

On the third day, she began to feel better, albeit still strange, as if half-drunk. Perhaps that was why she spoke candidly to Alice.

Alice removed her lunch tray with an approving look at the empty plates. She fussed with Robyn's pillows, then sat beside her. The room was full of flowers from Harold and a couple of would-be admirers, but from Sebastian there was no word.

"The night you were taken ill," Alice said, "did your gentleman friend stay the night?"

"Part of it," Robyn sighed. "I told you his name."

"Well, Mr Pierse hasn't called since."

"I know."

"I wondered... did he hurt you in some way?" Robyn didn't

answer. "Only I noticed a little mark on your neck, and you've been so..."

"Out of my mind," Robyn said softly.

"Don't tell me to mind my own business. I'm here to protect you, as much as wait on you hand and foot."

"I wasn't going to, you sarcastic beast. Yes, he hurt me."

Without emotion, Robyn told Alice everything.

The housekeeper turned her face away, looking sideways at her mistress with narrow, chiding eyes.

"You know, I don't care if you don't believe me," said Robyn. "I hardly believe it, either. I was attacked by a vampire who knew everything about me... and I'll tell you what it was: unfair!"

Alice blinked. "That's quite an understatement."

Robyn felt a flare of anger, a sign she was still alive. "No, I mean it. *I'm* the one who takes revenge. How dare he usurp that privilege? Did he think he'd leave me too scared ever to approach a man again? He's wrong. I won't give him the victory!"

"Madam..."

Robyn subsided, smiling grimly. "So, you think I've lost my mind?"

"I think," said Alice, unmoved, "that maybe you should see the doctor again."

"You don't believe me," Robyn said, with perverse satisfaction. "No doctor can help. But that's all right. I feel better; I'll get up tomorrow. And to think I expected to be bored when Violette and her friends left town..."

Karl reflected that he and Charlotte had experienced some of their most exquisitely happy moments during the Ballet Janacek's tour.

As the tour took them from Richmond, New Orleans, Houston and Dallas to San Francisco and other cities en route, Violette seemed completely fulfilled. Endless travelling, rehearsing and performing filled her days; she forgot her conflicts with Lilith and other immortals for a time. Karl was glad to see her at peace.

Meanwhile, he and Charlotte walked in deserts, ascended purple- and white-veiled mountains, watched great waterfalls cascading under the moon. They trod the length of the Grand

Canyon between its soaring red walls, made love in a glorious wilderness of rivers and giant redwoods. They captivated strangers and sipped their blood without guilt, feeding together as if all inhibition had magically lifted.

Their truce held. Karl and Charlotte rarely quarrelled for long. Now they were able to discuss Ilona and Violette without ill feeling, but sometimes he thought, *If only it were possible not to speak of them at all. No outside force should have the power to tear us apart, not even if that force happens to be Charlotte's friend and my own daughter.*

"I don't want to go home," said Charlotte as they walked along a cliff-edge by the Pacific Ocean. The world was burnt-gold and azure.

"Don't say that. Wishes may come true in most unfortunate ways." Karl took her hand, and led her into the Crystal Ring.

As they made the transition, their pale flesh turned darkly iridescent, like black opal or colours swirling on oil. The change still amazed him.

They ran together, almost flew, until they found a bluish, rippling path to the higher levels. It was as if they'd shed their earthly forms to reveal their true natures: slim, inky demons, their hair and clothes turned into glittering webs. Vampire beauty, pared to its feral essence.

Karl led Charlotte higher until coldness pricked their skin. He was searching for something. Wherever they were in the world, Raqia was still the firmament he knew: a wild skyscape of unearthly colours, threaded with ribbons of magnetism and shifting veils of light like an aurora. Overwhelming, terrifying... with an atmosphere of menace that grew stronger by the day.

Bronze hills rolled beneath them, as wild as ocean waves. The electric blues of the void darkened to bruised shades of violet.

"Raqia used to seem tranquil when you first brought me here." Charlotte clung to his arms as air currents tried to tear them apart. "Now it's always stormy. What's happening?"

"I wish I knew, beloved."

They climbed a chasm wall that would have dwarfed the Grand Canyon. Nothing was solid here, but they were near weightless, like fish in water. Below, the Earth was hidden in purple shadow.

Above, mist-veils diffused the fierce distant light of the *Weisskalt*. Between the upper and lower layers hung vast shining mountains of cloud.

Karl folded one arm around her shoulders and pointed upwards. "There," he said. "Tell me what you see."

"I know," Charlotte whispered. "It's everywhere we go."

In the restless cloudscape, a great raven mass appeared to hang in one place while ghost-mountains rolled around it. The sight filled him with dread.

"Describe it," he insisted.

"Every time I'm here, wherever I am, that huge black shadow follows me – as if it can be seen from anywhere, like the Moon from Earth."

"Yes," Karl said. "Everyone has seen it, but no one mentions it. Why not?"

Charlotte stared, alarm in her eyes. "Because we're afraid."

"And do we think that if we don't speak of it, the shadow will vanish? It won't. It's growing."

"But what is it?"

"I've no idea. I only know it's dangerous."

"And so cold," breathed Charlotte. "But you're right. We should explore, not run away. Isn't that why we're here?"

The structure reared above them like a fortress of obsidian. Such a thing had no place in the Crystal Ring. Karl, despite his unease, was fascinated. Even as he watched, it increased in size, drawing mass from wispy arms of ether that spiralled inwards towards its bulk.

They climbed. Judging distance was difficult in Raqia, but the structure was closer than it seemed. Charlotte drew ahead of Karl, her scientific curiosity overcoming her sense of self-preservation; a tendency that Karl both loved and regretted. "Be careful," he said.

"But I must know what it is."

The object became a black wall across the sky in front of them. Charlotte stretched out a hand...

"Don't!" Karl cried, too late. She touched the wall.

Seizing her free hand, he felt the impact like a glacier crashing into them. The shockwave flung them apart. Charlotte was spiralling towards Earth like a winged seed.

Karl caught her, slowed their descent until they landed feet-first on a lower layer. Charlotte seemed unconcerned that she'd fallen. She was staring at her fingers.

"It was solid," she gasped. "Solid. How can it be? If the entire Ring turned to black rock it would be dead to us... Gods, would we cease to exist?"

"Charlotte, don't," Karl said softly. The same questions were in his mind too. *Is the Crystal Ring dying, or turning against us? No, unthinkable!*

He guided her downwards until the world snapped into reality around them. They were in human form again, on a cliff with the Pacific Ocean glimmering cobalt blue below them.

"Hush," he said, clasping her hands. "Beloved, don't be afraid."

"I'm not, I'm all right." He held her, pressing her hands to his chest. Her fingers were frozen.

"But what's causing this change? How can something solid exist in Raqia?"

"I wish I knew," he said.

"It means something. Some event must have precipitated this."

"Kristian's death?" Karl said thoughtfully. "The creation of Lilith? Or her breaking of the angels' power over her, or my placing a dangerous book in the *Weisskalt* for safekeeping, or our scorn for God?"

"Karl!" she exclaimed. "Why is it our fault?"

"It probably is not."

"Then don't take everything onto yourself." She ran her hand over his cheek and through his hair. Her eyes of violet crystal were alight with curiosity, fear, courage; all the qualities that had drawn him to her. She added, "But what are we going to do?"

"I doubt there's anything we *can* do. The truth will reveal itself eventually... before it's too late, I hope."

"But everything's connected," she said, eyes widening. "And if this is because of Lilith – then it's my fault, because I made her. How can I live with knowing I caused this darkness?"

CHAPTER ELEVEN

SILVER, CLOSE AS GOLD

"I shall get up tomorrow," Robyn had said, but first there was the night to endure.

She lay half-asleep, delirious. The moon shone through the curtains, a white coin dappling the room with lace patterns. Her bed was a snowy plain, frozen under a moon in another world. She thought the floor was a river that she must cross or die...

A thin dark figure appeared against the moonlit lace. Her blood began to pulse through her head, slow and heavy.

"Alice?"

No reply. She lay there for an aeon with the faceless silhouette gazing down at her.

In a spurt of panic she cried, "Alice!" – or dreamed she did. There was no answer. She knew that no one was coming to help her.

The figure came closer. Robyn was confused. For a moment the creature was a hovering bird of prey, Odile in black feathers, the death crone in her most beguiling livery. *Violette*, she mouthed, but her voice failed.

When the shape moved again, it changed. Not Violette: too tall and masculine. Still no light on its face, but she recognised the shape of the hair and shoulders.

"What do you want?" she hissed.

Alice's chair was by the bed. The intruder pulled it back and sat down. His nonchalance was infuriating and unnerving. For an instant, as he sat, she saw his profile in the moonlight; the sharp beauty of nose and jaw, one dark soft eye turned obliquely towards her.

He crossed his ankles, rested his left elbow on the chair arm with his chin on his hand, and sat gazing at her.

"What the hell do you want?" She was angry now, breathing fast.

"To see you again," Sebastian replied.

Robyn groped to turn on her bedside lamp. The bulb burned, flickered, and failed with a *tink*. For one second, captured as if by a photographer's flash, she'd seen his face, his long, pale wrists and hands, the candid, heartless eyes. He wasn't smiling. The serious set of his lips alarmed her.

"Well, now you've seen me," she snapped. *Oh, God*, she thought, *hold on. Don't let him know how scared you are.*

"I can see you quite clearly without the light," said the soft voice.

"Who let you in?"

"No one. I let myself in. Vampires do that, you know."

She was unconsciously fingering her throat, trying to gather the collar of her nightdress like a fragile shield. "Oh, I love the way you sit there and admit it! Is this the end, then? You've come back for the blood you didn't steal before?"

He caught her wrist before she could evade him. He was so fast.

"If I wanted to," he said, "there's nothing you could do to stop me. Scream and fight all you like. If anyone comes to help, they won't stop me either; they could get rather badly hurt, actually, and I'm sure you wouldn't want that. Oh, Robyn, you're trembling."

He pressed her fingers and let her go. She snatched her hand away and cradled it against her chest. The skin felt ice-cold and numb. Yet her loins contracted and tingled with the memory of his body against hers.

"Of course I'm trembling. Wouldn't you, if you were about to die? But I suppose you wouldn't know what it feels like, since you only pick victims who are too weak to fight back!"

He was quiet for a time. His silence made her more wretched. Defying him was like defying a thunderstorm.

Eventually he said, "This is why I came back."

"Why? Why are you doing this to me?"

"I could have killed you, my dear. I meant to drain all your lovely blood... but I stopped. Why did I spare your life, do you think?"

"To prolong the torture? I've hardly left this bed since you were here. I've had such fevers and nightmares. I think I'm still dreaming now. But I guess you're happy to hear that."

"No. It's an unfortunate side effect for those we leave alive. Our bite causes madness, to one degree or another." Then he added, unbelievably, "I'm sorry."

"What?"

"It gives me no pleasure to see you suffering." Another pause. He dropped his hands to his knees, leaning towards her. "Do you want me to leave?"

"I – I don't know."

"I'm not here to prey on you. I only want to talk. I give you my word, though you may be disinclined to believe me."

But Robyn did believe him. Even if he'd said he wanted more blood, her answer would have been the same. "No, I don't want you to leave. I'm curious to know what someone – some*thing* – like you could possibly want to talk about."

"God, you're a hard one, aren't you?" said the vampire. "I spared your life, and I don't know why. And you want me to stay, even knowing what I am. This is an interesting situation that requires discussion, does it not?"

Robyn drew herself into a sitting position against the headboard and stared at him, chilled. "Do you always kill your victims?"

He shrugged. "I take what I want. If it kills them, that is their affair. What I mean is that I don't usually force myself to stop before my thirst is sated."

"And do you always make love to them first?"

"No, of course not. Far too much trouble. The blood is essential, sex only a pleasurable distraction. I do so quite often, I suppose... but no, not always."

"I think," she said, her throat in spasm, "that you are an utter fiend."

"And what about you, Robyn? You have a nice line in making men lose their heads over you. Are you any better than me?"

"I don't kill people."

"Just drive them to suicide."

"I don't rape them, either."

"Nor do I, my angel. I've never taken anyone who wasn't willing. And if I'm in a generous frame of mind, I ensure they experience so much pleasure that they're willing to die for me anyway. Isn't it so?"

"Ah yes, that," she said bitterly. She resented him for dissolving her self-control with rapture. Conflict raged inside her; how could she accept him as a vampire, an impossible mysterious demon – yet speak to him as if he were a man?

She knew the answer. Her scepticism had been eroded by Violette, Karl and Charlotte without her even realising. And Sebastian had torn down what remained of the veil. These demons were reasoning creatures who appreciated the weight of their own actions. Her mouth dry, she said, "So you – your kind – like to seduce before they attack, do they? Make the victim a willing participant, share the guilt. Subtle."

"You don't hate me for giving you pleasure, surely?" he said.

"Oh, I do. Manipulator *and* fiend."

"Have you not manipulated me?"

"How?"

"I'm here now against my will," said Sebastian. "I didn't mean to come back, but, well..."

She looked at the shadow-figure, motionless with his hands resting along the chair arms: a patriarch in a gothic throne. He looked solitary, tormented, lethal. Not a man she could dismiss like one of her lovers. A vampire haloed by the moon.

And yet so nearly human. A creature she could engage in battle, mind to mind.

"How did you come to be like this?" she asked on impulse. "Are you very old?"

"Not old enough. Too many questions, beautiful child. Don't expect me to shriek at the sight of a priest, or to catch fire in the sun. Can I see you again, when you're better?"

He was so charming, when he chose. Almost touching, the way he asked permission, as if he needed it. A wave of fatal excitement rose in her throat, capsizing all common sense.

"Can you make love to me without..." Her fingernails grazed the place where he'd bitten her.

"It's extremely hard not to."

"Then it will happen again."

"Every time."

"And will it kill me?"

"Eventually," he said very softly, "if we don't stop." He stood and leaned over her. "Well? Knowing this, do you still want to see me?"

And knowing it was suicidal, Robyn said, "Maybe once."

The vampire bent to kiss her. She stiffened; her terror was instinctive. But his mouth only met hers in the gentlest kiss, warmly tantalising. His hair brushed her cheeks. She slid her arms around his neck, only to find herself embracing air.

After Sebastian had gone – vanished – Robyn turned on her side and lay curled up like a child. After a while she fell sound asleep, undisturbed by fever or dreams.

In the morning, she woke feeling well and manic with excitement, as if she'd volunteered for some insane, exhilarating stunt, like flying on the wing of a biplane.

I'm going to see him again. He will not kill me, or even harm me. I shall get the better of him! What a challenge, to outwit him; not a mere man, but an actual devil!

Will he come tonight? A warm tremor of desire went through her. She danced around the room.

Then she noticed how late it was. Why hadn't Mary come in with her tea?

Pulling on a dressing gown, Robyn went onto the landing and saw that the door to Alice's room was still closed. Softly opening it, she found the room in darkness, the curtains closed.

"Alice?"

She looked at the figure in the bed, and shrieked.

Now she knew why no one had heeded her cry in the night. From Alice's room, she ran upstairs to Mary's, her heart racing and her mouth sticky with fear.

Like Alice, Mary lay unconscious and pallid, breathing in shallow sighs. And on her throat, too, were the fading crescent scars of Sebastian's fangs.

* * *

Cesare's plan took shape swiftly. Now, when he addressed his followers, he did so from the dais, one hand resting on Kristian's ebony throne. No one suggested that he was being presumptuous.

There was much to do before Violette returned from America. The date of her arrival in September loomed in Cesare's mind like doomsday. "When Lilith comes," was a phrase he often repeated to his flock. It always sent a wave of terror through them, like the backdraught of Satan's wings.

Cesare felt happy, fulfilled. Vampires were arriving at Schloss Holdenstein unbidden, alarmed by rumours, by the growing knot of blackness in the Crystal Ring, or by some instinctive knowledge of Lilith that rippled through the ether. His little band numbered twenty, and more would come. *They know they're in peril*, he thought, *and they're coming to me for help!*

Further proof that my leadership is ordained by God.

The need to survive had tamed even Ilona. Cesare was paradoxically grateful for her mischief-making; it had revealed Simon as less than perfect, thus enabling Cesare to be more forceful. The trinity was powerful – Cesare saw Simon, John and himself as fire, earth and air – but he was careful to keep slightly apart. John was right. He should trust only himself.

The plan was going well. More vampires joined the crusade every day, and Ilona was beginning the work she did so well. In secret, though, Cesare's happiness was tainted by doubt.

Despite Simon's assurance, "Not the first, but the best," Cesare couldn't force Sebastian out of his mind. He remembered Sebastian's visit in the last century; a vampire more wayward even than Karl, who'd dared to challenge Kristian. Cesare hated to think that Simon had asked such a rogue to take power.

And what arrogance, to have turned Simon down!

Sebastian became a shadow in Cesare's mind that had to be exorcised.

And then there was Lilith herself.

In moments of clarity, when his crusading fervour cooled, Cesare would sit alone in the inner sanctum and dredge through his deepest fears. *I'm bringing an army together, united by hatred of the Enemy – but what do I really know of her? How can I send them against her, when I haven't faced her myself?*

Am I a coward?

No! He clenched his fists on his thighs, but the words circled like a litany: *when Lilith comes, when Lilith comes...*

Cesare looked up to heaven and thought, *I must prove my courage.*

I must face her alone. Just once.

He called John and Simon and asked gravely, "How can we actually destroy her?"

"I don't think she can be destroyed," said Simon, "but she can be hurt and bound. Ask yourself what would hurt her most."

Cesare couldn't conceive of vampires caring for humans, so he couldn't answer. John, though, spoke at once.

"Destroy her ballet! She killed Matthew because he threatened her dancers."

Cesare was suddenly full of excitement and ideas.

"We can't touch her yet, but we can strip away everything around her," said Simon. "Take her ballet, take those who shelter her. Leave her alone, exposed."

"Alone and threatened, she'll be at her most dangerous," Cesare said, shuddering. Sometimes he felt the ache of long-faded scars on his back, childhood terrors.

"Yes, but also at her most vulnerable." Simon's gilded face showed no fear. "When she returns from her travels, we'll wait a while to lull her suspicions..."

"And then," Cesare breathed, "then we'll welcome her home."

Every Sunday, Robyn went to Trinity, the Episcopal Church in Copley Square. This was part of her pose, to seem more acceptable to Boston society; what could they say about a woman who attended church and did charity work? The word "hypocrite" sprang to mind, but she didn't care.

She wasn't religious, but she loved the church, with its Romanesque solidity, its arches, turrets and pointed roofs. The interior, all dark wood with a wealth of paintings and decoration, felt warm. She liked to sit in the gloom and study the glorious La Farge and Burne-Jones windows. To flood her senses with their stormy purples, bright greens and peacock blues was spirituality enough for her.

But this Sunday she prayed.

Please, God, let Alice and Mary get better.

Please forgive me. Let them get better and I'll never fall again.

To tease Robyn, Sebastian kept away for a few days; to tease her, and tantalise himself. Meanwhile, he explored the city, enjoying the separate worlds of wealth and poverty, the churches, burial grounds where he could seize a victim between the gravestones as befitted his true nature. From the grand bow-fronted houses of Back Bay and Vermont Street to the tenements of the North End, he hunted invisibly in the night; and then he'd walk along the harbour, staring past ships and ferries to the black-sapphire water. Clearing his mind.

Yet everywhere he went, he imagined Robyn beside him, sharing the silver beauty of the night... imagined himself driving his fangs into the tender flesh of her neck.

The worst she could do to me, he thought, *is to leave home and vanish by the time I go back for her. And she might do so to spite me... but I doubt it.*

One evening he crossed the Charles River to explore Cambridge and amuse himself among the students. There, as he wandered through the stately tree-filled squares of Harvard University, he realised he was being followed.

Strange sensation of dimensionless entities watching him, like the time Simon had found him in New York... And then, with a stab of alarm, he saw two glimmering figures, one pale, one dark.

If Simon found me, why not Fyodor and Rasmila? he thought. *But why?*

For a moment he was back at Blackwater Hall, two hundred years falling away... He took a step forward. The black shape resolved into a lamp post, the white one a sliver of light between two buildings. Sebastian stood aghast at the tricks of his own imagination.

Again he found himself thinking of Simon and Ilona – and of Violette. He loathed these intrusions. His gaze swept up, past a library's pillared frontage, past shimmering elms and beeches, to the night sky.

"If you interfere with my existence," he said softly to Violette or anyone; perhaps to the demons in his own soul, "you will regret it."

The sensation of being followed faded, but left him empty, unsettled, thirsty for more than blood.

That feeling drove him back to Robyn's house.

He stood on her terrace, watching her in the parlour: a glowing jewel-box of safety. She was alone and looked so innocent, curled up with a book like a little girl. But she kept breaking off to sigh and gaze at nothing.

Sebastian watched for a long time, motionless. Second nature for a vampire to observe as if he'd turned to stone, transfixed by the object of fascination.

Thoughts of other vampires left sourness in his mouth. He needed Robyn to wash the taste away.

Presently she put her book aside and walked around the room, adjusting ornaments. She appeared to sense something... And at last she came to the French doors.

By the time she opened the doors to the night, Sebastian was standing on the small lawn, beneath a lemon tree.

She started. He savoured the wave of nervous heat she radiated. Then she descended the steps towards him, demanding, "What the hell are you doing here?"

In a pyjama suit of ivory silk, her hair loose over her shoulders, she looked astonishing. Lustrous eyes wide with anger, one hand clasping the jacket at her throat, blood blooming in her cheeks. He could have devoured her. When he said nothing, she grew angrier.

"Have you been watching me?"

"Naturally. You are a very pleasing sight. Do you mind?"

"Yes, I mind. Damned right I mind!"

Clearly he'd underestimated her anger. She was alight with rage.

"I've been waiting for you to come outside," he said, smiling.

"Why the hell couldn't you knock on the front door like a normal man? You know, telephone first or leave a card. I've been going mad, wondering if you were coming back or not, you god-damned –"

"You said you wanted to see me." His tone was cool, and he knew how he appeared: too still and pale, his eyes hypnotic but unfeeling. He enjoyed his power to frighten her – yet her brave spirit intrigued him.

"That was before I found out what you really are!"

"I thought it was obvious."

"I'm talking about Mary and Alice!" she cried. "I found them when you'd gone. You went to them and – how *dare* you do that to them!"

Sebastian laughed. Robyn seemed ready to kill him.

"You have no cause to be jealous," he said.

"What?" She caught her breath. "*Jealous?*"

"I did nothing carnal with them. It would have taken too long."

Her mouth dropped, eyes opening wide. He continued, "I am joking, my dear. I have no designs on your servants. But blood is blood. It's the one thing I absolutely must have."

She glared speechlessly at him.

"You invited me back," he added, "knowing what I am."

"Don't you dare blame this on me!" She came closer, pointing a finger at him. "If you ever touch Alice or Mary again, I'll –"

"What?"

Her voice fell. "I'll never see you again. What can you do about that, unless you kill me? And that would kind of defeat your object, wouldn't it?"

Sebastian exhaled softly. She was right, and she'd won a small victory.

"I don't want to kill you, and there'd be no pleasure in forcing you. And I mind very much if you refuse to see me. You look cold, Robyn. Won't you invite me inside?"

"Oh, you need an invitation now?" She studied him, her eyes glittering. Then she relented. "All right. Come in."

He followed her, watching her hair swaying against her upright back, the rich curves of her hips. He closed the doors. Robyn went to a lace-covered table and picked up a small object, closing her hand so he didn't see it.

"Where are Alice and Mary?" he asked.

"Mary's in the kitchen. Alice, at a concert with friends."

Sebastian spread his hands. "So, no harm done."

"That's a matter of opinion." She turned to him. "They were both in bed for a day, not as sick as me, but bad enough. I don't think Mary remembers, although she jumps at every little noise. But Alice... She knows what you did. She won't talk, but I see it in her eyes." Head drooping, she pressed a fist to her forehead. "What am I doing, letting you in?"

Sebastian went to her. Her head jerked up. She looked dishevelled, flushed, wholly irresistible. Obvious why men lost their heads over her; almost shaming, that he wasn't immune. He longed to touch her, but sensed she would shake him off.

"Robyn..."

"Does this mean anything to you?" She opened her fist. In her palm was a silver crucifix on a chain.

"No." He regarded the cross, unmoved. "What does it mean to you?"

She bit her lip. The gesture was so unconsciously erotic that it was all he could do not to seize her. "My mother's Jewish, my father's Unitarian and I'm a cynic. And a sinner. So I guess it ought to mean something, but it doesn't."

"But you go to church."

"So?" Another flash of anger. "Have you been following me?"

He shrugged, leaving her to guess. "Well, I was once a Catholic, severely lapsed, so there you are," he said lightly.

"Oh, well." She let the chain slide through her fingers. "I wanted to see if you would scream and leap through windows, like Count Dracula."

"I can, if you'd find it entertaining." Sebastian was looking at her more softly now. Her fear was fading. "But not in response to a piece of metal."

He allowed himself the luxury of touching her. He rested his left hand on her shoulder and rolled strands of her brown hair between his fingers. She didn't flinch.

"You were trying to protect yourself. I don't blame you," he said gently, "but you can't."

Dull pain, laced with tenderness, fleeted across her face. She pressed his hand to her cheek, swallowing hard as if she wanted to stop but couldn't.

"I think we should go to my bedroom," she said. "Don't you?"

* * *

They dived through lakes of flame and smoky light, joined from mouth to loins. No bed beneath them, nothing of Earth to constrain them. Sebastian felt that he'd transported Robyn into the Crystal Ring and now they fell through the clouds forever, entwined.

This was even more glorious than the first time. They knew each other, but there was more to learn. This time, to his delight, Robyn didn't fight her feelings but absorbed him, craving sensation, passion, release. His body slid over hers; he loved her moist heat, all her natural scents. Her eyes were half-closed, her throat taut, fingers kneading his back, nails scratching him, her limbs and breasts heavy against him as they rolled over and over, striving to consume each other.

Robyn climaxed beneath him, blood rising in her face, her heart clamouring against his chest. All through him, he felt her heartbeat. Folding her elbows behind his neck she clung to him, rocking, almost weeping.

He followed her into the mindless light. Every sensation brought overwhelming pleasure, almost unbearable. *Robyn... ah, God... I am lost in you now...*

Her eyelids lifted, her expression changed. Eyes ringed white with anxiety, she whispered, "You don't have to – to feed this time... do you? Sebastian?"

He couldn't answer. It was too late.

White heat swept over him. He became dimly aware that she was resisting, trying to keep his mouth from her neck. When she realised she couldn't prevent it, she began to fight in earnest, squirming and hitting out and gasping.

Somehow she deflected him and his fangs sank into her shoulder instead. A taste of blood, not enough. He bit again, found a thick vein at last. Sucking hard, he quivered with bliss, while she went on struggling beneath him.

Stop now, said a subconscious voice. *If you want this to happen again, stop!*

One deep, delicious draught of her blood had to be enough.

The pleasure passed its red peak and ebbed away, leaving him weak with satiation. He rolled to one side, oblivious to Robyn's distress. So he was shocked when she delivered a powerful slap to the side of his head.

"You bastard!"

He caught her arm to prevent a second blow. She wormed away from him and sat against the headboard, clasping a pillow, her knees drawn up. Scarlet threads ran down her collarbone, matting her hair.

"I asked you not to. I said stop!"

"And I told you before that I can't."

Robyn, trembling with the after-shock, began to cry. She looked so lovely, curled up under the burnished veil of hair, that he wanted her again. But he could not feel remorse.

"It hurts," she said angrily. "It feels horrible."

Sebastian got up, brought a damp cloth and a glass of water from the bathroom. She glared. Giving her the water, he began gently to sponge the wounds he'd made.

"Look, Robyn," he said softly. "They're healing. Only faint marks, hardly there at all."

"Haven't you the remotest idea of how it feels?" she said bitterly.

"Of course I have. It's when they take all your blood, *all* of it, that you want to be worrying. How do you think I became like this?"

She froze. He watched the enticing rise and fall of her throat as she sipped water. "Oh, God, will it happen to me?"

"No. We're not infectious like the smallpox."

"But you bring death by degrees." Calmer now, she regarded him through narrow eyes. "What's your bed like, I wonder? Black, with a white lining?"

"No, I don't sleep in a coffin and I won't turn to dust when the sun comes up. Now, tell me –" he caressed her cheekbone "– do you feel as bad as the first time?"

"No. Just dizzy. I'm all right."

"Because I stopped, Robyn."

Her eyes flashed open. "What if a time comes when you can't stop?"

"We both take that risk."

"No, I take it."

"By your own choice." Placing the glass aside, he lay beside her, pulling her towards him. "I won't force myself on you."

"I just wish you would love me without taking my blood," she whispered. "Is it too much to ask?"

He pressed his lips to her warm, downy forearm, lifted her wrists to link them around his neck, and kissed her. She glowered dully, then gave a heartfelt groan and pressed herself along his lean body. He entered her again and she gave herself to him, liquefying.

"Listen to me," he said into her ear. Her breath was a warm cloud on his neck. "Don't fight me. Relax, then it won't hurt. I won't take much, I promise."

Then they were on fire, melting, falling like comets through space... and when the moment came, his mouth slid gently over the contours of her throat. Finding the place, he bit into her.

This time she only stiffened beneath him. Her breath ran out in a sigh and she lay unresisting but not passive; participating, in the way that she rested her cheek on his hair and stroked his shoulder, while emotion informed her whole body with radiance.

He kept his word, though it wasn't easy.

"Was it so terrible?" he asked afterwards.

She rubbed her thumb over his lips, looked at her own blood on her thumb-tip. Unconsciously she sucked it clean. "Not quite," she said faintly. "It was like floating." She almost smiled, her eyes drowsy.

Sebastian lay back, cradling her against his chest and stroking her hair. He wasn't eager to hear her thoughts. He just wanted to hold her.

As he did so, an inner voice spoke in horrified amazement. *What the devil am I doing, showing a mortal tenderness? Have I gone mad? Humans are below us, like animals, their sufferings transient and meaningless... and yet, I'm compelled to be careful because I do not want her to die.*

The feeling was close to panic. He controlled it, telling himself firmly, *Of course I'm not mad. It's expedient to keep her alive and pliant so that I prolong my own pleasure. That is all.*

Have I quite deceived you yet, my Robyn?

When the ship sailed from New York, bound for Hamburg, Charlotte was sorry to leave. The tour had been successful beyond Violette's dreams. Ballet Janacek had been feted across the continent. Most importantly, Violette seemed happy.

Throughout the tour, she'd been kind to her dancers, gracious to the press. She hadn't said a word about her usual concerns. Charlotte suspected that Violette had taken her advice, and was obeying the thirst instead of fighting it. She imagined the dancer slipping out each night to feed as neatly as a cat, in order to devote all her energy to the ballet.

She'll do that for her art, Charlotte thought, *but not for herself*.

Sadly, the idyll had to end. Crowds of well-wishers lined the quay as they sailed, cheering and waving and throwing flowers. They saw Violette as a living legend, already immortal.

No one, thought Charlotte, *has the faintest idea of the truth*.

Home drew them like a current sweeping across a mist-veiled sea. Charlotte was aware of her mood darkening, sensed the same in Karl. There would be no more wanton sharing of prey.

Violette took to her cabin, seeing no one but Geli. Charlotte began to despair. But one evening, as she stood at the rail watching the calm green sea at sunset, Violette softly joined her.

"Something's waiting for us at home," said Violette. "I don't know what... Something bad. Do you feel it too?"

"Yes," Charlotte admitted. "But if we stay away and ignore it, we'll probably make things worse."

Violette fell quiet. Other guests were strolling on deck, elegant in evening dress. A few glanced at Violette, but were kind enough to respect her privacy.

"While we were on the West Coast," said Charlotte, "Karl and I entered the Crystal Ring."

"You go there every day."

"I mean we went to look at... the darkness there. To investigate."

"Stop." Violette's face was white. The ship's rail creaked under the pressure of her fingers.

"Don't you want to hear what happened?"

"You're still alive, aren't you? How bad could it be?"

"Bad enough."

"And you think it's my fault?" Violette glared frigidly at her. "Some physical manifestation of my inner sickness, is that it?"

Charlotte exhaled, resting a hand on Violette's shoulder. "Of course not. But we should face it, whatever it is. You won't talk about anything."

The dancer looked away. "And you and Karl never stop. What good does it do? Please, Charlotte. I don't even want to think about this when I get home. All I want is to work on a new ballet."

"Immediately?"

"Yes, why not? A ballet about Lilith."

"Oh. That could be a risk."

"After *Dans le Jardin*? I know. Please don't remind me of that disaster. No, I've learned by my mistakes. This will be different: the themes will be subtler, and I won't use modern music or experimental sets. We'll dress it up as an old-fashioned, tragic fairy tale, another *Giselle*. It will be beautiful. But I have to do this, Charlotte. It's clawing its way out of me."

"What's the story?"

Violette brightened. "We'll have Adam and Eve again, but this time the Serpent is a woman, Lilith. I'll change their names, of course. A young man falls in love with a dark spirit of the forest, but when it's time for him to marry, he chooses an innocent, compliant girl as his bride. Rejected, Lilith curses them. She torments the wife, seduces the man; she murders their children and excludes their souls from heaven…"

"It sounds very dark."

"No, it will work," Violette said fervently. "The tale will be beautiful and tragic!"

"Do you see yourself in such a negative light?"

Violette met her gaze. "You know I do. That's why I need to explore Lilith. Josef told me to confront myself, after all."

"How does it end?"

"I really don't know. But I need Ute to dance the wife; if only I hadn't driven her back to her bloody father!" She looked at Charlotte, thoughtful. "I suppose you wouldn't consider…?"

"I can't dance."

"Yes, you can. I've seen you."

"That's mimicry. Cheating. It's only because vampires can imitate humans, not from years of training. It wouldn't be right."

"And Karl can't spare you." Violette sounded more sad than bitter. "No, you go back to Switzerland. I'd be unfair to keep you in Salzburg. I'll find someone."

"But don't make it too dark. Have the children kidnapped, not murdered, so there can be a happy reunion!"

Violette smiled. "You could write the story for me. All the steps are in my head. I'll begin rehearsals without the remotest idea of how the ballet ends."

Charlotte thought, *Does acting out your life save you from having to live it?* She didn't say it. Planning the new project made Violette calmer, at least.

"You won't dance because you're not human," Violette said presently. "Do you ever wish you were human again?"

"I think of it, but in all honesty I wouldn't go back," said Charlotte. "Would you?"

"I never felt human to begin with, so perhaps it wouldn't be very different. Only... I met someone who gave me hope, but I had to leave her behind. Now I wish I hadn't been so noble." Pain darted across Violette's face. "Is it possible to cross the Atlantic in a night, through the Crystal Ring? If only I could see Robyn one last time..."

"You can probably do anything, dear, but I shouldn't," Charlotte said gravely. "Leave her alone. What possible good can a vampire lover be?"

"You're one to talk."

"Exactly. I know."

"Oh, it's an idle wish. At least Robyn is safe. She'll never know the lucky escape she had! I think I wanted to escape into her, into a warm, comforting human, because I'm frightened."

Her face perfect between raven wings of hair, Violette looked anything but vulnerable.

"Of what?"

"Myself, of course. I'm terrified of my capacity for destruction. I can hold Lilith in check for a time; you've no idea how hard I worked to ensure nothing went wrong on tour."

"I can guess." Charlotte stroked her arm.

"But she'll have her way in the end." Her voice fell to a whisper. "And I dread to think what may happen when we get home."

CHAPTER TWELVE

SHADOW DANCE

Robyn had expected Sebastian to leave before dawn. Waking from a deep sleep, she was startled to find him still beside her. It was daylight, nearly eight o'clock. Half-asleep, leaden, she began to sit up.

"Don't move," he said. "I like looking at you. So lovely to watch you sleeping."

But Robyn was thinking of Mary and Alice about to bring her tea. She rarely let her "gentleman callers" stay the night. The last thing she wanted was for one of them to be confronted by their vampire attacker.

Too late. She'd barely sat up when the door opened.

Alice. Seeing Sebastian, she dropped the tray. As it hit the carpet with a crash of metal and china, Alice uttered an aborted scream and fled the room.

"You'd better go," Robyn said, hostile towards Sebastian again. "Get dressed!"

"Why? That was your housekeeper, not an outraged mother."

His beauty threatened to captivate her, the leaf-green eyes and soft dark hair making her want to eat him alive, but she resisted.

"She's also my companion. You scare her to death! I care more about her feelings than yours – so leave." She climbed out of bed, pulled on her dressing gown and tied the cord.

"Without even a bath or a cup of tea?"

"Don't be facetious," she snapped. Grabbing a hairbrush, she went to the dressing table mirror. The colour was high in her cheeks but otherwise her skin looked drained. She fingered the healed bite-marks on her shoulder and neck. Where he'd fed the second time, he had left a bruise and telltale blood streaks. Alice must have seen them.

Sebastian's face appeared in the mirror behind her. His long hands folded over her shoulders. *Thank God he has a reflection*, Robyn thought, *or I might just lose my mind completely.*

"Are you regretting last night?" he asked.

"I regret the whole damned thing."

"Don't." He pressed his mouth to her neck. She jumped violently, but he only kissed her. His warm silken lips made her tingle with echoes of their lovemaking. How carnal it seemed, in the judgemental light of day. Almost bestial. "When shall I see you again?"

"I don't know," she said, savagely brushing her hair. "How soon would you like to attend my funeral?"

"A few days," he said ambiguously, and turned away.

She heard him dressing. Eventually she swung round to say, "Don't go yet," only to find that he'd already disappeared.

Alice was in her room, staring out of the window. Robyn glimpsed the roofs of Beacon Hill, sea mist condensing on the humid air, treetops flying a gorgeous array of colours.

"It's okay, Alice, he's gone," she said.

Alice turned, looking pale but severe.

"What in heaven's name are you doing, letting that creature into your bed?"

"Are you all right?" Robyn asked meekly.

"Never mind me, answer the question!"

"I notice you assume I invited him."

"I know you, madam. No man makes you do anything – not even him. How can you let this happen, knowing what he is? It's obscene!"

Finding Alice outraged rather than cowering, Robyn's concern eased towards humour. "One good thing about this: at least I don't need to convince you he's a vampire."

Alice flinched, and one hand flew to her throat.

"When you read things in a storybook, you don't take

it seriously. But when it really happens – Lord, it's no joke. A stranger's face leaning over you in the middle of the night. His mouth open, the terrible sharp teeth... And it's agony, like being stabbed with knives... But the worst thing is the helplessness. An ordinary man I could have stabbed with my scissors, maybe... but his eyes paralysed me. If I was scared, how do you think poor Mary felt? It was obscene. So for you to be sleeping with him – that's evil, ma'am. Just plain evil."

Alice's passion rendered Robyn speechless. When she managed to answer, her voice was husky with shame.

"Alice, I'm so sorry. I made him give his word never to touch you or Mary again. I know you're afraid, with good reason, but it's all right. You're safe."

There was little conviction in her words. In truth, she had no control over Sebastian and didn't trust him at all.

"Even if we're safe, what about you? There was blood all over you!"

"Don't exaggerate." Robyn lowered her gaze.

"It was obvious what he'd done! And you let him?"

Robyn gave a single nod. "In a sense."

"For the love of God, are you *trying* to get yourself killed?"

"I'm being stupid, I know, but..."

"Stupid? Suicidal! What is he? I mean, we know he has a taste for blood, but what actually *is* he? You're being completely reckless! Why, for pity's sake? Why?"

"Because..." She paused, searching for words. "He's a wonderful lover." She touched her friend's shoulder, but Alice remained stony. "The only wonderful lover I've ever had."

She sighed at the memory. The searing, impossible pleasure that went on until she was a wrung-out rag, breathless... the frightening struggle against his blood thirst, then reluctant surrender... Unspeakably strange feeling. Lying there with his fangs impaling her, a piercing clamp on her throat. Yet the pain was bearable, pure and sharp like diamond, even heightening her pleasure. So weird, to give her blood as an extension of their sexual bliss. A bond between them. Cruel, unequal and unhealthy... yet a bond, all the same.

"I can't give him up," Robyn said. "And I hate him for that."

"Hate him?" Alice's face opened up with surprise.

"Yes, you know, for getting under my defences. I have to figure out my revenge, because he has no reputation to lose and doesn't give a damn about money. So until I think of something, I'm going to enjoy myself. Use him the way he thinks he's using me."

"You're crazy. You have to stop!" Alice seized Robyn and actually shook her. "Don't you realise he's probably murdered people?" Her voice fell. "There was a housemaid found dead in Marlborough Street, a young man dragged out of the river..."

"That's speculation," Robyn said, but cold gooseflesh ran over her.

"He should be jailed. He should hang. I'm going to tell someone."

"Who?" Robyn cried. "No one will believe you. Alice, please. Don't interfere."

Alice's usually serene face was hard.

"And what about your responsibilities to the people in this household? Not just to Mary and me and Mr and Mrs Wilkes, but to yourself. What would we do if anything happened to you? How d'you think we'd feel? Or your Uncle Josef?"

"Stop!" Robyn lifted her hands in exasperation, her mother's gesture. "Stop worrying. Nothing is going to happen to me."

Idyllic as America had been, Karl was happy to come home. He'd missed the crisp whiteness of the mountains. As he and Charlotte climbed the steep path to their chalet, the air was like cold wine infused with scents of peat and pine trees.

Violette had returned to Salzburg with her company. Karl was glad to have Charlotte to himself again. But as they reached the front door, they paused to look at each other.

"There's someone inside," said Charlotte.

Entering Raqia, they melted through doors and walls and emerged into the drawing room. A fire burned in the grate, and two blond figures were lounging on a sofa. Stefan was sitting up, Niklas lying down with his head on his twin's lap, while Stefan absently stroked his hair.

Seeing Karl and Charlotte, Stefan pushed Niklas aside and

leapt to his feet. Niklas rose beside him like a delayed reflection.

"I've been waiting days for you!" Stefan exclaimed. "I thought you'd be home by now."

"What's wrong?" Charlotte asked, placing her coat on a chair.

Stefan rarely let anything perturb him, but his sky-blue eyes were anxious. "We had visitors in London. Cesare, with a couple of underlings. He's changed, Karl. He thinks he's the new Kristian and he's taking the part rather seriously."

Karl's heart sank. He thought, *Could we not have had a few minutes' peace before this began?*

"What happened?"

"He's summoning all vampires to Schloss Holdenstein. He has something very important and exciting to announce: a crusade against Lilith. But here's the rub: anyone who refuses to join in will be considered an enemy, Lilith's minion." Stefan paced around the room, trailing his hand across Niklas's shoulder as he passed. Karl had rarely seen him so agitated.

"Surely he didn't frighten you?" Karl asked.

"Oh, but he did!" Stefan looked at Charlotte. "You didn't know Cesare in the old days. So quiet, he was like a piece of Kristian's medieval furniture."

"He would make excellent firewood," Karl said darkly.

"I can't explain, but he's acquired power. He threatened us, and he meant it."

"But you dislike Violette anyway," Charlotte said thinly. "Why would Cesare think you were on her side?"

"I don't dislike her." Stefan paced to the fireplace and back. "She makes me uneasy, but that's beside the point. The thing is this, and I beg you to take me seriously. Cesare's dangerous, and he's on the march. And I've had enough. Kristian, Simon, Lilith, Lancelyn – how many more would-be tyrants must we suffer?"

"I feel the same," said Karl. "I suspected we'd have someone like Cesare to deal with before long."

"Well, you can deal with him," said Stefan. "You're on your own."

Karl looked hard at him. Stefan stopped pacing.

"I don't wish to fight anyone," said Karl, "but if it's necessary – are you saying you won't help us?"

"That's exactly what I'm saying. Cesare's gathering an army. He'll become an immortal dictator and it will be, 'Follow me or die!' We can't stop him without creating an army of our own. What's the alternative? If we plunge in unarmed, we'll be overwhelmed and killed. No, thank you. I came to warn you – and to say goodbye."

"No!" Charlotte exclaimed. "Where will you go?"

"That would be telling. I wouldn't like to think of Cesare torturing my hiding place out of you."

Stefan's vivid eyes burned into Karl's. He found it difficult ever to be angry with Stefan, but this time Karl felt betrayed. "So, you're disappearing?"

Stefan went to Niklas and put an arm around his shoulders. Niklas went on staring into space with a faint smile and vacant, gold-glass eyes.

"Correct. We're running away. Call me a coward: water off a duck's back. It's not for myself, but for Niklas. He may be a vampire, but he hasn't the wit to protect himself. In a physical confrontation, all my energy would go to protect him, not to help you. The last time, I was nearly killed, and what would Niklas do without me? We can't live without each other. I don't want to be a fugitive, but I've no choice."

Karl sighed. He couldn't argue with Stefan's logic. "Do what you must. We'll miss you."

"You'd be wise to come with us."

"Perhaps." Karl met Charlotte's eyes. "But we must stay."

"Then be careful. I don't deserve such understanding friends. And I don't want to lose them."

Stefan clasped Karl's hand, and hugged him; then he went to Charlotte, kissed her cheeks and lips, almost with the passion of a lover. Charlotte struggled not to cry.

"I'll write," said Stefan. He placed his arm around Niklas and they vanished into the Crystal Ring.

Charlotte's eyes lit up with sadness and rage. "If Cesare thinks Lilith's so dangerous that he has to raise an army against her, he's an imbecile!"

"Without question," Karl said heavily. "However, I'll have to visit Schloss Holdenstein and find out what's happening."

"Alone?"

Karl usually suppressed his instinct to overprotect Charlotte, but for once his sense of foreboding won.

"This time, beloved, if you don't mind."

He spoke so gently and firmly that she couldn't argue.

Karl had never considered himself an idealist. What possible ideals could a vampire hold, who had forsaken all morality? Yet now, as he climbed the rugged slopes to Schloss Holdenstein, he realised that he'd envisioned a kind of utopia.

With Kristian dead, he imagined a world in which vampires were free to determine their own destiny, codes of conduct, relationships. No vampire would interfere in another's existence... Why should they, unless their behaviour reached unacceptable extremes?

And that was the trouble. Human or vampire, there were always some who went too far. There *had* to be laws, and someone to enforce them. Now he understood, with a heavy heart, how misplaced his optimism had been.

Something worse was rising in Kristian's place... but was it Violette, or Cesare?

He walked softly through the castle's dank corridors, gauging vampire presences around him. And... he hesitated, curious... humans?

He went into the windowless heart of the castle, where Kristian had held court. The atmosphere had always been stifling, heavy with blood and death. Now there was also a feverish note.

Karl wanted to see Pierre. He also wished to know if Ilona had come here after leaving Boston so abruptly. As he followed a winding corridor, Cesare stepped out to meet him.

Karl halted, resigned. He hadn't expected to reach his friends unchallenged.

Stefan was right: Cesare had changed. Physically, he remained pallid and deceptively boyish in his drab robe. But there was light in his eyes, new energy and confidence in his bearing.

Cesare grinned, to Karl's surprise, and clasped his right hand.

"Karl, how wonderful to see you. Have you come home?"

Does he imagine I ever thought of this as home? Karl regarded the pale-eyed figure with contempt. He'd once had a chance to kill Cesare, and now wished he'd taken it. He freed his hand.

"I am here to see friends."

"Be my guest," Cesare said with a broad gesture.

"Thank you," Karl inclined his head with icy courtesy, "but I don't believe I need your permission."

He walked past Cesare into the warren of rooms that clustered around the meeting chamber and the inner sanctum. He sensed Pierre's presence nearby...

A cell lay beyond a doorless archway, with candles flickering, stonework blackened by years of candle-smoke. Karl noted a table, a few ancient chairs, and a wooden pallet on which Pierre lay, entwined with a human: a well-built male with fair hair. The male was naked but for a cloth around his loins.

At the table sat a grotesque vampire, his bald skull a mass of scar tissue. This must be John... and the severed head perched on the table's corner was Matthew's. Karl felt a surge of horror and pity.

John sat writing with a feathered quill, ignoring Pierre's feast, but Ilona, perched on a stool, watched raptly. She leaned forward over her crossed knees, resting her chin on one hand. Her flapper-style dress was dark plum, like her hair, like the blood that escaped Pierre's lips to streak his victim's chest.

Karl caught the scent, and the musky-salty human smell that lured vampires with the promise of satiation. He responded, despite himself. His fangs slid half out of their sockets with the pressure of desire.

Ilona turned, her lips in a tight smile.

"Father! Join us, why don't you. Pierre, leave some for Karl." Her eyes were sultry from feeding, but she too had changed, Karl observed. Nothing definable: a dullness of spirit. He recalled, with a stab of pain, how she'd wept on his shoulder and fed from his throat, and he had a fleeting thought, *All this hideous misery was caused by Violette...*

"Thank you, I'll refrain," he said.

As Cesare joined him in the archway, Karl again sensed the fevered atmosphere that pervaded the castle.

"Cesare, aren't you aware that it's unwise to kill victims in your own domain? The castle has enough ghosts already."

Nothing, it seemed, could dent Cesare's good humour. "We do not kill them, and they are not victims."

"We have to bring Pierre's supper to him, because he won't leave the castle," added Ilona. "You wouldn't want him to starve?"

Pierre was oblivious. His eyes were closed, his mouth clamped to the man's neck, hands locked around the broad, naked shoulders. The man was conscious, rigid in the deathly embrace. Muscles stood out in taut curves along his arms. His hands wagged in the air, thick fingers splayed. His groans might be of agony or rapture.

"I wouldn't be confident that this victim will not die." Karl leaned against the archway, folding his arms. "Have you ever *tried* to make Pierre cease feeding before he's ready?"

"Pierre," Cesare said lightly, moving to the pallet. "Enough now. We must not damage him."

To Karl's astonishment, Pierre obeyed. He dropped the man, crawled away and knelt on the end of the pallet. He was dishevelled, as if he hadn't combed his hair or changed his clothes for weeks. Blood dripped from his lips. His expression was full of fear.

Karl was so shocked that tears sprang to his eyes.

"How long has he been like this?"

"Months," said Ilona. "Since before you went to America."

The human curled on his side, groaning. Ignoring him, Karl went to Pierre. "My friend," he said gently, "what happened to you?"

"I told you," said Ilona. "Violette happened."

Pierre rubbed his mouth with the back of his hand. "Nothing's wrong. Leave me the hell alone!"

"Violette seems to be happening to everyone," Ilona remarked.

"She is dangerous to those who cross her," Karl said in a neutral tone.

Ilona's face tightened. "I was with a victim. Isn't there some code of honour that forbids us from interfering with another vampire's kill?"

"She's dangerous to us all," said Cesare. "I hope you aren't here to defend her, Karl?"

"I came to see Pierre and my daughter."

"Is there hope for you, then? Can we persuade you to our cause?"

Karl didn't reply, but he knew an answer would be demanded eventually. The change in Cesare was alarming. No longer a mere acolyte, waiting passively for Kristian's second coming, he had found his own path. Cesare's new inner light had the power to draw followers to him. *To dazzle them so subtly*, Karl thought, *they never notice they're blind.*

A sound made Karl turn. Two more humans entered the cell, strong young men in brown robes, barefoot, both fair-haired. They bowed to Cesare, then went to the man on the pallet.

"Take him away, wash and feed him," Cesare ordered.

The newcomers helped Pierre's victim to his feet. He swayed, but he was clear-eyed and smiling. He gave Cesare a deep nod of respect, adoration in his eyes.

"Master," he said.

Cesare touched his cheek, and the man – big and muscular enough to break Cesare in two, had they both been mortal – looked as if he might faint with delight. "Go and rest. You have earned it."

Karl watched with a mild sense of revulsion.

"Be a gentleman, Cesare," came Pierre's hoarse voice. "Offer Karl a drink."

Cesare's expression tightened, but his tone remained gracious. "Let me not withhold refreshment from you." He gestured towards the two robed humans. "Take whichever you wish."

Karl wanted nothing from Cesare, but curiosity overcame him. Young, fresh-faced men in their very prime, their eyes held intelligence, respect and eagerness to please. Even Kristian had never kept humans in the castle. The rush of their blood drew him powerfully. It crossed his mind that this might be a trap, but he thought, *Cesare hasn't grown that devious – yet.*

He approached one of the men, who promptly relinquished Pierre's prey to his companion and stood as if for military inspection. He was as tall as Karl and much broader, with cropped hair and a tanned, freckled face. Sinews stood out in his wide neck. He showed no sign of fear.

Karl moved slowly, watching him. *What do you see as I*

approach? Do you understand what I am going to do?

Karl placed his hands on the shoulders, feeling their muscular thickness through the loose-woven robe. Perspiration broke on the man's upper lip. As Karl felt his tension increase, he thought, *You know what I am, yet you barely flinch...*

Karl struck. The blood hit him like a wave. He felt the hot clasp of flesh around his fangs, salt and fire in his mouth, the seductive softening of the victim's body against his own. How bestial, this pleasure.

A vampire could wrestle with his conscience for all time, but it would never be more than a shadow-dance obliterated by the throbbing reality of the kill.

The first surge over, he let the flow slacken, until he could bring himself to stop. Amazingly, the man showed no sign of weakness. He remained rigid, as if trained to withstand the assault. It was Karl who, half-swooning with pleasure, had to lean on him for a few seconds. This brief loss of control reminded him why he rarely fed in front of anyone, particularly Ilona.

Regaining control, Karl drew back. The man dipped his head – like a cat questing for his owner's caress – then collected himself and stood to attention. Karl studied him, trying to read his eyes. All he saw was the unquestioning obedience of a soldier.

"Who are you?" Karl asked softly.

"That's enough." Cesare's voice was like gunshots. "Brothers, you're dismissed."

Repeating the ritual bow, the three men left. Karl felt bemused horror, even while he floated on the crimson afterglow of feeding.

"What is this? Are you keeping captive prey, like dairy cattle?"

"Only the finest," Ilona said quietly. "Not cows, but magnificent bulls, actually."

Cesare cut across her. "We have nothing to explain unless you come to us wholeheartedly in the service of God."

Karl faced him without expression. Recalling Stefan's fear, he was angry that this creature had driven Stefan and Niklas into hiding. "Why would you want me? You know I destroyed Kristian. I made no secret of it."

"But I forgive you, Karl." Cesare's eyes glowed like a saint's. He clasped Karl's upper arms; a distasteful, over-familiar action.

"There are many here who rebelled against Kristian. More come every day. There are even vampires who escaped the *Weisskalt* when Kristian died. The past is forgotten. God instructs me to unite all vampires against the Enemy. If you join us, you'll be saved – but stay in the darkness and you will be friendless, an outcast for Lilith to devour."

"Is this what you tell everyone?"

"It's the truth," said Cesare. "You're no fool, Karl. You know how dangerous she is, don't you?"

Karl couldn't reply. He had been denying Violette's nature, but Cesare's words cut straight to the core of his fears.

"We met two vampires named Rachel and Malik," said Karl. "Are they here?"

Rachel had not been seen since she vanished after the attack on Violette, and the dancer's retaliation. As for Malik – a tall, stoic-natured vampire of African origins, who had emerged from the *Weisskalt* after Kristian's death – Karl had not seen him for months. He had no idea where Malik's allegiance might lie.

"No," said Cesare. "Not yet."

"And what of Simon, Rasmila and Fyodor?"

Cesare gave no answer. "Well, Karl? Are you with us or against us?"

"I'm not here to take sides," Karl said evenly. "May I speak to Pierre alone?"

"Impossible." Spines prickled through the fur of Cesare's voice. "If you can't give me a clear statement of your intentions, you'd better leave. Take time to think."

Ilona slipped to Karl's side. "Do as he says, Father. It's not worth arguing with him."

Ignoring them, Karl went to Pierre. Cesare followed, adding insistently, "Leave now and do not return until –"

He touched Karl's arm. Karl turned, furious, shaking him off. "Don't lay your hands on me. How long did your throat take to heal, the last time you tried?"

"I was weak then. I am strong now. This is your last warning."

Cesare had acquired a stunning air of authority. No doubt he'd become dangerous. But after what Karl had endured to win his freedom, he would submit to no one.

"Well, I'm going," Ilona said impatiently. "Karl, if you've any sense, come with me." She vanished as the Crystal Ring received her.

Karl turned to Pierre, who was now leaning against the wall, his long legs drawn up under him. "Pierre, I wish you'd come with us. I'm distressed to see you like this."

"Why are you so solicitous, suddenly?" said Pierre. "I've always done my best to make your life unpleasant. I hope you're not about to reward me with some nauseatingly sentimental speech about friendship."

"Call it curiosity, then," Karl said patiently. "Tell me what happened."

The curly brown head drooped. "Really, there's no point. I can't leave, and I've nothing to tell you. Do as Cesare says. Get out."

Cesare was watching, his smile a strand of wire. Then John rose and stood glowering at Karl. And in him, Karl saw, lay Cesare's real strength: a brutish power, glowing like hot iron from the gargoyle face and minotaur shoulders. John's once neat, slender form appeared to have been reforged in hell.

The horror of this transformation terrified Karl more than any physical threat. He had a nebulous thought: *What if the Crystal Ring can do this to any of us?*

"As you wish," he said evenly. "I shall consider what you've said."

Returning Cesare's gelid stare with a smile, Karl stepped into the Ring and went in search of his daughter.

The Bierkeller was a sweltering mass of bodies, noise and laughter, stewing in smoke and lager-yellow light. Werner was already drunk, but not too drunk to be brought up short by the sight of an incredibly beautiful woman sitting alone.

He'd deserted his student friends, sick of arguing politics with them, frustrated by their shallow refusal to listen. Intellectuals, they fancied themselves: not an idea between them. It broke Werner's young heart to see what was happening to Germany. Crushed by the Treaty of Versailles, lands and rights confiscated, inflation running wild, while incompetent bureaucrats floundered and squabbled. Werner couldn't bear to see his mother working herself to death to put a loaf of bread on the table. He wanted better for his ruined country... wanted more out of life.

Drunkenness gave the illusion of knowing all the answers; but he knew he'd wake tomorrow still in despair, and that made him want to drown his frustration in more beer... or in a woman's arms.

He wished he were not still a virgin, at eighteen. Girls liked him, but his mother had instilled him with the fear of God and he always backed away. He was ready now, but he felt so awkward. This angel couldn't possibly want him, or even notice...

She'd seen him! Werner froze, unable to believe his luck when she gestured with an unlit cigarette. Her stare was a magnet. As he wove towards her around lakes of spilled beer and damp sawdust, the cacophony of voices and music receded.

"May – may I join you, *Fräulein*?"

She nodded at the empty stool opposite, leaned forward for him to light her cigarette. He ordered drinks, but noticed she didn't touch the red wine she'd asked for. And her cigarette in its long holder was a mere accessory; she only mouthed the smoke before expelling it. The action was unutterably erotic.

Over her shoulder, Werner saw his friends – five flushed, raucous youths sitting a few tables away – giving him jealous looks and crudely suggestive signals. He ignored them.

Werner was shaking. He hoped she could not smell his sweat.

Her name, she said, was Ilona.

While they talked about nothing in particular, he could not take his eyes off her mouth. Deepest red, like her dress and her hair, her lips were dark petals against her shell-pale skin. The girls he knew – his sisters' friends – were attractive enough in a merry, rosy way, but this woman was different, as quiet and sure as an arrow.

"Are you from Austria?" he asked.

"Vienna," she replied. "A long time ago."

"I recognise the accent!" he said triumphantly. "You should be in a grand hotel with marble pillars and ferns, not this pigsty. You're too beautiful for this."

"Aren't we all? In our own minds, at least."

Ilona, he decided, was strange. She wasn't flirty, but caustic and distant. It never crossed his uncluttered mind that he might secure her services for money. He tried to act like a man about town making a heroic effort to seduce a movie star.

Soon he found her drawing out all his frustrations and dreams, listening as if he were the only man in the room – not shouting him down as his so-called friends did.

"And how would you change things?" she asked. "What would you do?"

Her interest was intoxicating.

"We need a good, strong leader, to kick this country's backside and give us a future. I want my mother to have a beautiful house and servants, my sisters to marry successful men, their children to have a future. We Germans need our pride back!"

Ilona listened, leaning forward on the table, her chin resting on her diamond-encircled forearms, her eyes like black tulips. He stared at her luscious mouth, entranced by the tips of her teeth. He was slurring his words, couldn't help it. *God in heaven, I must have her or die!*

Werner was in full flow when they were interrupted. A man appeared from the crowd and sat beside Ilona without a word of explanation. Werner went rigid, would have hit the stranger if he'd been less drunk.

The intruder gave him a glance, then turned to Ilona as if he didn't exist.

"What are you doing?" His tone was lightly quizzical. Ilona seemed annoyed.

"What does it look like? I don't know what you want, Karl, but go away."

"You asked me to follow you."

"To get you out of Holdenstein before Cesare lost his temper, that's all. I've nothing to say to you. I said it all in Boston, I believe."

Werner witnessed this exchange, outraged but powerless. *If this swine ruins my chance with her...* Then he felt the hairs rise on the back of his neck. Only by observing the man did he realise how extraordinary Ilona was – because Karl was the same. Luminous, elegant, darkly mesmeric.

That was why he couldn't find his voice to protest.

"I disagree," said Karl. "I'm sure you have a great deal to tell me."

"I've already told you too much."

Karl touched her upper arm with blatant affection. Werner was in despair.

"What has Violette done to you, to make you work for Cesare? I thought you despised him."

"I do," Ilona said crisply. "But when it comes to Violette, I happen to believe he's right."

Werner, hearing the words without understanding what they meant, rose unsteadily to his feet. "Get lost, sir. The lady is with me." He lunged at Karl across the table, only for Ilona to stop his fist in mid-air.

It was like hitting a wall. He sat down in shock. How could such a slender hand be so strong? "Don't," she said, pressing his hand onto the table. Her fingernails pricked his skin, as if to hold him there.

Karl's only reaction was a look of faint disdain. Werner thought, *Who the hell does he think he is?*

"He's perfect, isn't he?" Ilona said to Karl. "Young, strong, idealistic, handsome, a little naive. I have a very good eye."

"And Cesare wants them for Pierre?" Karl's eyebrows lifted.

"What else?" Ilona said smoothly.

"You tell me."

"What do you want me to do? Are you going to follow me about trying to save me from myself? Do you want to protect this young man from me? I don't think he'll thank you."

"Do what you will." Karl stood as he spoke. "I've never interfered in your affairs. But I hate to see you being used."

"I'm not! How dare you?"

"Cesare is using you. I never thought you'd allow that to happen." Karl inclined his head with cool politeness, and walked away. Werner watched him, but within seconds he'd vanished among the revellers.

The woman was distracted, her face hard. Werner was so distressed at this exquisite creature being almost within his grasp, only to be torn away, he forgot his manners.

"Who was he?" he demanded. "Your husband? Brother?"

Her attention swung back to him.

"No," she snapped. "He's my father."

"You mean... your priest?"

She started to laugh. He added defensively, "Well, he was hardly older than you!"

"No, he really is my father."

An obvious lie. Werner, agitated and aroused, had no idea how to proceed. "But what was he saying to you, what did he mean?"

"Nothing. Forget him." As she looked into his eyes, he felt something dimming and slipping away inside his mind. His train of thought evaporated. Her eyes were so softly moist, and she was still laughing...

"Can I share the joke?" he said, clasping her hand.

"One day. Don't look so worried. You are a dear boy." She tilted her face towards his, and with an immense rush of excitement, he knew that she was his. He ached to taste her mouth, her neck, her breasts... to leave boyhood behind.

"Now," she said, "are you ready to take me home?"

Alone, Charlotte tried to stop worrying about Karl.

Cesare, another Kristian? She couldn't believe it. But to frighten Stefan, of all people, Cesare must have gained *some* form of sinister influence...

She went out to hunt, losing herself in a river of fire and rubies that reminded her, with overwhelming intensity, how very far she'd come from being mortal.

Arriving home, two hours after midnight, she sensed someone in the house. A whispering, unseen presence, a column of dust.

"Stefan?"

She lit an oil lamp and replaced the stained-glass shade. In the dragonfly scatter of colours, she saw a tall golden shape hovering. Then he materialised fully and gazed at her with terrifying eyes. Cat's eyes of pale gold flame.

Charlotte caught her breath like a human. She took in the bright hair and handsome face of a gilded statue from Greek legend. And when she realised who he was – as if she could forget – her fear surged.

"Don't look so horrified," said Simon. "I'm here to talk."

"Karl will be back soon," she managed to say.

"Not too soon, I hope." Simon smiled. "May I sit down?"

"Can I stop you?"

"Don't be unfriendly." He went to the sofa uninvited, but Charlotte stayed on her feet. Somehow she managed to gather herself.

"The last time I saw you," she said, "you made strenuous efforts to kill Karl and most of our friends."

The fallen angel shook his head. His appearance was breathtaking, and the worst thing was that he reminded her of her brother, David. A man of openness and decency.

"Yes, we had quite a fight, didn't we?" he said without shame. "Especially Karl and I. And yet you survived, for which you earned my admiration. Can you accept my apologies? Let bygones be bygones, as humans say?"

Charlotte gaped at him.

"You came to apologise? It's hard to forget that you starved Karl close to death and tricked him into attacking Stefan and me. As for Violette –"

His handsome face showed no contrition. "Charlotte, my dear, it wasn't personal. We did what was necessary."

"Cruel to be kind?" She lit more lamps. Jewel-colours flared and overlapped, but no amount of light could exorcise this demon.

"Quite. You're so lovely in your tawny silk and lace. You and Karl are both so beautiful. You could have such power if…"

She took a few steps towards him, as on a tightrope.

"If we come with you?"

His eyes were all colours of the rainbow. "Yes, as lovers, friends, helpers, everything."

She swallowed. "What happened to Fyodor and Rasmila?"

"We parted, as I'm sure Karl told you. And doubtless you know that I've joined Cesare and John at Schloss Holdenstein? However…"

She hadn't known, but she believed him. Her imagination seized on dreadful images: Karl arriving at the castle, Simon and Cesare ambushing him… She pushed her anxiety away. If she pleaded to know where Karl was, that would only give Simon more power.

"What's wrong?" she said. "Aren't John and Cesare good enough for you?"

"Oh, they are useful, but they could never be lovers. They're immortal monks, with the sensuality of sackcloth. I need someone warmer. I need you."

"Why?" she whispered. She felt as if she were falling into his eyes.

"You know Violette is our enemy. You won't admit it, but you *know*." His words made her shiver. "We must join forces against her. I know Karl refused, but I'm giving you both a second chance. Join us, or..."

"What? Are you threatening us?"

"I don't need to. If you cling to Lilith, she will destroy you." Simon extended a hand. "Come and sit with me, Charlotte."

She resisted, but her own body betrayed her, pulling her towards him with threads of desire.

"I don't believe you're an angel," she said, an inch away from his fingertips. "To imagine that God has nothing more important to think about than the affairs of men – or vampires – is a childish construct. But it must be a powerful thought-current in the Crystal Ring, and that's why it has infected you."

"No, you're wrong." Simon looked irritated, which pleased her. "If this happened to you – you'd know."

"Safer not to let it happen, then. Otherwise you forget who you are, and lose your sanity. You become a mere cipher for the Crystal Ring – or for God, if you insist."

Abruptly he grabbed her hand and pulled her towards him. She couldn't break free. "You're too clever, Charlotte." With a swift movement, he dragged her onto his lap. "Too analytical."

He gripped her arms. Their faces were very close now. His eyes entranced her and she went molten with desire. His lips parted and she ached to taste his beauty...

Suddenly she realised what was happening, and jerked back, petrified. *Was I about to be willingly unfaithful to Karl?*

Not willingly.

"Don't pull away," said Simon, his hands tightening. "Whom will we hurt? Immortals are above earthly rules. When Karl knows you desire me, he'll come to me too. And you do want me, don't you? Lilith is death but I am life."

Charlotte's face flushed with stolen blood. Simon was stronger than her. If she fled into Raqia he would follow, and if she struggled, he would hurt her. And the dreadful thing was that she didn't want to resist. There was nothing to do but relax, and slide her arms around his neck, and open her mouth to a kiss as fiery sweet and honeyed as blood.

CHAPTER THIRTEEN

THE CLARET-COLOURED VEIL

In Sebastian's absence, Robyn tried to carry on as normal. She would not let him rule her life. The thought of languishing in feverish love-sickness between his visits was abhorrent.

So she attended the usual charity and social functions, lunched with friends, drove down to Cape Cod with Alice in hope that the sea would work its calming magic on her.

She continued to receive Harold as if nothing had happened. But she put off a couple of prospective lovers, no longer interested. Now there was only one man whom she wished to pleasure, torment and ruin...

Sebastian presented the temptation of an impossible challenge.

Kneeling astride Harold, coaxing him to his brief little spasm, she recalled why she used to find sex so depressing. Fortunately he was easy to please. He never minded what mood she was in, never chided her for being brusque. But afterwards, as he entwined his sweating body around hers, he said, "You got someone new, h'mm?"

"Maybe."

"I can tell. It's like you're not here."

"Sorry."

"I hope you're not falling in love with him."

She tried to smile, but her mouth wouldn't co-operate. "I left that nonsense behind at school."

"You're never past it, believe me," he mumbled.

"I'll always be here for you, Harold dear."

But she saw he was worried. Robyn wondered what she'd given away.

Alone, she thought about Josef and his relationship with Violette, Karl and Charlotte. *Does he know what they are? He must, of course! That would explain his evasiveness and strange remarks... "Some of these people are not so nice," indeed!*

And that time I found him in bed, hugging the covers around himself. Hangover, hell! Which one of them...?

She rubbed her forehead, trying to press out her frown. Worrying about Josef was pointless. He might be still in New York or travelling home. Even if she could telephone him this minute, what could she say? Warning him to be careful was only telling him what he already knew. Then he'd wonder how she knew... and she felt strongly that Sebastian must remain her secret.

Oh, there's so much I'd like to ask you, Uncle, she thought. *But you'll never tell me unless I explain why I want to know, and I can't.*

She tried not to dwell on Sebastian, but sometimes she found herself wandering through the house as if searching for something. Often she would turn cold with a sense of being watched...

Infuriating that he could do this to her. She felt she was performing for a ghost audience; always moving, dressing, undressing as if Sebastian could see her.

And thinking, *When will you come to me again?*

"Perfection," Simon breathed, his cheek pressed to Charlotte's as he held her on his thighs. "You and I and Karl. You can't refuse me, because you know..."

He kissed her again and Charlotte let him, aching. She had only one chance to stop Simon, she knew. One chance to control herself.

Even through the rushing drumbeat of desire, with his whirlpool eyes sucking her down, his hands plucking at the buttons of her dress, she knew what to do. She must seem to surrender. Relax into him, like a warm helpless nestling in his lap, so he didn't suspect...

While her mouth moved feverishly over his lips and cheeks, her mind stayed aloof, calculating. Assuming victory, Simon closed his eyes and sighed. Charlotte seized the moment. She drew back her lips and struck.

How strong and thick his neck was, like oak! She feared her fangs would break against his flesh – no, they were through, but she couldn't find a blood-vessel and his fingers were tightening on her arms...

At last she broke through a vein-wall, and blood burst into her mouth. It tasted strange, like red wine turned to vinegar: too strong, but she couldn't stop. This was the only way to weaken him.

"Not yet," Simon whispered, trying quite gently to prise her off.

He hasn't guessed I'm attacking him! she thought. She sank her fangs deeper, drawing hard to drink as deeply as possible before he realised.

She shook with apprehension, even through the bliss of feeding. *If he stops me too soon, he'll punish me and I don't even know if he will weaken like other vampires...*

"Don't," he said. "Charlotte, enough!"

Oh, he understood. She felt him go rigid, his desire swamped by rage. He began to resist, his hands so tight on her upper arms she feared the bones would break.

Simon's strength was great – but so was hers. She stole it from him with every thick, sour mouthful of blood. And even he could not break her purchase.

His hands released her arms only to creep around her throat. Vampires could live without breathing so he couldn't strangle her, yet the pressure still awoke a primeval terror. Charlotte felt the constriction tightening until she could barely force a trickle of blood down her throat... tightening until it seemed his fingers would crush her spine.

She could no longer swallow. Agony filled her skull, but she went on sucking at the wound, the blood escaping from her lips to bubble over her chin and his hands.

Just as pain nearly overcame her, the pressure eased. To her astonishment, Simon's hands slid away and his head tipped back. Charlotte paused. If he was faking surrender to trick her, she couldn't risk mercy. She drank again, wincing as she pushed blood past her bruised windpipe.

Red fire filled her, while Simon was slumped like a fainting human beneath her. Oh, his collapse was real after all...

"So beautiful," he sighed faintly. "I could die for you."

She was only sipping now, too caught up in the divine rhythm to stop. After a few seconds, she felt Simon's hands caressing her back... and she sensed another presence, very dark and definite, watching them.

Karl.

With a stab of dismay, she wondered what he saw. That she was defending herself from Simon, or making love to him? Because she wasn't entirely sure.

With an effort she wrenched her fangs free. Blood ran from her open mouth, soaking his collar. He was too weak now to prevent her escape. As she slithered off his lap, his hands fell away and he made no attempt to keep her there.

Purple-red blood drenched his hands and her dress. It was everywhere.

Charlotte fled to Karl, mortified. His face, half-shadowed, revealed nothing as he looked from her to Simon, who lolled as if someone had stabbed him where he sat. His golden skin was flat beige, all radiance lost.

Karl's arm went around Charlotte. Before she could speak, Simon pushed himself to his feet with a magnificent effort.

To her embarrassment, he kissed her hand and gazed into her eyes.

"Was it as pleasurable for you as for me?" he asked silkily. She'd expected fury, but this was worse. Simon looked at Karl and added, "As they say in the parlance of these times, your wife, my dear fellow, is a jolly good sport."

Karl merely looked at him, his expression frigid.

With that, Simon left – not through the Crystal Ring, but through the door. Charlotte emitted a sigh of relief and despair.

"What happened?" Karl asked coolly. With long, delicate fingers he brushed the drying blood from around her lips.

Charlotte told him everything, even how close she'd come to letting Simon seduce her.

"He wasn't violent, just *persuasive*. Gods, I'm so sorry. The only way to stop him was to feed on him. And he won't give up; I think he'll come back when he's recovered his strength, because he says he wants you, too."

Blood-heat suffused her face. To her own shame, she felt intensely aroused and unable to hide it. She pressed herself to Karl's body, feeling she would melt into him from head to foot.

"Karl..."

Rather than push her away, Karl responded, as if his sovereign compulsion was to please her. And this transition from detachment to passion, she found irresistible.

Later, as they rested on the bedcovers with the first glint of dawn turning their limbs to pearl, Karl said, "I hope you were not thinking of Simon."

"I hope you weren't, either," she said reproachfully.

Karl smiled, his lids half-veiling his eyes. "Love, do you think you have no power to hurt me?"

"I think," she said, looking down at their entwined fingers, "that I don't always like myself, therefore I sometimes can't understand how you can love me."

"Really? If you suspect my love is so fragile, would that drive you to someone else? Violette, Josef, Stefan – even Simon? That's my fear. If you are so unlovable, why do we all adore you?"

"I only want you, Karl," she whispered. "You know I'd die without you. Frightening, but true. Simon tried to tempt me away, but he never could."

"All the same, Simon is dangerous," said Karl. Their faces were close together on the pillow. "Why does he want us both, do you think?"

"To take the place of Fyodor and Rasmila?"

"Or because he thinks we're stronger than John and Cesare? Perhaps he wants us on his side because he's afraid of us."

The thought gave Charlotte, who'd often felt powerless, a thrill of excitement.

"You refused him," she said, "but he won't give up. Karl, I think he was trying to get to you through me. But I won."

Karl breathed out softly, looking grave. "*Liebling...*"

"What is it?"

"Rasmila once played a similar game with me. I was starving

and she gave me her blood, convinced me there was love or at least friendship between us. But her blood put me in her power for a time. Took away my conscience and willpower..."

Charlotte sat up, aghast. "You think Simon's done that to me? God, no, you're wrong!"

"I hope so," said Karl.

Remembering the magnetic evil in Simon's dazzling eyes, she shuddered, thinking, *I wouldn't put it past him to set such a vicious trap.*

"Look at me," she said, turning to Karl and stroking his cheekbone. "Can you see anything wrong? Because if you can, I'll go away. I won't stay and risk betraying or harming you."

Karl's face was lovelier to her than Simon's sun-bright beauty could ever be; his eyes, honey-brown crystal, were infinitely more alluring.

"No, don't leave." His tone was gentle, but the words were a command.

Her voice raw, she said, "But can you kiss me, and lie beside me, and hunt with me... without trusting me?"

The woman, Ilona, took Werner to a cheap hotel room. Once inside, she turned into a vampire.

Werner had never anticipated such pain, such pleasure and fear. His most lurid fantasies bore no resemblance to reality. Ilona rendered him helpless as if staked out for slaughter, and she led him into visions wilder than any fever.

She ravaged and hypnotised him. She dragged him through paradise and left him stranded on the other side, gasping, his body blood-streaked and throbbing with puncture wounds.

Afterwards, she sat above him like a cat, licking her lips. Huge, passionless, intent eyes... A cat seen from a mouse's viewpoint.

He wanted her again. Wanted her forever.

He told her, and she smiled.

"You're very good," she said. "For a virgin, perfectly incredible."

He hadn't admitted that, so his pride was dented. "What makes you think..."

"Never mind. Just be thankful you didn't disappoint me –

because you would have found out the painful way if you had."

Werner began to shiver, his teeth chattering. He seemed to see her through claret-coloured glass.

"But if you want this forever, you'll come with me and do everything I say."

"Anything." He was losing consciousness, pawing at her for help.

"And when I say forever – what was your name?"

"Werner."

"When I say it, Werner, I do mean *forever*."

Then came a long interval of oblivion. A few times he bobbed to the surface of awareness, just enough to gain the impression of being carried by soft-footed monks... Then blackness again.

When he woke, he was lying on the floor of a dungeon. A lone candle flickered on dank walls. For minutes, certain he was dreaming, he could only stare at the barred iron door. Then horror struck him. *God Almighty, this is real!*

Panic ripped through him. He sat up, only for an iron hammer to pound behind his eyes. He collapsed again, moaning.

"Ilona? Where are you? Let me out!"

"She can't hear you," said the dry voice of a spider.

The cell was full of shadows. Werner felt the same unreasoning dread that he'd felt as a child at night, fear of what lay in the dark corner of his bedroom. Now the dread was fulfilled, as a swathe of blackness detached itself and came towards him.

Bony hands grasped him, with nails like thorns. A ghastly face, all hooked lines of cruelty, glared down. Werner caught the abattoir stench of blood and stared in horror at the creature's naked, red-raw scalp and its pointed teeth.

"She delivered you to us," said the demon. "Do you fear God, human scum?"

Werner thought he was in hell, being punished by some mad demon-priest for the sin of fornication. The vampire's fangs were lengthening, as Ilona's had. He writhed in fear.

"Let me go!"

"No, you must repent. Do you fear God?"

"Yes, yes," Werner cried, but the vampire kept repeating the phrase, his voice rising to a frantic shout, the mouth moving closer to Werner's face, red tongue wobbling.

"Do you fear God? Do you fear God?"

Werner began to scream. He wet himself. Then, convulsing in the vampire's claws, he began to sob and cry for his mother.

Outside the cell, Simon and Cesare listened to the screams of their latest recruit. Cesare stood with folded arms, nodding in satisfaction. Simon felt nothing; no pity, no pleasure.

"This Werner is a fine boy," said Cesare. "Ilona chose well again."

"I told you she'd have her uses," Simon said without tone. His encounter with Charlotte had left him so despondent that he had no patience with Cesare's banality. Important, though, to maintain his angelic mask. Draining three victims had partly restored Simon's strength, but he still felt listless, frustrated.

The cries grew fainter but more desperate.

"A mother's boy," Cesare sneered. "John will knock that out of him. The more completely John breaks them, the simpler they are to reshape. Twenty so far; how many more, do you think, before we begin the transformations?"

"As many as you wish," Simon said, trying to sound interested. "But let's keep the number manageable. Thirty should be enough, not an army of thousands."

"Of course. I believe in moderation." Cesare's gaze slid sideways to meet his. "The thousands will follow in good time. They're not just an immortal army against Lilith; they are for the world *after* Lilith."

"The bright new day," Simon murmured.

"Quite so." Cesare's face shone with a soft, radiant smile. "Which reminds me, we should discuss the question of transformation. The order of initiation will be crucial –"

"Don't worry," Simon interrupted. "We'll talk later. All will be well."

Cesare looked reassured. Simon walked away, the human's sobs dwindling but still audible; an irritating noise, like a constantly whining dog. Even when he reached a small chamber at the top of the castle, he could still hear it. He stared out of a narrow window at the forest beyond.

"What you don't realise, Cesare," he muttered to himself, "is that unless we seduce Charlotte, Karl and even Sebastian to our cause, your dreams may never bear fruit. They are the crucial ones. By refusing to join us, they aid Lilith."

So close I came to winning Charlotte... The memory of her fangs piercing his neck burned Simon as much with ecstasy as humiliation. *The fact that she outwitted me only proves me right. With her on Lilith's side, an army of green fledglings will fall like grass to a scythe.*

The grey light rippled. Simon looked round to see two figures emerging from Raqia: his rejected lovers again, Fyodor and Rasmila. Pathetic waifs.

This time, however, they didn't rush to cling around his neck. Instead they greeted him with formal bows, self-controlled and dignified.

"We've given you time to reconsider," said Rasmila. "If you still insist that you no longer want us, we'll accept your word. You will never see us again. But if you'll give us a last chance to prove our love..."

She looked resigned, not hopeful. Fyodor's chalky face was gaunt, like a man facing the gallows. Yet their dignity touched Simon. Or... perhaps his contempt for Cesare and John made him more tolerant of his former companions' failings.

"Well, I make no promises," he said thoughtfully. "But there are matters in which you may be of use, after all."

Their faces lit up. They gasped his name, but he turned his back on their gratitude and incredulous delight. In the depths of the castle, Werner's sobs became the whimpering of an abandoned child.

Five days passed before Sebastian went to Robyn again. To his disappointment, her house was deserted.

He entered and wandered the rooms in darkness, imagining her everywhere, looking at silver-framed photographs on her polished sideboards. Four pretty young women in wide-brimmed hats, laughing in an open-topped car: Robyn and her sisters? A formal Edwardian couple: mama and papa, no doubt. A very young Robyn in a cowboy hat, sitting on a horse. A lean-faced, intelligent-looking man arm in arm with two women... this one had a caption. "Mommy, Josef and Lisl, 1902."

No photographs of the dead husband, no happy wedding scenes.

All her possessions looked expensive, gorgeous. Ornaments, vases of fresh flowers, creamy lace on dark wood. He breathed her lingering scent, imagining her in the parlour, or climbing these stairs... brushing her hair at this dressing table, stretching out on the bed... her tall voluptuous body dappled by moonlight.

Ah, I wish you were home tonight, my Robyn.

Yet he didn't wait for her. A pensive mood fell on him. To see her now would destroy the magic of haunting her empty house. It was as if Robyn, not he, were the ghost.

Sebastian recalled another house he'd loved. He felt the place calling powerfully to him, although it lay across an ocean. Perverse, that he felt more affinity with houses than he ever had with sentient beings.

But the thought of Blackwater Hall reminded him of Simon, Ilona and the others. He cursed. *Am I lingering here*, he thought, *to avoid their intrusions into my life? Perhaps. What of it? I don't want them, but I do want Robyn.*

When he left, he waited another four days before returning. He wanted to punish Robyn a little, for not being there precisely when he'd needed her.

Every knock at the door made Robyn's heart leap and drum in her throat. It was never him, of course. When had he ever bothered to announce his arrival?

Tonight – ten days since she'd last seen Sebastian – she jumped by reflex, then scolded her nerves into submission. *Let Mary answer it*, she thought. Unless it's Harold, I'll play the gracious hostess for fifteen minutes then get rid of them.

A minute later, Mary entered and announced two names that sent a chill through her.

"Mr Victor Booth and Mr William Booth to see you, ma'am."

Russell's brothers. The last people in the world she wanted here, but propriety demanded that she face them.

"Show them in," Robyn said, resigned.

Two young men, with close-cropped brown hair, entered with their hats in their hands.

"Mary, take their coats," she said, but the older one raised his hand.

"There's no need, ma'am. This won't take long. I'm William and this is Victor, my brother."

"Yes, I remember. It's a pleasure to see you," she lied. "How may I help?"

The two were of average height, thickset, as serious as detectives. Neither attempted to shake her hand. Their fleshy, shiny faces recalled their brother, although he'd taken the family's meagre share of good looks to the grave with him.

"You remember our brother Russell, Mrs Stafford?" said William.

Their eyes were dull and hard as gunmetal, accusing. Robyn's invisible armour slid into place. "I know. I was terribly sorry to hear of his death. Won't you have a drink?"

"We don't drink, ma'am," said Victor. His voice was weak, with a strangled note that people must love to imitate. "Neither did Russell, until he met you. Then it seems he drank himself to death."

She had a ghastly feeling of *déjà-vu*: Sebastian in the Booths' garden, insinuating that she was Russell's murderer. But surely Sebastian had no connection to these men? Preposterous... but what if he did?

"I'm afraid I don't know what you're implying, if anything." She spoke lightly, as if this was a friendly conversation.

"I think it's clear enough," said Victor. He was less sure of himself than William. She could take advantage of that.

"Are you suggesting I had something to do with his death?" she said in soft amazement. She moved deeper into the room, while they stayed by the door. Harder to hit a moving target, she thought. "That's unfair. I was fond of your brother. He was a nice guy, the best. We saw each other for a while, but he was so young..."

"Too young to die," said William. "Too young to kill himself over a whore like you. Don't act innocent, Mrs Stafford. Everyone in town knows about you."

"What do you want?" she said sharply.

"We want you out of Boston. Go, or we'll smear your reputation over any town where you try to settle. We will ruin you."

Robyn gave no sign that she'd heard. She pretended to be lost in thought, one hand playing with the slide that held her hair coiled on her neck. The slide came free. Sweeping her hair over her right shoulder – a gesture she'd perfected to seem artless – she was about to begin her appeal, only to be arrested by the certainty that Sebastian was nearby.

She ignored the feeling. Eyes downcast, she said, "Do you really blame me? I thought he'd get over it. I never realised... God, if it's true, I'll never forgive myself!"

She swayed. Victor started towards her, thinking – as she'd intended – that she was going to faint.

"I'm fine," she said as he hovered, looking confused. "What could I do, but end our relationship? I shouldn't have let it begin, I admit that. But what was the alternative to ending it? I hardly think your family would have approved of our marriage, do you?"

She was a faultless, natural actress. Victor was half hers already, so she focused on William.

"If I caused his troubles, I'm sorry. Folk say you're fair, Christian men who wouldn't dream of making such accusations against a widow on her own. Especially not ones based on rumour. You don't actually know me, do you?"

Even William looked less sure of himself. Not finding her the hard-faced witch they'd expected, they didn't know how to proceed. *A few more moments,* she thought, *and they'll be eating out of my hand – or drinking my bourbon, the miserable abstainers.*

Now she would invite them to sit, and she'd ask questions about Russell, perhaps cry a little. Favour one brother, create jealousy, divide them. Playing this game with two at once would be fun.

"Please, make yourselves comfortable," she began. "Whatever you want, let's talk first. You don't object, do you?"

"No, ma'am," William said with reluctance.

As he spoke, she heard a footstep in the hall. Then Sebastian appeared in the doorway. He wore a dark overcoat and looked forbidding, every inch a creature of subtly malevolent strength.

The brothers, still on their feet, stared at him.

"You'd better be leaving now, gentlemen." Sebastian's soft tone was a promise of violence. "If it takes two grown men to intimidate one woman, I think you should be crawling back under your stones while you can still walk. And if you ever come near Mrs Stafford again, you'll be reunited with your brother sooner than you hoped."

Robyn could only stare, incredulous, as William confronted the vampire.

"Whoever you are, sir, this is none of your god-damned –"

Sebastian's hand shot out and landed on William's throat. He appeared to exert no pressure. He fixed the brothers with gleaming eyes, but both men stared back as if he'd produced a gun. William turned grey.

"Out," said Sebastian.

Both men jammed their hats on their heads and fled.

Sebastian turned to Robyn with a look of amusement. "Well, that was easy," he said.

"How dare you!" she exploded.

"How dare I – what?" He appeared stunned by her reaction.

"Interfere in my life!" She felt livid enough to attack him. "You had absolutely no right!"

"Beautiful child, they were threatening you. They deserved the fear of hell putting into them, gutless pigs."

"I was coping perfectly well on my own, thank you! I didn't ask for your help and I don't need it. They came here hating me. They would have left thinking what a warm, wonderful and wronged person I am. Given time, I'd have sent them both the same way as their precious baby brother."

"To the grave?"

"To the bottle! Russell told me the reason they're both teetotallers is that Victor used to be an alcoholic. It would have been my pleasure to make him lapse. I love corrupting evangelists."

Sebastian gazed at her in wonder. "You truly have an evil streak, don't you?" He came to her and stroked her arm. "I thoroughly approve."

"I don't need your approval." She folded her arms. "I'm nothing like you."

"Yes, you are. You're exactly like me."

"Go to hell."

Without visible reaction, Sebastian turned side-on and gazed at the floor. "So, these men," he said. "Would you have gone to bed with them?"

"If necessary."

"Good thing I got here in time, then, is it not? And while we're on that subject, I want you to stop seeing that little old rich man who's always here."

"Harold Charrington?"

"Whoever he is – and although he's old enough to be your father, I assume he's *not* your father, unless you're even more perverse than I thought – you'll stop seeing him."

Robyn gaped at him. "You are absolutely unbelievable."

"Well?"

"You don't come near me for days on end – then you saunter in making ridiculous demands? What gives you the right? And why the hell are you so possessive, all of a sudden?"

Sebastian went quiet. His change of mood alarmed her.

"I want you to myself, Robyn. I don't want other men with you when I'm not." His eyes were enticing, but his possessiveness aggravated her. And she thought, *He could kill me. Just seize and murder me, if I say something he doesn't like.*

Defying him was coldly thrilling.

"You're asking too much. I won't change my life for anyone. And I won't stop seeing Harold. He needs me, I enjoy his money, and he's the only man I don't actively hate."

"Are you saying that you hate me?"

"Of course I hate you," she answered harshly. "What did you think?"

He grinned. He began to laugh.

"What's the joke?" she said, infuriated.

"The joke is this, my dear. The 'brothers grim' came seeking vengeance, when actually it was me who killed your young lover."

The floor sank under her. She felt dull horror, but not surprise.

"How?"

"I met him at the Booths' party. He was hiding upstairs and drinking himself into a stupor because you'd had the effrontery to turn up. When I told you I knew him, I lied. It was the first and last time we met. A young man alone, very drunk because the *Dame aux camélias* had broken his heart, needing a shoulder to weep on. Unfortunately, he chose mine. And I came looking for you afterwards, because his description of you so intrigued me. By the way, he didn't exaggerate."

She was stepping away from him, mouth open with denial.

"You sat and sympathised – then you killed him? And then you came hunting me?" She remembered Sebastian's silhouette in the arbour like a dark dream. "And you had the nerve to come and tell me Russell's death was my fault!"

"Ah, but I take such pleasure from telling lies and being cruel. Don't you?"

"So his death wasn't my fault." Her fingers danced over the back of a sofa as she backed away. "He didn't kill himself over me!"

"And that's all you care about, isn't it?" said Sebastian. "So don't stare at me with those great eyes like saucers. Haven't I made you happy?"

"Get out," she said.

"Oh, Robyn…"

"I mean it." She pointed at the door. "Out, now. Don't ever come near my house again!"

It was possibly the bravest thing she had ever done. She saw a flash of feral rage in his eyes that put her in fear of her life.

Then the look vanished. The vampire shrugged. "If it's what you want, beautiful child, I'll bid you good-night – and goodbye."

With a sweeping bow, he vanished.

She started violently; the trick never ceased to astonish her. Unable to believe he'd gone, she went into the hallway, but there was no sign of him.

Robyn returned to the parlour, walked around the room in nebulous distress. She hurt all over, inside and out. *What's wrong with me? Why did I tell him to go, if it wasn't what I wanted? But it was. I hate him. He's poison. I am right to end it now, before it's too late.*

She heard the front door opening. Every nerve in her body jerked – but it was Alice who came in, her brown coat and hat dewed with rain.

Robyn ran to her.

"What is it?" Alice hugged her like a mother soothing her child. Robyn told her.

"So he's gone for good?" Hope fractured Alice's voice. "We're out of danger? Oh Lord, I pray so!"

Robyn couldn't reply; guilt silenced her. Even knowing the peril she'd placed Alice and Mary in by seeing Sebastian, she hadn't let this stop her. "Oh, don't be upset, dearest. You did the right thing. Just be thankful it's over."

It was not over, Robyn knew.

Robyn couldn't eat, couldn't sleep. Even knowing what Sebastian was, and the vile things he had done, and the danger he posed – still she craved him.

What's he done to me to induce this infatuation? she thought. *It's irrational, disgusting. I won't give in.*

Oh, but to fight with him, to insult and torment and tear at each other – all of that was preferable to being without him.

The next afternoon, after a sleepless night and a miserable day, she went out alone and walked around the town until dusk. She wasn't looking for him, she told herself. She needed to clear her mind, that was all.

Should I employ a vampire hunter? I'm sure Uncle Josef must know one. If we stake him in his lair, will that free me from the curse? Good grief, what nonsense this is.

She walked through the wealthy areas of Beacon Hill and Back Bay. The tall houses with their bowed fronts seemed to grin at her in the gloom. She glanced into their lighted windows, seeing cosy family worlds from which she was forever excluded. She didn't want them, anyway. Their cosiness was an illusion; she knew the callous husbands, cruel parents, petulant sons and daughters who warred behind the facades. But their worlds looked warm and she was cold, even in her thick red coat.

Wandering down Beacon Street and into the Public Garden, she sat on her favourite bench by the lagoon. Squirrels scampered towards her, rising expectantly on their haunches; so dear, with their bright eyes and tufted ears, but she had no food to keep them around her. Instead she watched ducks on the water. The summer colours were beginning to turn; the beeches tipped with burnished bronze, the elms glowing, the maidenhairs edging towards gold. Time to go home, she told herself. But she remained there, huddled up in her coat, dejected. Her life, she realised, had no point at all.

And then he was there, standing beside her, hands in his pockets and his collar drawn up as if he were cold; his presence as natural and ordinary as that of any human.

"So here you are," he said.

"I'm often here." She didn't look round, but she saw his black coat from the corner of her eye. "It's my favourite place."

"I know. Did you hope I'd remember?"

"Maybe." She spoke quietly, all anger burned out, only relieved that he'd found her.

"If so, I'm glad," he said.

"Glad that I'm stupid?"

"Robyn." The vampire sat down a few inches from her. "Robyn, Robyn."

"Were you looking for me, after everything I said?"

"I respected your command not to come to your house. I don't believe you placed any restriction on meeting in the park." He sighed faintly. "It's hopeless, really, isn't it?"

His arms slid around her. She let him hold her, her gloved hands finding their way around his waist. The feel of his body through layers of material, his uncanny aura, the dark beauty of him, all filled the void. She wanted his soothing, seductive embrace. Needed it.

"Hopeless, keeping away from each other," he said.

She let the moment wash over her. *There will be no foolish admissions, no angry words*, she promised herself. Just this. A quiet relief, almost like sleep.

He moved to look at her. His expression was soft, concerned, sombre: lovely woodland light and shadows. The look seemed genuine, but she knew he was an actor, like her.

"You're a bad girl," he said.

"Am I?"

"Yes. You haven't been eating properly. I won't have you wasting away. Come along now, I'm taking you for dinner."

He stood up, pulling her with him. Not resisting, she laughed. "But who is going to be dinner? Me?"

"Funny."

"Shall I order steak *tartare*, to keep up my strength?"

They went to the restaurant on the waterfront where they'd met the first time. This time Sebastian made no pretence of eating. He simply smiled at Robyn while she worked her way through four courses, and finished them all. She'd been weak from hunger without realising. They hardly spoke. There seemed no need; their silent communication was continuous, a sort of resignation to their fate, edged with black irony. They were completely at ease with each other.

And both were thinking, *What the hell is going to happen now?*

Afterwards, they walked arm in arm through the old town, past the graceful buildings that had helped to shape history. When passers-by glanced at them, Robyn felt a delicious if reprehensible sense of conspiracy. *You don't know what Sebastian is but I do!*

"What does it feel like," she asked as they walked through pools of gaslight, "to drink blood?"

"Tell me what it feels like to drink brandy, or to make love," he said. "You can't."

"Better than sex?"

The corners of his mouth rose enigmatically. "Different."

"But how does it feel to know that they can't stop you?"

"Extremely exciting," he said candidly.

She shivered. "And it gives you special pleasure… to kill?"

"Now I never said that." He spoke sharply. "We have to feed. Killing, murder, whatever you call it, is not my object. The blood, the bliss of drinking, is what matters. If the source of blood dies, I take no pleasure in that, I assure you." He added, as if to eliminate doubt, "No pain, either."

"No guilt."

"Why should I feel guilty? Do you feel guilty about the bloody steak you just consumed?"

"Don't tell me your victims are no more than cattle to you," Robyn said acidly. "I don't play mind games with a bullock before I eat a slice of him. I don't go to bed with him, either."

"Where's your sense of adventure?"

She ignored his flippancy. "Well, am I merely food to you?"

"You know you aren't." His tone became low and tender. "You know you're much more than that."

"I don't know anything of the sort."

"Let me walk you home, anyway."

They went very slowly across the Common, where little white lights glittered in the branches. Behind them, crowds were emerging from theatres in Tremont Street. But the park and the night, the dome of the State House rising like a golden moon beyond the trees, belonged to them.

"I meant what I said," Robyn continued. "I won't be ordered around, and I won't change my life for you."

"And I meant what I said." He spoke with equal fervour. "I want you to myself."

"What's made you so possessive?"

He pulled her in a half-circle so she had to stop and face him. His pale hand moved over the fabric of her hat, along her cheek, coming to rest on her left shoulder. He looked human: full of conflict, tenderness, determination, indecision. His great dark eyes shone.

"What would you say," he asked, "if I told you I'm in love with you?"

"I'd say you're a liar."

He laughed. "Oh, you're cruel. Sensible, though. Vampires can't love. But I need to see you. Do you believe that?"

"Yes."

"And do you feel the same?"

"I feel," Robyn said quietly, "that I don't trust you."

"Not at all?"

"Not the merest fraction."

A silence. They walked on. Her hands were linked through his left arm, her head resting on his shoulder. Now and then his right hand moved across to clasp her hands in the crook of his elbow.

"Will you invite me in tonight?"

"Not tonight," she replied, although she wanted him desperately. "Why should I let you satisfy yourself then disappear for days?"

"You're right. I wasn't going to accept, anyway."

"Oh, sure."

THE DARK BLOOD OF POPPIES

"It's true. Because if I don't disappear, if I were here every night
– however much we want each other – it would not be long before
I lost you."

In his face, webbed with light and shadow, she saw a terrible
look that froze her. A look from a landscape of bleak hills, of
ice-winds blowing between dark standing stones. She'd thought
it impossible to feel any sympathy for him, but somehow her
sympathy slipped its leash.

"My God, you're lonely," she said, astonished.

"Oh yes. The myth of the lonely vampire." He kissed her
cheek with cold lips. The chilling look stayed on his face and self-
mockery darkened his voice. "Who can resist it?"

Sebastian stepped up to Robyn's front door with an armful of red
roses, so deeply coloured they were almost black. It was Mary's
night off, so the unfortunate Alice opened the door to him.

As Sebastian presented the roses, Robyn was very aware of
Alice in the parlour doorway, staring hard at her mistress. Her
face was waxen, her eyes brimming with horrified questions.
What is he doing here? You said it was over! You promised!

"Would you put these in water, please?" Robyn said, hurrying
to her. "Alice, don't look at me like that. It's all right. Leave us."

Alice gave the bouquet a glare of contempt. "Deal with them
yourself, madam. I won't touch anything of his."

She walked out with dignity, heading upstairs to her room. As
she went, Robyn bundled Alice's feelings into a closet in her mind,
and slammed the door.

"Your companion doesn't like me," Sebastian said ruefully.

Then he and Robyn fell on each other as if starving. His coat
fell, the roses fell. He began to unbutton her dress, nipping her
neck, his teeth growing sharper until he drew blood.

"No, no, not here," she said, fighting him off. "Come upstairs."

Their coupling was brief, ferocious, sharp as rose thorns. He
bit her just as she reached the peak of bliss, so she felt pain and
pleasure together. The sensation was like being drawn down a
silvery, glittering strand of barbed wire, dripping with poison and
narcotic crimson flowers.

When the fire subsided, they broke apart, gasping. And then they held each other and wept.

Summer became fall, turning New England to flame. Robyn and Sebastian drove out to the mountains of New Hampshire and Vermont to see rolling waves of apricot and gold, of bronze and toffee-brown and limpid yellow, preternatural tints of scarlet and deep maple-red, dazzling all the senses.

"You like this, don't you?" said Robyn, as if she could hardly believe a vampire could retain an appreciation of nature.

Then it was Christmas, which meant nothing to Sebastian and very little to Robyn, as far as he could tell. She paid a short visit to her family and returned to tell him that the gathering had been polite but strained. Meaningless. She was glad it was over.

Snow fell, wrapping Boston in luminous softness. The city glittered by day and glowed by night, as if it had drifted backwards into another, more idyllic time.

Sebastian loved the chilly New England winter, the rain and snow and the cold sea-scented wind. They reminded him of Ireland. He wasn't at home here, had never felt at home anywhere... except at his mansion in County Waterford.

He would have gone there now, if not for Robyn holding him like a magnet in this prim old-fashioned town. He'd been visiting her for months now, once a week or more often if he could refrain from tasting her precious blood. Sometimes, with cheeks as pale as magnolia petals, she would beg him not to feed on her that night. Sometimes he would acquiesce; at others, he would take her anyway, leaving her furious, or silently hating him, or languid and tender...

Every time was different. One night they tore at each other with hatred, the next with passion. That was why he couldn't leave.

Every day he would make a decision. *I'll kill her soon. I've teased her enough. It's time to leave.* Yet when the moment came, he couldn't. He made excuses: *I'll wait until I'm tired of her, so sated that she's no more than a husk.* Or: *she's not quite in love with me yet. There's still suspicion in her eyes. When she lets down her guard and trusts me completely – that's the time to strike.*

But now, with the snow falling in great flakes past her windows, they lay entwined in bed, warm as nestlings in down. The taste of her blood was lush in his mouth; the scents of her hair, perfume, skin, the natural musk of her body, all filled his senses. Her eyes were half-closed, sultry with pleasure. She hadn't resisted tonight. When he'd pierced the vein, she'd clutched him, as if thrusting herself deeper, finding a way to love the pain. And in the afterglow, she seemed content.

"Now, you're not finding this so terrible, are you?" he asked, gently teasing her.

She was happy, unguarded. "If you must know..." She stretched, the warm weight of her breasts sliding over his ribs. "It's kind of a masochistic addiction. Rather a dangerous habit to develop, isn't it?"

"Do you still hate me for it? Is hating men an addiction in itself? Have you found us all such monsters?"

"Of course. What else? My father, my husband..." Words began to flow out of her: her miserable marriage, how her injured soul hardened, scarred by rage into a cold, vengeful pearl. Sebastian spoke too – his words weaving through hers – of a love that turned to bitter wormwood, and his revenge.

"Her name was Mary, like your little maid. Her hair was fair too, and my Mary was beautiful, a tall fine woman. But we'd been married a long time with no children, and I badly wanted a child to inherit the estate or my work would all be for nothing."

"You're talking about a time when you were human?" The wonder in her voice drew him on, like fire-glow to a storyteller.

"At the end of the seventeenth century, beautiful one. In a country where religion is so real that people will persecute and kill each other for it. Centuries, my family fought to keep our property out of English hands. My father and brothers fled to France – but I stayed, and I did a very terrible thing. I converted from Catholic to Protestant, which entitled me to claim the estate. Do you understand? I betrayed my religion, my family and my people, in order to seize my father's demesne."

"So you had no principles in those days, either," said Robyn.

"I had ambition. For me, changing religion meant little, because I was never pious. My Catholicism was more instinct than belief... a feeling that there were sinister meanings behind the surface, that the saints were really older gods... But understand, it wasn't greed that moved me, it was passion. I loved that place too much to lose it, even for the sake of family loyalty. As for Mary, I thought we loved each other... but I took her for granted, I thought that to build a grand house was enough to prove my devotion. When she fell pregnant I was overjoyed, I thought that we'd be the perfect family in our magnificent new house. But the child wasn't mine."

"Oh," whispered Robyn.

"She said I was never there, that I couldn't give her children, so she'd taken up with someone else and she was running away with him." Even after all this time, he felt a twinge of old pain.

"What did you do?"

"I meant to kill myself."

"I can't imagine you contemplating that!" Robyn said, shocked.

"But I was human. Distraught. My future, my wife and child were gone from me, so there was no point in a new house. Blackwater Hall was a shell, mocking me. I intended to burn it down and die in the fire. But someone stopped me. They say Irish Catholicism is only a step away from paganism, that the faerie folk were never destroyed, only assimilated and made into saints so people could still worship without heresy. The old gods never left, only vanished into sea and stone, tree and sky. And that night, as I set about destroying my future, three of them came along and did the job for me. Three ancient gods with burnished skin and terrible fiery eyes. They transformed me."

"Why?"

"I don't know," he answered slowly. "They saw the makings of a perfect vampire in me, and it's hard to say they were wrong, isn't it? But the strangest thing is that they spoke as if the Old Testament God had sent them. That seemed wrong: surely they were gods even older than him? But they claimed to serve this God, insisting that vampires are legitimate punishers of mankind. Like plagues and floods."

"What an interesting point of view." Robyn's eyes widened.

"Theology was the last thing on my mind. I cursed them for changing me, but in fact they'd freed me from mortal weakness and conscience. Instead of destroying myself, I went after Mary and her lover."

"You killed them?"

"Yes. Showed Mary how much I loved her by draining her blood. And it was very easy, Robyn. I relished it. Because mortal passions no longer mattered, you see? And then I left Ireland. The house still draws me back sometimes… but only the house, nothing else."

"So you don't feel anything now? You just pretend… as I do?"

They were both saying too much. Their eyes met in a flash of mutual panic, and a slow recoil began.

"Oh, I feel, dear Robyn."

"Yes. You hate women and I hate men, yet here we are together…"

"But I have the advantage," he said, "because I hate men too. I despise them all, male, female, human, vampire."

"You care for me, though, don't you?" Her eyes gleamed: imperious, not pleading. "You spared my life. You protected me from Russell's brothers. You can't stay away."

"Don't you love me?" he said. "Just a little?"

"I'd never admit it if I did."

"So you do."

"And you're waiting for me to say yes, so you can seize the moment to destroy me?" The gleam hardened to a diamond sparkle. "Oh, I see through you, Sebastian."

"Because it's what *you* would do." The way she outguessed him was irritating. "Only bear in mind that you can't ruin my reputation, because I don't possess one. You can't break my heart, or my body. But, Robyn, you live or die at my whim. I only have to threaten your precious maids to put you in a fit of panic. But really, to break your heart, all I need do is to leave you."

Her face was sullen, her lower lip demanding to be kissed and bitten. When he tried, she turned her face aside, so his mouth met her smooth warm cheek.

"If you order me to leave," he murmured, "I might not come back."

"Are you so arrogant as to believe that I'm not just using you for my pleasure, as you're using me?" she retorted. "You say I have no way to protect myself. Well, you may be right… but there is Violette."

The name startled him, like sunlight flashing from a dark mirror. "Violette?"

"The dancer. You do know she's a vampire, too?"

"Of course." But he failed to hide his shock, and she grinned.

"But you didn't know that she was here before you." Robyn's smile became laughter. "You're not my first would-be vampire lover, you know. She didn't play games. She wanted me. She said that if ever I needed her help, just to let her know. I can get in touch with her very easily, Sebastian."

He remembered the night of the party; Robyn drifting past him in the garden... and another presence he hadn't registered because Ilona had distracted him. *Violette*! Inwardly cursing both Ilona and the ballerina, he said, "You're lying."

"I couldn't make this up, believe me. Are you afraid of her? Something tells me she's as strong as you. One telegram... oh, you'd have time to kill me before I even sent it, but if you do – she will know. She'll come after you. Maybe she'll bring her friends."

Sebastian, thrown off-guard, could not reply. He was furious. What Robyn said about Violette was true: she was almost certainly a match for him. He thought, *Now will I regret dismissing Simon's warning?*

"Very clever," he said at last. "So we're equal. But do you want her or me?"

Her eyes darkened. "You," she said. "Without the threats."

A terrible feeling filled his heart, like a trapped raven.

"Too late, my love." He stared down at her, letting the icy poison of his soul infuse his face. She blanched. Her face stiffened with terror and she strained to avoid him, but he felt no pity.

"Do you really think I ever felt anything for you but contempt?" he said.

He left her side without a kiss, dressed quickly and stepped into the Crystal Ring. Robyn, wide-eyed with shock, uttered no word of protest.

Sebastian had to leave before the fatal web of love ensnared him forever. This time he had no intention of going back, ever.

* * *

The demon-vampire, John, kept a severed head in the dungeon. Night and day, it grinned down at Werner from the sill of a narrow embrasure.

Each lightless day, John would enter and torment Werner; feed on him, inflict physical torture, mock him. Once Werner was a bedraggled heap on the flagstones, John would lecture him for hours about God.

Werner's terror, John insisted, was a lack of enlightenment. Weeping for mercy showed rebellion.

"Until you shed your fear," said John, "you aren't worthy to serve the great Leader."

What leader? Werner had no idea why he was being held prisoner. He was ill, starving, desperate to go home to his mother. *I've repented a thousand times but John still won't say what he wants of me!*

Then one day, it happened. Werner woke and found his fear gone. Washed up on the edge of insanity, he was crushed, empty, blank. He anticipated nothing but death.

The cell door opened and John's gargoyle face glared down at him. Werner waited indifferently for the torment to begin. "If it's God's will," he murmured, "I submit."

Nothing happened. Past caring, Werner drifted into sleep, only to wake again to a blinding light.

Only a lamp, but it hurt his eyes like the sun. Squinting, he made out a group of men around him, immeasurably tall, with radiant firm flesh and bright hair. Teutonic gods, they seemed. Werner stared, one hand flung across his forehead.

One was brighter than the rest, filling the cell with glory. *Lucifer*, a voice whispered in Werner's fractured brain. *Fallen angel, Star of the Morning.*

A smaller figure leaned down and took Werner's hand. Less dazzling but equally powerful, he seemed as clear as a diamond. A holy man with the world's future in his ice-grey eyes.

Werner was transfixed. This man carried the air of one who'd passed to a higher plane from which he observed the petty turmoil of Earth. His solid certainty of purpose lanced straight to the vacant core of Werner's soul.

"Poor child," said the saint. "How you've suffered. But you survived the test. Are you ready to join us with a pure heart?"

Werner's empty heart brimmed with hope. He was so grateful for a little kindness that he would give his life for this man. Leader. Saviour.

He reached out, his mouth open with yearning. *Yes, take me into your world, save my soul!*

"Patience," said the leader. He lifted Werner to his feet and kissed him on both cheeks. "I'm Cesare. These men will bathe and feed you. They are your friends; they've all been through the darkest night, as you have, and will help you to understand that iron must be hammered in order to forge it. You'll learn to serve alongside your comrades. A long path, but prove yourself worthy and you will be elevated to our rank."

Werner could hardly breathe for wonder. Not merely to serve, but to *join* them!

Cesare's promise healed all wounds. He realised that Ilona had not abducted but rescued him. This leader, with his clear-sighted strength, was the saviour of whom Werner had always dreamed.

There was a future after all. The love radiating from these glorious beings eclipsed what he'd felt for Ilona, even for his mother. What could compare? Overcome, he wept.

I've entered Valhalla.

Falling to his knees, he kissed the saviour's hands. "I am your servant, my lord Cesare, my king. I pledge you my life."

"Your pledge is accepted." The leader's voice was a sweet blessing.

All around him, the young men who shared Werner's dreams smiled in approval.

CHAPTER FOURTEEN

FIREBIRD

From the moment she conceived the new ballet, Violette was obsessed. It blossomed within her day by day, so in rehearsal she was explaining what she wanted of her dancers even as it came into her head. She didn't tell the truth behind the story. She named the characters Siegfried, Anna and Lila, with assorted peasants and forest-spirits.

Her instincts were true. The ballet was destined to be as magnificent as any of the classics. Elated from their success in America, the company generated an atmosphere of feverish enthusiasm. When she commissioned music for the project, the composer responded as if inspired by angels.

She called the ballet *Witch and Maiden*.

But there was an element missing. An ending.

Charlotte and Karl had gone home to Switzerland. Violette missed Charlotte, but at least she was not constantly reminded of her darker side. Some days she almost convinced herself she was human... until the thirst began.

One night Charlotte came to see her. They met in the studio, where oblongs of light fell through the windows to ripple with snow-light from the mountains, glass-green reflections of the river Salzach. The glow was infinitely lovely to vampire eyes.

"You're in danger," said Charlotte. She leaned against the barre, her dress of bronze silk and lace beautiful in the light. "Almost everyone you've upset is at Schloss Holdenstein, and Cesare's elected himself their leader. They want revenge."

Violette was unmoved, apart from a stirring depression. "How have I upset Cesare? I don't know him."

"But he knows of you. He's a fanatic. I'm sure it took no effort for others to convince him that you're the Antichrist."

"Who told him? Pierre and Ilona?"

"Yes, and John. Simon's with them, too."

"Simon." She felt a dull wave of foreboding. "And Stefan? Rachel?"

"No, Stefan's in hiding to protect Niklas. No one's seen Rachel. I hardly know her so I can't speak for her. But as for the others, I'm afraid they're planning to attack you."

Violette smiled. "Do you think they'd dare?"

"Don't underestimate them. The Crystal Ring can give us strange powers." Charlotte looked candidly at her. "It can take them away, too. We can't take anything for granted."

"Well, thank you for warning me."

"I'm serious. Simon came and tried his hardest to persuade Karl and me onto their side. Perhaps he succeeded, I don't know."

"What do you mean?" Violette's faint anxiety jumped to a higher pitch.

"I drank his blood. Karl fears it may have put me in his power."

"Any symptoms?"

Charlotte shook her head. "But how can I know? Something might happen without me being aware, or able to stop myself."

"You mean you might go for my throat? I don't think you'd win." Violette moved towards the windows. "I don't want to hurt you, or anyone. But it's what Lilith does when she feels threatened... I won't harm them, as long as they stay away!"

"I can't persuade them to do that. They're frightened. They seem to think you've been sent by God to test them."

"Perhaps I have," Violette said softly. Turning, she saw concern in Charlotte's eyes. "Are you sure you're right to defend me?"

"Yes. I brought you into this, and I love you. If they kill you, they can take me too."

"And Karl?"

Charlotte didn't answer. "I should go."

"Yes, go, Charlotte. I appreciate your concern, but all I want to think about is dancing."

Charlotte vanished, without a kiss, looking desperately sad. Violette was on the verge of following, but restrained herself. *I've no room for sentiment. I must think about the end of this ballet, nothing else!*

However, Violette couldn't get the conversation out of her mind. Images of violence plagued her. She remembered their terrified faces as she plunged fangs and nails into their flesh: Matthew, Pierre, Rachel, Ilona...

She needed to escape. Melting into Raqia, she left Salzburg behind and flew to the Alps. There she walked for hours, oblivious to the cold, relishing the wildness of the mountains. A bitter wind wailing from the peaks blew ice needles into her face, chilling her from head to foot. Numbing the pain.

She hadn't wanted to loiter in the Crystal Ring. It was too sinister, full of mysteries and accusations. No, the clean harshness of nature was the place to confront Lilith, to catch her black wings and bring her down.

What are you? Violette cried.

I am night, said Lilith. *I am blackthorn winter and the death of dreams. I am madness and cruelty and fever, I am disobedience and disappointment and disease. I am the laughter of demons and the tears of God and the Devil's bride. I am all your worst fears.*

You are many things, said Violette. *You are a demon lover, a storm spirit and a night hag. You exist in every mythology. You have always been here.*

Always, Lilith agreed. *And I have a special affinity for blood.*

But why? What are you?

Look harder. You're looking but you can't see me.

Violette tried. A great curtain of ink flowed across her mind. Searching for Lilith was like groping for the end of the ballet. But she was looking at nothingness. What she'd taken to be Lilith was only a dead end, a wall of blackness. The real Lilith moved somewhere behind the wall but Violette couldn't reach her, couldn't grasp the truth.

Why can't I find you?

I am a Black Virgin in a shrine, Lilith informed her. *I am a black stone in the earth. I am the end of all things.*

But who are you?

I am you, said Lilith.

"Then why can't I remember?" Violette cried. "How can I know I'm you, yet not understand?"

Because, said Violette-Lilith, *you are talking to yourself.*

Crouching beside a rock in her thin lavender dress, the ice storm battering her, Violette screamed her anguish.

No one heard. The storm and the mountains ignored her.

After a time she stood, entered the Crystal Ring, and surged through the rolls of liquid cloud towards the south.

Again she'd denied herself blood, even knowing it was foolish. Thirst unhinged her. Her mind filled with the flapping of ravens, the maddening enigma of Lilith. *Black because she is veiled...*

Violette thought of Lancelyn, the arrogant human mage who'd tried to unveil her. He'd called her the Black Goddess, bringer of wisdom, madness or death to those who penetrate her.

He'd been so certain of finding wisdom, but Violette had brought him madness. She'd destroyed him for his arrogance... yet the memory still needled her. What if he had been able to unveil Lilith's mystery? *It's obvious I can't unveil myself. If I'd swallowed my pride, let him make an altar of me – perhaps the ritual would have enlightened us both.*

But no, Lilith kept the veil closed. It was not what she wanted. And she must always have her own way.

Lilith was pulling her towards another horizon now.

Violette couldn't forget Rachel's visit, or the terrible sense of being hated purely for existing. She remembered Lilith's rage, which had made her tear off Matthew's head, compelled her to bite Rachel's long, slender neck and swallow her fierce blood.

How could they ever forgive her?

Violette felt the pressure of hatred building against her. She sensed it in the Crystal Ring, where every tremor seemed to express a human nightmare or a vampire's tortuous thoughts. Sometimes it happened that Lilith's sixth sense caught the wavelength of an individual... And now she was thinking of Rachel, a victim of Lilith who'd simply disappeared. So many questions Violette needed to ask... How to find her, though?

Let Lilith guide me, she thought. *Don't fight. Let go...*

She was a dark rag tossed on a sea of blue-black waves.

Crimson light dripped endlessly down the chasm walls above her.

This realm is made of the fragile energy of thought-waves, so Charlotte says. And every vampire is part of it, so we each leave a vibration, a trace of our existence here. She recalled an analogy made by Charlotte-as-scientist.

"Imagine the Crystal Ring as a cloud chamber. If human thoughts represent water vapour, then vampires are the atomic particles. Chains of bubbles form in our wake to mark our path."

Raqia flowed inside Violette-Lilith, indivisible from her.

She saw a statuesque man with skin like burnished coal, walking across a parched golden plain. A single African, walking under a vast sky, watched by lionesses... and she knew he was a vampire.

And that was where Rachel was. Africa.

A long journey, but Violette couldn't turn back. She climbed very high, almost to the *Weisskalt*, and travelled so fast that she terrified herself. *Perhaps*, she thought, *I could also travel to America in a night...*

She found them at dawn, as the sun bleached the hem of night. Insects sang in the grass. She saw a single white tree on the plain, and beneath it Rachel and the African were sitting cross-legged, like travellers sharing stories. They wore loose white garments to deflect the sun. Rachel's hair was an orange flame against the whiteness.

"Good morning, Rachel," said Violette.

The woman started as if seeing a ghost; she turned a shade paler, if that were possible. The man looked up as if nothing could surprise him. He was muscular, his skin burnished ebony; he would tower over her if he stood.

"Oh, my God," said Rachel.

"Not exactly. Try the other side." Violette knelt, facing them. A snake slithered away from under her knees, rustling through the dry grass. "Won't you introduce me to your companion?"

Rachel recovered herself and became cool, tense, self-controlled. "Malik, Violette."

"Malik. I've heard of you. You're one of the immortals who escaped the *Weisskalt* when Kristian died. One of the few who hasn't threatened me. Yet."

She studied his long, sombre face, his velvety eyes. He looked back serenely until she wondered if he spoke English. Then he said, "I have no reason to threaten you, Lilith." His voice was bass-deep, soothing. "You are no threat to me."

A hot wind sprang up, stirring grass and leaves. "Am I not? Do you mean that if we fought, you'd win?"

"No," he said. "I mean that I don't fear your bite. And you have no desire to attack me."

She gazed at Malik, trying to perceive what he meant. She realised he spoke the truth. He raised no anger in her whatsoever. Why was he different?

She turned to Rachel. "You're a long way from home."

"But Malik isn't. This continent is his home, the savannah, the desert, the jungle. He hates what we call 'civilisation'."

"What about you? Did you come all this way to escape me?"

"At first. I was afraid."

"Is that why you're not with the others?"

"What others?"

"Those who are plotting to kill me."

"I don't want to kill you," said Rachel. "I thought if I saw you again, I'd be terrified – but I'm not."

Rachel had changed, lost her acerbity and remoteness.

"I'm not here to frighten you," said Violette. "I only came to see what happened to you."

"You cared, after all?" Rachel's tension softened. "I thought you were another Kristian, but you're not. Malik and I are the same. We loathe Kristian and his kind, with their mania for power. I fled here out of fear, but I stayed because I belong here." She smiled, her mouth as red as her hair. "I love this solitude. The freedom to walk these great plains without fearing any hunter, whether they wield claws or spears."

"When did you discover this?"

Rachel raised her long fingers to her collarbone. "When you drank my blood. You stopped me dead like a wall and made me see that in making demands on you, I was behaving like Kristian. Don't you realise, Violette, that you can't merely feed? You change people."

"I know," Violette whispered. "Not always for the better."

"Nor for the worse." Rachel leaned forward and kissed Violette full on the mouth. "I'm not your enemy."

Violette felt a flicker of desire, a poignant echo of Robyn's presence. Lovely moment.

Rachel sat back on her heels and leaned on Malik's shoulder. They gazed intently at her, pale and dark like chess pieces. Violette was suddenly afraid.

"You two see something that I can't see for myself. What is it?"

"Darkness and evil are not the same thing," said Malik. "When you understand, you'll know more than I can tell you. But you must find the truth for yourself."

"You're right."

"Will you take Malik's blood, too?" asked Rachel.

Violette studied the tempting skin of his throat, so black it had a blue sheen. His calm eyes held wisdom she couldn't yet decipher. *Dive through the layers of darkness beyond the veil, let in the lovely silver light...* Her heart quickened, and she had to look away. "No," she said.

"Why not?"

"Because Malik does not need to change."

Violette had expected to meet an enemy and instead found – dare she think it? – two friends. Or at least, two who didn't despise her.

She raced northwards through Raqia, not feeling the cold.

Could I have persuaded them to fight with me? I doubt it. They don't want that, and neither do I. I suppose I could draw an army of adoring followers, throw them against Cesare's and watch them slaughter each other, as if I were some gloating goddess of war.

That's why I drive them away – because they'd love me so easily if I let them, and I would destroy them. Cesare and Simon are right about me, and that's why I must face my enemies alone.

Violette wished she could stay in Africa under the burning sky. Or in the desert, Lilith's wilderness. Impossible. Chains drew her home. *And,* she thought, *I might have grown to envy Rachel and Malik's love, another triangle from which I feel excluded.*

But why envy anyone, when I despise love and its lies?

She knew that the comfort she'd sought in Robyn was an illusion. *Yes, it broke my heart to reject her, but she would never have loved me fully, because her deepest desires are for men.*

Violette thought of Charlotte, who was generous with her affections, but who loved Karl more than her own life. She wasn't sure she could bear to see Charlotte again without seizing her and piercing her divine throat... spending all her frustration on a carnal wave of blood.

Again she pictured Robyn, and Malik's eyes telling her to follow her instinct. The ache of missing Robyn, struggling to finish the ballet, and fighting Lilith's thirst, were all one. She changed direction. Magnetic lines drew her like gold threads, westwards above the Atlantic. She felt she could travel forever without rest or blood.

Another night and day before I arrive home, she thought. *Two days of rehearsal lost. And my girls will worry...*

But the journey would be worth it to catch one glimpse of Robyn's face.

If only I can find an answer there.

Robyn felt cool, strong and in control. She told herself the feeling would last, and it did – for a full five minutes after Sebastian had left. Then she broke down.

It was like bereavement. Like falling, this hideous feeling of being gouged hollow, torn to shreds on a cold wind. She curled up, head between her elbows, hands folded on the back of her head. The effort of not crying was agony.

Come back, come back. What are we doing, why must it be like this?

Morning came. The day dragged and died. The night was eternal. And then it all began again.

Robyn carried on, but her spirit had gone. Alice fussed, the doctor came and went, Harold brought flowers and chocolates and diamonds; nothing mattered. She didn't want to eat, or talk, or sleep, or think. Somehow she forced herself, but the effort was exhausting.

She thought of Violette.

He's punishing me for threatening him with Violette. For how long? Oh, Sebastian, come back so I can live again!

One night, three weeks later, she dreamed of the dancer.

She came to Robyn, lily-pale in the moonlight, black hair loose around her shoulders. She wore a floating garment and walked *en pointe* out of nowhere. She stood looking down at Robyn, then extended her long slender hand to stroke Robyn's cheekbone.

"Don't be afraid," Violette said in the dream. "I want you and your blood so much that I could die... What would you say? Would you die for me too?"

Robyn couldn't speak. When their eyes met, Violette looked straight into her and saw all her secrets.

"You love someone else, is that it? But they've left you in pain." A spasm crossed her face. "Not in a million years could they love you as I do. When I left I thought the feeling would pass, but it hasn't. Why didn't I seize the chance? I can't bear to see you suffer at the hands of a callous lover... and I could end it, dearest. Make you forget everyone and be mine forever."

"Do it," Robyn tried to say, unsure whether she'd actually spoken. "Take away the pain."

Nothing ever changes, thought Violette, looking at Robyn's beloved face, her lustrous brown hair spread on the pillow, the lace collar of her nightdress cupping her chin. *I still love her. She's like the only house in a wilderness, the only fire in winter.*

But I can't do it. I want her to stay as she is, whole and warm, not broken by Lilith's savage caress.

Violette trembled, wishing she hadn't come after all.

I love you but I can never have you.

Any more than Charlotte could have me, or Karl could have Charlotte, without turning us into monsters. If Robyn became a vampire she'd no longer be herself, but as my human lover she'd go mad and die... So I must leave her. Even if some dastard breaks her heart, she must heal in her own way, live her natural life...

But love and desire drew her to Robyn's drowsy, sweet warmth. Lilith's fingertips touched the lace collar, and Lilith whispered, *Why hesitate? Just take her. She needs it.*

* * *

The night Sebastian finally surrendered and went to Robyn, he found someone there before him.

From the darkness of the bathroom, with the door ajar, he saw Violette by Robyn's bed. He watched from a dark lake of disbelief. Knowing, now, that he should have taken Robyn's warning seriously.

The dancer wore a smoky lavender dress with ragged points falling to her ankles, long wide sleeves, a design of poppies sewn in darkly shining plum beads. She looked exquisite. Sebastian desired her, hated her.

She appeared not to sense his presence. He saw subtle power coiled inside her: an unpredictable, chaotic power like that of a snake, a storm, a scorpion.

Something familiar.

"Forget everyone and be mine forever," she was saying. Seeing her rapt face, her seashell hand gliding over Robyn, Sebastian was overwhelmed by jealousy. Not since his human wife Mary betrayed him had he experienced such profound emotion.

And Robyn, although her eyes were glazed with sleep, whispered, "Do it. Take away the pain."

Violette's hand hovered on Robyn's throat. Any moment now she would pull down the collar and see the pin-prick scars of another vampire's fangs.

She's mine, Sebastian thought grimly.

He was poised to seize Violette and drag her away, when she looked up, eyes wide, all hair-trigger alertness like a bird. Not staring at him, though, but at an alcove to the right of the bathroom. He felt the flicker of a presence there.

Another vampire?

Anger transformed Violette's face. She turned, vanished in a dusting of mauve stars. The other presence also dissipated, leaving Sebastian to wonder if it had been real. *But*, he thought, *something scared her off, and it was not me.*

Sebastian crossed the bedroom to Robyn, who only sighed and turned over. She was asleep. She'd seen nothing.

Then he sprang into the Crystal Ring after Violette.

In a labyrinth of tilted walls and weird perspectives, he couldn't see her at first. Again he glimpsed another vampire above him, but it was faint, a mirage. As he climbed to a higher level, he caught sight of her: a black thread against the flank of a cloud-hill. She was fast! Sebastian ran like a cheetah to catch up, clawed feet slipping in the strange substance of the Ring as if in liquid ice. Growing closer, he saw how beautiful she was, even in her altered form. Serpentine yet feminine, gloved in black leather and jewels that threw sparks of red, purple, silver.

And there *was* someone else following her, a greyish figure some distance ahead of him.

Intent on Violette, Sebastian experienced a shift of perception and thought suddenly, *I know her!*

Samael and Lilith... the Devil and his bride. Deep in his subconscious, inky sediment stirred and took on amorphous shapes against a swirling bank of smoke and fire. Serpents dancing to a drumbeat.

His memories were impossible: unclear and nebulous, funnelling backwards long before his birth as if his life had no definite beginning.

I've always been here. And so has she.

I know her.

Robyn forgotten, he soared after her. Violette didn't look back at him, nor at the greyish figure between them. Eventually, though, she appeared to tire. She dropped out of the Crystal Ring over Canada, and Sebastian followed to find himself in a pine forest. Snow lay thick on the ground and trees. The world was luminous and bitterly cold.

He'd lost her again. Pulled by her aura, he ran, stumbling in thigh-deep snow. Then he reached a clearing and stopped dead at the edge of the trees.

She was on the far side. In the centre of the clearing stood a human, a big bearded man in thick furs, hat and boots. There was a rifle in his hand, a hound the size of a pony beside him. A few yards away, firelight shone in the windows of a log cabin. No one inside, Sebastian noted. This was a hunter who worked alone.

The man stared at Violette as if his eyes would spring from his head. Where had she come from, in the depths of winter, a delicate, snow-skinned woman in thin layers of silk?

Everything was stark, silvery, pure black on pure white.

"Are you all right, ma'am?" said the hunter. He clasped the gun, as if he'd seen such apparitions before, and had to shoot them. "You'd better come in –"

Violette was already on her way towards him, running lightly over the snow as if on stage. The dog barked, jumped into the air from all fours, and fled. The rifle fell from the man's hands. She leapt onto him like a cat, burrowing between his furs and beard to feed savagely. The giant could do nothing to stop this slender female from clinging around his neck and draining his life.

Sebastian watched, enraptured. The hound was barking frantically from a safe distance behind him. As the victim sank to his knees – Violette sinking with him, still feeding – Sebastian noticed a third vampire half-hidden among the pines, observing.

Violette dropped the corpse and rose as if dazed, her eyes blank, lips blood-red. As she stood there, the other vampire emerged from the forest.

A cherubic young man in a drab robe; physically unprepossessing, yet charismatic with self-assurance. Someone Sebastian hadn't seen for seventy years. Cesare.

The dog came back and snuffled at its master's corpse, whining. Violette ignored the animal. Glaring at Cesare, she asked icily, "What is this? Why are you following me?"

Her eyes were demented. Did Cesare know she was lethal? She must have seen Sebastian by now, but gave no sign of acknowledgement. He wasn't afraid of her. He felt they were equals. He was furious that she'd dared to near Robyn – but for the present, he was willing to be entertained by Cesare's imminent humiliation.

The witch waited in the snow, purple as dead blood, pale as the *Weisskalt*, black as oblivion. The dark trees framed her.

Cesare felt as if he were climbing a mountain. She seemed so far away. He felt like a mortal confronting Satan, a tiny child battling a monstrous mother.

He was so terrified that he felt elated. He knew God would protect him.

Cesare had vowed to confront Lilith before he asked his followers to do the same. This was a test he'd set himself: to find and follow her, even when her caprice led her across the Atlantic Ocean. Impossible journey, but he'd done it: proved himself Simon's equal.

Now all that remained was to confront the Enemy. If he survived, he would claim the right to ask anything of his flock. *If he survived.*

The presence of the dark vampire puzzled him. A friend of Lilith's? The face was familiar, but he wasted no time searching his memory because the dark one meant nothing. Only Lilith mattered. She filled Cesare's world with the wings and claws and writhing hair of his nightmares.

Although Cesare saw Lilith's beauty, he felt no desire for her. His nature was celibate, like Kristian's. The human weakness for sex, he believed, had no place in immortal lives.

However, Cesare decided that one day, he would rape her. Not in lust, but as a token of his victory over darkness. That would make the act acceptable in God's eyes.

"Madame, my name is Cesare," he said politely. "No doubt you have heard of me."

"Cesare, the great leader," she said in a flat tone. He hadn't expected her to be impressed, and she certainly was not.

"The leader of the holy fight against you," he said. "Your existence is an affront to vampire-kind. You have harmed my friends. Your acts cannot be forgiven. I come to give you notice that my purpose under God's will is to rid the Earth of you and your demons."

I've done it, Cesare thought in jubilation. *Faced her in the flesh. Now no one can label me a coward! And her friend, whoever he is, shall serve as a witness.*

Lilith frowned as if irritated. Shadows encircled her eyes, and her fangs were at full length.

"Who do you think you are?" she said, like a teacher to a naughty child. "Isn't it a little pathetic to gather a castle full of crusaders against one woman? I don't want to hurt you, but I will, if you and your friend don't leave me alone."

Cesare was in a turmoil of fear and triumph. She was trying to entrance him with her searchlight eyes, but he thanked God for creating him pure and strong. He kept his voice steady.

"Any threat you make, you will regret. Your dominion over the Earth will soon be over."

"My dominion," she said frostily, "is over one quite small company of dancers. And you are out of your mind."

Cesare heard the stranger laugh.

"Don't take my warning," he said. "Take the warning you will find at home."

With a brief glance of contempt, Violette leapt into the Ring, her form elongating as she vanished. Euphoric with power, Cesare followed. He must have the last word...

Then unseen hands clasped his arms.

Sebastian saw Violette melt into the snow-light, saw Cesare follow. Swooping after them, Sebastian seized the priest-vampire and dragged him back to Earth like a netted bird.

"What in God's name –" Cesare grunted as they landed in deep snow. "How dare you lay your hands on me?"

"I'm saving your life," said Sebastian. "She would have torn your head off. I've heard she does that." He rose, shaking snow crystals off his coat. Nearby, the dog still snuffed at the dead hunter, crying.

"Who are you?" Cesare said indignantly. "One of Lilith's minions?"

"I'm no one's minion. She must have thought I was with you. You have a bad memory."

Climbing to his feet, Cesare studied him until light dawned. "Sebastian."

"Correct."

"You were Kristian's enemy! So, are you friend or enemy of Lilith?"

Sebastian remembered Cesare as being doggedly submissive, unremarkable. The vampire who now stood before him now was a different creature.

"I heard how you rejected Simon," Cesare went on with fervour. "You're a fool, refusing to help us. Don't you know she will slaughter all those who don't turn to God under my guidance? You must come to us!"

Sebastian was taken aback by Cesare's apparent concern for his soul. But his thoughts had taken a darker turn.

"You were there in the bedroom. What brought Lilith to America, do you think?" Sebastian asked, putting an arm round Cesare's shoulder.

Cesare looked displeased by this overfamiliarity. "I assume that particular human has some meaning for her. I can't conceive of it myself, but I know there are vampires who develop affection for their prey, unnatural as it is."

"So would you consider disposing of the woman in order to distress Violette?"

"I'd consider anything, but there are mortals closer to her, easier to reach. This human is probably irrelevant... but why were you there?"

"Following Violette, like you," Sebastian answered. "I hunt in Boston; I don't care for competition. I'll extinguish that female anyway, just to be sure."

"So you have no love for Lilith?" Cesare's eyes shone.

"None," Sebastian said emphatically.

"Then come with me, join us!"

"One day, perhaps." Sebastian had no such intention, but he couldn't face an argument with Cesare. *If I have to destroy Violette*, he thought, *it will be over Robyn, nothing else.* And all that concerned him now was Robyn's safety. "You'd better go home and hope Lilith isn't lying in wait for you."

Cesare moved away, shrugging off Sebastian's arm. "Come to us soon," he said ominously.

"Cesare," Sebastian said with a chilly smile, "I've a message for Simon. Just one word. Samael."

"I'll tell him," said Cesare, frowning.

He was gone. Alone, Sebastian sighed and stared up at the heavy sky. He was full of quiet rage at both Cesare and Violette. How *dare* they trespass on Robyn's domain?

As he took a last look at the hunter's corpse, the hound swung up its large head and snarled, as if deciding, *Here is my master's killer!* It came racing towards him, muscular body bunched and wolf-teeth dripping saliva.

With a single punch to its skull, Sebastian killed it.

* * *

By the time he reached Robyn's house, near dawn, Sebastian had a searing thirst for blood, born of anger at the intruders. *To think they were here and might have killed her... To think that Violette might seduce her away from me, or Cesare use her as a pawn against Violette!*

He'd been calm before. Now he was shaking.

I have to take her away before those other vampires come back.

He stared at Robyn's troubled face, her hair richly tangled on the pillow, and felt he'd gone out of his mind. He was angry with her, too. *I must keep her*, he thought. *Punish her.*

He put his hands to his head. Fragmenting.

Raqia crystallised around him, enabling him to walk straight through the outside wall. Corridors and walls leaned eccentrically, and the stairs to the top floor went up at an odd angle, the treads like compressed bars of light.

Warmth and thirst drew him. He mounted the stairs, melted through a door, and entered the maid's chamber. A neat, pretty room with flowered chintz, a gleaming brass bedstead.

Mary had just got up. She sat with her back to the door, brushing her hair. She was in a loose white nightdress, her head to one side, her hair a wheat-coloured veil with the light shining through. As she brushed she hummed to herself, dreaming private dreams of which her mistress knew nothing.

Something alerted her and she turned, blue eyes wide, her hair floating with static. An ordinary face, pretty enough. Nothing to compare with the magnificence of that other Mary, the one who'd betrayed him, but no matter. She would do.

Sebastian went quickly to her, knelt and put a finger to her lips. He'd tasted her blood before but this time he wanted more. She was frightened, but one deep look and her pupils expanded with excitement.

"Shall we turn down the lamp?" he said.

The light shrank, shadows flowed in. Mary began to unbutton her nightdress, her eyes locked sightlessly on his, the tip of her tongue poised between her teeth.

He bent to kiss her breasts, and his blood gelled.

He couldn't do it.

Enraged at himself, he pulled her wrists behind her back and bit into her throat, sharp and brutal. She made no sound. But even her blood tasted flat. Not what he wanted. Holding the girl away from him, he pierced her eyes with his, erasing her memory. Then he flung her aside on the bed.

A footstep outside. A column of warmth.

Then the door flew open, and a harpy rushed at him, hair streaming, nightdress billowing, eyes wild. A line of steel swept towards his head. He moved just in time to avoid the blow, which caught his raised arm with sickening pain.

He twisted the poker out of Robyn's hand and held her wrist. Her other hand catapulted up and delivered a hard blow to his head before he could restrain her. She struggled, her face murderous.

"You do feel pain!" she exclaimed, gasping for breath.

"Of course. You almost broke my arm. I hope you're happy."

"What the hell are you doing? You promised not to touch Mary, how dare you –"

The maid was curled on her bed, unconscious.

"And you, with Violette," he whispered. "You were going to give in to her, weren't you?"

She went rigid. "But that was a dream."

"No, love, she was really here. I heard what you said to her. So I was going to take Mary and…"

"My God, so vindictive! You think you're gloriously evil but really it's petty spite!"

"True." He held her very close now, their breath mingling. His hands were light on her arms and she could easily have escaped. "I wanted to punish you, yes – but I couldn't do it, Robyn. I barely touched the girl. I don't want her. And I could slaughter you for that."

"For what?"

"For making me want no one but you. For souring all my other victims. For changing my nature."

She stiffened, as if she expected him to attack her. "What do you expect me to do about it?"

He embraced her suddenly, inflamed by her heat and scent. He kissed her cheek, held her earlobe between his teeth, nipped gently at her neck. She shivered. "I told you," he said. "I want you."

She touched her cheek where he'd kissed her, then stroked the skin beneath his eyes. Moisture shone on her fingertips. "Good Lord," she said faintly, "you're crying. Where did you learn that? You think you're winning, but you won't destroy me! How many more times do you plan to come back swearing devotion, then desert me again?"

"You did miss me, then."

A shudder. "It was unbearable. You've no pity at all."

"Have *you*? Robyn, no more, I promise. Come away with me."

"Where to?" she gasped.

"Back to Ireland."

"I can't." She was soft in his arms now, her desire for him – dare he think, love? – melting all her defences. "Do we have to talk about this now? Let's go to my bedroom before I die."

Violette wanted to cut Cesare and the stranger from her mind, but she couldn't. They haunted her thoughts all the long way home. Who was the dark silent man with Cesare? She felt she'd seen him before…

She thought of the hunter in the forest. Shivered with the echo of overwhelming hunger that had caused her to drain him dry.

He's the first victim I've ever killed outright. Or was he? I can't remember. But he called Lilith's judgement upon himself. If I'd been a human woman, lost in the forest, he would have raped me and kept me to breed and cook his meals, and all the time thought he was being kind. Such a man is fit only to keep a dog.

Hours in the Crystal Ring tired Violette. She travelled slowly now, feeling as heavy as marble. The currents buffeted her cruelly. Daylight in the world meant that a ghost-sun also shone in the Ring, high above the *Weisskalt*. It couldn't be seen, but its light dispersed through layers of azure, purple, umber.

As she descended, unexpected terror seized her, causing her to flounder and almost fall. A dark current caught her. The pull drew her towards its source: a massive concretion in the sky, a shimmering blackness that was now a towered fortress, now a mountain. A cliff, a wall, a prison. Or a house, groaning under the weight of a million crimes, tortures, murders...

She knew what it was. She'd seen it in Malik's eyes. This was Lilith's darkness made physical, the walls that shielded her from the blinding truth.

She twisted away and fell, arms across her face. An unbearable thought screamed through her.

This cancer in the Crystal Ring is because of me.

It is me. It's Lilith, the death crone. Cesare speaks the truth when he says I must be destroyed before I annihilate everyone else. But I'm being used by Cesare's callous God... and like Lilith, I shall never accept His will!

She fell to Earth a few miles from Salzburg and walked the rest of the way, to calm herself. She'd spent all day in the Crystal Ring. Night had fallen again, and the winter air was like iron.

She thought of Cesare and his companion, the dark silent vampire. Of the two, the dark-haired one disturbed her more. Was he in Robyn's bedroom too? She hadn't noticed, but now she was unsure. She'd fled to draw Cesare away from Robyn. What a mercy that she'd lured the dark stranger too.

And Robyn. How close I came... I should thank Cesare for stopping me. I won't go to her again.

She was in town now. The river slid past on her left, tall, elegant buildings on her right. The home of Ballet Janacek appeared in the distance, narrowed by perspective. As she drew closer, a sense of wrongness hit her. In her mind's eye were two humans, darting away behind the house, out of sight...

Violette sped the rest of the way through the Ring. As she reached the house, a smell billowed out to meet her.

Smoke.

Take the warning you will find at home.

The milky-green building towered over her, its windows black mirrors. She felt heat flickering inside, and the smoke stench was acrid like burning hair. Racing to a side entrance, she found the door ajar, the lock forced.

The fire was in the costume store.

A stench of paraffin mingled with fumes of burning wood and material. A wavering wall of heat struck her, matching her horror and outrage. *Who would do this to us?*

Flames danced between hampers, catching and running, silhouetting a costumed tailor's dummy for a second before catching the stiff layers of net.

Transforming Odile into a blazing Firebird.

CHAPTER FIFTEEN

AVATAR

Flames leapt, hungry to strip the bones of the old building. Upstairs, Violette's dancers and staff slumbered, more precious than her own life. She was the line between their survival and death...

Buckets of sand and water stood in the corridor, though she'd never dreamed she'd have to use them. Lifting the first two, she shouted at the top of her voice to wake the caretaker, who slept on the ground floor.

"Herr Ehlers! Fire! Herr Ehlers!"

Hefting the buckets inside the storeroom, she slammed the door, shutting herself in with the fire. Walls and ceiling were carbon-black. A great bubble of hot gas teetered towards the ceiling, burst into flames with a *whump*. Sheets of fire consumed the air and the smoke was thick with ash, but it couldn't touch Violette. Her unnatural body would not suffocate or burn. She faced the fire in semi-paralysed horror, as if about to witness a fatal accident happen to someone else.

She flung the contents of the buckets on the worst of the fire. Not enough. The flames only shied and flared up elsewhere.

Rather than open the door and risk unleashing the blaze, she entered Raqia to slip back into the corridor. She risked someone seeing, but it didn't matter.

"Fire!" she yelled. "Fire!"

A vampire's voice at full volume was piercing. The elderly

caretaker and his wife came shuffling down the corridor through clouds of smoke, pulling on dressing gowns as they came.

"Madame!" Ehlers cried, turning white. "What are you doing? Go outside immediately!"

"Call the fire brigade!" she snapped. Then she was past the couple, running upstairs to her apartment, shouting for Geli.

The maid opened the door as Violette reached the top of the stairs. Geli looked astonished. She held a hand to her mouth as her eyes began to water from smoke.

"Don't stand there!" said Violette. "Down the back stairs and out through the kitchen!"

The fifteen girls who formed her *corps de ballet*, and their ballet mistress, lived in the attic rooms. Violette woke those who hadn't already heard the commotion, accounted for everyone, ushered them downstairs and outside to safety. It was done in minutes. The girls coughed and clung to each other. Some were crying, others staring in amazement at the inferno, at smoke and ash whirling into the night. Musicians, the handful of male dancers, household staff…

Minutes, Violette thought, as she heard fire wagons trundling along the road, bells clanging, galloping hooves striking the cobblestones. *If I hadn't come home at that precise moment they could all have died. Fire would have roared up through the wooden floors. But if only I'd been earlier!*

Shock and rage hit her like the barrage of heat.

I could have prevented this. Caught the arsonists and torn out their throats. If I hadn't gone to find Rachel and Robyn, this wouldn't have happened. All the time Cesare was taunting me, he must have known!

The fire brigade took too long. Losing patience, she rushed back into the building. Behind her, people yelled for her to come back, but no one could stop her. The inferno engulfed her, but she was an ice-statue that couldn't melt.

Under the fire's crackling roar, she heard a tiny voice crying.

A commotion began outside. Figures loomed outside the storeroom and water jetted through doors and windows. Violette, meanwhile, began methodically to smother the fire with her hands and feet. It was the swiftest, most desperate dance she'd ever choreographed.

Her dress caught light and blossomed into flame. Violette cried out. Heat seared her and human terror kicked in. She beat frantically at herself, while the material fragmented and floated away – yet, when the flames were extinguished, she found her flesh undamaged: carbon-black, but whole and perfect underneath. Her fear fled, but she hated this: the stench and wanton destruction, the stupidity and waste.

Tears made trails down her sooty cheeks.

She heard the firemen shouting for her. *Now I've given everyone a heart attack, on top of this,* she thought. Water rushed in and drenched her, soaking the tatters of her clothes. At last the fire surrendered, leaving the costume store in saturated ruin.

The little voice grew louder. Something black and white darted from under a sink and leapt into her arms. A terrified and bedraggled cat.

"Which of your nine lives was that, Magdi?" Violette whispered. "And which of mine?"

Two firemen came stepping over the wet debris towards her, plainly relieved and shocked to see her. She was smeared with soot, nearly naked. Then they were businesslike.

"Come outside, Madame," said one, putting his coat around her shoulders.

As she emerged from the house, with the cat in her arms, the crowd gathered in the street gave a huge cheer.

Suddenly she was surrounded by her dancers, who touched and embraced her as they would never normally dare. "Madame, you shouldn't have gone back in! What if you were burned, your face, your lovely hands? You might have died! How could you risk yourself like that? So brave!"

Brave, Violette thought, extricating herself to escape the throb of their blood. *If only they knew... I drew this trouble.*

The fire brigade took charge. Violette and the others huddled outside, surrounded by what seemed half the town, watching the men pumping river water to drench the building.

The flames died. Wisps of smoke and steam carried a black stench into the night. Geli leaned on Violette's shoulder and cried, but Violette was numb.

The fire chief, a big stern man with an old-fashioned moustache and whiskers, wanted words with Violette. She gave Magdi to Geli, and turned to him.

"Doctors are on their way, Madame. The smoke is more dangerous than flames."

"I held my breath," she said truthfully. "I'm perfectly all right."

He looked sceptical. "All the same, you need an examination." He was stern, even furious in a controlled way. "It was foolhardy in the extreme for you to re-enter the building. It's a miracle you survived. Did it cross your mind you were putting my men's lives at risk?"

"I'm sorry," she said, gazing into his eyes, willing him not to question her any more. "I'm truly terribly sorry. But it's my ballet."

He cleared his throat. "I appreciate your feelings, Madame. And your prompt action on discovering the fire undoubtedly saved your girls' lives."

"Is it safe to go back inside?"

"Out of the question," he said severely. "The damage must be assessed. If there's structural damage…" He shook his head.

"Thank you," said Violette, and walked away.

All around, neighbours were offering her staff beds for as long as they needed. Such kind people, Violette thought. Once she had calmed her girls and ensured that they all had somewhere to sleep, she changed into a borrowed dress and coat and slipped away. Violet dawn was glimmering under the edge of night. The air was chilly. Ashes of anger were bitter on her tongue.

Cesare, you damnable cowardly pig.

Attack me, if you must. I can look after myself. But my dancers can't and you knew it, you bastard. You knew.

And I can't protect my ballet single-handed. It kills me to ask for help, but for their sake, I must.

Violette raced through the Crystal Ring. It was turbulent, the dreamscape flowing like indigo rags across a sapphire void. She sensed the dark knot in the Ring's fabric above her, a black moon trying to pull her into its orbit, a black sun radiating death.

Karl and Charlotte weren't at home. She paced around their drawing room until the grey dawn in the balcony windows brightened to blue. Appearing from the Crystal Ring, they greeted her with astonishment.

"What's happened?" cried Charlotte, rushing to her. Violette had washed hurriedly at a neighbour's house, but the fire-stench clung to her.

"I hate asking for anything." She clasped Charlotte's hands. "But I need your help. We had a fire. No one was hurt; I got them out in time, by pure luck. How can I admit the fire was my fault? I made the enemies who attacked us."

"You are sure it wasn't an accident?" said Karl. There was never kindness in his face when he looked at her – not that she expected any. Each resented the other's hold over Charlotte, and always would.

"No, it was Cesare. I met him and he virtually admitted his intention, only I didn't understand what he meant at the time." She told them about her journey to America and back. "I sensed two people running away from the ballet premises as I arrived. Humans, not vampires. He hadn't even the courage to start the fire himself!"

Suddenly she couldn't speak. Hurt rage. Terror of what might have been.

"Violette," Charlotte said, hugging her.

"Everyone thinks I have no feelings, but if anything happened to my dancers I should die."

She turned her face into Charlotte's shoulder. "It's all right," Charlotte said gently. "We'll help. It goes without saying."

Karl made no comment, but at least he didn't object.

"Cesare knows he can't touch me – but he can threaten everyone around me. That gives him complete power over me. Of course, that's what he wants. The fire was a warning."

A silence. Then Karl said, "He may be trying to provoke you into attacking him."

"He's making a fine job of it!"

"So don't take the bait."

"I suppose Pierre, John and Simon condoned his actions," Violette said acidly. "And Ilona? But why can't they fight their own battles? I never meant to make enemies of them – but their weakness is precisely what makes me despise them!"

Their shocked expressions took her aback. *Do I sound so bitter?*

"Forgive me," she said. "I forget I'm talking about your

daughter, Karl. You have every reason to be on Cesare's side."

"I am on the side of common sense," he replied with his usual cool restraint. "Charlotte, will you go to Salzburg with Violette? I am going to Holdenstein to have a word with Cesare."

"The damage doesn't look too bad," said Charlotte. "Will you go on with *Witch and Maiden?*"

Violette couldn't reply. How sad the house looked in the revealing light of day, the milky-green rendering blackened by smoke, the lower windows boarded up. *Perhaps it can be repaired*, she thought... *and then, will we have to make it a fortress?*

"I don't know," she said bleakly. "I'm not sure it's worth it."

Then, to her surprise, Violette saw a woman outside the front door, dithering as if she didn't know whether to stay or go.

"That's Ute!" exclaimed Violette, hurrying to meet her.

Ute was on the doorstep, suitcase in hand, looking distressed. Seeing Violette, panic came into her eyes.

"Madame, I want to come back," she said in a rush. "But no one answered, and I saw there's been a fire, and I was so afraid... Is there still a Ballet Janacek?"

"Yes, there is," Violette said firmly.

"Then will you have me back, please?"

Violette saw no fang-marks on the ballerina's neck, no trace of bad memories in her face. Yet the attack had effected a subtle change in her.

"What about your father?" she asked coolly.

"I decided to defy him. While you were in America I cried myself to sleep each night, knowing I should have been with you. I had time to think... and suddenly, a few days ago, I realised I'm not afraid of him anymore." Her eyes were large with hope. "Madame, is it too late?"

"It depends how much condition you've lost."

"I practised in secret every day!"

"Good. I have a role for you but you've missed so much rehearsal time," Violette said brusquely. Ute's face was radiant, but Violette couldn't afford to show any emotion. If she did, she would break down, or worse, express it disastrously as blood thirst.

"Madame, thank you. I don't know what to say – but where…?"

"We'll find you a hotel for now. Things will be difficult for a time; we need alternative accommodation and a rehearsal room until the building is repaired – but we will come back. *Witch and Maiden* will be performed as scheduled."

Violette glanced sideways to see Charlotte's brilliant smile mirroring Ute's.

"One thing," Violette murmured, "just one thing has gone right today. Ute, I never gave your place away."

"Tell me the truth, Pierre," said Karl. "Cesare isn't bringing young men here for your sole benefit, is he?"

"Like bringing grapes to an invalid?" Pierre sat at a rough-hewn table, reading by candlelight. In shirt-sleeves and grey trousers, he looked clean, at least. He seemed better, but shadows of fear lingered in his eyes. "Well guessed, Karl. If he was doing it for my benefit, he'd bring women. Actually, he'd bring Violette, on a spit, with an apple in her mouth."

"You seem more like your old self, at least."

"Sorry to disappoint you."

Karl sat on the bench beside him. "What does he want with these humans?"

"I can't tell you."

"I'll guess, then. I know Ilona is recruiting them."

"Of course," Pierre said sarcastically. "Young, strong, heterosexual men are what he wants."

"As slaves, worshippers, an army?"

Pierre shook his head, looking away. "Stop this, Karl. He'll hear us."

"Are you afraid of him? I'm not."

"You don't have to live here."

"Neither do you."

Pierre sighed. "Leave it alone, *mon brave*. What happened to your policy of non-interference?"

"I simply want answers. Cesare feels so threatened by Violette that he's forming an army against her. And sending human agents to terrorise her by setting fire to her property."

"I know nothing about that." Pierre hung his head, but Karl grabbed his collar and dragged the vampire around to face him. Pierre's eyes fluttered with alarm.

"Answer me."

"Why didn't you kill him when you had the chance?" Pierre burst out. "You let him live, so whose fault is it that he runs amok?"

"Well, he's a fool if he thinks a human army can protect him from Lilith," said Karl.

He released the collar. Pierre put his head in his hands and groaned. "Oh, Karl, Karl. Use your imagination."

Candlelight gleamed on Pierre's brown curls, on the pallid fingers entwined through them. Karl released a horrified breath. "*Liebe Gott*. He means to transform them?"

Pierre gave a single nod, not looking at him.

"All of them?" Karl was aghast. Right or wrong, he believed in preserving the exclusivity of vampires, both for their own benefit and that of mankind. The creation of even one vampire required grave consideration. His own pain, Charlotte and Ilona's suffering, Katerina's death, Kristian's megalomania and Violette's madness… all proved that the initiation of a single vampire could bring disaster.

"A few at first, but maybe hundreds by the time he's finished. Even thousands." Pierre sounded off-hand, but he was shaking.

"Do you approve of this?"

"Of course not, but what can I do?"

"The Earth can't support that many of us. What the hell is he trying to do?"

"Destroy Lilith, exterminate his enemies, conquer the world," Pierre said with a sneer. "Just the usual. Cesare's an evangelist now. Kristian liked to keep his little dark empire cloistered here, but Cesare wants to take it to the masses. Imagine it, a race of golden immortals, eager to do his will. What heady nourishment to the ego! The inferior mass of humanity to be kept as cattle, of course. Us and them, to the extreme."

A nightmare, Karl thought. Hell on earth. "Has he transformed anyone yet?"

"No, he's training them first. He's learned by Kristian's

mistakes. John breaks them, then Cesare becomes their golden saviour. A few proved unsuitable, so…" Pierre drew a fingernail across his throat.

"And he's using only men?"

Pierre shrugged. "He doesn't like women, does he? They're useless, except as tools to further his cause."

"He has to be stopped," said Karl.

"I've told you too much."

"Then leave here with me now!"

"I'm a lost cause, my friend."

Karl stood, put one arm around Pierre's shoulder and leaned down to his ear. "If you don't face whatever it is Violette has done to you, you're going to die. Is that what you want?"

Pierre shrugged again.

"Where is Cesare?"

"In Kristian's rooms. He's usually there." Pierre looked up suddenly. "Don't…"

"What?"

"Take any stupid risks."

Karl whispered so softly that even a vampire could not overhear, "I won't, my friend. I have unfinished business, that's all."

He found Cesare in the meeting chamber, as Pierre had suggested. There were humans guarding the door and flanking Cesare's carved ebony chair. No one tried to stop Karl. Cesare watched him approach, as if he'd carefully arranged himself in this relaxed posture – in Kristian's throne. *Obviously he knew I was here,* Karl thought wearily.

"I trust you had an interesting conversation with Pierre?" said Cesare.

"I'm sure you heard every word." Karl ignored his muscle-bound attendants.

Cesare's smile was one of benign wisdom. "Pierre told you a lot, and you may have guessed the rest, but the extent of your knowledge is irrelevant. You can't stop us."

That's true, Karl thought, *unless I break my vow not to interfere.* At this moment, killing Cesare seemed perfectly desirable. Whatever he felt for Violette, he couldn't countenance terrorism against her dancers, or other innocent humans. It stank of Kristian's methods. Blackmail.

Killing another vampire wasn't easy. To drain him of blood then behead him was the most straightforward method. Karl had found it nearly impossible to kill Kristian because he'd been so physically strong. But Cesare was weaker than Kristian, an easier target.

"You must realise that to create vampires in large numbers would be obscene," said Karl.

Cesare's expression was obdurate. "You condemn us because you don't understand. If I could make you see! Stay, Karl, and you'll come to realise…"

Karl sprang, swift as light, and pinned his wrists to the chair arms. Cesare seemed paralysed. His head strained backwards, eyes flicking back and forth under half-closed lids. A fist struck Karl's back and hands clawed his arms, but he ignored the men trying to protect their master. He nipped Cesare's smooth pale neck, feeling distaste. The priest-vampire's robe smelled musty, like the castle, but the blood in his veins was fiery enough.

"Violette is not the Devil," Karl whispered through the blood, "and you will leave her alone."

Cesare tried to escape into the Ring, too slow. Karl went with him, still feeding, and pulled him back into the real world.

Something changed. Karl sensed it even through his blood-frenzy. Radiance filled the corner of his eye, a new presence that lit the whole chamber.

Karl was wrenched off his prey and flung aside. He hit the flagstones with Cesare's scream filling his ears; his fangs must have torn the tender flesh. Karl landed on his back, gazing up at a golden-haired immortal, as splendid as a lion. Next to this being, Cesare seemed a colourless sibling.

Simon. Archangel, envoy of God, deceiver. And beside him was John, a scarred crimson bull of a man.

Karl made to regain his feet, only for Simon and John to lunge and hold him down. He struggled fiercely, but John's strength was bizarre, as if he were massively heavy. Simon caught Karl's throat and exerted vicious pressure, enough to break flesh, to snap tendons, crush the spine… to remove his head with one hand, if he chose.

No point in entering Raqia, because they would follow. As Simon smiled into his eyes, Karl experienced a fear that he hadn't known since Kristian's death.

"You won last time. Now it's my turn, Karl." Simon's nose was an inch from his. "Circumstances change. I used to be as weak as you, but now I'm stronger. Don't delude yourself; Cesare's right, you can't stop us. So if you've any sense you'll join us, you and the lovely, obliging Charlotte. You must become my lovers because you're too wise to be my enemies... aren't you?"

His eyes were burning amulets, hypnotic. Karl felt the onward rush of a terrible philosophy, a monumental change that could not be averted. Soul-destroying. He closed his eyes in despair.

Simon slid his hand over Karl's collarbone and under his shirt. Then he struck. Sharp pain pierced Karl's veins. He felt his vitality flowing into Simon, while the angel-demon pressed his body hard to Karl's, flattening him along the floor.

Over Simon's shoulder, Karl saw Cesare smiling. He resembled a boyish monk, his hair a crisp halo.

"You can't leave now, Karl," said Cesare. "You're ours."

Karl was floating in euphoric weakness, enmeshed in pain. Simon finished at last and raised his head, his mouth crimson, his eyes sultry flames. His body shuddered against Karl's like a fulfilled lover.

"Oh, Karl," Simon breathed. "I have wanted to do that for such a long time."

Charlotte was alone in Violette's apartment above the studio, arranging bowls of white roses in hopes of sweetening the air. It was a room of silver-greys, muted lavender and ashes-of-roses tints; soft, luxurious, melancholy – and tainted by the bitter-sour smell of dead fire.

The blaze hadn't reached the upper floors. No one was meant to re-enter the building, but there was no danger to vampires, and the fire chief would never know.

At this moment, Violette was downstairs, convincing the police and the fire brigade, as only she could, that the fire had been caused by an electrical fault.

And Violette was a fresh heroine for the newspapers. BRAVE BALLERINA FIGHTS FIRE TO SAVE THIRTY LIVES – AND CAT exclaimed the evening papers. Charlotte had been protecting Violette from reporters all day. The blood of three now sang sweetly through her veins.

She was waiting impatiently for Karl. She tried to resist checking the clock, but her anxiety was increasing. What kept him so long at Schloss Holdenstein? *He can look after himself...* But memories of the castle chilled her. *Even with Kristian dead, I still feel it's dangerous*, she thought, stripping leaves from a rose stem. A thorn pricked her finger. A drop of blood oozed out. She looked at the perfect red cabochon on the pearl whiteness of her skin, then absently licked it away. A tiny fork of lightning struck her tongue; strange, disturbing, that even the taste of her own blood could electrify her.

I should have gone with Karl, she thought. *If only Stefan had stayed, he could have helped protect Violette... Whatever he thinks of her, he would have done so for me. I wish Karl wouldn't insist on taking such risks alone! But I admire his independence, so I cannot complain.*

She watched the tiny puncture heal and vanish.

An unsettling feeling crept over her... A frosty, unnatural presence lurking behind a bedroom door. Waiting for her or for Violette? Charlotte went to the panelled door and turned the handle. The presence was radiant yet cold, and eerily familiar.

She opened the door and halted on the threshold, transfixed.

The being was white, obscured by a veil of opalescent light. Far from threatening her, it lay half on the bed, as if it had fallen and couldn't get up.

It stretched out a glowing arm and said, "Help me." A heavy accent, perhaps Russian. "Help me."

A trap? Charlotte approached cautiously, all her senses poised. She knew this creature... Through the glare, she made out a narrow face and long silver-white wisps of hair.

"Who are you?" she said.

"Fyodor," said the hoarse voice. "You know me, Charlotte, friend of Lilith."

So it was him! She remained out of reach, suspicious. Fyodor:

lover of Simon, enemy of Violette.

"Help me," he said again. "So weak. Took all my strength to find you."

Reluctantly, she gave him her hand. She was ready for treachery, but he only leaned on her, rose and collapsed onto the bed. His glow faded as if sinking back into his pores, leaving his flesh so white that hers was golden-pink by contrast. His white shirt and cream-coloured flannels were rags. Bloodless and emaciated, he resembled a blue-veined albino ravaged by addiction. The vampire she remembered, full of arrogant mirth, was gone.

"What do you want?"

"To talk. You created Lilith, so listen to me."

"Are your companions with you?" she said harshly. "Are you planning to kidnap Violette again? Why can't you leave her in peace?"

Fyodor held up his hands. "I'm alone. The trinity is broken. You could drain my blood, break my neck and throw me to the hounds of hell, Charlotte, if you wished. Since Simon left us, I have no strength."

She sat on the bed, arms folded.

"Do you expect sympathy? My God, you should kiss Violette's feet and beg forgiveness for the way you treated her!"

Rage glinted in Fyodor's eyes, a silver lash. "Love is blind," he said. "You are in love with a serpent, but a serpent can't feel love. It can only bite. We obeyed God's will!"

"When you half-killed us, coerced Violette into nearly being raped by Lancelyn – that was God's will?" Charlotte said bitterly. "What a charming God you serve."

His head tipped listlessly to one side. "I agree. That so-charming God abandoned us. You are so young, Charlotte, a baby in vampire terms, but Simon, Rasmila and I are very old. The older we grow, the closer to the Crystal Ring we become, too confident of our powers. That's when the Ring moulds us to its own designs. We become what it wants: angels, devils, gods. And when it's finished with us, it spits us out. Raqia has a use for Simon again, but no use for me."

"Oh," Charlotte breathed. Energy filled her, a revelation. "That's what I believe, too. God didn't make the Crystal Ring;

it's the Ring that creates gods! And you've found this out at last? You've lost your faith."

His silvery face creased with pain. "And loss of faith is our punishment. It hit Simon hardest. I could accept it, be a simple vampire again, with no reason for my existence except nature's caprice. But Simon can't let go. He needs power and influence, but he can't use Rasmila and me any longer, so he fastens onto someone new."

"Cesare," said Charlotte. "I know."

Fyodor sneered. "Cesare isn't enough for him. Simon still needs me but won't admit it." He touched her thigh, and the touch tingled unpleasantly. "I don't care about Lilith or Cesare. I want Simon back, that's all. I want Simon."

Charlotte moved out of reach, almost laughing. Lovesick, this poor creature. Simply lovesick. "What do you think I can do about it?"

Fyodor sat up, long milky hair hanging down to his lap. He was frail, androgynous, not the exuberant creature she remembered. "You are keeping him from me, you and Karl!"

"No, we're not," she said. "I gave Simon no encouragement. He tried to use us, that's all. That's not love. He has no soul. He's empty, and emptiness breeds mischief."

Fyodor appeared not to take offence at her judgement. "Simon gave you his blood," he said quietly. "Didn't that make you adore him?"

"No. I wish he *would* take you back and leave us alone."

Fyodor seized her hand, making her start. "Then come and fetch Karl!"

"What?" Waves of fear shivered over her.

"They're holding Karl at Schloss Holdenstein."

"Why didn't you tell me when you arrived?" Charlotte was on her feet, distraught. "We're wasting time!"

She was out of the apartment and running downstairs, not waiting for an answer. The scent of singed timber rose, choking her. On the landing, she met Violette running up from a lower floor, as if she'd heard Charlotte's cry.

Charlotte rushed back up to the apartment, Violette following, only to find that Fyodor had vanished.

"He was here," Charlotte said. "Fyodor. He said they're keeping Karl prisoner at Holdenstein. We must get him out!"

Violette was unmoved. "No, Charlotte. It's a trap."

"So? If Karl's in danger, I have to help him. Will you come with me?"

She was about to step into Raqia, but Violette said, "No."

Charlotte stared, incredulous. "You're refusing to help Karl? But he went there for your sake!"

"It's a trap," Violette repeated, "and if you've any sense, you won't fall for it."

Charlotte was floored.

"Don't you care? I know you and Karl don't get on, but what does it matter? After all we've done to help you, despite receiving nothing but threats in return? Maybe Cesare and the others are right about you. I'm the one who's blind, not them."

She couldn't look at Violette, couldn't bear her glacial eyes and heartless words. Furious, betrayed, but dry-eyed, Charlotte turned away and arrowed into the Crystal Ring.

John had wanted to lock Karl in a cell and torture him, but Simon, disgusted, wouldn't hear of it.

"You don't know Karl as I do," said Simon. "He's not one of your ox-headed young men. We'll win him only by affection and reason, not cruelty.

But it was torment, Simon mused, to treat Karl as they had. After Simon drained his blood, they took him to the meeting chamber and sat him on a low chair, with John on hand to prevent any escape attempts. They kept him there for hours, starving.

Few things caused more agony to a vampire than blood-deprivation. Yet Karl bore the ordeal with extraordinary composure. Simon was impressed.

Torchlight made the stone walls appear bathed in sweat. John stood guard beside Karl, while Cesare paced in front of him, expounding his beliefs with enough force to bring anyone, mortal or vampire, to his knees. Simon quietly watched.

The bliss of stealing Karl's blood had whetted his passion. Simon was in love. He knew now the mystery that made everyone love

Karl. He saw why even Kristian had lost all common sense over him. The secret was distilled in Karl's beauty: a poet's face, amber eyes like fire captured within the shadows of his brows and lashes. He was like a panther, caged without losing one mote of dignity.

Oh, why did you refuse me? Simon thought. *What a leader you would have made! Cesare will do – oh, but you with Cesare's vision, Karl! What perfection that would be. I'm truly sorry for causing this pain but I can't help myself...*

Simon's fingers played on the chair a hair's breadth from Karl's arm. Karl ignored him.

Then Cesare brought in the humans. Handsome recruits, with bronzed skin and blue eyes. Their tans were fading. A long time would pass before they saw the sun again.

Simon felt Karl tense as the mortals were paraded in small groups. Simon's own fangs ached and his body yearned towards their moist heat. How much worse it must be for his captive! But Karl remained immobile, expressionless.

"Are they not magnificent?" Cesare said. "What glorious immortals they will make! You don't begrudge them eternal life, surely?"

"They will turn against you," said Karl, "as Kristian's children turned on him."

"Never," said Cesare, "because I rely not on vague hopes of love, but on sure foundations of discipline. They are mine already, through life, death and eternity."

"Are they to have no thoughts of their own?" Karl's voice was steady but tense with thirst.

"What thoughts could they have that are better than mine?" Cesare asked. "Your misguided obsession with freedom leads to depravity and anarchy, the dark path to Lilith's domain."

"They'll begin to age unless you transform them soon."

"The time of transformation is mine to decide." Cesare looked reprovingly at Simon. "You haven't weakened him enough. He hopes to discover our plans. But it wouldn't matter, Karl, if you knew the time of initiation to the minute: you can't stop us."

"And it won't matter if you keep me here for a hundred years," Karl said flatly. "You will never persuade me to your cause."

"Will this not persuade you?" More human males came in,

bowed, walked away. Delicious blood-heat wafted from them. "Or this?" Another group. "Or this?"

Two vampires marched in, holding between them an exquisite young woman with dishevelled russet hair. She was afire with indignation.

Charlotte.

That, Simon noted with satisfaction, made Karl react.

When Charlotte saw Karl seated between John and Simon, his face gaunt with blood-loss, she broke free of her captors and ran towards him. John stepped forward and stopped her. It was like hitting an iron gate.

John's grotesque appearance shocked her. His hands on her arms were thick and powerful, like snakes. But it was the emanation of his soul that horrified most; there was nothing in his eyes, nothing but hellfire.

She could have fled into Raqia, but escaping would not help Karl.

No sign of Fyodor. She wondered, *Was he sent by Simon to trick me here?* Not that it mattered now.

"Karl, have they hurt you?" she said.

"You shouldn't have come, Charlotte." Karl glared at Simon, who waved John aside and let Karl go to her.

"How could I not?"

"But now they have us both prisoner. What does that achieve?" He stroked her arms, his expression as sombre as death. And Charlotte knew – as if she'd never believed it before – that she and Karl were not invulnerable, that Cesare's powers were real. The new order forming within the castle walls would roll onwards, an iron-wheeled leviathan.

"It achieves this," said Simon. "Time for you both to think. Time to accept that you can either join us or die. What holds you back? Pride? But a vampire's greatest priority is survival. And then... love."

Simon came too close, put one hand on Karl's shoulder, stroked Charlotte's cheek. She wanted to feel disgust, but instead she felt soporific. On the edge of surrender again.

She wondered if Cesare was jealous, as Fyodor had been.

"Did my blood call to yours, after all?" Simon asked, smiling.

"No. Your white-haired friend came and said you had Karl here."

"As I intended. Good."

"Let Karl go! I'll do anything, put myself in his place…"

"But we want you *both*." Simon's tone became persuasive. "I won't impose unreasonable conditions. You won't be separated or enslaved. No, you'll be treated as gods by our followers, like Cesare and myself. All we ask is that you listen. Is it really so wonderful to be out in the cold with only Lilith for company, when you could be with us, warm and loved and safe?"

Charlotte pressed her palm to her forehead, recalling Violette's refusal to help rescue Karl.

"What is it, *liebling*?" Karl asked, but she shook her head.

"Nothing. All of this." But she thought, *Maybe Simon's right. Violette is a monster. I've always known. She cares nothing for Karl or me. Why go on defending her, when we may be killed for our efforts?*

"May I speak to Karl alone?" she asked.

"As you wish," Cesare said graciously.

She and Karl went to a corner behind the ebony throne. She put her mouth by his ear, whispering so faintly that even vampires would not overhear.

"What if we appear to do what Simon wants? Pretend we're on his side, then seduce him away from Cesare?"

"No," said Karl.

"It could be our only chance. Win some time, set them against each other…"

Karl hugged her close. "You're probably right, but I can't. Yes, it worked with Kristian; I pretended to love him in order to betray him – and that's why I cannot do so again. It leaves a stain in the soul… And I can't watch you do that, either."

Charlotte squeezed her eyes shut, ashamed that she'd asked. "Either we prostitute ourselves, or we die."

"Not yet," he whispered. "We're too precious to Simon for him to dispose of us easily. If we stay, at least we may subvert others to our cause –"

"Enough," came Cesare's sharp voice. "How went the fire, Charlotte?"

"No one died," she said, turning to him. "Hard luck."

"I didn't intend anyone to die. It was a warning, as Violette knows."

"What else will you do to her?"

"Anything, everything. Whatever it takes. Simon insists she cannot be destroyed. But I say she must be contained. And one day she'll wither and die of self-loathing."

Charlotte took a breath. "Look, we can't escape, and Simon doesn't want us ill-treated. Couldn't you let Karl feed?"

"I could," said Cesare. "But not until he's expressed contrition and willingness to co-operate."

Charlotte looked at Karl. However well he hid it, she knew he was in anguish.

"This is inhuman!" she cried. Simon broke into laughter.

"No, it's simple," Cesare said serenely. "You can be tortured until Karl surrenders, and vice versa. John will find it no trouble: torture is his vocation. Or you could give in now, which would be less fun for John but easier for the rest of us."

Karl embraced Charlotte protectively, his face in her hair.

"Leave, while you can," he said.

"Not without you!"

Simon came and took Charlotte's hand. Karl glared icily at him, but as Simon drew Charlotte away, John seized Karl. Separated, they were bundled to the centre of the chamber. Charlotte was aware of Karl struggling, but he was powerless to prevent Simon putting his fangs to her neck.

"It's over," Simon murmured. "You're angry now, but in time… We'll be angels together, Charlotte." His fangs were icicles pressing her throat. "Am I not as beautiful as Karl? Can you love me?"

"A bottle of poison wrapped in beautiful paper looks like a desirable gift," she said. "But it's still poison."

His arms tightened savagely. She closed her eyes, waiting for him to strike, but the pain didn't come. He paused; then his mouth left her throat, and he looked up.

Charlotte felt the air tremble and the temperature drop.

The sound began like wind groaning around the castle. And

then the air was full of wings, beating at the air unseen. She froze in dread, as if all Kristian's victims had stepped out of the walls to take revenge...

Everyone was looking around, eyes glazed with alarm; Cesare, John, Simon, Karl, the unfamiliar vampires – one male, one female – who'd brought Charlotte in. Cries echoed from other parts of the Schloss. More vampires and humans came running in through the archways as if to beseech their leader for reassurance.

The walls shook. A mass of air was displaced as if by some vast primeval beast with ribbed wings. Night fell. Someone screamed.

When torchlight flared again, the female vampire and one of the human males lay dead. The vampire's head had been severed, still in its hood. The male's blood had sprayed everywhere.

And Lilith was in the room.

Charlotte's heart flew in loops. Mortals and vampires were crying out and clinging to each other, while Cesare crossed the chamber towards the ebony throne, stumbling as if he might expire with fury and fear.

The terror Violette inspired was tangible, like booming sound waves. Charlotte, though, was not afraid; she was inexplicably part of it. She thought, *Violette followed us after all! What else matters?*

Simon and John kept their grim hold on her and Karl.

Violette faced Cesare, her jet hair tangled with static, her eyes blue comets. Cesare stepped behind the throne, clinging to the back as if it were a shield. His voice, when he found it, was loud and commanding.

"Surrender to us," he said, pointing at Karl and Charlotte, "or your friends will suffer."

Violette blinked. Then she moved so fast that Charlotte hardly saw her, but somehow she had Cesare by the throat and was dragging him from his refuge. His attempts to shake her off were pathetic. His eyes bulged like huge grey pearls.

"On the other hand," said Violette, glaring at Simon, "let my friends go or Cesare dies. Perhaps you'd like him to die, I don't know." She squeezed. Blood oozed between her fingers.

"Do as she says!" Cesare rasped. "Let them go!"

Karl and Charlotte were thrown suddenly together.

Lilith's wings filled the chamber. She gathered Karl and Charlotte against her, and swept them into the Crystal Ring.

They had each tried to destroy the other, each tried to win, or at least to end the affair. Hopeless. Robyn and Sebastian remained fastened on each other, gorging on dark sensuality. A horrible and wondrous feeling, like opium addiction, wanton and irresistible.

"I'll take you away from here," he whispered, but she only laughed.

Sebastian began to despair of persuading Robyn to leave Boston. He wanted to free her from the chains of her past, her responsibilities, her lovers.

"No, this is my home, I belong here. Why should I move?" she would say, as if she had a choice.

He could not admit the truth: *"Other vampires know where you live. I must protect you, keep you to myself."*

If persuasion wouldn't work, it followed that he must use force. *Place her in a position*, he thought, *where she can't refuse.*

"I can't see you tonight; don't come to the house," she said one evening, but Sebastian went anyway.

He melted through the locked French windows, and found Harold Charrington, dressed up for an evening out, sitting in the parlour on his own. He was in an armchair by the fire, smoking a cigar and looking thoroughly at home.

If Harold had seen him appear from nowhere, perhaps he would have been less nonchalant. As Sebastian approached him, though, he didn't turn a hair. He merely looked the vampire over with a knowing, worldly air that infuriated Sebastian.

"So, you're the one," said Harold. "The other man, the young lover. Pleased to make your acquaintance, sir."

He rose briefly to shake Sebastian's hand, sank back into the chair. Sebastian thought, *How can she let those hairy, veined hands touch her?*

"And you, sir, must be Mrs Stafford's grandfather."

Harold laughed. "I may be well struck in years – but she ain't thrown me over for you, has she?"

Despising him, Sebastian sat down opposite. "Well, I'm glad of this opportunity to insist you stop seeing her."

Harold laughed harder.

"I'm serious," Sebastian added.

The old man shook his head in amusement. "Sure you are. When you get to my age, you learn tolerance. I know that to keep her, I have to accept she has other admirers." He chuckled. "You'll learn."

Sebastian stared, smelling Harold's musty body-heat, his pulsing arteries.

Harold threw his cigar stub into the fire. "I guess one of us better leave. Wouldn't want to embarrass the lady." He looked pointedly at Sebastian, then at the door. No doubt his iron self-assurance terrified his employees.

Sebastian stood. "Allow me to point something out." He beckoned. Harold rose, puzzled, the top of his head level with Sebastian's chin.

Sebastian seized him. Harold cried out. His spectacles fell to the floor.

"Wouldn't it be terribly embarrassing for your widow," said the vampire, mimicking his educated accent, "if you were to be found dead in the house of your mistress?"

Harold gaped like a flatfish.

The vampire struck, feeding swiftly and neatly. The old man's blood was thick with potential clots; his heart thundered, stumbled, exploded long before blood-loss would have killed him. When Sebastian dropped him back into the chair, he looked as if he had simply expired there. His expression was oddly indignant, his lips slate blue.

Sebastian replaced the spectacles on Harold's nose and left, silently, the way he'd entered.

"I'm ready, dear," said Robyn, entering the parlour in cream satin, with pearls in her hair: virginal, old-fashioned, just as Harold liked her. But Harold failed to leap to his feet. His head lolled and she thought, *I took so long he's fallen asleep.*

Then she saw his livid pallor. Saw two tiny marks in his throat, only because she knew to look for them.

"Mary," she said, her voice hoarse but steady. She fumbled her way backwards to the door, and called again. "Mary, get the doctor, will you?"

Robyn managed to stay calm throughout the doctor's visit, but inside she was in turmoil.

"He didn't look well when he arrived," she lied.

The doctor failed to notice the marks. They were flea bites, not gaping wounds. "Looks like a heart attack," he said grimly, frowning at Robyn. He knew Harold's family, and disapproved of infidelity. "Happens to men of his age, especially if they over-indulge their... appetites."

"Could you please arrange to take him away?" Robyn said sweetly. "He's not my husband, as you know. He really shouldn't be here. You understand."

Once the body had been removed and the grumpy doctor was gone, Robyn sank down on a sofa, head in hands. Mary hurried to make tea, but Alice stood over Robyn like a prison wardress.

"Well, you'll see sense now," said Alice.

Robyn looked up, aggravated. "What are you talking about? He had a heart attack."

"But you and I know damned well what really happened!" Alice retorted. "That devil almost killed me and Mary. Now he's actually murdered someone. He's killing you too. What will it take to make you stop?"

"Leave me alone," was all Robyn could say. "You're giving me a headache."

She went to bed and lay awake, waiting for Sebastian. He never came.

The next day Robyn was calm and controlled. *Yes, like someone walking a tightrope over a fire-pit*, she thought.

She hoped Harold's death would quietly be forgotten, but knew she couldn't be that lucky. The following days were chaotic. Harold Charrington had been eminent in the business community. The fact that he'd expired in his mistress's house could not be kept secret. Scandal broke and spread through the puritanical hierarchy of Boston society.

Robyn tried to brazen it out, but each day brought fresh horror. Reporters haunted her doorstep. Friends failed to call. The church congregation shunned her and she was discreetly asked to leave. The same happened everywhere she went. A hand on her elbow, the obsequious whisper, "Ma'am, your presence is causing, er, embarrassment so if you wouldn't mind... I'm sure you appreciate..."

Jesus, I hate this! she would rage in the privacy of her bedroom, withering.

One afternoon, Harold's widow arrived, hysterical and baying for blood.

Thankfully, Alice and Wilkes saw the wretched woman off and spared Robyn a confrontation. Robyn was being forced into seclusion, and she couldn't tolerate it. *Next the Beacon Hill Civic Association will be demanding I clean up the neighbourhood by moving out.*

I don't blame them. I blame myself. But most of all I blame you, Sebastian, you demon.

Sebastian hadn't reappeared, which was as good as an admission of guilt. He must know the trouble he'd caused, realised she was fond of Harold. In fact, she missed Harold more than she believed possible; even wept for him, once.

On the fifth morning, she slept late and came downstairs to find her parlour full of visitors. Mary, Mr and Mrs Wilkes, the doctor, several police officers and a minister from Trinity Church. At the centre, radiating the grim resolve of a woman who'd reached the end of her rope, was Alice.

"I've told them, madam," Alice said as Robyn halted in the doorway.

"Told them – what?" Her eyes raked over the grim faces of authority. She felt horribly exposed.

"That I believe Mr Charrington was murdered by your friend, Sebastian Pierse."

Robyn gaped. This was so hideous she almost laughed.

"Why is the minister here? Have you explained you believe Mr Pierse to be a vampire?"

The visitors stirred. Mary hung her head. The minister looked into the middle distance, betraying that yes, Alice had told him.

Robyn addressed the officials.

"I'm sorry you've had a wasted journey, but my companion

hasn't been well. She sometimes has... ideas that are only loosely connected to reality."

Alice glared back stonily. Now the betrayal was mutual. "I'm doing this to protect you, madam. I won't stand by and watch him destroy you!"

One of the police officers cleared his throat. "We need to hear your side of the story, ma'am."

"I assure you, officer, no one's destroying me," Robyn said firmly. She sounded calm, Alice the hysterical one. "As the doctor will confirm, Mr Charrington suffered a heart attack, which was unfortunate, but not uncommon. I'm grateful for you taking this trouble, but I don't want to waste any more of your time, so if you don't mind..."

"I'm sorry, ma'am," said the officer. "It's not that easy. This is a very serious allegation. Our duty is to pursue it until we're satisfied there are no suspicious circumstances."

"What can I say to reassure you? Mr Pierse didn't know Harold Charrington and had no connection to him. On the night of Mr Charrington's death, he was alone only for a few minutes while I was getting ready. The doors were locked, there was no break-in. And when Mr Charrington first arrived, I'd noticed he looked unwell."

The doctor nodded. "Mrs Stafford did say that."

Alice's eyes blazed with silent accusation. *Liar*!

"Well, how do you answer the allegation that Mr Pierse on one occasion assaulted both your housekeeper and your maid in their beds?"

Robyn shook her head. "Impossible. Mr Pierse is a gentleman. His visits were spent in my company. Mary, do you recall Mr Pierse ever entering your bedroom?"

Mr and Mrs Wilkes sat in silence, their chins drawn in with puritan denial. The maid's face was a mask of tense bewilderment.

"No, ma'am, I don't."

Robyn looked pointedly at the policemen, her eyebrows raised. "I hope this has cleared things up."

"Not really," the officer said heavily. "There may be an autopsy, and we need to question Mr Pierse. If you'd tell us where to find him?"

"I'm afraid I can't."

"It's not in your interests to withhold information, ma'am."

Fear and indignation slithered through her. She felt judged as an accomplice, if not a criminal. "I've nothing to hide, but I don't have his address."

Silent disapproval hung heavy in the room. She felt invaded, violated under her own roof.

"You were seeing a man," said a second policeman, "without knowing his address or circumstances?"

"He's a visitor from Ireland," she said quickly, knowing most of them had Irish blood. "You could check the hotels."

The police made to leave. "You'll be sure to notify us immediately if you see him, ma'am?"

"Of course, officers," Robyn said graciously. "If there's anything else I can do—"

"Don't plan any vacations. We'll need to see you and your housekeeper again."

Mary saw out the policemen and doctor, to Robyn's great relief. Her head ached. She sank down on a chair arm, rubbing her forehead. She couldn't turn her wrath on Alice because the Wilkes and the minister were still there.

"Mrs Stafford," the minister began in a voice of oak and honey, "I'm here to help you. Anything you wish to talk about..."

"There isn't, thank you."

"None of us is perfect, you know. We're all faced with temptation and it is only human to succumb once in a while. Satan has all manner of tricks, but God is merciful. You're a devout worshipper, Mrs Stafford. You know the church is always here to help."

Robyn shot to her feet, feeling homicidal.

"I came to church last Sunday and was asked to leave! There's no more to say. So if you'll excuse me?"

The minister left, looking grave and shamefaced. No sooner had he gone than Mr and Mrs Wilkes came to her and offered their resignations.

"You've been so good to us, ma'am," said Mrs Wilkes, in tears. "But under the circumstances – we're sorry, but –"

"I'm sorry, too," Robyn sighed. "Alice will arrange your final payment. A generous one to reflect your hard work and loyalty.

But I've a headache and I need to rest."

With that she left, barely glancing at the stunned Alice. In her bedroom, she sat at her dressing table, temples resting on her fists, trembling. After a few minutes, the door opened and Alice came in, her face as grim as thunder.

"You made me look a fool downstairs, madam."

"And you made me look like an accomplice to murder!" Robyn flared. "How dare you drag the police into this! Have you gone completely crazy?"

"But that creature really is a murderer!" Alice struck the edge of the dressing table, scattering perfume bottles like skittles. Robyn had never seen her so angry. "I'm trying to save you from him. But you, God help you, are trying to protect him! That *makes* you an accomplice to murder. So tell me, which of us is crazy?"

"Get out," Robyn grated. "If you want to lose your job, home and generous salary – you're going the right way about it."

"You ungrateful b–" Alice closed her lips on the last word. Eyes brimming, she marched out.

Robyn dropped her head onto her arms, drained. She was too depressed even to cry. *Why am I doing this?* she thought. *I'm mad, because I know Alice is right. Why am I protecting Sebastian and attacking her, when all this is his fault?*

She sat without moving for an hour or so. Mary brought a tray of coffee, set it down with trembling hands, and left without a word. Robyn roused herself to pour a cup, stirred in too much sugar and winced at the cloying sweetness.

That was when Sebastian appeared. She saw a dark movement from the corner of her eye and stood up to face him, livid.

"Have you the remotest idea what you've done to me?"

"What is it?" He moved like a shadow towards her, beautiful, gentle, self-assured, infinitely more real than her accusing visitors. "The idiots in your parlour? For the love of heaven, Robyn, don't let the likes of them upset you."

"They want to question you about a murder. The minister wants to save my soul. They know about you."

Sebastian shrugged. "I'm a jealous lover, child. You know that. I told you to stop seeing Harold. You didn't really care about him, did you?"

Her head ached to the bone. "Not as much as I should. I suppose that makes me no better than you."

"Those policemen are no problem. They could all have heart attacks, you know."

"Don't you dare! You don't understand how bad this is! By seeing you, knowing what you are, it's as if I murdered Harold myself – and there are people in this town who'd love to see me in prison. Even if they can't prove anything, there's the scandal, the newspapers. I've got away with a lot over the years, but beauty and charm wear thin if it's just too scandalous to be acquainted with me!"

"You're certainly a realist."

"Damn right I am. But I'm damned if I'll let them drive me out of my home. I won't let them win. I'm going to face them down."

"Why?" He pulled her onto the foot of the bed, his alluring eyes on hers. "Just come away with me, Robyn."

"I'd be admitting defeat."

"If you come with me, no harm will come to Alice, Mary or anyone."

"That sounds like blackmail."

"That's as maybe. They can't touch me or even prove I exist; you're the one who will suffer. I'd have no choice but to protect you. But leave with me now, and everyone will be safe. All this will fade away and be forgotten."

Robyn exhaled. For all her fighting words, she was surrendering. She lacked the energy for a day-to-day battle with the police, the church, Alice, society. Her crusade against men had turned sour. Only one man was left now against whom she could aim her thirst for revenge. Only one whose defeat would truly satisfy her: this creature of darkness who had ruined her life.

"All right. You've got your way again," she said. "Why do I feel I'm being abducted by the King of Elfland?"

He smiled. "Pack your suitcase. I'll come for you after dark. Let me show you what it is… to disappear."

CHAPTER SIXTEEN

A GHOST AMONG GHOSTS

Winter drifted down on Salzburg, an ermine cloak pricked by the black of church spires and treetops. Steel clouds pressed down. Icy gales blew off the Alps, whipping the world to pearl-grey nothingness.

Through the storm, Lilith brought them safely home.

Karl's skin was as white as Fyodor's as Charlotte helped him to a chaise longue in Violette's apartment. She offered him her wrist, and he was so famished that he didn't even try to refuse. How bitter-sweet, to cradle his head and kiss his dark, red-sheened hair, to be clamped to him by pain, his need pulling at her veins, pulling her into himself.

Violette paced behind them, as if restless to be somewhere else. "I don't want thanks," she said, businesslike. "I don't want to discuss it."

Nothing's changed, Charlotte thought sadly. *She rescues us but there's still no reconciliation!*

"But why did you save us?" Charlotte asked, exasperated.

"How could I not?" Violette exclaimed, as if that were sufficient explanation. "Do you still think I have any reason to fear Cesare? I could have snapped his neck. And if he comes near my ballet again – I will. God help me, I will."

Charlotte gently stopped Karl feeding before he weakened her. He let her go without protest and sat back, clasping her hand to his chest.

335

"Cesare's strength comes from Simon and John," said Karl. "He would be nothing without them. But Cesare's zeal is what holds them together. What kind of immortals his human flock will make, I dread to think. I don't think they'll be... ordinary."

"You mean the Crystal Ring will have unpredictable effects on them, as it did to Simon and –" Charlotte thought better of adding, *Violette*. "And John?"

"Possibly. Or their fanaticism gives them unnatural strength. The pure power of will. Perhaps it's the same thing. All I suggest, Violette, is that you don't take for granted that you are untouchable."

Violette became still. Charlotte glimpsed her inner pain.

"The time will come, I know," Violette said quietly. "Until then I must be left alone to complete *Witch and Maiden*. I'll protect you, if you help me protect my dancers against that fiend. But I must produce one last ballet!"

Violette refused to talk any more. Instead, Charlotte took Karl outside in the snowstorm to hunt. There was no one to see them in the whirling gloom, but on a mountain path behind the house, near walls of a monastery, they met a young novice monk.

Charlotte let Karl take the prey alone, watching with tears of desire in her eyes. After a time, unable to stop herself, she clamped her lips to the other side of the boy's throat. She and Karl held each other through a crimson storm as the boy died between them.

All through the feast, Violette's words hung in her mind.

One last ballet.

Afterwards, Karl fell to his knees in the snow as if in despair. Charlotte knelt beside him, her head on his shoulder. Both were shuddering with the sensual aftermath and stark awareness of what they'd done. No need to speak. The snow swiftly made the corpse an amorphous cocoon.

As they walked back to the house, Karl said, "Well, this has taught us our limitations, at least. Violette may be able to defy Cesare, but you and I cannot."

He seemed his normal self again. Charlotte was inexpressibly relieved. In a way she loved the exquisite tenderness of caring for him, yet to see him vulnerable distressed her.

"Will Cesare and Simon leave us alone, from fear of Violette?" she asked. "Or will it make them angrier?"

"As Violette said, the time will come," he sighed.

"What did she mean, 'one last ballet'?"

Karl shook his head. "If only we could vanish and live quietly, like Stefan or Rachel…"

"I wish we could, too," Charlotte sighed. "But we can't."

"We steal life to live," said Karl, "yet we still hold the principle of protecting life against tyranny. Who can fathom us? Well, we're not allowed to thank Violette, but…" He took Charlotte's hand and kissed the inside of her wrist where his fang-marks were fading.

"Beloved," he said softly, "thank you."

When the blizzards abated, the sun appeared as a pale yolk in a blue eggshell, and the town glittered under a crust of sugar. Children skated on the river. Enthusiastic tourists, muffled against the cold, were everywhere, taking photographs.

Karl watched them with pleasure, with detached, dual appreciation of them as objects of fascination and as potential prey. How lovely, the Austrian winter.

Violette had ensured that all traces of the fire were obliterated. Builders and carpenters worked flat-out for Madame Lenoir. Damage was repaired, walls scrubbed clean and repainted, inside and out. New doors with stronger locks, fire escapes and alarms were installed. Extra seamstresses were taken on to replace destroyed costumes. Then Violette brought her *corps de ballet* and staff home, continued rehearsals for *Witch and Maiden* as if nothing had happened. The fire, she told everyone, was an accident.

But the acrid smell of smoke lingered, and the atmosphere, Karl noticed, had changed. Joyful innocence had gone. Everyone was serious, loyal, and driven.

In the studio, the dancers wore woollen leggings and took greater care to warm up before rehearsal. Violette wanted no pulled muscles if the ballet was to open in early spring.

Karl and Charlotte had little to do but watch over the household, to cast their senses wide for human or vampire threats. Karl thought Fyodor might return to complain of Simon's heartlessness, but no one came.

Whether Cesare was too nervous to attack, or trying to make Violette complacent, Karl was unsure.

He'd lived too long to fall prey to prosaic boredom; but all the same, he wished they were not bound here by a sense of duty. He longed to leave Cesare to his games, take Charlotte far away and forget it all. But for Charlotte's sake, from love and loyalty and knowledge of what was right, Karl stayed.

"There's only one way to end *Witch and Maiden*," Violette said one day. "Anna and Siegfried trick Lila. Pretending to make up their quarrel, they invite her into their cottage, where she is trapped and killed. Children reunited with mother; everyone lives happily ever after. And a glorious death scene, of course."

"Sounds wonderful," Charlotte said, but gave Karl a dubious look.

Later, as he and Charlotte walked through wind-sculpted white streets towards the old town, Karl said, "The ballet is about Lilith, is it not? Lila is the witch and outcast, as Violette sees herself."

"That's what she told me," said Charlotte.

"Then you can read her fate in the ending she's chosen."

Charlotte looked sideways at him, her eyes large with anxiety. "In what way?"

"She isn't going to fight Cesare and Simon. She doesn't want to win. She wants, or thinks she deserves, to die. The last ballet, a blaze of glory, then…"

Charlotte said nothing for a long time.

"And an enemy trapped by a pretence of love?" she whispered eventually. Worst betrayal of all. Ghosts of Kristian and Katerina flickered between them. "Does she fear that from us?"

"Yes. I think that's why she sometimes provokes us so severely. Prophecy fulfilled."

"Why is she like this?" Charlotte asked softly. "Josef's explanation was plausible, but it doesn't ring true. There's something more." She caught Karl's arm. "How did Lilith and Simon become as they are? Could it happen to us, if we let it?"

"Beloved, don't."

"Perhaps it's already happened, and we're just playing out some role for the Crystal Ring."

"Or are we playing a role, simply in being vampires?" Karl

said thoughtfully. "No, I don't accept it. Saying free will is an illusion is like believing in Simon's and Kristian's God. It negates our independence, which would leave us no will to fight."

And in the bright crisp day he felt darkness; the crushing machinery of fanaticism rumbling towards them, like the dark tumour in the Crystal Ring.

There are ways to flee, or surrender, or die, Karl thought; *but no way to win.*

As Ireland's lush hills rose around her, as soft as cloaks, Robyn kept asking herself, *What am I doing here?*

Sebastian had his arm around her, but she was cold. He insisted on making the last stage of the journey on foot and she'd never before felt so invaded by the elements. Wind, mist, drizzle: at least it wasn't snowing – yet. Dusk faded through thick layers of cloud. The landscape was saturated, brooding, mystically silent.

He'd travelled the Atlantic with her from Boston to Cork. She hadn't expected his company. She knew he could move invisibly through some mysterious ether, so why was he on board the ship? He often disappeared on the voyage, and she knew he was drinking the blood of some poor passenger or crew member. The number of unexplained illnesses had been alarming.

This disturbed her terribly. When he came to her, she knew what he'd been doing... yet there was no clue in his appearance or his manner. He was composed, elegant in his mildly bohemian way, with the same candid, affectionate light in his eyes. Perhaps a faint flush of colour in his cheeks. And Robyn still couldn't resist him. Her own sinful knowledge almost unhinged her at times.

They travelled on false documents that Sebastian had obtained with no apparent difficulty. Robyn was now an Irish Bostonian called Maeve O'Neill. Vampires, it seemed, could seduce whatever they needed out of humans: blood, money or forgery. Now no one could trace them... Not a comforting thought, Robyn reflected.

Everything must be done in secret.

"After we disembark at Cobh," Sebastian had said, "no one will see us together. I shall disappear. Go and eat, then at dusk hire a car to Lismore in County Waterford. I'll meet you there."

"Where, exactly?"

"I'll find you," he said, smiling.

Uneasy, she did as he said. At Cobh harbour she found a garage with a garrulous, obliging driver willing to chauffeur her anywhere. She ate lunch in a public house, then passed the time wandering along the waterfront, gazing at the charming houses and the great silver-grey cathedral.

She had expected Ireland to feel like home, but it was a foreign country, she realised as the car carried her along narrow roads. The trees were leafless, but the pasturelands were a rich saturated green, the air like iced honey. They drove past low, white-washed cottages where she saw old men leaning on half-doors to watch the motor car go by, saw children's faces in windows no bigger than handkerchiefs.

Time and again they had to stop for slow traffic. Horse riders, bright carts drawn by donkeys, herds of cattle; everyone had all the time in the world. Robyn saw a girl in long skirts, carrying a baby in a shawl. She carried herself like a princess, not a peasant.

In the distance, the mountains were grape-blue against a vast sky.

The driver kept up a running commentary all the way, but Robyn was listening to something else. Music in an eerie key, emanating from the land itself.

They turned a corner and she saw a great castle poised on a forested rock. The castle floated on darkness like the moon, remote, enigmatic, silvered by the last trace of light. Its flanks fell, fold on fold, into the black-sapphire depths of a river.

"What is that?" Robyn gasped.

"Lismore Castle."

"Let me out here."

"Are ye sure? Is it not the town you're wanting?"

"No, here. I'm being met. It's all right." She gave him a large amount of money, enough to make his eyes stretch. "A little extra, to tell no one you brought me here."

The driver nodded and tipped his cap knowingly.

The car had barely turned and driven away, leaving her on the roadside by a wooded shoulder of rock, when Sebastian appeared beside her. She was relieved, and scared. It had taken two hours to travel thirty miles.

"It's a long walk, but there's no other way to reach Blackwater Hall without anyone knowing. It's easy for me to come and go, but not for you."

"I'm out of my mind," she murmured. "I'm alone with a vampire, and no one in the world has the remotest idea where I've gone."

Sebastian did not reply.

He took her past the castle, over a bridge to the far bank of the river, and into a dew-drenched field. The ground rose slowly. Robyn was soon out of breath, but Sebastian seemed disinclined to let her rest. He led her through a copse studded with rocks and treacherous hollows; she could barely see, but he guided her surely. They walked for three hours. The moon peeped through the clouds and the landscape changed subtly. Its contours were mellower, sure sign of man's intervention. There were sweeps of grass, magnificent lone trees, copses, a lake and river gleaming like milk in the vaporous gloom.

"We're on the estate now." Sebastian sounded excited. "You'll see the house in a moment."

Must be quite wonderful, thought Robyn.

They came around the skirt of a hill and there it stood: a great mansion, broodingly desolate and ugly. Three storeys with tall imposing windows, a soaring pillared portico. The walls were mottled and crumbling. The windows, fogged like cataracts with dirt, stared indifferently at long-neglected gardens and stables.

Robyn couldn't speak for disappointment. *What a hideous pile!* Just as well she didn't put this thought into words. Sebastian was clearly enraptured.

"Was this your home?"

"I never lived in it," he said, "and I don't legally own it. After I left – vanished, undoubtedly wanted for murdering my wife and her lover – the Hall was confiscated and given to some English Protestant family. But I built it. I still feel it's mine. It *is* mine."

He led her across a weed-infested drive and through an archway with carriage houses and storerooms on either side. The arch gave onto a courtyard overlooked by rows of grim windows. Sebastian led her to a small door of thick, aged wood. "The house hasn't been lived in since 1864. The last owner was an eccentric bachelor who left no progeny. So the distant relatives who inherited the place care nothing for it. Daren't even come here. Strange folk, that family."

He lifted the latch and the door swung open. Inside was a huge grim kitchen with floor-to-ceiling cupboards, a black range, a cracked sink full of debris; fallen plaster, broken glass, leaves, rust, cobwebs.

"It's colder inside than out," she said, hugging herself.

He turned away with a faint look of disapproval. "No one's touched this place for over sixty years. When the bachelor died, the executors locked it up and left." He went to the kitchen table, took matches from his pocket and lit candles in a branching candlestick that was more black oxide than silver.

"I shall have to get oil for the lamps," he said. "I forget humans need light, because we don't. But we find it pleasant."

He picked up the candelabrum and turned away. She followed him, shivering, through a narrow passageway. "How often do you come here?"

"Once a year, once every ten years, as the whim takes me."

"But you think of this as home?"

He glanced at her with a wry smile. Candlelight gave his face sinister illumination. "I'm the ghost, dear. I was the reason the family moved out."

They emerged into a square hallway with a stairwell looming up into the shadows. As Sebastian led her up the first flight, candle flames threw a spectral glow over dust-covered banisters, wooden panelling, portraits in thick gold frames on discoloured walls. On the half-landing, light gleamed on the treacly wood of twin double doors. Sebastian opened the left-hand door and ushered Robyn into the room beyond.

A cavernous space opened around her; a room of eerie grandeur with a ceiling of carved and painted plaster, two storeys high. An impressive fireplace at the far end was surmounted by a coat of arms. Two rows of long windows filled the right-hand wall, one above the other, the lower ones hung with dusty-red velvet curtains. Faded rugs lay on bare floorboards. She saw a full-sized billiard table covered by a sheet, glass cases full of posed dead animals. One, directly in front of her, contained a huge crocodile skull. All along the walls were the antlered heads of stags, staring out with black marble eyes. And countless dark portraits of ancestors, fixing their painted gazes on hers.

"This is the salon," said Sebastian. "Or the madman's museum." Placing the candle holder on a table, he began to light more candles around the chamber. She walked slowly through the great room, fascinated and repulsed by this surfeit of taxidermy. Case after case of finches, owls, birds of prey, and gulls lined the walls; and then mammals, reptiles, amphibians. Astonished, she forgot everything else. Then she came upon butterflies. Even in half-darkness they glowed with preternatural intensity, sulphur-yellow, electric blue, iridescent green... faerie creatures pinned in rows.

She opened the drawer of a cabinet and found scores of monstrous beetles attached to cards.

"Sebastian."

He didn't answer. He was brushing dust from a display case. The dust, though thick, was nothing compared to the grime of the kitchen. It struck her that this place had not been entirely neglected for sixty years. Someone had looked after it.

She circled the room, finding new treasure in every cabinet: shells, minerals, fossils, birds' eggs. The journey was haunted, grotesque, filled with the whispering of all the unknown lives on the walls above her, a thousand eyes watching from the darkness. And the vampire in black, his face lit from below by wavering flames, his pale hands resting on the dark glass; expressionless, aloof, his lowered eyelids forming two black crescents against the fine skin. Death in repose.

When she came to his side, she looked through the glass that he'd cleaned and saw hundreds of ancient coins on bottle-green velvet.

"Who brought all this here? Not you?"

Sebastian was contemplative, as if he'd forgotten she was there. Perhaps he wished he was alone.

"Not me. The whole family was eccentric. The last one to live here was an obsessive collector."

"So all these things were left here when he died?"

He nodded. "And after his heirs deserted, I decided to look after the place a little."

He walked away. Robyn followed. He looked completely at home here. She could imagine him in sombre Victorian clothes, or in an eighteenth-century tailcoat, white lace at his wrists, drifting from room to room; the solitary lord of the manor, eternally in possession, while the other inhabitants were mere tenants – and knew it. She imagined their insecurity, their paranoia. A woman's voice, low and frightened.

"He was there again in the library, Father. I didn't see him but I felt him. This house is so cold. It hates us!"

Now Robyn was the one who felt utterly out of place.

Another double door led to a drawing room that was insistently golden; wallpaper, frames, curtains, the scrolled woodwork of chairs, all gold. Sebastian pulled off dustsheets to reveal chairs lush with needlepoint roses, tapestry stools and fire screens. Too many ornaments: clocks, statuettes, stuffed birds under glass domes, black onyx elephants. More glass cases filled with shining semi-precious stones. More paintings and huge mirrors rimmed with gilt.

"This is how the family left it," said Sebastian. "I rarely move anything."

He led her through a library with floor-to-ceiling bookshelves, a fireplace flanked by two chaises longues, paintings of racehorses on the walls. Beyond lay a snug, a room more ugly than cosy with its green wallpaper mouldering and falling away, its velvet hangings turning grey with age. There were cabinets full of porcelain that Robyn guessed was priceless.

"The family's taste was lamentable," Sebastian murmured. "The house is not as I would have had it, but after all this time it would seem sacrilegious to change anything."

He led her in a circuit through a grand dining room with marble pillars, a smaller breakfast room, and back to the salon. Everywhere was the same decaying grandeur. The house smelled of damp and mildew, emanating a dank chill that seeped into her bones.

She would rather have settled in the gilded drawing room, which had a semblance of homeliness, but Sebastian seemed to favour the salon. Standing in front of the fireplace, he faced Robyn and removed her hairpins so her hair fell loose over her shoulders.

"There are old clothes here, too. I hate modern clothing. I'll find you something to wear, a tight bodice and long skirts…"

Her throat went dry. She looked into his eyes, which glowed intently under his soft dark hair. His hands were firm on her shoulders. "So I can't run away?"

A shadow creased his brow. "Why would you be wanting to run away?"

"Just a joke. It's quite… extraordinary here."

"I'm glad you think so." He glanced at the wedding-cake ceiling. "By the way, don't go upstairs for the time being."

"Why not? Will I find the skeletons of other women you've brought here?" Her attempt at grim wit didn't seem remotely funny. Fear clenched a fist round her throat. No joke at all. Sebastian could tell any lie, assume any disguise.

He seemed distracted. He didn't react to her remark, and his attention was still on the room.

"You are the first and only person I've brought here," he said softly. "If you want to go up, you can. I've done no work upstairs, so you'll find it damp, dirty and generally unpleasant. That is all."

"Worse than down here?"

She realised that the easiest way to offend him was to insult the house. "I appreciate that this is not the luxury you're used to," he responded icily.

She was afraid, and then she was angry. "Do you intend us to stay here?"

He let his hands fall away from her shoulders. "Yes."

"How do you expect me to live? Is there any food here?"

"Of course not. I have no need of it."

"Well, I can't live on air, nor on –" She couldn't say the word, *blood*. "Is there a village nearby?"

"Four miles away. But you can't be seen coming and going, and we can't ask tradesmen to call because we're not meant to be here."

"Otherwise you'd be happy for me to walk eight miles to fetch the milk, is that it?" she gasped. "For pity's sake, Sebastian, there is no water!"

"There's a well in the garden."

"You're not listening. There is no functioning plumbing at all,

345

is there? Human beings have certain inconvenient requirements, in case you'd forgotten. You may have dispensed with them, but I haven't!"

He looked straight at her. "Then find a suitable receptacle, and acquire the habit of feeding the roses. I don't care what arrangements you make."

Robyn was close to hitting him. "Why do we have to stay here at all? You could take me to a hotel!"

"But I love this house."

"What does that make me? Another ornament for your collection? You could have me stuffed and put in one of those cases, all your problems solved!"

He turned away. "I'm tempted." His callousness stabbed her. "You don't have to stay, Robyn. Leave. Straight down the drive, turn right; the villagers will point you in the direction of Cork."

"I'm tired," she said. "My feet hurt. I'm cold. If you can't say anything helpful, at least let me make a fire. Don't tell me: we can't have a fire because someone might see the smoke?"

He exhaled. "I always have a fire. If anyone comes... well, it won't be the first time. I set their minds at rest and send them away." His tone was sinister. "Didn't you notice the logs on the hearth?"

"If they're not too damp to light." She went down on her haunches, pushed her coat sleeves back, and picked up a log. Dust blackened her hands. "The least you can do is help me! Are those newspapers to light it?"

Sebastian crouched beside her, very close. He took her face between his hands and kissed her.

"Beloved child, I'm only teasing. I can't resist it. But you're right, I am a fool; I'd forgotten that humans don't live on... air. Will you forgive me?"

"Will you bring me something to eat?"

"Of course. I don't want you to leave. Forgive me."

He crumpled up brittle sheets of old newspaper – with headlines about Lloyd George's treaty with Ireland – and piled logs on top. Damp or not, the wood caught light magically for him. Sparks flew, scarlet light danced. And at last she felt warmth brush her palms. Unfastening her coat, she knelt on the hearth rug and watched the fire blossoming.

Sebastian knelt beside her. Sliding his arm under her hair, he kissed her again, deeply and tenderly, his tongue tasting hers and lighting the nerves all through her body; simply went on kissing her until she turned fluid, like mercury.

"Well?" he said, after a time.

"You're forgiven," she said, "conditionally."

He stood up, lifting her with him. "Depending on my future good behaviour? Stay here and keep warm while I'm gone. I have been many things but never a grocery boy."

"But it's the middle of the night!"

"So? I don't want anyone to see me. I'll take what we need and leave the money. They'll think the faerie folk have been a-visiting. Now, what would please you?"

"I'll make a list," she said grimly.

While Sebastian was away, she sat huddled on the edge of the hearth, aware of the age and immensity of the mansion around her. She longed for her cosy home in Boston. Perfect madness to come here.

I've never been the same since the first time he... she rubbed her neck, where many wounds had opened and healed. *Do I love him? Is this what it feels like? Am I sitting in this godforsaken hole for love?*

Half an hour passed. She was bored and uneasy, an unpleasant combination. She tried to sleep but couldn't; too many dead eyes were staring at her. Everywhere she looked were birds, mammals, painted humans, all dead and staring in accusation.

I wonder how Alice is? Hope she's forgiven me for leaving just a brief note to say, "Sorry." Hope I left them enough money.

She stood up, wrapped her coat around herself, and went to explore. From the half-landing, she mounted the stairs, the candelabrum in one hand. The treads, covered by worn carpet, creaked alarmingly under her feet. Rosy-cheeked, wooden-looking children in eighteenth-century dress stared at her from paintings. They looked little adults.

One flight up, she found a gallery that overlooked the salon. Dust, moonlight, a view of the estate from the murky windows. How bleak the landscape looked. She found bedrooms with four-poster beds draped in rotting fabrics, wallpaper curling off the walls, more paintings, priceless furniture, an obscenity of neglect. One room contained no bed, only an oblong shape covered by a dust sheet. A huge coffin? She lifted the corner of the sheet. Nothing more sinister than a packing case. Further on, she found a four-room apartment that was a treasure trove of junk: more glass cupboards full of shells and stones, stags' heads and framed pictures in disarray, boxes full of tools, books, toys and military regalia. Nothing, it seemed, had ever been thrown away.

The topmost floor was disappointing. Narrow, dilapidated corridors with paint and plaster flaking off the walls. Servants' or children's rooms, some empty, some filled with drifts of clutter, all unspeakably depressing in their starkness. Their windows overlooked the central courtyard. The flagstones were overgrown with moss. The mottled walls could have been those of a prison.

Don't go upstairs, indeed! He must have known his words would awaken her curiosity. Don't open the box, Pandora.

Then she found a nursery. A large room, barely lit by moonbeams through a single big window. No echo of childish joy; the chamber was cheerless, grey, haunted. On naked floorboards, several generations' worth of toys were shored up against discoloured, peeling walls. Robyn picked her way through the room, looking at rusty prams, doll's houses, a rocking horse on massive green rockers, waiting in vain for a small rider. She touched its grimy mane, saw that its legs and neat Arabian head were riddled with woodworm. Dolls lay among wooden guns and toy soldiers like eyeless babies.

This house was haunted. Desolate with loss and regret.

Robyn began to weep, unable to help herself. She wept for the children who no longer filled this place with life; she mourned the children she had never borne, because God had seen fit to tear them prematurely out of her. *No, it was my husband who destroyed them... or maybe I did it myself to spite him, because I wouldn't perpetuate his bloodline.*

She sobbed without restraint. Desolation everywhere.

If Sebastian were my husband instead, could I have happily given him sons and daughters?

In response, she felt sexual warmth spread through her

abdomen. She fell to her knees. *Oh God, so I do love him. Oh God, oh hell.*

Carefully she put down the candelabrum. She leaned on the rocking horse's foreleg, her breath quietening. A foolish spasm. Over now.

In the darkness that lay heaped in a corner to her left, something moved.

Robyn jerked backwards. A scream rose into her throat and caught there, fluttering.

I must be seeing things...

The shape moved again.

She leapt to her feet, nerves shrieking with the urge to flee. Yet she froze. The thing that unfolded and groped towards her was human-shaped. A glossy black head. Slender dark limbs.

It looked up, and she saw black irises ringed with white.

Fleeing would not make it go away. Her instinct was to keep the thing in view, but she dared not bend down to pick up her source of light. Very slowly, she began to back away towards the door.

The apparition stretched its hands towards her. Then it spoke. The sound of its voice made her catch her breath in shock.

"You have forgotten us."

Robyn collided with something soft behind her. An arm came round and gripped her across her chest; her heart almost failed, and she cried out.

A second later she realised that it was Sebastian who held her. Ambivalent feelings assailed her. Was he trying to protect her – or had he lured her here to throw her to this demon?

The first feeling won. She swivelled in his arms and clung to him. In that instant, she realised that the apparition was addressing Sebastian, not her.

"I have not forgotten you," he said.

Robyn forced herself to look round. Now she saw that the creature was female, brown-skinned, naked but for a mass of blue-black hair. And she also had an unearthly vampire glow about her... Yet she seemed vulnerable, huddling among the debris, stretching imploring hands towards Sebastian.

"What is she?" Robyn whispered.

His arms were firm and protective around her. She felt his breath on her neck as he answered with a soft sigh, "One of my ancient gods."

Charlotte was not unhappy, but… unsettled was a better term. The Ballet Janacek's home had become a fortress, there was constant tension between Violette and Karl, and the looming threat of Schloss Holdenstein. *But things could be worse*, she thought. *We might have been prisoners of Cesare, or dead. At least we're alive and free – for now.*

"Charlotte?" Violette's voice made her start. She and Karl were in the dancer's sitting room, talking, but Violette had left only ten minutes earlier to supervise morning practice. "My secretary just gave me a letter addressed to a Mrs Charlotte Neville-Millward. Is that you?"

Charlotte took the ivory envelope and sat on a chair-arm, too shocked to speak. Karl's gaze followed her, darkening with concern. "Er… yes. Or used to be."

"I thought your surname was Alexander," Violette said crisply, "but… I suppose we all pretend to be someone we are not." She glanced at Karl. "Well, it's none of my business, so if you'll excuse me… Rehearsal, for which I'm now late."

She left, closing the door behind her. Charlotte stared at the firm, neat handwriting on the envelope, the British stamp. *Mrs Charlotte Neville-Millward, c/o Ballet Janacek, Salzburg, Austria.* "Who could possibly know I was here?"

"Do you recognise the writing?" Karl asked, looking over her shoulder.

"It looks like Anne's."

"She has certainly taken no chances with your surname."

She opened the envelope with apprehension. *My family are trying to find me again*, she thought in dismay. *They still can't give up.*

My Dear Charlotte,
With no other clue to your whereabouts, I am writing to the Ballet in the faint hope that this letter may be forwarded to you. It is clear

that you want no further contact with us. I'm sure that's for the best. However, if I owe anything to the years of our friendship, it is to tell you this. Your father is dying. If you still care, if your goodbyes were not as final as they seemed, you may wish to come home.

Yours sincerely,
Anne Neville.

The abrupt style was alien to the warm, irreverent Anne she remembered.

She thrust the letter at Karl and waited for him to read it. Shock washed slowly over her, like some vast invisible horror descending from outside. *Not my father*, she thought. *It's impossible, he must go on forever. Father, no.*

Karl said something. She looked up in a trance.

"Will you go?" he repeated.

"How can I? I can't possibly leave with things as they are. And you'll tell me not to."

"I would advise you against it, with all my heart." As Karl spoke, she had a vivid image of him in her father's house; his lethal charisma, radiant against the comfortable banality of the life she knew. Inevitable, her seduction. "Vampires shouldn't care, yet we still do. Caring baits the trap for us. Our loved ones change. They grow old and infirm and they die, leaving us behind. And because we haven't been part of the process, we can't accept it. They won't be the same, Charlotte. They won't know you. What can you do, except cause them more pain?"

"Then why did Anne write to me?"

"A sense of duty."

"But what if Father's asking for me? How can I not go?" Anguish seized her, an iron spear in her heart. "I said such bitter things when I left, and so did he. I resolved not to go back, but…"

Karl's hand rested on hers. "Life consists of unresolved pain."

"But they've offered me a chance… I don't expect forgiveness. It doesn't matter what they think of me. Just to be with him… but how can I leave Violette? It's impossible."

"Charlotte," he said gravely, "if you want to go, you must. It's your decision. I'll watch over Violette. If anything happens, I'd rather you were out of harm's way."

She narrowed her eyes at him. "I'm sure you would, because that has always worked wonderfully, hasn't it? We're stronger together."

"Unfortunately, you can't be in two places at once," he said dryly, "unless you happen to have a *doppelgänger*."

"I have to go to him, Karl," she said. "I'm sorry."

"You owe me no apology, love." He stroked her hair, and she leaned into him. "Go swiftly, come back safely: that's all I ask."

"Gods, I wish you'd come with me, so they could see…"

"That I'm not the Devil? But by their standards, I am. It would do no good. They think we both belong to Satan, Charlotte, so be very gentle with them."

Telling Violette was harder than she anticipated. Charlotte caught her alone in her dressing room after morning rehearsal. She thought the dancer would be unmoved, but to Charlotte's dismay, she looked panic-stricken.

"No, you can't go!" Violette exclaimed.

"It's only for a few days."

"Or weeks, or months."

"No. It's my father, Violette."

"But what will I be without you?"

"What do you mean? You don't need me that much!"

"Don't you know?" Violette caressed Charlotte's shoulders and arms. She looked exquisite, her hair a soft silken mass, ruffled from dancing; but she was also Lilith, seductive and terrifying. Suddenly she kissed Charlotte full on the mouth, a lingering, sensual kiss, charged with all her yearning. Then she clung to Charlotte, trembling from head to foot. "Where do you think my strength came from, to save you from Cesare? It came from you. Without you, I'd be lost."

Stunned, Charlotte could only hold her, but Violette was a creature of thorns, impossible to comfort.

"A few days," Charlotte promised helplessly, and fled before she gave in.

Robyn watched the goddess kneeling among discarded toys. She was naked, hair cloaking her like a midnight waterfall. Against the dusty grey clutter she was a polished, nut-brown icon.

"Is this why you told me not to come upstairs?" Robyn said. "How many others are there?"

He spoke quietly into her ear. "Robyn, I had no idea she was here. I have not seen her for more than two hundred and twenty years."

Putting her gently aside, he went towards the creature. He was now dressed exactly as she had pictured him; dark tailored cloth, white lace. Her heart jumped. She pressed herself to the door frame and watched in bewilderment.

"What do you want?" said Sebastian.

The woman's eyes were white crescents, tipped up towards him. "You have even forgotten my name, Sebastian."

"No, never." He crouched in front of her. "You are Rasmila."

She nodded. "Though I have had other names."

"Haven't we all?" he murmured. "So, why after all this time –"

Her hand shot out to rest on his collarbone. He gripped her wrist, and Robyn thought, *He's afraid of her!*

"I've been waiting for you. I know you always come back here. I have nowhere else to go, no one…"

"I've seen Simon. He told me you'd fallen out. He wanted to use me, as if I were just a wind-up doll you'd set in motion all that time ago, but I told him no. I've nothing to offer him. Nothing to offer you, either, and I don't want you here."

"You can't deny what you are!" said the woman, shaking him. However alien she seemed, her despair was genuine.

"I never asked you and your friends to do this to me."

"But you wanted it." She rose onto her knees and pressed her lips to Sebastian's. The kiss lingered. Robyn's jaw dropped. "We gave you the gift; now you must help us in turn! Our power is diminished…"

Sebastian pushed her away and stood up. "I don't care. Leave my house."

Rasmila sank down again, head bowed. "I won't go until you listen to me."

"Rot here, then."

Ushering Robyn out of the nursery, he shut the door and led her downstairs to the saloon.

"Who is she?" Robyn demanded.

"I told you, one of the vampires who made me."

"Why wouldn't you listen to her?"

"It was their choice to transform me. I'm not in debt to them, and I don't care what problems they've brought upon themselves." He threw logs on the fire, stabbed at them with a poker.

"But she seemed distressed," Robyn said cautiously. "Can't vampires suffer?"

"We can. But she was more…" He stopped without elaborating.

"So you've no compassion for her?"

"She's not an orphan in the storm. It's a miracle she didn't attack you! Lack of blood makes us weak, but it can also make us horribly strong."

"You think she was just hungry? I don't think so."

"She is not my concern! I want her to leave." He held out his hand. "Come on, you need to rest."

Robyn was eaten up by curiosity, but he refused to answer her questions. She wasn't tired, but as soon as she sat on a couch that Sebastian dragged near the fireplace, she fell asleep.

Sebastian's hand on her arm woke her. She groaned. "Leave me alone, I only just closed my eyes."

"No, you closed your eyes eight hours ago," he said, "and we have work to do."

Robyn only believed him when she saw light in the windows. Full daylight made the room look bleak and grey, revealing every mote of dust, every moth-hole. Cold and dispirited, she shook herself awake.

"Is Rasmila still…?"

"I'm afraid so," he said. "Never mind. Come on."

Together they drew water from a well in the overgrown garden, carried containers into the kitchen, and cleaned an old tin bath. Sebastian even managed to light the kitchen range. She wondered if he would have been so industrious if he hadn't been trying to ignore Rasmila's presence.

She heated water, scoured cooking pots, plates and cutlery. The cupboards were packed with china. She could almost feel the ghosts of maids, cooks and footmen moving around her… and she cursed at having to do this menial work herself. Oh, for Mary, Alice and Mrs Wilkes…

I have twenty thousand dollars' worth of diamonds in my suitcase, and here I am...

At last she was able to make a pot of coffee. Back in the salon, she drank cup after cup with cream and sugar, and made toast over the fire. Half an hour of heaven. It was the first time she'd felt warm since the previous night.

She stared around the cavernous room. A thousand pairs of eyes stared back. *This place was designed for vampires,* she thought. *I can't live here!*

She found Sebastian still in the kitchen, wearing a voluminous old-fashioned shirt in which he looked irresistible. He was filling the bath with buckets of hot water.

"If you love this house so much, why don't you buy it back legally?" she said. "Then we could restore it. If I want coffee I like to ring for Mary, not break my back for three hours."

Sebastian looked coldly at her, as if she'd uttered heresy. Again she felt like a trespasser. And she hated him for it, as he sometimes seemed to hate her. "Your bath, madame," he said aridly.

She undressed quickly and stepped into deliciously hot water. To her surprise, Sebastian knelt beside the bath and began to wash her, as if she were a little girl. His hands felt wonderful, sliding all over her body on a layer of soap. He seemed enraptured by the way her limbs gleamed through the lather, by the flashes of light on her glassy-wet skin. His long, green-brown eyes were contemplative under half-lowered lids.

"Do you really hate it here?" he asked.

"It's – magnificent. Not what I'm used to, that's all."

"Be patient."

He helped her out of the bath, wrapped her in a towel and held her. She found it madly arousing, to be all but naked while he was clothed. But when she began to respond and kiss him, he held her away and smiled. "Later."

She looked up, thinking of Rasmila. "Is it because...?"

"We have more work to do to make you comfortable."

Refusing to put on any heavy, ice-cold Victorian garment that had lain in a chest for sixty years, she dressed in the warmest clothes she'd brought: a skirt, sweater and cardigan of russet wool. While she made another attempt to render the kitchen usable, Sebastian fetched more water and chopped logs. He'd even brought extra candles, matches and oil from the village.

While he was outside, Robyn loathed being alone in the house. The shadows seemed to move. She couldn't stop thinking about Rasmila, brooding in the ghastly ruins of the nursery.

It was dark by the time they finished. Robyn, finding the library the least unfriendly room, had lit a fire there. Now she was glad to collapse on a chaise longue in front of the smaller fireplace. Sebastian leaned on the rolled back, hands folded.

"Is she still here?" said Robyn, glancing at the ceiling.

"Yes." He sighed.

"She's making me uncomfortable."

"I don't want her here any more than you."

"So do something! At least find out what she wants!"

He was silent, pressing his fingertips together. *God*, Robyn thought, *does he have to be such an enigma?*

"Very well," he said. "Stay here. I'll try a little persuasion."

When he'd gone, Robyn fetched her coat, which she'd left on the billiard table in the salon. Returning to the library, she wrapped herself up and settled down to wait in her nest of warmth.

Why did I let myself in for this? Alice, I wish I'd stayed home with you...

Her thoughts sank into the red glow behind her eyelids. She slept.

"So, Rasmila," said Sebastian, "I almost did not recognise you. Such a long time."

"Your memory is poor," said the figure in the shadows.

"My memory is perfect. I hardly saw you when you transformed me, if you recall. It was dark, and you all three had a glow that made it hard to look straight at you. I thought you were gods. Beautiful pagan spirits. You, Simon, and the pale one."

"Fyodor," she said. She was kneeling as he'd left her, like a statue. A Hindu goddess, perhaps. He'd felt almost nothing for Simon, but Rasmila aroused painful and incomprehensible emotions.

"And where are they now?"

"Our trinity was broken. We served our purpose as angels to

guide Lilith, but when she rejected us, our power was gone."

"I've seen her," he said darkly, thinking of her leaning over Robyn's bed. "Violette Lenoir." He rested a hand on the rocking horse's head. Even to his sensitive eyes, everything looked grey, decaying in the musty air.

"We were meant to be shepherds, too," Rasmila continued. Her accented voice, calm and precise, conveyed her deep sense of loss. "I chose you. We should have stayed to mentor you – my mistake, to think you could find your way alone – but you wanted nothing of us. We tried to guide Kristian, but he was betrayed by love."

"I heard. Tragic."

"And Lilith, who should never have been created, and Lancelyn, who overreached his powers."

"A catalogue of misjudgements."

She spread her hands, palms upwards on her knees. He saw the triangle of black hair gleaming between her thighs, and sudden memories flowed and burned.

"We let God down, so He abandoned us. Simon blamed Fyodor and me and cast us aside. But Simon still needs us, if only he would admit it."

"So, are you no longer a goddess?"

"I never was. I am a vampire. I've existed for a thousand years. I carried heavenly messages to and from Earth... but God is now blind and deaf to me."

"And Simon?"

She paused. "If Simon, too, rejects me forever... that would be far harder to bear."

Sebastian smiled. "So, what do you expect me to do about it?"

"Help me. I am afraid."

"You? You came to me clothed in the night, like Kali."

She bowed her head onto the floor, trailing her arms behind her. Her hair made a raven shawl over a shoal of broken toys and dismembered dolls. He watched her, enthralled despite himself.

"You are too proud," she said. "You refuse to acknowledge any vampire but yourself. You wish you were the only one, but you are not! You must accept this."

"Why?"

"If Lilith has not touched your life already, she will."

Sebastian couldn't answer that. He saw images of Violette and Robyn in the garden, heads close, whispering secrets; the dancer hovering by Robyn's bed in her icy, silk-veiled beauty. Robyn threatening him with Violette! Ilona, Simon and now Rasmila with that name on their lips, affecting to despise her while their terror was painfully naked.

"Simon and Lilith are both dangerous," Rasmila went on. "They will try to destroy each other."

"So leave them to it! Isn't that what you want?"

She raised her chin and glared at him. He leaned down to her. She hesitated, then accepted his hand, letting him lift her to her feet. Her satiny dark skin enthralled him.

"All of this is Lilith's fault! She sundered us from Simon. Without divine guidance he is too headstrong, uncontrollable like her. They will disrupt the Crystal Ring. The damage has already begun. Have you not noticed?"

The hostile storms of the Ring, the knot of darkness... Sebastian had noticed, but tried to ignore the changes.

"Of course, but there's nothing I can do, is there?"

"Help us against Lilith. Help us show Simon that he cannot defeat her without us!" She pressed closer to him. "We created you for the benefit of immortal-kind. Why do you refuse to understand?"

"I do understand. However, I refuse to be used."

"We made you! We never choose at random."

"You chose badly, all the same."

"You are betraying us," she said, stroking his cheek. "Running away from your responsibilities."

"I have none. I'm not in your debt."

She slid one leg around the outside of his. "Don't you remember how it was when we transformed you?"

He remembered. The dark cellar. Three fallen angels, capturing his soul and delivering him into a state of undeath... and in the darkness, Rasmila drawing him to her. Naked beneath her robe. Blind lust possessing him... the absolute, wanton sweetness of her, making him forget Mary and all that went before.

Now her mouth and eyes shone as she unfastened buttons one-handed and pulled at his clothes. Her legs went round his waist, supple as a temple-dancer's. Weightless, she impaled herself on him and he thrust to meet her, sinking down onto the floor with her limbs entwined around him.

The aching compulsion was almost painful. He gasped with wonder. His body and the whole room came alight with jewels. Rasmila clawed at him, uttering a soul-deep cry. Sebastian dropped his head into her shoulder as a sharp, soundless explosion convulsed him.

Now he was tearing into her throat, streams of light on his tongue. The pleasure was less focused but more intense, unearthly rapture taking him so far out of himself that only the pain of Rasmila's bite could bring him back.

The divine exchange of blood... something Robyn could not give him. He drew hard on her, merciless, but every drop he took, she stole back. Neither could win. Sated and in equilibrium, they ceased and lay still, smiling at each other.

Then he felt bleak. She was not Robyn.

"Now my blood is in you," Rasmila said. "You can't deny me."

"You don't know me," he said pleasantly, refastening his disarrayed shirt and breeches. "When you changed me, I felt I'd become the Devil. Of course you could not 'mentor' me, nor could I ever share your beliefs."

She shook her head. "No, you are not the Devil, Sebastian." She sat up. "And you've given me something after all: your blood, your strength."

Rising to her feet, she was magnificent against the window. A deity, Hindu or Celtic, there was no division: Kali and Cailleach were the same goddess.

"I hope you're suitably grateful." He stood up, brushing dust from his clothes.

"You are involved, whether you wish it or not," she said. Her expression was sweet, but as strong as steel. "And so is your lover."

"This has nothing to do with Robyn," he said grimly.

"But it will, if you turn your back. Are we enemies?" Rasmila touched his cheek.

"No."

"I came to warn you, not to threaten. I am not Simon, demanding acts of heroism. I ask only for friendship, a little help in protecting us all from Lilith. I'm going to find Fyodor now;

we've been apart too long. Help us, and we'll help you in turn."

"I need no help."

Her serene face showed amusement. "But if you change your mind, call and my blood will hear you."

Rasmila moved away, seeming more an icon than a living being. In a column of smoky-bronze light, she stepped into the Ring. He was alone.

He stood among the detritus of long-vanished childhoods, feeling like a ghost among ghosts. *Now I need to hunt*, he thought. *I need a human struggling in my arms and their hot blood... and then the solitude of the Crystal Ring.*

Robyn was in his mind, but she was an abstract image, not a breathing reality.

"Do they feed on each other's energy, as we do?" Cesare asked. "Karl, Charlotte and Lilith?"

His eyes were red, like those of a man who'd been working frantically for days and nights. His face shone with mania. "If she were separated from them, would she become weaker?"

"Possibly," said Simon. They were in the sanctum with John: the supposed triumvirate. Lilith's attack had petrified everyone. It had taken all their energy to keep control of their terrified human disciples. Something had been lost. John had sunk even deeper into his need for vengeance, while Cesare clung to the very lip of sanity.

Simon regarded Cesare with despair. *If you were Karl*, he thought, *you would be rational, not crazed; and if John were Charlotte, we might have constructive suggestions in place of baleful silence.* "I felt power between her and Charlotte."

"There is nothing to do with Karl and Charlotte but kill them," said Cesare. "An execution for the good of the majority."

Would you extend the threat to me, thought Simon, *if you saw that behind my smiling mask, I actually despise you?*

"Killing them won't stop Lilith," Simon said wearily. "We've seen her strength. It's a wonder she didn't decapitate you on the spot, Cesare."

"You urged me to anger her! 'Kill the humans she loves,' you said. 'We are God's fire. Annihilate her ballet, and Lilith will be nothing but a cloud of wailing anger!' But her damnable ballet is still intact, while two of my flock are dead at her hands!"

"I hope you aren't insinuating that it's my fault," said Simon. "We made her angry; wasn't that the aim? In that, we succeeded admirably."

Cesare lowered his head, collecting himself. "Simon, I don't mean to rail at you. But we must bring the transformations forward. I need my army. Lilith frightened them, and I cannot afford to lose them to mortal fear."

"The transformation is a simple matter," Simon said. "It can be done whenever you wish, all in one day, one hour. However… neither Karl, nor your new army, is central to this."

"Then what, precisely, is central?" Cesare asked icily.

"You've already given me the answer yourself."

"Have I?"

"Sebastian's message," said Simon. "One word. Samael."

"Just a name. What does it mean?" How desperate Cesare sounded.

"It means that only one vampire is capable of destroying Lilith. And that vampire is Sebastian. He's like her: Samael was the Devil, Lilith's husband. Her equal and opposite."

"Who refuses to co-operate." Cesare exhaled.

"But who thinks he can use this knowledge to manipulate us. He was trying to show he is cleverer, more knowledgeable than us! Well, let him think that. All we need is for Sebastian and Lilith to loathe each other, and to meet."

Simon had expected to impress Cesare with this insight, but the leader only folded his arms and spoke with scorn, "How could you hope to arrange that?"

"It's already in hand. Rasmila is assisting."

"Rasmila, who has no thought in her head but you?"

"Exactly. She will do anything for me."

"But I've met Sebastian. As I said, he and Lilith have no interest in each other. He cares for nothing but himself. No, Simon, forget him." Cesare gazed at Simon with the fervour that had swayed his disciples. "He's like Karl, an unreliable, useless subversive. Such men are powerless because they throw power away! But we three understand. Simon, if you and I and John lack the strength to defeat Lilith, what are we worth?"

Simon examined his perfect fingernails. There was something in what Cesare said.

"If only Charlotte and Violette were not joined at the hip," he murmured. "If only Charlotte would leave her... and come to me."

Cesare seemed not to hear him. As if possessed, he lunged forward and shook Simon, his eyes burning white.

"What if Samael and Lilith came together and created something *worse*?"

A sound disturbed Robyn's sleep: the echoing cry of a woman in pain – or extreme pleasure. Her eyes snapped open. She stared at the embers of the fire, slept again.

When she woke properly, it was light. The fire had gone out and her coat had fallen to the floor. Numb with cold, she ached all over from sleeping in one position.

For a moment, she had no idea where she was. Thousands of books in faded reds, blues and browns towered around her. A mirror above the fireplace reflected a window framing a cloudy sky. Figures in oil paintings stared at her. *Oh, this place*, she thought, feeling sick at heart.

She sat up stiffly, swearing.

"Your language doesn't improve," said a voice.

She twisted round and saw Sebastian, a graceful silhouette against the window.

"How long have you been there?" She was angry at first; then, seeing the look on his face, the feeling deepened to suspicion.

"Not long." He came to the chaise longue.

"Why didn't you wake me?"

"I love to watch you sleeping," he said. His eyes were very soft, too tranquil. "Are you cold?"

"Frozen."

"Then I'll attend to the fire." He began to move away, but she caught his wrist.

"Have you been gone all night?"

His eyes slid sideways under lowered lids. Shame? "There were certain things..."

"So you just left me to sleep on a couch again?"

"I meant to prepare a bed, but certain matters intervened. Forgive me, Robyn. I'm still unused to considering your needs before my own."

"Damned right you are." Her breathing quickened and her blood rose. He sat beside her and stroked her hair, but she folded her arms.

"And now you are angry with me," he said ruefully.

"Has she gone, your uninvited guest?"

"She's gone."

"So you persuaded her, did you?" Her venomous tone appeared to startle him. "Your powers of persuasion are as impressive as ever. I hope you enjoyed it as much as she did."

"What are you talking about?" he said quietly.

She could have screamed. Pulling away, she grabbed her coat as if it, too, had wronged her. "Don't treat me like an idiot! You had her, didn't you? I won't even grace it with the term 'seduction'."

His lips parted, ready to deny it. Instead he hesitated, frowning. "How did you know?"

"I just *know*. I saw how you were with each other; there was a bond between you, two hundred years separated or not. It's all over your face, damn it, that shameful glow."

He seemed bemused. "I never thought you would be jealous."

"And you're amazed by that?" She buttoned her shoes, rose and threw on her coat. "You are absolutely amazed."

"What are you doing?"

"Looking for my purse." She found the purse under the chaise longue, checked how much money she had. Enough. "My God, all that garbage about not sharing me with Harold!"

She hurried through the door and into the salon, her footsteps ringing. She was more than hurt. She felt annihilated.

Sebastian followed her. "Robyn, don't leave."

"No, I've had enough."

"Where do you think you'll go?"

"Cork. Home."

"Stop, will you?"

She halted, three-quarters of the way across the room, keeping her back to him so he wouldn't see her crying. Beside her, the crocodile skull grinned in its glass case.

He said, "Anything between Rasmila and myself is separate. I won't insult you by saying it meant nothing, but it was to do with blood, which I can't explain to a mortal…"

"And I don't want to hear it! You're a monster. You must take me for such a fool."

"Please don't leave." His voice almost broke. He sounded desperate.

"You've got yourself; what more do you need?"

Without looking back, Robyn resumed her walk to the door. She took four steps; she neither heard nor felt him move, but suddenly he seized her from behind, his arms locking across her ribs.

She struggled, outraged and terrified.

"Don't go!" He turned her round in his arms, holding her with unholy strength. "I should die if you left me!"

She almost wriggled out of his grip, but he thrust her against the closed door and held her there.

"Why the hell should I stay?" she cried.

He spoke fervidly into her ear. "This morning I came in from the outside world and the otherworld and the arms of a vampire where it was bitter-cold, and I saw you lying by the fire and you were warm, you were a living fire, the most beautiful sight I'd ever seen, with your hair like brown flames. And I realised you are all that matters to me, your heat and your precious life. All Rasmila wanted from me was blood. She is like ice and I could never love her, because –"

She waited for him to go on, her eyes tight shut. "Why can't you say it?"

"I'm telling you that I cannot endure my life without you."

"It's not enough! Let go of me!" She fought him, but he held her. "What's the point, when you won't say the one thing –"

"Do you want blood from me?" he whispered.

"Say it!"

"If I do, will it make you stay?"

"Nothing else will."

He went quiet, his mouth in her hair. She felt his grip loosening, his whole body softening. "Have my blood, then. I love you, Robyn."

Her breath whooshed out in a laugh of sheer astonishment. "Now, will you please stay with me?" he said.

Not a struggle between them now, but an embrace. "I'll stay," she said. They clung together, lost to each other and ashamed of it, pinioned by the dreadful joy of surrender.

But I won, Robyn thought in bitter-sweet triumph. *I've changed him, I've soured all his other victims; I made him fall in love with me and I forced him to admit it.*

I won!

PART THREE

Sometimes the Earth Goddess cried out in the night, demanding human hearts, and then She would not be comforted until She had been given human blood to drink.

MAYAN MYTH

I am all that has been, and is, and that will be
No mortal has yet been able to lift the veil that covers me.

INSCRIPTION ON THE GODDESS'S TEMPLE AT SAIS

CHAPTER SEVENTEEN

VAMPIRE IN BLACK

Charlotte found it deeply unsettling to be in Cambridge again. Over two years had passed since she'd left, and she had heard little of her family in that time. She had placed them in a doll's house in her mind, where they remained frozen as she had last seen them, like vampires: reassuringly the same forever.

The idea of never returning seemed inconceivable, but her dreams of doing so had been vague, fantastical. The reality was both disturbing and oddly banal.

How strange to see the big greyish-cream stone house behind the high wall. To push open the gate, feeling the wrought iron damp and flaky under her fingers. To cross the drive, noticing how the shrubs had grown, the changing pattern of moss on the stones. Even the great trees had subtly changed shape. All looked familiar and yet strange, as if memory and reality were in static conflict.

She rang the doorbell. The maid answered. Dear Sally, the same as ever; tall and thin, with a vaguely worried air and untidy brown hair hanging in wisps around her spectacles.

"Miss Neville!" Sally stared until she was swept aside by a dark-haired woman.

"Go back to the kitchen, dear, I'll see to this."

Charlotte took a moment to realise the woman was Anne.

The maid obeyed, bewildered, glancing back over her shoulder. Charlotte could imagine the gossip in the kitchen. Then she and Anne were alone, gazing at each other.

Charlotte saw changes in her immediately. Still young, attractive, warm-hearted – but there were fine lines around her eyes, a look of maturity. She'd put on a little weight and was dressed staidly in a skirt, blouse, cardigan and long strings of pearls. A county wife.

Charlotte also saw the strain that tugged at her mouth.

"You'd better come in," Anne said at last. No display of emotion. "You got my letter, then."

"How did you know where to find me?"

"Simple," Anne murmured with a half-smile. "I'll show you later."

On the threshold, Charlotte hesitated. "Is David here?"

"No, he and Elizabeth went out for some air. They needed a rest from the sickroom."

So her father was still alive. She wasn't too late.

Relieved that she wouldn't have to face David immediately, she entered the hall. The way Anne stepped back, as if Charlotte were infectious, saddened her. That was why Anne had sent Sally away: to protect her.

"Madeleine's here, though," said Anne.

Her heart twisted. She didn't want to see Madeleine either. *The worst thing of all*, she thought, *would be seeing Henry*. He'd been their laboratory assistant, much-loved by her father, no more to Charlotte than a comfortable acquaintance until he'd declared his feelings for her. And when Karl vanished, believed dead, she had married Henry simply because nothing mattered any more. Married him, then betrayed him the moment Karl came back.

To see Henry again would be excruciating.

"How is Father?" she asked quietly.

She thought of times when she'd arrived home from an outing and her father had come into the hall to greet her, hands distorting the pockets of his tweed jacket, delighted to see her yet gruffly annoyed that she'd been away. How empty the hall seemed when he didn't appear.

"Not well." Anne's mouth twitched down at the corners. She made a marked effort to control her voice. "The doctor doesn't think he has much longer. Days, at most."

For a frozen instant they stared at each other. If they'd still been friends, if Charlotte had still been human, they would have embraced and wept. But Charlotte couldn't move. To feel her friend recoil would make this even worse.

"What's wrong with him?"

Anne's shoulders rose and fell. "His heart, his lungs. He's been growing weaker for months. David says he's never been completely well since the influenza in 1919. And my father says the stuff he worked with in the laboratory may have been dangerous. Radium, wasn't it?"

"Yes, radium," Charlotte replied, her voice faint.

"Of course, losing you and Fleur didn't help."

Charlotte said nothing. She wanted to see him straight away, but the words would not come out.

"You may as well come into the drawing room," said Anne.

As she opened the door, Charlotte was arrested by the scene inside. There was her sister Madeleine on the carpet, playing with a boisterous blond toddler; or at least, trying to stop him destroying a wooden train. The boy took one look at Charlotte and began to yell.

Charlotte stayed in the doorway. She didn't rush as a human might, only observed, as was her vampire nature. Madeleine's gaze flicked to her, registered astonishment, then went back to the toddler.

"He's been grumpy all afternoon, Anne," she said, standing up. "I can't do a thing with him. I'm afraid he'll disturb Father."

Anne picked up the wriggling child. "I'll have Sally put him to bed. He just wants attention; he knows things aren't normal."

Passing Charlotte, she paused. Charlotte studied the boy; even red-faced and grizzling, he bore a clear resemblance to her brother David. How plump with blood – Charlotte shut off the thought, horrified at herself.

"This is my son, George. Eighteen months old. Say hello to your Auntie Charlotte, George."

The child responded with an ear-splitting bawl and turned his face into his mother's shoulder. Anne smiled tiredly. "It's not you. Don't feel obliged to say anything nice about him; he's the most objectionable child in the universe. David's sure he's a changeling. But we love him. Don't we, George? Most of the time."

She went into the hall, calling for Sally. Charlotte remained where she was, staring past Madeleine, thinking, *My God, Anne had a baby and I didn't know.*

Then she recollected herself, and went in. Nothing had changed. The cosy sepia room was still full of Victorian clutter, her father's collection of clocks ticking madly.

Madeleine smiled hesitantly.

"Charlotte, I can't believe it's really you! Oh, look, no one's taken your coat. Let me."

Charlotte was reluctant to take off the garment; it was like shedding a protective barrier. But she obeyed, also relinquishing her hat and gloves into her sister's hands.

"Isn't it lovely?" said Maddy, admiring the coat. "I love this swirly figured velvet. And beautiful colours, russet and gold, like your hair. It does suit you…" Her voice gave way on the last words. She half-ran into the hallway, reappearing almost immediately. She was as Charlotte remembered; all nervous energy and charm, strikingly pretty with her shingled copper-red hair. But Charlotte noticed changes. She'd lost her sharp corners, her self-absorption.

"Do sit down. I can't believe you're here." Maddy settled on the couch, Charlotte in an armchair. "I don't know why you waited until Father – oh, it's too awful, Charli. Why did you stay away so long?"

"You know why," Charlotte said gently. Her sister looked sideways at her, as if struggling inside. Charlotte hated adding to her pain.

"Yes, well, that's all in the past now, isn't it? I know it was awful when you left, and David and Father were angry, but I'm sure they didn't mean you to stay away forever. You could even have brought –" She clearly couldn't say Karl's name. "Well, you know, you could have brought him with you. I'm sure they've forgiven you." Her face froze suddenly and a wild look came into her eyes. "He's not with you, is he?"

"No."

She gave a small gasp of relief. "But you're still…?"

"Together. Yes."

Madeleine seemed at a loss, not knowing whether to be pleased or dismayed. She, too, had fallen under Karl's spell, but the shock of discovering he was a vampire had almost destroyed her. Obviously those memories haunted her. How could they not?

"But where have you been?"

"Switzerland, mostly. And America, and Austria."

Maddy looked stunned by this prosaic answer, as if she'd expected Charlotte to say, *Hades*. "Switzerland? Good Lord, we went there on honeymoon two years ago."

"You're married?" Something else she hadn't known.

"Yes, to a simply wonderful man, Tristan."

"Any children?"

"Not yet. We're hoping. We're trying like mad." Madeleine took a ragged breath. "I wish it could have happened before Father got ill."

Charlotte took a risk. She moved to the couch and sat beside her sister, knowing she might recoil. Her recollection of Maddy jerking away in terror, when Charlotte had tried to say goodbye, still burned.

This time Maddy didn't move. Charlotte touched her arm, then folded her hand around the tender flesh, suppressing with all her will her desire for the hot, sweet blood pulsing under the surface. Her arm slipped around the bony shoulders and Madeleine leaned into her, hungry for solace. Their closeness emphasised a gap between them, where their older sister Fleur should have been.

"I do miss you, Maddy," she said. "I often think about you."

"You never wrote."

"How could I?"

"But it's all right now... isn't it?" Madeleine looked up, her sweet face close to Charlotte's. She was pale with anxiety. Charlotte understood.

Maddy could not bear the knowledge that Charlotte had become a vampire. Her mind wouldn't accept it. Instead she denied the truth, let herself believe that the intervening years had magically cured Charlotte – perhaps cured Karl, too – making her human again. That was why she let Charlotte touch her. To convince herself.

"It's not all right," Charlotte said gently. "I shouldn't have come back. But don't be afraid of me, Maddy. I love you more than I can say." She cheated a little as she spoke, allowing her eyes to work their spell, calming Madeleine's fears. Let her keep the illusion. Forcing the raw truth on her would be cruel.

"What does it matter at a time like this, anyway?" Maddy said. "We're still sisters. I'm so glad you're here."

They were sitting like that, arms around each other, when Anne came back. A look of grave suspicion clouded her face. Charlotte winced. *Don't you trust me one tiny bit, Anne? But... why should you?*

"I've spoken to the nurse," Anne said. "You can go up and see him, if you wish."

An unexpected wave of fear hit Charlotte. She didn't want to see her father. She wanted to remember him as he used to be. Pacing the laboratory in his shapeless jacket, his tie askew, propounding some new theory to her and Henry, his thick white moustache tinged yellow from cigar smoke. Bluff in manner, short-tempered sometimes, but the kindest of men underneath. Too possessive, he'd made Charlotte suffer in many subtle ways, but he had adored her – until the day she ran away with Karl.

Then he'd disowned her. And she had said such cruel things in response, words that could never be taken back.

"Are you sure he wants to see me?"

"Ask him yourself," Anne said grimly, folding her arms.

"You know how we parted." Charlotte stood up. "He told me I'd ceased to exist."

"Well, you have in a way, haven't you?" Anne's lips thinned. "I thought it was impossible for you to turn any paler – but you've gone quite white."

"Why are you doing this?"

"Whatever is happening now, Charlotte, you were the instigator."

"Has he asked for me?" she said desperately.

"Go and find out for yourself."

Floored by Anne's obduracy, Charlotte strode out of the room and went to the stairs. The house was deathly quiet. Daylight hung like dust in the stairwell. Every move she made unleashed memories. There was the door to the study, half-open onto silence. There was the door to the cellar laboratory, where she'd spent her days assisting his experiments. Shut and locked now, perhaps forever.

She ascended the stairs. She'd walked up these stairs with Karl, once... climbed them thousands of times without him, but always remembered that one time she'd led him to her bedroom...

She knocked lightly on the panelled door to her father's room, then let herself in. The curtains were drawn. There was a shape under the bedclothes, wisps of grey hair... she couldn't look. The stale smells of illness hung in the air. On the near side of the bed sat a plump woman in uniform and starched white cap. She stood as Charlotte entered.

"Good afternoon, madam."

"I'm his daughter, Charlotte. How is he?"

"Resting. He's comfortable," said the nurse, telling her nothing at all. From her calm manner, she knew nothing sinister about Charlotte. "I'm pleased to meet you, Miss Neville. I'm only sorry it's under such circumstances."

"Quite, er – would you leave us alone, please? I'm sure you must need a rest."

"Well, I wouldn't say no to a cup of tea. Just call if you need me."

When the nurse had left, Charlotte approached the bed. Her mouth was sour.

There was her father's dear face against the pillow, eyes closed, mouth open. How sunken his cheeks were. She stared at his neck, his wrists protruding from the sleeves of striped pyjamas, the narrow ribs rising and falling under the covers. How had he become so thin? He'd always seemed robust. She had known for years that his health was delicate, but she'd put it from her mind, never entertaining the possibility that he might die. Ever.

She remembered blue specks of radium glowing in darkness, tiny flashes of light hitting a screen as her father patiently counted them. She imagined those minute particles raining into his eyes, his body. *Is it radiation that's ruined his health – or grief?*

She took his hand. He frowned a little in his sleep. How dry and loose the skin felt, but the hand beneath was still strong. The hand of a man who had years of life and brilliant thought left in him. He wasn't much older than Josef. But his face was grey, appearing closer to eighty than sixty. The wheeze of every shallow, drowning breath hurt her ears.

"Father," she said, but he didn't hear.

She thought of another sick-bed she had attended; that

of Josef's sister, Lisl. At Josef's request she had relieved Lisl's suffering, gently sucking her blood until the end came. *I could do that again...*

Or... could I take him beyond death forever? I could find Stefan and a third vampire to transform him, quickly, now, before it's too late.

Her head dropped. She knew she wouldn't do it. Becoming a vampire was the last thing her father would want; how grotesque even to think of it! And if the process failed and he died – how hideous, far worse than dying with natural dignity. She could never bear the blame, the guilt.

No. She would do neither of those things. She would simply sit with him, the dutiful daughter.

Then, a small revelation. *Anne let me come in here alone! In her heart she does trust me, after all.*

"Father," she said again. "It's Charlotte. I'm so sorry I hurt you. You don't have to forgive me. I only want you to know that I still..."

His eyes opened. He blinked at her. Light gathered in his face, and he smiled and grasped her hand. "Oh, you came back!" he said.

Her heart sprang with relief. "Yes, dear, I'm here."

"It seems a lifetime since I saw you, my darling. I'm so glad. I knew if I waited –" He broke into a spasm of coughing. She supported him, mopped his mouth with a handkerchief. Blood soaked the white cotton. The vivid colour and ripe scent seemed to invade her physically. She threw the handkerchief aside and gave him a drink of water.

"I knew you'd come back," he said.

He looked so joyful. He held her hand between both of his, and she thought with a rush of happiness, *He's forgiven me! Not that it matters, all that matters is that he doesn't die thinking I hate him.* "I'll stay with you now, for as long as you want."

"Yes, stay with me," he said. "Dearest Annette."

Annette was her mother's name.

She sat down in the nurse's chair as if pinned by a lead spear, still holding his hand. He thought she was not his daughter but his wife, twenty-five years dead.

Charlotte was numb. Tears burned and overflowed her eyelids.

Now it made sense. *He must have been asking Anne for Annette, not for me.*

He never got over losing Mother, she thought. *He always saw her in me; now he believes I am her, and if it makes him happy, let him think it.*

She leaned over to kiss his forehead and his cheek, tasted a lingering trace of blood. He smiled. "I won't leave you," she said softly. "Dearest George."

"Madeleine grew into a fine young woman, you know," he said. "But where are Fleur and Charlotte? Will you bring them in to me?"

He'd forgotten that Fleur was dead, and that Charlotte had left him.

"Later, dearest," she whispered. "When you're stronger."

"Later. I am rather tired." His eyelids fluttered down, but his grasp on her hands did not weaken. "It's so good to have you with me." He went on talking, rambling about old times, confusing past and present. His words made little sense, but he required nothing of her except her presence. Finally she lay down on the bed beside him, one arm over his wasted body, her head on his shoulder. No blood thirst plagued her. His shallow breathing and the tap of his heart hypnotized her. She was human again, a child curled around him.

"You know, Annette, I feel a little better today," he said suddenly, almost in his normal tone. "I could quite fancy some eggs. Yes, eggs and toast."

Those were the last words he spoke. She felt his heart stop. She heard the last breath gurgle out of his lungs. And when it was over, she went on lying there so he wouldn't be alone. What hurry was there to tell anyone? She stayed there, eyes wide open in the gloom, because if she moved she would break down.

She was still there when the nurse came back, ten minutes later. Then she got up calmly and said, "He's gone." And she didn't cry after all, although a strange force was trying to lift her heart out of her chest.

The nurse was quiet and methodical as she attended to the body and pulled the sheet over his face. She uttered words of sympathy, but Charlotte barely heard her; ghost-like, she wandered across the landing to the top of the stairs. Then she saw Anne with David and her Aunt Elizabeth in the hall. They'd just come home and they didn't know...

So it was Charlotte's responsibility to break the news. But she was numb, and couldn't find any gentle way to tell them.

"He's dead."

Their faces swivelled towards her, aghast. She started down the stairs. "A few minutes ago. I was with him. At least someone was with him..."

And now, she thought bitterly, they are going to think I killed him.

Elizabeth hurried upstairs, passing her with barely a glance. She was muttering in anguished rage, "Oh, I knew we shouldn't have gone out! I knew this would happen if we left him. He might have waited!" – as if her brother had been simply inconsiderate.

David's face kind, strong face lost its colour. He came straight to Charlotte. She braced herself mentally, thinking, *Please don't let him be angry now. If he blames me for everything, I can't bear it.*

To her complete amazement, her brother threw his arms around her. He almost lifted her off her feet.

"Charlotte," he said into her neck, muffled. Then he wept.

While the doctor came and went, and the family and servants comforted one another, Charlotte waited alone in the darkened study. How desolate it seemed, never again to be animated by her father's intellect. In the past she had often sat at that desk, in a pool of lamplight, typing out his papers and theses... Never again.

She had told the others how he died: happy, because he thought Annette was with him. And they believed her, but she saw sorrow and confusion in their eyes. They must be wondering, *Is she a vampire or is she still Charlotte? How odd that he died while she was with him and we were not... our fault or hers?*

She couldn't blame them, but their suspicion flayed her. So she had left them to it. Now she sat in darkness, too shocked to grieve, aware of the years carrying her away from them.

She had been at the typewriter one rainy night when she realised, with a heart-stopping thrill, that Karl was in the room with her. He had been sitting on this leather couch, where she now sat alone. When he invited her to join him, against her better judgement, she couldn't resist.

She visualised Karl beside her now; lean, shadowy, enticing beyond reason, with tantalising glints of red light in his hair and eyes. She could almost hear the rush of rain. That evening, under a guise of kindness, he began to seduce her. So deep had she fallen under his enchantment that he could easily have taken full advantage of her there and then. He might have feasted on her blood – he'd told her, long afterwards, that he was sorely tempted – yet he held back, out of compassion. Love.

How young, how naive and full of hope she'd been. No one knew he was a vampire, of course, and by the time she found out, it was too late. Ironically, it was his kindness that had kept her fatally in love with him. If he'd proved to be merely a charming monster, her infatuation would have died and then perhaps her family would not have been torn apart, and her father and Fleur would still be alive...

Her human life had not been so bad, she reflected. *Yes, I felt oppressed and trapped – but as much by my own choice as by Father's demands. It was a shelter as well as a prison, a cocoon woven around me by my family. So divinely sinful to have a forbidden affair with Karl under their very noses!*

Falling for him had been a time of innocence and thrilling discovery... at least at the beginning. Never had she dreamed it would lead to alienation, to living on human blood, heartlessly seducing and attacking people to steal that blood... even killing them.

God, I've even done that. I was a guileless, wide-eyed girl... and now I'm a murderer. How did it happen?

The sheltering cocoon had been ripped apart. The idyll hadn't ended the day she discovered the truth about Karl, nor even when Ilona tore out Fleur's throat, and David struck Karl's head from his body. No, it had ended when Charlotte became a vampire, and she'd come back to say goodbye; hoping for forgiveness, finding only hostility and pain.

Karl, by the magic of Kristian's dark skill, had been restored to life, but Fleur lay in the cold ground for eternity. And Charlotte now treated her murderer, Ilona, like a sister. That was the ugly reality beneath the romance.

The house was dead, life and laughter extinguished. A frigid black wind blew in through the windows... that was how Charlotte felt. So cold. Slowly unravelling.

Father, she cried silently. *Father*.

After a couple of hours, Anne came in. She closed the door, switched on the desk lamp, and stared at Charlotte. She looked red-eyed, exhausted. Then she sat down beside her.

"Well, it's over," said Anne.

"How is everyone?"

"As you'd expect. Upset. Drinking tea and pretending to cope. I don't think David can forgive himself for not being there at the end."

"David never was good at forgiving himself for things that were not his fault."

Anne gave her a sharp glance. "It's strange, isn't it, that Dr Neville went so quickly after you'd gone in to him?"

White-hot anger consumed Charlotte. She sat forward a little, her eyes burning.

"How can you say that?" She managed to keep her voice low. "How could you even think it? My own father! What do you think I am?"

"I don't know." Anne flinched, putting up a hand as if to ward Charlotte away. "That's just it, I don't know!"

"He was waiting for Mother, that's all. When she arrived, he could sleep. If you think so ill of me, why did you invite me here?"

Anne's head dropped. "You're still his daughter. Right or wrong, I decided to trust you. I could have made a dreadful mistake."

"You thought that if you put anyone in danger, you'd be to blame? Well, you haven't." Charlotte's anger cooled to sorrow. She'd sometimes dreamed of meeting Anne in a gilded scene of reconciliation, but reality was jagged and difficult. "I'm still myself, I still have feelings. If anything, our feelings are more intense, like knives. If you think it meant nothing to me to see Father, you couldn't be more wrong. It means everything."

Tears overcame her suddenly. Anne looked shocked, at a loss. "I'm sorry."

They could have embraced each other then, but Charlotte saw

rejection in every line of Anne's body. If she held Anne in her arms, she would be all too aware of her blood pulsing like sap through a succulent and infinitely precious fruit...

"I'd better go," said Charlotte.

She began to rise, but Anne said, "Wait, please. I want to speak to you, but it's difficult."

"Just talk to me as you used to. I told you, I'm still the same."

"But you're not. That's the trouble. Look at yourself in the mirror – if you can. You haven't aged a day, and your eyes... I didn't realise I'd find it this hard."

"Neither did I." She touched Anne's wrist; Anne flinched, so she withdrew her hand. "How did you find me, anyway?"

Anne went to the desk and opened a drawer. Returning, she placed a newspaper on Charlotte's knee, turned to an inside page. A photograph showed a group of passengers at a ship's rail, smiling and waving. In the middle was Violette, with the *corps de ballet* girls alongside. Just behind her, clearly recognisable despite the smudgy grey print, were Karl and Charlotte. Charlotte was smiling, a sweet-natured, carefree girl; Karl was inclining his head towards her, as if whispering in her ear. Her hand was on Violette's shoulder. LENOIR SAILS TO CONQUER U.S.A. said the headline.

Charlotte gasped. This had been inevitable. Her real shock came from realising that she had never seen a photograph of Karl before.

"How do you think I felt when I saw that?" Anne said angrily. "How do you think David felt? We managed to hide it from your father."

"It's just a photograph, Anne. We sponsor the ballet. Help with the business side."

Anne looked stunned, as if unable to believe that vampires could do anything so human. "Does Miss Lenoir know what you are?"

Charlotte verged on laughter. "Oh yes, she knows."

"*What on Earth have you been doing?*" The question exploded out of her.

"I wouldn't know where to start."

"I can't imagine seeing Karl again. The whole thing was a bad dream." Anne looked obliquely at Charlotte. "I don't understand why talking to you makes me feel as if I'm losing my mind."

Charlotte dropped her gaze. "For heaven's sake, don't be afraid of me. I've so wanted to talk to you. I know you're the one I upset most, apart from Father. Elizabeth understood my reasons but didn't care; David and Maddy cared, but didn't understand. But you did, and you want to forgive me, but you can't. And I'm sorry."

Anne pushed back her hair, folded her arms. "You're not the centre of the universe, Charli. David and I are happy at Parkland, and when we've mourned the Prof's death, we will be again."

"And Maddy's happy too," Charlotte said, to deflect her sharp words.

"Is that what she told you?"

"Yes. Why?"

"She married Tristan for his money, that's why. She lavishes his wealth on charity work to ease the guilt she feels for her privileged upbringing. And meanwhile she dotes on someone else. She's so besotted with this other man that she has him living with her and her husband."

"What? And her husband puts up with it?"

"Yes, because he worships her. She gets away with anything. She couldn't marry this other man because he's a semi-invalid, mentally unstable. He couldn't have provided for her. She simply looks after him, out of love."

"Oh God," Charlotte whispered. "Edward."

"Yes, Edward. Remember him? David's dearest friend, who nearly died and was fit only for a mental asylum after Karl attacked him? He's lucky to have Maddy and us, but he'll never be really well. And you wonder that I'm upset, when David sees Karl's face in the paper, and you with him, laughing!"

Charlotte shrank under the pressure of Anne's distress. *How can I defend myself, when she's right?* The Anne of her daydreams was the friend she used to know; lively, confiding, forgiving. They kissed like sisters, and exchanged a sip of blood as a bond... Of course Charlotte knew the dream could not come true, but nothing had prepared her for this mature, angry, harassed woman.

"It should have stayed a dream," Charlotte murmured, "coming to see you."

"Why? Do vampires feel guilt? Karl's gone, but the things he did stay with us. They almost wrecked our lives. You knew, yet you went with him anyway!"

The words struck like fangs.

"I was selfish, I know. But I loved Karl to the point of madness and I still do."

"Damn it," said Anne. "I swore to myself, no recriminations. Not at a time like this."

"But if it wasn't a time like this, I wouldn't be here." Charlotte's tone was gentle, cool. She was drawing away. All she wanted was to be alone with memories of her father. "I'm grateful you asked me here. So glad I was with Father. I only wish…"

"Don't we all. But wishing won't bring him back." Another hard glance. "And it won't bring you back either, will it?"

"No. I can't become human again."

"Would you want to? That's the question."

Charlotte didn't answer. "Would you mind – would the others mind – if I came to the funeral?"

Anne's stark expression revealed that this was an appalling prospect. Charlotte knew Anne would never accept what she'd become. Yes, she might use vampiric influence to change her friend's mind – but it wouldn't be real. Charlotte couldn't do it. She waited.

"You don't need my permission," Anne said after a moment, her tone not exactly kind, but resigned. "It's your right."

Dressed in black, heavily veiled, Charlotte arrived late at the chapel and sat alone at the back. She knew her presence would disturb her family, and she didn't want to worsen their grief.

She'd spent the intervening few days in Cambridge, exploring the city she loved so dearly, avoiding anyone who might know her. She telephoned Karl every day; all was quiet in Salzburg. She longed to see him, but it seemed important not to leave until her father was buried. A mourning ritual, of a sort.

The chapel was full of eminent people; fellows from Trinity, her father's colleagues from the Cavendish, many of his former students. Seeing how well loved and respected he was moved her to tears. She wept silently behind the veil. The eulogies were unbearable.

I wish Karl were here, she thought. *He would hold me steady against this terrible greyness.*

As they walked to the cemetery afterwards, she recalled another burial: that of Janacek, whom she'd killed in order to free Violette. She had felt detached then, completely in command of herself. Now she felt vulnerable, as if made of glass: not of the same flesh as her family, but hard and fragile.

Earth fell on the coffin. David and Anne cried, leaning together. Elizabeth held Madeleine. Henry was there too; her father's assistant, virtually a son to him – and once, for a brief time, Charlotte's husband.

She didn't look at him, nor he at her.

When it was over, she meant to slip away – only to find her family all around her, Maddy's hand through her arm, and David's sombre voice in her ear.

"Will you come back to the house, please, Charlotte?"

"We thought you should know," David said, "that Father cut you out of his will. There's nothing for you, I'm afraid."

Charlotte felt a dart of misery – for the loss of her father's affection, not his property.

"It's all right, I didn't expect anything. I hadn't even thought about it."

They were sitting around the breakfast room table; David, Anne, Henry and herself, while Elizabeth and Madeleine played host to mourners in the drawing room. Henry had aged visibly, well on course to becoming a bumbling professor. A bulky, bespectacled figure, pompous yet shy and embarrassed by emotion, he was just as Charlotte remembered. So far he hadn't said a word to her, though it was obvious her presence made him acutely uncomfortable.

"Why did you come back, then?" David said with sudden sharpness. Tired and distraught, he ran a hand over his fair hair. She saw a few silver strands.

"Do you think I loved Father any less, because of the decision I made? How could I not come?" She gazed at her brother, knowing the gleam of her face and eyes disturbed him. "I know I'm making things difficult. I'm sorry. But why on earth did you try to find me? I don't mean now... I mean last year."

David cleared his throat. Anne glanced at him, then at Henry, who was looking anywhere but at Charlotte.

"About eighteen months after I left," she went on, "you sent a private detective called John Milner to find us. And he did."

"We know," said David. "Not because he told us, but because he was found wandering in Dover with no recollection of how he'd got there. He was ill for a time; said he was having weird, wonderful dreams of a woman who looked like you. And there were marks on his neck, so faint that most people wouldn't notice. So we knew, Charli, even though he couldn't tell us anything. That's why I didn't try again, until we saw the photograph. It was too dangerous."

"But why did you try at all?"

"Because I was worried sick about you!" David exclaimed. "Why d'you think? You're still my sister; I couldn't help thinking what that – that man might have done to you!"

"His name is Karl." From the corner of her eye she saw Henry shudder and put a hand to his face. "All he did was help me become myself."

"Oh," said David, "so the kind, shy sister I loved was really a demon all along?"

"David," said Anne. She touched his arm and he subsided. Anne, it seemed, had already said all she needed to.

Charlotte sat with cruel revelation pouring over her. How they'd changed in such a short time. They had a child already and there would be more; they were growing older, drifting away from her. As Karl had once said, a vampire was like a stopped clock on a landscape: she stood motionless while they travelled without her. The gulf between them felt like a grave. Terrifying.

"You're right to feel betrayed, David," said Charlotte. "I did wrong, but love is stronger than reason. I can't repent. If you want me to say it was all a mistake and I'm coming home – I can't. It will never happen."

"I see," David said wearily. "Just tell me one thing. Does he – does Karl treat you kindly?"

"Of course he does. He always did."

David sighed. There was an uncomfortable silence. Their unease distressed her, but she couldn't enchant them into accepting her. They must love or hate her of their own free will.

"Henry wants to say something," said David.

She turned her gaze to Henry. He could barely look at her, and his voice shook. "I – I have become friendly with a pleasant young lady. We – we want to marry."

"How nice for you," Charlotte said frigidly. She could imagine the woman; a prim little Methodist, approved of by Henry's mother.

"But I can't marry her, can I!" he exclaimed, slapping the table with both palms. "I'm still married to you! I – I want a divorce."

A smile frosted Charlotte's mouth. This became more ghastly by the moment. Thinking she'd lost Karl forever, she'd married Henry only to keep him from walking out on her father. But Karl had come back. She felt cruel, completely a vampire.

"As far as I'm concerned, we were never truly married."

"Well, as far as the law's concerned, we ruddy well are!" Henry turned crimson. She felt a sudden ache in her canine teeth.

"Do you really think I'd waste my time, sitting about in court? How can you cite Karl, when the police think he's dead? I suppose one of us could pretend to commit adultery in a boarding house while some private detective takes notes; David has a friend who does that sort of thing." This dig caused her brother to blush. "It's ludicrous. Do what Karl and I do. Live together."

She knew her words would horrify him. Henry seemed close to exploding with outrage. "This isn't Bloomsbury! It's out of the question!" He stood up suddenly. "You are a monster, Charlotte! The Prof was never the same after you left. It should have been you in that coffin instead! You killed him!"

Her fingers tightened on the table edge. She stared at the shine of her taut white knuckles. "I think we'd better continue this conversation in private, don't you?"

Henry harrumphed. "I suppose so."

Anne and David looked uneasy. Charlotte said, "Go on. It's all right."

They left. Charlotte's presence seemed to have undone Henry's composure entirely. Alone with her, he became rigidly correct and unapproachable, but he dabbed his upper lip with a handkerchief.

His hands trembling. From the way he stared she knew, with dismay, that her vampire allure was affecting him.

"You can say what you like now." She stood up as she spoke. He edged away to the window. "Go on. I'm a monster and I killed my father?"

"You look –" he stammered. "You look just the same."

"What did you tell people, when I left?"

"The truth," Henry said gruffly. "That you'd run off with another man."

"That was brave. Most men would have felt too humiliated."

He turned on her, pale with anger. "How could I be any more humiliated than I already was?" As his anguish came pouring out, she could only stand there and let it wash over her. "You were – *intimate* with Karl while you were engaged to me! How could you? You seemed so shy, so virtuous, Dr Neville's perfect daughter. It was out of the question that I'd do more than kiss your cheek until we were married, but with Karl you – I still cannot believe what you did!"

"Hurt your pride?" His pain roused only mild sympathy, mixed with irritation.

"That is not fair! I loved you!"

Charlotte looked down. "I did you a terrible wrong. I only married you to please my father, not you or myself. The woman you thought would make a quiet, unthreatening wife wasn't me. My fault, for letting you think it was. But Henry, what were you offering me?"

The question seemed to dumbfound him.

"A respectable marriage," he said stiffly. "A family."

"But what about passion? You say you loved me, but the few times we consummated our so-called marriage, neither of us enjoyed it. It was just our duty, and I must be a scarlet woman for wanting anything more! Everything, duty. How could you expect me to live like that?"

Henry's face coloured. "You are a heathen, Charlotte. In a previous age you would have been burned at the stake."

"And you would have lit the fire; not enjoying it, just doing your duty to God. I wish you could understand why I gave myself completely to Karl, again and again, and why I left you for him."

She was provoking him now, relishing his discomfort. "I wish I could make you feel just one moment of that passion!"

As she spoke, desire ignited beneath her heart. With excitement dancing through her, she went to Henry, pushed him into a chair and sat on his knee. Too stunned to stop her, he caved in beneath her as if he'd lost all his strength.

Even when she twined her arms around his neck, she knew he was dying of embarrassment. He'd put the fact that she was a vampire out of his mind, because he couldn't believe it. While he was rigid with outrage, she sensed his puritan nature warring with his secret dark impulses, with the fact that he was and always had been her slave.

Her lips found the artery beating beneath the salty skin. Mouth wide, she bit down, felt blood and salt rushing onto her eager tongue. The red starburst convulsed her. She hugged Henry to her, experiencing perfect happiness, laughing through the blood.

Henry uttered a single cry, as if a wasp had stung him. Then he was silent, passive; not touching her, not resisting, as if he'd found a very deep, dark place inside himself that only her bite could touch.

It was the first exchange of genuine, unfettered passion that had ever passed between them. First and last.

Charlotte found it easy to stop, to slip lightly from his knee as if nothing had happened. Henry's head lolled forward. He took off his glasses, squeezed his eyes shut and pinched his forehead.

"I wish you joy of the dear little Methodist you wish to marry. She'll never do that to you. Or will she? Appearances can deceive. One day she may tire of making afternoon tea for Cambridge dons and develop a taste for their blood."

Now he was staring blankly at her, as if his memory had already erased the unacceptable.

"What?" he murmured. "I feel dizzy. Bit of a headache."

"You'll be all right." She crouched down beside him with the easy affection she felt for her victims. "Henry, listen to me. Go and join the funeral feast, have some tea. When it's over, come back and I'll give you my answer."

He blinked at her. "Answer?"

The solution was obvious. It invaded her, with Henry's blood, like a kind of insanity. Amid the desolation of her father's death, the funeral, her family's grief, the answer was like a jewel, a polished moonstone in a perfect setting.

"I'm going to set you free, dear."

Charlotte waited until the guests were leaving as darkness fell. Then she went into the hallway to share the goodbyes and expressions of sympathy, for all the world as if she were still part of the Neville family. The least she could do for her father was to show his friends that his daughter had loved him.

Once they'd gone, she followed the others back into the drawing room: Anne, David, Henry, Madeleine and Elizabeth, all in black. No one sat down.

Feeling calm, Charlotte saw them as if through a lens. How distant they looked, like figures in a play. The ghastliness of her plan infused her like cold madness. Perhaps she had gone mad; there was no better explanation.

Karl had said, "Be gentle with them." She tried to speak kindly, but her tone could not shield them from her stark words.

"I don't want to stand in the way of Henry's happiness," she began. "And he said he wanted to see me in a coffin. Well, so be it."

"What are you talking about?" said Anne.

"I'm thinking of Henry. His family are strict churchgoers. A divorce would be scandalous and messy, and might sour things between him and his fiancée. But if I were dead, everything would be simple, wouldn't it?"

Henry stared at her, sweat beading on his flushed face. She thought, *I really should not have fed on him... but his blood was irresistible.*

"You can't just pretend to be dead," said David.

"I'm not talking about pretending," she said. "I'm talking of a legitimate death certificate and a real burial. Strictly speaking, I'm not really alive anyway. At least, no longer human."

Henry sat down heavily on the sofa. David said hoarsely, "For God's sake, Charli, what are you proposing?"

"The doctor pronounces me dead. You place me in a coffin and bury me. Henry's free to remarry. Well, why not?"

They looked stricken, as if this were some black joke. She saw their faces as if through gauze. Mentally she was travelling away from them, cutting the chains.

"Stop this," David said. Madeleine's eyes were round with disbelief.

"It sounds a perfectly good idea to me," Elizabeth said acidly.

"A few conditions: hold the funeral as quickly and quietly as possible. I'll pay, of course. And don't let the undertaker touch me. I wouldn't appreciate being embalmed."

"How – how –?" Henry stammered.

"Like this," Charlotte said softly. She sat beside him and composed herself, arms at her sides, head tipped back. She made her slow heartbeat stop completely. She remained like that, not breathing, not blinking, until they began to edge nervously towards her.

"Charlotte?" said Anne. She shook her arm hesitantly, then gripped her wrist. "My God, there's no pulse!" Anne shook her, but Charlotte was a glass-eyed rag doll in her hands. "Charlotte!"

Their horror was tangible. With a gasp, Madeleine backed away and ran out of the room.

Charlotte looked up at Henry's white stare, Anne and David's consternation. Only Elizabeth's supercilious face was blank. Then she stirred and sat up. They all started violently.

"Do you see?" she said. "The doctor will be convinced I'm dead. Tell him I fell ill after the funeral. When you bury me, I won't really stay in the coffin, of course. I'll vanish."

David stood frowning, battling to maintain his composure. Eventually he said quietly, "I'm going to see how Maddy is," and he turned and walked out.

Anne ran after him. "David!"

"I refuse to have anything to do with this grotesque charade!" he called over his shoulder. Anne hesitated in the doorway, swore under her breath, then marched back to Charlotte.

"You can't mean to go through with this!"

"Why not?"

"It's too horrible! And the doctor will want an inquest on a young woman who dies for no reason."

"Oh no, he won't. I'll see to that."

"I think we should let her do it," said Elizabeth. Her hard brown eyes met Charlotte's. Although there was little affection between them, they'd long ago reached a truce. "For Henry's sake. I'll make the arrangements, if the rest of you can't face it."

Anne was shaking her head, her face a mask of dismay. "But you won't really be dead, will you?"

Charlotte spoke gently. "No, but you can forget me then, or at least let go. Let yourselves *believe* I'm dead. Because actually I am. Undead." She touched Anne's cheek. "It's for the best."

Anne, for once, permitted the touch. Charlotte closed her eyes, feeling madness rushing around her, like a gale through a dark cathedral, like the earth walls of her father's grave. And she thought, *I can't make them accept me but at least they don't hate me. That will have to be enough.*

CHAPTER EIGHTEEN

SWALLOWED IN THE MIST

Alone in the library, Robyn dreamed. She seemed to be in the nursery again, with figures whispering around her. Everything had the understated malevolence of a nightmare. The light was flat grey on heaped shadows, while the walls and ceiling tilted at terrifying angles. In the greyness were two ghosts. One was Rasmila, the other a slender man as pale as Rasmila was dark.

They whispered urgently to each other, their words nonsensical but unspeakably sinister.

"She is the one Lilith loves. If she comes here... jealousy... he will destroy her, he will break her wings... *He can do what Simon cannot.*"

Then she dreamed she was breaking glass cases, tearing birds off their perches, snapping their reed-like bones and shredding their feathers, weeping bitterly because she didn't want to destroy their beauty, even if it was dead beauty.

"Robyn? Such groans!"

She started. Sebastian was there, holding her hand.

"Oh, I was having awful dreams," she said, annoyed at her own imagination.

"Don't dream in this house," he said wryly. "It might come true."

"I'll bear that in mind." She got up, shaking off the nightmare. In retrospect it seemed a waking dream, a bizarre train of thought into which she had drifted while waiting for Sebastian. "Where have you been? You told me to stay here because you had a surprise for me. That was four hours ago!"

Sebastian only smiled enigmatically. "Surprises like this can't be prepared in ten minutes. Come along."

He led her upstairs to a large bedchamber. Robyn remembered the room as being semi-derelict, nothing in there but a big packing case under a sheet. Now she found the place transformed. There was a fire in the marble grate; even the ancient wallpaper took on a bloom of luxury in the light. Bright Persian rugs lay on the floorboards.

The sight that stopped her breath, however, was a magnificent bed that had appeared from nowhere. A four-poster draped in lavish canopies, it looked pristine, too new for its surroundings.

Robyn held the fabric between her fingers, marvelling at the embroidery. A cream background, hand-sewn with flowers in jewel colours and gilt thread. And swathes of dark blue Chinese silk, sewn with dragons, deer, and storks. Months, if not years of work.

"Do you approve?" Sebastian enquired.

"Wonderful... but where did it come from? It looks old, yet brand new."

His smile was one of unaffected pleasure. "You saw the packing case? The bed was delivered to the house in 1735, a wedding present that was never used. So it is old but perfect. I never had a reason to assemble it, until now."

"The colours are so bright!" she said. "Silly, but I imagined antique furniture being as faded then as it is now."

"Well, it wasn't," he said. Amazing to think that he remembered those times. That he could be so old, yet eternally young... "It ought to be christened, don't you think?" Taking her hands, he pulled her on to the bed. "Or whatever the infernal opposite of christening is."

"Wait," Robyn said, laughing. "Fold back the covers first. It would be sacrilege to damage this beautiful embroidery."

In their ecstasy, they allowed themselves to experience happiness. For once, they held nothing back. This was perhaps the first time they had loved each other without artifice.

Robyn was almost out of her mind with joy. She never wanted this to end; to stroke Sebastian's beautiful body and his dark hair, to have those seductive eyes endlessly on her; to have him all around her and inside her, flesh soldered to flesh. And more, to know that his passion was as desperate, ravenous and blissful as hers. To inspire such fever in him...

She was grateful to Rasmila now. That experience had taught him, as nothing else could, that it was Robyn he really wanted.

Climaxing in lightning, in rains of fire, Robyn drew his head down to her shoulder. She wanted his mouth on her throat, wanted the pain. She would have given him anything. She had no virtue left to sacrifice, but she could give him this: the deeper sacrifice of her life-fluid.

When Sebastian lifted his head at last, he seemed overwhelmed that she'd given her blood willingly. And for that look of wonder, she could forgive him anything.

"Is it over, then?" she whispered as they lay together in tangled sheets. Her fatigue was so heavy she thought she might never move again.

"What?"

"The war between us."

"If you want it to be."

"Where was it getting us?" she asked. "Trying to ruin each other, break each other's heart... what was the point?"

"To nourish our pride," said Sebastian. He'd never looked more desirable; his hair disordered, his face coloured by her blood. "It seems pointless now. Dry, dead, unimportant."

"Shall we call a truce, then?"

"Only a truce, my lady?" he said. "A peace treaty, at the very least."

Sebastian stood watching Robyn as she slept. She was sleeping more as the days went by. Too pale. However careful he tried to be, each time they made love her languor deepened.

He was troubled. The emotions aroused by the mere sight of her face disturbed him. *Do I worship her, or only her human life-energy?*

There may be other women prettier, younger, or sweeter in nature, he thought, *but none of them is Robyn. No, I need Robyn for herself. With all the faults that make her so like me, in all her magnificent warmth, she is unique. No one else will suffice. Ever.*

The knowledge made him feel agitated, terrified. *In loving her I'm acting completely against my instincts. How has she done this? She's changed me, and in doing so she's destroyed what I was.*

She made me admit my feelings, but she has never once said, "I love you," in return.

So she has won the game. All I can do in retaliation is to keep her here, and thus control her... but for how long? Until she grows old? Will I still love an old woman, out of her mind because a vampire has kept her prisoner for years?

Verging on horror, he reached down and stroked her hair. Robyn pushed her head against his hand, smiling in her sleep.

No bad dreams now.

After Charlotte left, Karl half-wished he'd gone with her. He had no fear of the Neville family's wrath or their opinion of him. *For Charlotte's sake*, he thought, *to prove she hasn't deserted them for a fiend who tricked and ruined her, but for someone who truly loves her, I should have gone. And for the respect I owe Dr Neville, and the affection I once felt for them.*

Yet here I am, putting Violette before her... again, for Charlotte's sake.

Charlotte telephoned with the news of her father's death. She would stay for the funeral... But when it was over, she called again to say she was staying a while longer.

"I can't explain over the telephone," she said, sounding too calm, not herself. "I'll be a few days, that's all. There's something I have to sort out with my family."

Dr Neville's death saddened him. Karl had nothing but fond memories of his time in Cambridge and at Parkland Hall, until Kristian's wiles had caused him to betray himself. Neville had been a kindly man, generous enough to welcome a foreigner, Karl, into his home. *For which I thanked him by stealing his daughter, drawing other vampires to the family.*

Still, Karl dwelled for a while on memories: their long philosophical discussions in which Dr Neville had treated no theory as too outlandish. Even speculation of the Crystal Ring's existence.

Karl was in Violette's apartment, aware of every human in the house and those who came and went. He could hear dancers in the studio, the pianist starting and stopping, Violette's crisp voice giving instructions. And on lower floors, seamstresses, set designers, kitchen staff at their work... even the quick warmth of a cat, twining around the legs of a delivery boy. Normality...

Then Karl sensed shadows, presences poised on the threshold between Raqia and reality. He looked up as they coalesced before him.

Two angels, swathed in long hair: midnight and ice-white silk.

"Rasmila, Fyodor; this is unexpected." Karl rose to greet them, startled but careful not to show it.

"Oh, I think you knew we'd come back," said Rasmila. Her eyes were spheres of obsidian, lit by white comets and blue stars. Karl still found it difficult to look directly at her.

"Fyodor got his wish," said Karl. "Lilith removed me from Simon's presence, to the relief of all. Did that help your cause?"

Karl guessed, from the tightening of their faces, that they still hadn't found favour with Simon.

"You've no cause to mock us," Fyodor said sharply. "I can't see you as an enemy, however hard I try. I asked Charlotte for help and she obliged. I'm grateful."

"We are not Lilith's enemies, whatever you think," said Rasmila. "We want to help her."

"I believe your 'help' is the last thing she needs," said Karl, "but would you come to the point of why you are here?"

"Lilith-Violette has a particular interest in a human female, does she not? An American."

Karl regarded them warily. *How on earth have they found out about Robyn? I thought only Charlotte and I knew, unless these creatures are omniscient, acting as Simon's spies.* Then he remembered Violette's story; that when she'd paid a visit to Robyn, Cesare had followed her.

"Where did you hear this?"

"Rumours," said Fyodor.

"I couldn't possibly comment," said Karl, "on rumours."

"You don't have to." Rasmila came closer. In her sari of indigo sewn with tiny mirrors, she seemed to float. "Someone is on his way to see you. Someone very upset and desperate. When he has gone, we will come back and explain."

The air opened and closed to receive them.

Karl could only think, grimly, that this was some plot of Simon's.

Moments later, a human came running to the door, knocking urgently and entering without waiting for him to answer. Violette's maid, Geli.

"Sir? There's a gentleman to see Frau Alexander. I told him she's not here, but he won't go away. Madame's working, I can't disturb her."

Karl felt Rasmila and Fyodor still present, invisible. Spying, without question. He must warn Violette.

"I'll see him, Geli. Who is it?"

"Dr Josef Stern," said the girl. "He's downstairs."

"Tell Madame anyway. If she's annoyed, tell her to shout at me, not at you."

Karl found Josef in a small office. He was stood with his hat in his hands, his thick silver hair in disarray, his face lined with anxiety.

"Ah, Karl," he said uneasily, "forgive the intrusion. I gather Charlotte is away."

"Yes, for several days." He shook Josef's hand, cold and formal. "Can I help?"

"I'm not sure. I really don't know what to do."

"What is it?"

Josef hesitated, then apparently decided to trust Karl. He took a letter from his coat pocket and offered it, seeming close to tears.

"It's my niece, Robyn. You met her in Boston. She's disappeared. I received this letter from her companion, Alice. I might have thought Alice deranged, if not for what I know... about *your kind*." His voice sank on the last words.

It must take courage, Karl thought, *for him to approach me, knowing what I am.*

The letter spoke of a vampire named Sebastian Pierse. The language was wild, barely comprehensible. Robyn had taken this vampire as her lover and apparently lost her sanity. He'd attacked Alice and the maid, Mary; he might even have murdered Robyn's lover Harold. Now Robyn had vanished, leaving a curt note. Alice concluded that Sebastian had abducted her.

Karl absorbed all this, incredulous. *Sebastian. God help Robyn, if it's true.*

As Karl read the letter a second time, Violette entered in her grey practice clothes.

"Dr Stern," she said. "What's wrong?"

Karl raised his eyebrows in enquiry. Josef nodded, so Karl passed the letter to Violette.

She said nothing at first. But when she looked up, her face was transformed by silent, devastating fear.

"Do you know this Sebastian Pierse?" Josef asked.

"I met him once," Karl said, "a long time ago."

Violette's lips parted but no sound came out. Karl gently prised the letter from her hands.

"Who is he?" Josef cried. "How could this happen?"

"I have no idea," Karl said.

"How was it possible for him to be in Boston, without you or other vampires knowing he was there? Why did you not warn us?"

"Did *you* warn Robyn about us?" Karl asked. Josef subsided, looking grey. "We didn't know. Vampires usually sense each other from a distance, but some have no detectable aura, or can shield themselves. Sebastian, as I remember, was like that. Unless we physically saw him, he could keep himself invisible."

"And is he dangerous?"

No point in giving Josef false hope. "Do you think I am evil?" Karl asked.

Josef's larynx rose and fell. "Yes, I'm afraid I do."

"You didn't trust me with your niece, although I would not have laid a finger on her, out of respect for our acquaintance. Sebastian, unfortunately, has no such scruples. If Alice's letter is true, I'm not optimistic."

Josef looked as if his heart would fail. He said hoarsely, "Can you help me find her?"

Karl groaned inwardly. Secretly he was mortified by the news and half-blamed himself, but he never let such feelings rule him.

"I would if I could, but Robyn could be anywhere. We have troubles of our own here. I'm sorry."

"Of course, I should have known better than to expect concern from you," Josef said bitterly. "After all, she's only a human being. I thought Charlotte might have cared, that's all." Josef put a hand to his face, hiding tears.

"No, you're mistaken," Violette exclaimed. "I care. We'll help you find her."

Josef's gaze caught hers like a hooked fish. He reddened and dropped his eyes. *As if*, Karl thought, *he knows the nature of Violette's feelings for Robyn.*

"We can make no promises," Karl said quickly. "I suggest you write to Alice again and obtain clearer information. But if we discover anything, we'll let you know."

Karl gently but firmly brought the meeting to an end. Looking drained, Josef retrieved the letter and made for the door. "I'd be so grateful. I'm sorry to have troubled you." He gave a crisp, Viennese bow. "Madame, *mein Herr*."

When he'd gone, Violette began to pace the room like a starved tigress.

"Another vampire with Robyn!" she breathed. "I thought she was safe!" She turned on Karl, eyes blazing. "*I left her* to keep her safe! How could we miss this other vampire? How did he get to her? God, if only I'd let her come with us!"

"Violette, try to be calm," said Karl. "I understand your feelings, but while we have the threat of Cesare over us, there's no chance of searching for Robyn."

"Do you think I don't know that? This is all I need! Who is this Sebastian?"

"I barely knew him. He once came to Holdenstein and made trouble with Kristian. Some of us hoped he'd become an ally against Kristian, but he would have none of it. He seemed to despise all vampires equally." He thought sadly of Ilona, with whom Sebastian had toyed for a time. "And I understand he's cruel with his victims. He likes to play before he kills them."

"And now he's playing with Robyn." She shuddered. Then her eyes opened wide. "Wait, I've seen him! When I was in Robyn's room, and realised Cesare was there, and I fled to lead him away – another vampire followed us! I thought he was one of Cesare's followers, but he wasn't. He was alone. Tallish, slim, very dark.

Aloof, as if everything were beneath him and amusing."

"That sounds like him," said Karl.

"I never sensed him in Robyn's room – but what if he was there? Yes, her face... as if she was suffering. She actually said, 'Take away the pain.' And I didn't. I failed her. Again."

"Violette, come upstairs," Karl said gently. "Rasmila and Fyodor are here to see you. I think it's about this."

Violette glared at him, but said nothing.

"Be careful," Karl added. "Anything they say is probably designed to trap you."

"No one is more wary than me," she said aridly.

They were waiting in Violette's living room, like polarized twins; Fyodor silver-white, Rasmila a carving of rosewood and jet. She had once provoked lethal tenderness in Karl, given him her blood when he was starving, only for the blood to put him in her power like a drug. She would not take him in again.

"I thought I'd seen the last of you," Violette said. "How dare you come here unannounced? What do you want?"

"To help you," said Rasmila.

"How?" Karl said. "Why should she trust you?"

"Why should I trust anyone?" said the dancer. "Karl cannot bear me, although he's too well-mannered to admit it. And you two have brought me nothing but misery."

"That's in the past," said Rasmila.

"Is it? We've heard tales of woe from Simon and Fyodor. But you are the worst, Rasmila, with your pretence of passivity. You condone the lies with which women destroy themselves. You delivered me to a man who almost raped me, and called it God's will!"

"But God's will is that –"

"Whose god?" Violette cried. "That of the Catholics, or the Jews, or the Hindus, or Kristian's god? They are all different beings. I don't know which one you worship."

"There is only one God," Rasmila said, unmoved, "as you should know. Please listen. We don't hate you, Lilith. We're only protecting the Crystal Ring from what it will become if you do not surrender to God."

"The Crystal Ring," Violette said softly. She turned away and perched on the arm of a chair. "Yes, the storms are my fault, and the black stone mass that hangs there like a tomb..."

"Do you want to destroy vampire-kind?" asked Fyodor.

"Destroy my own children?" She gave a thin, humourless smile.

"Mothers do," said Rasmila.

"What's your justification for blaming everything on Violette?" said Karl. "The strange object in the Ring could be unconnected."

"No," said Violette. "It's connected to me. I feel it."

Karl said, "But this artefact – what is it?"

Rasmila shrugged. "A mystery. I've tried to discern its nature but I cannot lift the veil. All I know is that it is deadly to us."

Karl remembered trying to approach the dark fortress with Charlotte, being flung away by its cold, leaden force... Rasmila spoke the truth, but this didn't answer his question.

"So, Cesare's right to want me dead." Violette's voice was low, sinister. "Should I take my own life, to save him the trouble?"

"No. Lilith cannot die. She's been here from the beginning."

"Like the Devil, I know, but what would you have me do?"

Rasmila moved closer to Violette, with Fyodor hanging back behind her. Karl watched in apprehension. Violette could attack like lightning.

"Come with us to Simon. If we deliver you to him, he'll accept us again," said Rasmila. "If the three of us were reconciled, God would give back our angelic status and lift the veil. We want peace in heaven. Not war."

"And Simon and Cesare will win, with Lilith back in chains," said Violette. Karl expected contempt from her. Instead she sounded bleak, as if she'd already surrendered.

"For the good of all. Lilith may not want peace – but you do, Violette. In your heart."

"And what shall I receive in return?"

"We'll tell you where to find Sebastian and Robyn."

"I could find them myself."

"But not so swiftly. And if we warned him – never."

Violette went ash-white. Karl, concerned, placed a hand on her forearm, but she shook him off. "I find your threats repellent – but I agree, all the same. If I find you've told me the truth, I'll do anything you want afterwards."

Fyodor and Rasmila exchanged joyful looks. Their relief was

tangible. Karl felt only foreboding. "You promise to come with us to Simon?"

"Yes, I promise."

"Good. You will find them in Ireland. County Waterford, in a great house called Blackwater Hall."

Violette raised her head with the dignified resignation of someone walking to the gallows. "How is Robyn? No, don't tell me. I only trust my own eyes."

"We'll be watching," said Fyodor. "To ensure you fulfil the bargain."

A rim of Crystal Ring light shone briefly round the two immortals, azure-bright against the dull lavenders of the room. They bowed, and disappeared.

"I must leave at once," said Violette. "I need only a minute to change my clothes."

"Violette, do you know what you've agreed to?"

She paused with her hand on the door to her dressing room, blinking as if she'd forgotten Karl was there.

"No. Do you? If I save Robyn's life, nothing else matters. And if I don't, nothing matters anyway. They think I can heal Raqia by surrendering to them – and who's to say they're wrong? Even you half-believe it, don't you? So don't start a lecture about falling into traps."

Not reacting, he asked, "Would you like me to come with you?"

"No!" she flared. "No, thank you. I'd like you to protect my dancers. But you don't have to. Leave, go to Charlotte: I don't care."

Her fangs shone, indenting her lower lip. She seemed on the verge of fulfilling her threat to feed on him, transform him and destroy his soul. Karl turned cold, but didn't move.

"Why do you drive away everyone who wants to help you?"

"I don't need help."

"Or you think you don't deserve it."

"*You* think I don't deserve it," she retorted. "Duty to Charlotte: that's the only reason you're here."

Karl was weary of arguing with her. Hurt, she was impossible to console. He was inclined to take her at her word, and leave.

"Is duty such a repellent concept to you?" he said. "Yes, I think you are harmful to Charlotte, but I can put aside my personal doubts and do what is correct, because there is no point in doing otherwise. I am not your enemy. I couldn't possibly compete with the loathing you feel for yourself."

White fire sparked in her eyes, then died. "Two good things have happened to me," she said, more evenly. "I learned that Rachel has forgiven me, and my best dancer Ute came back. But I'd fed on them both. Some of my victims respond with love, others with terror and hatred. Of the two, it's love I can't cope with. I feel such rage, Karl, and fear. And the simple truth is that no one can help me. Not even you."

"Well, I'm not leaving," Karl said dryly. "Go to Robyn. I'll look after your dancers – out of love for art, if nothing else."

The closer the ceremony came, the uneasier Pierre grew. He longed to leave. He wanted the bright lights of a city, theatre crowds, potential victims thronging around him, not a care in the world. But if he left, Violette would pounce and finish him. He knew it.

So instead of the old life he wanted, he had Cesare and his insufferable henchmen, Simon and John; a castle full of sombre fanatics and wide-eyed gullible youths. And now there were yards of white and blood-red satin, being sewn into robes by conscientious Maria and her helpers. He felt he was trapped in the wardrobe department of some insane theatrical company.

"How can this transformation work?" he asked Cesare. "Three vampires to change one human; that was Kristian's way. The only way, so I was told. More vampires would be superfluous, but fewer than three would lack the power to make it work."

"This will work," Cesare said with the tranquil self-confidence that Pierre found so irritating. He sat behind the table in his cell, his hands folded. "One vampire, one human. A necklace of power. Simon assures me that it was done in ancient times. Besides, it's more than an ordinary transformation. It will be a ceremony ordained by God."

Cesare could go on like this for hours. Pierre groaned inwardly, thinking, *I wish I'd never asked*. When Ilona walked in, he was pathetically grateful. She was the only source of entertainment in this wretched pile.

"You wanted to see me?" she said.

Cesare nodded, and beckoned her closer. "I want to thank you for your efforts in recruiting our disciples. You've done well."

"I brought the best I could find," she said, with a light shrug. "But if you want my opinion, they'll still be no use against Violette. Any lumbering mammal can be killed by a little snake."

Cesare's manner turned glacial. Pierre loved the way she provoked him. "You misunderstand. They are for the world after Violette. She will be gone by then."

"Always so serious, Cesare," she said. "Don't you ever smile? Or think about anything but your great plans?"

Mon Dieu, she's on dangerous ground, thought Pierre, watching in delight as she went around the table and sat on Cesare's lap. She ruffled the cropped hair, kissed his forehead, moved suggestively on his thighs. "Why don't you relax?" she said. "You can't always be this dull, surely."

The leader froze. He looked revolted and furious. His hands came up to grip Ilona's arms, clearly hurting her. She went white, and fear misted her eyes.

"We are not beasts," he rasped. "Humans may couple like grunting pigs; immortals do not. Blood is all we need. Carnality is a degrading sin and you, child, are no better than a whore."

"How dare you!" Ilona exclaimed. "How d'you think I lured your beautiful young men here?"

At this, Cesare jerked her wrist to his mouth and bit. He ripped the flesh and fed brutally. Pierre watched in amazement.

Cesare tore her wrist out of his mouth as if tearing flesh from a chicken leg. He leapt up, dumped her off his lap onto the floor. Ilona glared up at him, her eyes spitting fire.

"Get her out of my sight," said Cesare.

Pierre helped Ilona up, and took her back to his own cell. He cradled her torn wrist as they went, licking it clean, watching the miraculous healing process.

"Well, that was one of your more spectacular efforts," he said.

"Shut up! Don't speak to me!"

When they reached the cell, Simon was there, to Pierre's annoyance. Seeing him, Ilona ran into his arms. Simon sat down with her on the edge of Pierre's pallet.

Matthew's head, which got about, watched from the lid of a chest. Most of the flesh was gone from it now, leaving an ash-caked skull.

"Cesare is inhuman," she complained. "Worse than inhuman! How dare he call me names, after all I've done!"

"What did he call you?" Simon raised his gilded eyebrows at Pierre.

"I wouldn't dare to repeat it," said Pierre.

"Oh, Ilona, you're not happy, are you?" Simon said chidingly. "You thought helping Cesare was a game but it isn't. You can't wrap him around your finger as you could with Kristian."

"That's a joke," she said. "Kristian was completely sexless as well. I tried everything!"

"Cesare isn't Kristian. You cannot mock him and walk away as you please."

"Can't I? So who is in charge; you or Cesare?"

"Cesare, of course." He added under his breath, "For now."

"There's something wrong with men like that."

"Don't be angry." Simon stroked her hair with his golden hands, kissed her face. "Don't run away. We need you."

Ilona let herself be consoled. Their kisses grew deeper. Pierre put his head in his hands. Couldn't bear to watch, too apathetic to leave.

If I'd known my coming here would spark Cesare's madness, he groaned inwardly, *I'd have crawled back to Violette and begged her to finish the job.*

Karl was aware of humans going about their business: a few dancers lingering in the studio, others in the changing room or in their bedrooms. He could even pick out threads of conversation: the rehearsal pianist complaining to the ballet master that the piano was out of tune. The kitchen bustled with activity as the cooks prepared the evening meal.

A noise penetrated the murmur. Quick footsteps, someone crying.

Karl stood up. Geli rushed in without knocking, a heap of black and white fur in her arms. Seeing Karl, she stopped.

"Oh – isn't Madame here?" Tears were rolling down her face.

"She had to go out."

The cat in Geli's arms hung limp, foam streaking its open mouth. "I'm sorry, sir. I was taking some clean linen from the airing cupboard and I found Magdi –"

"Lie her on the sofa," said Karl. Geli obeyed, but he knew the animal was dead before he touched the cold fur. "It's too late to help her, I'm afraid. Take her to the caretaker and ask him to bury her."

Geli broke into sobs again. "Do you think she ate rat poison somewhere? We've four cats, I'm worried about the others now."

The word *poison* electrified Karl. "When was she last fed?"

"I don't know. I can ask in the kitchen, sir."

He gathered the creature in his arms. "Come along." Geli followed, trusting Karl completely, as unsuspecting humans so often did.

Karl left Magdi's corpse outside, entering the kitchen by the back door. The room was full of steam and cooking smells, which he found repellent. Three cooks and four maids turned to look at him, their faces red and shiny with heat.

The other cats were fed at five, one of the girls told him, but Magdi hadn't turned up with them. "She hangs around miaowing for treats when the butcher's boy comes. I always give her a bit of sausage.. And she rarely misses her meals, so when she didn't appear this evening, I thought I'd given her too much and spoiled her appetite."

"What meat did the butcher bring today?" Karl asked.

"The usual," said the head cook, a bony woman with grey plaits pinned around her head. "*Bockwurst, Bratwurst*, chicken and pork."

She indicated the big central table, where girls were shovelling sausage and sauerkraut onto plates.

"Has anyone been served yet?"

"No, we're only just ready."

"Then stop."

The servers stepped back as if they'd been burned. Karl took a knife and sliced open a *Bratwurst*. The thought of consuming this dead object was alien and vile; vampires lost any pleasure in food at the instant of transformation. Still, he was capable of scientific objectivity. Under the fatty aromas he caught a false note. He touched his tongue to the cut surface and caught a malign flavour, some metallic chemical.

"Throw all this food away," he said matter-of-factly. "Tell the dancers to eat in the town tonight. Madame Lenoir will reimburse them."

The kitchen was in a mild state of uproar as he asked the horrified cook to show him the rest of that day's delivery. In the pantry he prodded chickens and slabs of meat, tasted the watery blood oozing from the flesh. All contaminated.

"Was this brought by the usual butcher?"

"No, sir, a new boy. Never seen him before. Handsome lad, fair hair; could have been a dancer himself."

How did I miss this? Karl wondered. But looking back, he knew. Tradesmen called at the house every day; he'd barely registered the visit of a delivery boy.

And if Geli had found the cat even five minutes later...

"This must all be disposed of."

"I don't understand," said the cook.

"Someone meant to make the dancers ill. Fetch all the food yourself from the market for the time being."

"But who would –?"

"I believe I know," Karl said, walking away.

He overtook the culprit near Ulm, halfway between Austria and the Rhineland. A young man riding a motorcycle along a snowy, tree-lined road in darkness. From the whispering shadow-world of Raqia, Karl saw him as a narrow yellowish-silver shape: an aura as plain as a signature. All the young men at Schloss Holdenstein radiated the same light: pure, fierce, devoid of compassion.

Karl swooped. He snapped into the real world on the rider's pillion, hands gripping the leather-clad shoulders in front of him.

The young man screamed, lost control of the machine and swerved off the road. Hitting the snow-banked verge, the motorcycle somersaulted. The man was flung face down into a ditch and Karl fell with him.

The ditch was thick with snow. A pine forest rose on their left, black and silent. Karl snatched off the man's goggles and helmet then pressed his face into snow, twisting one arm up behind his back. The man grunted with pain.

"Well, butcher," said Karl, "who sent you?"

"Sent me – to do what?" he rasped, defiant.

"To poison a houseful of innocent young men and women."

No answer. Karl jerked the arm. The socket popped, the man shrieked. "Was it Cesare?"

"Yes! Cesare sent me. Let me go!"

Karl turned him over and saw a handsome freckled face under straw-pale hair. It was the man on whom Cesare had let him feed. He clearly recognsed Karl, but his stoic pride had vanished.

"If you answer my questions. Are you hoping to become one of us?"

"Yes. Cesare promised!"

"Has he transformed anyone yet?"

"Not yet." He grunted and struggled, but Karl held him down.

"How many does he plan to initiate?"

"Thirty."

Dear God, Karl thought, *thirty new vampires!* "When is he going to begin?"

"I can't tell you – he – argh!" This as Karl pressed a thumb into his throat. "He will transform us all at once."

"How? That's impossible."

"Not for Cesare. He knows a way. I don't know how, but he does."

Karl believed him. "When?"

"Soon. Stop, stop! In three days' time. Midnight. Please, it's the truth!"

"Three days," said Karl.

"And then I'll be like you. I'll come after you and make you sorry for this!"

"That's not the cleverest threat to make at this moment."

"You can't defeat our leader! Thirty of us will become sixty, then a hundred and twenty, then –"

"I can add up," said Karl, dread descending on him. "When will he stop?"

"When he sees fit."

"The idiot means to conquer the world – but then it would be a vampire world, not a human one. But I like the human world. I wish to be a shadow in the darkness, not a daylight tyrant, an object of terror and loathing. Everyone will regret this, mortal or immortal."

"He was right about you! You're weak. No use to the new order. Now I've answered your questions, so let me go!"

"After what you've done?" Karl said icily. "I don't think so."

"You promised, if I told you –"

"You should know better than to trust a vampire."

The young man pulled feverishly at his jacket collar. "Take my blood," he pleaded. "You know how good it tastes. Take what you want, only let me free."

Karl looked at the tendons gleaming through the skin, the sheen of sweat, the pulse ticking madly, and felt only distaste. "Your blood would be as polluted as the meat you delivered."

"*Please.*"

Karl gripped the head at the chin and the crown. The man tried to resist, eyes bulging, but he might as well have tried to shift a boulder. With a deft motion, Karl broke his neck.

If anyone from the castle finds him, Karl thought, *they will take this as a warning – or provocation.*

"I have often felt pity for my victims," he said aloud, standing over the corpse. "But for you, none."

Charlotte lay couched in satin like a rosy-lipped angel, but no one looked at her. The coffin had stood in the drawing room for three days; they were waiting now for the funeral cortège, for the undertakers to screw down the coffin lid. Charlotte, hearing the murmur of unhappy voices somewhere in the house, drifted in a trance of quiet insanity.

The charade had passed off smoothly, as she'd predicted. A sudden illness, a doctor who readily believed that Charlotte had collapsed with grief after her father's funeral. Anne's voice shook as she told the story.

"We couldn't wake her this morning. If we'd known she was so ill, we would have called you sooner!"

Charlotte wondered, as the doctor probed her cold flesh, if

he found Anne's edginess suspicious. No, he simply assumed she was upset.

"People do die of grief," he said, "but she's so young, I'm afraid there may be an inquest…"

Charlotte's eyes, glass slivers under half-closed lids, caught and held his. *Sign the certificate, and leave.*

He wrote the cause of death as pneumonia, and departed.

Afterwards, Anne was furious at having to tell lies, but Charlotte remained deadly calm. Madeleine was upset, while David simply washed his hands of the matter, which aggrieved Anne more. Even Elizabeth was on edge. The house seemed shrouded in greyness, full of ghosts and cobwebs.

Charlotte hated inflicting such distress on them, but she couldn't stop. It was a form of madness. The moment her father died, she had lost her reason.

Three days to the funeral. The coffin lay empty, its lid in place so that their servants and visitors did not suspect. Charlotte vanished, haunting Cambridge for victims. That night she went out to the fens; the night was chill, flatly colourless. Dropping her unconscious victim, licking his blood from her lips, she thought, *I rose from a coffin tonight and I shall return to it, in the best tradition.*

She shook with laughter. She was close to screaming.

Sometimes, when the others were in bed, she sat in the drawing room staring at the coffin.

Mine, she thought. *I'll never need it. If ever I die, I'll be left to rot in some forest or I'll vanish into the* Weisskalt. *No one but a vampire can know what it's like to lie in their own coffin and actually be buried.*

The night before the funeral, Madeleine crept in and sat with her, as if they were holding a wake. In a way, they were: for their father, and for Charlotte's lost humanity. She put her arms around Maddy's thin shoulders and consoled her.

"It's only for Henry," said Charlotte. "Only for legal reasons."

"Then why's everyone so upset?"

"They don't understand what I am. I didn't mean to disturb them so badly. Please don't be afraid, Maddy. No need for nightmares."

"I had enough nightmares about Karl," Madeleine whispered.

"I'm past all that now. But they won't actually bury you, will they?"

"Of course not. David will weigh down the coffin with a rug or something and they'll bury that. It won't be real."

Madeleine seemed content with that. Charlotte stroked her hair, breathing the lovely fragrances of shampoo and soap and perfume, forcing herself to ignore the pulse of her blood. At least she could reassure Maddy. It was too late for the others.

When Madeleine left, there was silence. The clocks had stopped without her father there to wind them.

But what would it be like, she wondered again, *to be buried?*

She was going to go through with it. To punish herself for the pain she'd caused her family. To atone, a very little, for Fleur's death.

She heard cars outside. It would be a modest, private affair, as befitted a fake funeral. No flowers.

Under the shroud, she wore a dress of coffee-coloured georgette, so she could discard the shroud afterwards. They'd wanted to know how she would escape. Anne suggested that they screw down the coffin lid before the undertakers arrived. The idea of Charlotte being shut in the coffin seemed to horrify her family more than anything.

But she said, "No, I want them to see me as they fasten me in. So there's no doubt in anyone's mind. We'll sew lead weights into the corners. As soon as the lid's fastened, I'll escape. I can walk through walls and vanish. Nothing can go wrong."

But now the undertakers in black were here, sliding the lid over her, turning the screws, she experienced wild panic. Her heart, which she'd stilled, began to beat madly. She nearly gave herself away, on the verge of screaming, "No, don't shut me in!"

That would have felled them all with heart failure.

She mastered herself and lay like stone. Petrified.

"She hardly weighs a thing," said someone, as her wooden cocoon swayed into the air. "Shame, when they go so young."

A short car journey. She was lifted and carried again, set in place. She heard the service, but sensed no one in church beyond the minister and her immediate family: Elizabeth, David, Anne, Madeleine. No one cried. It was a drear and depressing sham, like her supposed marriage to Henry.

In the cemetery now. She was being lowered in short, jerky

stages; it felt like falling backwards, out of control. The priest's voice receded. Eyes closed, she was aware of the lid barely clearing her forehead, wooden walls confining her. She braced her hands as if to push the coffin sides apart, to brake the downward motion.

The air turned clay-cold. Scents of soil and decay wormed in. When the coffin came to rest, there was terrible stillness.

Opening her eyes, she saw dim woodgrain above her nose. Her eyes were attuned to wavelengths beyond the visible, so the interior was not quite pitch-black... but dark enough. She thought, *What if I can't enter the Crystal Ring from here?* Faint panic. *I should try now, if it's not too late...*

When the first clod of earth hit the coffin, she jumped. Her mind stretched out instinctively for Raqia, touched only blunt nothingness.

What if the Ring doesn't extend underground? I can't escape!

Her heart, which she'd halted again by willpower, exploded into a wild rhythm. She pushed frantically at the coffin sides. It seemed the lid was made of glass and she saw black walls of soil, an oblong of daylight high above, the figures in black looking down. Then one leaned over her, screaming, *"You can't bury her! She's not dead!"*

She forced the hallucination away. *Keep still. Wait until they've all gone.*

There were no screams above her, only a murmur of voices. Anne whispered, "She can't still be in there, can she?"

Somehow she forced her panic to subside. *I must see it through. This is my penance.*

Madness. And I pulled my family into my craziness with me, because I love them and – being a vampire – my love can only suck them dry and leave them insane.

Soon she sensed a massive weight of earth building up. The mourners had gone. Once the gravediggers finished their task, they, too, left. She imagined twilight gathering between gravestones, dew silvering the grass. And now she almost dared not try to escape, in case she truly couldn't.

She relaxed, concentrated. She felt the wooden prison dissolve, soil holding her like concrete. She moved upwards with ghastly slowness, like an earthworm floundering through the sticky embrace of clay. At last she broke free into the mauve, dully glittering landscape of Raqia's lowest circle. Gravestones and winter trees were warped ghosts of themselves.

Suddenly aware how very cold she felt, she wrapped her arms around her waist. A shock, to see her own form transmuted by the Ring: her arms snake-slender, the shroud a webbing of black strands. As if she'd been so far out of her mind that she'd forgotten this would happen.

Shivering so hard she could hardly move, she began to walk. Two human auras appeared, large and small: a mother and child, placing flowers on a grave. As she passed, she heard the child exclaim, "Mummy, that lady!"

"There's no one there, dear," replied the mother.

Charlotte looked up into the firmament. She saw charcoal clouds moving across darkness. All light had bled from the skyscape. No heart-lifting sapphire blue voids, or dappled bronze hills rising into towering ships of the air. All was stormy. Malevolent.

The Crystal Ring doesn't want me, she thought with a rush of terror.

She was wholly unhinged now. Possessed. Something had made her act out this grisly charade of death, a grim tendril of the Ring crawling into her mind and loosening the bonds of reason. Forcing herself to the macabre journey's end, taking her family with her, had achieved nothing good. No, it had been an act of pure evil, sealing her insanity.

There must be something of Lilith in me.

She threw off the shroud and watched it billow away, as if it had a life of its own.

She began to run, her teeth chattering. *I can't go home. I'm not Charlotte any more. I can't take this gibbering shell back to Karl.*

Charlotte rose through Raqia, caught by stormy currents. All her thoughts and memories were streaming away. She was a ragged skeleton. The only way to keep her psychosis at bay was to flee as hard as she could, an ice-thread lost between infinite walls of cloud.

CHAPTER NINETEEN

DEATH AND THE MAIDEN

One morning, in the winter-light of dawn, Robyn realised that she was dying.

She was alone in bed, Sebastian out bringing death or nightmares to some victim in the dark. For the past two days, she'd been too ill to get up.

They had been making love far too often over the past weeks. She knew Sebastian took as little blood as possible – how much was that, she wondered, half a pint, a few sips? – but even those small losses were too much. Repeated nearly every night, how could her overdrawn system possibly keep up?

They both knew, but gave in to their insatiable obsession anyway.

She was cold. *Get up and stoke the fire*, she told herself. She tried to sit, only to fall back, dizzy. Hammers pounded inside her skull.

She lay shivering. After a time the spasm passed and she lay impassive, eyes half-open. The bed canopy, the fireplace and the walls hung dimly across her vision, seeming to blur and shimmer.

She was even losing her eyesight.

There were ghosts in the wallpaper, whispering to her. They peeled themselves off the wall and danced around the room.

Sebastian hadn't touched her since her condition worsened. He was solicitous, but seemed frightened by what was happening to her. He sat with her constantly, except when he went out to feed.

He brought her endless supplies of tea, soup and food to tempt her failing appetite.

"We must build up your strength," he would say, incongruously, like a doctor. "Rest and eat, and you'll soon be better."

They both wanted to believe it.

Only this morning, with no particular emotion, had Robyn realised it was too late. She couldn't eat or face more than a few sips of tea. Anaemia and starvation compounded each other. She had a cough, too, an infection she couldn't shake off.

Perhaps a blood transfusion would have saved her, but even that seemed pointless. It would only delay the inevitable.

Spectres wove and fluttered in the walls. Robyn lay on her side, staring into the malevolent shadows, her teeth chattering. This room wished her ill, but there was nothing she could do. Only lie here in quiet despair. Sinking down into the cobweb dark.

For a while, she thought she was home in Boston. The bright cosiness of her own bedroom... Alice and Mary to attend her, admirers at the door with gifts. Showered with love, she'd responded with contempt... but her needs now were as simple as a child's. *To be home, Alice holding my hand.*

Then she roused from the hallucination, and saw where she was. This dark, empty, freezing, godforsaken house!

Drifting in fever-dreams, Robyn had no concept of time. At some stage she became aware of a figure beside the bed.

Fear shook her to a higher state of awareness. Not fear of dying, which she'd overcome, but the abstract terror of a nightmare.

"Oh, Robyn," a voice murmured. The figure fell onto its knees beside her. A slight shape under a veil of black hair.

Robyn thought this was Rasmila, come to impart some dreadful revelation.

"Sebastian?" she cried, her voice almost gone.

"Why do you call him for help," said the voice, "when he's the one who brought you to this? Oh, God, Robyn, I could –"

The stranger rose and moved away. She lit a candle on the bedside table. As the light flared, hurting Robyn's eyes, she saw that the visitor was Violette. The dancer looked far from gentle.

"Why are you doing this?" Violette's voice was a serpent hiss. Rage turned her face bloodless, like opal with white fire burning inside. Tears ran down her cheeks.

"What?" Robyn painfully lifted herself onto her elbows.

"Embracing death like a lover! Why have you let him do this?"

A surge of adrenaline came to Robyn's aid. She sat up, head spinning. "Because I love him."

"Don't make me sick. Even I would never have used you like this! Love, what love has he shown you?"

"You've no right –"

Violette's hands flew down and pinioned her. "It's not because you love him, it's because you hate yourself. Your obsession is to punish *yourself*." The dancer's face was livid, terrifying. "Don't fight me, Robyn. I see right through you. You think you're punishing men, but really you're only hurting yourself, because in your heart you still believe everything your father and husband told you. You believe you are worthless and evil!"

Robyn was shaking uncontrollably, fighting for air. Suddenly she felt very much alive.

"I'll cure you of 'love'!" Violette snapped. She opened her mouth. Her canines, fully extended, were thin, wet and sharp.

"Don't!" Robyn cried. All she could think was how Sebastian would feel, when he came home and found her dead.

"Why not?"

"I can't die without seeing him one last time."

With a moan of anger, Violette attacked.

She flung back the bedcovers and leapt onto Robyn, welding herself from breasts to ankles. Violette's body in the soft black dress felt divine, almost weightless, yet it also felt leech-like, sucking Robyn's life from every pore.

The dancer's breath was hot, scentless. A veil of black hair brushed Robyn's face and its perfume was exquisite: roses, lilies, rosin dust. She would never forget that scent...

Then came the pain.

Savage pain, like thick needles driving through her neck, exploding in her skull. She thought she was used to it, but this wasn't Sebastian's gentle bite. This was a lamia in the throes of demonic rapture.

Robyn couldn't breathe. The pain sang coldly on, but the slender body against hers was warm, vibrant.

She felt herself falling backwards. She clawed at Violette's arms, clinging on for safety.

They fell together, locked, sobbing.

Light erupted between them. Searing diamond light.

As it faded, leaving Robyn in a different universe, she saw an overblown vision in crimson and black; a phantom of herself, drawn in rippling ruby light, being born from Violette's mouth.

The ghost-Robyn dropped softly to the ground, still attached by a red string that went from its throat to the dancer's lips: a grotesque umbilical cord. Violette stood facing the blood-red shape, her hands on its shoulders.

Violette spat out the end of the cord. Then she slid her hands over the spectral Robyn's collarbones and, with a quick, pitiless action, snapped its neck.

Robyn felt something break and fall inside her, as if some vital organ had collapsed. Painless, but horrible.

Then the crimson ghost seemed to collapse and dissipate, like a bubble. Nothing was left on the carpet but a great splash of blood.

"It's kinder that way," said Violette, as if she'd simply wrung a bird's neck.

The vision ended. They were back on the bed, limply entangled, exhausted.

Robyn lay staring up at the canopy, while Violette lay across her, drained and trembling. "Robyn, Robyn..."

"Get off me," said Robyn. She felt unreal, hollow like glass. Everything around her was changing shape with the rumble of an earth tremor... She realised she was hearing her own labouring heart. "Get off!"

Violette obeyed, raven hair hanging over her face. As she swept it back, Robyn saw that her expression was sombre now, devoid of rage. Tender. Robyn, breathless and shaken, didn't know what to think or feel. The dancer's bite had changed everything... but she couldn't grasp how, or why.

"Forgive me." Violette touched Robyn's cheekbone. "I knew I'd do this when the time was right. I almost left it too late. Only I didn't know it would be so... No, don't say anything!" Robyn had parted her lips to speak. "Rest. Don't speak until you understand."

Violette poured water from a jug and gave Robyn the glass.

Robyn drank, holding the vessel tight to steady her hands. Her thundering pulse quietened. The trickle of cold water down her throat anchored her to reality. She felt...

"When did you last eat?" Violette asked, sitting on the edge of the bed.

The question startled her. "Oh... yesterday."

"And how do you feel now?"

Robyn shut her eyes, taking deep, tentative breaths. Her heart beat strongly again. Her headache was gone. Strength returned to her limbs. Most amazing of all, she felt clear-headed. Sebastian's feasts always left her languid, but Violette's attack had scoured her like a clean, icy wind. She felt almost her normal self: the last stand of her spirit before death?

"Confused," Robyn said shakily.

"You weren't made to be a martyr," said Violette. She took the glass away and placed an apple in Robyn's hand. "What is wrong with you, that you won't look after yourself?"

Robyn ate the apple, ravenous for its sweet juice. Violette's lovely eyes rested on her. *Is she hypnotising me? As if she needs to.*

"What have you done to me?" Robyn asked.

"That, you must find out for yourself," Violette said gravely.

"How did you find me?"

"You can't hide from me." The idea of Violette as clairvoyant seemed only natural to Robyn. "Your uncle is worried about you."

At that, a wave of devastation shook her.

"Oh, Lord. I never thought – I should have written. My God, if I died and Josef never knew why..."

And she began to realise how Violette had changed her.

"You are not going to die," said the dancer. "I won't allow it. You will eat and you will live. But ask yourself, what has Sebastian done to you? He's made you a victim. You were strong before you met him, weren't you? You controlled your own life. Now he controls you. This is what love brings you to!"

Robyn's mouth fell open. Her breath quickened. *Yes.* She saw the self-destructive insanity of her own behaviour as if looking on from outside. "How do you know this? I told you too much, that night in Boston!"

"No. One look was all I needed to know everything about you."

Robyn resented Violette for compelling her to face what she had been doing to herself... Yet even resentment was a sign of emotional rebirth. She found herself regaining self-control, confidence. To find her soul stretched naked before Violette was both unsettling and eerily soothing.

"What about Sebastian?" Robyn asked. "How much do you know about him?"

"I've never met him, but I know him through you. He can't face the strength of his own passions, so he walls them away. That's why he brought you here. To wall you away."

"Oh, God," said Robyn, putting her head in her hands. "Yes, that's exactly what he was doing." *Only*, she thought, *I was too infatuated to admit it.*

She felt easy with Violette now, as if they'd been friends for a lifetime. Yet she recoiled from the vision of Violette strangling the blood-red ghost, casting her into darkness.

"Tell me what you've done to me," said Robyn, her voice raw. "Help me understand."

As Violette's dazzling gaze met hers, Robyn saw her as a divided entity; half goddess, half angry, passionate human. She spoke softly.

"I've changed you. Strangled the sickness in your soul so that the rest of you, the adult woman, can live. I am Lilith, destroyer of children: destroyer of infantile needs and obsessions, if you like."

"Are you calling my love for Sebastian infantile?"

"No. But your need to hurt others before they hurt you, and your willingness to sacrifice your life to the first real love you found – that was a form of sickness."

Robyn looked down at her own hands lying on the embroidered silk. So this was Violette-Lilith's magic. Although she still loved Sebastian, she was no longer mad enough to die for that love. She felt calm and self-possessed. All she wanted was to live out her natural life. Nothing more.

And for Violette, now, she felt simple tenderness.

"If I was sick, am I cured? You must be an angel."

Violette's expressive face became bleak. "I envy Sebastian because you love him instead of me. That's rather too human, isn't it?"

"I offered to come with you! If you'd let me, I'd never have seen him again!"

Regret suffused Violette's face. The look moved Robyn to tears.

"If only." She stroked Robyn's face, her fingers achingly delicate. "I wonder if he was sent by my enemies, to seduce you away from me?"

"Enemies? Who could hate you?"

"Almost anyone. Lilith is an evil demon, didn't you know?"

"And a paranoid one, maybe," said Robyn. Violette looked startled. "I met Sebastian the same night I met you, at that party. How could anyone else have known? It was a coincidence, Violette. These crazy things happen."

"I suppose you're right. I like the way you say my name. Say it again."

"Violette. Lilith."

The dancer breathed out softly. "And I'm grateful to you."

"Why?"

"For showing me that I'm capable of love, when I believed I wasn't. And for proving the absolute hopelessness of it."

"Hopeless... because you would do to me what Sebastian's done?"

"And because you don't share my feelings. Either way, I can't win."

Robyn was at a loss; she had no idea what to do if the dancer wept. "We can be friends," she said lamely.

"But friendship is not what I want."

"I'm confused," said Robyn. "You assume I prefer men, but I felt nothing for men until I met Sebastian. And I felt very little for women until I met you."

She sat forward and embraced Violette. Couldn't help herself. The dancer was so slender she was hardly there at all, and yet she was warm and divinely firm to touch; so lovely that no one, male or female, could resist her.

"Lilith," she said in a kind of ecstasy, into the black hair. "How could anyone not love you? We were lovers when you took my blood. We are lovers."

For a few minutes, Violette held her so hard that Robyn thought her spine would break. But it was the dancer who ended the embrace. She kissed Robyn full on the lips. Electric warmth. A taste of blood and clear fluids like the sweetest nectar... then she drew away.

"You were never cold-hearted, Robyn, only wounded. You're gentle and kind, but... don't lead me into fond delusions. Don't pity me." Her face was composed, with formidable willpower shining behind her eyes.

"Pity you?" Robyn gasped. "That would be like pitying a goddess."

"But you pity the Devil a little, don't you?" Violette smiled, disentangling Robyn's hair with her fingers. "And talking of your lover, what would he say if he came back and found me sitting here – or lying beside you?"

The thought froze her. Her feelings towards Sebastian had changed, but they hadn't died. "He'd want to kill you."

"He would have to join the queue," Violette said tartly. "It's more likely that I'd win."

Robyn was horrified. "Oh, you must leave! He could be back at any moment."

"Are you still defending him?"

"Of course!" she said fiercely. "Don't you see? I love you both. I couldn't bear you to fight over me. Go, please."

"I'd like to break his neck," Violette said in a chilling tone. Lilith's ruthless soul burned in her eyes.

"He could have killed me months ago, but he spared me out of love. I've changed him, too – more than you've changed me."

The hard light dimmed. "Well, there's something of me in you," Violette murmured. "In all my daughters, I suppose... All right, I won't harm him – but only for your sake."

Robyn wilted in relief. "And my blood is in you. It's a bond, isn't it? So you'll remember that I love you, even when I'm not there. But you really must leave."

"Come with me."

"I can't." She added under her breath, "Not yet."

"Robyn, I haven't come all this way to leave you at his mercy again!"

She sat up straight, angered. "What is this? You complain that I'm too much in Sebastian's power – then you start telling me what to do? I'm not one of your students."

"I want you out of danger, that's all."

"I'm not in danger! Try to understand. I need to see Sebastian just once more. To say goodbye. I cannot walk out on him without explaining."

They argued, but Violette was obdurate. Eventually Robyn said lightly, "This is our first quarrel. First of many?"

"I'm sorry," the dancer sighed, relenting. "I've no right to bully you. I trust your judgement. I would wait for you but I can't, I have business at home."

"I must face him alone," said Robyn. "I'm not afraid of him. I don't want to remember him as a vampire, but as a man, my lover."

"Enough," said Violette. "I understand."

She kissed Robyn again. Overcome, Robyn grasped Violette's hand. "You live in Salzburg, don't you? I'll come to you as soon as I leave here."

"Don't. I might not be there. I made a promise that I can't break."

Lilith dissolved into the shadows as she spoke. Her hand crumbled to dust and stars in Robyn's palm.

When Sebastian returned, Robyn was in the library with her stockinged feet on the hearth, a cup of cocoa resting in her lap. He rushed to her side with a genuine delight that almost broke her heart. She'd made her decision, but was still nervous of his reaction.

She feared he might suspect something wrong immediately, but he seemed oblivious. Perhaps he'd stopped looking at her too closely, in case he saw imminent death in her eyes.

"You're up and dressed," he said, covering her face and hands with kisses. "Are you feeling better, beloved child?"

"Yes, much better."

"And have you eaten?"

"An obscene amount," she said. "Fruit, porridge, eggs and bacon."

"But this is wonderful." He sat beside her on the chaise-longue. "And there's colour in your cheeks again. If I had a God to thank

I'd be on my knees! I was so afraid…"

"You thought I was dying? I was. But this morning, I woke up and decided to live."

His hazel eyes were rapt with love, but she felt tranquil and distant. Then she saw his eyes cool suddenly, as if he suspected a change. She said, "You love me, don't you?"

"I don't know what more I can do to prove it."

"You could prove it… by letting me go."

He frowned. "What do you mean?"

She shook her head. Her throat ached. "You're killing me, dearest. I'm not such a fool as to die for you. I love my life too much to make that sacrifice. I want to live, for myself and for you, so that you don't end up hating yourself for taking my life."

He said nothing for several seconds. When he spoke, his voice was cold. "So, you want to leave me?"

"I must."

Another silence. He looked at her strangely, then lifted her chin and rested his gaze on her throat. "You've changed," he said. "Why?"

"I've come to my senses, that's all."

"No… Someone has influenced you." His tone began to alarm her. "Someone came while I wasn't here. Was it Rasmila?"

"No, no one."

"Don't lie to me! These marks on your neck, tiny silver-pink flowers that even a doctor would overlook, were not made by me. Who was it?"

She jerked out of his grip. "All right! It was Violette. Don't be angry with her; she probably saved my life. And she didn't 'influence' me, just made me see sense."

"Made you cease to love me?" His tone was murderous. His eyes lanced through her.

"Sebastian!" She clasped his arm. "Don't blame her! I was dying until she came. And that's where it will end if we don't stop!"

His rage diminished to brooding menace. He stood up and paced about. "Let us leave Violette aside. Are you saying that you refuse to see me anymore?"

"No, no." Her confidence returned. "I'll sail back to Boston. If there's still trouble about Harold, I'll sort it out. I should never have left. I'll live in my house as before, and you can visit me, maybe two or three times a year…"

"It's not enough," he said grimly.

"Why? It's all my body can take! Why is everything so extreme with you, why is it all or nothing? If you truly cared –"

"You've made up your mind, obviously."

"We can still be lovers. Not so often, that's all."

He didn't answer, and she could find nothing else to say. She was no longer sure what she felt for him. One thing was certain; her obsessive craving was dead, strangled by Lilith. All that had made her vulnerable and dependent – dead.

Yet she didn't want to hurt him – assuming such a monster could be hurt. She thought, *If he tells me he faked his love for me… I wouldn't blame him, but I couldn't bear it. Does he care or not? Is he still playing games?*

Robyn was calm, but far from happy. *I was ready to die for him; now I'm not. That's all. But to lose that incredible passion… Has Lilith done a miraculous thing to me – or a terrible one?*

When Sebastian finally spoke again, he sounded different. He was very controlled, almost impersonal. His formality turned her cold. "When do you want to leave?"

"I should go as soon as possible. Tomorrow, I suppose."

"Do you want me to come with you?"

She thought of her intention to visit Salzburg before returning to America, but knew it was only a dream. *I might not be there*, Violette had said. Robyn had a powerful, heart-rending feeling that she would never see Violette again.

I'm on my own now. That's the whole point.

Managing to control her voice, she said, "It's up to you. I told you, you're welcome in Boston, but if you don't want to come with me now, I understand."

"Well." He sat beside her and took her hand. He changed again, becoming gently forgiving, but she didn't trust the soft look in his eyes. "There's no real hurry for you to go now, is there? Tomorrow, or the day after. Stay a little longer with me, beautiful child, for old times' sake."

* * *

When Violette returned, Karl told her about the would-be poisoner. He expected her to react with rage, but she became unnervingly quiet. She sat down at a table and lit a thick white candle. Behind her, curtains of watered silk in lavender and silver hung closed against darkness. In the glow, her face was a delicate white shell, her eyes lakes of violet glass overflowing with light.

Fyodor and Rasmila stood nearby in the shadows, listening. They had come for Violette, again. Karl sensed their hunger. In the dark tension of that moment, he felt they were all gathered on the edge of an abyss.

"This is the end," said Violette, staring at the candle flame. "How could Cesare do this, when I already *know* I'm fated to surrender? One small concession was all I asked: let me finish *Witch and Maiden*, then I'll accept my fate. But Cesare can't wait, he must have me there *now*."

"There's no time for you to finish the ballet," Rasmila said softly. "But we regret the poisoning attempt. We had no hand in it."

Karl sat opposite Violette. He said, "I doubt that Cesare knows about your agreement with Rasmila."

Her dark eyebrows jerked up. "No?"

"And I doubt Simon knows, either. I think it was Rasmila's and Fyodor's own decision to approach you. They mean to present you to Simon as a *fait accompli*, Lilith in chains. They think he'll fall on their necks in gratitude. Meanwhile, Simon and Cesare being unaware of this plan, Cesare tries again to force the closure of your company." Karl looked at the pair. "Is it so?"

Their expressions were rigid. They said nothing.

Violette stood up and faced them. "Come here," she said softly, and they obeyed as if under a spell. "Tell me the truth."

She was an ice-flame, a sorceress. Angels or not, they were in thrall to Lilith, Karl saw. He almost pitied them, struggling to master an elemental of which they were mortally afraid.

"The truth?" said Rasmila.

"Every word. What is going on?"

Rasmila looked at her companion, then turned her kohl-ringed eyes to Violette.

"Yes, we're working for Simon, out of love, to prove ourselves worthy. He left us to do as we wished. Of course we know what he expects of us – to bring you to him as a captive. But he doesn't know about our bargain with you. Nor where Sebastian and the woman are."

"You will *never* tell Simon about Robyn," Violette hissed. "And Sebastian – is he on your side too?"

"He follows no one," said Rasmila. "Simon believes he's as dangerous as you, Lilith."

"Does he?" Her gaze burned into Rasmila. "And is he?"

A shadow darkened Karl's thoughts. Sebastian might prove as icily ruthless and strong as Kristian. He'd never sought power, but what if he changed his mind?

"Simon believes so," Rasmila said, as if this made it true.

"Cesare doesn't," said Fyodor, "but Simon despises Cesare, tells him nothing."

"Does Simon mean that Sebastian could destroy me?" Violette asked, frowning.

"Perhaps," said Rasmila. "At least overpower, weaken and imprison you."

"Ah... So you lured me to Robyn in hope that Sebastian and I would fight over her? But if that didn't work, you'd deliver me to Simon instead. Either way, I was caught."

"Of course; what did you think?" Fyodor exclaimed. "We have our quarrels, but on one point we're all agreed – even Karl, if he'd stop being too chivalrous to admit it. Lilith is the Enemy of all. We have to do this!"

"For your good," Rasmila broke in with feeling, "because you cannot live as you are, an outcast, can you? We must bring you back to God!"

The dancer's face was blank, crystalline. "Isn't it time you shed the idea that you're Semangelof, God's messenger? It's a delusion."

Fyodor replied with a white-lipped smile, "Not while you remain the incarnation of Lilith. How is that a delusion, when you feel her in every cell of your being? See, you cannot answer. What we are, for now, is *real*."

"Can you compel me to go to Simon?"

"No, but you gave your word," said Rasmila. "You pledged to come in exchange for us telling you where Robyn was."

"How can I keep my word, after Cesare's despicable attack on my company?" Violette said frostily. "You claim you didn't know, but the fact is you have no influence on Cesare or Simon at all. You're scrambling to get back in favour and they're using you!"

Rasmila and Fyodor stared malignly at her. Karl was coiled to intervene if they attacked her, but no one moved. He, too, was incredulous that they expected Violette to keep the bargain after they'd made such admissions.

To his astonishment, Violette said in a low voice, "However, I did promise."

"Yes," said Rasmila, her eyes glittering.

Violette went still, blank-faced and desolate. Looking into the abyss.

"What will Simon do to me?" Fear tinged her voice. "No, don't tell me. I ask one favour; give me until tomorrow afternoon. Then I'll come to the castle with you."

Their faces, umber and pearl, brightened with amazement, triumph. They had the sinister kindness of warders about to lead her to an execution chamber.

"Tomorrow, then. And you must be ready."

The angels bowed solemnly to her and vanished.

Violette sat down again, her shoulders drooping, ebony hair hiding her face. Karl studied her, full of grave misgivings.

"Do you know what you're doing?"

She stiffened. "Do you care? You always play devil's advocate, Karl. For all I know, you're on their side!"

"Violette, I am not." As always, her hostility saddened him.

"I've decided. I'm going to send away all my dancers and staff and shut the premises. They'll only be safe with me out of the way. Don't you agree?"

"It's wise, but what will you achieve by surrendering?"

"I don't know, but I can't accept that Ballet Janacek is finished. Someone must carry on after me. Ute, perhaps, or Mikhail... I've been a fool, of course." Violette stared through him, her eyes burningly desolate. "I should have seduced and flattered my way through this un-life, and had everyone at my feet instead of at my throat... but Lilith is not a hypocrite. She can't lie."

"So you're putting her out of her misery?" said Karl. Her aloof chilliness made it difficult to feel compassion for her – but for a second, something caught hard at his throat, and loosed its hold reluctantly. "Can't I persuade you not to go?"

"Too late," she said.

"It's the new ballet, isn't it?"

"What do you mean?"

"*Witch and Maiden*, Violette. You could end it in any way you wished. Instead you chose to end it with your character's entrapment and death."

"What else is there for me?" she hissed. "This agony, this hatred all around me and the thirst – I cannot endure it any longer!"

Karl, pinioned by her will and her terrible beauty, was at a loss. Nothing he said or did would influence Violette. It wasn't that he wanted to control her, only to help – because Charlotte loved her. But she was a bird of prey, alone, impervious to advice or compassion.

Then she gave a barbed-wire smile. "I promised to present myself to Simon. I said nothing about not ripping off Cesare's head on my way."

"Will that solve anything?"

She leapt to her feet and shrieked, "He killed my cat, my Magdi! If I go to hell, he's coming with me!"

Her outburst took Karl aback. An explosion of simple outrage – and she sounded so human. Wholly, heartbreakingly human.

They stared at each other. Violette looked as shocked as Karl felt. "I suppose you're amazed that I care about such things," she said harshly. "So am I."

"Well, it's the first honest anger you've shown," said Karl. He remembered her last visit to the Schloss, vampires and mortals quaking in terror beneath her sweeping wings.

"If you choose to fight," he said, "they'll stand no chance against you. And we may prevent the transformation of at least thirty vampires."

"We? I don't expect your help."

"If you go, I'm coming with you."

"That's very noble," Violette said. However, she didn't refuse. Suddenly Karl perceived her lucent glow as fragility, not strength.

"Are you afraid?" he asked softly.

"No."

"Then why are you shaking?"

"Because Charlotte isn't here." She clasped her arms hard across her waist, but her trembling grew worse. "I'm not the same without her, but we can't wait for her. I won't take her into danger just to feed my strength."

"We agree on that, at least," Karl murmured.

"That's why I must walk in barefoot with downcast eyes, like Lila of the forest going into the cottage... To set Charlotte free."

Karl closed his eyes, couldn't speak. *Yes*, he thought, *I want Charlotte to be free of her... Does it follow that I want Violette to sacrifice herself while I stand and watch?*

"You're afraid, aren't you?" said Violette.

"*Natürlich*. I don't relish the prospect of being ripped apart and beheaded. And I'm thinking of Charlotte."

"I'm frightened, too," Violette said very softly, "of Lilith. If she is the Mother of Vampires, it's in her power to destroy as well as create her offspring. To take them all with her when she falls."

And that, Karl thought, *is what I fear*.

Sebastian stood on the slope of a hill, trees massed behind him against a wild sky, a banshee wind tearing through their branches. Below him stood Blackwater Hall; cavernous, dusty, empty-eyed. Yet magnificent. His home. A casket to contain the rarest of jewels, his blood-red diamond, Robyn.

Who no longer loved him.

He entered the Crystal Ring and the wind sliced through him like a sword. The trees turned to shivering crystal and the house leaned like some distorted cartoon. Above him, seeming close enough to touch, a mass of darkness seethed like an emanation from hell.

"Rasmila," he whispered. The ether seemed to vibrate in response. "Kali, Semangelof, my Cailleach; can your blood hear mine?"

They came to him through the twilight, sable and gossamer, and wound around him like cats.

"We knew you'd need us," said Rasmila. She stroked his hair, while Fyodor leaned on his shoulder. "What can we do?"

He told them.

"And if we help, will you reward us?" Her voice was a dove's. "Because we need you, Sebastian. You are more than Simon can ever be. We love you."

Sebastian barely heard them, or felt their feathery hands sliding over his body. In his desperation he would agree to anything.

"Help me, and I'll sell you my soul," he said. "Again."

Surveying the recruits who stood like soldiers for inspection, Cesare was overwhelmed by pride. Thirty perfect humans, ripe to receive the Crystal Ring's gift. Fit, powerful young men with blond hair and blue eyes, all soundly drilled in the discipline of obedience and loyalty. Men who worshipped their vampire leader as God.

There was Werner on the front row, one of Cesare's favourites. An idealist, a bright star.

Another thirty had been eliminated as unworthy. Some had never recovered from John's attentions. A few had been wilful, threatening to run away and tell the human "authorities" – for all the good that would do. Others had fallen ill from the over-enthusiastic feeding of vampires. Of course, some were bound to fall by the wayside. They were only mortal, after all. The ones who'd passed were exceptional.

Cesare's pride was tempered by sad anger. One of his best men, sent to poison Violette's precious ballet, had not returned. Cesare suspected that either Karl or Violette had killed him. The mission had failed, but even the death of a cat was a small victory.

Their spies brought a fragment of good news, too. Charlotte was no longer with Violette.

Simon believed her absence would weaken Lilith. But Cesare did not fully trust Simon. He trusted Fyodor and Rasmila even less. They lurked on the fringes, even though no one wanted them, and who knew what schemes they had? Still, their obsession with Simon made them unlikely to cause trouble.

The humans were grouped in the centre of the chamber, flanked by immortals. Simon and John were behind his right shoulder, Pierre in the audience to Cesare's left. Everyone waited eagerly to hear Cesare's last speech before the transformation.

Cesare was profoundly moved. He thought, *This is too much*

happiness for anyone to bear. I've been called insane but how can I be, when they share my vision and love me for it?

Standing on the dais before Kristian's throne, he began.

"Tonight you'll wear the white robes of initiates, while your initiators don the red robes of immortality. Consider the symbolism of the colours; the white of innocence and the red of knowledge, of blood."

He smelled the heat of the men's excitement. They trembled to be elevated alongside their ruthless, jewel-eyed masters.

"Our father Kristian rejected the drinking of blood as a carnal act, asking that we deny our natural desires and exist only on life-auras. But I say that the appetite for blood is a gift to be used wisely. Use it only to subjugate your prey. Never indulge for pleasure, for that way lies ruin. Carnality is a human weakness that you will soon leave behind forever. Sin has no place here!" On these words his stare pierced Ilona, who was at the rear of the chamber with the remaining female vampires, a minority now.

"Devote all your love to your leader and to God; devote every act of feeding to God, shun the weakness of flesh, and we shall rule the world." Cesare leaned forward, directing a steel glare at them. "Do you think I exaggerate? Consider this: God set us above men. He created us to punish their sins. We have divine ordinance in the form of Simon, His envoy. The time is coming when He will set us to rule mankind!

"Tonight, thirty new vampires will be created. Next time, sixty, our numbers doubling each time. Think how swiftly our numbers will increase! We will inhabit new castles, a network of strongholds across Europe. First there will be infiltration of human institutions, then their destruction and replacement by vampire law." His voice rose to an ecstatic shout. "That is the work we begin here tonight. An immortal empire, ordained by God!"

Their cheers were deafening. Cesare nodded in thanks, arms clasped across his chest, tears escaping over his lashes. He left the dais and moved among his flock. They clasped his hands, crying, laughing, as if he were their messiah.

As Cesare neared the back, however, he noticed that Ilona contributed no more than polite applause, so half-hearted as to be an insult.

Cesare loathed Ilona. She didn't share his ideals. She was of the old guard, a slave to carnality, her only motive for helping a desire for revenge against Violette. She'd been useful, but his new world held no role for her. After the initiation, he decided, she wouldn't survive long.

He stopped short of the female group. They looked disappointed when he turned away, especially his pet, Maria, but he ignored them. What female could he trust, when all were tainted with Lilith's power?

Cesare's utopia held no place for sexuality or for death.

His ideals were nothing new: they were ancient, tried and tested. But to him, as he breathed in charged excitement of his disciples, they sprang eternally fresh, like gospel truth.

Pierre caught his arm, speaking rapidly. "What if Lilith comes again? Last time, she filled the castle and swept Charlotte and Karl away like dolls! Aren't you afraid?"

"No such word exists here," Cesare said icily. "And if I hear that name mentioned again, the speaker will be permanently silenced."

Pierre glared back from sullen eyes.

"She'll come," said Simon over Cesare's shoulder. "She won't be able to stay away. I promise you, she'll come."

Pierre looked down, shuddering.

There is too much of the female and the decadent in all these older vampires, Cesare thought as he mounted the dais again. *They'll have to be stamped out in time.*

But tonight was for the celebration of life. Not the faintest shadow of fear touched him as he surveyed the shining faces of his acolytes. He had never felt more serene.

Then, with humble grace, he seated himself in Kristian's dark throne.

The roar of approbation shook the walls.

Robyn had fallen asleep with her head on Sebastian's chest. When she woke to darkness, she was alone in bed.

He's gone out to feed, she thought with her eyes still closed. *To suck out someone else's life so he can spare mine. How long could I have gone on, knowing that?*

Well, not for much longer. Guess that salves my conscience. She stretched and turned over in bed, feeling warm, cradled in cream and blue silk. *Today I start for home. I mustn't even think about Violette. Alice will be glad to see me, at least.*

But the thought made her uneasy. *Can I go back to my dull old life, after knowing Sebastian?*

Light moved across her eyelids. She opened her eyes to see Sebastian staring down, his face a carving of candlelight and shadow. She could appreciate his beauty now in a detached way, unmoved by insatiable longings and fears. Such a relief. Violette's gift.

"You startled me," she said. "I thought you were out. What time is it?"

"Time doesn't matter here," he said. His tone sent a flicker of panic through her. He sat on the edge of the bed and gave her a warm look that verged on a smile. "So, you're off on your travels today."

"I have to go."

"No need to sound apologetic. After all, if you no longer love me, there's no point in you staying. On the other hand, maybe you never loved me at all. You never said it."

"I told you I still want to see you," she said gently.

"Do you, now? Have your cake and eat it? But what if I don't agree? If I said, 'Leave me now and you'll never see me again,' could you bear it?"

Be strong, she told herself. "Blackmail won't help. I'd have to bear it, wouldn't I?" She took his hand. His skin was cold, like quartz. "Don't take it badly, dear, please."

"There is nothing to take badly," he said, "because you are not going anywhere."

She tried to sit up, but he held her down. At first, still confident, she felt indignant. Then fear filled her in a rush. His eyes consumed her; soft, leafy, soot-fringed, they were ciphers of a single-minded and merciless will.

Her words tumbled out. "We've discussed this, I thought you understood."

"What is there to go back to?" he broke in. "Can you resume your old life, after knowing me? I don't think so."

Robyn flinched. "I'll find something."

"No, you won't." Gripping her arms, he lifted her half out of bed. "You forced me to admit that I love you, I love you to the exclusion of all others." Suddenly he slammed her back against the headboard. She cried out, more in shock than pain. His fervour terrified her. "You can't do that without taking the consequences! You can't reject me now. You've got to accept it all!"

As she gasped for breath, straining uselessly to evade him, she saw two figures at the foot of the bed. One she knew: Rasmila. The other was a long slender being like a snow-covered willow, his skin and hair pure white. The two vampires shone with unnatural energy, their eyes bright with hunger and unknown intent. She saw no trace of humanity in them. *Demons.*

She managed to say, "What do they want?"

"Rasmila and Fyodor are here to help me." His face was too close to hers, his eyes glittering.

"To do what?"

"To make you the same as us."

Her heart bucked with terror. "Why?"

"So you'll never grow old, beautiful child. So your earthly life won't matter. So we can stay together forever."

She couldn't take in what he'd said. The prospect filled her with absolute revulsion, with denial in every cell. She knew, with complete certainty, that this must not happen.

"I don't want it," she said when she could speak. "I want to grow old and be a grand old lady. I don't want to live forever, not at your price. I can't become some unnatural thing that drinks blood, I just can't. I wouldn't be me!"

Sebastian tightened his grip, lifting her out of bed as he spoke. "Yes, it is terrible, but you don't understand. It's also wonderful. I'm taking you into the Crystal Ring because I can't let you go, now or ever."

Robyn went on fighting and protesting, but her strength was nothing against his. After the tenderness he'd shown, she'd forgotten how physically powerful he was. Nothing tender about him now. His love was as dazzling and fierce as that of a god.

She fought for her life while he whispered in her ear, his hands numbing her arms. Realising this was hopeless, that no amount of protest would deflect his will, she became more frantic.

"I'm going to take your blood and your life now," he was saying, "but don't be afraid, because the Crystal Ring will give back what we take. My friends will help you. We'll hold your hands and form the circle of un-death. You must trust us."

"This is against my will," she said, sobbing now. "Never forget, you did this against my will."

He clasped her hard, his mouth hot on her throat. She felt her ribs creak and thought they'd break. Over his shoulder she saw the other vampires drifting closer. Ghouls with staring, white-ringed eyes.

"Robyn." Sebastian's voice was muffled, raw with emotion. "You must love me, or I'll die."

His pain caught a nerve deep inside her. She wanted to say, *I never said I didn't. If I don't love you, why does it hurt so much that you can treat me like this?* His anguish almost won her back, despite Violette... if only he'd given her a chance to speak.

Too late. The familiar, sensual thrust of pain obliterated her thoughts. He sucked hard and savagely, convulsing against her, strangling her.

For a time there was only the steel ache in her veins. She held him now instead of fighting, her hands locked around his back. Then a horrible greyness invaded her brain, a dust storm. She couldn't see or breathe. She was sinking. Her limbs were weightless, as if she were made of some strange loamy substance that floated away as all the liquid drained out.

She was bone-cold, shivering. Mad with fear, her mind was a panicking, trapped bird. Dying.

Everything tipped sideways. Sebastian had let her go. She had a vague impression that he was holding her left hand and Rasmila her right, while Fyodor – a spectre floating before her – completed the circle. But she couldn't feel her hands. Reality vanished. Only fear remained.

There was one last jolt, like a small but essential fire being sucked out of her.

Then darkness.

* * *

The building that housed Ballet Janacek was empty and silent, a great desolate shell around Violette.

Only she and Karl remained there now. With regret she had postponed rehearsals of *Witch and Maiden*, called everyone together, and told them that for personal reasons she must close the ballet for a few days. Rather than lie, she told them nothing, simply asked for their patience.

"Go home, take a holiday, whatever you wish," she told them. "All your wages and expenses will be paid. Your jobs are not in peril. Please bear with me."

Secretly she'd left a sealed letter with her solicitor, to be opened if she did not return within seven days. It gave instructions for Charlotte, Ute, and her most trusted staff to run the company.

It didn't occur to Violette that they might not want to go on without her.

The mass departure that morning had been subdued, unhappy. Violette still couldn't be sure her people would be safe. She could only hope that Cesare lacked the resources – or the spite – to track down individuals.

They wanted to stop me dancing, and now they've got their wish, she thought. *But they will pay.*

Now it was afternoon, wintry and overcast, luminous with snow. Nothing to do but wait for Fyodor and Rasmila.

She saw a recurring image of herself, walking barefoot and downcast between them, being presented to a triumphant Simon. This was no longer to do with God: it was personal. Surrender, humiliation, death… or worse, eternal life in some prison of the spirit. *Out of other vampires' hair, but forever a torment to myself.*

She felt the pressure of their will like ever-increasing gravity. *Vampire and human alike, all want me dead.*

No, stop this, she thought. *You forced me into this, Lilith. Don't desert me now!*

But the hours dragged by, and Rasmila and Fyodor failed to appear. Dusk drew in.

"I can't bear this waiting," Violette said finally. "Why haven't they come?"

"I wish I knew," said Karl. "They were so eager to have you, I can only think something's stopped them. Perhaps Simon doesn't want you after all. He may have thought they were idiots for bringing their most dangerous enemy into the castle on the eve of the grand transformation."

"What shall we do?"

Karl looks so sure of himself, she thought, *so calm, even if he is not.*

"Fetch Charlotte and disappear," he answered without hesitation. "To Africa, New Zealand, or wherever Stefan's gone, and hope Cesare forgets us. I'm not a coward but I am also not stupid."

"I know that, Karl," she said dully. "But it's no good. I have to keep my promise. With or without an escort, I must face my enemies. You don't have to…"

"I told you," he said with a faint sigh. "If you go, I'm coming with you."

They were dressed in simple clothes, for ease of movement; Violette in a loose greyish-mauve dress, Karl in white shirt and charcoal trousers. And she had stockings and plain solid shoes, not the bare feet of her visions.

"You haven't fed enough," Karl said as they moved through the grumbling storms of Raqia. "How will you have the strength to fight Cesare if you keep yourself in this permanent state of hunger?"

I wish I were alone, she thought. *Lilith is a solitary creature; I don't even want Charlotte. This is my battle and I don't need Karl to be the voice of my conscience.*

"I'll take Cesare's blood," she said savagely. "And Simon's. I'll take yours!"

Karl said nothing. His eyes were dark with concern.

"Don't look at me as if I'm mad," she said. "I drink as much as I can bear to. I'm not going there to fight. One execution – then I let them have their way."

On the banks of the Rhine, they broke from the Ring to survey the undulating flank of the hill rising from the river, the ancient trees with their roots twisted around rocks, and on the ridge, the brown, turreted bulk of Schloss Holdenstein. No sign of life, no one coming or going. Yet at the sight of the castle, Violette felt agitated, as if frozen fingertips were dancing over her skin. Lilith's easy rage and power deserted her.

If I go in there, I'll never come out.

"Let me appear first," said Karl, "I'll create a diversion to give you a chance of attacking Cesare. Simon took me by surprise last time, but he won't again."

"Yes," said Violette. "Come on."

The Schloss, seen from the odd perspectives of Raqia, had curious delicacy and a strange ochre cast. Steeped in centuries of vampiric power, it seemed to exist in both worlds at once. The walls impeded them like clay and honey as they passed through.

Inside, the castle was as dank and unwelcoming as she remembered. But the atmosphere was intense, shimmering with the massed glow of torches, lamps and candles.

"I've never seen so much light here," said Karl, "nor so many vampires, since Kristian died."

Humans were everywhere. Vampires and men worked together, trying on robes like friends dressing each other for a carnival in a mood of frantic excitement. They glimpsed Ilona and Pierre, assisting Maria with the dressing. Violette and Karl moved through the castle like shadows, flitting in and out of the Ring, and everywhere they saw the colours of those robes; pure white and arterial red.

Entering the heart of the castle, they came to the inner sanctum, Cesare's den. Seen from the Ring, the unlit chamber looked flat and unreal.

Cesare was not there.

"He's not in the castle," said Karl, "and neither are Simon or John. I can't sense them anywhere. Can you?"

They slipped out of Raqia and stood in darkness, perceiving with vampire sight the subterranean glimmer of the walls, reaching out with all their senses for life and danger.

Then Violette felt something. A great weight above them, unseen powers descending like three huge, muffled figures gliding down from an immeasurable distance...

Karl, too, was staring upwards. She grabbed his sleeve. "Karl!"

They leapt into Raqia, too late. The whole world tilted sideways. For a split second, Violette felt an uprush of coldness, disorientation, the Crystal Ring sifting down like snow. Then she and Karl slammed into a wall of light.

They were back in the sanctum with torches and candles blazing around them. Violette hit the floor and lay like a bird twitching its useless wings, Karl beside her. Looking up, she saw John, Simon and Cesare gazing down with reptilian smiles.

The room shook in time with her heartbeat as she climbed to her feet. Her anger and power dissipated. She thought, *What am I doing here? What did I think I could achieve?*

Karl stood beside her and cupped her elbow in a protective gesture. Normally she hated to be touched, but now she barely noticed.

They surrounded her, faces full of contempt: Simon the gilded sun-god, Cesare a choirboy with the steely eyes of a general, John a scarred mass of hatred. They'd accumulated massive powers, she realised, absorbing energy from the ancient walls, from the blood of luscious youths and from storms of the Crystal Ring. They fed each other with self-importance.

All Lilith's strength withered before theirs. *I knew this was a mistake*, Violette thought. *I can't kill Cesare – but I won't submit either! It's the same as with Lancelyn. I thought I could, but I can't.*

Her most powerful instinct was to flee. She felt defenceless, as she once had in the hands of Senoy, Sansenoy and Semangelof. And Lilith's nature was to fly free, not to stand and fight.

"There's no need for violence," said Karl. "We entered in peace."

"But where are Fyodor and Rasmila?" said Simon. "They were meant to accompany Lilith. Fulfilment of destiny…"

He looked puzzled, disappointed – *As if*, thought Violette, *his rejection of them was a huge, cruel test. Arrogant of him to be so certain they would understand and pass. Yet he was right. In spite of his cruelty, they still tried. Idiots.*

"We haven't seen them," said Karl.

Simon's expression tightened. Violette thought he would attack Karl. "Have you not?"

"No. We waited; they failed to keep the appointment," Karl said sardonically. "Do you think we killed them? Would you care?"

"Yes. I would care, very much," Simon said thinly.

"Why are you here, Karl?" said Cesare. "There may be unsettled scores between us but you're no longer of any importance. She's the one we must deal with."

He pointed at Violette but didn't grace her with a glance. Trying to reduce her to an object.

"I'm here to witness your actions," said Karl. "After all, only Sebastian can vanquish her. Isn't that what you believe?"

"An unproven theory, Karl," Simon replied. "Samael and Lilith are equal but the same, destructive, whereas we represent the Right-Hand Path of God. Whose side will you take? Would you give your life to save Lilith? What a waste. She hates you. She corrupts Charlotte, kills and mutilates your friends, despises your daughter. What reason have you to make noble sacrifices for her?"

"Simply to stop the madness of creating a new race of vampires," said Karl.

"You could have recreated the world, Karl," said Simon. "You had your chance, and turned it down."

"If I'd agreed," Karl said coolly, "I would without doubt have been as mad as John by now."

"Not you," said Simon, "my love."

"So you're using Cesare instead, despite the fact that you loathe him?" Violette said with contempt. "Are these God's instructions? You couldn't control me, so now you try to do so through Cesare. God's envoy? You're nothing, a parasite feeding on anyone foolish enough to fall for your lies." Cesare and Simon only regarded her with bland arrogance, John with the mindless menace of a bull. "You're all poison."

"No," Simon replied. "You are the snake, Lilith, the venomous serpent in our garden of immortality."

Cesare approached her, coming so close that his metallic eyes almost hypnotised her. "We revile your dark destructiveness. We want a bright, golden future and the dominion over mankind that is rightfully ours."

All she had to do was to seize him and stab her fangs into his neck. But she couldn't move. She thought, *Why am I afraid instead of angry? This is not me, not Lilith.*

"Leave her alone," said Karl. "You've made your point."

Too late, she realised that Cesare's approach was a distraction. Movement – then John's hands clamped on her shoulders like red-hot iron, while Cesare grabbed and pinioned her arms.

All her once-boundless strength deserted her.

She saw Karl leap at Cesare, fangs extended, fingers clawing at the leader's throat. Saw Simon lash out and knock him aside, so violently that Karl hit the flagstones. Simon swooped, pinned him down and buried his face in Karl's throat.

Violette was borne down to floor. In shifting his grip, Cesare released her, and she took the chance to slash John's face with her nails. Then Simon loomed, pressing her legs to the floor while Cesare and John held her arms. John was like a boulder on her, as if his small form held a ton of invisible muscle.

I killed Matthew as a cat kills to protect her kittens – can't you see?

Karl was silent. She couldn't turn her head to see what had happened to him.

Simon stared intently at her, his fingers like vices on her knees. The conquering warrior. And she knew, with absolute horror, that he intended to rape her.

"You should have let Lancelyn do this." He pushed her legs apart as he spoke. "But you were too proud. You'd destroy a man sooner than let him invade your so-perfect body. You'll be damned for your pride, Lilith. I want the wisdom you denied to Lancelyn." His tone was sneering. "Let me break the veil and enter the sanctum of the Black Goddess. Then you won't mind doing the same for Cesare, and John, and Pierre, and all the others, all these virile young mortals."

Her revulsion hung fluttering on the edge of insanity. Stopping Lancelyn had been easy. But Simon was no weak, sweating human. This was a ruthless, heartless intelligence whose strongest desire was to humiliate her.

Simon moved a hand to her thighs, pushing up her dress to her stocking-tops. With her free leg she kicked out, caught him hard in the chest, then spun away into the Crystal Ring, twisting as she went so they couldn't keep hold of her. The chamber turned dark and distorted like the depths of a lake. Violette soared up towards the light, with their demonic hands catching at her, clawing, wounding. But she evaded them and flew.

They were pursuing her. How many times had this happened, Lilith flying from her three pursuers? They were close, barely a few inches behind her, their fingers tangling in the webs of her hair. She glanced back in panic. Cesare's form in the Ring was a drab grey streak. John was a deformed crimson bull. Simon glowed, no longer golden but the baleful orange of hot coal.

Losing Fyodor and Rasmila had diminished him, but his lust for power had corrupted his soul.

No, she thought. *His failure to subdue Lilith diminished him, and he'll never forgive me. It's not just power he needs, but* purpose.

The skyscape swivelled past in a blur. Directionless, she strove for freedom, swimming through a hostile ocean.

"Run, Lilith," said Simon. "Flee as if the Devil were on your tail."

They were laughing at her.

Then she knew. They were letting her escape. Worse; they were driving her.

The substance of the Ring thickened around her. She floundered through sand and slush. Looking up, she saw the vast midnight fortress ahead, the hellish accretion that had begun to afflict Raqia from the moment of her creation. It hung across the sky, a rootless mountain with forests flowing from its skirts. And they were forcing her towards it.

She found herself stumbling into a nightmare forest. The trees were close-set, carbonised spikes that shifted and murmured around her. They terrified her, but she was forced to run between them, like the dryad Lila in the ballet, pursued by hunters in the shape of hell-hounds.

Now Violette was running on all fours, like a wolf. She climbed a black slope that ran with blood – but when she bent to lap at it, it tasted of nothing, like glass. She cursed God as she ran, but she didn't weep. These monsters would never make her weep.

They ran her to ground against the wall of the fortress. Her back was pressed to the basalt wall. The three hounds of hell panted around her, their eyes red embers.

"This is the end," said Cesare. "Surrender!"

"Never."

"You must," said Simon. "This is your place of exile. You have nowhere else to go."

Following his gaze, she looked upwards over her shoulder at the fortress towering out of sight.

"Yes," said Cesare. "Go inside. You created this monstrosity, Lilith. It's fitting that it should be your prison."

"We never wanted to destroy you," Simon added with mocking sweetness, "only to contain you. What will it be? Defilement or exile?"

Pressing herself back, she felt the wall softening beneath her. She glared into their arrogant faces, projecting all the impotent fury and hatred she felt. If she chose the prison, she would be alone forever – but at least her spirit would be intact.

"Exile," she whispered.

"So be it," said Simon.

John nodded; not with glee, only with satisfaction. He said calmly, "Now Matthew can rest."

"Go then," said Cesare. "Go inside and reap the harvest of your nature."

Violette gave up, and the wall drank her into herself. She dissolved as if falling slowly into a lake of ink, welcoming the utter darkness as if it were a lover, her other-self, the black hag of death.

Robyn seemed to be moving... yes, rising. Light gleamed above her. Colours of incredible beauty, stormy heliotrope and amber fire.

All her fear was gone. She knew the three beautiful demons were with her, although she couldn't see them; there was only light, and a wonderful sense of anticipation.

Something I meant to do... Oh, to tell Alice and Josef I'm sorry... to tell them I'm all right...

The thought faded, and ceased to matter.

Every earthly concern relinquished its hold on her.

Now she saw swirling blackness coming towards her, like angel wings or a great cloak. Violette! The beautiful Dark Mother was winging across the sky to save her.

Robyn turned over in the sea of fire and lay along Sebastian's body, her arms around him, her head on his shoulder. She couldn't see him but she knew he was there. No more conflict between them, only perfect tenderness and peace. Nothing to do but wait for Violette. She was close now, her silky black feathers all around Robyn, filling her world.

She smiled and let go of her last breath.

Fell into the kind darkness of Lilith's wings.

Sebastian didn't feel the Crystal Ring's chill as they drew Robyn into it. He was on fire with her blood and her life-essence, wildly determined, fiercely excited.

They formed the enchanted circle: three immortals sharing their strength to draw a mortal, on the point of death, into the other-realm. The Crystal Ring flowed like blood to fill desiccated cells with bright energy, dark hunger. Ah, the miraculous change from human to vampire.

Robyn's body hung between them, bluish-white. Her hair drifted like sea wrack. He watched for the change, for whiteness to blush into rose and down through the deepest reds to ruby-starred ebony. He waited. He was aware of energy flowing from Rasmila's hand to his, a tingling current that would channel life into the initiate's body...

Arctic bitterness zinged on his face.

He felt the current flow from his hand to Robyn's, and stop.

The Ring held her but did not enter her. Her form should have been a sponge in water but instead it was a stone, smooth and impervious.

All this seemed to take place slowly but in fact was very brief. Sebastian's disbelief as he realised that nothing was happening – and then the electric shock between his hand and hers, flinging them apart.

In panic he tried to seize her again, but she slipped through his fingers like melting ice. Then she vanished. Winked out of the Ring as if she'd never been there.

Rasmila stared at him across the gap where she'd been. Ghastly, the knowing look in her eyes.

Sebastian dived back to Earth. He found Robyn beside the bed where he'd taken her life. She lay on her side, one arm flung out on the rug, the other folded across her breasts, her legs softly bent. He fell to his knees beside her.

A second later, Fyodor and Rasmila reappeared.

"Help me!" he cried, seizing Robyn's limp wrist. "Form the circle again!"

They looked gravely at him. Then they obeyed with maddening slowness. "Hurry, God damn you!"

But the moment was lost. Robyn remained tethered to the world, slipping out of their hands like soaped marble each time they tried. The Crystal Ring would not accept her.

A long time passed before it dawned on Sebastian that he was acting hysterically. He realised then that Fyodor and Rasmila were helping him, only to prove that it was hopeless.

He lay over Robyn's body, kissing her waxy cheeks, trying to will the life back into her. She was so white, so heavy. He had done this to her. He began to weep bitterly, his tears running over her closed eyelids and into her open mouth.

"What did we do wrong?" he cried. He glared up at the others. "You – you betrayed me, you bastards!"

Rasmila pressed her hand to his wrist. "Sebastian," she said calmly, "we did nothing wrong. Sometimes the transformation does not work. You knew that before we began."

"But why?" He kept staring at Robyn, touching her, sobbing uncontrollably. "Why?"

"Many reasons," said Fyodor. "She told you it was against her will. I've never known anyone resist the transformation by will alone, but –" he shrugged "– there are some the Crystal Ring won't accept."

"It's Violette's fault," Sebastian said, his voice hoarse. "She turned Robyn against me."

"More than that," said Fyodor, leaning against a bedpost. "The changes she caused as Lilith in the Crystal Ring may have prevented –"

Sebastian leapt up and seized the thin material of Fyodor's shirt. Fyodor winced, turning his blanched face away. "Is that what it comes to?"

Rasmila tugged at his arm. "What, Sebastian?"

"You *made* this go wrong, to set me against Violette! Killed Robyn in order to use me like your tame warrior in some grand cosmic battle!"

"No, no," she said soothingly. She went on pulling his arm until he let Fyodor go. "We did not, I swear. Lilith is already ours; we had no reason to harm Robyn!"

But they didn't care, he knew. He wanted to rip them apart for their indifference. And suddenly he understood. "*You* told Violette where to find Robyn! Jesus Christ! Nothing matters to you, does it? You act but you don't feel. You are reptiles, not angels. God forbid I should ever become like you!"

"Every pain and every loss you suffer will make you a little more like us," Fyodor replied.

"Get out," said Sebastian. He got up and thrust a poker into the embers of the fire.

"You don't mean this. It's grief speaking," said Rasmila. "We warned you about Lilith. We tried to help you. If this is Lilith's fault, don't blame us!"

"And she's going to pay for it," Sebastian said grimly. "But on my terms, not yours. Now get out of here before I kill you."

"Don't send us away. We are forsaking Simon for you!" Rasmila persisted, her tone musical, soothing. "When we take Lilith to Simon, and he is overcome by our dedication and begs us to return, then we'll laugh and tell him it's too late, we belong with you instead. How beautiful our revenge will be! You promised us that we three would be together, a trinity more powerful than ever we were with him."

"I lied. I used you."

"No," she said fervently. "Your grief will pass. This is a new beginning, not –"

Sebastian spun round and drove the poker, red-hot and smoking, into Rasmila's breastbone. She uttered a shriek, the most hideous he'd ever heard, but he bore down with such force that the poker went through her ribcage and into the floorboards beneath. She lay there, pinned, shrieking.

Sebastian grabbed a firescreen, a heavy sheet of brass with embossed patterns and thick, blunt edges. Fyodor flung himself at Sebastian, clawing wildly and screaming curses in Russian. Ignoring him, Sebastian slammed the metal screen down on Rasmila's throat and saw her head roll aside in a gout of crimson.

Her eyes gleamed up at him. Comets and blue stars, dying.

She had meant... something to him.

Sebastian uttered a single sob. And then he saw Fyodor fleeing through the doorway.

Racing after him, Sebastian caught him within six paces. They ran two steps in the Crystal Ring, then Sebastian hauled him back into the real world.

As Fyodor twisted around to fight, Sebastian shoved him backwards into one of the big windows. Glass shattered and rained on the courtyard below. The angel's thin back caught hard across the window ledge. Sebastian heard and felt the dull crunch as the spine broke. Curses became screams. Crazed, Sebastian shook the screaming vampire. He broke his neck against the window frame, slit his throat on broken glass, dropped him head first so that his skull smashed onto the cobblestones thirty feet below.

Blood oozed, like yolk from a diseased egg, red into the silver hair.

Sebastian stared down at the angel's corpse, shaken. *I have killed my own gods*, he thought. *So much energy and rage... and none of it has brought Robyn back to life.*

Calmer now, he returned to the bedroom, lifted Robyn's body onto the bed and sat beside her for a long time, stroking her face and talking to her.

"Well, if you weren't dead, I'd murder you. Look what you've done to me. I wanted no company but my own, until I met you. Then you worked on me and turned me against my own nature until I couldn't exist without you – and then you go and leave me. That is cruelty, Robyn. I thought I was the master, but you've surpassed me on every count. I see you're smiling a little there in your sleep. And you never once told me you loved me. You never surrendered. I admire you for that. So you won after all, and I concede defeat for the first time in my life – but I'm a bad loser, beautiful child. A very bad loser."

CHAPTER TWENTY

HIEROS GAMOS

As Simon bore Karl to the floor and sank hooked fangs into his neck for a second time, their minds touched.

To Karl, Simon seemed a red-gold entity, a lion-god of ancient power who believed himself omniscient and yet did not fully know himself. Always seeking wholeness through others, never finding it. Forever feeding, discarding the drained husks – Fyodor and Rasmila, Cesare sometime in the future, Karl and Charlotte if he could – but afterwards, always, still hungry.

Clamped in the red embrace, Karl felt Simon's emptiness but could find no sympathy for such ravening self-obsession. Even to be "chosen" by God was not enough for Simon.

"I thank God," Karl whispered into the blond hair, "that I am not like you."

The words fell like drops of acid into milk, curdling passion to hatred. Simon raised his head, fangs slicked with Karl's blood, his eyes wheels of metal, sparking.

"You had your chance; you are nothing to me now."

Karl waited, rigid, for him to feed again. Instead, Simon stood up. As he did so he wrenched Karl's arm and flung him aside.

The pain, as muscles tore and immediately began to heal, was so searing that Karl couldn't move. Struggling, he turned his head to see Violette being held down by Cesare and John – and Simon poising himself above her in the ultimate arrogant expression of conquest.

Her head was back as she strained to avoid Simon's mouth, her own mouth open and her fangs extended. Karl willed her to strike, but she appeared defenceless, as if Raqia had withdrawn its fickle strength and poured it all into Cesare's triumvirate. Her naked grief burned into Karl's soul. *This obscene behaviour is for humans, for brutes*, he thought. *We should be above it.*

With a surge of will, Karl got to his feet. He looked for a weapon against Simon, anything, even a lit torch – too late. Violette vanished into Raqia, and the brutish trinity dived after her.

Simon had taken only a few mouthfuls from Karl, not enough to weaken him. Ignoring the explosions of fire running from shoulder to wrist, Karl plunged into the Crystal Ring.

He saw streaks of darkness against the firmament: Violette was a ragged arrow, with the others nearly close enough to catch her. Yet they did not. They let her flee, as the soot-black fortress above them drew her like a whirlpool.

Karl saw Violette and her pursuers swallowed by a strange forest. Seconds behind them, he plunged between the weird obsidian trees. The surface beneath him was slick yet rock solid, sheened with ruby redness. Glacial air enveloped him. The silence sang.

What is this place, he thought, *and what's happening to Raqia?*

He lost all sense of time. The pursuit seemed eternal, mythical, taking place on a mountainscape in a dream.

He saw Cesare, Simon and John – three demons, grey, dull orange, crimson – catching Violette at the base of the coal-black wall. She pressed against the wall like a pinned moth, or a crucified figure. They were talking, but he couldn't hear the words until he almost reached them.

Then he heard Violette say, "Exile," and Cesare's cold words, "Go inside."

Karl made a desperate effort to catch up. But when he reached them, moments later, Violette had gone.

Cesare and his comrades turned to look at him. They appeared dangerous and grimly self-satisfied, triumphant knights who'd taken the first victory in a holy war.

They wanted me to follow them, Karl thought. *That's why Simon didn't disable me completely.*

"Always the hero," Simon said, laughing. "Why are you so

frantic to protect the witch? She treats you with nothing but scorn. She would have brought death to all if we hadn't contained her."

Karl ignored his taunts. "Where is she?"

"In the darkness, where she belongs." Simon waved a radiant hand at the wall. "Will you go after her?"

"What is this place?"

Simon only smiled. "Her prison. She brought a tomb into the immortal realm. Now she's trapped inside. Fitting, isn't it?"

"You can't carry out your plan." Karl spoke quietly, gazing straight at Cesare. "You cannot overrun the world with vampires. Mankind can't support us. We're meant to be solitary, unseen predators, not a brazen army. We are Lilith's children – not yours."

"Sentimentality traps you in the decadent past," Cesare replied. "The world is changing, and you can't stop it. You owe us your life – for murdering Kristian, for defying both Simon and me – but you're not worth executing. You are pernicious, but weak. The Crystal Ring, the mind of God, favours its chosen ones. Who are you to argue? We have brought vampires back to God and defeated Lilith! We're going home to Schloss Holdenstein now. You have a choice: come back as our prisoner, or go freely after Lilith."

Karl knew Cesare was right. He couldn't defeat them, nor could he leave Violette to face the darkness alone.

"Go," Simon said with venom. "Then I can have Charlotte to myself." Karl looked stonily at him and Simon added, "What should I do – send her to you instead?"

Karl thought of Charlotte, coming back to find the dancers gone and no sign of him or Violette, searching, never finding them... But he knew she wouldn't want him to desert Violette. *She would do the same herself*, he thought in despair.

"Go on, then." Simon flourished a hand. "Follow her. I said you'd go to hell with Lilith; am I not a prophet?"

Not bothering to answer, Karl touched the wall. Although granite-hard at first, it liquefied under his fingers. Dread chilled him, froze his heart. Whatever lay beyond, he knew he could never go back...

Karl stepped forward into sable nothingness.

For several long moments, the wall held him like a fly in molasses. Then the substance relinquished him. He was inside a space, in darkness so intense that not even vampire sight could penetrate it.

He walked slowly forward, blind. His arm throbbed, but the injury was healing. Pain was nothing compared to his concern for Violette. That, and fascinated terror.

Then he saw faint white flames ahead – Violette's face and hands. She must have been standing with her back to him, then turned to see who was following.

"Violette!"

Relieved, Karl hurried to her. The surface beneath his feet felt hard but yielding, like wood. Odd illusion. As he faced Violette, her eyes were huge, swimming with light and fear.

Realisation hit them both at once.

"My God," she exclaimed. "We're back in human form! But we're in the Crystal Ring, aren't we?"

"We were," said Karl. "Now I don't know where we are."

She frowned. "Why did you follow me? I didn't expect or want you to do so."

"My choice was between this, or going back as Cesare's prisoner," he said patiently. "If I were you, I would rather not be here alone. Are you all right?"

"I don't know," she said briskly. "I'm cold, exhausted, furious and frightened. Other than that, yes, I'm perfectly all right."

Karl thought, *I should have learned by now that it's hopeless showing any concern for her*. "Then we'd better try to find a way out."

"There isn't one." A tremor came into her voice. "That's the point, there is no way out for me. Nothingness forever. Exile, starvation, but never death. That's why I'm scared, Karl. I don't know why you had to walk in after me. That must have delighted Cesare! Why is it I can hurt someone like Pierre, who is nothing to me, yet I can't touch tyrants like Cesare or Simon? Still, it's too late to rage about them now."

Karl looked around. Blackness, in every direction. Terror plucked at him with insistent fingers, whispering inside his skull. He perceived their prison as an infinite construction, groaning under its own weight and age. An oubliette of all human malice and nightmares.

"I suppose this is what I wanted," she murmured, "to be out of harm's way... but where did all this hatred come from – mine, and theirs?"

"I wish I had an answer," said Karl.

"If Josef's right and Lilith exists only in my own mind – why do others see me as Lilith too? They believe I am Death. The Black Goddess. So now they think they've banished Death... but that is impossible. It's a ludicrous notion, but they need to believe it because they hate me simply for existing... and I don't know why."

Her words sent a chill through him. Irrational, but nothing here held logic.

"Nevertheless, we can't give up yet," he said firmly. "Let's search for a way out."

He moved away from her, seeking the outside wall, but Violette remained where she was. Karl looked back. "We should stay together. It's too easy to lose each other in this darkness."

"No, wait," she said. Her face floated like an opal on a dark mirror. "Not that way. We must go further in."

Turning, she walked directly away from him. Karl had to follow, or lose sight of her. In doing so, he felt a subtle shift as if he'd surrendered his fate to hers: as if he'd willingly become the servant of the dark goddess who possessed Violette.

Although Karl couldn't see the walls around them, he sensed them by the subtle movement of the air. He felt they were in a cold, haunted room, with a high ceiling and corridors leading from every corner. Then his outstretched hand made contact with an object at waist height. An edge, a flat surface, rough and dusty under his fingertips. A table, an altar?

Violette moved ahead of him, and he almost lost sight of her. Hurrying after her – relieved to see the glimmer of her arms again – he felt the walls closing in. They were in a tunnel. The air stank of damp stone and mildew, like a deserted house.

He touched a wall. How strange it felt, rubbery and gelid yet brick-solid, all at once. He searched for a door, found none.

The tunnel gave way to a square void in which a cold draught sank from above. Violette began very slowly to climb unseen stairs.

Karl groped for a handrail in the blackness, and found one. The treads felt solid beneath his feet.

"Whenever anyone tries to pin Lilith down," Violette said, "she flees. Gilgamesh drove her out of the willow tree. Adam drove her out of the garden and she fled to a desolate place... This is desolate enough, isn't it? But it isn't the desert."

"What desert?" Karl asked.

"When Charlotte transformed me, I found myself in the most beautiful wilderness. Sand like dried blood, rocks like rubies. I imagined the place, I suppose, but I belonged there. It was as pure as fire. That is Lilith's home, a wasteland among wolves and owls..."

The stairs bent at a right angle and ran up to a landing. There Violette stopped, touching something in the darkness. Karl went to her side and felt panelling under his hands.

"A door," she said. She found the handle, and the door swung open without a sound.

A huge chamber lay beyond. The blackness was no longer absolute; Karl made out faint shapes sketched in dust. Chairs and sofas, the hint of a fireplace at the far end, framed paintings on the walls.

Violette caught her breath.

"I've been here before," she said.

They walked onward. The darkness weighed on Karl like fear. There were strange objects everywhere, tauntingly hard to see. Angular silhouettes: furniture, cabinets? Demon heads, with curling animal horns?

In this surreal place, he became convinced that the unseen faces in the portraits were those of all his victims, staring at him in blank accusation. And he was trapped with them, for eternity.

You'll go to hell with Lilith.

In rising panic, Karl went to the wall on his right. He found an alcove, felt some cobwebbed fabric like a curtain. Behind was a smooth surface. A window?

He struck the surface with his fist as if to break the glass and touch the outside world. The blow jarred his arm, re-igniting pain. No glass, no window. Only the nightmare stuff of their prison.

"What are you doing?" Violette sounded anxious.

"Just exploring." Swallowing dread, he went back to her.

"I know this place," she repeated. "I've made this journey before."

"So, where are we?"

She led him across the chamber to another door. Beyond was a further cavernous room, more strange shadows on the inky air. He touched carved chair backs, traced the shapes of candlesticks on a sideboard. Everything he touched seemed to radiate sighing evil... like the ancient tunnel where Kristian had met his death.

"It's where Robyn..." Her voice faltered. "It's like the house where I found Robyn."

"But it isn't," said Karl. "It can't be, can it?"

More rooms. Doors everywhere, but none to the outside. A long, bare corridor. He could see Violette's face and arms, her hair a raven shadow against the white flesh, but their surroundings remained obscure.

More stairs. Violette ascended like a sleepwalker, slow but sure of her purpose. Karl said, "You seem to know where you're going."

She stopped and glanced back at him. "This is my journey, Karl. You don't have to come."

"But I will, if you've no objection."

"Only you could sound sardonic in this place."

"But where is this journey leading you?"

"I've no idea," Violette said with a shiver.

Night lay all around them. The house was labyrinthine, infinite. *We can never escape*, Karl realised, *because we are walking through Lilith's mind*.

At the top of the stairs were more corridors, endless bare rooms. They opened a door and saw a rocking horse formed of dust in the darkness, glaring at them from black wooden orbs. Doll's houses, toys, prams, the debris of a hundred lost childhoods lay heaped like ashes.

The nursery, for no clear reason, filled Karl with terror. Violette's face mirrored his fear. Her hand hovered near his arm, as if she were on the point of seeking physical reassurance.

She caught a sharp breath; he thought she was going to weep. Such grief hung in this room. Ghosts crying soundlessly for lost children.

But she only said, "We must go on. This is the way through."

Another door led from the nursery to a narrow passageway. Violette guided him like a candle-flame until they reached a small lobby. The air seemed warmer here, but it was the warmth of airlessness, suffocation.

Over Violette's shoulder Karl saw an arched doorway leading to a room so immense he could sense neither walls nor ceiling. But there was a hint of light. A pewter glow sifted down from above as if through a high cupola, like dusty blades of moonlight illuminating nothing.

Another mystery. He felt they were moving towards the heart of the maze, where some fearful revelation waited to unleash itself.

Violette stopped in the archway.

"Karl," she said, "I have to go on."

Was she asking him to stay behind? Her eyes were black with fear, the pupils huge in rings of lapis. "Alone?"

"It's your choice. But if you come with me... you can't go back." Her breath quickened, as if a tiny lightning fork had stabbed her. "I want you to come with me."

"As you wish." He spoke impersonally, but the midnight air echoed with warnings. This threshold was a point of no return, like a cliff-edge. If he crossed the boundary, something would happen that could never be undone.

Violette took his hand. The act was out of character, a voluntary touch of reassurance, not conflict. Karl was so startled, so transfixed by this web of mystery, that he went with her.

They walked to the centre of the chamber, into the pool of coppery phantom light. The doorway vanished in darkness behind them. Facing each other in the heart of nothingness, Karl and Violette were the only creatures who existed in the universe.

"It's here," she said faintly. "Here is the place where it ends. There is nowhere else to go... except into each other."

The eerie look on her face unnerved him. He tried to remain impartial.

"What do you mean?"

"Don't speak to me like Josef." Her voice shook a little. "I mean that where we go is irrelevant. It's what we do that matters." He said nothing, unable to believe what she was implying. "Karl, do I have to spell it out?"

Karl froze. An inner chill seized his heart and crawled along his limbs. Denial. She moved as if to touch him, but he caught her wrists and stopped her. "You are not yourself. You don't mean it."

"I do," she said. "We must."

"Why?"

She stared at him like a wild creature, Lilith rising to obliterate Violette. "To open the gates. So I can become my true self. This is what the goddess demands, that I face my fears and dive through the veil. If I don't, I will *never* see or understand the truth."

"But... you have no desire for men."

"That's irrelevant. This is symbolism, energy, magic. Lilith's mystery."

"But I saw how you were when Simon and Lancelyn tried to violate you. Your revulsion. It almost killed you! I can't – you cannot ask me to inflict such misery upon you."

He hoped to deter her, but she persisted. "That's why it must be you, Karl. There's no one else I trust not to use me."

"My God." He released her wrists and turned away, at a loss. She moved round to face him again. He thought she had lost her mind.

"Am I so disgusting to you?" she said.

"You know you are beautiful. You don't need flattery to convince you."

"Beauty? What has that to do with desire? You've always been so cold to me, Karl, so indifferent. No lustful looks behind Charlotte's back."

"I hardly think you would have appreciated it," he said coolly. "You should know by now that a vampire's desires are never simplistic or random."

"Again, that's why it must be you. No man forces himself upon Lilith. *She* chooses."

The burning force of her will alarmed him. Whatever he did now, he could not win. His only defence was reason.

Even as a human, Karl had hated the tawdry heartlessness of coupling without love. That sensibility drew women to him, unaware they were offering him the temptation of blood, not sex. But Charlotte, who woke every possible desire in him, was his soul's companion. He wanted no one else.

"What would Charlotte say to this?" he said. "She is your friend. Don't ask me to betray her."

"I am not asking for betrayal, but *transformation*. Charlotte would understand."

"I doubt it."

"Then you don't know her. This is what Lancelyn tried to do, but he couldn't, because he was the wrong one. This is not a prosaic act, Karl, but sacred magic, the alchemical wedding, *hieros gamos*."

Violette shed her clothes as she spoke. Her dress, shoes, silk stockings and undergarments of ivory satin. She stood naked before him, long velvet-black hair slipping over her shoulders. Her body was white, slim, long-limbed, the perfectly-honed dancer's body in which she'd entered reluctant immortality. Despite himself, Karl could not take his eyes from her. Heart-stopping, the lines of her neck and shoulders and her small, rounded breasts tipped with coral. The curve of her hips outlined an alluring symmetry; the dark jewel of her navel and the shadowy triangle between her thighs.

Perfectly artless, she seemed, with her flower-pale skin, innocent violet eyes and the rippling fall of her hair. Karl forgot that he'd ever thought her too perfect to be desirable. This was wrong... but they stood outside reality; the dark goddess possessing him in a dream, like a succubus. He tried to steady his breath but his heart was burning, his whole body liquefying. *Oh God...*

She slid her hands over his chest, and began to unbutton his shirt. He stood absolutely still, although the feel of her flesh against his clothed body was unbearably arousing.

He said, "I cannot do this if you hate it."

"Vanity, Karl." She slid off his shirt and cast it away, outside the pool of light. And she bit his chest, not enough to draw blood, just hard enough to hurt. His hands came up to enfold her back. Her skin felt smooth over the firm muscles. "It would hurt your ego not to please me, that's all."

"Violette." His control became precarious. Heat prickled a path from his heart to the bitter-sweet pressure at his loins. Unable to look at her, he lowered his head and felt his hair brush hers. "Stop now, or I will not be able to stop."

"Good. This journey is all we have." Her fingers, slim and

warm, plucked at his trouser buttons. "Will you please help me?"

He met her eyes, and was shocked by the depth of fear there. For all her insistence, the human part of her dreaded this. His arms went around her and he held her against him, pressing his lips to her neck. "Don't be afraid," he whispered.

She stiffened and pulled back. "Listen to me with your conscience; this is nothing to do with your love for Charlotte, or with infidelity. It's completely separate. Now I'm going to lie down. You wouldn't walk away and leave me there in humiliation, would you?"

He could have done that. His only chance to escape was the moment she lay down in the lake of blood-red light. But she looked so vulnerable, stretched out like a lily on obsidian. Like a sacrifice. The black void thrummed with the pressure of its unvoiced designs. He was caught in a dream, a sacred rite.

Quickly he finished undressing and lay beside her. The floor was cold but Violette felt warm. The heat of her flank against him was delicious. He recalled Josef's description of Lilith as a seductive witch whose embrace brought disaster. It was Lilith who lay before him now, offering an act of magical transfiguration – or threatening the death of love between him and Charlotte.

No one attacked by Lilith was ever the same again. She'd turned on Lancelyn before he could consummate the act, drained him and left him insane. Karl knew she would take his blood, too. She was leading him into the very act he'd dreaded.

Then he knew. Simon had stopped short of raping her, because he had been afraid.

Unknowable darkness waited, yet Karl could not hold back.

His hand travelled over her from neck to thigh, gentle as feathers. Her wide eyes held his; her tongue was poised between her parted lips. He cared passionately that she should not find the act odious. But as he rose over her and kissed her, Violette went rigid.

Shuddering violently, she turned her face away and said, "Just do it."

He stopped. Lilith was also Violette, forcing herself with every mote of her formidable will through a nightmare. He couldn't comprehend what it cost her, to put herself at his mercy. She was all willpower and defiance. But behind the glaze was a frightened, human girl, whose dread filled him with sorrow.

"No," he said. "You're still expecting me to violate you, and I won't. Come here." He sat her up with her back to him, and began to stroke her shoulders. She remained tense under his hands. "Unless you can bear me to touch you, there is no point. Has no man ever treated you with tenderness?"

"Never."

"Then life has been cruel to you, but we are not all cruel."

She spoke in a low voice. "I hated and feared my father, but I didn't *want* to hate him. I danced on Janacek's grave, but I felt no pleasure. I drank Lancelyn's blood, but I didn't want to! They all forced me to fear them. I can't forgive that. I believe some part of me even wanted to love them. So why, if they couldn't treat me kindly, if they could only bully and abuse me, why couldn't they leave me alone?"

"Control," said Karl. "Possession. And I agree with you, it isn't love."

"I don't require you to love me," she said. "You despise me, so don't pretend. I'd rather have honesty."

"Look at me," he said. She looked sideways over her shoulder. As if she'd passed the peak of fear, she leaned into him. His hands slid over her long, flat stomach. The tension between them was formidable, their words running together like the heat and rhythm of sex. "I never hated you," said Karl. "All I feel for you now is tenderness. All I'll show you is tenderness. If you can read the truth in people's faces, you must believe me."

"I thought I could bear it with Lancelyn, but at the last moment I couldn't, because like all men he only thought of himself. His urges, his ambition."

"Too many make that mistake, but I learned long ago always to put my lover before myself. That isn't pride, Violette. Simply the way things should be."

"Your hands feel nice," she said. "Gentle."

"When we become vampires, being male or female loses its meaning. We change. Our desires become the same. We are outside the human race but we grow ever closer to one another. So, can you see nothing feminine in me? Nothing you can forgive?"

She almost smiled. "Don't ask too much."

"But how can there be transformation, unless we both lose ourselves to pleasure, and to the darkness?"

"Oh," she whispered, her eyes intense. "Oh, you do understand."

"And you will be in control, so there's nothing to fear." Karl lifted and turned her to sit on his thighs with her legs around his waist.

Of her own accord, she slid forward, clasped her hands behind his neck, and kissed him. The kiss was electrifying. After a moment, her tongue quested hesitantly into his mouth. Desire surged, a sword of crimson heat, a weight drawing him breathless towards the edge of a chasm. He thought of Charlotte as the ritual drew him past the point of no return.

He found the moist folds within the soft hair between her thighs, stroked her there. She caught her breath. Ending the kiss, she rose up to guide him. Now he was poised against the tender portal. She lowered herself, easing onto him until he felt the tight flesh yield; and she slid onto him, and he was inside her.

Violette gasped. Her eyes were glazed sapphires, blank but for a faint etching of anxiety. He clasped her head, made her look at him.

Something changed. A new current flowed between their eyes. A rueful kind of acceptance; he couldn't define the feeling, but it came with an intense mutual wave of compassion. They shared this with tenderness as intense as grief.

They sat still. Enveloped in her fire, Karl was suspended between peace and the divine ache of need. The moment was golden, wrapped in sorcery.

Words from another time unspooled a filament of dread. *Those who dare to unveil the Black Goddess receive wisdom, or madness, or death...*

Violette's arms glided over his back. Karl dropped his head and they clung together hard, almost weeping, overwhelmed, as if mortal enemies clung together in a shipwreck: the only survivors.

As they embraced, she began to move tentatively against him. If somehow he could feel nothing, if he could let the pleasure be solely hers, perhaps that would absolve him... impossible. Trails of exquisite fire spread upwards to his throat and the tips of his fangs.

Violette stared at him, her palms resting on his back. She

showed no emotion, no discomfort; only detached curiosity, as if she were thinking, *So this is the mystery.*

The sensations were burning now, excruciatingly sweet, building by degrees as Karl forced himself to hold back and let her have her way. Her warmth and her subtle perfumes wove around him. Her presence engaged all his senses.

Violette. She was lovely, so lovely.

Then something happened. She gasped. Her face tautened and flushed, her gliding movements grew stronger and more insistent. He smiled to see her ambushed by her own capacity for pleasure; her complete amazement.

Blue-black energy ignited around them, softly sparkling. Their tension became incandescent. Karl's consciousness slipped, as if he'd entered Violette's mind, and she his. They undulated together in a dark, infernal realm, serpents swaying to a primal drumbeat.

Abruptly she pushed him back, making him lie flat. Kneeling astride him, hands on his shoulders, she thrust onto him with increasing intensity. Her face was savage.

Karl closed his eyes. In an agony of need and pleasure he surrendered, letting her sweep him towards the fire...

He *was* Violette. Her emotions crowded into him: her earlier dread, the instinct that nevertheless forced her down this dark path – and then a softening, a trust of Karl's gentleness, enabling her to follow Lilith's quest to its end.

Then the unexpected, devastating surge of lust. She had expected a mechanical act. Not this. Wonderful beyond description. And essential... Without mutual pleasure, the rite would be for nothing.

And behind everything rose her true self, Lilith. As hungry and accurate in her flight as a horned owl.

Now the anguish of bliss held them both, too much to bear. Karl opened his eyes and saw her above him. He witnessed her eyelids falling shut, her face contorted. Then her whole body went into spasm and she cried out, head falling back to expose her long throat.

Her rapture brought him to the edge. He spilled over, all sensations converging to a searing, perfect, fire-tipped arrow of release.

It seemed to go on forever, unwinding into the darkness.

He seized her arms by reflex to drag her down towards him

– but she was already swooping, her lips drawn back, fangs fully extended. The pain as she struck was as violent as a second orgasm. Somehow, out of his mind, Karl twisted his face into her neck and found a vein.

Her blood was a wave of light; indigo, garnet-red, sharp as silver, intoxicating. His pleasure surged again, unending. Lilith caught him, flung him spiralling into the realm of visions.

In the ring of blood-crystal, toothed serpents mated.

They were equals, their joy and love untainted by subjugation. A woman and a man, entwining like bejewelled snakes. The goddess and her consort.

Rain fell. Wheat ripened. Red rain… blood spilled upon the earth, running between the ploughed furrows.

Blood gushed from the mother-goddess as she laboured to deliver new life. The blood of her consort, the sacrificed king, flowed out in emulation of her magic.

Rain washed the blood into the earth. Saplings sprang up, becoming a dense forest as time flowed at manic speed.

And then a woman was running through the forest, pursued by faceless hunters. Her hair was wild, her face wrought with fear, anger and terrible knowledge.

They caught her. They burned her alive.

Karl writhed, feeling the flames on his skin, sharing her agony.

Lilith's rage flared brighter than the flames. She burst out of the fire and soared into the sky like a meteor.

Never again, she vowed. *I'll hide in darkness. I'll come to you in nightmares. Deny me, reject me, use all your power to destroy me, I'll still be waiting for you at the end of all. No man, however righteous, has yet escaped the judgement of the Crone, the Black Goddess of death…*

The vision ended.

Violette collapsed on Karl's chest, breaking the circle of blood. Her hair spilled over his arms. He put his arms around her and held her.

Presently she looked at him with solemn eyes. "This isn't finished," she said.

"I know."

"We've lifted the veil, but we're still on the threshold. We need the courage to go inside... to look full on the face of the Black Goddess. We need light."

Karl sat up, lifting her with him. He had not died, and wasn't sure that he'd received wisdom either... He realised he could see, and that the room had changed. Although still dark, there were definite features and dimensions. He felt a carpet beneath him, and saw the bulky shadows of a wardrobe, a dresser, chairs, a large bed.

A hint of Regency elegance and lush fabrics; the resemblance to the guest room he'd once occupied at Parkland Hall was uncanny. The bedroom where he had first seduced Charlotte... but that was impossible.

So, he thought, *does this mean the remaining possibility – that I've gone mad?*

"We should find somewhere more comfortable to talk," he said.

"Talk?" Violette blinked at him. Her eyes were magnificent. "You always want to talk, but it won't help us now."

She rose and went to the bed. Karl watched the pale curves of her hips and buttocks, closed his eyes briefly. He felt warmth for her, but said nothing. To express the feeling was pointless, and a deeper betrayal of Charlotte that he could never make. Violette showed him no affection and seemed to expect none in return.

He thought, *Where can this lead? Of course, if we can't escape and I never see Charlotte again, it's academic. But if we do... Too late to undo this. We have not merely lifted the veil but rent it, and it can never be repaired.*

"We need..." Violette whispered, pulling back the bed covers. Karl went to lie beside her on the clean white sheets. A blade of grey light fell through the curtains, but he had no desire to see what lay outside: the Earth, the Crystal Ring, or limbo. He still feared that Violette would regret what they had done, but when he put his arms around her she relaxed against him.

"Give me your blood again," she said. He lacked the will to object. He simply lay still as she lapped softly at his throat. *Too late now*, he thought, caressing her wondrous hair.

Has she changed me? I don't know... but nothing can be the same after this.

Karl felt visions of blood, flight and rejection crawling through the back of his mind, a pressure that must be released before the spell would break. But what more was there to do? He had encountered the Death Goddess. Now he lay with her in his arms and was not afraid. All he wanted was to sink into her rose-red core again, and if he died there, if he went mad, he didn't care.

Violette raised her head. "We need light," she said again.

He kissed his own blood from her lips.

"Wait," she whispered. "We need Charlotte."

A profound sense of ceremony permeated the castle. Werner felt proud, excited and nervous, like a soldier going into battle. The same look blazed in the eyes of the young men all around him.

The meeting chamber was ablaze with torch-flames. The air was hot, golden, smoky, sweltering with the heat of mortal excitement. Ten minutes to midnight; the transformation was imminent. Soon Werner and his comrades would no longer be novices but initiates, steeped in the mysteries of the Crystal Ring.

Werner thought of his mother. John had tried to stamp her out, but he still kept a small shrine for her in his mind. *If only she could see me now, how proud she would be!*

It did not occur to him that she might have been horrified. He saw nothing but perfection in immortals.

The vampires, all dressed in scarlet satin, were awe-inspiring, like fallen angels in cardinals' robes. The humans were in white. Empty vessels to be filled, Cesare said.

Gathered in two separate groups, they waited for Cesare to enter. Werner's eyes were moist, his breath shallow. No one said a word. Vampire thirst pressed on the air as heavily as the novices' apprehension.

There was a stir. The Leader, at last! Cesare entered, flanked by Simon and John, all three in red. Their arrival generated a bow-wave of power; solid, certain, absolute.

A cheer rose as Cesare seated himself in the ebony throne.

Werner saw him as a vessel of pure light, a prophet, a messiah. Such love shone from his silver eyes!

Werner was overwhelmed. *Under such leadership*, he thought, *I shall want for nothing, I'll never stumble and fall. This is the first day of the future, a new world, for ever and ever.* Moisture gathered and spilled from his eyes as Cesare raised his hands and began to speak. Simon and John, standing on either side, were smiling as Werner had never seen them smile before.

"Some news, my friends, before we begin," said Cesare. "For too long, our brotherhood has laboured in the shadow of the Enemy, Lilith. Lives have been lost in the fight against her. However, tonight... It's my joy to inform you that threat is over. Lilith came here tonight, as predicted. John, Simon and I overpowered her, bound and destroyed her. She surrendered because she knew –" Cesare had to shout over the exuberant swell of voices "– she knew that her time is over! God was with us and we did His will. All of you helped defeat the Enemy through your devotion! And now the future is ours."

An explosion of cheering; Werner shouted himself hoarse. How terrible that day had been when Lilith invaded the castle. This news was almost unbelievable, the end of a nightmare.

With a gesture, the Leader instantly changed the mood to one of solemnity.

"Conserve your energy, my friends," he said. "Never in history has our gift been bestowed on mortals in such numbers. All of you stand here now because you proved worthy to enter the Crystal Ring. Well, there's nothing more to say. The time is here. I hand you to Simon. You have an abyss to cross – but God will go with you, and I will be waiting on the other side."

Utter silence. Suddenly Werner was very scared. He looked at the man beside him but his eyes were fixed ahead. Each of them was alone.

Simon stepped off the dais, and the humans flocked around him. He was like a winged archangel and yet so warm, so benevolent.

"Place your trust in God," he said in reassurance. "Each of you will be paired with an immortal who will take your blood and your life. There's nothing to fear, because you'll receive it back, and more. Then we shall form one great circle, a rosary, if you'll excuse the analogy, to generate a flow of power and lift you into the Crystal Ring. A process so simple that there's only one thing more to say: God be with you."

Werner was trembling as the vampires, who'd been allocated

their partners in advance, began to move among them. The leaders themselves were taking part. Werner prayed to be paired with Simon or Cesare – anyone but John.

Instead he found himself looking into Ilona's eyes.

A thrill went through him. He hadn't been allowed to see her for weeks. How perfect that it should be Ilona!

Werner smiled, but her darkly burning eyes looked straight through him. He was puzzled, thinking, *Doesn't she know it's me, doesn't this mean anything? It must!*

She placed her hands on his shoulders. Around them, other couples were doing the same, as if about to begin a bizarre courtly dance. Her lips, satin cushions in which two daggers nestled, were as red as her robe. Werner's pulse drummed so hard he thought he would faint.

Then, at some unheard signal, Ilona struck.

A violent shock of coldness and pain. Werner had anticipated pleasure: receiving none, he was stricken. Instead he felt he was in a cage of freezing iron bars, and Ilona was a winter sky looming over him, or a crone, pushing his cage under the surface of an icy black flood.

He felt her lips on his neck, taut with the urgency of thirst. Her slender body was hard against his, no consideration in her mind beyond her own need.

Werner was choking, drowning. Then, with a hideous sense of disconnection, he found himself floating near the ceiling, watching the scene from above.

He saw his comrades, each in the same lethal embrace, faces turning bluish-white, eyes closing, mouths opening. Some fought, some were passive, others responded like passionate lovers. All were dying.

Then, as one, each vampire released their partner and joined hands, with their own victim and with the one nearest, until a great circle was formed; red, white, red, white, like rubies and pearls on a necklace. The vampires pressed shoulder to shoulder to hold the wilting men on their feet. Werner could see himself, pressed between Ilona and Pierre. Oh, and some lucky soul with Cesare and Simon.

He felt no emotion. Only curiosity.

An invisible string tugged him. With a rush, he was back in his body. Still alive, barely. His vision was a mosaic of colours and faces. His heart and brain felt ready to explode. The hands that held him were stone.

Then emotion rushed back. Wild panic, black terror. *Mother, help me, what am I doing here, I didn't mean to* –

Ilona sucked out what little remained of his energy.

The chamber swirled and vanished.

And the visible world rolled back to reveal the fires, the writhing smoke-clouds and the livid red chasms of hell.

CHAPTER TWENTY-ONE

THE CHALICE OF CRYSTAL TEARS

Charlotte raced through the Crystal Ring, so far beyond sanity that it was as if she'd ceased to exist. Her madness was not a prison of mortal anguish, but a complete loss of her *self*.

She soared between mountains, arms outstretched, rising away from the Earth. Raqia flowed around her: lava and blue flame. A dazzling light drew her upwards; she was nearing the *Weisskalt* but she was beyond fear. Even the cold could not touch her.

Faint doubts played a counterpoint to her mania. *But the* Weisskalt *means death. Am I like a human, throwing herself from a cliff in the crazed belief she can fly?*

Charlotte couldn't stop.

She ceased to be aware of her body's dimensions. Her skin was no longer a membrane separating her from the Crystal Ring. Its energy flowed freely into her, until she encompassed the whole firmament...

This is what Simon has done to me, she thought.

Or am I doing this myself? Simon's voice: *We'll be angels together, Charlotte. If it happens to you, you'll know...* And her own words: *You forget who you are. You lose your sanity. You become just a cipher for the Crystal Ring.*

Dear God, it's happening.

Heart-stopping, wondrous, terrifying. And she had no power to resist.

The snowy blaze of the sun drew her. Its searing light filled the sky, a veil between her and the ineffable light of heaven...

Charlotte arced high above the electric white plain of the *Weisskalt*. She was a comet with a tail of glittering ice-dust, and the cold was no more than dew sifting over her.

She pierced the veil. Blinding radiance possessed her.

This was the light Simon called God. She understood now. Knowledge came like a clear, purposeful voice. *You cannot change what you have done. It is past. There are others who need you now, and knowledge to be discovered. Seek. Your only purpose now is to unlock the truth.*

A revelation – but not of God. To Charlotte, the light revealed not one presence, but a billion. There could be no deity in the light because it had no prejudice, no chosen ones, no judgements to make. It was pure energy, the impartial fire of wisdom, life.

She saw stars, planets, galaxies whirling in the void. She touched the edge of the universe.

The brilliance began mercifully to fade. Passing the apex of her flight she curved downwards, out of the *Weisskalt* and into a sea of storms. She noticed that her demon-form had changed from dark to bright. Her limbs and body were glistening alabaster, webbed with rainbows of opal and palest gold.

Yet all this seemed natural. As if in a dream, Charlotte observed without analysing. She was out of her mind, but fearless.

Descending, she saw a dark mass floating below her: the amorphous fortress that she dreaded. No surprise to feel a powerful emanation, pulling her down until the vast sable bulk filled the world. She dropped clean through its fabric into absolute darkness.

Angel, goddess, cipher: whatever she had become, she was afraid.

Black walls enclosed her. Although she could see nothing, she felt a profound change in the atmosphere. This wasn't the Crystal Ring, nor Earth... more like some strange limbo in between.

A wash of light appeared. Charlotte was in a corridor with soft carpet beneath her feet, paintings on papered walls.

Instinct made her look down at herself. She was in human form again! Two selves at once; the immortal, and the innocent girl, walking along this corridor to an encounter with Karl that would leave her changed forever...

Karl was waiting for her, she knew. The knowledge filled her with anxiety and delicious excitement.

A door stood ajar, and through the gap fell the glow that drew her. She pushed open the door, and there was Karl, caught in the evocative flicker of candlelight. He was naked, his body a long white flame on the darkness. A lean, beautiful sculpture, exquisitely lit and shadowed.

In her trance-state, Charlotte's mind asked no questions. Their meeting was inevitable and perfect. The sight of him brought an intense thrill of anticipation, as if they'd never met before. His gaze, absorbing her, was dark, reflective, sad, fiery, alluring, all at once. And Charlotte knew that if she had changed, so had he. They were strangers to one another... yet there was a deeper recognition between them. No need for words.

Karl took her hand and led her into the room. She made out detail and lovely soft hues in the shadows; damask, brocade, Regency furniture. She caught her breath. So like the bedrooms at Parkland Hall... exactly like Karl's room, where they'd seduced each other that first, magical time.

This could not be Parkland... but the goddess inside her accepted this strange magic.

Charlotte saw a large four-poster bed. On the disordered covers lay a lily-pale figure. Violette. With a languid hand she brushed her raven hair out of her eyes and looked up at Charlotte.

Then the dream began to twist and darken. Charlotte felt incredulous, fearful, confused. *Karl would never betray me but... Violette in my place? Violette and Karl?*

Looking enquiringly into their faces, she saw no guilt in their eyes, no apology; only dark intelligence. Tender, seductive invitation.

And she knew that Violette had fed from Karl. His unnatural flesh had erased the scars, but a single bloodspot remained on his collarbone like a birthmark. And it showed in his face: a haunted look. Of course she had fed.

So Lilith has finally had her way, Charlotte thought, in a state of weirdly calm horror. *All her threats... "How strong is your love, if it can't survive my bite? I'll take you away from Karl... and you'll never see me coming."*

And Charlotte hadn't seen. Violette had got to Karl first. Intense love brought intense fear of loss, and sometimes Charlotte had wanted that agony to end. To detach herself from Karl, not to care so desperately. In reality, losing that passion would be infinitely worse, it would be hell, but now it was too late.

If Lilith had drawn Karl down into Hades, Charlotte had no choice but to follow.

Without a word, Karl drew Charlotte towards the bed. Violette stretched out her arms and spoke her name. Her tone was raw with need. "We've been waiting for you."

Karl kissed Charlotte's neck from behind and began to undress her. He lifted her dress over her head and threw it aside, and with the garment she shed the lingering horror of the burial. Karl and Violette no longer seemed the people she knew and loved, but strangers with enigmatic, sinister intentions.

Even through her fear, she was wildly excited. The new power inside her asked no questions but simply drifted along, accepting, welcoming.

Naked, Charlotte lay on the bed between Violette and Karl. Their hands flowed lovingly over her, their hair brushed her skin. The beautiful sensations made her weep.

She bathed in memories like fire. Ah, the first time, when she'd come to Karl's room in innocence, only to find she couldn't leave... That imperative passion heating the air between them. Both aware it was wrong, but knowing, deliciously, that they couldn't stop. And the breathless miracle... no longer to behave as decorous strangers, but to lie mouth on mouth, flesh on flesh, melting into each other, sated and insatiable.

Now they lived it again. And how strange and wonderful that Violette was here with them, that they could all share this without jealousy or guilt.

None of this can be wrong, she thought, *when my whole life has been leading me to this place.* Charlotte sank in ecstasy. Karl was inside her, where he belonged, his face soft with rapture. Violette's mouth and hands were travelling over her. Incandescent pleasure.

Charlotte's lips found the dancer's neck. She bit down. First taste of her blood for such a long time. The wine of purest love. Charlotte cried out through the blood. More than love, this was sorcery.

Then came the moment Charlotte had dreaded.

Lilith's devastating, transformative bite.

Her words again, "*I'll come back for you and Karl. I'll do it. I'll take you away from Karl and you won't care...*"

In her bliss Charlotte had half-forgotten the threat. She'd been trapped, seduced into this, yet it had to happen. There was nowhere else to go.

Except into each other.

"Do it, Violette," she whispered. "If Lilith's taken Karl, you can't leave me behind. I know you've always wanted this."

Writhing against Charlotte in her own bliss, Violette's canines stabbed into her throat. Charlotte gasped. Karl's hands held her shoulders and his body was pressed to hers, their legs entwined. Violette's arms went around her waist with her hands resting on Karl's flanks. The three of them spiralled outwards on the crest of enchantment to a different level of consciousness.

A single, slow heartbeat. Their faces and crystalline eyes floated close to hers. And in their eyes – amber and violet jewels – visions floated, layers of mist peeling away to reveal forgotten histories.

Karl and Violette hovered on the edge of truth, but seeing only darkness they hesitated. They had lifted the veil but they had not entered the shrine. *They waited for me*, Charlotte thought in joyous amazement. *They needed me and they waited for me!*

Now she understood. Losing her mind in Raqia, she had absorbed the persona of a goddess, just as Violette had become Lilith. Charlotte was Isis, empowerer, interpreter, light-bringer.

I'm ready. Don't be afraid.

Clasping each other, they became a thorned circle; Violette feeding on Charlotte, she on Karl, he on Violette. And they gave themselves up to the darkness and let Lilith have her way.

Terror, falling, great wings beating like a storm.

Warm darkness surrounded them. They were travelling down into the Earth. Lilith became Persephone, leading them through the underworld to the primal womb that was also a tomb. Karl and Charlotte became the god and goddess who must descend before they can rise again.

Whatever ancient power Simon had drawn from Raqia's subconscious currents, Charlotte found something far older, history's deepest secrets, concealed for thousands of years. The wisdom of Isis was a cool diamond on her forehead.

She saw serpents dancing in a circle of fire: Lilith and her consort, Samael. She saw men cutting their own flesh so their blood soaked into the ground. She saw Lilith as a seductive witch, then as a terrified woman fleeing through a forest.

And then a million images came, raining down like blood-drops.

Lilith lives in the night, haunting human dreams. She is in exile but won't submit; defying every attempt to suppress her, her fiery rage echoes down the aeons. She is the Black Goddess of sexuality and wisdom, terrifying to men – but why is she so feared?

The cool diamond poured light into the shadows of Lilith's soul.

Goddess and god, Charlotte and Karl walked the underworld: Charlotte like Kore, walking freely into the darkness; Karl like Osiris, sacrificing his blood as a penance. Their blood flowed into the mouth of Violette-Lilith-Persephone, Queen of the Underworld.

In turn they fed on the fruit of Persephone. The pomegranate bled, its red crystal seeds bursting on their tongues. The fluid of life.

Persephone's fruit changed them, making them one with darkness forever. But they understood the darkness now. They drank its beauty. They met Lilith-Persephone not as destroyer or ruler, but as friend, healer, lover.

The chamber that contained them was the fruiting head of a poppy, life-in-death. Scarlet petals flamed around them.

Then the luscious ruby-red vision faded. They were in the bedroom again, wrapped around each other, their blood wholly mingled from their mutual feast. Drops lay scattered like garnets on their throats and breasts.

How beautiful it feels, Charlotte thought, *to be touched in absolute love.*

Violette looked exhausted, the ends of her hair plastered to her breasts as if by sweat or blood. Charlotte felt too drained to move. She looked at Karl. He was dishevelled, his eyes drowsy.

They lay gazing at each other, shipwrecked on the far side of their journey, at peace, metamorphosed. After a time, Violette sat up and looked at Charlotte.

"Tell me what you learned," she said quietly.

With an effort, Charlotte sat up and leaned on her drawn-up knees, her hair trailing over her thighs. "Lilith isn't evil," she began. "She never was. Men demonised her as a scapegoat for their own fears. Thousands of years ago, before they created God in their own image, there was a Goddess. She was all-powerful, like a mother to a child. She could create life or destroy it. She was the first trinity: Maiden, Mother, and Crone, but one based in the reality of nature: birth, life and death."

Violette nodded, her eyes closed and her face a mask of relief. "Yes," she said, "but men turned against nature."

"Because the goddess was too powerful," Charlotte went on. "Men envied her magic. They could only emulate her life-giving blood of birth by cutting themselves. Lilith – any woman – represented sexuality and wisdom, prophecy, knowledge, beginning and end. She contained everything, good or bad. Men feared her powers. They began to associate her with death, their greatest enemy. The Great Mother became the destroyer, Kali, the black crone."

"And of course they were desperate to escape death," said Karl, resting his hand on Charlotte's hip. "They fashioned an ultimate god to offer eternal life, a linear existence of life, judgement, heaven. And invented our friend, the Devil, to explain away all the world's evils. I've always felt this to be the truth."

"But you didn't see the other side, until now," said Violette. "In elevating the male, men rejected everything female, twisting all that's sacred in menstruation, sex and birth to seem filthy and bestial. They split spirit from nature. Men were spiritual, women mere flesh, like beasts. And all their natural gifts of sexuality and wisdom came from the Devil and must be reviled!"

"Lost. Wasted," Charlotte said bitterly. Tears flowed down her face. She felt anguish at the madness of it all. "Did they mean to cripple the world by diabolising half the human race?"

Karl exhaled. He sounded weary and deeply sad. "All religions have sanctioned men's disdain of women. The church was always about power. God's name is used to sanction any atrocity, yet death is blamed on Eve's disobedience! I haven't believed any of this since I was six years old. Myths, all of it."

"But with symbolic meaning," said Violette. "Josef was right about that. When Lilith in her serpent form tempted Eve, she was telling her to rediscover the goddess's wisdom before it was lost forever! Too late. The goddess was split in two. Eve the mother, who submitted to punishment and slavery, and Lilith the witch, who would submit to no one. She's everything women are not meant to be."

"Lilith personifies the rejected goddess," said Charlotte, to reassure Violette she understood. "That's what the vision told me. Her flight into the desert symbolised the end of matriarchal authority."

Violette's eyes were alight with conviction now. "The Holy Grail was the lost cauldron of the goddess, the womb of rebirth. God provides a fantasy of life after death; the goddess reveals the inescapable truth that everything dies and decays – even us, one day. That's why she was rejected."

She leapt off the bed and paced about in sudden fury, her black hair rippling. "How dare they turn me into a demon! Why are women feared and suppressed, unless we have true power? The goddess subjugates no one – she simply tells the truth, which men can't accept. This God of theirs – with his plagues and floods and eternal damnation – he's infinitely worse than the Devil. I curse him!"

Karl propped himself on one elbow to watch her. Turning to glare at him, Violette said, "Have you anything to say in God's defence?"

"You know I haven't. What was Lucifer's crime, beyond challenging God's autocracy – like Lilith?" Karl looked steadily at her. "I've no sympathy with Simon, Cesare and their kind. And Kristian represented the ultimate denial of flesh; he was a vampire who refused to feed on human blood. Now I know why. It was for the same reason that some men despise women. Fear. I was afraid of you, Violette, but I've walked through the darkness with you. You don't need to ask."

As they gazed at each other, Charlotte shivered with a thrill from head to foot. The feeling was not jealousy, but sheer relief.

"The truth is this," said Violette. "No god, no power in heaven or Earth, can rescind the cyclic law. The goddess symbolises the blackness at the beginning and end of life. The infinite void. The shadow is terrible but mankind – and immortals – must learn to face it. They cannot live by rejecting Lilith!"

Her anger spent, Violette came back to bed and rested her head on Charlotte's shoulder. "Now I know who Lilith is, I'm not ashamed. I'm at peace with her."

"But she's still in you?" asked Charlotte.

"Always."

"I don't know how I found you," Charlotte said thoughtfully. "When I left my family, I went insane. I felt transparent... and Raqia possessed me. It was neither good nor evil, and it certainly wasn't a deity of any kind. It's what I suspected; the ebb and flow of mankind's subconscious. But that doesn't make us helpless vessels. We can take what we need, and filter out the destructive aspects, if only we stay *aware*. Something in me knew that you needed light. This bond..."

"Who was she?" Violette asked softly. "The one who entered you."

"Like Lilith, she has many names. Such as Isis."

"Only the goddess herself!"

"I'm no deity," said Charlotte, "but I believe I understand why we're driven to drink blood. Blood is the source of life and wisdom: women bleed in childbirth, men in sacrifice. This idea is so deep-rooted and powerful that it saturates the Crystal Ring. That's why the Ring creates vampires. The ancient reverence for blood."

"So mortals still offer their blood to deities?" Karl said wryly.

"More than that." Charlotte was excited by the revelation. "I believe we evolved slowly, after men began yearning for eternal life. After they suppressed their blood rites until all that remained was the chalice of altar wine."

"The chalice," said Violette. "A remnant of the cauldron of life and death."

"But we're not gods," said Karl. "We shouldn't even think it, or we'll become as deranged as Simon or Kristian. In my opinion, the Crystal Ring has a deeply perverse sense of humour."

"And now we know," Violette sighed. "I was insane because I was divided against myself. But now I'm whole." She smiled coolly. "I may still *seem* mad, but be assured, I know what I'm doing. And I think we should go home." She stood back, looking at Karl and Charlotte. "Well, has Lilith's bite cured you of being enslaved to each other?"

Charlotte met Karl's eyes, and knew, with a rush of joy, that nothing had changed. His lovely eyes held sadness and wisdom – and deeper warmth than she'd seen there for a long time.

"I don't think so," she said.

"No," Karl said emphatically.

"No," said Violette, "because it wasn't meant to. The transformation was to destroy fear, not love."

Charlotte smiled. "You brought me back to Earth. I was out of my mind when I walked in here."

"And where, precisely, is here?" Karl asked.

"Wherever it is, it can't hold us now," said Violette. "But before we leave..."

She held out her arms to them. They rose, and went into her embrace. As they did so, Charlotte's perception of the room changed. Not luxurious after all but threadbare, damp and neglected. Not Parkland Hall.

"I was right to reject Lancelyn," Violette went on. "He could never have shown me the truth. It had to be you, Charlotte... and you, Karl." She stroked his face. "I needed you to stop me being afraid."

"Of what?" He looked candidly at her.

"Of God, of men, of myself. You taught me that men are not gods or demons. They're only human. Even immortals are only human."

She smiled, but she was still the Black Goddess, covered in a veil so bright that no mortal could look upon it. She slid closer, her arms enfolding them. "The wisdom concealed by the Goddess's veil is knowledge of the future. Do you dare to look?"

Charlotte recoiled – but Lilith would not be denied. One last trial, before the underworld would relinquish them.

"Hold me tight," Violette said. "Don't let me bear it alone."

They held each other, and visions came.

The relentless march of patriarchy.

The dark concretion in the Crystal Ring was not of Lilith's making. Rather, it was a concentration of mankind's thought-energy, an evil movement powered by fervid ambition. A new future, a new pure race, enemies annihilated – Cesare's words. Trembling, Charlotte saw an endless flow of images.

Streets glittering with broken glass. Innocent people vanishing in the depths of the night. Armies on the move, families driven onto trains like cattle, smoke and flames rising. Cities in ruins. The sky aflame. Untold suffering.

She was looking at a world in which vampires were irrelevant, because men could create far greater horrors of their own.

Violette broke the link and the visions stopped. They stood speechless for a long time, bodies pressed together. Then Charlotte felt the change Lilith had created in her, and heard the same in Karl's voice: new strength, an ability to watch human folly from the outside.

He spoke calmly, his sardonic tone drawing them back from the brink of despair.

"If Lilith has taught me something that Kristian never could, it is that vampires cannot change the future. We are not *meant* to change anything."

"And we're at the mercy of humans," said Charlotte. "I always thought so."

"I know what this place is now," said Violette, looking around the dilapidated walls, "and it can't hold us. It's the heart of remembering and forgetting. This is where mankind shed their ancient memories in new pursuit of power. And it's where we had to come to remember."

"Simon didn't know that, when he forced you here," said Karl. "He was blind, as are mortals."

"Is it too late to make them see?" asked Charlotte.

"We can't stop the tide," said Karl.

"And now they need no more of us," Charlotte whispered. "They can create enough nightmares of their own."

Werner clung to dreams of glory throughout his horror. Impossible. But, with all his might, he tried.

Clouds of fire, streaked with crimson, swarmed across his vision. He was flayed, boneless, raw with fear. He'd expected heaven and found hell.

So cold now. Shivering. Helpless. His hands were numb and he couldn't feel Ilona or Pierre holding him. The circle hung in the void, ruby-clad vampires darkening to jet, the humans remaining pearl-white. Their hair and garments floated. Empty vessels, waiting for the rain of life to fill them...

Werner heard a drumbeat from a great distance. No, not drums. Marching feet. An army, bearing down in legions. Thousands of booted feet advancing, shaking the infernal skyscape, making the whole world tremble. Magnificence beyond his wildest hopes –

Precisely and deliberately, Ilona let go of his hand.

He didn't realise she'd done so until he found himself tilting backwards, like a corpse in water. He saw yards of empty air between her hand and his. Caught a glimpse of her face. Pure evil in her searing eyes and malevolent smile.

Betrayal.

He saw his comrades, deathly white, floating like driftwood. He felt Pierre jerk his arm, as if in shock. Then, one by one, the humans began to wink out of the Ring.

Werner saw the immortals staring at each other in consternation. Their alarm was infectious. Unmanned by terror, he began to scream without sound.

The unseen army trampled him underfoot.

Hysterical, he sobbed for mercy. As marching boots passed over him, leaving him crushed in their wake, he glimpsed the amorphous shape of the future.

Horror and pain ground him to nothing. He couldn't even cry out for Cesare. When the castle walls congealed around him once more, no glory awaited. All promises were broken. Lying untended on the flagstones, with his last breath running gurgling from his mouth, Werner died.

As they dressed, Violette became aware of how real the room felt. It was shabby, cold and haunted – but obstinately solid. This was not the Crystal Ring.

Charlotte slipped into her dress and Karl buttoned it for her, his eyes tender. Watching them, Violette couldn't believe she'd had such a violent urge to tear them apart.

I'm glad, she thought. *I never wanted them to be unhappy.*

Lilith, too, had changed. She was less cynical, more tolerant. Just a little.

When Karl and Charlotte turned to her, she smiled. No guilt, no regret. Warmth flowed between the three of them, the delicious bond of shared secrets. Sweetest of transformations.

Outside the room, they found a narrow corridor with a high ceiling and bare, flaking walls.

"This is the real world, without question," said Karl. "How did we get here?"

"I don't know, but I know where we are," said Violette. All Lilith's calm strength was suddenly upended in turmoil. "It's the house where I found Robyn. If she's here, this time I'm taking her with me. And if she's gone, I'll find her!"

Dull grey light filtered through windows along one side. Looking out, Violette saw a courtyard with crumbling yellowish walls.

"Oh my God," she breathed.

"What is it?" said Karl over her shoulder. Then he and Charlotte saw what Violette had seen. The long, thin white corpse of a vampire lay sprawled like a broken crane fly on the flagstones. The head was still attached, only by ribbons of flesh; the skull was crushed, the spine obviously severed.

"That's Fyodor," said Karl.

Without speaking they walked the length of the corridor, dusty floorboards creaking under their feet. Although Violette sensed no presences in the house, human or vampire, as they turned a corner she stopped in her tracks on a wave of dread.

"What is it?" Charlotte asked.

"Don't you feel something?" Not waiting for an answer, Violette walked on.

The next corner angled onto a wider corridor that led to the master bedrooms. Violette recognised it. Her step slowed; the corridor seemed endless. In the wintry light, she saw, at the far end, the doorway to Robyn's bedroom standing ajar.

She had no sense of Robyn's presence... *So why does the atmosphere feel so wrong? I perceive no one, yet I'm sure there's someone here.*

Violette went on, the others behind her. When they reached the door, Karl said, "Let me go in first."

Charlotte placed a gentle hand on her shoulder. Violette quailed, thinking, *I can't go in. What's the matter with me? I must!*

With Charlotte beside her, Violette entered.

The curtains were drawn, the only light coming from a dying fire and an oil lamp. An odd shadow like a discarded coat lay near the fireplace. Violette took in the canopied four-poster, draped in lavish embroidered silk of cream and dark blue, saw Karl in silhouette inside the doorway, and another figure beside the bed. The stranger was a vampire she'd seen before, tall and dark-haired with a softly luminous beauty about him. His hands were folded and his head bowed, as if he were standing beside a deathbed.

The vampire said softly, "Don't come in. Please don't."

The plea was half-hearted. Nothing could stop Violette. She walked past Karl and looked down at the bedcover.

Then she fell apart. Her composure, her very soul disintegrated. She flung herself down at the foot of the bed with a raw shriek of pain.

She knew Robyn was dead, without studying the pallid face or touching her stone-cold hands. Robyn's lovely warm life-aura was gone.

I should have known, Violette thought in anguish. *Oh, Goddess, why didn't I stay with her?*

Grief flattened her with iron chains. No one spoke, no one touched Violette as she remained on the floor, clinging to the bedcover, fingers crushing the delicate fabric. Her shock was so extreme that she couldn't speak or move. *Robyn Robyn Robyn...* She could only stare at the body that had once been replete with luxuriant life. Then she turned her gaze from the waxen mask to the dispassionate face of the vampire who had killed her.

Sebastian.

In a cat-leap, Violette flung herself over the corner of the bed and seized him. His expression flashed into rage; madness swam in his eyes.

"You did this!" Violette screamed. She was Lilith again and she was going to rip open his neck, snap his spine and tear off his head as she'd done to Matthew a lifetime ago–

But he was strong. He fought back, gripping her wrists, straining to reach her throat. Grief weakened her and strengthened him.

"No, *you* killed her," he snarled. "You turned her against me."

His fingernails tore like scalpels into her throat and chest. She lunged, slit his cheek with her fangs – then someone grabbed her from behind. Charlotte was trying to pull her away, while Karl got between them and forced Sebastian backwards. For a few moments Violette and Sebastian continued fighting like maddened dogs. Then they were dragged apart, struggling to reach each other across a space magnetised by hatred.

Two feral demons, fighting to the death. Lilith and Samael.

"Stop!" Charlotte yelled. "This is what they wanted! This is what Simon, Rasmila and Fyodor wanted!"

Her words sliced the air like a bright sword. Violette froze.

In the silence, from the corner of her eye, she saw that the shape near the fireplace was a vampire corpse. Its severed head gazed at the ceiling from a pool of blood.

Rasmila. Violette felt nothing; she had nothing left.

"What happened to Robyn?" Karl asked, his voice icy calm.

"What do you think?" Sebastian snarled. He bit Karl's restraining arm, but Karl only flinched and held on.

Violette hissed, "Murderer!"

"No!" Sebastian said furiously. "We tried to transform her but it failed. The Crystal Ring refused to accept her."

"So you blamed Rasmila and Fyodor?" said Charlotte. Her voice was ragged, but her hands on Violette were firm. "Was it their fault?"

Sebastian pointed a pale finger at Violette. "It was *her* fault. She came here and poisoned Robyn against me."

"I made her see the truth, that's all," Violette retorted. But she thought, *If I hadn't, would she still be alive?*

"Truth? What the hell is that? She knew she'd die if I didn't transform her. That's why I tried, so she wouldn't die!"

"But you killed her," said Violette. "She died because she didn't want to be like you."

"If that is so, it's still as I said. *Your fault.*" Sebastian made another lunge. Karl hung onto him with deadly strength.

"No," said Charlotte. "There's disruption in the Crystal Ring.

That may have prevented her transformation. It doesn't always work, anyway; you must know that! It's no one's fault."

Sebastian, motionless in Karl's grip, said, "If there's disruption, Violette is the cause."

"If anyone is the cause," Karl said bitterly, "it's Cesare, Simon and their like. They're the ones who corrupted Raqia – not Violette."

"Cesare," Sebastian said flatly. Violette saw his hazel eyes go dull, like claws drawn in. Like her, he was hanging from wires of grief, but she felt no sympathy. His self-pity only inflamed her hatred.

Violette put a hand to her throat, to stifle a scream that threatened to tear her mind out of her body.

"I did not kill her," Sebastian said quietly. "I wanted her to live."

"So did I," Violette whispered.

"Come away from here," Charlotte said into her ear. "Come on."

She began to coax Violette away. Violette resisted, then gave in, letting herself be drawn towards the door. But the scene branded itself on her mind; Karl in shadow against the wall, Sebastian's hatred and grief searing into her, Rasmila's pitiful corpse lying ignored.

And Robyn on the bed with all the dear, precious life bled out of her. Never to stir or speak or smile again.

"All my power," Violette said faintly, "all Lilith's power, and I can do nothing to help her. What use is it, when I cannot bring a single soul back to life?"

CHAPTER TWENTY-TWO

WHITE TO CONTAGION, PRESCIENT TO FIRE

Torn from the Crystal Ring, Cesare pitched forward onto cold stone, dragged down by the two corpses who still gripped his hands.

He couldn't open his eyes. He knew what he'd see. Couldn't bear it.

He heard voices around him, groaning, crying. Death was a leaden grey emanation in the air.

Cesare looked. He saw heaps of blood-splashed white satin in a deformed circle around the meeting chamber. Vampires in red were rising unsteadily to their feet as if they'd taken part in an exhausting ritual slaughter. Cesare got up and stood swaying, seeing everything as if through water. Nothing seemed real.

This could not be real.

With a scream, Cesare fell to his knees.

His heart was broken. All these young men who should now be standing before him in proud splendour – instead they lay drained and lifeless, mouths open, faces blue. And he almost despised them, because they were not immortals: they were only dead humans.

They had let him down.

Yet he wept bitterly, because they'd been so beautiful and full of hope. They had not deserved this.

All round the chamber, his followers were crying out in disbelief, some shaking the humans as if to force them back to life. A few lay weeping on their partners' breasts.

Four of his flock rushed at Cesare as if they'd lost their minds. "Father, what are we to do?"

Cesare rose from his knees and pushed them away. "Don't touch me!" Tears of rage and grief flowed down his face. "Calm yourselves. This is not the end! We'll start again!"

All the vampires looked at him as if he were crazed.

"It is the end," said a voice. Cesare turned and saw Simon standing like a statue amid the devastation, unmoved.

"You told me this would work!" Cesare raged.

"It should have worked. Nothing went wrong, but –"

John came to them, his outstretched arm trembling with tension. "It was her," he said. "She broke the circle!"

John was pointing at Ilona. She stared back in defiance, hands on hips, her eyes like blood-drops. And Cesare knew. His anguish was magnesium fire flashing through him. *Never, never should I have trusted her!*

All Cesare could say was, "Take her away."

John strode to Ilona and seized her. Pierre, in a rare burst of chivalry, tried to protect her, but John only shoved him aside. Ilona let herself be led out of the chamber without protest; only looking back at Cesare with a cold smile.

"You had to blame her," Simon said in scorn. Cesare turned to him, burning with suspicion.

"Do you care more about her than *this*?" He swung round and snapped at his followers, "Don't stand there! Lay out the bodies in some dignity. Attend to it!"

They obeyed slowly, casting sullen looks at Cesare. He turned back to Simon and lowered his voice.

"They think I've let them down. But we'll try again!"

"I don't think so," Simon said woodenly. "I could have told you it was a mistake, trying to make so many vampires, but you would not have believed me without proof. So here is your proof. It's no one's fault but yours, Cesare."

Cesare stared, incredulous. For a moment he felt like a child, betrayed and abandoned. He howled with inward rage. But the flame of self-belief came to his rescue.

There is something wrong with Simon, he thought. *Not with me.*

Simon's topaz eyes were empty and coldly mad.

"We'd better have this discussion in private," said Cesare.

"No, let them hear," said Simon. "You are finished. You were never more than a poor substitute for a leader. When Ilona said you were my last choice, she was exactly right. Fifth-best, tenth-rate."

"I was right not to trust you," Cesare retorted, enraged. "You used me!"

"Yes, of course! I never wanted you, I wanted Karl and Charlotte! I needed to absorb power from you to win them."

"A vampire who preys on vampires? Is that all you are?"

"All?" said Simon. "Don't you know why I need such power? Power is light to illuminate the hidden wisdom of God. But all you care about is your earthly empire. You're a creature of clay, Cesare, a blind mole."

Cesare didn't understand. He didn't want to. "Liar," he said. "Traitor. I'll go on without you. I don't need you!"

"Blind, Cesare." Simon's voice was hollow. "Or you would have seen, while we were in the Crystal Ring, that we are all finished."

In a copse on the long green flank of a hill, Charlotte held Violette and kissed her dry cheeks. Violette was ashen, but Charlotte knew she didn't really want sympathy. She wanted Robyn. And Charlotte thought, *How am I going to tell Josef?*

"You should have let me kill Sebastian," said Violette.

"Perhaps, but it won't bring Robyn back," said Karl.

Sebastian had let them leave the house without argument. Now they were in the countryside, half a mile away.

"How wonderful." Violette's tone was softly bitter. "I know all about taking life but nothing about giving it back. I'm certain Robyn didn't want to become one of us. She let herself die, rather than let it happen. Why couldn't I have died, too?"

"Don't," said Charlotte, anguished.

"The Crystal Ring decides," said Karl. "It's as arbitrary as nature."

"We should go home," Charlotte murmured.

Violette mastered herself, and clasped their hands. What had passed between the three of them could never be forgotten.

Sensual magic, shadowy with grim wisdom, had changed them for all time.

"Oh no," said Violette, with a demonic, chilling smile. "We have unfinished business at Schloss Holdenstein."

Charlotte had been prepared for a battle. Instead they found the castle in deathly stillness.

As they walked along corridors to the heart of the castle, they heard soft voices, moans. Scents of congealed blood and sour human excretions met them, but no sign of life.

Entering the meeting chamber, they found carnage.

Human corpses everywhere. Thirty young men in white lay like scythed lilies, leopard-spotted with blood, bathed in dying torch-light. All of them drained of blood, cheated of eternal life.

There was a sudden weight in Charlotte's chest. Mingled with relief she felt sorrow for the waste of life, the betrayal.

There were some thirty vampires in the chamber, all Cesare's flock. Some were dragging corpses into rows, others sitting dazed on the floor. Pierre was with a group in a far corner, talking quietly. Charlotte saw one yellow-haired male vampire clinging to a corpse and weeping steadily. She thought of Robyn and tears came to her throat.

Cesare and Simon were near the ebony throne, engaged in a quiet but rancorous argument.

Karl, Charlotte and Violette entered softly. For a moment, no one took any notice. Simon saw them first but barely reacted, only gazed flatly at them and stopped responding to Cesare's words. After a few seconds Cesare froze, and turned to see what had caught Simon's attention.

Cesare staggered backwards, tripped on the dais and rescued himself on the arm of the throne. His face turned the horrible colour of the dead mortals around him.

"How did they escape? You told me they were trapped there forever!"

"A misjudgement," Simon said dully.

"What? How can you claim to be from God when you've failed me in *everything*?"

"Can't you understand?" Simon said viciously. "They are the new leaders, not you. That's why we can't contain or destroy them! They are the future!"

"If only," said Karl.

Cesare looked so heartbroken that Charlotte sincerely pitied him.

Violette walked to the centre of the chamber and looked around. This time she came not as a storm but as her quiet self. Yet everyone stared and backed away, as if she had died and risen again from the underworld.

But that's what we did, thought Charlotte. *They're not only frightened of Violette, but of us all.*

"Well, which of you shall be first?" Violette said conversationally. She was a goddess of ice-crystal, her hair the night sky, her eyes arctic violet-blue. "Simon?"

Simon walked to her as if he couldn't resist. *What's wrong with him?* Charlotte thought, chilled. His eyes were like glass: dead.

"Your friends were killed," said Violette-Lilith, taking his hand.

"Friends?"

"Fyodor and Rasmila. By Sebastian. Do you care?"

Simon only frowned. "How did you escape?" he asked.

"Let me show you."

"Yes. Show me what I already know."

No one moved as Violette stood on tiptoe and pressed her lips to Simon's throat. He stood like a gilded figurine in his blood-red satin robe. Her arms went around his shoulders, the widow's veil of her hair half-covering them both. Simon's face became immobile, his eyes hooded, lips parted. A frown indented the skin between his eyebrows.

Cesare clung to the throne, aghast.

In the silence, Karl said, "Where's Ilona?"

Pierre rushed forward and tugged at Karl's arm. "I'll take you."

Charlotte watched them pass through the archway. Then she looked at Cesare. He approached her, lips parting to reveal his fangs.

"Don't touch me," said Charlotte, putting up her hand. Cesare stopped. She thought, *Do I have power over him, like Lilith... or Isis?*

"This will never be forgiven," he said. "God will be your judge."

"It's not our fault the transformation failed," she said angrily. "This is all a lie! Fanaticism is a human disease. We should know better."

"We failed because we were betrayed!"

"No, you failed because the Crystal Ring has more sense than you." Charlotte walked past him and went to look at the bodies. The other vampires watched her expectantly.

"Well?" she said. "You were all there; didn't you feel what was happening? The Crystal Ring itself won't allow so many immortals to be created. Something worse than you is coming, Cesare. The world can conjure its own nightmares without your help."

"Liar!" said Cesare, frantic, helpless.

"We've seen the future," said Charlotte. "Earth has no place for you and your empire."

She heard the rustle of a robe behind her. When she glanced back, Cesare had disappeared.

Charlotte looked at the others. "Do you still love him? Still believe him?"

No one responded. The yellow-haired vampire, still clinging to his dead friend, looked up at her with piercing black eyes but said nothing. Sighing, Charlotte gazed with sad detachment at the corpses. Trying, like Karl, not to turn away in horror.

I have been sealed in a coffin and buried and I'm still alive...

One of the bodies twitched.

She bent down and felt a pulse, a weak life-aura. His face was drained, his breathing shallow – but he was alive. Still human.

"What's your name?" Charlotte asked in German.

The man's eyes fluttered, trying to focus.

"Werner. Am I in hell?"

"More or less." She knew she must get him out of the castle before someone decided to stamp out his tenuous life. "Get up," she said, holding his arm. "I'll help you."

He was well-built, but she had the strength to half-carry him along narrow twisting corridors until she found a door to the outside. Like the others, he was blond, handsome, not very bright. He had worshipped Cesare and yet, for some reason, Charlotte wanted him to live.

She dragged open the door and thrust Werner out onto the

hillside. He stood blinking at her, confounded.

"Go on!" said Charlotte. "It's a miracle you're alive! Just go!"

The youth went, stumbling, into the darkness.

Then the stench hit her.

The warmth of other humans, steaming from below. The sourness of sweat and excrement. Charlotte ran down a spiral stair, wrenched open a cell door, and saw three dozen pairs of eyes glaring through the dark in terror and supplication.

She gasped, holding her throat. She knew what they were. Victims, held ready to feed Cesare's new-fledged race of immortals.

"You're free," Charlotte said, almost losing her voice. She pointed. "Up the steps. The door is open. Come on!"

"What happened?" Karl asked as Pierre led him to a passageway lined with iron doors. Kristian had used to lock up recalcitrant disciples here; Karl had been imprisoned here more than once. He shuddered, thinking, *If John has harmed Ilona, he'll think I am Kristian, come back from the dead…*

"It all went wrong," Pierre said with a shrug. "John and Cesare blamed Ilona for breaking the circle."

"Insane, trying to transform them all at once."

"Simon swore it would work. Maybe he knew it wouldn't. He admitted he's been using Cesare. They had a glorious argument. And what now?"

"You tell me," said Karl.

Pierre caught Karl's elbow. Their eyes met; Pierre looked exhausted and afraid for his life. "My friend, you're the one who brought Lilith here again. I don't know what the hell you are playing at! Since she nearly destroyed me I've thought of nothing but how to escape her."

Without sympathy, Karl said, "Have you considered facing her instead?"

Not answering, Pierre brought him to the open door of a cell. Inside, Karl saw Ilona confronting the grotesque figure of John.

"Daughter of Lilith," said John, his voice the whisper of an inquisitor. "You betrayed us. You are a serpent."

Ilona smiled at him. "Flatterer," she said.

She was unhurt, Karl saw in relief. She and John were like wolves circling, each waiting for the other to attack first.

"Shameless whore," said John.

"You couldn't afford me."

"Witch!"

"And you are scared to death of witches, aren't you?"

Karl walked in and seized John's arm, making him growl in pain. He glared at Karl with hellish strength, rage seething in his disfigured face. Yet he'd lost some spark of courage. His jaw dropped, and he vanished into Raqia.

Karl looked at Ilona. "Are you all right?"

"I hate you, Father," she said, her mouth sulky. "I was enjoying that."

Then she ran into Karl's arms.

As they returned through the corridors and stairways, Karl asked, "Did you really sabotage the transformation?"

"Oh, yes," said Ilona. "I broke the circle and I did so on purpose. Also, I didn't quite kill my partner, so he would block the energy."

"Why?" Karl said in astonishment.

"Because I'm Lilith's daughter in spirit." She smiled thinly. "I have my pride; I never thought anyone could break me until I met her, and I wouldn't admit I was broken until I found myself being used by Cesare. By then I was too busy hating Violette to care."

"What changed your mind?"

"Realising the perfect insanity of Cesare's plan. My God, to think I was helping that halfwit become a tyrant, just to revenge myself on her! Eventually I saw that Violette acts as she does because she's exactly like me."

Karl and Pierre shared a look of surprise over Ilona's head.

"I couldn't face what she'd done to me," Ilona went on. "She makes you look at yourself and it's not a pretty sight. Is it, Pierre?" She grinned at him. "I thought I was being clever, not giving in to her. But my idiocy lay in coming to Cesare, instead of facing the truth. Still, unlike some, at least I came to my senses."

Back in the main chamber, there was no sign of Cesare or Simon, Violette or Charlotte. The vampires in scarlet lingered restively.

Karl saw one he knew, Maria. She stood passively, head bowed and dark gold hair escaping the hood of her robe. "Where are Cesare and the others?" he asked.

"They left separately," she replied tonelessly. "First Cesare, then Charlotte. And when Lilith let Simon go, he walked away, speaking to no one. Then Lilith vanished. But they are still in the castle, I believe."

"Why don't you leave?"

"Where would we go? Only Cesare can protect us from Lilith."

"We're waiting," another vampire said acerbically, "for Cesare to tell us what to do."

"Why do you need anyone to tell you?" Karl said, exasperated.

"We need answers!"

Turning away, Karl moved through the grisly scene of devastation, compelled to look at every corpse. Such young faces, no longer plump with health but drained, empty, discoloured. Life cared what it looked like; death did not. He took in their slack mouths and sightless eyes, their outflung hands. Crimson maps stained their virginal robes. Not just their own, but also the blood that had spurted from their comrades' torn arteries. No survivors.

He saw visions of past and future: thousands of young men felled in their prime to fulfil the ambitions of ideologues...

A small group of vampires huddled in a corner, weeping. One had collapsed over a corpse as if all his hopes lay dead.

Some of them believed in this, Karl thought. *Some of them truly cared.*

He was aware of Ilona and Pierre watching him. Then, making him start, Charlotte touched his arm. "Karl? Don't brood on this. It's not your responsibility."

"Where have you been?" he asked.

"One of them was alive. I set him free. And some prisoners. Captive prey."

"One," Karl echoed. "Did Cesare explain the risk? Did they know he was gambling with their lives?"

"That wouldn't have stopped them," said Ilona.

"I wonder if he'll give them a decent burial," Karl said darkly.

"Should I feel guilty?" Ilona asked. "For my sabotage?"

Karl shook his head. "If Cesare had succeeded, this would have been a disaster of a different order. But the transformation would probably have failed anyway."

"Oh, don't tell me that! At least I tried."

"I'm sure Cesare blames you, anyway," said Charlotte.

"Oh, he must have someone to blame." Ilona laughed. "Oh yes, let him think that I had the power to ruin him! By the way, don't tell Violette what I did. I don't want her thinking she's won me over. My pride won't allow it."

"She'll know," said Charlotte.

Pierre broke in, "And you're going to let her run amok? Your worship of Madame's artistic talent has blinded you to the fact that she's insane! She tried to kill me!"

"Pity she failed," said Ilona.

"You're a perfect bitch."

"At least I'm perfect. There's always one who can't or won't face the truth about themselves."

Karl gave Pierre a cold look. "Violette made mistakes. Which of us hasn't?"

"Pierre's trouble is his illusion that he's strong and pitiless." Ilona went to Pierre and leaned on his shoulder. He looked sour. "How dreadful, to be confronted with your own weakness – with the truth that you regretted your first victim being your mother, after all."

"Ilona, shut up!" Pierre said savagely. "Violette didn't change me. She's a fraud, an evil fake like Kristian. Do me the courtesy of letting me hate her, without patronising me. What brought about your change of heart, Karl? Did she offer something more than her blood?" He glanced at Charlotte, sneered. "You should restrict your appetites to blood, my friends. Otherwise you start acting like sentimental humans."

"Heaven forbid," Karl said dryly.

"Don't be miserable, Pierre," said Charlotte. "You're still alive. Just be thankful Lilith didn't take revenge on you for helping Cesare."

"I didn't help him," Pierre retorted. "And I hope she tears his eyes out."

Ilona came to Karl and laid her hands on his chest, tilting her face up to his. "Father," she said quietly, "I don't want you to regret transforming me for the rest of your existence. Once it would have killed me to admit this, but I can say it now: I'm not sorry. Tormenting you was fun, but such amusements pall in the end. You don't regret changing me... do you?"

Her need to know was almost childlike.

"No," Karl said heavily. "Even knowing what would happen, I'd do it again tomorrow."

Smiling, she bowed her head onto his chest. And Karl still didn't know if her change of heart was genuine, or another manipulation. Unable to speak, he rested his head on Ilona's hair. But his hands remained at his sides.

Cesare knelt in the inner sanctum, praying. All the doors were closed, candles lit. Although he was terrified, he was determined not to flee.

A sword lay before him. A heavy broadsword that had hung on the wall in one of Kristian's rooms.

To see Simon lose his mind and surrender to Lilith had unhinged Cesare. He prayed. *She won't take me. Dear God, have mercy on your servant, forgive my sins and failures, only lend me your strength against the Enemy! I kneel before you as the last bastion against the dark, and I swear to fight to my last breath...*

He felt the air change. Felt a hand on his shoulder, a long slim claw.

It was her. Lilith.

"You're mine," she said, as dispassionate as a cobra. He couldn't look at her. He knelt under her claw, dying of fear. "Let me kiss you, as I kissed Simon. Let me enter your soul and show you the truth."

Cesare scrambled to his feet, grabbed the sword, and ran, flinging back the doors in his path. He stayed on Earth, because to face her in the Crystal Ring would have been worse.

Smiling, Lilith glided slowly after him, a snow-maiden in blood-spattered lavender silk; an owl gliding towards her frantic, earthbound prey.

Simon knew the truth before Violette pressed her icy lips to his flesh. That was why he hadn't fled. Lilith's lash of fire, as painfully revealing as it was, was almost a formality.

He'd known, the moment that the mass transformation had failed. Raqia itself had wrecked their ambitions. The veil of light had split to reveal, not heaven, but the dazzling face of the Death Crone, who did not discriminate between male and female, king and peasant, saved and damned.

Reality.

Live ten thousand years, Simon. The fantasies and ambitions of your tiny soul will still be no more and no less to me than the life of an ant.

Raqia had inspired him to believe he was an archangel with a calling to unite vampire-kind. Just as abruptly, it tore his status away. And Simon couldn't bear it. The simple pleasures of Earth, of love, blood and flesh, weren't enough for him. He needed the absolute, the eternal: the linear process of birth, life, elevation to heaven – not the cycle of death and decay.

Simon needed to be a god.

He'd come so close! To find it was all illusion... That was unbearable.

When Lilith had finished with him, and his soul hung tattered and raw, Simon left the chamber and climbed the twisting stairs towards the highest castle balcony.

He thought of the *Weisskalt* but it was not final enough. To him, oblivion in the *Weisskalt* would be no more than a light sleep.

On his way, he took a hand-scythe from a wall and tested its sharpness. He also found a length of rope.

Reaching the balcony, Simon loosened a block of stone with his bare hands. The mortar was old, his fingers as hard as steel chisels. At last he lifted the block out of the waist-high wall and secured one end of the rope around it, tightly parcelled so it wouldn't slip free. Next he gouged channels on either side of the breach he'd made, working feverishly, his nails crumbling the stone like cheese. Then he placed the scythe across the gap, resting blade-upwards in the grooves.

With the loose block sitting atop the wall, he tied the other end of the rope into a noose, slid it over his head and tightened the knot beneath his chin. He worked single-mindedly, as he had at everything. He felt no fear.

Simon didn't know that the weightless feeling in his chest was overwhelming grief. The spectres of Rasmila and Fyodor were beloved presences in his mind, calling him, but he ignored them. Too late.

Kneeling, Simon bent forward and rested his neck in the curve of the scythe. The edge nicked his skin but he welcomed the silver-sharp pain. Below, the wall dropped sheer into the steep hillside.

Simon pushed the block off the wall. He saw it fall with the rope rippling behind it. When the rope reached full stretch, the block jerked and dragged Simon's head down onto the scythe. The blade crunched straight through the tissues and bone of his neck. The stone went on falling, tugging his severed head behind it like a child's balloon.

Yet his consciousness persisted. He felt the stump of his neck as a circle of acid fire, saw trees rushing up to meet him. One second of annihilating horror...

Then, like a flame, he expired into the kindly oblivion of Lilith's wings.

Cesare seemed more enraged than terrified as he fled Violette. She followed him along the tortuous corridors of the Schloss, kicked off her shoes and ran barefoot. Lighter and faster than him, she could have caught him at any time, but she let him stay just ahead. Teasing him.

He made no attempt to enter the Ring. Perhaps the castle gave him an illusion of security.

She ran him to ground in the meeting chamber. A crowd of vampires, with Karl and Charlotte among them, stared and gasped. Violette thought, *Cesare's come back here thinking that his acolytes will protect him.*

In the centre of the chamber, before Kristian's throne – which had never truly been Cesare's – he stopped and faced her, brandishing the sword.

"Mortal weapons against Lilith?" said Violette, sweetly poisonous, aiming all her grief and rage at Cesare. His power-hunger had disrupted the Crystal Ring, and that made him at least partly to blame for Robyn's death.

She stepped towards him. The blade wavered at her throat.

She gazed along its length to Cesare's face; he had the look of a schoolboy, debauched by premature knowledge and power. Strangely innocent, though. His pale grey eyes were awash with tears. Only evil in that he was passionately deluded.

"But these delusions are infectious," she said aloud. "They will oppress and slaughter millions."

"You are filth, you don't deserve to live!" Cesare exploded. "Whore, impure female, witch, hag –" A stream of insults washed over her and faded. The sword shook in his hands. He took a step back and cried, "If Kristian were still alive –"

"Oh, I should like to have met Kristian! He was worth a hundred of you. That's what they say, although it isn't saying much."

Violette grasped the sword and wrenched it out of his hands. The blade cut her palms, but she barely noticed. She flung the weapon down behind her. Cesare let out a short scream. He seemed petrified by her eyes, racked with horror, knowing this was almost over.

"Let me alone," he said, his voice trembling. "I'll go away. I'll live like a monk, anything you say, only don't –"

"I'm not going to kill you – yet."

"I know!" he cried in anguish. "But I'd rather die than be infected by your evil!"

"Poor Cesare," she said softly. "How hideous to live without the comfort of your fond illusions. But I can't spare you."

She reached for him, quite languidly. The spell broke; he fled towards the side-wall of the chamber, arms outstretched as if to launch himself into Raqia.

Pursuing him, Violette saw a dark shape materialise between Cesare and the wall. She stopped. Then a great weight brought her down from behind.

Flattened by the impact, she couldn't fight back at first. A hard, leathery body pressed her down, thin hands gripped her like talons. She smelled damp mustiness and stale blood. Then a dry mouth scraped over the back of her neck, fangs pricking the skin, sending a wave of cold revulsion over her.

She twisted furiously, and from the corner of her eye saw John above her. A sneering demon face, the veined bulb of his head, his eyes like hot embers pouring hatred over her. Soulless eyes, as rabid as the medieval, devil-obsessed age that he'd never left.

"You are dead, serpent-witch," John whispered. His fangs sank into her neck. Pain froze her to the spot, as if the sheer force of his hatred equalled Lilith's power. Her fingers clawed the flagstones, trying to pry her way into the Ring.

Pain leapt to a crescendo of agony, then the weight abruptly vanished. Through a crimson mosaic, Violette saw shapes moving around her. Someone had wrenched John off her, but his fangs had ripped holes in her flesh.

Her vision cleared, agility returned. With one hand pressed to the wound, she found her feet, crouched ready for another attack. She saw Karl, his eyes amber fire, the sword in his hands glistening with blood. And John lay at her feet, his head severed.

As she watched, Karl struck again. The head rolled into two grisly halves.

Violette straightened up. Karl dropped the sword and embraced her. No word was spoken. He turned her, with his arm round her shoulders, and Violette saw what was happening to Cesare.

She'd seen a shape appear, a split-second before John's attack. That shape was Sebastian. Unable to stop, Cesare's momentum had carried him straight into Sebastian's arms.

And now the dark vampire was feeding on Cesare, the pair side-on to Violette and Karl. As they watched, Sebastian lifted his head, his lips peeling back from long wolf-teeth slicked with blood. Holding Cesare at arm's length, he stretched out his free hand, fingers hooked like talons. He thrust straight through Cesare's robe into his stomach, plunging deep into the internal organs.

Cesare hung there as if flattened against a sheet of glass. His silent agony throbbed in the air. Violette could only stare as Sebastian worked his hand deeper, up beneath the ribcage. Blood oozed around his wrist. Cesare's eyes strained in their sockets and his mouth hung open, but no sound came out.

Sebastian grasped something, twisted and wrenched. There was a sucking, snapping noise. Sebastian held aloft a trophy: Cesare's heart, glistening and pulsating.

Cesare hit the floor like a felled tree. Undying, he writhed, clutching the bloody pit of his abdomen. A whine rose from his throat, the worst noise Violette had ever heard. But Lilith, the dispassionate witness, held her motionless.

Sebastian crouched over Cesare, brandishing the heart. "This is what you've done to me," he said in a low voice. "How does it feel?"

Cesare plainly had no idea what Sebastian meant. Feebly he shook his head.

"How long will it take you to die while I tear you apart, piece by piece? A long time, you bastard. Everything starts to heal and regenerate, ready for me to rip it out again and again. We could have quite a little family of your hearts here. It could take forever."

Cesare's whine rose in pitch. He began to sob, an animal sound. "I wouldn't waste my time." Sebastian squeezed the heart, letting gelatinous drops fall onto the deposed leader's face. Then he flung it away.

Cesare's sobs became words, hoarse but vicious. "Fool, Sebastian. You have all eternity in front of you but you live in the past, thinking of nothing but yourself! At least I thought of the future. At least I acted for all vampire-kind, not just my own narrow life!"

Leaning down, Sebastian bit hard into Cesare's trachea, gashing a deep wound to silence him.

Finding her voice, Violette said, "Leave him."

Her tone was commanding but Sebastian ignored her. He seized Cesare's head, snapped his neck. Then he went on biting through fibres and vessels until he reached the spinal column.

Leaving Karl, Violette ran forward and seized Sebastian's arm. It was like clutching granite. She couldn't stop him.

She heard the rasping crunch as his teeth closed through bone. The head came free and rolled aside. Cesare was dead. His eyes contemplated oblivion with the same impervious fanaticism they'd shown in life.

Violette dropped down to face Sebastian across the gore-soaked body. They crouched like two black-haired harpies squabbling over the kill.

"Why?" she said.

He met her gaze. His face was colourless, hag-ridden. "To avenge Robyn."

"So you had to blame someone."

"Yes! As did you!"

"Did you have to kill him?"

"Holy Mother of God, what's made you go soft?"

"I haven't," she hissed. "Don't you see what you've done? He died with his illusions intact! My punishment would have been far worse. His physical pain couldn't compare with the horror of finding his whole life was a lie! And you've taken that from me."

"Then you're as bad as me," he said. "So don't lecture me, Madame. Go back to where you belong. Go to hell!"

Sebastian straightened up, glared at the others. "If anyone wishes to take issue over this," he said thinly, "you are welcome."

No one moved. Someone shouted, "We don't want another Kristian. We won't accept you!"

"I'm not offering," Sebastian replied. "And all of you, too, can go to hell."

Sebastian turned his back on them and vanished. An uprush of voices released the tension. Violette put her hands to her temples and pushed her fingers into her hair, not realising she had blood all over her: Cesare's and her own.

The other vampires gathered to stare at the bodies of John and Cesare. And most of all, they stared at her. Charlotte came and stroked her arm, her eyes sombre.

The acolyte who'd spoken out – the male vampire with yellow hair and black eyes, who'd wept bitterly over his human comrade – said, "We don't want revenge. Today I lost a human friend whom I loved. Cesare let us down; he led us on with false promises and broke them. We conclude that those who try to rule us have had their day. They demand sacrifice and reward us with betrayal! We've had enough. Lilith – I don't know how to address you – Lady Lilith, no one wants to avenge Cesare – but we do not want you in his place!"

"Good," Violette said fervently. "I'm not setting myself up as queen of vampires. I'm not your enemy, whatever Cesare said. I've acted harshly at times, but I've done nothing that was undeserved. If you approach me in friendship, I won't harm you. But the truth hurts – and some find me too honest."

She sounded cold, and knew she looked like an ice-witch; ebony, snow and blood. But she could force no warmth into her manner.

THE DARK BLOOD OF POPPIES

It was Charlotte who redeemed her, bringing light and compassion, as she had when they'd entwined with Karl. Resting a hand on Violette's shoulder, she said, "You don't understand who Lilith is. She will to teach us to face the darkness without fear. Don't drive her out. That's the mistake men made for thousands of years and will go on making. But we don't have to be like them. Let her in, welcome her. Listen to her."

Another vampire said, "Is this a new theology to replace Kristian's?"

"No, it's not doctrine." Charlotte was fervent. Violette sensed them thawing, perceiving her as sincere. "We've seen something of the future. Raqia, which isn't God's mind but the subconscious of mankind, won't let us create more vampires. Not for now, at least, because their minds are turning to a future that will bring more horrors than ever we could. The disturbances in the Ring are caused by thought-movements on Earth. Not by Lilith. It's a wave that can't be stopped."

A hush fell, electric.

"My God," said Pierre, "does this mean we'll die?"

"No, I believe we'll live. But there'll be fewer of us. So we must face this darkness together, not at each other's throats! The Crystal Ring lends us power to be angels, gods, monsters, anything. But be careful. The transforming energy is born of mankind's fears and desires. Raqia is a sentience without conscience; it can use and consume us. And if we go too far..." She paused, smiling a little. "Lilith is the power that says, 'Enough.'

"Let me say something else. We're not human. We don't need leaders, we can each rule ourselves. Clinging to the past is hopeless. You must leave this castle. It's destroying you. The pain of your victims soaks into the walls, and one day it will come back to claim you. It's an illusion that humans are at our mercy, because in reality, we are at theirs. But in recompense we have these wonderful abilities! Don't squander them on false prophets. Don't waste these gifts. That's all."

Silence. Charlotte looked at Violette and shrugged, as if to say, *Has that made any difference?*

Then the black-eyed vampire came forward. He kissed Charlotte's hand and bowed to her, paid the same respect to

Violette, then inclined his head to Karl. After him, one by one, all the others followed suit. Even Ilona, though she did so with a cynical edge. All except Pierre, who remained obstinately apart, staring at Violette with hollow eyes.

Nearly last came Maria, handmaiden first to Kristian, then to Cesare. Instead of bowing she threw back her hood and offered her throat to Violette. She looked like a saint in scarlet.

And Violette-Lilith took her; a sharp embrace, a few passionate mouthfuls, just as she'd taken Ute not long ago. "Now you know," Lilith whispered, putting Maria away from her, "that you need never be a slave again."

Maria walked away without speaking and followed the others leaving the chamber. She was dazed, Violette knew, but she would recover.

Now only Pierre and Ilona remained. Charlotte put a hand to her forehead and released an astonished laugh. "They listened to me!"

"Yes," said Karl, kissing her. "They listened."

Then Pierre came forward at last. With reluctance he approached and stopped a stride from Violette.

"Well?" she said.

"You will be the death of me!" Pierre exclaimed. "After all you've done to me, Violette, I fear I'm still hopelessly in love with you. Humiliating, is it not? But I don't want to stop being terrified of you, ever. It's heaven within hell. And I'm nothing, if not a colossal masochist."

Alone, Karl searched for Simon. He'd slipped away unseen and left no sense of his presence in the Schloss, yet Karl was driven to know what had become of him.

Exploring the upper levels of the castle, Karl reached the highest balcony overlooking the Rhine. The stars were bright. By their evanescent light he saw the body: blood-red satin contouring a magnificent form, the sinewy neck reduced to a crude stump.

Karl saw the scythe wedged across a gap in the wall, the blade smeared with blood. He knew then that Simon had taken his own life. Not easy for a vampire to decapitate himself... but not impossible. Karl groaned.

Some could cope with the truth revealed by Lilith; some could not. Despite the hostility between him and Simon, Karl felt sorrow. *Given time*, he thought, *perhaps we could have become friends... perhaps not. The most elevated fall the hardest.*

Karl took a step towards the body, halted. Two translucent figures were twined around Simon, sobbing out their grief; one dark, like ultramarine and umber, one albino. His breath caught. *Do vampires leave ghosts? Or can these "angels" never truly die?*

He moved, and the figures vanished. A trick of the starlight.

He looked over the balcony, down into the tangle of trees and bushes and rocks. He sensed movement down there. And he thought, *Dear God, the head!*

Karl launched himself over the balcony and jumped.

Plunging downwards, he entered Raqia so that branches and rocks would not tear him to pieces. He landed in undergrowth with the hillside rearing above him, trees like spiderwebs of frost. A sprinkling of snow covered everything, but the Rhine was a black sword. Karl searched urgently through the bushes for Simon's head.

Again, he saw the two shadows.

They were drifting towards him between great snow-silvered rocks. Then Karl saw, lying in his path, a rock unlike the others. A rough cube, tied up with rope...

Karl dashed towards it, determined to reach it before the phantoms. He followed the snake of rope with his gaze, saw the head like flawless pale gold marble, lying in a frosty drift of leaves.

Karl lifted the big square stone and dropped it onto Simon's perfect visage. The skull crunched like an egg. He pushed the stone aside with his foot and saw the crushed mass of white, gold and crimson; a ghastly mosaic. Karl sighed, horrified, relieved, and drained.

When he looked up, there were no grief-stricken shades of Fyodor and Rasmila watching in recrimination. There was only a human. A youth, Ilona's protégé , the only survivor. His face was colourless and he gaped at Karl as if immersed in a nightmare.

"It's essential to destroy the skull," Karl said, feeling he must reassure the youth by explaining. "Otherwise we can come back to life."

The young man only went on staring as if Karl were insane; which, in that moment, Karl felt that he was.

Werner could not take his eyes off the vampire or the crushed head of Simon. He was dizzy and there were weird gaps in his memory. He couldn't believe he was alive; more likely he was in some hellish afterlife, a rippling world of spun silver where madmen thought severed heads could come back to life.

The vampire, tall and mahogany-haired, shook his head as if mortally tired. Then he vanished into thin air.

Werner was alone. *I am ill*, he thought, shivering. *Must get help*. But he was lost and couldn't seem to gain any distance from the castle...

Then they came. A train of women, children and men, down the steep path he'd taken from the Schloss. Not strong golden youths, these, but dark-skinned gypsies, the kind of imperfect lowly mortals that Cesare had taught his flock to revile.

Werner could no longer despise them. Their piteous state floored him with empathy and anger. Rage filled his chest, stopped his breath. *Who could do this to these poor souls?*

The answer came. *I could.*

I'm going home, he thought, wiping his eyes, feeling sick revulsion at the memory of Cesare. *I was spared! On my mother's life, I swear I'll never fall under the spell of such a dictator again. I shall fight tyrants, with all that's left of my soul.*

Violette had had no chance to say goodbye to Robyn. So, after they left Schloss Holdenstein, she slipped away from her friends and returned to Ireland alone.

In Raqia, the inky fortress still seethed. It would grow worse, she knew, before it began to dissipate. But here was Blackwater Hall, the house of sorrow, cupped in lovely green hills. A mansion of ghosts, discoloured like old bone.

The bedroom lay in darkness. Violette's preternatural vision filtered out the rich bed-curtains. The only colour she saw was Robyn's hair, richest brown, like wood from the tree of life.

The face, though, was no longer Robyn's. It was sunken and discoloured and the jaw had dropped. Her hands, folded on her chest, seemed to have shrunk.

But I am the funerary priestess, Violette thought. *I see the dying through death and beyond. This holds no horror for me. Robyn's body will nourish the earth and the wheel of life turns.*

She walked around the bed, taking in every detail, forcing herself to accept it. She was trembling. Her emotions were so extreme that she couldn't define them as mere grief.

Rasmila's body by the fireplace had gone. She took this in without interest.

"Could we have been true lovers, dear?" she whispered. "Or was I just dreaming, torturing myself?"

She found a pair of scissors in the bedside cabinet and cut off a lock of Robyn's hair. As she put the skein in a pocket, she became aware of another vampire in the room.

Sebastian. She turned to see him in the doorway, an immaculate dark figure, like a clergyman who'd never lifted a finger in rage.

"What are you doing here?" he asked quietly.

He was the last person she'd wanted to see. But now he was here, she lacked the energy for another fight.

"I'll tell her Uncle Josef where she is," Violette said tonelessly. "Then he can come and take her home."

She expected Sebastian to object, but he said, "That's only right. It's a shell, after all. It isn't Robyn."

"I expect he'll have to notify the police, but that's nothing to do with us."

"I buried what was left of Fyodor and Rasmila," said Sebastian. "No one will be looking for them."

"No," Violette said indifferently.

She meant to say a final goodbye to Robyn, and leave. But as she stood there, a great weight seemed to crush her ribs. Unable to help herself, she sank onto her knees, clawing at the side of the bed, and began to sob uncontrollably.

A few minutes passed, though time lost clarity. Then Sebastian slid down behind her. Folding his arms around her, he held her tight, his forehead resting on her shoulder blade. And she didn't mind. She was glad.

They remained like that for a long time, weeping together.

"Simon is dead, too," Violette said eventually. "He killed himself. I didn't shed a single tear for him."

"He was one of my creators," said Sebastian. "It should be like losing a father, but I don't feel a thing. Why did he do it?"

"I showed him the truth. He didn't like it."

"Truth?"

"That he needed his God in order to deny death. That older beliefs were diabolised, in order to destroy them. All out of fear."

"Oh, Violette." She felt his breath on her neck, as warm and consoling as his arms. "I could have told you that. We didn't all lose the old religion. I am part of this country, after all. Last century the supposedly Christian folk of County Waterford worshipped at a well with a figure described as looking 'like the pictures of Callee, the Black Goddess of Hindostan'. They can't erase our memories of the Dark Mother so easily. But I murdered Rasmila and Fyodor in my rage. My own creators. What have I done? Destroyed two treacherous vampires, or slaughtered gods? Surely I'll be punished."

"I think," said Violette, "that we're being punished enough. Rasmila was part of me; an aspect of Lilith in some way. But she didn't know me, because she couldn't see past Simon's illusions. I wish I'd had the chance to make her *see*. She could have borne the knowledge."

"Can you bear this?" he said softly, looking at Robyn.

"Sometimes I can," she said, "and sometimes I cannot."

"Well, I can't," he murmured.

"Do you still blame me?"

"No," Sebastian said heavily. "Not you, not Cesare. Only myself. And now there's nothing left but to place myself in the *Weisskalt*."

His words shocked her. She hadn't realised – or been able to admit – the sincerity of his grief. "Why?"

"I blame Robyn a little, too. She changed me. I was as evil as it's possible to be, I was the Devil incarnate, and I was perfectly content. Then along came Robyn and I fell for her like an idiot. Oh, Lilith, I don't need you to be my mirror; she's done a fine job of wrecking all my self-delusions. How can I live with myself now? How can I live without *her*?"

Violette folded her hands over his. "Don't."

"How did Simon destroy himself, by the way? We can come back from the *Weisskalt*. I'd like something final."

"Stop this!" She turned her head to look at him. "Don't think of it."

"Why not?" he said dully.

"Too many of us have gone. If I can live, so can you."

And she felt him yield to her. "As you wish, madame." They were quiet for a time. She exhaled, leaning back into him.

Sebastian said, "Rasmila once told me you hated men. Couldn't stand them touching you."

"I don't mind this. It feels comforting. It was another sort of fear, the opposite of Cesare's, I suppose. I had to overcome it."

"Well, at least I've been of some use," he said.

"Oh, it wasn't you." Violette was past caring what she said. There was nothing between them but tenderness, shared grief. No hostility, no secrets. "It was Karl. I let him make love to me. No – I didn't *let* him, I persuaded him into an act of magical transfiguration."

"He needed persuading? The man must be made of ice."

She half-smiled. "So am I, so we were well-matched."

"No, you're very far from that. Oh, but why Karl?"

"What?"

"You should have waited for me." He sounded only half-serious. "Weren't we married once? Lilith and Samael."

"I don't think so."

"Lilith was the bride of Samael, the Devil. King and Queen of hell. Have you quite forgotten me, my dear? You're not the only one who's felt the timeless weight of other lives."

Something dark shifted within her. "What do you remember?" she asked.

"Silhouettes. Serpents. Black vines with red flowers. Fire and drums... not memories, only knowledge."

"The Crystal Ring plays games with our minds."

"Ah, but such wickedly dark and rich games," he said. "And the same with both of us?"

"Sebastian," she said coolly, "you must understand that it was a single event with Karl. A sacred act, not an expression of desire.

I only love women. I'm not sure there can be anyone after Robyn, but my feelings haven't changed."

"And you must understand," he said, his tone equally cool, "that I also want no one after Robyn. Do you really imagine I thought you could replace her?"

"No, that's not what I thought," she said. Too sad to argue. How eerie this felt, comforting yet bleak.

"Whatever was between us is in the past."

"Perhaps we weren't husband and wife," Violette said gently, "but brother and sister. That endures."

"Then stay, just for a little while, dear sister," said Sebastian. "Not to weep alone. That's the most we can ask for."

They were at home in Switzerland, within a circle of red-gold firelight; Karl in an armchair beside the fire, Charlotte curled on his knee with her head on his shoulder.

"Have you changed?" Karl asked. "Am I to share you with an overexcitable deity?"

He spoke lightly, but now they were alone there was a filament of anxiety between them.

"No," said Charlotte. "I'm just me. A little older and wiser, that's all. And you?"

"You must understand," Karl said, very quietly, "that Violette and I... I wish it hadn't happened. It wasn't love, it was not even lust."

"Dearest, you don't have to explain. I was there; I joined in, if you remember. It was sorcery."

Karl half-smiled. "Well, you have my word that it won't happen again."

"No, I suppose it won't," Charlotte said, rather sadly. "We've no reason to feel guilty; it was a sacred ritual, not a sin. All the same... I want you to myself. Always."

"And so do I," said Karl. "The danger was that I'd lose you to Violette."

"You won't." She met his gaze. "But must she be alone forever? I wonder if the effect of Lilith's embrace was to remove us even farther from humanity. I should feel guilty about the horrors I inflicted on my family... I meant to show them love and gave them nightmares instead, yet I can't bring myself to agonise about it."

"Perhaps you've realised the pointlessness of agonising. And I should be horrified at your rashness, but... I think I've grown used to you, *liebling*."

Charlotte stared at him, indignant. "So you expect me to behave badly?"

"But you are never dull," Karl said, lips curved. "Write to Anne."

"Yes." They were silent for a time, gazing into the fire. Presently she said, "Then there are things we still can't talk about. The sharing of victims."

His eyes slid towards her under his long lashes; amber shadows with points of blood-red light. "We can talk about it if you wish."

"I think I'm less human than you, Karl. After we'd taken prey together I only remembered how beautiful it was, but you hated yourself."

"It was a singularly hateful thing to do. Would you prefer me to glory in it?"

"No, but... we are vampires. You are such a gentleman and you expect me to be a lady; if a human came to our door and offered himself this minute, you would very politely send him away. I love you for that, but... I don't want you to torment yourself. We're vampires."

"Whom Lilith has made a little crueller," Karl said softly.

"No, more accepting of our nature." Charlotte gave up, leaning her head on his chest, one hand in his hair. Still hopeless to speak of it. "Violette's talking of leaving Salzburg and finding new premises in Switzerland or England. She wants the company to have its own theatre and ballet school. I'm so glad. I thought she'd give up after Robyn."

"She's too strong," said Karl.

As he spoke, someone knocked at the front door. They looked at each other, surprised; then she slipped off his knee and followed him along the hall to the door.

Karl stood in the doorway, an elegant silhouette against the deep dusky-blue of mountains, forest and sky. Facing him, on the wooden porch, were Stefan and Niklas, their blond hair like moonlight. Between them stood a human: a male of about twenty-five with curly black hair and rosy cheeks, slightly drunk, happy and friendly and completely innocent of what his new friends actually were.

"We couldn't stay away," Stefan said apologetically. "I felt dreadful for deserting you, and I couldn't help wondering what we were missing, and, what's worse, I was bored."

"Your timing is immaculate," Karl said sardonically. "It's all over."

"Oh." Stefan looked, Charlotte thought, more relieved than disappointed. "Well, then you can tell us all about it." He placed a fond hand on the human's shoulder. "We brought... refreshments."

Karl and the young man regarded each other. Then the man's smile vanished, and his pink face turned deathly white.

"Come in," said Karl.

ENVOI

FLAME TO ICE

By the opening night in Vienna, Violette had given *Witch and Maiden* a very different ending. The dark spirit Lila, rejected by Siegfried in favour of the pure Anna, curses them and abducts their children. As her curse unwinds, Siegfried repents and lies dying of love for Lila. In desperation, Anna goes to Lila and asks how to lift the curse. Lila replies that instead of rejecting her, she and Siegfried must invite her in. The two women – Violette and Ute – dance an exquisite duet; then, by a stunning special effect, the two become one: Lila-Anna, danced by Violette in a wonderful costume of black, white and gold. Siegfried comes back to life, the children are restored, the divided goddess becomes whole.

The ballet was magical: unsurpassed, Charlotte thought, even by Violette's previous creations. The audience responded ecstatically. *Witch and Maiden* was a new classic.

Charlotte had invited Josef to the ballet, but he didn't appear. Afterwards, Charlotte slipped away from the post-show party – leaving Violette to her rapturous well-wishers – and went to his apartment.

She found Josef sitting at his desk in shirt-sleeves. With a pen in his hand, a blank writing pad before him, he was gazing at nothing. Crumpled balls of paper lay around him. Seeing her, he started and almost smiled. Not quite. His face was calm but his eyes were dark, half-dead. He looked older.

"You didn't come," she said softly. "You missed a wonderful evening."

"I was in no mood to enjoy anything."

"Was I tactless to invite you? I didn't know what to do for the best. I thought it might take your mind off..."

"Nothing can do that. Not even time." Exhaling, he put down his pen. "I was trying to write to you. Hopeless."

She went to his chair and knelt beside him. "Why?"

"To tell you what happened about Robyn. To say – ah God, I don't know. I can't find the words."

"Tell me now."

His strong face looked beautiful in the glow of his desk lamp, silver hair and eyebrows dewed with light. "It went as you'd expect. I informed the police that I'd been told – anonymously – where she might be. They found her. There was a post-mortem, then the body was returned to Boston for burial. Now the Irish and American police wish to question one Sebastian Pierse about her murder. And I should like to kill him with my bare hands –" He stopped, raw pain suffusing his face. "They'll never find him."

"Of course not."

"And her death is my fault."

"No!" She grasped his arms. "Don't you dare say that! How could you possibly be responsible?"

"Because I befriended vampires, Charlotte." He looked candidly at her. "I failed to protect her from them. This is the result, and it was bound to happen, and I should have prevented it – but I didn't."

"That's nonsense," she said vehemently. "She met Sebastian by coincidence. There was no dark plot. We didn't know him, or even know he was in Boston. You couldn't have prevented this."

"But would she have succumbed, if she had not first been enchanted by you, Violette and Karl? You left her yearning... and, God, I know how she felt. Now I cannot help thinking that this is my punishment."

"For what?"

"For my arrogance. Thinking that you and I could be friends. How can we be? It's against nature, against God. There was bound to be retribution."

"You don't believe that," she said, distressed.

"Intellectually, it is of course nonsense." His tone was arid.

"But I cannot persuade my heart. I'm too exhausted to try. I was writing also to suggest we should not see each other again."

"I see." She stood and walked slowly around the study. Rows of books. Silver-framed photographs of Robyn, in all her radiance. "Perhaps you're right. I've caused you nothing but distress."

Silence. He rested his head on his hands.

"But before I go," she said, "I've something to tell you. Violette achieved the wholeness you said she needed…"

"Individuation."

"But to find it involved taking apart everything we believed and looking at it from the inside. Do you remember telling me how the Adam and Eve story was based on misinterpretations of an earlier myth?"

"Charlotte, please. I haven't the energy for theology."

"I'm sorry." She paused. "All that was leading to something important. A warning."

He stirred tiredly. "What warning?"

"Within the next few years, I don't know exactly when, Austria will become dangerous for you. You'll have to leave."

At that he straightened up, more indignant than alarmed. "Leave my home? Whatever for? Will vampires come to take revenge on me?"

"Not vampires. Men. Violette saw the future and it's very ugly. I can't tell you any more. But unless you leave and go somewhere safe like England or Switzerland, your life will be in danger."

Josef's only reaction was another sigh. "I don't know why. I've offended no one."

"But millions of people who have offended no one will be persecuted, all the same," she said quietly. "It's happened countless times in the past. It's bound to happen again."

"A tragedy for those others," he said, his head bowed. "But a threat to my life fails to wake any trepidation in me. It doesn't matter so much."

"Josef!" She flew to him, dismayed. "I'm serious. You won't feel this grief forever. You'll want to live. I want you to live."

He looked up and took her hand, smiling. "Well, I'm being selfish, thinking only of myself. I didn't notice how sad you look. What is wrong, Charlotte? Not just pity for an old man?"

A touch of his usual spirit and humour lit his eyes. She leaned down and rested her head on his shoulder, her head touching his.

"My father's dead," she said. "My leaving made him ill. So I've been blaming myself as well."

"Oh, God, poor Dr Neville," Josef said into her hair. "I didn't know. He was a good friend, many years ago. I am so sorry."

His sympathy was unforced; he didn't stop to wonder how a vampire could care about her mortal family. In that moment she felt hopelessly human.

"You've lost a niece who was your daughter in spirit," she said, "and I've lost my father. I miss him."

They held and comforted each other, off their guard. And the inevitable happened. Charlotte felt the soft, lined skin of Josef's throat under her lips, and she bit down. It was an act of desperation, not thirst; a need to purge her feelings, to connect with another being. The luscious flow of blood was a lightning strike.

At once she realized what she was doing, and pulled away, horrified.

Josef fought her, straining to keep her teeth in the vein. He wanted her to carry on. But Charlotte won. Gasping, she fought free.

"No, I won't! I said I want you to live and I meant it. If you want to die, it will not be my doing."

"But there's no other way I wish to die, Charlotte." He spoke intensely, gripping her hands. "Don't forget that. When my time comes, you had better be there. It would be kind, not cruel, can't you see that?"

She nodded. "Yes. I know."

He released her. His voice dropped. "To bring such love to me and then to take it away – that is the real cruelty."

She kissed his forehead. "Forgive me," she said, but he was like stone to her touch.

When Charlotte returned to the party, she said nothing of her meeting with Josef. Violette's bite had given her detachment, at least. She could experience sorrow without being crushed; she could believe that all grief eases with time.

The party, in an opulent hotel near the theatre, was almost over. Violette must have dismissed all her human guests. Only vampires remained: Karl and Ilona, Pierre, Violette, Stefan and Niklas, a handful from Schloss Holdenstein. How elegant and lovely they looked in their evening clothes, their opalescent skin, lustrous hair and eyes gleaming in the diamond light of chandeliers. Charlotte felt a rush of dreadful excitement, knowing she belonged with them.

Then, to her shock, she saw Sebastian. He hadn't been at the ballet – or had he? He might have been in the audience unseen, a shadow. And Charlotte thought, *Thank goodness Josef didn't come after all!*

As she crossed the room, Karl turned to her with the warmest look she'd ever seen. He'd missed her; her reappearance brought light to his eyes. To know she was so wanted made her weak with happiness.

The same feeling enlivened the whole room. She sensed unity between the vampires that she'd never felt before.

"Is this a truce?" Charlotte said as she reached Karl's side.

Ilona gave a wry grin. "Us against the world, dear," she said.

"It seems foolish to go on arguing amongst ourselves, if the world's decided it will support no more of us," said Stefan.

"A truce," said Violette. She seemed gentler, less aloof yet more vivid; radiant, graceful and strong. "One that will last, I hope."

"We should drink a toast," Stefan remarked. There was a murmur of laughter, then a pause. A change of mood.

"Well, why not?" Ilona said. And she went to Stefan, put her arms round him, and bit into his neck. That initiated the chain, a languid, magical ritual that seemed to Charlotte like a dream. She and Karl exchanged sips of blood with passionate tenderness, kissed with the blood still on their tongues; then Stefan was pulling her away, Violette embracing Karl. And they all passed from one to another, giving and receiving sips of life-fluid as if in a slow-motion dance. It was the most extraordinary experience of Charlotte's life. An unholy, absorbing, loving, utterly enchanted sacrament.

At the end, she found herself between Ilona and Violette. They clung to her and covered her with kisses; she almost died for joy. *That we can do such ghastly things...* she thought. She looked across the room to see Karl with Sebastian, two darkly handsome figures, fatally alluring to their prey. *Such appalling, unconscionable things, all of us, and yet still love each other so deeply. What can it mean, this miracle?*

Karl and Sebastian were the last to meet. They exchanged a look of mutual reluctance to taste each other's blood. Yet they did so anyway, and when it was over, the tension between them had vanished.

"So," said Karl, "you chose not to follow Simon's path?"

Sebastian shrugged. He was calm, but with a spectral quality, a lack of vitality. "Violette asked me not to. Who am I to argue?"

"She can be very persuasive."

"So I heard," Sebastian said dryly. "You must understand, there is nothing between us. Only our love for Robyn."

"That is a stronger bond than many."

Sebastian's eyes held a brief look of abstraction. "Could you live, if you lost Charlotte?"

"I don't know," Karl replied honestly. The idea was something he couldn't contemplate.

"You'd live for blood." Sebastian's voice sank harshly on the words. "There is nothing else."

"Then why are you here?"

Sebastian made no reply. Karl looked at Charlotte, an enchanting tawny-haired sylph between Violette and Ilona. The affection between them as they hugged and caressed one another was spellbinding. And he had the strangest feeling that it should have been Robyn with Charlotte and Violette. They formed the goddess-trinity of his vision, and Robyn was the rightful third member. Instead, Ilona had taken her place. This was not wrong... yet Karl felt, all the same, that they'd lost something. Robyn had been taken, not only from Sebastian, but from them all.

Strange to realise that he no longer feared Violette. Not that she'd become safe, or predictable: no vampire was ever that. But for tonight, at least, there was peace.

Violette detached herself from her companions and spoke.

"Whatever the future holds, we can't change it. Sebastian is right when he says that our purpose is a selfish one: to live for the blood-hunt, to bring pleasure and nightmares to mortals. Not to change the world. The Crystal Ring itself won't let us do it. That's why Cesare's ambitions failed: to make way for something worse. I fear we have drunk to a very dark future.

"Everything men do is in denial of death. They wish to live forever. But no man can avoid his fate, no mortal can escape Lilith. That's why they created God: to annihilate her. But a few, just a few take the risk of embracing Lilith and accepting her kiss."

"And we become immortal?" said Pierre.

"We live a little longer," said Violette. "That's all."

"But we will live," Sebastian put in. Karl saw his gaze lock with Violette's. Her lips curved as if he was taking the words out of her mouth. "Mankind turns his back on the great mother of all... but she will come anyway, dressed for battle like the Morrigan, and take her revenge for being rejected. Then we shall feast like vultures on their folly."

As he spoke, a ghastly vision struck Karl: cold mist drifting over the mud and trenches of a battlefield. A memory of moving from one dying man to another, as if by taking the last drops of their blood, immersing himself in their suffering, he could somehow understand why it had happened. Bridge the chasm, be reconciled to his guilt.

But never again, Karl thought. *I will never let human folly torment me like that again.*

"And when it's over," said Charlotte, "we will still be here."

Karl meant to complete the last task alone, then decided he would prefer company. He had less of a taste for solitude of late. *So*, he thought, *even immortals can change – as if I didn't already know that.*

Besides, his friends would want to witness this purging act.

So one night he took Charlotte, Violette, Ilona, Pierre, Stefan and Niklas on their last visit to Schloss Holdenstein. In the stench-laden chamber where the young men's corpses still lay, they made a funeral pyre with branches. They went through every room, dousing the walls and furniture with petrol. Six vampires who still huddled there, the remnants of Cesare's flock, tried to stop them, but Karl and the others brushed them aside. Eventually the six acolytes fled.

And then came the glorious conflagration. Karl stood on the riverbank, his hand on Charlotte's waist, their friends grouped around them. The Rhine flowed on, changeless. Above, on top of the ridge, the castle floated in plumes of apricot fire. Great bubbles of flame and smoke surged through the doors and windows, crackling and roaring towards heaven.

The walls were turning black. Heat cracked the stone. Balconies charred and crumbled, roofs collapsed with a whoosh like soft thunder. The smell of roasting meat filled the air, and was swallowed by smoke and heat.

In an uprush of scarlet flame, in columns of firefly sparks, Schloss Holdenstein shrank to a weightless black skeleton and died, taking its ghosts with it.

No one wept. Charlotte embraced Karl, transfixed; Violette leaned on Charlotte, and Ilona clung to Karl's other arm.

After a while Charlotte said, "All the visions we saw, the lost secrets of the goddess – no one would believe us. Particularly not men of power. No church or no political body could afford to let it become common knowledge. There's too much power at stake. How could they ever give up their authority by admitting it was based on lies? So the secrets will remain hidden, except to a few. Such a loss. They'll stay hidden forever."

"Always in the shadows," said Violette. "Like us."

Sebastian watched the fire from a distance, with no desire to join the others. *That should be Blackwater Hall aflame*, he thought. *But I've no will left to finish what I started before Simon first came. Let it rot. It's not my house any more.*

After a time he turned away and entered the Crystal Ring.

We will live, he'd said to the others, but the words had tasted flat in his mouth. People all around him, vampire and human, teeming crowds of people to provide him with endless fountains of blood until the end of time... but none of them was Robyn, none of them would ever, ever be Robyn.

It's not just the loss of her, Sebastian thought as he rose through the cloudy mountains of Raqia. *It's not knowing whether she ever truly loved me. That's what I can't bear. And now I'll never know.*

I am alive and you are dead, beautiful child, but you won. You spoiled my pleasure in being a vampire. You taught me to love and you tore it away. Oh yes, you won a victory so complete that you might as well have annihilated me and held victory celebrations on my grave.

But was it what you wanted? Robyn, does your soul look down on me now with pity or with heartless glee?

If only you had given me an answer. I cannot live forever without an answer.

Lilith, my sister, I'm sorry – but I cannot.

So he left it all behind. Sebastian passed from flame to ice, to the *Weisskalt*'s dazzling eternal winter; embraced the very extremity of the solitude that he had always held so dear.

ACKNOWLEDGEMENTS

As with *A Taste of Blood Wine* and *A Dance in Blood Velvet*, there are many friends old and new whom I'd like to thank for their help and support with this book and my writing in general over the years – too numerous to mention without the risk of leaving someone out!

Thank you in particular to my agent, John Berlyne, and to Natalie Laverick, Cath Trechman and all at Titan Books, not least their wonderful design team.

Special thanks are also due to many wonderful writers on female spirituality (as named in *A Dance in Blood Velvet*) for inspiring me with tales of Lilith... and opening my eyes to hidden worlds that we still rarely see. Eternal thanks also to Stevie Nicks and to Horslips, for the inspiration of their music. I hope I don't need to point out that I wrote *The Dark Blood of Poppies* at least fifteen years before the film *Black Swan* appeared... but the slight similarities of theme are certainly interesting!

I'm very grateful indeed to all the readers who have emailed me longing to know when the Blood Wine books would come back into print. It's been a long wait, so thank you for your patience!

ABOUT THE AUTHOR

Freda **Warrington** was born in Leicestershire, UK, where she now lives with her husband and mother. She has worked in medical illustration and graphic design, but her first love has always been writing. Her first novel *A Blackbird in Silver* was published in 1986, to be followed by many more, including *A Taste of Blood Wine, Dark Cathedral, The Amber Citadel,* and *The Court of the Midnight King* – a fantasy based on the life of the controversial King Richard III. As well as the *Blood Wine Sequence* for Titan Books, she writes the *Aetherial Tales* series for Tor. Her novel *Elfland* won a Romantic Times award for Best Fantasy Novel. She can be found at www.fredawarrington.com

THE DARK ARTS OF BLOOD
Freda Warrington

In the turmoil and glamour of 1920s Europe, vampires Karl, Charlotte and Violette face threats to their very existence...

Fiery, handsome dancer Emil achieves his dream to partner the legendary ballerina Violette Lenoir – until his forbidden desire for her becomes an obsession. Rejected, spiralling towards madness, he seeks solace with a mysterious beauty, Leyla. But she too is a vampire, with a hidden agenda.

Is Leyla more dangerous than the sinister activist, Godric Reiniger? When Karl and Charlotte undertake an exotic, perilous journey to rescue Emil, they unearth secrets that threaten disaster for vampire-kind.

The long-awaited, brand-new fourth novel in the Blood Wine Sequence.

Available October 2014

For more fantastic fiction, author events, exclusive excerpts,
competitions, limited editions and more

VISIT OUR WEBSITE
titanbooks.com

LIKE US ON FACEBOOK
facebook.com/titanbooks

FOLLOW US ON TWITTER
@TitanBooks

EMAIL US
readerfeedback@titanemail.com